*"To those who strive for good in this world,
to the people who love this planet and wish to expel all evil therein,
to those who are bold enough to follow their great dreams and visions
into the unknown,*

this Odyssey, is for you."

Duncan William Gill

Notes to the Reader

Thank you for purchasing, borrowing or stealing this book. If I were in your company I would shake your hand regardless of how you acquired my material. One of the greatest feelings as an aspiring writer is knowing that there are people out there like you, reading my work. It really is so very touching, whether you hate it, love it or land somewhere in between, it matters not to me, your time is important, never forget that. The fact that you have decided to indulge in a fantasy story today, is greatly appreciated.

Before you embark on this epic adventure, I would like to share with you a few details that do need addressing to perhaps spare any confusion. I'd like to point out that each book/episode, has three Volumes to its name, and what you are about to read is the first of the three Volumes belonging to Episode One: The Ancestral Odyssey - The Utopian Dream; formatted into this wonderful Paperback Edition. Episode Two will consist of a further three Volumes of Four, Five and Six. Episode Three will be Seven, Eight and Nine and so on. This pattern will persist until The Ancestral Odyssey is completed. Alternatively, you can download each Volume onto a Kindle device or if you're feeling strong and brave, you can pick up the Hardback aka The Paradise Edition that contains all three Volumes. Don't worry, whether you download it onto Kindle, purchase this copy or decide on the glorious Hardback, the content is exactly the same.

Inside this book, you will find my world map of Equis. Over time, after future releases, the map will grow and expand, more locations will be added as the adventure progresses and the story deepens, perhaps the graphics will also improve as I am constantly working to enhance my craft. Be aware that the world map acts as our geographical guideline, even I still refer to it from time to time and I created this mess over a number of many years.

The acknowledgements page will not appear until the end of Episode One, which is after Volume Three. So, for those of you who know me personally or have helped me throughout this process, I do promise you an acknowledgement at the end. Thank you again for reading, and I really hope you enjoy the story. If you have any questions you'd like to ask me, about my books, future projects or anything within the realms of writing, feel free to e-mail me at taotome@outlook.com.

Please check out my Blog at www.taoscribe.wordpress.com if you would like some insight into how this project came about, and some interesting reads into other topics. Follow me on Twitter @MegasTeque for quotes and updates. I get a lot of e-mails and messages, if you don't hear back from me right away, please be patient and I'll try my utmost to get back to you.

See you at the end.

Paperback Edition
Episode One - The Ancestral Odyssey: The Utopian Dream. Volume 1

Printed and bound in the United Kingdom
Paradise Edition Paperback Published 14/09/2018

ISBN: 978-1-9997844-0-9

Book fonts set in: Felix Titling and Times New Roman.
World Map fonts set in: Anke Calligraphic FG, Ameno and Anlin

Edited by Michael Lumb
Cover design by D.W.Gill and James Van Nguyen
World Map created by D.W.Gill
Graphics by James Van Nguyen
Copyright © 2018
All rights reserved.

Published by Taoteque Publishing.

EPISODE ONE
THE ANCESTRAL ODYSSEY

THE UTOPIAN DREAM VOLUMES 1 - 3

By
D.W.Gill

"What happens when dreams become real and a place of peace and paradise is within grasp?
Afterward what is left to be achieved, what then does life have to offer? I'll tell you."

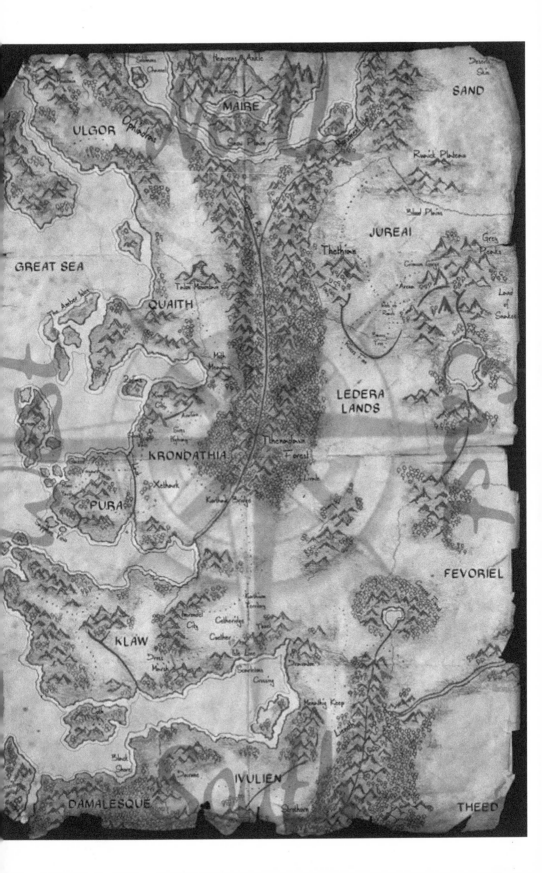

Contents

History and Prophecy

Humanity has always been a mystery.

When humans first came to the lands of Equis, their intentions provided for a working order and a fair society, where men and women of different cultures could together live in harmony, working towards making Equis an even more wonderful place. The Circle of Six was soon assembled; the first council to rule over the common people, who needed direction and leadership. These rulers were glorified, wealthy, noble lords who had united peacefully under the name of Requorn. Together they helped make this dream of an equitable, well-maintained world a possibility. Thus, the Age of the Six was born, the first great age of Equis, when the six tribes of Norkron, Renasark, Muligoro, Desaru, Dovidian and Liarath shared the world.

So began the genesis of mankind; each tribe had enough land, food, and resources to support their future generations. Communities grew and culture was cultivated. The world of Equis flourished with life, joy, and happiness. All was not well, however; tensions between the noble lords gradually grew. Arguments flared in their meeting chambers, and slowly but surely, through humanity's weaknesses of greed, irrationality, and lust for power, the Requorn Council of Six broke the societies apart, segregating their populaces, destroying shared traditions, eroding them until the tribes grew apart and separated themselves completely, continuing to evolve independently of the influence of their neighbours. What came after this separation was not only the end of the first age but the birth of a second; one ruled by jealousy, hatred, dictatorship, and war. It was the first war mankind would wage upon its own kind, but certainly not the last. So, came to pass the Time of the Warlords, the second age of Equis.

For hundreds of years, the tribes fought one another, conflict after conflict, battle after battle. The people called it The Never-Ending War. Countless generations lost their lives to the will and demands of the sinister warlords, a position passed down from father to son. Each vowed to his people that he would end the war, but these promises swiftly turned to lies, the lies turned to deceit and chaos continued to reign.

Throughout this period, the Norkron Tribe bred an army through discipline, and dedication to their cause, whole-heartedly believing that they were the strongest and noblest tribe of all and that they deserved to have the world all for themselves. This army was not based on savagery and barbarity, rather each member embraced justice and honour, traits which had long since ceased to prevail in the present time. They unleashed this unstoppable force upon the world, crushing all who opposed them. The Honour Guard, as they were known, were never defeated, and quickly struck fear into the opposing armies of the age. The other tribes eventually submitted to peace, after failing time and time again to stand in the way of the mighty Norkrons. Four tribes surrendered, one after the other, complying with the terms of their conquerors, swearing complete loyalty to the victors, adopting Norkron culture as if it were their own. All vowed to serve the Norkrons, save for the Dovidians, who fled further afield, evading the attacking forces, venturing deeper into the south-eastern lands, delaying any engagement until forming a resistance.

Over time, the battle-weary Norkrons came to accept the Dovidian people, and instead of igniting yet another conflict, they learned to live together, remembering what it was to show endearment and compassion. The Norkrons and Dovidians met on the field, their strongest armies facing off in opposition for the last time and lowered their arms together after agreeing upon fair terms. Thus, they became allies once more, rekindling a long-forgotten friendship. The Dovidians could keep the south-eastern lands for themselves, forming the country now known as Ivulien. The Norkrons, remained in the north-western lands, which came to be known as Krondathia. The Eldor, head advisor to the Norkron Warlord, was displeased with the actions of The Honour Guards, bitterly disappointed that they had allowed the Dovidians to retain their own territory. Nevertheless, the war was finally over, and peace returned once more.

So the Dovidians existed in peace and built upon their kingdoms in Ivulien, while the Norkron people did the same in their own lands, continuing their research into the resources of the earth, having always held a keen interest in the history of Equis. The ruins, the ancient architecture that littered the land all around the world, gripping the imagination of the people and drove the Norkron people toward studying the lost history of the world. It was not long before a great explorer, named Hallow Diases, unearthed the lost knowledge of the mythical twelve higher powers. The Norkrons were unearthing something, something that they could not possibly understand without guidance.

One widespread, though unpopular belief system of the time was known as Starillia. Small pockets of the Norkron populace suddenly became enthralled by the idea that something out there was looking down on them, believing in twelve Gods that commanded the seas, air, earth, and fire of Equis, possessing powers that outmatched anything mankind could master themselves. Diases understood that Starillia was incomplete; that before it could truly shine a Chosen would have to be born to lead its followers, a female leader who would show the enlightened ones the path to their destiny. A path to a greater world, one of beauty, a utopia.

Times changed. The Eldor now ruled over Krondathia, in accordance with the dying wish of the last Norkron Warlord. The Eldor had been sworn to forfeit all powers of leadership to the prophesied Chosen, upon her eventual arrival. After many long years of anticipation, finally, she was born among the Norkrons, though the Eldor did not give up his power over the people willingly. Quickly the Chosen was hailed as the people's light, the people's hope, the people's saviour. Regina Corah, the first Star Caller of Equis, took her rightful place as the new ruler of Krondathia with the Eldor at her side. With her birth began the third great epoch of Equis, The Awakening Ages, and with it came the discovery of Omnio, a strange pearl born of the earth, encapsulating unique gifts that humans could wield and perfect over time. Regina visited twelve ancient shrines, shrines housing the resting places of the elemental Gods, traversing unforgiving lands and enduring perilous challenges along the way. Upon her arrival, she would awake the God that lay there in slumber and ask it to serve mankind, to fulfil its purpose. She named these twelve The Celestial Souls.

Before her death, another baby girl was born and blessed with Regina's holy gifts. Ashleigh Hauckos was swiftly named the next

Star Caller, to take Regina's place at the head of the country of Krondathia. With this, The Fourth Age, The Passage to the Great World, unfolded. The line of the Chosen grew ever longer, Regina's descendants maintaining peace and prosperity through the whispered wisdom of the twelve Celestials, also known as The Holy Ultimas, which to this day provide comfort and direction to all those who follow the Norkron ways of Starillia.

Their promise, written in stone, will never fade or be forgotten. The promise of salvation for those who believe, who thrive for happiness and the answers to the hardest of questions; Why are we here? What is our purpose? What is the meaning of life itself? As we join the story in the present day, this prophecy remains to be fulfilled. It is The Fourth Age of Equis, and revolution is nigh.

On the throne sits a young and gifted Star Caller: Isabelle Verano, the 23rd of her line.

The year is 1512

Introduction

Our story begins. The sun will rise anew.

Endless crystal blue seas stretched as far as the eye could see. A quiet storm had rapidly worsened developing a bitter temper. The waves rolled over themselves, looming high as the wind picked up, skittering over the crumpling blue fabric of ocean. A dark speck swooped down from the sky, stretching out its wings, surfing along the tempestuous gale. The black dove landed upon a smooth, silver stone, unhindered by the throws of heavy waves breaking at its base. A strange yet distinctive symbol had been carved into the stone's face; two vertical lines joined through the centre by a single horizontal slash. The small bird rested for a short while atop the rock, glancing from side to side every so often with optimistic eyes, contemplating the next step of its great adventure. Eventually, it leapt off the rock and soared gracefully into the wind, catching the updraft, taking off into the sky, clearing itself far away from the curling blue waves.

Armies of golden sand dunes burned brightly under the searing sun. The ground grew harder with every mile the bird left behind, transitioning into an endless plateau of earthy brown rock. The small creature glided between large chasms, swooping through the cold shadows of deep gorges. The valleys and canyons of the area once flooded with watery streams and mighty rivers now lay dry and seemingly devoid of life under the intense heat of the glaring sun. Onwards, the bird flew toward its distant location, shaking off its weariness. Finally, escaping the tortuous confinement of the valleys, the black dove found itself once more faced with a desert, its surface made of crimson earth.

The new day was miserable. A cold wind blew over the green countryside, over empty woodlands, and icy rivers while in the distance, were the peaks of a great wall of ominous silver mountains. Still, the black dove kept its eyes open, on the lookout for anything of interest, food, predators, its route home. The small bird hunted for shelter from the cold, in desperate need of rest. The grey clouds overhead had gathered to block out the clear sky and the sun's glorious gaze. Finally, the bird found peace within an old rodent's home, within the open bark of a tree. It settled itself for a time within the warm space before it set off. The dreary clouds would eventually move on and so would the black dove continue its own journey. For now, however, it patiently watched and waited from inside the tree. The wet and windy weather persisted for hours, and only seemed to be getting worse as darkness crept in, so the bird nestled deeper into the tree, further away from the opening. The dove would now have to wait until morning.

When dawn came with a cold sun and a light wind, the bird left the shelter of the tree, spreading its wings as it flew. The clouds had yet to part, though the weather was now peaceful. The black dove head towards the cliffs which swiftly grew tall and menacing as the bird drew nearer. The steep bluffs were simply too high to fly over, so instead the bird plunged into a small cave behind a crack in one of the mountains. The darkness that quickly surrounded the bird soon gave way to bright lights rising from the floors of the cave. The dove flew confidently through the shadows at great speed, darting through hundreds of these fountains of light, each releasing plumes of colourful gaseous energy. These strange structures illuminated a crumbling, ancient, forgotten city, resting in silence deep underground. A haunting groan breathed through the mountain's passageways a shuddering tremor rocked the very walls. The dove spotted an exit through the roof of the cave, nothing more but a pinprick of hopeful light upon a canvas of black. The little bird made for this target, tucked in its wings as it passed through only to open them up as it emerged outside, returning to the great outdoors.

As the bird soared gracefully over golden meadows, it spotted a thick smog beating out into the sky. Hundreds of abandoned siege engines, the shapes of fallen men in armour littered these pure lands attracting savage scavengers. Swamp mist and charred smoke birthed noxious fumes, fumes which stung the senses of the living. A once magnificent human city of Equis lay shrouded in black cloud having been reduced to a fragile, skeletal frame. Destroyed with fists made of stone and by breathes of incinerating fires, the city was dead! Falling into ruin before the eyes of the bird, the structures breaking into thousands of pieces. The dove plummeted to the ground and carefully perched itself upon one of many decorative banners, a banner of the red serpent, its black cloth swaying to the side against the poisonous wind. The bird rest at its destination, having wanted to see the carnage for itself, fixing its dark eyes upon the wreckage.

Footsteps approached from behind, the dove caught sight of a lonely man wandering through the mist in charred silver armour. When the two made eye contact, the black dove flew away, off the banner with urgency, catching an updraft of air using it to prolong its flight elsewhere.

<u>Chapter 1 - And So It Ends</u>

Present Day. Year 1512. Amid the death and destruction, survivors rise from the ashes of a ruined city.

A slow mist invaded the charred plains of faded grass, floating ponderously over the surface of the land. The air was moist, the light from the sun masked behind thin streaks of cloud. The old day was dying, the golden sun sinking below the horizon. Gusts of soft wind blew a faint, stale smell through the breeze, teasing the multitude of ragged banners stuck haphazardly into the ground. All over the field, they stood, bearing strange symbols, the patterns of various clans, tribes, and armies. Arrows pierced the floor and dead alike. The gleam of bloody metal lit up the plain riddled the armour, weaponry, and all manner of tools dropped beside the bodies of their fallen owners, doomed to grimace eternally with their twisted expressions of pain and misery. Time passed ever so slowly; clouds rolled by, occasionally exposing sunshine, lighting up the land with orange rays. Menacing structures crudely fashioned from wood and metal lay dormant in the mist, still damp from the last rainfall. These large, complicated machines were still arranged in formation, all facing the same direction. Their arms were long and thin, with what resembled a gigantic ladle affixed on the end. The devices were mounted upon large carts that had partially sunk into the grassy earth, treading deep tracks behind them for miles. Nothing was whole. Some of these catapults had been smashed completely by heavy chunks of stone, while others had collapsed inwards, rendered useless even as their operators still lived. Some had been charred, having been set alight over the course of the previous days. Shrill cries and shrieks whistled through the air; scavengers stealing the flesh from the dead. Greasy feathered vultures gathered over dead steeds. The sharp-beaked pillage's squabbled over the contents of soft underbellies, peeling off the hairy skin, digging into the nourishing innards. They played with the stringy pieces of meat and tendon within, until they had stripped it bare, exposing parts of the hard skeleton.

Before the mist ravenous swarms of flies and midges attacked the fallen, crawling over faces, emerging from eyes and ears, finding their way into every crevice of their unmoving prey. They came in countless numbers for an easy meal, and to lay their eggs for future generations. When disturbed they flew away in an angry cloud, filling the air with their aggressive buzzing.

Across the plain, a more dignified movement could be witnessed. The participants wore long, dark brown, crusty cloaks, draped over their shoulders, so long that they stroked the ground as they moved, attracting mud, sweat and blood alike. With the hoods concealing their faces, these cloaked figures traipsed awkwardly over the obstacles of bodies and the debris of war machines, carefully checking the faces of the dead. They worked carefully but efficiently. On rare occasions, a shout would echo across the field and others would come running to the aid of the wounded, to carry them to the nearest healing tent before continuing the search for more survivors. The calls and whimpers of grieving women and children rang out; here and there a ruined family knelt beside a crumpled suit of armour, clutching their hand and holding the lifeless head, whimpering and talking into the limp, empty vessel. Faint prayers were whispered by a wandering priest clothed in a worn, white robe. He walked by, sometimes losing his footing, treading on a lost arm or leg. Those who wandered, searching for life, looked upon the corpses; some lay horribly disfigured, mangled beyond belief. A man in silver armour tarnished with dirt approached out of the fog between the long lines of heavy large catapults.

Any conversation between the survivors was bland and repetitive. Those who had survived the siege were exhausted and yet unable to rest, agonisingly tormented by the events of the previous days, constantly pestered by the broken families in search of those dear to them. Desperate people would run up to them and cling on, tugging and pulling on their armour aggressively, shaking and yelling out questions about their brothers, uncles, sons, husbands, and fathers. As irritating as it became the surviving soldiers tried their best to help. Deep down they knew they could not replace what had been taken; deep down they knew they were powerless. Many desired in these moments to simply disappear. They would step back and remain silent, trying to find peace in their minds. Suddenly the

cries of a tied up white horse fitted with a decorative blue saddle -
bearing the symbol of a high-ranking guild of knights - awoke and
startled the nearby wounded. More dying men were being carted into
the makeshift tents every minute. Space was limited; the beds had
long since been filled, blankets were running low and many of the
worst cases had to be abandoned in favour of those with some hope.
Squashed up close in the cloying humidity, the men were shrouded
in the stench of sweat and worse. Under these white shelters, screams
of blistering pain could be heard as the surgeons in their gore-coated
leather aprons tended to the dying, attempting to prolong lives in
vain. There was little that could be done for most; resources were
limited, and for the majority, it was a choice of heavy stitching,
amputation or a quick, clean and painless death performed with a
small chisel and mallet to the back of the head. The terminal cases
rested on grubby blankets stained with grit and grime, their gaping
wounds festering with flies and dirt. Ants also took advantage of the
fallen, carrying tiny pieces of flesh to their underground nests. Few
men cared for life having suffered and resolved to ignore the pain,
giving up the struggle to stay alive, too ill, too devastated to even
notice when their injuries became infected.

Overlooking the horrific chaos, the smoking remains of a once-
mighty city cast its shadow over the battlefield. Its massive metal
gate, tinted with silver, its doors carved into beautiful
representations of the old world, had been smashed in. One of these
massive slates of metal, hung off its great hinges, whilst the other
lay to the side having detached completely. The city's proud smooth
wall had too suffered greatly, looking as though it had been
pummelled repeatedly by small fists of fire and stone. Hulking
chunks of rocks and rubble were piled at the foot of the wall, along
with wooden ladders bound by rope, sturdy enough to hold dozens
of men at a time, some lay in pieces, shattered and splintered among
the debris. Two mighty siege towers loomed high above the layer of
mist, reaching even beyond the wall's highest walkway. Only two of
many had survived the assault, but in the end, that was all that had
been required to capture the fortification. Misshapen bodies lay
buried beneath boulders, distorted limbs poking out of the mounds
of debris. Arms hung out from between rocks, bearing witness to
futile attempts to break free from their concrete prisons. The cloaked
men scoured this wreckage, gently feeling the limbs of those soldiers

who had tried to escape. Some went about with shovels, scraping away the thick dust in the hopes of finding a survivor. Others wheeled around light equipment, providing workers with tools and flasks of spring water. Instead of pulling out survivors, they dragged and carried away broken bodies. The wide path atop the wall was obstructed by yet more corpses, put to rest by the blade and arrows. A few groggy survivors wandered the long stretch of pathway, while others sat drinking wine or water out of leather flasks, whatever they could get their hands on in this dire time. Out to the horizon, they gazed, thankful to be alive but full of sorrow and loss with what had been witnessed. They had survived the terrible ordeal and would never live life in the same manner again.

Cylindrical towers enveloped in mist, came into view with a drawn-out gust from the belly of the sky kingdom. Entire streets and districts of the great city lay fractured under the hammer of war. Ash rained heavily in some more densely populated areas, dissolving amongst the wreckage. The buildings crafted with holy intent had sustained heavy damage; rooftops had been whipped clean off, walls had given way to the forced elements. The cracks and crevices in the streets were full, running red, saturating into possessions thrown out into the road. The smell of burning wood and cloth stung the noses of the survivors, assaulting their senses, making them wrap scarves around their faces. Distraught citizens staggered through the destruction, while others gathered around unattended wildfires, burning freely. Like a hungry animal, they ate away at homes and turned stone black. No man, woman or child had the strength or will in them to put out the blazes; it wouldn't be long before they would die, rain would soon come the thunder foretold, and the people would have the cold to do battle with when night arrived on the pass of the day. They made use of the heat that tore through their city and the light, as long as it would last. Already some were preparing for nightfall, claiming whatever shelter they could find. Fights frequently broke out, no longer was there any sense of law and order, the people of the ruined city were quickly resorting to primitive habits, obeying basic instincts. Desperate and homeless, the citizens of this once-proud stronghold were forced to sleep amidst the glowing embers, rising and falling with their history echoing; What to do next? That was the question a conscious few were discussing.

Someone would have to lead them someone would have to save them!

The brown cloaks worked on and on, spreading themselves along the plain, searching through the sea of corpses, stumbling upon both enemy and friend. One stopped what he was doing and pulled back his hood in total disbelief; he had seen someone, a man widely reported to have been killed who now walked by unscathed. No sword, spear or arrow had touched this man, only the bite of weariness had found its way through his defences. As the figure made his presence known, he could sense their stalking eyes. He came into view of the city, behind him the cloaked men had stopped work, were talking quietly to one another, catering to new feelings toward the unwelcome guest. Unable to catch what they were saying, he turned back and stared in grim silence. With this they quickly got back to work, sifting through the dead. This lonely man moved slowly around the fallen, staring into their lifeless eyes and pale faces. As he paced, his gaze caught a glimpse of someone familiar. He hurried over to the fallen person, who lay slashed and bloody on the ground. He knelt by the corpse for a time, lost for words, taken by grief. Fighting back the flood of tears threatening to overwhelm his heavy eyes, the pain of loss drained him, almost too great for him to bear. Finally, he rested his hand on the shoulder of his fallen friend, picked himself up and continued toward the city. As the figure passed by in his blood-spattered armour, a cluster of survivors cleared a path. Moving through a wide grey column, the armoured man finally witnessed the true carnage and saw his beloved home all but destroyed. Before returning he had prepared himself for a sight like this, yet still, he found himself shocked and breathless by what he saw; nothing could have adequately prepared him for the carnage. His body language, however, betrayed no sign of reaction, though the man was tearing to pieces on the inside. Unwilling to move on, yet compelled to do so, he observed the ruins. *This place has no future*, he thought. It was nothing but a pile of burnt-out rubble. In his right hand, he held a shining sword with a broad hilt and a long metal handle wrapped in a soft, light blue fabric. The blade was coated with a thin crust of dry blood. His armour tried desperately to show itself off under the layer of mud and dirt. He stepped up onto a heap of rubble that slid gently under his feet; standing silently, he heard someone approach. From the corner of his eye, he saw one of his soldiers, a man without armour, his undergarments stained with dirt. He approached the foot of the rubble, hoping to be noticed by the one who held the gleaming, silver sword. Speaking with a stern look, he called up to the man:

"Lethaniel, Sir?" The one addressed as Lethaniel, watched a trail of thick smoke rise into the sky and into the distance. He answered, speaking quietly:

"I always knew it would come to this…" His head sank as he made his way down the charred pile. "It was only a matter of time." The man in the cloth followed his face.

"Sir… What now?" Lethaniel gazed out once more towards the wrecked city, turning his head and ignoring the question.

"There's nothing left. The city is destroyed. We lost."

Turning around completely, Lethaniel distanced himself from the man. People stared at him as he went by. One man saw him and hastily got up before pointing and snarling.

"You could have prevented this. It is your fault. YOU HEAR ME?! YOUR FAULT!" Attempting to gain support from amongst the scattered crowds, his shouting made others turn their heads to see what was occurring. A middle-aged man of average build with a round, red graze over his eyebrow, heard the commotion and hurried over to Lethaniel, staring into the eyes of his abuser as he shook him by the collar.

"Back!" the older man snapped and firmly pushed away the heckler, pulling Lethaniel away, clearly having taken the remark to his heart. He was taken away by his friend, who said not a word, his face as damp and dirty as his green shirt. His short, brown hair was sodden, spiking up in places. "You're still alive…" he stuttered, "We all thought you weren't coming back."

"They are dead, Jerhdia." A moment of sadness gripped the pair.

13

"What happened to them?" Lethaniel could find no words; what had happened, had happened, and there was no changing it now.

"Does it matter? I could not stop them. They have destroyed us," he replied, his tone, bereft of all hope.

"Along with thousands of others, and the great city itself. There was nothing you could have done here. All this death, all that has happened since we set out, we were fighting the impossible, though we did not know it," Jerhdia comforted, putting his hand on his friend's shoulder, stopping him in his tracks.

"If only we had realised that sooner, but it is too late now. Everyone is gone, including countless innocents, all because of me. If I…"

"Don't think like that! You are still alive, aren't you? None of this was your fault."

"We're all that remains by the looks of it," observed Lethaniel with a dry throat.

"Not everyone is gone," replied Jerhdia, getting ahead, glancing at the floor and observing his surroundings.

"I don't think many see things the the way you do, my friend," Lethaniel replied softly, looking out again upon the tableau of death. With that, they found themselves at The Main Gate. "Did Letty and Kathina get out in time? Tell me they did."

"Yeah, Letty got out. As for the rest, well…" The man shook his head, biting his bottom lip in anger. Lethaniel remaining quiet, lifting the hand that gripped the blue sword hilt, staring at the golden ring on his finger, a red-crested jewel set in its centre. "What happened to your arm?" asked Jerhdia. For the time being, no answer was forthcoming.

Both men stood by the broken gate, walking in small circles and pondering what to do next. Jerhdia handed Lethaniel his flask of water.

"They will be moving steadily now, to the northwest, we'll find them without their siege weapons. They will cross the border under a fortnight. We cannot depend on our strength to defeat them. We are faced with a choice: either we fight with a flawless tactic in mind and hope that we pull through, or we... We lose, accept defeat and surrender to their control for as long as we live."

"If we surrender, we forfeit our lives," Lethaniel groaned. Under the dull light, he dangled his sword to the floor, tapping its sharp tip on the ground, thinking.

"They left the dead this time. Why?" Lethaniel mused.

"I think they want to finish what they started. It matters not...And we have no idea if we are still defensible at Korthak Bridge. The weight of their entire army will be bearing down on those few stationed there. We put up a fight here but let us be realistic; we only made a dent in their ranks." As Lethaniel's expression turned from vulnerable to thoughtful, he raised his head suddenly, staring at something in the distance. His eyes fixed upon a shadow in the mist. He steadily returned to the plain outside the city, coming to the long line of black assault catapults, where the enemy had once stood. Slowly, he approached one of the machines and touched it. He moved around to the rear of the device, studying it with his eyes. Backing off, he looked from left to right, counting how many he could see; the mist had begun to irk him. Not too far away, about two hundred yards at the most, he spotted something else. Larger and more complex trebuchets in their hundreds, sitting derelict at the far end of the battlefield. Mightier and far more destructive than the ruined trebuchets within the city limits, these models could be moved great distances with little effort. Eager to investigate the abandoned machines, Lethaniel's mind was drenched with ideas and possibilities. His attention was drawn to the fluttering of wings; a bird, a black dove perching on top of an enemy banner, a red serpent woven through black fabric, symbol of The Salarthian Clan of Jureai. The strange, ethereal black dove went about its business until it spotted Lethaniel, observing the bird as old thoughts returned to him; images of friends long gone, past times entering his mind as though he was telepathically recounting his story to this dove, looking at him as if it knew him. He tried to make sense of the past, tried to understand some things that failed to conclude. Squinting his eyes and rubbing his forehead, he thought harder, dug deeper and rummaged further. A headache was setting in, though it was not the only thing washing through his consciousness. Could it be hope?

Lethaniel sheathed his longsword, the scrape of metal startling the dove. It took off in haste. He knew now what must be done, knew what to do, to end it all at last!

Chapter 2 - Paying Respects

Sometime earlier, in a world called Equis.
Year 1511. Early spring.

"Elaso fiin Isabelle, elaso fiin an ute fiin tressa"

"Isabelle, it is time? The crowds have gone and it's late" a voice said. The long strands of colourful beads fell back in the doorway. Within the small room, an assortment of curved bookcases and stylish furniture was artfully arranged. Books filled the shelves; some in order, some left open at a specific page. Atop a single desk sat flickering candles, providing a warm glow. Some had worn down to their wicks, their meagre flames struggling to stay alive. Crisp, old papers filled with neat, black handwriting lay on the desk, mixed in with brown scrolls, unrolled and draped over the edges of the table. Large maps in dark wooden frames rest on the floor. Smaller parchments outlined certain areas of the world in greater scale, though some of the regions were all but unknown to humanity. Twelve small models stood in a glass case fixed on the wall, black marbles statues depicting creatures not of Equis. Sculptures of divine beings were located on three shelves, one above the other. A bronze key hooked into the door of the cabinet fell out of its home and hit the stone floor. Standing up from an unmade, fluffy bed, a woman walked over to the cabinet, knelt, and picked it up with a sigh of frustration. Isabelle pushed it back into its slot firmly and clicked it into place. She made her way back to the warm bed and sat down, continuing her reading. As the young woman stared deeply into the pages, her hand made her way to her forehead and rubbed impatiently. She dropped the book flat onto a side table, straightened her back and stretched her neck, letting her long blonde hair fall in exquisite curls. Looking up at the plain-beamed ceiling, she released a sigh of breath from her thin, dry lips. Relaxing back into position, she peered inside the glass cabinet containing the statues. They stared back at her. She got up and walked over to the cabinet, glancing at the twelve sculptures, one by one. Without warning, she found herself interrupted by a voice, causing her to close her eyes, slowly. "Isabelle, please, you must come." The blonde girl turned around and looked at her unwanted visitor, shielding her true feelings with a sweet smile and a nod, she made her way to a tall, wooden wardrobe. In its centre was a circular mirror, through which she now observed her reflexion. Hanging from around her neck, glinting in the candlelight was her golden locket she carried with her everywhere she went. Its contents were most precious to her. She tucked the locket into her blouse, pulled out a robe at random while gazing into the mirror, noticing her pale skin, wishing she had the time to bathe in the sun like most women her age. Unfortunately, she could not spare much time to work on her appearance. Losing herself in the mirror for a moment, she touched her cheek with the outside of her fingers. It felt cold and lifeless, her nails brittle and uncomfortable. Finally, she drew away and began to dress.

    Isabelle emerged from her hut. The day was already half gone; the wind had picked up, curling back her hair. A priest wearing a robe of black and white came to her and handed Isabelle her dark blue long coat. Taking it, she slid it on as she walked passed the crowd of people, shrugging off any offers of help. She was puzzled by the sight of the saluting Glyph Wielders, who would also be escorting her today, but she threw her hood over her head regardless and continued down the narrow path. As the group left the decorated huts, they walked through the countryside on a dusty, light brown track. The day was chilly, a fresh wind blowing softly, making the trees sing and shuffle. Small birds danced around the road, quickly flying off as the party approached. As they walked, the group passed an array of beautiful structures. Majestic buildings with dark emerald green and violet windows that arched out from the sides of the cathedrals. Skilfully crafted, smooth rock ran through the stone of every temple they passed, every door was wide and tall, every window ledge and rooftop uniquely made; however each cathedral had one thing in common; a frontal tower that grew out over the door, stretching high, tapering to a sharp point. Frequently the doors of Cathedral Alley, as it was known, would clank and creak open. Holy men would appear clutching shiny, mesmerising relics; these were the servants of the temples under the employ of The Priest who owned the cathedral, some of the holiest men in the world. They bowed as she passed by and priests recited a prayer from a book, loud enough that only Isabelle could hear it. People saluted, flooding the pathway; some drew a little too near making her guards enforce a protective circle around her. To keep her safe.

"Hail, the Conductor is here," someone cried. She focused on the road, trying hard to block out the calls and pleas of the onlookers. People rushed out of the buildings, crying out for The Star Caller. More and more joined the group as they passed by simple homes, flowers of every colour were thrown over the circle of Glyph Wielders and priests. One made its way directly in front of Isabelle, immediately drawing her attention, it was a blood red rose. Approaching it, she swiftly picked it up and held on to the stem tightly. Across the shiny meadows and woodland areas, the large band of people followed Isabelle under trees and over small stone bridges spanning streams of gushing water. The path soon merged into a greater one, becoming a rocky road large enough for carts. The hills rolled over to reveal a small village. Isabelle looked up at the old, wooden signpost; it signified that this was the village of Penstrive. Small and built for convenience by the servants of the island, it was a grey place and quite lonesome.

The group made their way through the quiet community. Locals had noticed the visitors and were staring at Isabelle with envious eyes as she strolled passed. Women were washing priests' robes, while the men worked on a stone tower of another cathedral and the children carried water from a well. They all slowed and stared, though Isabelle ignored the whispers and looks that became unwanted. The village although small had many residents; it consisted mostly of buildings of work, storage sheds squeezed between average-sized households not leaving much room for places of leisure, but for a single inn that stood out. It had a large sign above the door, proclaiming its name: The Chanting Inn. Looking back, she could see that people had dropped whatever they were doing and were now following her group with haste, having to jog to catch up. She turned to a priest who rushed forward, eager to listen or carry out a command.

"I thought you said the crowds had left the island?" she asked.

"Sorry milady, these people must have come late, or they just wanted to see you." With that, the priest bowed and stepped back. Isabelle knew she should not show the smallest sign of weakness; these people had taken the time and effort to travel from afar just to get a glimpse of her! She felt honoured and guilty at the same time because she had no wonderful words for them, no new stories or gossip of the Gods. Putting on a heroic face, she walked down the path towards the group of people, organising themselves to split, giving her a pathway to the gates of the cemetery. Her priests and Glyph Wielders stayed behind her as she approached the gates. Suddenly, a stranger hurried to the front of the crowd, pushing passed the people, and stumbling forward in full view of everyone. Isabelle caught his eyes, wondering what he was doing. She then understood as he pulled open the gates for her, to which they squeaked horribly. He pulled them open enough for six people to pass through, then stood aside and bowed low with respect.

"I think they need some oil" suggested Isabelle giving a slight nod of acknowledgement and walked on through into the cemetery.

The people moved forward, eager to follow, but the powerful Glyph Wielders stood in their way. The wind picked up as she made her way up the steep hill. Gravestones set in the earth yearned for attention; she had perused the names of each one before, though some she could not read because they were too worn from the weather over the long years they had stood. The path wound its way toward the top of the hill where a large statue came into view. It depicted a woman dressed in long robes, clutching a magnificent staff pointing to the sky kingdom. Her hair was long, falling over her hips. Her eyes were hypnotising, her face beautiful, ethereal blessed with wisdom. It was rumoured that a woman with power, ruling over one of the five clans of Jureai, residing in the northlands, had been born of a Celestial, inheriting certain features that could bring any man to his knees. This statue had been placed on a large, square, concrete plinth decorated with trees and vines, twisting, and curling around its fine edges. This was someone who had made history, a woman with a name everyone had heard. Intricate patterns worked their way around a circular plate laced in silver and gold that read:

Here rests the soul of Regina Corah, the people's hope, the people's light, the people's saviour.
May her magnificent example continue to lead our kind until the very end of days.

Regina Corah
First Star Caller 0718 - 0768

Isabelle approached the statue towering over her and gazed up at her face and into those eyes set deep in thought. She walked over and brushed the dry leaves away from the foot of the plinth, all the time wondering what this ancient woman had been like in person? Stroking the foot of the statue she looked down at the rose she had collected earlier. She felt a sharp sting in her middle finger; a thorn had pierced her, yet she had failed to notice until now, drawing droplets of blood. The cry of a horse made her turn her head; she recognised the man riding toward her upon a great, black steed. He was accompanied by two others; both were equipped with heavy, distinctive armour and brandished great war hammers. Their banner was predominantly green and blue, with hints of yellow. This was the Norkron flag and the symbol of Krondathia, a marvellous pattern of a mauve jewel encased in plated scales. The scales wrapped around the holy gemstone, but not entirely leaving a gap. She knew who it was. Turning back to the statue and clearing her mind she placed the bloodied rose at the foot of her ancestor, kissed her two fingers and rested them lightly on the petals of the flower. She paid her respects to the life of the greatest woman to have ever walked the world of Equis, a true believer and her only inspiration. The wind blew hard, pulling back her hood to reveal her face liberating her long blonde hair. Questions entered her mind about why the rider upon the black stallion had come? She moved away, puzzled, and head back toward the vast crowd, still watching from the foot of the hill. The gates were opened for her, this time by two men, bowing respectfully just like before. Isabelle traversed the corridor of admirers and was about to return from where she had come when a Glyph Wielder called out to her. At the sound of her name, she looked at the Wielder, then at the man who had recently arrived on horseback before passing them both by. The newcomer followed, giving a gesture to her escorts. Isabelle was safe in the care of this armoured man from Krondathia. With a hint of satisfaction, she moved away with him once he had dismounted his companions staying among the priests and the people upon their horses.

It was cold, whipping through the pair as they walked away from the crowd at the cemetery. The man was tall, well over six feet, with broad shoulders, thick arms, and a stacked chest. Far larger than Isabelle was, he was a hardened soldier dressed in fine clothes. As they walked side by side in silence, the moment they fell out of sight behind the hill, she released a desperate breath and broke the silence with a complaint that had been boiling up inside. "I hate this. Since I returned, I have had NO rest. It feels so good to be alone. Sometimes I need solitude." The large man kept walking at her side, matching her pace; he appeared to be listening though his face was hard to read. "I don't understand. Why all the protection when there is no danger? I am now being guarded by the Glyph Wielders, some of whom I tutored with Glyph myself." Still, the man kept up, listening, keeping an eye on the road but not contributing to the talk. "I can't even walk to the cemetery by myself or pay my respects in peace. This island could not be safer." Her voice was getting thinner and her throat dryer struggling to find the proper words for how she felt, but instead only the moans of a young girl could be heard. "What am I supposed to do, to end this charge?" The man quickly glanced behind their position, then looked at her, letting out a sigh; he was still forming his own thoughts while she raved. "I can't do this anymore. I hate this!"

"That's twice now. Do not let anyone hear you say that, do you understand? You cannot show these people any weakness or frustration with what you have been given. Remember, you are imperative to the running of the country and the morale of our people," he reminded her.

"I know..." Isabelle responded feebly, "I'm just, confused, burnt out and really could have used the time to rest."

"It's alright; I won't take up much of your time, I want the same thing, when it comes it will come. Oh, and you were not charged with anything, dear, you were chosen, it's what's expected of you." The two continued steadily along the path, eventually coming to a watchtower, its triangular roof built on a wooden circular house, with four openings facing north, south, east and west. Isabelle swiftly got to the point.

"I believe you have some sort of message for me. That is the reason you came, so what must I know, Thao?" She paused to see to the tiny hole on her finger.

"It can wait," he replied, handing her a clean cloth designed for polishing armour. Isabelle laughed.

"Imrondel sends out its best Honour Guard, the greatest of them all, to deliver a message for me, The Star Caller, and you say it can wait?! It must be important, or they would not have sent you. What are the other two guards for? Protection?" She knew that was not the answer.

"Arthur and Scarto are two of my best Honour Guards, Isabelle; there is little we cannot accomplish together. No, my girl, I came because I wanted to travel here and deliver the message personally, I have not seen you for a while, besides, I got the message while stationed in Xiondel."

"Why? It's still a fair distance between us and Xiondel."

"There are people I need to see, some old friends in these parts who I have not seen for quite some time."

"Friends... I forgot you have friends in this world; all I have is the company of books and the teachings of this...Somewhat incomplete faith. You have no idea of the works we have in progress right now, learning of new things that the human mind can achieve, expeditions to the far east and northwest, all in search of the origins of Glyph. Oh, and figuring out where our own ancestors came from; we still do not know how we arrived on this planet. Can you believe that? It does get so very tiring."

"Has that cathedral been rebuilt yet? You know? The one that burned down to the ground all those years ago?" asked Thao, attempting to change the subject.

"No, it has not. Apparently, the priest who owned that temple ran out of assets; he says his wealth and everything he possessed was stolen, though of course no evidence was found in the rubble. The priest still owns the land, however, but does not yet possess the resources to rebuild," Isabelle replied, spotting the site over the hill in the distance, not putting much more thought into it.

"You never did find out who or what caused the fire, did you? Strange that. Someone must know something about it," commented Thao.

"I wouldn't know what to do if I met the arsonist face to face. Probably have a guard arrest him and lock him up, I imagine."

The Star Caller and Honour Guard walked at a steady pace, secretly enjoying one another's company amidst the peaceful scenery. Isabelle did most of the talking, posing questions about the world and its people. Thao had answers for almost everything she threw at him; he spoke only when spoken to, knowing that he could not get a word in even if he tried. Soon the pair slowed down, and Isabelle came to a halt while Thao kept going. He walked to the edge of the grassy hill and stood upon a mound, looking out in awe. Behind him, she folded her arms and smiled, not nearly as impressed by what he saw, though she respected his feelings and was happy for him. She understood that he had not seen the sight in a long time. Slowly she strolled up behind him and muttered:

"Incredible, isn't it?"

"I yearn for the day when I am permitted to enter. Tell me, what's it like inside?" Thao asked, staring out across the hillside.

"What do you think it's like inside?" she fired back, letting her arms drop down by her side, examining the hole in her finger.

"Wondrous, holy, special... A place of peace, no doubt, the home of our twelve Celestial Souls, somewhere of infinite knowledge," he gushed in marvel.

"Then that's what it's like," she answered. Thao gazed out towards the distant white road that cut through the green grass. Along both sides lay round, unlit, golden basins, dwarfed by smooth statues of important holy people, each sculpted with a different pose. Each figure clutched a long staff, all dressed in similar fashioned robes, long dresses, chest pieces and coats. Most significantly, ALL were female. These were The Star Callers of Krondathia, shieldmaidens of the faith, rulers, mothers of the country, possessors

24

of unique and astounding abilities. As the latest in the line, Isabelle would one day have her own statue along the path to the temple; one day she too would become part of Equis's history.

The white road ended at the foot of a set of steep, black steps narrowing as they neared the enormous triangular, temple door. The colossal Column Temple was a grant pillar that almost touched the roof of the sky kingdom, an immense tower of black rock melted with streams of molten gold. To perfect for any human hand to craft, one of the many wonders of Equis. Forbidden from public entry, only a select few could enter, Isabelle being one of them. The pillar appeared to consist of twelve blocks resting one on top of another, each with its own unique decoration and intricate pattern. This made the temple very distinctive and dynamic to examine from top to base. Over time the round blocks that made up the tower would move ever so slightly. As a result, the temple was said by some to be alive. Why this structure would twist and moved a fraction with each day that passed was but one mystery alongside dozens of others left to be understood.

Regina Corah the 1st
0718 - 0768
Ashleigh Hauckos the 2nd
0758 - 0782
Hackney Beau the 3rd
0775 - 0813
Anazerath Relarnd the 4th
0802 - 0864
River Lye the 5th
0852 - 0896
Coppelia Velen the 6th
0890 - 0908
Ursula Cerrin the 7th
0904 - 0949
Ebony Heart the 8th
0943 - 0996
Melisa Nightsky the 9th
0987 - 1038

Atira Unasia the 10th
1000 - 1028
Selphie Olopoly the 11th
1020 - 1061
Iris Senatre the 12th
1050 - 1111
Kiera Atalisa the 13th
1101 - 1156
Melony Vel the 14th
1142 - 1174
Scarlet Siatas the 15th
1169 - 1197
Liandra Liola the 16th
1188 - 1244
Stella Verl the 17th
1234 - 1280
Penelasio Floras the 18th
1270 - 1331
Angelica Helii the 19th
1324 - 1378
Lexi Enil the 20th
1370 - 1418
Thespany Kayla the 21st
1414 - 1452
Freya Delmesca the 22nd
1448 - 1492
Isabelle Verano the 23rd
1485 -

Thao and Isabelle made their way to the white road. The mighty Column Temple was straight ahead. She approached with no sign of awe or wonder; she knew almost everything there was to know about this place, about the statues of her predecessors, about the history and prophecies of the Celestials Souls who resided within. Thao, on the other hand, kept looking from the steps to the top of the tower, admiring all the different levels and layers of beauty.

"Has anyone ever been to the top?" he asked.

"No. But something must be up there."

"This is yours?" Isabelle turned to see Thao standing next to an empty plinth set into the side of the road.

"Yes, that is where mine shall go, one day," she confirmed, walking on. Her statue itself had not been fitted on the block yet; it was still in the early stages of construction. Engraved within the fine stone Thao took a closer look and read her name and birth date; the date of her death had obviously not been filled in.

Chapter 3 - The Temple

Can a commoner understand true selflessness? For a Star Caller, there is no attribute more vital.

Intrigued by the exquisitely crafted statues, Thao kept up with Isabelle's steady pace, the temple of magnificence growing even greater as they neared. Despite his enthusiasm, he was forced to stop directly at the foot of the stairs, which Isabelle made her way up in no hurry. Awaiting her arrival were three of her priests, who appeared different to the usual black and white-robed servants. These three seemed far more sanctified and wiser than the common man; the opulence of the fabrics and ornaments that hung off their backs was evidence enough that these were of special blood. Each wore similar outfits that differed only in colour and other subtleties, all according to status. One High Priest waited halfway up the stairs and greeted Isabelle with a smile and a small bow; he was wrapped in a heavy, red, layered cloak, his arms concealed by long sleeves, the graceful thick cloak touching his feet, though it showed no sign of damage or wear. Behind him another High Priest stepped forward, this one dressed in the same style of cloak, yet thinner and less extravagant. Its marine tones of blue and green matching his eyes. The third was dressed in a leaf-green cloak. His height was considerably less than the other two, but his width certainly made up for it. Thao recognised these three important men: the most celebrated and respected priests in Norkron lands. These three served The Eldor, the father of Krondathia, from their place within the great temple. They studied The Books of the Early Past and other significant relics, believing in nought but the ways of Starillia, their faith keeping them alive, blessing them with a sense of great purpose and meaning. Thinking about the ways of The Priests' Order, then wondering about his own responsibilities, Thao could relate. He respected their beliefs and passion for their chosen lifestyle, feeling that their morals and those of The Honour Guards were very much alike. Both lifestyles required loyalty and strict devotion. From what he witnessed now, they bowed gracefully, gladly made small talk with The Star Caller until Isabelle made her way up toward the entrance of The Column Temple. He managed to catch some of the words at the end of a sentence: "*...he is expecting you.*" The High Priest in the blue cloak spotted The Honour Man listening in, noticing he had the tip of his foot on the first step. Hurrying down the stairs in a panic, closely followed by the rotund priest, they put their hands-on Thao, pushing him away and asking him to leave. Their anxious voices stated that the temple had no need for one such as him. As they tried desperately to move him along, the red priest told his fellow believers to withdraw, explaining that the visitor meant no harm. This one clearly held superiority over his two companions. He approached and placed his cloaked arm around Thao's shoulder, explaining in detail the rules of The Column Temple, telling him about the boundaries to the common folk, and that even high-ranking individuals such as himself were at risk of disrupting the slumber of the spirits within. Neither offended nor embarrassed, Thao listened to the elderly man as they walked back along the white road together. They spoke of religion and business in the city of Xiondel, as though they had known each other for years. The High Priest knew how to talk; clearly, he was the eldest of the trio and had a lot more experience in diffusing such situations. They exchanged stories and news; the soldier had much to say about the great changes that Xiondel City was undergoing; notably to the central palace, as well as the assignments he had been charged with of late. The High Priest listened intently and politely, responding intelligently when his turn came.

The day was preparing for nightfall and the basins under each statue were being filled and tended to by the servants. Thao turned his head back toward the entrance of the great temple where Isabelle was standing, who faced the massive triangular door that stared down on The Star Caller. Huge black hinges had been set into the stone, holding the doors together like a root to the earth, the entrance featured a pair of weighted black round handles. The metal canvas had writings all over its steel sheet, gleaming in shiny ink, markings had been etched into it by an inhuman clever hand. To the ordinary eye, they would mean nothing; they were nothing but beautiful pictures and symbols, but to Isabelle and The Star Callers before her, it was a map of the sky, locations of the stars and planets. She pulled on the handles and opened the wide door. Moving inside, she slowly faded into the shifting shadows of The Column Temple.

Isabelle closed the doors behind her, pressing her entire weight into them, for they were rather heavy. She locked them shut and a loud thud echoed through the temple's chambers. Pulling back her blue hood, a long lock of golden hair fell over her forehead. From further ahead came the soft glow of flickering firelight. She walked through a cold, stone corridor, freshly lit torches were on either side, stopping as she came to the end of the corridor, where she found herself before a wide, open chamber. This was the ground floor of The Column Temple. It was dark, so she raised her hand, at which all the torches brightened and illuminated the temple in all its wondrous glory. Along the sides of the great round room stood a series of twelve arched doorways, leading to other areas of the temple. Now able to see properly, she wandered into the main chamber, with the echo of her heels stalking her steps. The dark-bronze stone-paved floor was decorated with fine, flowing artwork of the elements. The black marble walls had been perfectly crafted with strange and beautiful features. Profiles of gargoyles frozen in stone grew out from the sides, some apparently in the process of climbing the wall. Other majestic, mythical beasts scaled their way around the walls as though struggling to find a spot of their own. Each doorway led to the quarters of an individual Celestial Soul; each was decorated in its own unique style as if it had been designed, moulded, and crafted by the Gods themselves. Peculiar symbols were engraved around the arches, though they spoke their own language, which few humans could read and understand. Each portal was cleverly detailed and fashioned to match its own God and their favoured element. Outside each, sat stacks of rich offerings from everywhere around the known world of Equis: chests of gold, pots, and cases of colourful jewels. Artwork of all kinds, from paintings to tiny sculptures, littered their porches, cluttering up the entrance ways. Isabelle, having seen it all before, was unmoved by the priceless offerings. Located directly in the centre of the temple was a perfectly round glass floor, as smooth as a frozen pond. Underneath the thick surface hovered the curled-up shape of a divine wing, spiralling down into the murky depths. No man or woman had ever descended into the bowels of The Column Temple, so no one knew what lay below or even how to break the impenetrable glass. Too great to be that of a bird and too elegant to belong to a reptile, the wing boasted every colour of the rainbow, and had lain undisturbed ever since the discovery of this holy place. A little further on was a great wave, frozen in a shining, transparent crystal. This was known as The Zephros Pedestal, the name coming from a widely forgotten period history, which described Zephros as a living rock that reacted with certain types of Glyph magic. Some believed that an entire city made of Zephros existed, The Crystal City. A place where knowledge and memory had once gathered, an archive of history stored in crystallised networks far out at sea. This was, of course, an old story, a myth told by men, women, and children when the world was far younger and its inhabitants less cynical. The pedestal was very tall, reaching far above the tips of the arched doorways lining the sides of the temple. It grew up like a water spring bursting from the ground within the temple, albeit one that had frozen over, trickling down to form sharp-pointed icicles. The sole purpose of this object was simple: The Star Caller simply had to insert a Calling Orb of one of the Celestials into its central groove. Once the Calling Orb was in place, this would ease the transition for the Celestial to cross over to the mortal plain. The Star Caller would then perform a ritual, depending on which Celestial she wished to call, for they all were different, and all had different luring requirements. Aries, for example, would necessitate the performance of a certain dance, while Cancer would require her to sing him his favoured tune. Celestials could, however, be called upon without the use of a Calling Orb. The Star Caller would have to expend three times as much power, but eventually, the soul would hear and gather its energy to rise wherever The Star Caller was at that time.

Several grooves had been etched into the stone floor beneath the pedestal. These indentations served no apparent purpose and were simple decoration to those of holy ilk. The Column Temple was a lair of mystery and riddles, its main chamber littered with a multitude of tiny details still unknown to the Norkron people. Isabelle approached a set of steps centred between the twelve arched doorways, dividing them equally, six to each side. Two lit basins stood at the foot of the stairs, which led up to a square doorway, the entrance permanently enclosed by a dark curtain. These were the quarters that belonged to a man; the one Isabelle had been asked to see. She stood awaiting a welcome, but it never came. She stood formally, like a soldier would, ready to salute his Commander.

"What troubles you, my dear?" A wise, yet weak voice hymned out from the dark room atop the stairs. Aware that the hidden speaker could sense her torment and sadness from his room, she responded in a normally, before bowing in respect.

"I know not of trouble, Sire. Starillia has been good to me. I have been blessed. I need not complain, Sire." Despite her own recognition that the answer was dishonest, it mattered not, for she knew that the one shrouded in darkness lacked any great power of the kind she possessed; only an attuned human power, of no real match for hers. She could see nothing of the man but knew that he was looking down on her from the darkness and could see right through her.

"Please, as you were, my child. I know your will is set, and your loyalty is admirable." Isabelle relaxed her form, though she realised with embarrassment she had nothing to say in response to this praise. A moment passed and a thought crept into her mind; she sensed an atmosphere of unease looming in the shadows, ready to catch her off guard. Still, she stayed quiet. "Put your mind at rest and let us talk of business. How was your journey?" Finding herself slightly relieved at the easy question, she replied:

"Long, but that was anticipated." Evidently, the unseen interlocutor could sense that she was holding her tongue.

"Speak free, young one; what is on your mind?" Reluctantly she jumped to a matter of great importance, yet upon opening her mouth she immediately knew that she could have waited for a later date. She simply could not hold in her concerns any longer.

"Sire, Davune has changed, drastically since my last visit five years ago. I was unaware that things could develop so extensively in that time. It is far greater and, dare I say, more advanced than our own civilisation. Not that I desperately wish for things to change here, but we do not seem to be making any significant steps toward enriching the lives of our people. Unlike the Dovidians, who care deeply for the comfort and lifestyle of their populace. It troubles me deeply, Sire, that I live comfortably while there are places where Norkron men and women struggle to find clean drinking water and food for their families. I want to help those more unfortunate than I." She knew her questions would be answered in time, and she eagerly awaited a response. All she received, for the time being, was the disappointment, born of deathly silence and the uneasy feeling that accompanied it. Now growing impatient, Isabelle threw out another remark: "Sire, I think that we should stop wasting our manpower on remote research in the east and Starillia, and focus instead on what we have here, especially in Xiondel City. Before you ask, Sire, the performance went well, very well in fact, but I feel like something is happening in the country of Ivulien... With its authority." Another short pause followed before she flung out another concern of hers; this was getting out of line and she knew it. "Change has also occurred in their council; a new member who I was unaware of until I arrived there. He was present at my performance and demonstration; he also sat with me while I ate with Desa and The Dovidian Leaders. He made me feel...Uncomfortable. He did not look like a politician or a man of leadership, more like a mercenary of some sort, but he was far too young for that kind of work. I don't know more of the matter, Sire, but I thought you should hear it." She felt like she had gone too far and forced herself still. The frail voice soaked up the silence and answered:

"Loyal you are my, child, my Conductor. Your courage and power are admirable, but you speak not the truth to me. I forgive you. Your abilities stretch far beyond those of anyone else; you are divine in many ways, able to give voice to your soul and show a strength that only you possess. Every Star Caller before you have given themselves to Starillia, and in time so must you. The statues outside are there to remind us of their great talents and deeds. All are missed, but will forever be remembered as perfect saints, holy maidens, childless mothers to the civilised world who maintained faith and belief in Equis. They strived for something we so desperately long for. I need not tell you what it is we ALL strive for. One day that world of perfection will come, Isabelle, whether it be on your watch or that of another, it will come, somehow." She listened on as the voice grew a little louder the next time it spoke. "You ARE complaining, my dear, and do not deny that you are not troubled. Clearly, you must see that your words do not reflect contentment or peace of mind. You are distant from Starillia, the faith that has been so good to you, that has given you a life of honour and beauty. Tell me, Isabelle, daughter of Zellah, what is it that troubles you besides the well-being of our people?" Her voice shaking as if wounded by the words he spoke, she replied:

"Do you not know that? You seem to know me quite well, Sire."
A shuffling noise alerted her ears as soft footsteps emerged from the
darkness. Slowly, a shape emerged; it stood on the threshold of light
and dark, its face thinly veiled in shadow. Isabelle could make out
the fine, cream cloak lined with gold. He stood at the top of the stairs
in silence. Even without seeing, she knew that he stared into her
green eyes, feeling again that horrible sense of dread.

"Have you seen anything, my child? Has an ill Vision struck
you with grief or sadness?" The voice spoke with sympathy toward
the girl, in a manner that invited a kind reply. Isabelle bowed once
again and quickly apologised.

"I will not speak to you in that manner again." She relaxed and
directed her body to fully face him once more. "To answer your
question: no. I have not had a Vision for some time. I think the
absence of this blessing has led me to jump to conclusions about my
faith, Sire." A figure emerged from the darkness with a sigh and a
smile. An old man with round, deep eyes, thin, white hair and an
innocent face, his frame not much bigger than that of The Star Caller,
began to descend the steps. As he reached the bottom, Isabelle
backed up giving him some room to move, though he ignored this
acknowledgement and shook his head from side to side.

"It is not the city of Davune that worries you; it's not that
council member either. This land has always been a mix of wealthy
and poor, it is a problem which will be dealt with in time once our
other priorities are managed. Understand that when you gain as
much power and grace as you have, my child, the faith of Starillia
never leaves you. You know this. You have been taught well;
however, I wish Freya were here, we could use her help right now.
Star Caller to Star Caller, apprentice to master." She felt scared that
he knew so much of her ignorant feelings and held her breath, trying
hard not to allow the smallest sign of change in her body language.
"No, I do not know what you feel; it is rude to look into one such as
yourself and it's not my place, it's not anyone's place in fact. I can
trust you, we can all trust and put our faith in you, that's why you
are who you are." *The worst is over*, Isabelle thought to herself. His
next words put the fear back into her mind immediately: "But can
you trust me?" he demanded with a look of intense seriousness.
"Isabelle, we are one. We are one: us, Starillia, the might of the great

34

Celestials. We govern this great land and we must protect it should the need arise. If one fails, so do the rest, which is why it is important for us to share our secrets, to forget the embarrassment if there is any and to open your mind to me." Isabelle's eyes shifted passed his to the doorway above the stairs from whence he had come; she could sense another presence, the slightest hint of a Glyph scent. "We are necessary, my child; be at rest. Davune has grown, but then so have WE; you just have not seen the progress we have made recently. Already Xiondel is making massive changes to its palace. Imrondel is working on employing new forces, looking to raise a flying force so that we may rule the skies as well as the earth. We are taming the dragora, and soon this dream of flight will be a reality to us, and the high places of Equis will be able to share with us their stories. Who knows what we will find on the roof of the world? We also wish to someday mobilise a gantuuar unit; for construction purposes, but in time we will train them for other uses. Despite our differences and beliefs, the Dovidians are our allies, and to suggest otherwise would be foolish. I realise that it is natural to compare our prowess to theirs; in fact, I have done so myself on occasion and drawn a smile afterwards, but we have nothing to fear from them, for we have Glyph. We have you." He backed up and strolled passed Isabelle, walking away towards the centre of the circular room, where he stepped from the stone paved floor and onto the glass that caged the strange divine wing below. The old man soon reached the crystal pedestal that rose out of the floor, weaving around itself up into a spiked wave.

"Come," he ordered. She followed and found him staring up at the frozen pedestal. Yet again she was lost for words and waited for him to make the next move. "As leaders of this country, you and I have many duties to attend to. We give up our luxuries, along with our privacy, so that the rest may live in assured peace. You are the twenty-third Star Caller…You are just as important as all those who have come before you, you are a significant part of our way of life, and it is my job to look after you, until the very end." Stung once more at being reminded of her responsibilities, her chest ached mildly, though she tried desperately not to let it show. Holding on to some strength, she protested:

"I do, Sire. I understand." The elderly man approached her slowly, having just remembered something of significance. Isabelle took a step back and raised her head, looking at him strangely.

"The High Priests outside informed me that messengers had arrived earlier. Thao himself has come bearing a message. This would not be the first time he has met you, that your paths have crossed before, is this so?"

"This is true, Sire," she admitted, wondering what was behind the invasively sincere look he had on his face. Once again, his expression demanded a quick response.

"Tell me, what did The Honour Guard want with you?" She answered honestly:

"They haven't told me yet, Sire. I will deal with whatever issue has arisen and inform you once it is done."

"Integrity I see in you, it is in your eyes, eyes your mother gave you, a gift she granted you at birth greater than the Glyph power you are blessed with now. Make her proud. I know you will not let me down. It's just a shame about your father's disappearance," he murmured, placing his hand on her cheek gently.

"I wouldn't know anything about that, Sire," she confessed.

"He would have been a great man, I wonder what gifts he passed to you...You may return to your quarters, Isabelle, and remember, our country is nothing without the brilliant minds that have come before. By history's teachings, we can learn more of the present and learn of what is to come." Bowing low, she made a hasty retreat towards the double doors, her long fine coat trailing behind her steps. "Lady Verano, before you go, I must ask. Have you found one who is capable?" Isabelle turned around. "Have you named a successor, Isabelle?" She thought about the question, momentarily confused by its meaning. It seemed too soon for her to be naming or even looking for an apprentice.

"Pardon, Sire, I have not...I am only twenty-six, isn't that a little early to begin my search?" she replied politely.

"Yes, you are still very young, but keep in mind that Coppelia the sixth was just a teenager when she named her successor."

"I'll keep my eyes open, Sire" she conceded, opening one of the doors, letting in the fading light and swiftly exiting the temple. The Eldor watched her every move with a concerned look on his face. When the echo of the door finally silenced, he glared at the fallen curtain that concealed the doorway to his quarters at the top of the stairs. Someone small and noticeably young hovered behind the fabric, staring down at him.

Back outside in the fresh air, a red sun hovering upon the horizon, Isabelle trotted down the stairs and began back toward the path where Thao patiently awaited her. She stood in front of him as he asked quite eagerly and excitedly:

"How fares The Eldor? How is our Sire?" She gave him a cold look and did not respond, folding her arms. Finally, with a sigh, Thao told her what he had come to say. "I came to tell you, on behalf of the Norkron Court of Imrondel City and by the request of The High Council of Xiondel City, you are to attend a meeting in the capital. It seems that the Dovidians are asking too many questions. We want you to help decide on a plan of action. I think you will be sent on our Sire's behalf." He spoke with an important tone as he handed Isabelle a thick envelope. This was obviously an assignment letter detailing an important task. "Will you be there?" he asked, holding the letter out with one hand. She sighed quietly, taking the letter, feeling its weight. She replied:

"Like I have a choice. When do we leave?" Thao's companions came galloping toward them both, holding the reigns of his mighty black horse. The big man smiled as he mounted his steed.

"The day after next. It has been good seeing you, Isabelle." With that he sped off along the white path, followed closely by Arthur and Scarto, his two favoured Honour Guards. The horse let out a cry, and soon Thao had disappeared into the evening. The basins before the statues slowly came to life, as two servants lit them methodically. Ambers arose as they burned away, the warm yellow glow magnified the statues and lit up the path. Isabelle walked the road once again, joined by marching Glyph Wielders, who escorted her all the way back to her encampment.

Chapter 4 - Rules Are Made to Be Bent

Like wild animals, humans should not be controlled or imprisoned. No matter how much discipline you force upon them, they will still break free of their bonds.

The room was warm and soft; fresh candles and lanterns flared, casting shadows. Outside, the wind whistled, and Isabelle could hear it. The wind flow distracted her from her studies. She was alone, accompanied only by her thoughts. Pushing away the beads and folding back a woven wooden door, she peeked outside. From within a hut not too far away from her own, perched upon a slope of grass, glowed a flickering candlelight. The faint conversation of her priests fluttered over. Uninterested and in no mood to listen in as she sometimes did, she noticed movement directly in front of her; two Glyph Wielders were on patrol, half staffs sheathed at their sides. They were dressed in their typical uniforms of finely cut robes coloured with many hues of white and cream, tied and held down with golden flaps of armoured fins. Slipping back into her room, clothed only in a few loose layers, Isabelle pulled another book from the shelf and placed it on top of a larger tome before sitting down, preparing to continue her reading. Turning over a page, she spotted the sealed envelope that Thao had handed her earlier, on her desk. She thought to herself that she really should open and read it; so far, she had stopped herself from doing so because she wanted to remain in blissful ignorance. Inside might be other assignments and responsibilities, duties that could take months to complete. Unlikely though it seemed, it could, of course, be good news of some kind. She had never liked opening letters for the negativity they could cast upon a day she had been enjoying. She picked it up, flipped it over after reading the front, then threw it to the floor. Frustrated at the thought of more long nights of travelling, being escorted, protected, and catered to around the clock. She continued a passage from her book, to change her train of thought. The cabinet key dropped to the floor once again; Isabelle heard the metal clang but did not move to place it back in the hole. Tiredness was slowly setting in; she could feel her vision blurring and her eyelids blinking for long periods of time.

Time stood still. The candlelight clouded over after every blink she took, the warmth holding and swaying her gently. Isabelle gave up herself to the weariness and tiredness that tugged at her eyelids, escaping from the real world where blackness crept through her mind. Was this a dream? She could not be sure. Looking in circles and walking with an echo behind her as if stepping upon hollow stone, she moved into the nothingness that went on to nowhere. Lost in the emptiness of space, there was no ground, just more and more blackness; she walked upon the air before suddenly she feeling a tremor and heard a threatening boom. The noise bellowed out from the darkness again, this time louder. She saw nothing but began to run in fear anyway; faster and faster she ran into the void, while her head span with thoughts of familiar faces. Soon it became hard to run, as though a thick mist was pulling on her. The heavy beating sound had gone, and a tight, cold clasp clenched her. Somehow, she had run into a severe storm. Coldness took her now; she could see her warm breath puffing out before her. Something in the distance came into view, a conspicuous block of a wall. Jogging over to the lonely structure amidst the emptiness, she examined its swerving lines and the familiar symbols and patterns carved into it. She knew this wall; she just could not place it exactly. With a blink, the stone wall enclosed her into a corner. Desperately she pushed and scrabbled at the stone. The horrendous, thunderous beat was behind her once again, but with a great effort she forcefully broke through the stone and collapsed onto the other side. Falling forever through a strong wind, she hit the floor hard on her back! The pain was too much; her back had split in half, but her senses were firing, desperately clinging onto life as she lay paralyzed on a crop of short grass swaying in the wind. Blood ran down the side of her mouth, her eyes swelling as they stared up at the distant grey clouds. Her heartbeat slowed gently as she lay still. As the sound of her life whittled down to a final halt, something whispered in her ear: *Elaso fiin an ute fiin tressa.*

Springing upright, back in reality, she knocked the wooden desk legs with her knees, the burning candles toppling over, spilling hot wax over a few sheets of paper. Quickly she stood and scrambled to her desk, crammed with books and papers, the terrible memory of her dream flashing back before her. *What did it mean?* Calming herself down with a sip of cold water and a few breaths of air, she convinced herself that it was only a bad dream, that this could not be one of her Visions. It was too unclear, too vague to mean anything, yet she knew that it had felt like a Vision. The kind that only Star Callers experienced. Visions would appear once a Star Caller reached a certain age or period in their lives, to help guide their path and that of others, who followed her and prayed for her. Putting it behind her, she tried to return to her books, but it was not long before she became bored and restless, unable to lose herself in the pages, fixated on what had happened. Flicking back a few pages and reading passages she had read a hundred times over, something suddenly triggered in her mind, and she found herself teasing an appetite she figured had been put to bed. The only thing keeping her at her desk was the risk of getting caught; it was too great, and the consequences of her misbehaviour would be dire. Seemingly independent of her thought process, her hand slapped the book shut, and she threw on her most casual of clothing from her wardrobe, choosing not her classic blue long coat, but a black coat with a patterned white streak sewn through the middle of the wide hood. Pressing out the candles, save for one, she caught a glimpse of herself in the mirror. The pause gave her time to think. She stared at the strange reflection; she really did look like a common girl, yet still, something was missing. She tied her golden hair back with a band; working girls did not usually have time to tend to their looks, so her beautiful hair was a dead giveaway. She killed the light of the final candle and sneaked off into the night, heading straight for the nearest woodland area, all the while wondering what had come over her?

Loud music was being played by crude stringed instruments. Bright, fiery lights and big bonfires stocked with dry wood lit up the darkness, pushing smoke up out into the air. Wooden stands drew the crowds, raring to get merry and out of line. People flocked to the town in their hundreds; some sat on wooden seats, while others gathered on the cold stone paving outside public houses. Carts towed by horses ferried in goods and hitchhikers leapt off from the back to join the dawdling mobs. Meat turned and roasted on the spit, dripping with juices, before it was sliced clean and served to hungry onlookers. Multitudes gathered around the blazing fires, chatting together, clutching mugs filled with ale; still more came out of the stone inns and taverns to be outside in the cool air under the starry night sky. On the hill, three stallions galloped up the road fronting the small town, where they stopped and waited a while. Three men observed the movement from a distance checking out the scenario. The black horse in the middle trotted forward. Thao, upon its back, glanced back at his men, waiting for him to speak.

"Ditch your armour and weapons at our encampment; there is no need for them tonight. If you wish to return and relax yourselves feel welcome but be aware and remember to prepare for anything. Always stay vigilant." Arthur and Scarto bowed their heads together and abandoned the road to the east, riding through the tree line and disappearing into the dark. Thao spurred his horse with his ankle and rode along the path toward the town of Harbour's Edge. The seafront settlement was renowned throughout Krondathia for its many bars and social gatherings. The road cluttered as Thao drew closer, the loud and noisy crowds making way for him, though few people recognised his face and gave him more than a glance but stared at him with the respect he deserved. Some saluted him or wished to shake his hand, for which he did. He eventually came to a large barn that had been converted into a stable where he dismounted his horse, leading the animal inside. Thao's horse happily trotted over to the golden hay within, allowing him to shut the wooden door. He was about to leave the stable when he heard a sound of crunching and chewing from another stall. Curious, he walked further down the wide hall and spotted a familiar white horse tucked into an open stable, its door wide open. Thao pushed it closed, but as he did so he glimpsed a saddle draped over a nearby bench. The leather was detailed with a sewn-on emblem, a symbol easily recognisable in the land. A spherical jewel, shielded by scaled plates that broke off before completion; it was the seal of Krondathia, the same seal Thao wore on his own armour and fabrics. The thick saddle was coloured a cold blue, with an outline of shining white, with space for weapons, though they themselves were nowhere to be seen.

"The decision passed." Thao knew the voice and acknowledged the young man, sat in the opposite stable, clutching a pint of ale, dressed in fine black clothes. A bowl of fresh apples was at his feet. Thao replied with a stern look:

"If it were up to me, I would have named you sooner, but you know how things are. Tell me, does the record still stand?" The man nodded and raised three fingers.

"Three hundred straight victories? That is impressive. Though I must warn you, overconfidence is a weakness; you must taste defeat in order to improve. Sometimes retreat is necessary."

"Undeniably true…" the man began, swinging backwards and forward on his short chair. "But..." He stood up. "Confidence, determination, self-belief; they all enable you to endure the fight. Trust in your abilities, and they will be sure to look after you. I do not speak for the masses, but I am living proof that this method works." Thao squinted his eyes at this contest of knowledge.

"You push yourself too far. Don't you think it is time to halt while you are ahead? It is only a matter of time before you meet your equal. Carry on as you are and you will end up walking only one path: not the path to salvation or freedom, but the path of death. It's an inevitable fact. I do speak for the masses, those who are no longer able to speak. We only get one life, that we know of anyway, so do not throw it away trying to prove yourself to others." He rolled down his collar and revealed a scar below his shoulder; it trailed on to the upper part of his bicep. "I have tasted defeat before, and no one would dare challenge me. As will you…" The man in the stable slowly clapped his hands while nodding. "A word of advice, Lethaniel: when you repeat your old General's words, make sure you use them on someone who didn't serve with him." They laughed, clasped hands, and pulled each other into a warm brotherly embrace. Pushing back, Thao beamed: "It has been too long. What have you been up to, my boy?"

"Single-handedly uncovering Equis, of course," boasted Lethaniel.

"People don't care about that nonsense; they care about your record. Three hundred is a proud number," praised Thao.

"Three hundred, give or take a few," muttered the younger man.

"Did you bring me something back from your travels, or am I going to have to beg?"

"Nothing but knowledge."

"All the knowledge I need is right here, in the mind of a young girl – sorry, a young woman - who goes by the name of Isabelle," Thao chuckled, pretending as though Lethaniel didn't know anything about The Chosen.

"I know who she is; I've known her for a great deal longer than you."

"Yes, but you have not guarded her for as long as I have. In your absence, she has changed much."

"I did not drop off the face of the earth for two years, Thao. Isabelle showed me a path, but it was not her words I found to guide me, nor was it her books or your father's counsel. I saw many faces, but one I will never forget." The Honour Guard placed a large hand on Lethaniel's shoulder.

"You must introduce us to him someday. Where did your travels take you?"

"To a mountainous area," teased the young man with deliberate vagueness.

"Well, that narrows it down. Why don't you tell me your story later over a drink?"

"That I could deal with," accepted Lethaniel as he was led out the stable by Thao.

"Agreed, my boy agreed."

As they walked out of the stables, Thao remarked honestly:

"I must say, I am shocked, how much you have learnt since last we spoke. Normally my little speeches riddle everyone; your teacher must have been wise."

"I was young when you and I last spoke, I am not that boy anymore...Anyway, since when does an Honour Guard retreat from battle, or surrender for that matter? I always believed that your troops were invincible." Thao gave Lethaniel a look of mild humour.

"Your horse - the door is open, won't he escape?"

"Oh, it's fine; Seridox doesn't like being tied up or shut in. He gets grumpy if you try. He will be fine, trust me. That beast is smarter than you, I am sure of it." The two walked fast toward the busy town and into the crowds. As they walked, Lethaniel drank the rest of his ale and placed the empty mug on a table, before lifting two fresh beers off a tray being carried around by a barmaid, handing one to Thao. The two men were glad to see each other; it had been a fair time since they had last spoken or gotten together like this. Usually, they avoided the drink, as it did nothing but slow their bodies, which always needed to be fit and healthy. However, on some occasions, they had to be men. "How have your own travels been going of late?" Lethaniel asked.

"I have just arrived, and I will be leaving shortly enough. Got to report back to Imrondel City. I have greater issues to be concerned with than drunken festivals. Don't worry though; I won't miss The Festival of the Awakening."

"You're concerned? There is nothing to be worried about these days, Thao." The big man remained quiet, thinking back on Isabelle's behaviour. "I think we should find a place. I am meeting someone in The Traveller's Corner Bar soon. Would you care to join us?" Thao glanced back in disappointment.

"The Travellers...Can't we go to another? I don't plan on staying here too long."

After a brief wander around the town, the two made their way indoors, finishing off their frothy beers, leaving the cups on a window ledge outside. They sat at a table close to a crackling fire loaded with black coal dug from the nearest mine a few miles away to the west. The chairs were made of soft, green leather, while the pub itself was empty and dimly lit, though it was pleasant and tidy at least. The barmaid, who was strangely attractive, came over with two mugs filled to the brim with ale. The young woman returned to the bar where she continued to go about her duties. Shadows of drunken fools stumbled passed the foggy windows, muffled chatter and noises fading in and out of frame now and then.

"You have been to Davune recently; how are the Dovidians?" Lethaniel asked Thao, taking a swig of ale.

"As a country, Ivulien is much larger than it was five years ago and very advanced compared with our cities. Davune, well, I can only say that it has changed. I guess that is the way of things." Drinking slowly from his mug, Lethaniel casually added:

"And Izzy?"

"Who?"

"I mean Isabelle. I've not seen her for some time," Lethaniel stuttered with a timid laugh. Thao remembered the way she had acted the last time they spoke, and he told the truth but neglected to mention some of the more personal comments she had made about being a Star Caller and how unhappy she was under her collected surface. There was a pause and they both stared into their mugs before he changed the subject again.

"When you were named General, what happened to Kaaz? How did he take it?" Lethaniel nodded, remembering.

"Syen Kaaz... Not entirely sure what happened to him. Out of the lot of us boy soldiers, it was a choice between me, him or that Ermak fella with the posh accent from Cuether. Syen was named through the fault of my own. I saw it coming. Did not expect him to give up the position."

"What happened?" Thao was quite eager to know, for Syen Kaaz was an exceptional soldier indeed.

46

"Not too sure. He left the day after his promotion. He even left his bow and arrows along with his armour in his tent. I haven't seen him man to man since."

"He's a good man, Lethaniel; he may not have a title or a distinctive reputation like you, but he is still a worthy man. I hope one day we meet him again." They both went quiet until the heavy door was pushed open and a man stepped inside, drinking some strong-smelling concoction from a small, silver canteen. He recognised Lethaniel and waved with two fingers, beginning the walk over. Thao could tell he had been on the road for quite some time. The man did not smell bad, but the scents of earth and grass clung to his clothing. They shook hands and he sat down.

"Why are you drinking already? This is what this place is for," complained Lethaniel, signalling to the maid to bring one more ale over.

"Just arrived in town. I saw Seridox in the stable. Fed him an apple. I thought I was early," the newcomer said with a hiccup. Lethaniel introduced the man as Braygon Augiene, a name that rang a few bells in Thao's head. The maid came over once again with the fresh mug; he thanked her before speaking with a slight excitement, though he tried to hide his thrilled tone "And you must be Thao Hikonle. It's always a pleasure to meet an Honour Guard, for you always have something interesting to say, unlike some…" Used to this sort of attention, Thao nodded, bowing his head once. "I'll get the next round in, it's on me," offered Braygon, getting the attention of the barmaid who peered over the surface of the bar top. The three men sat in comfort next to the fire, making small talk with one another and sharing some laughs before Thao addressed Braygon directly.

"I've heard your name before; Commander Sious spoke very highly of you. You are his protégé, are you not? What's your rank?"

"Captain Augiene of The Seventh Company, Scouting Rangers. We are the second unit after Mathias Sious and his Norfoon Scouts. Kind of like a back-up team."

"Ah yes, I know you now; you're just like Lethaniel," replied Thao.

"How so?" Lethaniel and Braygon chimed in as one.

"We are all in an elevated position where no one seems to ask us or come looking for us should we not show up for work in the morning, everyone assumes we are working when actually we are just taking our time. What I mean is that you frequently leave someone else in charge, someone you hold in trust to watch over your unit while you take your leave whenever you see fit. It just seems a little strange to me is all," Thao noted, taking a large gulp of ale.

"That's an interesting point," admitted Braygon, unsure whether the man was criticising him or trying to be humorous.

"We are all guilty of it; Lethaniel here didn't show up for work for two years and no one seemed to care." With that comment, the relaxed atmosphere returned to the table.

"We all have our orders, I suppose; sometimes we are required not to talk about where we go or what we do. You have your secrets too, I guess, and we all do as we are told, most of the time," said the Captain. "Would you care to enlighten us?" Thao wrinkled his forehead. Lethaniel decided to remain quiet for the time being. This argument was not about who was better than who and was not intended to be malicious, however, Braygon enjoyed a challenge and this was not the first time Thao had been asked to explain his actions. "I speak for myself, but I am sure I also speak on behalf of many other bewildered citizens…How DID you end the civil war?"

"If you don't mind me saying, Braygon, that story deserves the respect of a sober mind" said Thao. Lethaniel looked at him out of the corner of his eye but said nothing. The pub was still empty; the maid behind the bar was eyeing Lethaniel and Braygon, choosing her time when to work so she could hear what they were talking about.

"I am sorry, I didn't mean to impose. I have my business and you have yours, it's the way of the world, you don't have to answer," apologised Augiene.

"It's alright; I don't need your apologies. I will admit I am not proud of what I have done, there is not a day that goes by that I don't ask for forgiveness from those I took from. The true story of the civil war was drowned out by the celebrations of the victorious. The sorrows were buried and ignored. I hope that satisfies your curiosity. Mathias has mentioned you before, says he offered you a rank of Commander; surely, it is better than a Captain's routine. Why didn't you take the job?" Thao enquired.

"I didn't deserve it and I don't need it. There is little that I truly deserve. The world is a big place, and if I can get by on a little then that means there is more for everyone else."

"He also told me you have not seen your home in many months, which raises another question. Why don't you return?"

"It's been longer than that, I think," Lethaniel intervened.

"How long?"

"A few years, three, I believe," answered Braygon, getting the feeling he was being cross-examined. "There are people where I live who have their work cut out for them, just surviving. That is where they will remain, that is where they will die. My interests lay far away from there; there is a lot of uncharted territory yet to be explored."

"And you wish to be the one to discover it? Don't think you are the first to attempt it, son; it's been tried many times before. Men have become wealthy and famous simply by chance. If I were you, I would take my chances on securing a life surrounded by allies. If that is your goal and view on success. Better that than risking your life with the unknown," preached Thao wisely.

"You're right, people have found old stones and relics that could support them for several lifetimes, but there are rewards that pay greater than gold and silver." Thao sensed no threat or confusion in Braygon, he was a man worth having as a friend, or at least that's what Mathias and Lethaniel had said about him.

"So where are you from, Captain?" Lethaniel choked down a laugh.

"Good luck with that, Thao, no one knows where Braygon is from."

"Thanks, Lethaniel, that saves me the hassle of having to tell him" chuckled Braygon.

"You keep it a secret?"

"I don't keep many, but I do like to think of home as a secret."

"This won't be the last time I ask you of this. Keep in mind that a person is linked to his home in more ways than you can imagine. I'll find out where you're from," Thao vowed.

"Fair enough," Braygon grinned confidently.

Upon the deck of a recently moored transport boat, sailors loaded boxes, barrels, and other miscellaneous supplies onto the lower decks. Men scurried around, busy at work; they covered supplies up with blankets to help them last the night in case it rained, sealed crates by hammering them shut, all while passing around a bottle of liquor. The one in charge of the dock was a fat man who juggled the lantern and a bottle for himself. Barely able to stand up straight or even walk properly, wobbling from side to side, blurting out commands to his workers that made little sense, he oversaw the work being carried out. Drunk as he was, he knew the routine about the shipments going to and from The Zodias Island. The long, packed boat gradually grew quiet as sailors and workmen left to join the celebration in town. The dock lost its chatter and turned dark and silent. It became a maze of wooden crates, narrow corridors of supplies tied down or balanced on top of one another. A warm anxious breath released itself somewhere within a crate surrounded by others, all packed up against themselves. The shuffling of fabric and the rub of cloth came from inside one of the wooden boxes. A roof suddenly popped up with a scrape, the lid sliding off slowly to the side, and a hooded figure poked its head up out of the crate, filled with black robes and white belts destined to become priests uniform. Someone clambered out of the box and managed to reach the floor without raising much sound. Not yet out in the open air, she was concealed under a thick blanket that sheltered her figure. She knelt to the floor, trying to spot movement or hear sounds of activity. Listening hard, she started to have second thoughts about the whole trip and forced herself to move on, ignoring all logic and common sense that willed her to turn back. Squeezing out from under the tight waterproof blanket, she emerged into full view on the deck. The hood blew back, and her blonde hair were exposed. Isabelle had made it across the sea; she had arrived at Harbour's Edge. From here on she was free from all security and protection for the first time since she could remember. Keeping low and moving with soft steps, she manoeuvred in and out of the many obstacles that cluttered the deck. On edge and wide-eyed, she stuck close to the darker shadows. Peeking around a corner, a yellow light gleamed on her. Isabelle snapped away and merged as best she could back with the dark. After a short time, she faced the corner again, looking around it slower this time. She could see it was nothing more than a young boy fishing off the dock with a bright fire lamp. Sneaking passed him with ease on tiptoes she hopped off the vessel, jogged quickly over the wooden planks of the dock and happily ran down the road toward the town, from where the music and lights still blared.

Before continuing along the stone pathway, Isabelle stopped and paused whilst looking at the boat she had come in on, and then again at the pathway towards the town. Was this a mere sense of ill-logic, disobedience, and guilt? Or was this a Star Caller's gift when faced with a dilemma? She was confronted by a difficult choice between the road that led into town or heading back to the crate to ensure safe passage back to the island in the early morning. Her senses spoke to her, something was amiss, but this odd feeling soon passed, and she made her choice. Instead of taking the stone road, she made haste through the thickets and woodland, using her sight as best she could. She followed the growing light and sounds of the town that pierced the trees and vines. Scraping her way through the hedges, she found her way to a clearing in front of the town; Utilising stealth she ran low to the last tree that would cover her entirely. With her hood up, hands shaking, she spied upon the towns people for a time. *Amazing,* she thought, *everyone is having fun, everyone is happy.* She calmed herself and left the tree line behind, from where she walked over the grass and encountered the revellers. She quickly stepped aside to the nearest wall, pulling her hood down further over her face and backed up, yet they didn't look at her twice and just carried on casually, talking with one another. Isabelle tried hard not to make her presence known, and dodged the people who drank carelessly, who were way too merry for their own good. People bumped into her as they passed by; everyone was taller than her, it seemed. She felt naked, her power had gone, and she missed the company of her guards. A tune, however, lured her in from the street. A band playing old instruments she was unfamiliar with sat at the side of the pathway opposite the many stands and pubs; they fiddled and plucked away at the strings, belting out joyous tunes. Isabelle had to stop and watch couples dance around in circles to the music, the crowds clapping them on. It reminded her of the dancing she had learnt, yet this type of dance was strangely appealing to her. It had no set pattern, no footing or instruction; it was just random, whereas her dance methods were dictated, far more professional and required endless practice and perfection to perform. A group passed her by, and a gentleman offered his lady a dance. Isabelle could hear his words clearly; the woman took his hand and they both joined in with the dancing, getting into the swing of things very quickly. No one recognised her, but she still would not dare to take away her veil; she said to herself she was simply curious about everyday folklife, but deep down she was desperate to break free of her restraints as a woman of supreme power. *Strange,* she thought; she had seen the town of Harbour's Edge before, but not like this, it was on fire with movement and life. Minding her own business, she passed by a short man who was cutting meat off a lump that was turning on a spit over a roaring fire. He turned to her:

"Miss, I say young miss." Isabelle looked around, having not entirely realised he was talking to her. "Would you like to have some?" He handed her a plateful. Isabelle, bewildered "It's cooked very nicely, I'd say, would you like an ale as well?" Stunned to be spoken to in this way, she found herself speechless, though with delight rather than awkwardness, as she took the plate and moved closer. She watched as the man opened a fresh barrel of ale and handed her a full mug. "This stuff has been selling as if I was handing out zeal; it's the fourth-barrel tonight!" Isabelle, not really listening, was already wolfing down the dripping meat and tearing at the fluffy roll. "You like it, huh? It's nice, isn't it? Try the ale; this year has been brewed especially well. I don't know why, don't know what they done to it, but it tastes just fine." Clasping the mug with both hands she gulped down a mouthful, pausing a minute to accept the bitter taste. She then drank down the rest a little too fast, some trickling down her mouth. Handing the mug back to the kind man with a hiccup, she thanked him kindly. "You're welcome," he beamed, returning to offering meat to other people passing by. As she moved on away towards the centre of the town, he called after her: "You take care now you hear me young miss." Now in the centre of town and feeling a little bit more comfortable with the surroundings - or maybe it was just the ale taking its effect - Isabelle leaned on a wall to catch her thoughts once again. Further up the path, on the ground, lay a brown sewn pouch. It caught her attention, just sitting there unwanted. Glancing up at the people for a second, she picked it up, swiping it off the floor. Looking in the small brown pouch as she went, the glint of metal and tapping of coins came from inside. Isabelle had struck golden zeal! There was enough zeal in here to last her a week or two. She continued along the streets lined with sharp roofs and dark green windows.

"I apologise that Mathias could not make it here tonight," Braygon announced surrounded by empty mugs and brown bottles. Lethaniel remained next to the fire, quite comfortable. Thao, having had the least to drink, sat opposite Braygon, whose head hung lazily, slowly slurping down one more ale.

"When did you see him last? You were with him, I presume?"

"The last time we were together, we were stationed at the Korthium Outposts. Then he was gone; a guard told me he saw him, and few others leave, heading east most likely, towards Thnel. He could be anywhere in that direction right now," explained Braygon, the pungent scent of alcohol on his breath. The pub that had been empty started to welcome a few more faces, as the maid then cleared their table and got busy with other customers. As the place filled up and the chatter grew louder, Thao decided it was time to leave, so he stood up.

"The day after next I head for Imrondel City with our Star Caller…" As he spoke, he pulled on his gloves and buttoned up his collar. "Being now a General of Krondathia and a great example to the Norkron army, with a perfect record and reputation, I believe you are invited to this meeting everyone's talking about."

"Of course," replied Lethaniel. Thao got ready to go and walked around the table close to where Braygon was sitting.

"If you have no further tasks, would you like to help me escort her?" Drink in hand, Lethaniel replied:

"Of course, it is why I made the trip from The Silver City" Thao scratched the stubble on his chin and remembered something he needed to point out.

"Thieves and bandits are not our only concern here; Dark Rogues have been reported recently, wandering the roads and woods. Truly they should know who they are up against by now. I'll see you later," he smiled, throwing down a handful of silver zeal to pay for the drinks. Thao nodded at Lethaniel and left the pub. Lethaniel scooped up the coins and pushed his empty mug away from himself. Trapped in between the fire and the lightly dozing Braygon, he looked over at him for a moment and then began to count the silver zeal Thao had left.

"You, uh, haven't found any of those priceless stones or relics laying around recently, have you?"

"Nooo…" murmured Braygon, more than a little drunk.

"I thought not…" said Lethaniel in disappointment, picking up his ale. "Let me know when you do?"

Strolling through the town, remaining cautious, Isabelle decided to wander a little more before going into a pub. She found a shady spot away from the crowds at the edge of a field next to a fire; it was out in the open breeze, overlooked by a cloudy night sky. The heat of the blaze comforted her cold hands; she felt it stroking her face and warming her clothes. As she watched the flames rise and quell, Isabelle slowly opened her palm, her iris's glistened with a glow of green, and a stream of fire whisked over her hand, which she contorted into elegant shapes.

"Mommy, mommy where is it!?" Isabelle let the flames go, jarringly and they returned to the fire as the couple approached. A mother carrying a little girl away from the crowds.

"This is where you had it last" said the mother, who looked roughly the same age as Isabelle, around her mid-twenties. The little was sat on the ground while the mother searched the area. Feeling something under her foot, Isabelle found a soft toy, she picked it up and showed it to the girl.

"Is this yours, sweetie?"

"Thank the Celestials. Now say thank you to the kind lady" the mother encouraged.

"Thank you."

"You're welcome, I know what it is like to lose something loved." Isabelle returned the sweet smile and returned her attention to the fire. Soon she found herself thinking of her future, as a woman and as a Star Caller. Reminded by the weight of the small fortune in her pocket, she decided to make her way indoors. She passed by many pubs and inns; she wanted a place that did not draw too much attention, but that wasn't completely distant wither. The Traveller's Corner Bar caught her eye; not too big or crowded. She decided to go inside. Shuffling her way through a dense crowd, she found a seat at the bar.

"What can I get ya, honey?" the barmaid asked her.

"Oh, can I please have a small uh…One of those please," she stuttered, pointing at a light red bottle sitting on the far counter among others of various sizes and shapes.

"Pond or lagoon?"

"Lagoon…Please." The maid shook the bottle and added a few other clear liquids to it and slid the glass across the bar surface to where Isabelle caught it. The feelings of loneliness and insecurity haunted her again; intimidated by so many these strangers. She thought that maybe back at her hut reading was where she should be after all, it sounded like luxury after being in this hot, almost unpleasant atmosphere. Having gotten this far without detection, it seemed the right time to be heading back to the boat, though she didn't look forward to spending the night inside a box. That was the sacrifice of sneaking around, she figured, every action came at a cost. Surprisingly, the drink tasted nicer than she thought it would, refreshing, but sweet on the tip of her tongue.

She made for another sip, but just then noticed a stranger as still as a statue under a clean, hooded cloak at the opposite side of the bar. He appeared to have been watching her. Leaning on the wall, arms folded with a mug of ale hanging off his finger, his shape was lean, unlike most of the other men in the pub, who were wide, oafish, full of more than enough food and drink to last them a week. He did not move or flinch. People walked back and forth passed him and obstructed Isabelle's gaze, so she looked away with a sudden move and tried to act as if she had not seen him. Yet she felt compelled to look back to see whether he was still staring at her, and he was! It dawned on her with horror: she must have been identified or followed from The Zodias Island. All her worst fears fell into place in her head and clouded her focus; soon she would be exposed and then worse, a tarnish on her reputation. The eyes hidden under the darkness of the hood held onto her from the opposite side of the room. Then with a little luck: somebody walked passed him holding a brightly lit lamp on a tray with some empty glasses and mugs, his face was finally revealed to her. Her anxiety relinquished, and she felt calm, almost comforted in a strange, mysterious way. She looked at him closely and began to think logically once again. If he had been a spy from The Zodias Island, then he would have at least got up and arrested her by now. She had not seen anyone like this before in her life, but his presence and stare did not alarm her anymore. If she felt threatened then her state would change and the Glyph inside her would flare, having instincts of its own. Unable to look away, she nodded at the stranger with a pleasant smile. To her amazement, he returned a hint of acknowledgement. Isabelle finished her glass, keeping an eye on him, on his face especially; his eyes were clear and brown, his features slender and his long, straight, dark hair fell across his brow, some of it folded and tucked behind his ears. She guessed he was younger than she was, but not THAT much younger. Isabelle's heart pounded; she had never felt this way before; she welcomed the attention. She hesitated for a second and began to pull away her black hood. An unwise move, she knew, yet she felt like she should. He casually signalled an alarm, and just then a voice that she recognised rudely interrupted the moment. She pulled her hood back over her head quickly; Before he knew it, she had taken off, leaving a single gold zeal coin spinning on the work surface. She hurried towards the door, knocking a man's ale out of his hand in the process, spilling it down his front. Lethaniel, talking to Braygon, saw and heard the fuss, before a woman in a black coat whisked by them. After a second of thought, he went after the woman, following the distinctive white streak trailing down the middle, but struggled to find a way around the larger, drunken men who blocked the exit. Pushing passed the people obstructing his path, he finally burst out of the bar, checking the roads and paths. Not a sign of the girl in the hood, leaving him to ponder for a while.

"What was that about?" Braygon asked, emerging from The Travellers Corner Bar.

"I'm not sure."

The Captain shrugged. "I think we should call it a night. Are you settled in an inn or are you camping?" Lethaniel hung around outside for a little while longer, looking up and down the streets, searching for subtle movements, but there were none.

She crept out from an alley close by The Traveller's Corner Bar, safe from detection for now, though she knew Lethaniel would be searching for her on the streets. She was glad to see him looking so well after the two years he had been away, but she had to avoid him, at least until tomorrow, and then deny that she was ever here if his suspicion had be roused. Eventually, Lethaniel and his friend took off and blended in with the people. She took the opportunity to dart out of the alley and ran back to the clearing, feeling pleased with herself as she disappeared into the tree line. She had gotten away with it! A very minimal act of disobedience, a foolish act admittedly, but it made her smile and laugh as she navigated the woodland. Isabelle could see the road just beyond her; the dock was close; her final escape lay waiting beyond. A sense of joy came over her, a sense that made her not care too much about tomorrow or the day after. She knew what it was that made her happy; it was that face she had seen, the face that had picked her out from the crowd, yet it remained without a name. Isabelle needed to know. These thoughts stopped her in her tracks, and she kicked herself knowing how rudely she had behaved, taking off without even a friendly word. The shift of a shadow passed by and the scrape of booted feet upon loose gravel drew her eyes and alerted her ears. Like a flash, she knelt to the floor and froze. The stranger walked on and became clearer. It was the shape of a man walking along the road. Isabelle positioned herself, so she could get a better glimpse of his face, upon which she saw who was there. It was Thao, and he was walking back in the opposite direction to her. The darkness and tree line were the only things that separated the two. She would be in one messy situation if spotted; she would have a great deal of explaining to do. Being as quick and as quiet as she possibly could, she ran out after he had moved further up the road. To her delight, she found the docks free of people. Getting back on board and under her blanket with the crates would not be a problem. The lamp shone brightly on the dock; the boy was still fishing, though from the looks of it he had only made a few catches. Wriggling under the blanket and lying down on the deck next to her crate of robes, Isabelle breathed deeply with relief and exhilaration. She thought further about the nameless stranger, his face soothing her to sleep as uncomfortable as it was. Tomorrow she would get busy again, tomorrow she would return and try to put a name to the face, after her duties were attended to and completed first.

The night of celebration was over, and the taverns cleared out its customers, pouring them onto the streets, closing their doors and windows after them. It was late as Lethaniel and Braygon left the small town and walked the path cutting through the trees. Now that everyone was gone, they felt free to talk to each other, unlike earlier when they had had to restrain their voices. Now they could relax.

"I thought for a second you were going to reveal too much," muttered Lethaniel.

"Don't be ridiculous, I would never do that," protested Braygon.

"I thought after six ales and two bottles people might seem easier to trust," the General pointed out, clearly not having failed to take note of his friend's impressive tally.

"It matters not how much drink you put in me; I am sworn to secrecy, and I hope you are too. Do you ever plan to return to that place?"

"Yes, I made a promise."

"You mean to her? Or do you just want more of that wine she gave you?" laughed the Captain.

"Speaking of *her*, she has a message for you. She never got to say goodbye. She wanted to, but you left before she woke on the day of your departure. So, I want you to come back with me when I do decide to return. Perhaps we can go and talk with Tudor again," Lethaniel suggested.

"Yes, maybe one day, but we have business out here in the world to take care of first. Once we finish our duties and Krondathia has no more need of our kind, which hopefully will be soon, then we can return."

"I fear Krondathia will always have need of us; too many good things have been happening of late, it all seems too fast, you know? Change takes time. I always thought I'd be an old man when real peace was declared...But we can always hope. You haven't told Thao anything of this, have you?" asked Braygon, getting back on topic.

"No, of course not, why would I?"

"Because you trust him"

"He is trustworthy, Braygon, and he is an old friend who's never done me wrong," Lethaniel told his friend what he knew about The Honour Guards and of their ways. "They live by few rules and keep to the old code written around the time when people realised that they needed a reliable leader to maintain a noble society. Thao, as you know, is the leader of The Honour Guards, descending from a long bloodline going right back to the beginning. They might represent the highest rank in soldiery in our lands, but before you ask, the answer is yes: I have fought and defeated some of these men before, one at a time, but just so you know, they are unbeatable when together. Fighting one in the training yard is not the same as taking them on in a real battle," he explained.

"That is all well and good, but nothing that they have done or how hard they have trained can lead me to believe that they can fight as well as the average man defending his home and family. Believe me, I've seen this courage, things that you would not believe if I told you," Braygon insisted, clinging to the past and the old ways.

"Thao and his squad of soldiers protect all who need protecting, including our twelve High Councillors of Virtue in Xiondel City and The Lower Council of Law. They protect The Chosen Star Caller Isabelle, The Eldor. The Courts in Imrondel sometimes require their guard for long journeys, though they prefer to depend upon their Glyph Wielders. The Honour Guards are strong and trained intensely from birth. Together as a single unit, they have devastated armies in the past. We both know that they silenced the dispute between The Thunderhoofs and The Tulkan Knights."

"I wonder how," Braygon muttered under his breath.

"You asked me once, why The Guards wear armour crafted around a creature," the General began, holding his horse by the reins, feeding him an apple core that he had finished with.

"I have an idea why…"

"This creature is said to have inspired the Norkrons in The Time of the Warlords. Nowadays, the state of an Honour Guard's armour is a statement of how skilful he is in battle and how well he has served Krondathia. Thao has a full suit, of what they call Organix

Armour. He alone has achieved such a distinction. Do you know of the creature, Braygon? Do you remember the tarthais?"

"How can I forget? So, their armour is inspired by a feline?"

"Yes. Why, I am not sure, but the story of the tarthais is history entwined with the history of The Honour Guard," added Lethaniel.

"Thao must have done something remarkable," pondered Braygon.

"Or terrible…" Lethaniel noted. Just then, the men came to a crossroads, where Braygon took his leave.

"I will see you in Imrondel City."

"See you there. Are you sure you cannot come with us? We are taking the woodland paths, the quickest route through The Silent Vale, the location of the mysterious lagoon that only appears somewhere at night. Doesn't that sound appealing? Not even you have seen it," teased Lethaniel, who could do with his friend's company on the long road.

"I have my orders, as tempting as it sounds, but I will follow within the week." With that, they said good night. Braygon headed toward another part of the town while Lethaniel got back to his shelter and tended to a dying fire. His horse, Seridox walked away but did not stray far. The sky was blanketed with thick clouds, the wind was soft, and the breeze was cool. The small fire came back to life and ate away at the twigs. An owl called out somewhere in the dusky wood close by, standing out from the slight rustle of trees and plants. Lethaniel took some time getting to sleep. The night sky reminded him of a moment long before in Xiondel City. Looking up at the stars, holding his necklace in his hand, he thought back to old memories, which brought a faint smile to his face. He knew he would return to The Silver City, but she was waiting for him in the capital, in Imrondel City. It had been so long since they had seen each other, he wondered if he would recognise her after all this time.

Chapter 5 - Hawk from The South

One does not choose where he is born, but he is free to choose whether to make that place his home. Northland, in the warm country of Jureai.

Dawn broke and the air hung heavy and humid over the Bevork encampment. As the sun's rays shone over the red lands, smoke drifted from the tips of hundreds of tents pitched beside a deep, twisting ravine. The clear sky that had sparkled with countless stars was stolen away by the rising light. With the arrival of the morning sun, the northlands awoke. Young, dark-skinned men emerged from their tepee's. What little cloth they wore had been woven from animal skins. A few made their way to the closest well where they gathered water from dozens of wooden buckets nearby. Some were not truly awake just yet and had to rouse themselves properly from their slumber before they began their exercise routines or prepared their meals. Everyone had their own way during these early hours. This camp was one of the largest in the area, though others like it existed all over the northern country of Jureai.

Not everyone had opted to rise early; most remained curled up with their women, lying half asleep on the floor, resting cosily on soft, furry carpets. The shadows gradually distorted as time passed, as the sun rose. An entire clan were waking from a peaceful night. Thicker strands of smoke began to drift from the tops of the tents as men crushed up herbs and boiled water over fires, fed by their plentiful supplies of wood. Within the tepee shelters, families controlled larger fires, built directly below a smoke flap in the roof. Pots were suspended over the heat, cooking delicious stews consisting of wholesome ingredients foraged from the lands around them. As the water boiled, herbs were added, infusing the mix with flavour, creating a deliciously enticing aroma. The younger men congregated outside a central fire, the biggest in the camp, sharing an enthused conversation. Talk stirred around the camp, excitement stirring about the selection process and the tournament. The camp grew busier as the hours went by, seeing the arrival of more clansmen, all of them dressed in dark brown leathers, coiled cloths, though each boasted his own distinctive array of hawk feathers. The men had prepared themselves well, having trained for many years for the chance to be listed in the tournament, which at that very moment was being organised by their order. The warriors had overseen the creation of their armour for this important day, as well as the making of their own weaponry and shields. It was not just The Bevork Clan who would be competing, other clans from across the red lands of Jureai were preparing to participate in the games. In the distance, beyond the tents, a courier could be seen riding toward the small encampment. He entered and rode to the edge of the shelters, where he dismounted his tulkan bull. His cloth was clean and plain, displaying no vibrant colours, marks, pattern, or decorations of any kind. His appearance reflected his neutrality as an envoy under the employ of the five Chieftains of Jureai, also known as The Chimera Order. A young Bevork lad offered the messenger a drink of water. The older members greeted him warmly, touching their brows while closing their eyes as he approached; the traditional Bevork salute. The messenger did the same; he was a friend, well known among this clan. He spoke out to the congregation once ready.

"You all know what this day brings…" The small crowd looked on eagerly as he delivered his message. "A day for commencement or contentment. Consider yourself warned: the love swayed you has been cast from the bosom of Jureai." His voice dropped. "If your Southlander is to grant victory once more, don't expect to be celebrated as you once were." Silence reigned for a moment as the messenger drank his water under the rising heat and backed up to his bull, placing a hand on the reins. "The Tournament of Leadership will take place today. Go, and fight with honour!" A cry of excitement arose from the crowd of men and women, clapping excitedly, raising their hands and weapons into the air. The envoy mounted his tulkan bull and belted off into the distance, trailing dust behind him to the camp over.

Further north of the encampment, everyday life was proceeding as usual. Dust wafted into the sky as dark-skinned men worked around the site, digging up the earth, chopping wood and mining stone, shrugging off the hot stare of the sun. Men carted tools along winding dirt paths, ferrying equipment and resources of all kinds to those that needed it. Earth was removed by the men using short-handled pickaxes. The deeper, wider holes were used for collecting much-needed water. Fallen trees were cut away, stripped into thin poles by skilled carpenters to construct shelters, spears, bows and arrows. Women wove their magic under shacks in groups of twos and threes, safely away from the dig sites, stitching together fabrics to create exquisite patterns for their clan. Artists would then take this material and carefully dye shades of white, gold and brown over their symbol, the hawk, the sigil of The Bevork Clan. Women could often be seen accompanied by young children, usually young girls, who practised weaving and sewing together in social groups. They would not just focus on making clothing, but would also work on banners, flags, carpets, and blankets. Even the leather armour and battle suits of the clan's warriors were made by skilled, Bevork seamstresses.

Far out on the plains, Bevork warriors tutored young boys on the intricacies of hunting and fighting techniques, using blunt spears and wooden swords. Here, they would learn the foundations, the simplest forms of combat, practice for which included wrestling and weapons training, as well as learning how to do battle in a skilful and efficient way. Older lads with more experience could be seen in the distance, riding the mighty tulkan bulls, often falling off and generally having a good laugh rather than taking in any knowledge from the lessons. Elders of the clan could be found in the larger, rectangular tents, teaching classes of many young minds the ways of the world; the workings of nature, how to survive the heat and how to eat and live healthily, but most importantly, they taught their young how to mature and transform into an independent hawk of the wild. Education was central to The Bevork Clan; they believed that it was the key to a successful community.

The men worked away on the plains, digging out the stone and chopping up wood with crude tools, under the constant bombardment of heat. The dig sites overlooked the construction of further tents, shelters, and structures, with dozens more being pitched each day. Tall, thin but sturdy watchtowers surveyed the sites, from the very tops, a watcher was posted to warn of potential threats. A second Bevork encampment could be seen in the distance far beyond the deep valley set between them, they often communicated via reflected sunlight off sheets of metal panels.

What stood out above anything else in the encampment, was The Chieftain's Nest, sitting high atop a rocky hill. The roof of the building was made of a hollowed-out shell, suspended on a vast collection of thick tree trunks. The Bevork Clan believed that the first of their kind, long ago, witnessed a majestic golden hawk delivering this rooftop to them, setting it upon the supports, thus completing its nest and sheltering the first families as they built their society up using the resources provided by the red earth of Jureai. For three months, this golden hawk was said to have watched over them from atop its perch, protecting them from hungry reptilian eyes, until it was safe to fly back into the sun, from whence it had supposedly come. To the present day, the clan always made sure to thank the golden hawk, which they called Sun Feather, even long after it had faded into legend. This was the home of The Bevork Chieftain, El Raud, who was also the current Supreme Watcher of Jureai. At this moment, El Raud was not present; he was away with the other four Chieftains, arranging The Tournament of Leadership, the sole purpose of which was to select a new ruler. Of course, if El Raud's chosen warriors were to emerge triumphant during the tournament, then HE would be allowed to remain in The Five-Headed Throne for another three-year term.

The sky was clearing and the temperatures rising, though the day had just begun for The Bevork Clan. Uniformed clansmen and renowned warriors arrived on the plain; it seemed as though they were looking for someone. They began to spread out and search, bedecked in their battle colours of brown, white and gold, brandishing curved talon blades with light, wooden shields strapped to their forearms. One such warrior gave orders to the others, and while some carried on with the search, others made for the ranch of tulkan bulls. This warrior was of very dark skin, even more so than the rest of his tribe, and his frame was muscular, fit for the hunt. He brandished a spear with a fierce point crafted into a hawk's beak. He stopped to ask a nearby worker a question, who in turn pointed toward a hole in the ground. With a nod of acknowledgement, the spearman sighed in disappointment as he made his way over, pausing at the edge of the hole in the ground. A healthy, tanned man was swinging away at the earth with a pickaxe. Looking at his bronzed back, the spear-wielding warrior knelt and called out in his thick accent:

"Why aren't you ready? The selection is soon." The man in the hole appeared oblivious to the intrusion, continuing to dig away at the earth. After a few more swings and scrapes, he replied without looking up or even turning his head; obviously, he was more interested in what he was doing.

"Do I have to be present?"

"It is our tradition," insisted the spearman. The man finally ceased his work and looked at the warrior standing over him through dark brown eyes. Coated in dust, wearing a red breathing mask, the digger squinted under the bright blue sky, trying to come to a decision, his long strands of dark, sweat-soaked hair stuck across his face. He dropped his pickaxe and climbed out of the hole, only to be replaced immediately by a fellow worker. Sitting at the edge of the hole, he lifted his face mask, rubbing his mouth and face, before standing up and pointed to a finely built stone well. It brought water from the ground in a clay jug pulled by ropes, swivelling the jugs upside down, tipping fresh water into a smooth, hollowed-out tree trunk. The water ran down the wooden slide and through a thin, woven sheet, filtering the water into yet another large container, where the stream gathered and would eventually be collected for distribution and consumption.

"We finally got it to work. What do you think?"

"Are you coming to the selection or not? They will not wait forever." With a little frustration in his voice, he repeated his question. "Othello! Are you coming or are you not?" Silence gave the spearman his answer. Othello watched his friend walk away to his tulkan, waiting patiently. He drank from the well that he had helped build and paced around it in a circle, looking at the work site, briefly considering jumping on the back of a tulkan and going after the riders. He had made his decision though, and he swapped his cup of water for the pickaxe his replacement was using in the hole. Othello would not only dig for water; he would also assist others when they asked for his help. He had erected several new tepees that day, delivered work tools and ferried water to his fellow clansmen. Admired for his ambition and his endless desire to help others, he had grown popular among the clan. Of course, they also enjoyed his company, for he was a good friend to be with, asking for nothing and forever giving. Every so often, Othello would find time to rest himself, or to play with the excited youngsters of the clan, who would themselves one day become Bevork warriors and workers.

Othello was in the middle of a playful stick fight with a youngster when the spearman returned from the selection. As his attention was diverted, the youngster saw his opportunity and seized it, poking hard at Othello's side. In good humour, Othello responded with a tap on the head that sent the kid running away laughing. The Bevork warriors waited for him to join them, mounted upon their hulking tulkan bulls, looking as if they were ready for battle. He approached the spearman who had hopped off his bull, listening as he listed out some names:

"Malek. Karn. Vontarg and myself. I thought you should know." As the spearman left, Othello called out:

"Dingane. Who is the fifth?" Dingane continued to walk away.

"Kenjii is willing to take your place if your hole is not finished in time. It is his first tournament. Can you believe it?" The man mounted his bull. "Most of the country will be there. You draw quite a crowd, Othello. Most will want to see you fall, but wouldn't it be lovely to disappoint them? I will see you after it's all over." The tulkans waddled away down the path after Dingane, leaving the dusty plains. Othello tapped his stick on the ground for a moment, recalling the exhilaration and atmosphere of the tournament experience. Having been up and working since before the sun had even risen, a little rest was what he needed; it had been a long, tiring morning and now it seemed he had an important decision to make. Finally, Othello made up his mind, though not before once again being hit in the back by a child wielding a stick, back for more practice.

After carrying his last bucket load of water to a nearby stone table, full of materials and working gear, Othello rolled off his work gloves and handed them into the old man whose job it was to manage all of the work-related tools on site. They exchanged some friendly words before he went on his way. He visited a nearby shack and approached an elderly lady, who thanked him kindly for his hard work.

"Off so soon? Not like you, my boy" she noted, handing him his neatly folded, white shirt from the back of the shelter, which was packed with all kinds of hanging clothes.

"I'll be back before you know it," Othello promised.

"I hope so. Where are you going?"

"Just something minor I have to take care of."

"Thank you so much for the well; I knew I could rely on you to get it working again."

"No problem at all. If you need anything else done or if anything breaks, be sure to let me know, I'll be there." With that, Othello left the work site. On occasion, men who were enjoying a well-deserved rest in the shade stood up and saluted as he passed by. He always stopped to thank them politely, every time he did this, he explaining to them that it was not necessary, but the Bevorks had built up a great sense of respect for their foreign, Southlander friend. Eventually, he came to an alley of open shelters, a place for mothers and children. The aromas of incense reminded him of the feeling of home. The clanking and dragging noise of work could still be heard in the far distance, but here the tension and stress had given way to a far more relaxing atmosphere. This place was tranquil, peaceful. Young curious children often stopped and stared at him, questioning him about his paler skin colour. Othello was nicely tanned but compared to a common Bevork clansman his skin was far lighter. He took no offence to the curiosity of the children and simply teased and played back.

He passed by many tents where young mothers and elders alike cared for new-borns. Babies learned to walk here, crawling around inside their tents with their families close by. He spotted a wandering baby girl, picked her up very carefully with both hands. The little one must have been a fast learner, successfully escaping her mother's grasp. Othello held her close, gently talking to her softly as he found the mother, opening her arms for the pair.

"Thank you, Othello. I thought something was missing. This little one is keen to get away," she beamed, giving him a kiss on the cheek. She had a powerful Jurean accent.

"Just like her mother then…" he replied charmingly, as the baby tangled up in his wooden necklace. He took the chain off, gave it to the baby and handed her back to the mother. "She can have it." The young mother caught him staring down a sloping path with a look of concern on his face.

"He has not come out all day. I am worried about him," she said.

"No need to worry…May I?" he asked, pointing to a few items for sale at her feet.

"Of course, of course, help yourself. Anything you need, I am never far away. You have been so kind to us; many of us wonder how we can return the favour. Some of the girls your age have a few ideas…" He grinned with blushed cheeks. "You've given us so much since you came here," she continued her praise, handing him a bushy, green herb.

"I appreciate your help. I do intend to pay you back. I promise," he assured her, picking up a wide jug of water made at the pottery stalls further away in the camp, and a small pestle to grind the herbs, items he had made.

"Oh, don't worry about it, my darling, you work hard enough here already, harder than anyone else I know. You're a good man and we bless you for your charity every day you are with us."

"I still remember the day I made this…I'll see you again," he called, waving, and set off down the rocky slope.

Othello stepped inside the tent. The small area was dim, a little smoky and a warm air was adrift. The fire in the centre was calm, its ambers glowing red. He moved inside, stepping over the blankets covering the floor. Sitting down next to the elderly man sheltering beneath the sheets, who was half asleep and breathing soundly, he looked around the tent. It was in a bit of a mess; old things had been pulled out of place, clothing and small wooden drawers had been rummaged through. His father must have been looking for something. Othello lifted a box that he recognised from when he had first arrived here. It had been opened and emptied, to his disappointment. "Do you know of the other worlds?" asked the old man, his eyes firmly closed.

"Do you know of the lands to the south?" Othello nodded once; he did know of them, but he did not wish to speak of them. "It is a world of two nations: the Norkrons of Krondathia and the Dovidians of Ivulien. A fragile alliance has lasted for a long time, dating back to The Awakening Ages, when Regina Corah set out upon her quest to awaken the twelve great Celestials. Of course, you remember the stories I told you when you were just a boy. Since then, peace has driven men to do great things. In the south, one man can make a difference, can give meaning to his own life, become something that he never thought possible. It is a beautiful place, and it will stay beautiful so long as there are people there who continue to serve and maintain the balance. My son, I know I said, what seems like a lifetime ago, that we would return home one day, but I cannot come with you. You know you must go on alone." Othello drew a little closer.

"You will get better; just take the medicine and you will heal."

"It is worse now than ever. I won't improve, you know this. Never lie to yourself, Othello, face the truth, confront it, deal with it and beware of those who lie. Rise above them when you return and live to do good."

"Father, what of the others?" He was talking about his father's old friends.

"No need to deliver them any message, I will do it when I see them. I don't have time anymore like I once did, Othello, but you, you have time, time to show the world what kind of man you are. The Eldor of Krondathia rewards his finest. Wealth and gold in your eyes have no meaning, I respect that; the corruption power brings has no hold on you like it does others. Serve in Krondathia and you can make a difference to other people's lives, just as you have done here," the old man lectured, laying back down, breathing heavily.

"What about the tournament?" Othello asked, his eyes sinking to the floor.

"Go to the tournament, win it for The Bevork Clan one more time, keep the hawks in power, then come back here and I will tell you of…This." He held up a golden ring engraved with a red crest. Othello marvelled at the ring, then looked at his father for answers regarding its importance. "I have enough time to see you accomplish this last task, and ride away to the horizon, back to the south, back to where you came from. That will make me proud." As his father spoke these words, Othello mixed up some medicine using the pestle he had borrowed. He added water from the jug and carefully pressed it up to his father's mouth. The elderly man gulped it down with difficulty, breathing in deeply; the taste was not pleasant. "You must leave this place, son, head for home, head to Imrondel City. I know you do not want to, but you must, for the sake of your friends and all Bevorks. I know you had no intention to leave. Yet the other clans fear you and very soon that fear, that jealousy, will turn into hate. You will be killed along with all those who try to defend you. Don't allow that to happen, you have already outstayed your welcome."

"I understand, but I can't turn away. I can't abandon them. I cannot leave them in their time of need. The Bevorks are the smallest of all the clans. Who will protect them if not me?"

"This country is Jureai, a whole land of clans. They have never looked kindly upon the south. Power, true power lies in the majority and it always has; never has it resided in the strength of one man. Go, I will be waiting for you here." Othello gave a reluctant nod.

"Very well." He moved a cup of water to his father's side and fed the fire with a piece of wood.

"Go, son, and don't lose your way, do not become all that you fear and hate."

Othello left the tent and strolled down the path. It had been a long time since his arrival to these lands; so much had changed since. He was just a boy when he first met The Bevork Chieftain. He could still remember his very first meeting with El Raud, along with Dingane and Vontarg. It must have been twenty years ago, in the year of fourteen ninety-one, when he first became a part of the clan. He was still only twenty-seven, but it seemed like it was only yesterday when his father was a young man, far stronger and fitter than he was now. Othello could remember the journey; his memory had always been good; he had always been able to remember the little details that triggered more detailed pictures in his mind. Twenty years ago, he and his father had left the great and holy city of Imrondel. He thought back to one favoured memory. They were nearing the end of their travel, on the final route to the northern reaches of The Ledera Lands, where it grew hotter and hotter with every day that passed. Othello's father, Enemar, had not left alone; he had brought with him a carriage that sheltered many of their possessions. A few soldiers journeyed with them; one was the carriage driver, who Othello did not recognise or know the name of. The other two were familiar, good friends of Enemar. Their names were Kespar Lanara and Sebastian Sious. All were Norkron born and experienced riders. They would not be staying in Jureai; however, they were simply escorting and were good company. Not that Enemar needed protection; he had proven himself to the Norkron people on more than one occasion, he was perfectly capable of holding his own. Unlike Sebastian and Kespar, who held titles and owned land in Krondathia, Enemar had refused such privileges and remained independent, open to the free world, believing strongly that great wealth and riches held a malicious power over men. He simply denied himself such rewards, not because he could not use or manage them, but because he wanted no ties, no bonds, nothing holding him back. As an honourable soldier, he believed that the less he had to sacrifice and lose, the less his enemies could use against him as bargaining tools. This belief made him stronger in the mind.

"Where are we?" asked young Othello. Enemar looked across at his son while riding his horse and answered.

"Our journey is nearly over; we will be in Jureai soon enough."

"Why did we leave?" The young boy was full of questions today. Sebastian was keeping pace with them, listening in on the conversation, but did not interrupt.

"We would not have left if it wasn't important. Just know that this trip is more for you than it is for me." Othello did not understand and creased his face. His father grinned as he spotted the reaction.

"Not so long ago you asked me about where I grew up and where I learnt to do the things I do. Krondathia trains some of the finest soldiers; every boy must learn how to fight, it is essential, but you will be different, you will learn how to fight, learn how to live, but more importantly, you will learn how to think for yourself."

"And Krondathia cannot teach him those things?" interjected Sebastian. Enemar glanced over at his friend.

"Norkrons are capable; it's just different in Jureai, as you know."

"Why don't you remind me again?" Kespar requested, pulling up his horse on the other side of the carriage.

"It's far less complicated," stated Enemar bluntly, ending the conversation, giving Othello a quick wink. The young boy looked ahead and saw a small settlement of tall tepees gathered around a hill, with a great hut sitting proudly at the top. "That is The Chieftain's Nest. We will meet with El Raud when we arrive. Then we shall feast and rest ourselves." Othello wondered what this El Raud was like? His father had spoken of him a lot on the journey, saying that he was a very fair and wise man. He felt uncomfortable as the carriage rolled closer; he could see children his own age staring at him and his group from afar. Enemar galloped ahead to meet with the clan, for he was anxious to get settled in. The carriage came to a halt and The Bevork Clan gathered around, recognising the older man and his friends. Othello was left alone, sitting in the carriage, waiting for someone to approach and talk to him. El Raud stood atop the hill. Enemar spotted him and waved.

"HELLO!" called the Chieftain, stretching out his arm, waving his hand around.

"Othello, come!" All eyes fell on him; everyone watched him as he stepped out of the carriage. It was time to meet El Raud. He joined his father at the bottom of the slope, standing before the large hut. As he moved steadily toward The Chieftain's Nest, he could feel the invasive eyes of the youngsters of the clan. Enemar put his arm around his son as he got closer, preventing him from looking back at the children. He could see that Othello was uncomfortable, so he got down on one knee and made eye contact with him. "Something troubles you?"

"I don't belong here," came the nervous reply.

"It's natural for them to look upon us with suspicion, we've another shade of skin. Norkrons have done some terrible things in the past. This is their land, this is their home, and they want it to remain that way, so caution is understandable. The Bevorks will soon learn to trust you if you do right by them. Gaining the trust of El Raud is the first step. Once the leader believes in you, the rest will find it easier to accept you among them. Now come up the hill, let us make that first step together." The man held out his hand and the boy took it, only letting go as he neared The Nest at the top.

Othello hung outside the doorway, not too keen on knocking, but Enemar ushered him on. Othello opened the door to a spacious room with several large, wooden totem poles decorated with carvings of the twelve Celestials. A few wooden tables lay at the far end, alongside several opened chests and caskets. It seemed El Raud was in the process of moving in his belongings. Bevork servants were removing items and precious glass materials from such chest, placing them carefully on the floor. The Chieftain was supervising his servants; these were some of his most treasured possessions. He saw Othello, standing there silently.

"Greetings, little master," he smiled warmly. Enemar entered and the two men shared a brief Bevork salute, before taking a hold of one another's hands, which turned into a friendly hug. "Glad you made it here on time, old friend," said El Raud, sounding pleased.

74

"Yes, and as you have already seen, I did not come alone." El Raud smiled, picked up a small box that lay close to his feet and approached Othello, who did not move, desperately trying to appear unafraid.

"So, this is the son I've heard so much about." He measured the boy up, comparing him next to his father. "He is yours, alright; he has your strength, perhaps even more than you…Even at this age." He threw a cheeky smile at the boy.

"Indeed, he has no fear."

The Chieftain approached young Othello and stood over him. Enemar just folded his arms and watched the pair.

"I ask no loyalty of my subjects, no man is bound to me, the world binds us all together. All I ask is one thing." He then got down on one knee, looking the boy dead in the eye. "Will you help me make this world a better place? For those in need, for those less fortunate than us? Will you stay with us?" Othello felt an instant rush of respect, an instant feeling of being needed and wanted. Unlike his experience in the cities of Krondathia, where he had been treated like an insignificant child who would lead a narrow, mundane life of servitude, here he felt valued.

"Answer him, son. Remember that you always have a choice," his father advised, leaning his head to the side. Othello did not need to think for very long; he wanted to get to work right away, to meet the other clan members and get acquainted with those his own age.

"Are you ready to make a difference, Othello?"

"Yes, I guess I am," he replied.

"Then may the guard of the hawk watch down on you from above," announced El Raud, quoting a common motto belonging to his people. He clicked open the hinged box, the outside of which was square, with strange marks and colours both light and dark dyed into it. Inside the hollow box was a board, and a collection of small figurines for two players. El Raud took out the most important piece and began to explain the rules. "The game is called Take. It can be played in many ways. Depending on who you play, you will have to justify and assert your actions accordingly to defeat your opponent." He opened the box out fully, revealing all the individual figurines. "These pieces represent every human being on the planet; it is up to you to decide which you will be, not I. Will you be a Grunt?" He held up a piece with a little round head and tiny arms. "Will you decide to follow your faith?" This piece was called an Acolyte, wearing a pointed hat on its head. "Or maybe you will decide to take up arms?" El Raud revealed the proud model of the Knight; of course, this appealed to most young boys and it had the same effect on Othello. He took the piece with both hands and examined it carefully, looking upon its large shield and longsword. El Raud backed away a little and continued his speech. "Figuring out who you will become is just one of life's trials. Understand who you are, understand your place and you will soon understand your purpose, your path and your true calling in life. You may never find it, but here you stand a better chance than in the south…That is what I offer," he finished, standing up, leaving the box at his feet. Othello knelt and picked up a figurine with a crown upon its head; this was the piece that gave all the others orders.

"I want to be everything," he announced confidently.

"Say again, young one?" the Chieftain requested, looking a little startled.

"Why does one man have to stick with just one ambition or calling? Why can't he excel in more than one aspect of his life?" El Raud beamed at Enemar, who returned the expression.

"Not only does the hawk watch down on you, Othello, but I too will watch over your training with much interest," said the Chieftain, equally as proud as his father, giving the young boy a pat on the back. Othello placed the Emperor piece back in its place and folded the box up, sealing it with its hooked lock.

Chapter 6 - The Chimera Order

Differences can be settled in many ways, but an uneasy alliance may fall to a single misunderstanding.

Mounted upon the hulking backs of tulkan bulls, five Bevork Hawks travelled over the broad, red-hot wasteland of Jureai. Each man was similarly outfitted, equipped with traditional brown leather armour buckled across their chests, loose strands of cloth hanging off their waists and feathers flicked from their elbows, shoulders, and knees. Dingane led the way, holding his clan's banner with pride in his right hand. The banner was coloured with earthy, tanned dyes, boasting the symbol of the hawk. A long spear was strapped to his back, its head as lethal as a raptor's talon. Next to Dingane rode Malek, of the same build yet not quite as dark skinned as his banner man, he wielded a two-handed sword. Of the five he wore the most material and cloth, including gloves, a helmet that concealed much of his face, and heavy boots. Quiet in nature, with a reputation for having the worst luck in the tournaments, this would be Malek's third competition in a row. Not too far behind the two, rode a heavily stacked, menacing-looking man, strapped up with an abundance of leather armour, all held together by a wide, circular buckle in the middle of his chest. Bald on top, a long, dark ponytail trailed from the back of his head. His name was Karn, a gentle giant who had a history with The Honour Guards of the southlands. He was a man of great stature, clearly the muscle and heavy weapons expert of the group. Vontarg rode next to him; intelligent and light in weight, he nevertheless boasted an impressively muscular frame. He wore a sheathed sword around his belt and a dagger hung at his side. Latched around his arm was a small crossbow, skilfully made by the weaponsmiths in back at camp. Usually, he was the advisor of the group; he had previously escorted competing hawks to and from the tournament. This time, however, would be his second attempt at competing in the tournament, having performed admirably the last time around. Kenjii, the youngest, rode side by side with Vontarg. Pushing nineteen years of age he had wild, bushy hair. It seemed strange to some that Kenjii was chosen in the selection; there were plenty of other skilled warriors with far more experience, but regardless, he had been chosen over them for a reason. Kenjii must have shown distinctive ability to have ever stood a chance of being selected for the tournament.

Following The Bevork Hawks on foot was their clans supporters. They travelled light, and in great numbers, with the turn-out being the largest crowd of Bevorks the tournament had ever seen. Under the sky and intense heat, the tulkans and men trudged on, talking casually as they went.

"He is the best amongst us. I heard a rumour that he cannot be wounded; that is what the other clans say. He is the reason why El Raud has sat atop The Five-Headed Throne for so long. Before he came, it was Kronix and his Salarthian Snakes who ran things, and Jureai lived under the shadow of fear, fear of Xavien and his blood-tribes," Vontarg explained to Kenjii, keeping an eye on the road ahead of him.

"Why is he allowed to compete if he is from the south? I thought The Southlanders were unwelcome here."

"Not unwelcome…"

"What then?"

"The south is wealthy, its lands rich in Glyph and myths, though its people take what does not belong to them, without thought, without care. They will spread to Jureai again, the moment their own land's resources dry up, they will come and drive us out, pushing us into The Desert's Skin, into the ocean of Sand, where we will not be able to survive. People from the south behave this way."

"They will not push us out, we will stay, but if that day comes, we will find a way to cross the desert. There must be a way," insisted Kenjii.

"No one has ever crossed the width of the desert in the far north, and I mean no one. Who knows what lingers in the dunes and beyond? One day, the south will come here, and on that day, we must be prepared, not fighting amongst ourselves."

"So, if The Southlander was not welcome, to begin with, then why was he allowed to compete?" Vontarg breathed in deeply before he answered.

"Curiosity. A young boy of sixteen from the south, competing in the finest tournament against some of the most skilled and dangerous warriors in the world. Kronix had the throne at the time; it was he who allowed The Southlander entry to The Arena. The Salarthian Chieftain wanted to see the boy humiliated at the hands of his own Snakes. That was a grave mistake."

"What happened?" Vontarg thought back to the day; it really had been a thrilling and exhilarating sight to behold.

"Not only did he win, putting the smallest clan in power of The Five-Headed Throne, but his methods were unbelievable. He made a mockery of his opponents, winning with ease, turning the strongest, most feared men into weeds before him. There aren't many who care to try their luck against him now." Dingane glanced back at the group, listening in on the history lesson.

"You would think someone out there could take him on; his tutor or his own blood perhaps?" Kenjii suggested.

"No one can take him. His only living blood relative is his father. You were too young to remember, but when he arrived, he was put straight into training, as we all were. At first, he was reluctant to do anything, but then something changed inside him and he began to fight back. I was there, I saw it all."

"Did you ever fight him?" Kenjii asked curiously.

"Once, and yes, I was soundly beaten. He did not even feel the need to draw his fighting stick. He wrestled me to the floor using only one arm and one foot," laughed Vontarg.

"I heard that Kronix is competing today." The others had also encountered this rumour.

"Kronix is the Chieftain of The Salarthian Clan, NOT a combatant. There is no way he will be allowed entry into The Pit."

"But what if he is?" Kenjii asked quietly. Vontarg had an answer for this too and it satisfied him to be able to say it with such confidence.

"Then our man from the south, Othello, will tear him apart." With that he gently spurred his tulkan, catching up with Dingane who had called him up to the front. They rode close together alongside Malek.

"Do you think he will come? Do you think he will fight?"

"I don't know," responded Dingane, "El Raud has made a daring move by making Kenjii a hawk today. It is not like him to gamble, but to my understanding, our Chieftain purposefully made an unwise decision, in hopes that Othello will step in and correct it."

"Othello will show up. El Raud knows his best hawk's conscience is what controls him."

The group rode slowly, maintaining speed in keeping with the travellers behind them.

"I never thought that I would be selected for this trial again," Vontarg noted, changing the subject.

"You're skilled and you're fast; our leaders saw this in you last time. Be thankful, you may not get selected again," Dingane pointed out.

"I sometimes wonder about our ways. The question I often ask myself is: *why*? Why do we have to display a show of violence to determine a new leader for The Five-Headed Throne?" The question was certainly thought-provoking; Vontarg was now doing what he did best, taking up his place as the philosopher. "Why is violence and the ability to use a sword so important? Intelligence, wisdom, honour, integrity, even mercy; these are what a leader needs to be fit to rule."

"So how do you propose we measure these traits?" Karn asked him, in a far deeper voice than the rest of the hawks.

"I can think of a few ways without the need for a sword, but why ask me? I'm just a grunt."

"I took you more for the Acolyte, but you're a clever grunt who tends to think way too much…"

"This is true; you do think yourself into confusion far too often," laughed Dingane.

"Shut your beaks," Vontarg protested.

"A grunt that must see these days through," Karn added.

"These days? HA! These days of peace will last, so long as Othello is in our nest."

"You're aware of the rebellion rising in the south then?" Dingane interjected.

"Of course I am" said Vontarg.

"And this does not worry you?" asked Karn upon his snorting bull.

"What's the matter? Does the thought of rebellion scare you Karn? If it does, then the list Dingane and I are making of your fears has grown to an enormous two." Dingane smiled at the reminder.

"What was the other thing that scares him? Say it out loud so all can hear, come on." Vontarg shook his head, refusing to answer Dingane.

"I am sorry, I can't divulge such secrets, if I did then I would be going into this tournament with a dent in my head," he laughed, looking over at Karn, who had his hand on his hammer, tapping the tips of his fingers across its grip.

"What scares him?" Kenjii asked, eager to know, missing the private joke. He then turned around to see Malek, hoping he would fill him in, but he didn't. Malek did not seem to be paying any attention to the conversation at hand, riding at the rear of the group, a cluster of women walking next to him, trying to catch a glimpse of what he looked like under his helmet. This attention went by equally unacknowledged.

The Bevork Hawks travelled on over the red lands, closely followed by their clan. The empty road widened and eventually split off into many different directions. These paths clearly led to other significant areas in Jureai, though no one was interested in visiting them today. Everyone was heading northeast from The Web of Roads, the centre of Jureai. A short time into their journey, Dingane spotted another, significantly larger clan. They too were heading north. It was the Nexius, who, like the Bevorks, proudly paraded their own banner, with the emblem of a seahorse, held high upon a trident by the champion. Both parties kept their distance, but each was aware of the other's presence. The Nexiuns on foot whispered to one another, slowing their pace to get a better look at their rivals. Vontarg spotted his opponents, mounted upon camels, leading their clan; these were the ones he would likely face in The Pit of The Arena. He dropped back to the rear of his group, to speak with Kenjii. Instead of waiting for the young man to ask, Vontarg got the obvious out of the way first.

"The man in front, the one holding the banner is the Champion Seahorse; his name is Thollin. The one to his right is Taolou, and the other three I have never seen before. The Chieftain's name is Ukthoth." The Nexius Clan appeared to be searching for Othello, for he usually was the one holding the banner of the Bevorks.

"Why do they dress in cold skins?" Kenjii asked Vontarg as he observed the Nexiuns' livery, capes of silvery skin glinting under the sunlight, sea plants and pieces of silk covering any gaps. They wore accessories made of shell necklaces, pearlescent rings, and bracelets of sparkling coral stones.

"Long ago, before the establishment of The Chimera Order, settlers known as Jureans discovered a channel far to the west. A mystical isle was found where countless relics have since been unearthed. West of The Ophiadras Mountains, passed The Clawed Mountain, lies Monument Isle, where the Jureans ceased their journey. The descendants of those explorers would become The Nexius Clan. Compared to where we are from, they live in a relatively cool place."

"So, The Jureans that traipsed The Blood Plains and stopped under the great mountain of Thethian became The Red Stone Clan?"

"As history teaches us, this is true, but the story of Red Stone dates back further than any one of the clans."

"How much do you know about it?"

"Enough," answered Vontarg, taking a breath before beginning his tale. "The Red Stone Chieftain in power today is named Kollag Mel Thung; his son Darados Mel Thung is competing, as the Champion Rhino. Long before them, their ancestor was a man named Lillien Thethian, often referred to as Lil because of his small stature. Lillien travelled afar, not just within the boundaries of the red lands with which we are so familiar, but also into the southland, documenting his findings as he travelled. Thethian, though greatly admired for his vision and ambition of constructing a Jurean society, was never a true ruler; he left many of his political decisions to his followers. Towards the end of his life, the Jureans could not decide who was fit to rule this hot land, so Lillien suggested The Tournament of Leadership, a fair system that brought the entire population together. Upon his death, his followers took control of the four clans scattered throughout The northland: Bevorks, Salarthians, Vantarquinns, and the oldest, the Red Stones. The Nexius Clan formed shortly afterward when expeditions found Monument Isle. The Chimera Order was established in The Arena during the first tournament. That is how it all began, Interesting, no?"

"Who was victorious in the first tournament, Vontarg?"

"The Starillia believers were, the Vantarquinns. Then, years later, the Salarthians took the throne from them."

"The Vantarquinns are passionate about the beliefs of the south; are they as committed to the faith as their ancestors were?"

"I'd say so, though they never worship in the southlands"

"Why not?"

"Distance and the civil war. It never ended, regardless of who says otherwise; hatreds still exist."

"The Civil War for the Unicorn's Independence? The elders taught me of this; the crimes committed on both sides were unforgivable," noted Kenjii, recalling his studies.

"The Vantarquinns were once well connected with the southland, and members of the clan became devoted followers of Starillia, basking in its traditions, even practising The Glyph Arts. As history goes, The High Priests of The Column Temple were impressed with their firm commitments towards Starillia; as a result, they were granted seats in The Palace of Xiondel City, Xiliac. This honour allowed them a say within The Lower Council. It is a respected place to be, The Lower Council, though not secure, for it is forever changing, growing smaller each year. The Thunderhoof Captain of the time, with his legion of horse riders, part of The Regular Norkron Army, saw this as an insult, as they had served for far longer, with loyalty and obedience. When talks failed and the politicians refused the horsemen a seat on The Council, this sparked the harsh civil war, breaking out into the streets of Xiondel. The Thunderhoof Riders and Vantarquinn Tulkan Knights waged a bloody feud. It never ended; the only difference now is that it is fought in the shadows, out of sight. The Honour Guards of Krondathia had something to do with the dispersion of the belligerents, but I cannot be sure. After a year of bloodshed, eventually, The Thunderhoof Riders won their seats, becoming part of The Norkron Army, just like The Tulkan Knights. Though The Vantarquinn Clan withdrew, returning to their real home in Jureai, they brought back their faith, hand in hand with their hatred of the south." Kenjii knew a little of the history between the Vantarquinns and the Norkrons from the south, but not nearly as much as Vontarg, who continued. "The Vantarquinns follow a girl named Isabelle Verano, worshipping her under a petrified Celestial shrine."

"She is important to the Norkrons; I've heard of her. The stone embedded in rock is one of the twelve shrines. They call this one Capricorn," stated Kenjii.

"A Demi-God of the earth, representing independence. Apparently, it has a second name, an older name, which I have forgotten."

"*Capradius* is the name you are looking for."

"Capradius, that's it, well done, boy. The Vantarquinns live around the foothills of The Grey Peaks, far from here in the northeast. Their Chieftain, or Chieftainess as it were, is Reneeia Talaka. Her Champion Fox, Sarb, is one of the few in her clan able to harness the power of Glyph. There is no rule, as far as I am aware, that states you cannot wield Glyph when in The Pit" Vontarg recounted.

The Chimera Order
El Raud - Bevork Chieftain of the Hawk
Kronix - Salarthian Chieftain of the Snake
Kollag Mel Thung - Red Stone Chieftain of the Rhino
Reneeia Talaka - Vantarquinn Chieftainess of the Fox
Ukthoth - Nexius Chieftain of the Seahorse

The clans of Nexius and Bevork remained separated for the time being, as the desolate plain of hot earth seemed to stretch on forever. They took shelter under the shade provided by a sparse crop of trees. As the Bevorks rested, they quenched their thirst and tended to themselves and their mounts. A few approached the resting Nexiuns, also taking advantage of the shade. The Bevorks offered a small supply of water, which the rivals gladly accepted, without quarrel. Malek dismounted and led his bull to the shade, where Dingane was sitting, observing the behaviour of the two opposing clans. The common people were communicating on some levels, but the warriors and champions from both parties stayed distant, keeping themselves busy with the weight of their gear and the intense heat. Karn handed Dingane a pouch of water, which he drank from, before saying:

"It's a good day, yes?"

Karn looked up at the sky and nodded.

"Better than the last tournament at least." He sat down next to Dingane under the tree in the shade, stretching out his legs. Vontarg had drawn his dagger; its hilt was wide and curved with a smooth, light grip, tinted with a faint fabric of violet. The bronze shone in the sun; he reflected some sunlight into the face of Kenjii, who had been staring at The Nexius Champion, Thollin, an energetic looking man. The young Bevork squinted, then sat down next to a chuckling Vontarg.

"It is rude to stare," Vontarg admonished, cleaning his dagger thoroughly.

"If Othello comes, I will gladly forfeit my place for him. I know that El Raud has put me in this position to get him to fight. Not sure I agree with the move, but the last thing El Raud and many others want, including myself, is to see The Salarthian Snakes sit atop The Five-Headed Throne once again."

"That's wise of you to say so," praised Vontarg, "Othello will come, and if not, then The Salarthian Clan will certainly take the throne once again."

"How can you say that!? Are you saying that no other clan has a chance of winning? That we have no chance unless Othello shows?" Kenjii argued.

"Champions and warriors have died in this tournament. Every life The Arena has claimed, the Salarthians were the ones responsible. They are killers, not warriors; they are the most ruthless of all the clans of Jureai. Worse yet, they are in league with Xavien." Upon finishing his sentence, Vontarg tied his weapon to his belt. "Xavien was once a part of The Salarthian Clan. Before Othello arrived, the brute was the unbeaten Champion Snake, the most feared man in the land. He viciously slaughtered every opponent he ever met in The Arena, ignoring all the rules and laws, becoming a monster or, as some describe him nowadays, a Demon Man. Now, Xavien has not been sighted for quite some time, which is a growing

86

concern within The Chimera Order. When he was exiled from Jureai, The Salarthian Chieftain, Kronix, needed a new Champion Snake. Simultaneously Othello came of age and entered the tournament, beginning his winning streak. From then on, Othello's legacy surpassed even that of even Xavien's. The Bevork Clan is in power, and as it follows Jureai prospers, which the other clans happily acknowledge. Thanks to Othello, Jureai is balanced."

"I know about Xaviens search for The Blood Angel. He and those who follow him - The Blood Marauders - Truly believe that such a creature exists. I hope this is not true," murmured Kenjii.

"I have heard this too, but it is a rumour that must be put to rest before it is too late. However, no one I know, not even Othello, is bold enough to hunt down Xavien and his Blood Marauders; not after El Raud forbade it."

"Why would he forbid such action from being taken against Xavien?"

"The Blood Marauders sent The Chimera Order a message, written in blood, delivered in a hollowed-out skull."

"What was in the message?" asked Kenjii.

"Xavien has been hailed a King amongst his people, a King speaking on behalf of The Blood Angel itself, who will one day seize The Five-Headed Throne if it is not first surrendered to him. If Jureai does not comply with the terms, then they will suffer the same fate as those who stood against him in the south. The Chimera Order did not take the threat seriously, until Xavien started a guerrilla war with the Dovidians, rallying hundreds, if not thousands to his cause. Frightening to think that so many share his vision of chaos. Playing on the element of fear, I hear he takes off the noses and sometimes the jaws of his enemies. Besides his pursuit of power, I don't know what Xavien is planning. I do not believe in The Blood Angel, though his passion for brutality that he wants to inflict on others is apparently part of a ritual. Of course, the Dovidians are keeping this rebellion all hush hush; I do not think they want this to escalate into a war. If war is declared, then it won't be long before Krondathia steps in." The Bevork and Nexiun clansmen started to gather up their supplies. Malek mounted his Tulkan, as did Dingane, who took up the banner of the hawk and continued to lead the way.

"Not far to go now," promised Vontarg, offering Kenjii his hand, helping him up to his feet. The clans broke and continued trekking on under the sun. The Nexius Clan maintained their distance once again. Thollin and his fighters rode upon camels that had taken them far from their western home of Monument Isle; no horse or bull could travel that far of a distance without being consistently tended to. The camels they were mounted upon had made the journey before, back and forth between Monument Isle and The Arena, and they were well-accustomed to the conditions.

Chapter 7 - The Five-Headed Throne

Successful cultures often thrive off the most dramatic and vibrant of traditions. The Tournament of Leadership.

The Arena came into view. Built generations ago by Jurean settlers, before a great range of mountains, dwarfing the red landscape. A shadow splintered through the rocky wall where a narrow gorge ran through, creating a thin pathway. Shaped like a magnificent golden chalice, The Arena stood out in front of the enormous mountains. From what the travelling clans could see, they were not the first to arrive. Many had come to witness the spectacle, the most famous tradition in the land.

"There it is. The great Arena," Dingane said with awe in his voice, "I wonder if they have arrived yet? Malek, keep a lookout, we can do without any violence before the games." Malek, silent as ever, stared at the swarms of people through his helm. As the two clans drew closer, the Nexiuns broke away from the Bevorks. Thollin, however, rode up next to Dingane, holding out his hand as a sign of respect.

Thin but sturdy wooden structures made shade for travellers, warriors, and champions alike, shielding them from the beating sun. A multitude of strange, wild, and wonderful animals were cooped up in cages for the attention of tradesmen. Salesmen carted around the smaller beasts, along with anything else they wished to sell, mainly skins, fabrics, garments, hunting gear, weapons, tools, and other ornamental items. Clansmen and common folk gathered around certain vendors, standing tall upon raised platforms, auctioning their stock. The place was mad, bustling with movement. Members of the crowd held up their pieces of copper and silver, shouting over the top of each other, trying their best to be heard, to make a deal. The roads and paths were gridlocked. Tensions were slowly rising, and still more people flooded in from afar, seeking shelter, food, and a place to rest after the hard journey. The Bevorks arrived in the thick of it all; a pathway seemed to clear itself for them as they walked through. The clan dispersed in various directions, though The Hawks, Dingane, Malek, Karn, Vontarg and Kenjii, stayed together in a tight unit. Large, round wells offered cold refreshment for those being worked non-stop. Food from the seas, the mountain valleys and farmlands had been generously provided by each clan. The Arena was not only a place for ancient traditions but also a hotbed for profiteering. Farmers, travellers, miners, jewellers, cooks, teachers, old and young; all had come for work and pleasure. Salty scents wafted through the air, tickling the noses of The Bevork Hawks. One of the Nexius tradesmen, working hard behind his stand selling meat, generously offered Karn a juicy serving, wrapped up in a bag. He reached over from his tulkan and took the meat with a grateful acknowledgement. Exquisitely outfitted stalls offered idols, figurines, and statues; even Glyph Pearls were for sale, albeit in minimal quantity, though it was against the laws of Jureai, punishable by banishment. It was likely that these tradesmen did not know what they possessed. Most people did not inquire or even know the risks involved, taking the Glyph Pearls in their ignorance, unaware of what they were, and what effects they could cause to the rare few. Vontarg trotted up to one such stand, nestled in between two larger ones selling bread, picking up a colourful strand, examining a faint yellow bead carefully. He then spoke quickly and quietly to the young, naive seller:

"Is this only for decoration, or for proper use?" The seller, a young lad of about thirteen, addressed the warrior directly.

"My owner bought these beads for a high price from a Vantarquinn. Tells me I should sell them at the cost he has given me." Vontarg shook his head in disappointment and amazement at the ignorance shown in the face of such danger. He decided to educate the lad.

"This is Glyph...You have no idea what it is, do you? Have you seen what these pearls can do to a man? If anyone with any authority catches you selling these, they will hold YOU responsible, not your master." He hastily reached into his satchel and pulled out a bundle of gold talon coins "Here, take these, put away the Glyph. If your master complains, point him in the direction of The Hawks. These pearls are dangerous if not managed carefully." The young lad did as he was told, hastily throwing the orbs into a sack under the surface of the counter. Vontarg picked up a string of three pearls the boy had missed before making his way back to his group, where Malek had been watching the incident. Dingane came over and confronted Vontarg, who was staring into one of the pearls.

"Are you sure it's Glyph?"

"I am certain. The boy was being used by his master to sell these Glyph Pearls, trying to hide it with a masking substance to block out their true colour. It must have fooled many, passing for innocent decorative beads. If only they knew how devastating this power can be." Vontarg wiped the yellow pearl with a rough cloth, removing some of the polish. Where it had been scrubbed clean, the small pearl emanated a soft light. "This is dangerous magic," he groaned.

As The Bevork Hawks passed below the boundary of The Arena, the crowds grew thicker and the marketplace denser. The latter boasted an exquisite array of tools and armour at fair prices, laid out upon tables under the sun. Wild and rare species of plants had been stocked in great pots and hung from posts. Usually, those fewer in quantity were deadly poisons or expensive medicines, suspended from the roof supports, out of the reach of young children. Dingane could sense the attention directed his way; no doubt it was a result of the fact that he was the one bearing his clan's banner, rather than his more distinguished colleague. Over recent years, Othello had become one of the main reasons to attend the spectacle. Not all came to witness his success, of course; many hoped for the chance to see him fall. The settlements started to thin out as they came to the far end of the road, emerging amidst an area of ready-made shelters, space for them to tie up their tulkan bulls and rest before the tournament began. All combatants had their own private area set aside, for they needed time alone to psyche up and discuss strategy. They all dismounted, with Vontarg helping Kenjii to secure the bulls. Dingane got the fire going; Karn handed him some equipment, then the leg of meat he had been given earlier. Malek took the banner Dingane had been carrying, burying its tip into the ground. Under the grey shelters, the smell of herbal tea and roasting meat lifted the spirits of the five Hawks, who sat in silence, keeping themselves to themselves, save for Malek. Neither enthusiastic nor tempted by the cooking food or drink, he remained motionless outside in his leather armour and helmet, keeping a hand on his sheathed sword.

"What is he staring at?" Kenjii asked Vontarg, slicing off some of the cooked meat for them to share.

"The Crimson Gorge." The group ate and relaxed in the heat, while Malek still watched over the gorge in the distance. "That path splits the great mountains apart. It is about three or four miles long, a winding road of dark red rock, forever in the shade until the earth says otherwise. Beyond it is Salarthian territory; The Land of Snakes. I think they are yet to arrive, at least I didn't see any of their kind while passing through the markets." Kenjii fixated on t the dark passage. The Salarthians would soon cross through here, and when they arrived, they would meet the Bevorks before anyone else. The Snakes had no love for The Hawks; even before Othello's arrival, they had always held a hatred for them. When the foreigner from Krondathia did arrive, going on to win The Five-Headed Throne, taking leadership away from the Salarthians, it only caused a greater upset, amplifying their contempt for the smaller clan. The men sat comfortably for a while, until a high-pitched shriek echoed from the gorge, followed by another shortly after. Kenjii, with a puzzled face, asked:

"What was that!?"

"That was a copper hawk, they nest somewhere in the mountains. Beautiful birds they are, and right at the heart of our very culture. Keep a lookout, you may see one." Kenjii kept a sharp eye, hoping to spot one of these fabled creatures. Another sound came from the passage, a ferocious wail, evidently from a creature much larger than a bird of prey.

"That sounded odd…" said Kenjii.

"That was no copper hawk!" said Vontarg, sounding nervous, grabbing a hold of his weapon.

"That was a ptriva strider" Dingane observed, reaching for his own spear. Something was coming. Calming his companions down, Dingane spoke: "Hold on to your weapons. Do not let them fly. Don't strike. Vontarg, lower your crossbow but keep it latched. The Salarthians and their Snakes are here." From the red darkness of the gorge, mounted upon a fearsome war lizard, came Kronix, The Salarthian Chieftain, holding high the black banner of the red snake. The strider, larger than some of the biggest horses, had strong, muscular back legs, padded feet armed with curved claws, and thick, scaled skin. The lizard's snout stretched forward as the beast snarled with a mouthful of razor-sharp teeth, gleaming in the sun. Its tail grew thinner toward its end, flicking up at the tip. The heavy beast plodded forward, away from the shadow, carrying Kronix toward the camp. Four more ptriva striders followed, presumably carrying the other combatants. All were heavily armed with metallic spiked armour, their faces concealed beneath reptilian helmets, clutching fearsomely long weapons, blades that would slip through flesh without much resistance. The Salarthians had indeed arrived; a clan of dark-skinned men and women not dissimilar to those of The Bevork Clan now followed their banner bearer to The Arena. Hundreds, if not thousands of Salarthian clansmen appeared from the gorge in a seemingly endless, parading stream. Their skin was pierced and scarred to form fearsomely dark, strangely beautiful markings. Their accessories, bangles, bracelets, necklaces and jewels, had been styled around the various reptilian species of Jureai, the favourite, of course, the snake. They bore tattoos of black ink, highlighted with shades of red. The Salarthians, the greatest and most feared clan in Jureai, had once had the country pinned under its oppressive rule. They had lost this position of power to the Bevorks several years before, through the stunning moves of Othello, who thereby acquired the prestigious title of *Champion of the Hawks*. The loss had never sat well with the Salarthians, and Kronix's pride had never recovered. He was a brute of a man, built for the fighting. Not only had he lost the throne to a clan he despised, but it had been to a Southlander that he himself had allowed to compete. His skin was slightly paler than that of his clansmen, his hair and braided beard loose and wild, fading into grey with age. He wore heavy shoulder armour made from hyena fur, while his wrist pads, leg armour and parts of his chest armour were solidly bolted together with straps and leather belts. Strapped to his back, he had brought with him a round, heavy shield of immense size. On his right and left were scabbards holding a pair of swords, one he had named Trident Fang, for at the blade's end were three prongs, crafted in the likeness of snake teeth. The other sword was a simple great sword, stretching five feet in length. No one had travelled to The Land of Snakes for quite some time, and for good reason. If one was not a Salarthian, then one would not be welcome in those parts of Jureai. It was a ruthless place to exist in, even in the more civilised parts nature reigned over wanderers. The wild animals that inhabited those scorched lands could not be ignored; packs of hyenas, snakes, scorpions, brazen lions, and other creatures, some unknown to the clans and so referred to as monsters, all spread fear among the populace of Jureai.

The spear Kronix wielded had the red Salarthian Snake banner strung to it. A feared and powerful Chieftain, he had earned the right to lead the Salarthians in The Arena, proving himself through barbarity and strength, killing all who laid claim to his position. He had come to win The Five-Headed Throne, to avenge his clan for their previous loss. Yet he had remained unsuccessful, this time he had a plan to ensure victory. As the Salarthians came closer, Kronix spotted The Bevorks and signalled to his clan to hold. He steadily plodded over to them upon his ptriva strider, stopping a few feet away. His ptriva could smell the scent of the Bevorks; its tongue washing in saliva, tasting the air. Kronix steadied the lizard with the reins, saying nothing to his rivals; his face showed no sign of emotion as he stared at Dingane and his men. A copper hawk's cry echoed from somewhere within the gorge.

"Kronix, Chieftain of The Salarthian Clan…" Dingane began, making eye contact with his foe, stepping forward, "Move on in peace." The copper hawks were singing.

"The hawks are restless, I hear. Who are you?" Kronix grunted in a very rough and deep but authoritative tone, commanding instant respect. "Ah, I remember now; you're the ones who cower behind The Southlander. Unable to fight for yourselves, so you depended on another. You don't only disgust me with your inability to survive; you make me feel ashamed. Ashamed to know that we were once brothers of Jureai. Dare to adopt such methods again and things will surely change." He dismounted his strider, walking straight towards Malek, who held his ground. Dingane rushed toward them both, getting in between the two. "Othello… The Champion of Hawks. A puny Southlander he may be, but a worthy opponent, nonetheless. He is a man worth killing, but you… You are no more formidable than the tulkan beasts you ride on." Karn watched on, hidden in the shade alongside Vontarg, who had his finger on the lever of his crossbow. Kenjii folded his arms, waiting. "There will be no killing just yet. Not yet, but my Snakes are hungry. Ask yourselves: where would you be without your champion? What would become of you if he were gone?" Kronix demanded, now within arm's reach of Dingane, whose hand remained rested on the hilt of his blade. "Do you know what Xavien would do to you and your clan if your Champion were gone?" Dingane decided to ignore most of what he had just heard.

"So Xavien does fear Othello? That's good to know; when I see him, I'll tell him…" Kronix grinned a toothy smirk, as Dingane dug into him with more words. "Many fear you, this much is true, but know this: WE do not! And Othello certainly does not fear you or your blood thirsty maniac, so back off! Or I'll make you wish you had!" The Chieftain responded with a scratchy chuckle.

"If I am to spill your Bevork blood, I'll do it where all can see, but you, I'll pull out your tongue."

"Move on, we will meet in the tournament to settle this."

"Unlikely. Snakes are deadlier than hawks." Just as he was about to mount his ptriva strider, cries of joy erupted from the distance. Dingane smiled, baring his teeth. From among the gathering crowds of cheering Bevorks, Othello rode towards the Salarthians, showing no fear. His tulkan bull skidded as it came to a halt. Dingane handed Othello the Bevork banner, placing it into the hands of its rightful owner. It was only then that Othello acknowledged Kronix, hustling his tulkan over to him. The beast invaded his personal space and snorted, before trotting away, where its reins were taken by Karn. Othello dismounted and greeted the entire, gawping Salarthian Clan. The Snakes had all frozen on the spot, having stopped to wait for Kronix to give the orders. There he stood before them with his indescribable aura, his presence, a respect built up so high that no one else could hope to match it. The fierce Salarthians eventually moved on, to find their own space amongst the settlements, leaving Kronix alone on the plain before The Crimson Gorge. He sniggered, with a hint of satisfaction in his eyes, as if he had wanted Othello to show himself today. Eventually, he too plodded off on his strider, with the foul lizard giving off a croaking growl by way of farewell. When the threat had finally passed, Othello addressed his friends and fellow combatants. The people were still cheering and chanting his famous name, from the settlements to the marketplaces. The Hawks were clearly delighted to see him. It had not been the same without their champion.

A short time passed as the Bevorks finished up their drinks and food. They witnessed the crowds thinning out as the spectators head off to The Arena to view the spectacle. The Bevork Hawks, now reunited with Othello, would enter the structure shortly after, via a series of side passages guarded by tough, neutral Jurean guardsman, dressed similarly to the messenger who had arrived at their camp that morning. They wore no colours and bore no symbols of any kind, nothing to suggest allegiances with any clan. From there the tunnel descended, leading under The Arena. Torches lit the way to guide the six Bevork Hawks. As they descended, the echoing clank of hammers beating upon metal rung in their ears. They entered a dark, stony chamber filled with a great many Jureans, all working on weapons and armour. These were obviously blacksmiths, servants of Jureai, loyal to no clan though paid generously for their services. Chains and shackles were fastened to the walls, alongside suits of armour of all shapes and sizes. Some men approached The Bevork Hawks and lifted their weapons away from them, storing them in cages along with other personal effects. Walking in single file, they soon came to a dozen or so wooden racks, filled with a variety of swords, spears, shields, helmets, and quivers, as well as crossbows and longbows. War hammers and other weapons that could easily cripple a man with a single swing were not permitted in the tournament, though there were many around. Instead, wooden clubs and bats took their place, if such a warrior sought to use melee weapons. Karn lifted one club that fit his size and admirable strength. From the far rack, Vontarg grabbed a quiver of slug-headed arrows for his crossbow; he also drew a short sword. Malek pulled down a polearm, and then a battle dagger; he had no need for armour, for he had brought his own, which had been approved for use by the officials. Meanwhile, Othello remained seated on a nearby bench, waiting for his group to ready themselves. He was joined by Kenjii, who had just come down from the seating areas above them.

"The settlements outside are empty, as are all the markets, they have been closed up, nearly every one of them. Everyone is inside The Arena. They await the Chieftains, then it shall begin, the first act," the young man gasped, catching his breath. One of the officials snatched Vontarg's short sword away from him and took it to some hand-powered machinery. He rubbed its edge against a small spinning wheel for a time, before running the blade up and down his bare forearm to ensure that it left no mark and drew no blood. It was then handed back to its wielder, and the process was repeated for Dingane's weapon. After everyone had been inspected, The Bevork Hawks came together, gathering around Othello, who still had to find himself armour and a weapon. The crowds could be heard well above them, chanting their favourite names, excited for the tournament to begin.

"Bevorks, brothers of the hunt, I trust each one of you with my life. Let us show these Rhinos - these Seahorses, Foxes and Snakes – let's show them how lethal we can be. We are predators!" The Hawks grunted together, stamping one foot. "Never lose sight of your opponent; you are faster than they are, smarter than they are. Give yourself distance, allow yourself time to think before you strike down upon them, and do not stop until you are on top of them. This is not a battle to the death, so focus. Exploit your opponents' weaknesses, use what you know best against them, and tear them to pieces!" Another grunt followed by a stomp. "The terrain here is flat, it won't compromise your movements, stay strong, don't give them anything and soon enough this will all be over in our favour. Hawks, fight well, and, if need be, fall well." They moved closer and pushed their heads together for a moment. The armoury grew quieter; the blacksmiths were now washing their hands, removing their dirty aprons, and heading upstairs to watch alongside the excited crowds. The clank of metal ceased; now all that could be heard was the muffled noise of thousands of men and women, chanting, shaking the ground above them.

The Chimera's Pinnacle, a towering structure nestled at the very top of The Arena, was where the Chieftains gathered. They were seated around a metal table resembling a mighty shield, engraved with a diamond pattern. At the tips of the diamond's edges were the symbols of the hawk, snake, rhino, seahorse and fox. Ancient Jurean stories told of a creature known as the Driad, a giant beast that roamed the wastelands, searching for the foe responsible for exterminating its entire race centuries before. Four chairs were arranged at each of the table's points. The Supreme Watcher sat in a chair befitting his status. The ceiling above bulged inward; hanging from the roof was an unlit, bronze basin. The stone heads of former Chieftains dotted the spacious room, whilst skull trophies had been hung all over, and wooden totems depicting Jureai's myths, such as the golden hawk Sun Feather, and the Driad Wanderer, cluttered the floor space. Sitting in three of the four chairs, all facing The Sovereign Watcher - El Raud, Chieftain of the Bevorks - were the leaders of the clans Vantarquinn, Nexius, and Red Stones. Their expressions did not look at all enthusiastic about the upcoming event.

"Chieftains, clansmen, friends. We must agree. The people are waiting as you can hear…" El Raud began. His appearance reflected his power; dressed not in poor cloth or dull material, but wrapped in a shimmering, patterned robe, with two wings hanging off his arms. Around his neck was a chain of wood, with a handful of golden feathers strung upon it. Placed on top of his flowing, black, braided hair was a bronze band, his crown. Set into the centre of the crown were a pair of ruby-red eyes. Ukthoth, Chieftain of The Nexius Clan, was seated to El Raud's left, wearing the vibrant colours of the seas. His cloth was light and scaled, fashioned from an unknown creature of the deep. The blue ink tattoos on the left of his face depicted the beautiful seahorse. Next to Ukthoth sat Kollag Mel Thung of The Red Stone Clan, easily the oldest of them all. Strands of white hair fell from the top of his head, all the way down to his temples, draping over his bulky shoulder pads. Kollag's beard had been tied together with hollowed out marbles; beneath the beard one could just make out a necklace, adorned with the fossilised horn of a rhino. His dress was plain and heavy, though ancient. To El Raud's right sat an empty seat, then a woman of unknown age, the first female clan leader to exist, entered. Her name was Reneeia Talaka, Chieftainess of the Vantarquinn Clan. Believed by her people to be a living myth, the daughter of the Celestial Scorpio herself, she was the image of passion. Her elegant figure could not be ignored. Her hair was as black as night, floating down over her shoulders. Her eyes were sharp and delicate, full of life and love, while her face bloomed with passion and mysticism. Her most noticeable aspect, however, was not her perfectly slim, cared-for physique, but her skin; skin so divine, so thin as if made of pale silk woven by a Celestial spider. No one in the land had touched her; she had remained pure all her life, though many, men, and women alike, had dreamt of doing so.

The fabrics she wore were revealing. A misty cerise dress was slipped over her, resting on her shoulders, allowing her skin to shine through. Her jewellery sparkled in the minimal light; a rock mined from a rare crystal hidden in a cave under the remote mountains of Jureai close to her home. She wore one earring on her right side, her only piercing, a tiny, violet pearl shaped like the curl of a fox's tail. The leader of The Vantarquinn Clan was not only well respected by her people, but loved dearly, for she had been the one they had followed out of Krondathia and back into Jureai. She had been hailed as their saviour.

"Before the horn sounds, we must agree…" No one spoke a word. "If that is your answer, then I will speak for you. Not that I want to, but you leave me no choice. Since Kronix lost the throne, I think we can all agree that Jureai has prospered, not just for my clan, but for all. Reneeia, your clan is free to travel to and from the Celestial sites to worship in peace, without the need for guards. Ukthoth, your trade with Ivulien partners has never been so profitable, at least to my knowledge. And Kollag, my wise old friend, you and your family have enjoyed many undisturbed nights since the true colours of the Salarthians were revealed. They won't trespass or threaten to take your lands anymore; that goes for us all. We no longer have to sleep with one eye open. Our people, our food and water are our own. Jureai has never flourished to such an extent. Yet I must remind you that this can all change today, fellow Chieftains. It was not I who felt it necessary to ignore the laws of our lands, to bend them for my own pleasures. I never allowed Othello to compete when he did all those years ago, making a mockery of Kronix's Snakes. No, that mistake belongs to Kronix himself. So long as I' am in power, he will live with that mistake."

"If you were in our position and Kronix was where you sit, and he had an undefeated Snake from the southlands securing the throne for him time and time again, would you allow it to continue?" Ukthoth demanded, receiving a cold look from Reneeia.

"I will not allow Kronix to compete. You cannot justify a mistake he made in the past by committing another; its madness and it does not make sense. What is done is done, Ukthoth, and suspending Othello from the games now is not the answer. We have allowed him to compete ever since my clan won the throne from the

Salarthians; deep down I believe that you had your hearts in your mouths as Othello walked into The Arena last time. None of you supported the Salarthians that day, and you cheered when the boy took the victory."

"It was a glorious day, El Raud, a day worth remembering, but please try to see it from our point of view, acknowledge the dilemma and respect our feelings with wise thought. We are not here to fight, but to debate our situation, and to do what is right for the people of Jureai," put in Kollag Mel Thung in a mellow voice. El Raud rubbed his face, trying to come to a decision with haste. The clans of Jureai were waiting right outside, chanting for entertainment. Ukthoth spoke next:

"You are in a position to do anything you wish. Use your power, mighty Sovereign. Othello is a Southlander, a foreigner from the land of empire building. He doesn't belong here, and yet he is able to compete in our grand tournament. It's against our law, it's against Jurean tradition, and it's an insult to our people," he began, placing a firm finger upon the documents on the table. "Would Krondathia allow US to take part in their sacred ceremonies? Even the Vantarquinns, faithful followers of Starillia, are not welcome!"

"Ukthoth speaks the truth, El Raud. The people desire change. Othello no longer provides entertainment, only resentment," Kollag added, for once agreeing with his counterpart, for Ukthoth was radical, of a different generation altogether, with much to learn. Silence reigned, giving the head of the clans' time to reflect.

"Othello is one of us. I have known him since he arrived, since he was a child. He has not been a threat to anyone, save for the one we all fear; Xavien. The man contributes, works and could not be any more loyal to me. He bears no threat, and if the people cannot see that, then they should be made to." Ukthoth immediately interrupted.

"He is a Southlander; he is not welcome in our lands anymore. I say we vote again on his excommunication, right now!" Kollag put his hand on Ukthoth's shoulder, attempting to calm him down, while at the same moment, El Raud slammed his own hands on the table, standing up angrily, yelling:

100

"XAVIEN THREATENS US ALL..." His rage quietened Ukthoth's tongue. "You speak of Othello being unwelcome, while an exiled Snake, Xavien, a Demon Man murders, tortures and slays our people for his own sick pleasure. He is out there now, starting a war on a country that has never once threatened our lands. Xavien is a man I got rid of, by your own advice, and look at what he has become...Something far worse than he EVER was before. He is a twisted man, Ukthoth, a man that I will deal with in due course. Once we find him, that is! Can you not understand? I cannot rid myself of Othello, I simply cannot. And I will not, because he may be the only one with the skills to stop this beast." El Raud lowered himself back onto his chair, calming his thoughts. "More than that, much more, he is a friend to me, a friend to our people, regardless of our ethnic differences. Othello is one of us; he stays as long as he desires" He fell back into his chair. "If you feel what I am doing is wrong, speak now," he invited, looking at the other three Chieftains, all avoiding eye contact, except for Reneeia, who stared right back at him.

"This problem should have been addressed at a different time, my Sovereign. We can all see your dilemma." Kollag's words were cut off by the opening of the door. Kronix marched in, walking to the table where he placed both his hands and demanded:

"Do you know what I think you should do, Chieftain?" He ignored the others, speaking only to El Raud. "I think you should permanently forfeit your place, right now, and hand it to the winner of this very tournament." The others heard his words and expressed no hint of protest. They turned, expecting a good response to this solution from El Raud, who removed his hand from his face.

"You want me to grant you a place?"

"If you do not abide by these conditions, then there will be war; a civil war. It is inevitable."

"Othello will compete as usual, if he so wishes..." Kronix grew angry, clenching his fists. "Kronix, before you throw another tantrum, which I am frankly growing sick of, I will allow you to compete. Though it may go against the laws of old, whether the people agree and regardless of the fact that it goes against almost every rule we have, you people obviously think that two wrongs make a right. I don't, but I'll do what it takes to keep the peace. But never again will this come to pass, and never again will this be spoken of amongst us. Kronix, I grant you permission to compete, but so will Othello. Disagree with your Watcher's decision and you will wander the desert wasteland, where you'll likely become a meal for the sand sharks." Kronix loosened up, giving El Raud a stiff look before barging his way back out, slamming the door behind him, almost breaking it off its hinges. Ukthoth, struck with disappointment, left more peacefully. After him, Kollag Mel Thung arose, pleased with the result of the verdict, he too bowed and then left. El Raud was instantly regretting his decision, breaking yet another law to appease the masses, turning a Chieftain into a combatant. If one law could be ignored so easily, how long would it be before the others collapsed? Reneeia, now alone in the room with The Sovereign Watcher, spoke gently. She never said much; she was more of a listener than a debater, but whenever she did, El Raud would always listen. In just as strong a Jurean accent as his own, she said:

"You are much like the famed hawk of your culture, Sun Feather. You fly gracefully over the land, spreading your wings, ruling, watching, protecting, keeping an eye out for prey, but unlike most predators, you do not strike at what you see first. You display acts of tact." She unfolded her legs, stood up slowly and steadily approached him, moving along the curved edge of the table, sliding her white fingernails over the surface. "You are one who evaluates your targets, asking yourself what it is worth killing. And if a target merits the kill, instead of striking such a threat, you find the root cause...." She made her way around the table, drawing closer to El Raud, who hoped her story had some useful meaning. "There are two kinds of predator in this country that hunt this way; do you know what they are?" El Raud nodded his head; he did know, she was describing an old tale of Jureai, a tale largely responsible for the bitter rivalry between the Bevorks and the Salarthians. "The snakes and the copper hawks. They use this hunting method on each other. Maybe you should find out which came up with it first, for it may help you rule. Was it the snakes, or was it the hawks? Everyone knows that both...Species...Loathe one another, but who started the feud?" Reneeia was a quiet ruler over her own clan but was wise enough to put peace before conflict. She could see that El Raud was under stress. "I will help you, my Sovereign. You are a hawk, and you are soaring now over the land, surveying it. Choose wisely who to strike, choose very wisely, for I have heard that even the wisest hawks have died as a result of an ill decision."

"You think I've made the wrong choice? Is that all the advice you have for me? A mere story?" Reneeia opened the door to the light and noise of the gathered clans.

"I am helping you as best I can. Unfortunately, you are confused. I do not speak of this day, or of this little tournament. I am talking about a day that has not yet come, and I will not always be here to help you. Think of this as a…trial run… before the actual storm begins. Remember what I have told you; do not become the prey." Intrigued, El Raud remained seated. As she exited, she left him with some parting advice. "Find out who the snakes are and strike at them quickly, for the rest of the body cannot attack without its head. Everything has a purpose." He watched her leave and reflected for a moment on what she had said. Scratching his beard, he asked himself a question he often pondered: *was Reneeia a Glyph Wielder*? At that moment, a Bevork servant entered through the door Kronix had almost broken.

"Is The Five-Headed Throne ready?" El Raud asked the boy.

"Yes, my Sovereign. The clans await you."

"Very well. Take up your place."

"My Sovereign, it has been an honour serving you for all these years." Strange how the boy chose that moment to speak those words as if he believed that this would be the last time El Raud would be in power. If Othello were to lose, then the Salarthians would surely be the ones to rise and take The Five-Headed Throne, for they were the better fighters, caring for nothing else, training all day and every day for this one moment.

Thunderous roars chanted, songs arose from the crowds of thousands above, shaking the empty, dark armoury. Chains rattled, dust falling from the ceiling as someone sat alone on a wooden

103

bench, dressed for a harsh encounter. He sat still, listening to the noise, catching his name being called from time to time. Othello psyched himself up for the spectacle, taking several deep breaths, relaxing as he exhaled. After a moment of this silent meditation, his eyes opened and he stood swiftly, tightened his wrist bracers. Smearing grit onto his hands for added grip, he clapped a number of times and faced the rack of weapons. It was time to choose. He ignored the heavy weapons, brushing passed the cumbersome sticks fitted with long chains and awkward spikes and spotted his preferred weapon nestled deep inside one of the packed crates. Reaching in, he pulled out a remarkably simple, standard sword, layered with dust. The silver hilt was small, with space enough for just the one hand. Holding the dull blade out in front of him, he spun it around several times, picking up speed, getting a feel for it, practising a few combinations alone in the minimal light, just him and the old sword getting accustomed to one another. Satisfied, Othello was finally ready to compete, slipping the sword between the belts on his waist. Ascending the wooden stairs and exiting the underground blacksmith, he jogged down a stone corridor towards the light of day. It was time to represent The Bevork Clan. His clan.

El Raud left The Chimera's Pinnacle, stepping through a loose-hanging quilt and into the light. A roar of excited cheers erupted from the people of Jureai as The Sovereign Watcher came into view at the very top of The Arena. They stood with thunderous applause, whistling, waving, saluting him in their own ways. He looked down upon the populace from his raised stone balcony; it was a grand sight to behold, one that very few had the privilege to witness. Lifting both arms in the air, he exposed the cloak he proudly wore, designed to resemble a pair of hawk wings. The Arena was full, packed with the clans of Jureai, not a single space was left unfilled. From the outside, the grand structure took the shape of a chalice. Inside it was circular, a giant ring with its spectators filling the inside edges of the cup. In its centre was a flat plain of earth called The Pit; this was where the Hawks, Foxes, Snakes, Seahorses and Rhinos would soon be competing against one another for the throne.

Three Chieftains were already seated, observing the gathering, each with their own individual banner draped around their shoulders.

Etched into their triangular, stone seats were the insignia of their own clan. One chair, however, the one bearing the engraving of a curled snake, remained empty. El Raud made his way up a small set of steps, where the banners were raised high upon poles for all to see; the highest was that of the current clan in power, the Bevorks. El Raud took up his own splendid seat, The Five-Headed Throne. Far taller than a man and wide enough for two, this throne was the symbol of power throughout Jureai, a prize that everyone yearned for. Yet only Chieftains would ever have the chance to claim the seat, made of smooth stone mined from a place few knew of; The Ruaick Plateau. Not only was this throne a relic of Jureai's society, it was symbolic of every clan's culture. Set into the foot of the seat were snakes, slithering up from the stone block toward the fox tails armrests, curling over into the heads of seahorses. Above El Raud's head, perched upon the tip of a rhino horn, was a hawk, spreading its wings as though swooping in for a kill. El Raud gave a signal to a spokesman, who stepped up, holding his arms up high and calling for silence from the gathered clans. He then proceeded to address the impatient crowds. Everyone could hear his bellowing voice.

"THE DAY HAS COME!" Excited applause rippled around the stadium. Once again, he raised both hands before continuing. "THIS DAY IS A DAY OF HONOUR. A DAY OF COURAGE. A DAY FOR US TO REMEMBER HOW MIGHTY WE HAVE BECOME." The excitement was becoming unbearable for the clans. "AT DAY'S END, EITHER WE WILL BE GRANTED A NEW SOVERIGN WATCHER OR WE WILL BE CONTENT WITH THE ONE WE HAVE. LET US ENJOY THIS DAY TOGETHER. LET US SUPPORT OUR CONTENDERS, BUT ABOVE ALL ELSE, LET US GIVE PRAISE TO THE CHIMERA ORDER AND CELEBRATE THE FUTURE OF JUREAI!" As an ecstatic cheer filled the air, he cried: "LET THE TOURNAMENT OF LEADERSHIP BEGIN!" The clans then threw themselves into the air, creating an earthquake-like atmosphere within the ringed walls of The Arena. The spokesman lowered his arms, having delivered his lines perfectly. Around The Arena were five wide basins; one of these was now lit, the flames burning gold, signifying the beginning of the tournament. Round One would soon be underway. Within The Pit, directly opposite one another, were two identical, black gates. They now slid up simultaneously, with the clank of rusty chains rattling after them. The first competitors made their appearance.

Kenjii sat with his clan within the ringed seating area and remembered what Vontarg had told him about the first round. It would be a skirmish, designed to establish which warriors were skilled enough to get through to the next contests. He leant over to a Bevork clansman, who was staring at a thick piece of russet paper. "Pardon, may I have a look?" he asked politely. Taking the sheet, he read the stylised, black handwriting…

The Tournament of Leadership

Round One
Clans- Bevork. Vantarquinn. Red Stone. Nexius. Salarthian. Two warriors from each will compete in The Arena. Ten men, equalling five individual duels. Five will progress. Another ten will then duel under the same conditions in The Pit, leaving five more victors.

Round Two
The ten winning warriors from round one will pair off and duel until five more warriors are victorious. These men will then rest for a period until round three is to begin.

Round Three
Warriors who have not yet competed in The Arena must now do so, pitted against the previous five victors. Ten men will once again fight, including the Champions, to determine the final five.

Round Four
Each fighter must now draw. Whoever draws a female kylic beetle will be allowed to rest, while the four other warriors will pair off and duel, leaving two winners. Both winners will then draw as before. He who draws the female must now fight the rested warrior.

Round Five
(The Final)
Two warriors will be allowed to rest with water and have an opportunity to change their choice of weapon. They will be granted the entire pit as their boundary. The duel will last as long

as it takes, until there is a victor, either by the rules of swordplay or submission.

The victorious warrior of - Bevork, Vantarquinn, Red Stone, Nexius or Salarthian, Chieftain or Chieftainess, shall become The Sovereign Watcher of Jureai and be granted The Five-Headed Throne for a term of three years.

Kenjii read it through carefully. Taking a breath, he stared out across The Pit to the opposite side of the ringed Arena. No stone space was vacant; no gaps could be seen in the crowds. More than sixty thousand people had gathered in this one spot to see their clans compete in the finest spectacle Jureai had to offer. The golden fire had been lit, the public was seated, the Chieftains were all present and the stage was set. Only one thing remained; somewhere inside the walls, the fighters of each clan were preparing, having selected the first pair to represent them in round one. *I wonder who will fight first; Vontarg or Karn?* Kenjii asked himself. *Or will Othello show up to start the show?* Neutral servants of Jureai now appeared in The Arena. They emerged from the gates, equipped with sharp swords sheathed at their sides and bucklers strapped to their wrists. Their colours showed no allegiance; they wore plain shadow greys, their instructions only to maintain order, and to ensure that the tournament followed the rules. Behind these guards, the first competitors made their way into The Pit. In the distance, Kenjii spotted Vontarg, and to his surprise, Dingane jogging in beside him. Before separating, the two men clasped hands, spoke some words to one another and pressed their foreheads together gently. Each man then paired off to face their opponent. It seemed that Dingane would be fighting a Red Stone Rhino, who wielded a typical sword and shield, his armour flat and thick, running down his chest, leaving both toned arms exposed. Vontarg faced up against a Nexius Seahorse wearing the traditional, scaled armour of his culture, allowing him to move more easily than chain mail or thick leather would. Carrying a long, curved sword and a machete, Vontarg appeared confident. As the crowd quietened, the warriors faced their opponents and assumed their defensive stances. Dingane donned his helmet and steadied his hand, ready to assault. Vontarg had his hand rested on the leather of his quiver; he remained focused, crouching low, ready to strike like lightning when given the go ahead. Each man in The Pit ignored the sound of the crowd, ignored what their fellow partners were up to;

everything else seemed meaningless, other than the man standing in front of them. They listened to the sound of their hearts thumping inside their chests, feeling the droplets of sweat running down their backs and chests. They waited patiently for the horn to sound. The spokesman upon the balcony awaited El Raud's order. Finally, The Sovereign Watcher rose from The Five-Headed Throne and walked to the edge of the balcony, Reneeia's words still fresh in his mind: *Did the hawk strike first, or was it the snake?* Finally, with a quick click of his fingers, the battle commenced.

Reacting swiftly, Vontarg attached a blunt-headed bold to his crossbow, aimed, and fired. Unfortunately, the Nexius Seahorse saw it coming and managed to dodge the projectile with a spin. He ran up to Vontarg, who threw down his crossbow, hastily drawing his short sword to block the high, incoming assault.

Dingane and his opponent were both equipped with a sword and shield. This fight would be decided by whoever had the finest technique. They charged towards one another as soon as the horn was blown, trailing dust as they battered their shields into one another. Seconds in and Dingane had already made a fatal mistake! No one should ever charge a Rhino head-on; everyone knew that one would not emerge triumphant from such a clash. Red Stone Rhinos trained this way; charging had always been their best strategy. After realising his error as he was battered away upon initial contact, losing his sword, Dingane had no choice but to block the Rhino's heavy sword hits with his shield. Forced to back up frantically, he began to swing his shield against the incoming blade, knocking away the powerful strikes and enabling him to retrieve his weapon from the ground. When the right moment came, he broke his foe's defence and struck out against the Rhino. Dingane could feel the heat, the intensity, the panic, and sheer will to win. He let his instincts take hold, allowing them to guide his actions and reactions. He would need them against this brute of a Red Stone man.

On the other side of The Arena Vontarg, armed only with a short sword had retreated from his opponent. He had both hands on the hilt of his blade, awkwardly parrying attacks, maintaining a low, crouched posture. Suddenly, the Hawk ceased his retreat and put up a defence. As the Seahorse moved to within arm's length, slicing out with his sword, Vontarg bent backwards. As he did so, his foot connected with his foe's blade. As the sword flew away, the Seahorse placed both hands upon his machete, defending himself from the surprising speed of the Hawk.

The Red Stone Rhino breathed in heavily, tired, while Dingane remained collected and fierce. The warriors tangled their swords time and time again until finally, the Hawk seized an opportunity. He pulled away from the Rhino's shield, digging it into its owner's stomach and smashing him across the face, thus creating a few feet of distance between them. Shield-less, Dingane knew he had to be the better swordsman. He slashed the Rhino across the arm, drawing a small trickle of blood. In desperation, the Red Stone warrior made for another charge, hoping his size would overwhelm the lightly built Hawk. Dingane manoeuvred out of the way, moving into a perfect striking position. As the Rhino turned to see where his opponent was, it was already too late; he received a shield's edge to the face and a sword hilt to the back of the head. The Red Stone hit the dirt. The Hawk grasped his opponent's arm and lifted it up; the arm was limp, so he let it fall back down to the floor. Sheathing his sword, having won the fight, he placed the back of his wrist to his forehead. Before leaving The Arena, he glanced over to see how well Vontarg's duel was going. The three other fights had also finished, and the victors were making their way back down to their quarters. Eyes were now was on the last Hawk and Seahorse.

The Nexiun reassumed his crouched position, though this time he used it to defend himself as Vontarg tore down on him, ripping up his wrist and shoulder armour. The Bevork Hawk hopped back, deciding that this was not the way he wanted to win; he preferred a cleaner victory, a knock out rather than a submission, so he allowed the Seahorse to recover from his ball-like position, and let the man attack. The Seahorse was gullible enough to fall for the trap and made for a wild slash. Vontarg fell to the floor, getting a grip on the crossbow, using the butt of the weapon to clip the chin of his foe. The Seahorse staggered back, falling over onto all fours as he gripped his bleeding chin. Vontarg loaded his bow and patiently waited for the Seahorse to rise. When the Nexiun finally stood, the Hawk placed a sturdy shot right into the man's chest. At long last, the Hawk had emerged victorious. Vontarg wiped his sweating forehead with his sleeve, picked up his short sword that lay in the dust, and reclaimed the bolts he had spent during the fight. As he made his way out of The Pit, he held his crossbow high to the applauding crowds, celebrating his win. El Raud and the other Chieftains also showed their appreciation.

"Your Hawks are impressive," praised Ukthoth, "Tell me, does Othello train them?"

"I would think so. Though no one can fight like Othello, and I mean no one."

Once The Pit was clear, the next set of ten men stepped out. Kenjii saw the mighty Karn walking alongside Malek, his face still hidden under an enclosed helmet. They shared no words, their grim faces and offensive postures spoke volumes; they were ready. Applause and praise gave way to a thundering wave of cheers, as Kronix emerged. Kenjii folded his arms as the Salarthian chant, sung in the familiar Jurean tongue, overwhelming the support of the other clans.

"Sarpher. Sarphians. Karrsh. Karrsh. Karrsh karrsh sarphians karrsh karrsh."

Each clan, as different as they were, shared one thing in common; the language used by the first settlers of Jureai, who later became the first of the Jureans, their traditions living on through their descendants. As before, the fighters paired off, spreading themselves out across the floor of The Pit. Malek was confronted by a member of the Vantarquinn Clan, a Fox whose chest armour was smooth and slated, painted a dazzling white, sneaky trick. Black leather was wrapped around his torso and waist, though his biceps and a small part of his abdomen were left exposed for flexibility purposes. Hanging off his shoulders was a small, bristling red cloak. The Fox wielded a pike, thicker and heavier than Malek's polearm. Karn would fight Kronix. This would be a battle of the heavyweights, as both were extraordinarily strong men, wielding the most cumbersome of weapons. If Karn defeated Kronix, then it would greatly demoralise the rest of the Snakes. The official blew his horn, and the fighting recommenced. The multitude of spectators roared with excitement, suppressing the Salarthian chant.

Malek stood his ground as his opponent came at him with his pike. As the Fox neared, the Hawk parried the pike with the end of his polearm. Malek had a very peculiar way of fighting; his stance was very reserved, as were his movements. After each defensive action, he rested his pole horizontally over the back of his head along both shoulders, though occasionally he had to swerve while in this relaxed pose.

With the other fights well underway, Karn and Kronix had still not broken eye contact, nor had their weapons connected. This was the most significant fight taking place. The crowd's eyes homed in on them. Both men boasted heavy builds; they had to be careful not to make any wrong moves. Their power and weight alone would grant them their victory if utilised properly. Karn tightened his grip on his club and pointed it at Kronix, who appeared unmoved and unthreatened. The Hawk got within striking distance and swung for the head of his foe, who blocked it with an uprising counter of his great sword. Circling each other, Karn closed the gap with a sudden rush of speed. His club raised high, bringing it down upon the Champion of the Snakes. Kronix parried while side-stepping, in such a way that it sent Karn stumbling forward. After another failed assault, with the same predictable results, the Bevork warrior put a stop to his slide with an angled foot, and flung out an addition swing of his club, using just one hand, only to be blocked easily by Kronix's great sword. The big Snake saw his chance, and took it without hesitation, driving a fist into the face of the Hawk. Recovering as fast as he could from the blow, he came at Kronix, this time fuelled by pain and rage, attempting to deliver a crushing blow from above. What the Hawk received in response was a cold knee to the stomach, and a hard punch across the face. As he came crashing down to the floor, dropping his club, falling to his knees, Kronix wrapped a second clenched fist around his opponent's face. Karn spat blood, knowing it would soon be over, though Kronix did not finish the fight just yet; instead, he backed up, looked down at the Hawk's club, and kicked it back over to him.

Over on the other side of The Arena, Malek had both hands spread apart on his polearm. The Vantarquinn Fox used his pike like a sword, whipping its end at the Hawk. The pike smashed through the tip of Malek's weapon, forcing him to draw his dagger and lunge at his opponent, who defended himself skilfully. For a moment they held their distance, concentrating on their breathing. Malek took the opportunity to retrieve his main weapon. They came at one another again, except this time the Bevork won the first strike, deflecting the pike, connecting with a high kick to his foe's chest. As he made for his final move, the Fox pounced back, leaping on to the Hawk, vigorously grappling with his arms. Malek fell onto his back, with the Fox on top of him. He tapped the side of his dagger on the exposed flesh of his opponent's stomach. The Vantarquinn had no choice but to yield, and Malek stood up victorious.

Karn's struggle had gone from dire to humiliating. Nevertheless, he would not surrender, and Kronix lived for fighting, especially against wounded Hawks. The Bevork had suffered many head wounds; his face was plastered in blood. Having grown bored of toying with his foe, Kronix caught Karn's wrist mid-swing and delivered a series of punishing blows to his skull. Using the hilt of his great sword, Kronix dealt the final blow, driving it into the Hawk's forehead, placing him firmly on his rear. The Salarthian hordes exploded with applause for their champion. As he left The Pit, he caught a glare from Malek, who was on his way to check on his fellow Hawk, motionless in the dust. Dingane too rushed in along with several Jureans, checking that Karn was still breathing.

Othello stood still in the corner of their restroom, while Malek paced around, clutching his dagger by the blade. Vontarg knelt next to Karn, laid out on a wooden bench, unconscious. Dingane then opened the door and entered. He was about to say something important when he was interrupted by a knocking behind him. Going back to the entrance, he opened the door once again and Kenjii rushed in.

"We were expecting something like this to happen. No one walks away from this tournament unscathed." Dingane knew full well that Othello was the exception. The men were concerned about their friend. "We cannot falter now. The first round is over. If we keep this up, we can win…" he continued, trying his best to maintain a positive atmosphere. "We fought well, and we still have our Champion." Dingane sat down near the feet of Karn. Vontarg, the healer of the group, had cleaned off the blood with water and was in the process of stitching up the split in Karns forehead, with a needle and thread.

"How is he doing?" Kenjii asked.

"It's hard to say. He is unconscious. Might wake up soon, or maybe in a day or two. Head wounds are…Complicated." Kenjii leant forward, fascinated with the medic's skill with a needle.

"Anything you need?" he offered.

"Possibly. We can always try using a zethek thistle," Vontarg suggested to Dingane, who nodded in agreement.

"I saw some in the market; if we are lucky it may still be there for sale." Vontarg turned to Kenjii.

"Go outside The Arena and try to get your hands on some zethek."

"What is it going to do?"

"It may wake Karn up, so go, now!" Kenjii exited the room in a hurry, the door slamming closed behind him.

"What do we do about Kronix?" pondered Vontarg. He made eye contact with each member of the group, but no one said anything. Save for Othello, they were all thinking about the strength of Kronix, and how easily he was able to deal with Karn, their largest, toughest fighter.

"If you're asking for a strategy, our plan hasn't changed," stated Othello, breaking the silence.

"Then how do we defeat him?"

"The same way we defeat the others." Vontarg did not look too optimistic. "What? Do you really think his bite is filled with venom? That he is made of rock or metal? He is the same as the rest of his clan, and the same as us. He can and will be beaten." Othello's talk didn't exactly help, but he did speak the truth. The Hawks resumed their silence; they could not picture anybody defeating the might of Kronix, they found it hard to picture even Othello knocking him to the ground. The roll of a drum above their heads signified that Round Two was about to start. Malek walked straight out of the room with a distinct sense of purpose. Vontarg finished up with Karn and cleaned his hands off with a towel, before picking up his own gear. He was about to leave when Dingane said:

"I received the draw before I came down. Malek drew another Vantarquinn Fox, and I am up against one of The Nexius Seahorses. Which means Vontarg, you have been matched with Kronix." Before responding, Vontarg strapped on his sword and tightened his belts.

"Like Othello said, they are just men, and all men bleed the same."

"Right," replied Dingane, pressing his forehead into that of his friend. "I wish we all shared your skills," muttered Dingane, to Othello as, Vontarg left, making his way up to The Pit.

"No, you don't."

Another bronze basin had been set up on the far side of The Arena, directly opposite the one burning golden fire. This one was now lit, and crimson flames rose from it, signifying the start of Round Two. Once again, ten warriors entered The Pit, and the crowds sang their usual songs of praise for their representatives. Malek was tossed a new polearm as he moved towards his next opponent, another Vantarquinn Fox, this one taller than the last, and

114

wielding twin curled blades. Dingane marched on towards his own foe, a Seahorse draped in scaly skins, glinting in the sunlight, spinning a lengthy trident around his hand as he waited for the horn to bellow. Kronix drew his great sword as he paced toward Vontarg, who threw a devious smile toward The Chieftain and Champion of The Salarthian Snakes. On Kronix's back was his heavy round shield; he had not needed it against Karn. The other two Bevork Hawks were concerned for Vontarg after what had happened to Karn, though they had to focus on their own fights. The warriors readied themselves, the crowds silenced, and the mighty horn played its tune.

With his shield held close to his chest, Dingane steadily approached the Seahorse. The trident flew in from above, landing hard on the raised, wooden shield. The Nexiun did not hesitate, pulling the blade out from the shield and attacking again. Dingane was fast with his defence, and even faster with his sword, striking with a high offence, landing a blow between the trident's prongs.

Coming at Malek with speed, the Vantarquinn played with his curled knives, taunting Malek, who lunged in with his polearm. The Fox was an agile opponent, darting passed every assault the Hawk made.

Vontarg removed his quiver of arrows, dropping them to the floor along with his loaded crossbow, before drawing his short sword as he took up his defensive stance. Kronix approached with great sword in hand, three times as long as Vontarg's blade. Even the act of parrying would be enough to result in death or serious injury. Thus, Vontarg hopped back as the tip of the great sword landed in the dirt at his feet. Kronix lifted the weapon once again, bringing it around for a second attack. This time the Hawk ducked underneath it, getting dangerously close to the heavy body of his foe, striking him as he passed by. Kronix repeated his tactic once again, the Bevork crowd gasped in amazement, witnessing Vontarg landing a second blow. Kronix's approach changed immediately; he adjusted his footwork, moving in at an angle instead of head-on. Yet again Vontarg side-swiped the great sword and a follow-up thrust, opening his opponent for another attack. This time he was able to catch him by surprise, landing the knuckles of his sword hand on the jaw of the Snake.

Malek spun away in disarray as he failed to maintain an offence against the Vantarquinn Fox, who bounced around the Hawk, never remaining in one place for long. The Fox knew how to fight effectively, far more so than the last. This Vantarquinn was confident; he seemed to be having fun, while Malek momentarily took a knee to recover lost breath. His opponent briefly turned his back on the Hawk, to show his appreciation for the cheers of his clan. Raising his knives high in the air and skipping into a dance, he did a remarkable job of rallying up the excitement of his supporters. Unfortunately for him, this overconfidence proved to be his undoing. Suddenly a polearm whistled through the air at great speed, smashing its way into his chest armour, its blunt head shattering into fragments. With his foe thrown to the floor, Malek came over and pointed his knife at the throat of the Vantarquinn, claiming victory. The good spirits of The Bevork Clan were reignited as they burst into both laughter and thunderous applause. Malek was now in need of yet another weapon; he threw the splintered shaft of the old one down in triumph.

The Nexiun rushed forward, constantly on the offence with his lengthy trident, trying desperately to get behind the defences of Dingane, the master of the shield. The Seahorse pushed him back until he had nowhere else to back off to. Dingane met the ringed wall of The Pit, entering the stretching shadow around the extreme perimeter. The crowd above in the first few rows of seats hurried to look over the edge, to catch a glimpse of the Bevork warrior, struggling to block against the ferocious Seahorse. Hastily, Dingane threw down his sword, having had enough of defending, and put both hands behind his shield. As the trident drove its way toward him, he deflected with a slightly more aggressive swipe, denting the points of the three-pronged weapon. Granted a little more space to move, he waited for the Nexiun to make his next thrust. The Hawk gripped the trident's pole and dragged the Seahorse toward him. Lodging the pointed ends of his foe's weapon into a crack in the wall, he twisted it, leaving it stuck. The trident would not budge as the desperate man pulled and shook desperately, trying his best to dislodge it. Meanwhile, Dingane had found his own sword and came to gently tap the edge of the blade on the Seahorse's neck. His opponent let go of the trident and put his hands up in the air, accepting defeat.

Vontarg could no longer conceal his growing exhaustion. He tightened his grip on his hilt and wiped the sweat from his brow. Kronix had made sure not to overexert himself, once he had figured out the Hawk's hit and run strategy. While Vontarg had been utilising his speed, the Chieftain had preserved much of his energy, although he had been having difficulty with the young, agile Bevork, having suffered a handful of knocks, it was nothing the Snake could not absorb.

"If my blade were sharp, you'd be dead by now," taunted Vontarg, as Kronix powered into him, waving his great sword, driving him back Vontarg. Their blades crossed again; the Bevork short sword slid down the longer blade of the Salarthian and connected with the hilt. The Snake hit Vontarg in the chest, knocking him to the floor, all the air being forced from his lungs. Gasping for breath, the Hawk crawled on his knees, spotting his short sword glinting in the sun. Stretching out his arm, he pulled it to him. With all his strength, he rose again, blade in hand, ready for a final attack on the Chieftain of The Salarthian Clan. Just then a blunt-headed bolt, fired from Vontarg's own crossbow, punching him in the neck. Kronix brought the bow down onto his knee with force, letting the shattered pieces fall through his hands. It was over, and the Salarthian spectators resumed their chanting as their hero drew closer to Vontarg, once again on his knees and struggling to breathe. The Chieftain spotted Othello behind the gates, watching intently. "What's wrong? Did I clip your wings little hawk?" Kronix snarled, kneeling next to the Bevork warrior, taking a hold of his throat, squeezing the life out of him with one hand. "Struggle and I'll snap your neck. Listen to what I say, and you will live, little bird. Your choice…" Vontarg let go of Kronix's thick wrist; he could not compete with this man's muscle. "Jurean law protects you, we can exist side by side, but only after I've broken your champion. Be a good boy and pass on the message; would you do that?" Vontarg nodded. "Good," smirked Kronix as he released his grip. Othello's gaze met the Chieftain's once more before the Snake disappeared into the darkness of his own tunnel. Vontarg staggered to his feet, picked up his short sword, and exited The Arena on a limp.

Taking one quick glance around the room, Dingane noticed Othello, Malek, Vontarg and Karn. He re-opened the door and waited for a short moment, clearly expecting someone. When no one came, he shut the door, ready to address his clansmen, only to be interrupted by the sound of light footsteps and knocking. With a frustrated sigh, he opened the door once more, and Kenjii entered.

"I got it!" he gasped, holding up a few long weeds wrapped in a thin piece of crinkly paper. Dingane closed the door for the final time, as the young man hurried by.

"Thank you, Kenjii, put it over there please," Vontarg instructed, while Malek tended to the bruise he had sustained on his neck. Once Malek had finished with Vontarg's wound, he handed him the zethek thistle. As the healer unwrapped it, he noticed a note between Dingane's fingers.

"Is that the draw?" Dingane nodded. "Let's hear it then."

"I am to fight Thollin, The Nexius Champion. Othello, you are up against a Snake, and Malek, you...Heh heh heh... You are to fight your third Fox of the day. Don't worry, this one will be a real challenge for you; his name is Sarb, the champion of his clan, Reneeia's favourite." Malek shrugged. "Be careful, it's rumoured that Sarb can wield Glyph," warned Dingane, screwing up the note and tossing it aside. "In terms of The Red Stone and Nexius clans, their Champions are all that remain. Our clan is tied with the Salarthians. The Vantarquinns are down to one warrior and their Champion." He flopped his arms down to his waist with nothing more to announce. The draw had been made, and now all they had to do was wait to be called back up to The Pit. Othello picked up the ball of paper and unravelled it, reading for himself. Peeling away one of the pouches of the zethek thistle, Vontarg squeezed out some brightly coloured, yellow seeds. He squashed some of them and rubbed a sticky liquid between his fingers until it became waxy and dry.

"Kenjii, come here would you." The boy came over, as the others in the room suppressed their grins. "Tell me if you can smell this." Vontarg placed the waxy substance on the tip of a dagger. Kenjii took one small whiff of the mix and immediately jolted back, rubbing his nose, and sniffing violently. The others laughed at his reaction; every Bevork had been tricked into sniffing zethek once or twice. "Let's hope it has the same effect on Karn, shall we?" said Vontarg, placing the dagger's end under the stricken man's nose. Nothing happened. "Maybe if I increase the dose?" A rolling drumbeat interrupted him.

"It's time" Dingane stated solemnly. Malek stood up. Othello dropped the paper and tightened his wrist bracers; this time he too would be entering The Pit. Dingane held the door open for his men to go through first.

"Aren't you coming to watch Othello fight?" Kenjii asked Vontarg excitedly.

"He is our healer," explained Dingane.

"Don't worry; I've seen him fight many times before. You go with Dingane, Kenjii. I will stay here with Karn."

"This is turning into a tradition," said Dingane, turning to Othello.

"You never let me enter The Pit without a lecture; maybe that is what has kept me winning all these years," replied the young man, though he was not at all superstitious.

"It's not my lectures that are responsible for your skill; that comes from within you. I do not pretend to know how you do it, but you always know where the sword will land, and you know where to put yours."

"And where is that?"

"Where it hurts, Othello, everywhere" The two shared a laugh before heading off up the steps. "I know what you want to do out there though," Dingane added, speaking a little more seriously this time. "I've seen it in your face like you enjoy fighting. This I do not understand."

"When a challenge comes along, maybe I'll take it seriously."

"That day may be today," warned Dingane.

"Unlikely."

"Kronix is out there and he wants to fight you, to get revenge for what you did to him."

"I did nothing to him," Othello argued, having heard all of this before.

"You took the throne from him; you humiliated his Snakes and have continued to do so ever since. He wants your blood..." When Othello didn't answer, Dingane placed a hand onto his shoulder and continued: "I know what you want to do to men like Kronix; all of us want to do the same, but we don't, because we are not like them, we are not Salarthians, Othello, we are Bevorks, and Bevorks choose their battles. Here we are forced to fight, so we keep the violence brief. Make it quick, Othello, do what you must but do not seriously injure your next opponent. He probably has a wife he wants to hold when he gets home or a couple of children who would like their father to come home unscathed. You are a swordsman, the best swordsman I know, so be a swordsman today, do not stoop so low as a Snake, soar over them instead. Was that lecture enough for you?" he asked.

"That'll do," smiled Othello, disappearing up the steps.

The ringed Arena thundered as the Champions walked out into The Pit for Round Three. As before, a third bronze basin was lit, the flames burning with a terracotta colour. Kenjii saw Dingane from where he sat and recognised Thollin from earlier, only now he was dressed for battle, wearing grand, black armour, indented with the blue, skeletal structures of the seahorse. Beneath his armour was a tight suit of scales, covering him from head to toe. Thollin's armour shimmered in the sunlight, looking as if it had just been dipped into a pool of cold water. His weapon was a wide, wavy, longsword. In his left hand, he bore a round shield, its front decorated with his clan's colours and emblem. On his head, he wore a blue headband, designed to keep his flowing black hair neatly in place. A few metres away, Malek confronted Sarb, the best of the mysterious Vantarquinn Clan. Sarb's armour was of the same style and colour as that of the previous Vantarquinn Foxes, though he had chosen to remove his fur coat, and had placed a helmet on his head. The back of this peculiar helm grew into a spike. The Fox wielded the standard weapon of the Vantarquinns, with a few notable additions; a sturdy pike with a bushy tail wrapped around its end. Kenjii got a look at the Champion Rhino, Darados Mel Thung of The Red Stone Clan, about to face up against a Salarthian Snake. Darados was middle-aged, broad, muscular and full of experience and wore a chest piece of what appeared to be solid rock. He wore no undergarments, choosing instead to show off his toned body, his skin smeared with a clay paste that offered a protective layer, toughening the skin without reducing his movement. Darados' weapon of choice was a club as long as a sword, with a silver orb at the end. Kronix entered, to the same chant of;

"*Sarpher. Sarphians. Karrsh. Karrsh. Sarpher. Sarphians. Karrsh. Karrsh.*"

Othello emerged into The Pit to be welcomed by a resounding Bevork cheer. Equipped in simple, light, leather armour worn over a white shirt, he held nothing but a standard Jurean blade. While his supporters in the crowd sang his name, the other clans shared a common silence as they watched his every move, his every step, every breath he took. Judging by the cold reception from the other clans, Othello had outlived his welcome in Jureai. Among the Salarthian supporters, many had already started to heckle him, shouting out a variety of insults including "*Southlander scum*" and "*Exile to the trespasser.*" High up on the balcony of The Chimera's Pinnacle, the four Chieftains watched and listened with immense interest. The hopes of Ukthoth and Kollag Mel Thung rested only with their Champions now; if Darados or Thollin were to lose their duels, then The Five-Headed Throne would elude their leaders for another term. Reneeia Talaka, not quite as enthusiastic as her counterparts, sat in her chair, crossing her long legs. She relaxed her chin in her palm, her elbow rested on her armrest. Sarb gave her a

Vantarquinn salute, pressing two middle fingers to the centre of his brow and dipping his head. Sitting comfortably in the throne, El Raud was eagerly anticipating this next round; he knew what Othello was capable of and was totally confident of a Bevork victory. With Othello as his main man, THE greatest warrior he had ever known, they could simply not lose. El Raud's attention was drawn to the outlying ring of The Arena, the Salarthians had become somewhat angry, agitated by the presence of the reigning champion, while the other clans seemed less excited than usual. The Watcher slumped back as he sensed the grey atmosphere; by allowing Othello to take part, he may well have pushed the clans too far this time. A storm was coming his way, a storm he doubted he could come through unscathed, let alone quell.

"My Sovereign," prompted the horn blower. El Raud snapped out of his thoughts

"Sorry. Please, proceed." The horn sounded and once again the duels began.

Dingane sank his blade into the dirt and donned his helmet before grasping the hilt of his sword, pulling it from the earth, steadying it out vertically in front of him. Thollin wasted no time, striking at an obscure angle, reaching for the Hawk's sides. Dingane awkwardly managed to counter these attacks with a combination of his sword and shield, and in doing so switched to an offensive stance. Thollin's wave-shaped blade made it difficult for the Hawk to bring his blade back away and maintain his momentum. Both men were extraordinarily skilled swordsmen. Both warriors wielded their shields efficiently, keeping a careful eye on their footing and their opponent's actions. The duel, at that point, could have gone either way, forever switching between Hawk and Seahorse.

On the far side of The Arena, Othello bowed his head respectfully to the Snake, and adopted his surprisingly simplistic stance, holding his sword delicately, pointing its tip at his opponent. The Salarthian, knowing full well who he was about to fight, carefully edged his way over, striking at Othello at an angle. The Hawk broke his stance and struck at the Salarthian's blade, hitting it hard, close to where the hilt merged into the blade. Upon impact, the Salarthian lost grip of his weapon and lost sight of Othello! Taking the legs out from under the Snake with a leg swipe. The stricken Salarthian hit the floor with a thud. Before he realised where he was, Othello already had the tip of his sword pointed at his eye. The Salarthian held his hands up in defeat and The Bevork Clan applauded the fastest victory seen in this tournament. Kenjii's jaw dropped in amazement. Othello was already making his way out of The Pit.

Meanwhile, Malek stuck his polearm in the ground and grasped the dagger in his belt. Cautiously, he approached Sarb, who had been circling him like a shark. Suddenly the Hawk burst forward, slashing his dagger at his opponent, who had one hand in the middle of his pike, cleverly using both ends to deflect the Bevorks strikes. As Malek struck one end, the force he inflicted pushed the opposite end of the pike around, allowing for another, almost effortless counter. Sarb never stood still, fooling Malek to chase. The Champion Fox swung his pike into the dangerous right hand of Malek, before spinning around on the spot and releasing a lifted leg that powered into the right cheek of the Hawk's helmet.

Dingane struggled to get around his foe's defences, though Thollin too had found little success. They came at one another again and again, with the clash of metal ringing out; every once in a while, one of them would block with their shield or risk a bold move, which would get the crowd on their feet. This fight remained anyone's for the taking.

Kronix toyed with his Vantarquinn adversary. With a cheer from his clan behind him, he smashed the foolish Fox with a mighty blow from his great sword, breaking through the middle of his pike, impacting with the warrior's chest armour. The Fox yielded, though Kronix was not finished yet. Dropping his sword, he stood over the Vantarquinn, got a hold of his collar, and punched him in the face, until he found himself surrounded by Jurean guardsmen with real spears. As he picked up his great sword, the Jureans backed off, making way for the Champion Snake to exit The Pit. Reneeia had risen from her seat atop The Chimera's Pinnacle with a look of concern on her face; it appeared Kronix had seriously injured one of her warriors. Before she left to see to her Fox below, she scowled at El Raud; it was, after all, his decision to allow this Snake to compete, and thanks to that choice, one of her men had been almost battered to death.

Sarb drew close enough for a spinning kick that bounced off Malek's stomach. The Hawk staggered back, taking a knee, recovering from his exhaustion. The crowd sensed an end for the Bevorks' streak; even Kenjii knew that Malek could not get around Sarb's brilliance. The Fox was simply far stronger and wiser than his opponent. Malek removed his helmet for the first time in the tournament, his crop of hair soaking in sweat. His complexion drew many a female's gazes, and not just from The Bevork Clan; no wonder he had received so much attention earlier from the women. Bleeding from his eyebrow and a split lip, he was not going to yield just yet, not while he had some fight left in him. Sarb misjudged the distance between them and Malek rose to his feet, smacking his foe in the head with his helmet. The Bevorks roared with amazement at the sudden change of pace. Sarb found his balance again and lunged at the Hawk, who was just able to duck the attack, responding with a thunderous uppercut, sending his opponent hurtling to the ground. Malek dropped his dented helmet, found his polearm in the dust, turned, and threw it as hard as he possibly could at his target, who had just staggered back to his feet. With otherworldly reflexes, Sarb pushed out a flat palm in defence. The end of the polearm shattered, splintering on an invisible force field. The wooden pole flew back at its owner, who had to crouch to avoid it. All who witnessed the act were left just as stunned as Malek, now completely out of ideas. Both men remained motionless for a brief moment. Sarb rubbed away the blood running down from his mouth before darting towards his opponent, pike in hand, curling it around his wrists and arms. Malek, unable to keep up with the man's speed, hesitated for a crucial second, and for that mistake received a blow to the chest, draining him of the little strength he had remaining. Finally, he could not take any more punishment. The Fox used the butt of his weapon to knock the Hawk to the dust. Sarb flipped his pike over, the fierce end pointed at the back of Malek's head. It had been a glorious run, but it was over now without a doubt. Sarb discarded his pike and gave

Malek a hand up to his feet. The two men locked wrists in a sign of respect before the Hawk surrendered the glory to the rightful victor, the Fox claimed victory.

Dingane fought against Thollin's offence, dodging a move, and deflecting the waved edge of the Nexiun's blade. To his satisfaction, the Hawk had now turned the fight around; he was the one pushing back against his opponent, striking from a higher stance. Dingane thrust his sword hard at the shield of the Seahorse, tricking the arm into opening the body for attack. The man stumbled back in defence; Dingane clearly wanted to end this quickly. He drove his sword into the shield once again, piercing the line where the wooden planks met but was unable to retrieve the blade. Thollin threw the shield away, and with it went the Hawk's primary weapon. As sword and shield bounced away, far out of the reach of the combatants, Dingane held his own shield with two hands: his only practical option in this situation. Thollin thrust, swung, struck, and lunged, but the Bevork man had always been remarkable with a shield. The other fights had already ended; The Arena was fixated on the final two men, The Champion Seahorse and The Bevork Hawk. Dingane deflected one of Thollin's straight thrusts to the floor, lodging the blade between the earth and his shield. Behind his opponent, he spotted his own sword, gleaming in the sunlight. Using his shield to knock Thollin to the floor, he hopped over the stricken man, who stretched out his sword at the last minute, catching the Hawk's feet, causing him to fall to the floor. Dingane reached out, his fingers barely touching the blade's hilt. He heard the Nexiun nearing. In a stunning move, the Hawk wrapped his legs around the shins of his opponent, grabbed his chest plates and pulled him down to his level. Reaching over, he lifted his sword and placed it over Thollin's jugular. Victory at last.

The crowd erupted, applauding the spectacle. Dingane, however, suddenly felt the blunt tip of Thollin's sword softly nestled between his hip bone and ribs. Both men remained in this position, staring at one another; neither knew who had won. Eventually regaining their breath and helping each other to their feet, the two men stood face to face, breathing heavily, sweating in the sun. If it had been a real fight, both warriors would be dead, or dying. As the decision was being finalised, Bevork and Nexius clansmen loudly shared their own views on the situation. Before long, both clans were arguing across The Arena, while Dingane and Thollin stood amicably, side by side in the middle of The Pit, waiting patiently for the verdict to be announced. Atop The Chimera's Pinnacle, fresh scrolls were being unrolled and handed to the spokesman, who read them carefully with a magnifying glass in his hand.

"My Sovereign…" he began.

"Do you know who may claim victory?" asked El Raud from The Five-Headed Throne.

"I do."

"Then announce it to the people." The official appeared before the clans, lifted his arm to the crowd, and cried:

"PEOPLE OF JUREAI!" The crowd slowly quietened to hear the verdict. "UNDER THE CONDITIONS OF WHAT WE HAVE WITNESSED, IT IS FAIR TO SAY THAT THOLLIN, CHAMPION OF THE NEXIUS CLAN, TAKES VICTORY OVER THE BEVORK HAWK, WARRIOR DINGANE." From the Nexius side of The Arena came a thunderous combination of applause and laughter. Dingane walked out of The Pit for the final time, waving at his supporters.

As Dingane entered the restroom below, he immediately found a grin spreading across his face.

"Look who I caught taking a mid-morning snooze," Vontarg chuckled, taking a drink from a flask. Karn was conscious, sitting up on the bench. He had a neat bandage on his head and a few stitches above his eyebrow, though otherwise, he did not look too worse for wear.

"How do you feel?" Dingane asked, "You had us all worried for a while there." Karn took a drink before replying.

"I saw you in The Arena. You fought well. I only wish I could have done better for you all."

126

"Believe me; we all know what you're capable of. You have nothing to be ashamed of or to prove; you are still the mightiest of us all." Malek sat in the corner, his helmet removed, wiping away a small amount of blood from his mouth with a wet cloth. Sarb had hit him hard, but it was nothing that wouldn't heal in time. Kenjii was playing around with Vontarg's short sword, the one he had earlier used in The Pit.

"It's not even late and I feel like I've been here forever," Vontarg moaned, raising his head, "Once this is all over and we've won, I am going to get back to my house and sleep for a week."

"Doesn't that go against one of your mistress's rules?" joked Dingane, loosening the straps around his footwear.

"She didn't want me competing today, not after hearing what Xavien has done. Who wouldn't be worried? Word spreads fast in Equis. The man has lost his mind."

"Those days are over; Xavien has been banished. We may have lost plenty back then, but now we are the predators, and they are the prey." The men relaxed in their chamber; they were lucky, for none of them was seriously hurt, or noticeably scarred from the fights. Competitors were expected to get hurt, even though the tournament was made as safe and regulated as possible. Although their participation in the tournament was over, they all came to realise that they were in the same situation as they were three years ago. Once again, they were dependent on Othello. They had no doubt in their minds that he could win it for them. Kronix was not even a part of the equation; they just knew that their man would defeat him if it came to it.

"When we get back, what will happen, what will we do?" Kenjii asked.

"Return to normal life. Do the things we like doing most."

"So Karn is going to be drinking himself into oblivion every night?"

"Kid's sharp…" Karn muttered, raising his eyebrows; he knew it was probably going to happen the moment he got back to camp.

"What about you, Dingane? What do you plan to do after the celebration tonight?"

"Dingane is all for the quiet life," laughed Vontarg, "He doesn't touch a weapon until six months before the tournament, then he transforms from a farmer into the warrior hawk you saw today." Standing up, Dingane rested an elbow on the wall; he had only just noticed that their Champion was not present in the room.

"By the time we get back to camp, the food will be ready, and the work fields will be empty. The central fire will be lit, and the sun will be sinking. Everyone will be gathered around, free and in peace." He shifted his arm and leant his back up against the wall. "When the sun finally falls, I will be there. I will see the stars reveal themselves, out in the open plain of my homeland, with many years yet to look forward to. Just as our ancestors did, protected by Sun Feather, who flew into the sun's rays." The other men pictured the portrait painted by Dingane's words. They had all been so caught up in the tournament, the fighting that they had forgotten what it was all for. Dingane sometimes had to remind them. "I want to hold on to our Jurean traditions; the people before us built our ways of life, fighting for a land and its inhabitants, balanced with nature. We must never lose our way like the Salarthians have lost themselves to greed. There was a time when the clans were united when we were all Jurean settlers. It's hard to imagine those days, but I can picture reunification in our lifetime." Karn shook his head in disagreement, while the others remained totally silent. "Realise, my Bevork Hawks, that our peace, our freedom, were forged through one man, who is not of Jureai. We owe this man everything." A quiet noise came from behind the closed door, though no one got up to see if anyone was behind it. They sat in silence until the drum roll sounded above them once again. The tournament was nearly at its end. Four Bevork Hawks had been eliminated; only their Champion remained. They made their way up to the seating areas of The Arena, to watch the last two rounds together.

The Hawks found their reserved seats just in time to catch the spectacle. After receiving words of praise from their people, they braced for themselves before a clear view of The Pit. A fourth bronze basin had already been lit, the fire burning sapphire blue; only one more remained to be set ablaze. When Othello walked out from the tunnels below, the entire stadium echoed his name, though once again only Bevork voices were heard. He joined Sarb, Champion Fox of the Vantarquinns, Thollin, Champion Seahorse of the Nexius and Darados, Champion Rhino of The Red Stones. Kronix, Champion Snake of the Salarthians, was last to appear. All five Champions presented themselves before The Chimera's Pinnacle, before Reneeia, Ukthoth, Kollag and El Raud. The Arena was reduced to silence when Jurean guardsmen came out and circled the final competitors. It was a rare thing to see all five Champions in the final round, but not unheard of.

"When was the last time such a thing happened in Round Four?" Kenjii whispered to Vontarg.

"Last time it happened, Xavien was involved. He ended up killing a Nexiun and the Vantarquinn Champion, winning the tournament, giving Kronix The Five-Headed Throne. His barbarity resulted in his banishment but did not overturn the Salarthian term." One of the guards in The Pit presented a bag to Sarb, who put his hand inside. Vontarg touched Kenjii's arm, getting his attention.

"You asked earlier about Karn's second fear. Well, you are about to find out what it is," he winked. Sarb pulled a pale shell from the bag, holding it in the palm of his hand as the beetle uncurled itself. Tiny legs appeared by its sides, as it found its way around Sarb's hand, letting out short squeaks and clicks.

"That's it?" Kenjii blurted out, unimpressed, "That's what Karn is so afraid of?" Vontarg nodded. The young Hawk looked back at the kylic beetle, scurrying around the Fox's arm, then looked at Karn, double his size and strength "And I used to call him The Mighty Karn." Sarb stepped aside, putting the beetle into an empty bag held by another Jurean. Thollin was up next, again drawing a pale shell. Othello's turn: he too pulled out a pale kylic beetle. Kronix grabbed the sack, stuck his hand in, and pulled out a beetle. Opening his hand, he saw that the shell of the beetle was pale, with a dash of pink. With a grunt, he dropped the creature back into the sack and walked off, but did not exit The Pit, instead he remained in the shade. The four men who had drawn pale shells positioned themselves in front of their opponent; it was to be Othello against the wise and experienced Darados Mel Thung, while Sarb stood before Thollin. The Arena remained quiet on all sides as the crowd revelled in the anticipation. El Raud raised his arm, then let it drop, giving the signal, and the horn blew its tune.

Thollin and Sarb charged towards each other without hesitation. The former did most of the striking while the latter concentrated on defending, using the same method he had employed against Malek; deflecting the blade with both ends of his pike. When an opening presented itself, Sarb spun the pike around and thrust out its end.

Several feet away, Darados had instantly backed away from Othello, who bowed his head and assumed his favourite stance. He stayed where he was, sword outstretched, with a look of boredom on his face; it did not matter how careful his opponent was, the result would be the same. Even with this sense of pointlessness, Othello practised his patience, opting to wait, allowing Darados to circle him, just as the Salarthian had done. As the Red Stone came closer, he held his club up high. Othello waited for the right moment, keeping a close eye on his foe's footing and distance.

Thollin's attacks continued to meet with nothing but air or, at best, Sarb's pike. Drawing nearer, he drove his foot into Sarb's chest, shunting him backwards, but he didn't fall. He then adopted an aggressive stance, as Thollin lunged with a sudden upward strike, disarming his opponent, the pike bouncing to the ground.

Darados pushed out with his orbed club, narrowly missing the Bevork warrior. Othello pulled the shaft of the club towards him, causing his opponent to stumble forward underestimating the Hawks strength. The Rhino took a hard-left hook to the jaw and a swift right-hook beneath the cheek. When he came to his eyes stung, for the sun's rays were dazzling. Darados caught a glimpse of Othello walking away claiming an even faster victory than his last. High above on the stone balcony, Kollag Mel Thung sat uncomfortably in his seat, with a look of disappointment on his face. His Rhinos had now been eliminated from the tournament; his last remaining hopes of becoming the next Sovereign Watcher had fallen with Darados, taken away by Othello, the foreigner.

Thollin and Sarb fought on, alone in The Pit. The Fox backed away quickly, moving in circular patterns, while his foe held his shield high. Sarb's jabs were easily countered, and the Seahorse disarmed him with his shield, knocking him to the ground with a boot to the chest. Crawling away on his knees, he realised that Thollin had adjusted his strategy, drawing him in close, weakening him until his strength waned completely. He decided it was the time that he too tried something new, as he fiddled with the middle of his pike, covertly detaching something from it. At that moment, Thollin lowered his shield ever so slightly. Sensing his opportunity, Sarb darted forward, crouching low, and flicked his wrist, releasing a spinning disc. In blocking the spinning disc, the Seahorse took his eyes off Sarb, leaving his front vulnerable. He was tackled to the ground, the wind knocked out of his lungs and finished with the blunt end of the pike driven into his nose. Dazed and bleeding, Thollin realised that he had been tricked and beaten by the Champion Fox. Ukthoth scratched his chin as the crowds hailed the victory. He gave El Raud a grim stare and reluctantly joined in with the applause. Reneeia did not participate; she merely sat there with a smile, tapping her fingernails on the armrest of her seat.

After a short rest, Sarb and Othello stood next to one another and drew again from the bag of beetles. The Fox reached in the bag and pulled out a pink kylic beetle. Kronix walked back out to The Pit, while the young Hawk walked off to the shade and found his seat. As their paths crossed, Kronix kept his eyes on Othello, but the Bevork man did not deign to acknowledge the Snake. Sarb handed the beetle back to the Jurean official and joined Kronix in the centre. The horn sounded and right away Kronix swung his great sword at the Fox, who was already on the move, his disc at the ready. Once a gap had grown between the two, Sarb let the disc fly. It curled through the air, spinning rapidly, but deflected off Kronix's wrist brace.

"HA!" mocked the Snake. The Fox did have more than one trick up his sleeve though; he stretched his arm out at Kronix and opened his fingers, revealing a silver ring with a pearl set into it. Sarb's blue eyes were engulfed in blue flame. A loud crack of thunder silenced the thousands of spectators as a bolt of forked lightning, ripped passed the Snake's head, drawn into the pearl on Sarb's finger. It took a moment for the crowd to understand what had just happened. Glyph was not unheard of in Jureai; rather it simply wasn't commonplace, feared as it was for its infamously devastating powers and the corrupting effects it had on men and women alike. Krondathia, in the south, where The Star Caller Isabelle resided, was where Glyph was commonly practised, mainly in The Glyph Domes. The bolt of light had missed Kronix by inches, even scorching away some of his thick shoulder pad. Smoke rose from the damaged armour as it sizzled in the air. Feeling lucky to be alive, he ripped off the pad and hastily charged his opponent. Sarb ducked into a roll under the giant's swing and countered Kronix, both men lit with rage. They fought as professionals until finally, Kronix broke his sword through Sarb's pike, burying the blade deep into the Fox's skull. The fight was over! The Snake let go of his weapon and the Fox fell to the ground, the great sword lodged deep within in his head. No one cheered.

An hour rolled by as deliberations took place in The Chimera's Pinnacle. Sarb's body was removed from The Pit. The fifth basin had been lit, its violet fire signifying the impending start of Round Five. Whatever deliberations had taken place over the gruesome death were now over. The final had come at long last, to the relief of many in the crowd; the day was growing late, and the tournament had already lasted many hours. Any hopes of a Nexius, Vantarquinn or Red Stone Sovereign were now out of the question; either leadership would pass to Kronix and his Salarthian Clan, or power would remain in the hands of El Raud and his Bevorks. After the incident, Kronix had been sent to the Chieftain's room in The Pinnacle and had yet to return. Othello had retreated below, to cool off. His four other Bevork teammates and Kenjii had remained seated amongst their people. Kenjii was talking to Vontarg, while Karn and Malek sat in silence, reflecting on the tragic end of Sarb. Karn felt all the luckier that he had only been punched in the head a few times; far better than being all but beheaded by a great sword. He had decided it would be acceptable to start the drinking early that day.

"Sarb was a good man. Death does not belong in The Arena. Reneeia will want Kronix punished for this." opined Vontarg.

"He was a Glyph Wielder, wasn't he?" wondered Kenjii. His fellow clansman sat upright to answer the question.

"He was, though whatever he knew about the art form died with him. May he return to the earth and help the land to blossom."

"How many forms of Glyph are there?"

"I don't know exactly. A lot. It depends on what you combine them with, I think, and how determined you are to learn. I will lend you a book of mine when we get back to camp, it is from the south.

"How could Kronix do such a thing?"

"I don't think he did it on purpose," replied Vontarg, oddly siding with the Salarthian.

"How can you know that?" argued Kenjii.

"His reaction was perfectly natural, wouldn't you say? At least for someone who nearly lost his head to magic moments before." Kenjii shut his mouth, not uttering another word; the death had shaken him, he had never seen someone die before. "Kenjii, listen to me, my brother, and listen well: no matter how safe we try to make these games, people will always get hurt. Stepping into The Pit is a risk, but we all acknowledge the danger before we enter, Kronix is the same, he gets scared just as we do, and we should not condemn him for Sarb's unfortunate death, but we shan't forget" Dingane leant over to Vontarg, placing a hand on his shoulder.

"Seeing as we apparently have a moment to wait, I'm going to talk with Othello."

A cool draft of air flowed through the dark corridor of stone, causing the yellow torch lights fastened to the wall to flicker. Two figures stood in the darkness; one was pacing around, spinning a sword rapidly, while the other leant more casually on the rocks. Their voices echoed as they spoke hurriedly; time was running out.

"This is it. Are you ready?" Dingane asked, handing his friend a flask of water. Othello did not answer, instead focusing on quenching his thirst with the water and continuing to spin his blade. "Kronix wants you dead!"

"Oh really? I wouldn't have guessed." spat Othello fiercely, scraping his blade off the rocky walls. "He killed Sarb to send me a message."

"We don't know that, but" argued Dingane, stroking his chin.

"I know it; I saw the look in his eyes."

"What are you going to do out there?" The sword spun faster and faster in the Southlander's hand.

"What do you think I am going to do, Dingane? Kronix didn't have to kill a man to send me a message. I know he hates us, he always has, all because we represent a balance of power, whereas HE wants it all for himself. The real power lies with the masses. I am going to send him a message, to give the Salarthians a show they'll never forget," Othello vowed.

"The Salarthians ARE the masses; if they want him to rule, should we just give it to them?" pondered Dingane. Again, Othello didn't answer. He didn't look at all worried; he just hung around in the corridor, psyching himself up, curling the hilt of his blade around his fingers time and time again. "That temper of yours, it always makes me nervous…" Before Dingane could finish his thought, the drums rolled above them. He looked up to the ceiling and tapped his friend's leather chest armour with his fist. "Be the better swordsman today Othello. Please do not lower yourself to a snake's level; soar above them, be the Hawk that we know you are."

Othello entered The Pit, stepping into the light towards Kronix, who waited in the centre, his round shield in his left hand, the great sword in his right. The blade had not even been cleaned of poor

Sarb's blood. Up in the seating area, Dingane took his seat with the other Hawks and thousands of others. El Raud left The Five-Headed Throne and leant forward on the ledge, standing between Ukthoth and Kollag. Reneeia had chosen not to attend the final, not after what had happened to her Champion. The Bevork leader had never doubted Othello's skills, though when he was stood so close to The Salarthian Chieftain, he could not help but feel a little uneasy. If the Snake were to take victory on this day, then The Salarthian Clan would take power once more, and Kronix would become Sovereign Watcher of Jureai for a term of three, long, fearful years, years in which basically anything could happen should he allow it. On the other hand, should Othello be victorious, then El Raud, Chieftain of The Bevork Clan, would remain Sovereign, as he had been ever since The Southlander had arrived, turned seventeen and been approved by the current Sovereign of the time, Kronix himself, to compete in his first tournament nine years ago.

All the bronze basins around The Arena were now lit, burning the five symbolic flames of gold, crimson, terracotta, sapphire and violet. It had finally come down to this. The final fight between two bitter rivals. Bevork against Salarthian, Champion Hawk against Champion Snake. The Salarthians let loose once again with their battle chant: "*Sarpher. Sarphians. Karrsh. Karrsh. Karrsh karrsh sarphians karrsh karrsh.*" Over and over it repeated to raise Kronix's morale and lower Othello's seemingly unshakeable confidence. The Arena froze as the countdown to the duel began. Othello tightened his wrist bracers and dipped his head at the Chieftain. Kronix did nothing but stare at the Bevork warrior, even after the horn had bellowed, as the crowds roared and his Salarthians chanted their praise. Inside The Pit, the young Hawk, equipped only with a simple sword walked a slow, circular path around Kronix, who readied his shield.

"Do you hear that?" the Snake asked, pointing his sword at the clans. He was no amateur when it came to swordsmanship; he could see what Othello was trying to do. Many experienced fighters had fallen to the very same tactic. So many duels lost due to wrong-footing or misplaced balance. Kronix was fully aware of this and remained still, refusing to be baited. Finally, he found a defensive position and edged his way out of the circle his foe had made. The

Snake twitched his bladed ever so slightly, another technique used to distract the eyes and damage the opponent's concentration.

"Do you know what that means, Bevork?" Othello jabbed his blade forward and Kronix, parried it aside as if it were nothing. The strikes made by the Hawk were quick, decisive, and would certainly have been lethal if they met with flesh, but Kronix would allow no such opportunity. Almost twice the size and weight of Othello, he used his shield to his advantage, able to get close enough to drive away the younger man, who retreated, finding his own space again. The Salarthian spectators were growing confident, audibly overwhelming the minority Bevork Clan, drowning out their calls of support. "*Sarpher*, it means snake…" Othello made for his first hard strike at Kronix. Their swords met in the air several times, but Kronix countered each attack as it came at him, using his shield to take the hit. "*Sarphians*, means snakes…" The Hawk went in for another thrust, but Kronix manoeuvred his gigantic frame away, twisting to the side. As his opponent hurtled passed him, he stretched his great sword out; the swing of the cut would have taken Othello's head clean off, had he not ducked in time. This lowered the tone of the crowd's voice. "And *Karrsh*? It means, shed!" Othello had never gone this long in a single fight before; it worried a fair few, including El Raud. Kronix stayed his ground after another brief meeting of steel, with the Bevork man forced once again to retreat, and pace around in a circular motion. The Snake did not move, his confidence growing by the second. As Othello had not beaten him within the first minute or two, Kronix felt assured of victory. "I've shed my skin, Othello, and I am stronger for it. Time to hand over the throne."

The Hawk ceased his circling, took a deep breath of air, and loosened his grip around the hilt of his sword. His gaze left Kronix's face and found the sky kingdom. Gulping down the fresh air, letting it fill his lungs, he put his mind in another place, a place where a snake could not reach. Kronix charged and Othello spun his sword around into his left hand, springing out of the way of the marauding ogre, letting him pass safely by. As Kronix stumbled passed, his sword was deflected away by a snap of his foe's blade, and the Hawk ran his blade across the Chieftain's back, from shoulder to shoulder. The Salarthian crowd had been cut to silence. El Raud clenched his fingers around his sweating palms. Dingane stood, the only one in the Bevork section to do so. Kronix stumbled over, unsure of what had just happened. Flexing his back, he struggled to find his balance. Othello had his back to him, his eyes closed, though he listened intently to the shift of dirt. The Snake had lost his mighty strength and dropped to his knees, falling to the floor, grinding his teeth together, fighting off the lashing stings of agony. Othello sighed and opened his eyes. All the Bevorks in The Arena leapt out of their seats, screaming with delight. Dingane slumped back down into his seat as his clan arose around him, smiling as he saw his friends celebrating. He let out a soft, joyous laugh and said to himself: *Not bad sword master, well done indeed.*

"WOOOOO HOOO!" Kenjii screamed, imitating a crazy, squirming dance his clan were doing. Vontarg got Dingane's attention and pointed at Kenjii dancing about like an idiot, rallying up the Bevork supporters. Atop the balcony, El Raud turned, looking at the faces of Ukthoth and Kollag.

"Hail Sovereign Watcher El Raud," the pair announced in unison. The matter was settled.

Down in The Pit, Othello turned to see Kronix crawling away. The Hawk hovered over the Snake, throwing his blade into the dirt next to Kronix's head. The Snake rolled over on to his back, facing The Southlander.

"Overconfidence was your undoing," began Othello, taking a knee next to his fallen foe, blood soaking the earth as his clan sung his name in voices full of pride and glory. "I love my clan, and I respect yours. We can co-exist, you know. Leave us be and we will do the same for you." With that, he retrieved his sword, pulling it from the ground and walked away.

Kronix snarled "You will NEVER be a Bevork, Southlander, NEVER! Your blood is different, your blood is white! And Jureai is MINE BY RIGHT! IT'S MINE!" Othello ignored the pitiful protests and left with his dignity intact, having risen above the Snake as the Hawk he was. Now it was time to head home.

The Arena, so recently packed full of clansmen and women from every tribe, had now begun to clear. The Salarthian Clan could not accept the defeat; many remained stunned, shocked by the swift end to the fight that they had believed to be theirs. The Bevork Clan's celebrations would go on for days. Othello, the undefeated master of the sword, exited The Pit to the sound of his name. He gave one final wave to his clan before disappearing below.

Chapter 8 - Bane's Tree

How daunting it can be to make a decision that changes everything.

The sun fell, the breeze picked up and The Arena lay silent and peaceful. The Tournament of Leadership was over, and The Bevork Clan had emerged victorious once again, for the third time running. The clan, and Jureai could look forward to another three peaceful years under Sovereign El Raud's rule.

"Next time you see it, Kenjii, it will be your turn to compete," promised Vontarg, gripping the reins of his tulkan. Kenjii took one last look over his shoulder before The Arena disappeared to the distance. The colourful basins were still lit; time would see to their extinguishing until their time to flame would come again.

The tired Bevork party, consisting of Othello, Dingane, Vontarg, Malek, Karn and Kenjii, head home, back toward their encampment in the south-western regions of Jureai. They would not stop for rest until they arrived. The small group did not talk, choosing to ride in silence, enjoying the beautiful blood-red sunset, washing together with intermittent bursts of orange light. Each man thought about what he would do with his evening and the following day, each with his own idea about the true luxuries in life. Othello, on the other hand, was not thinking about hot food, drink, or the comforts of a woman; he was still faced with a decision, one that had to be made before the day's end. The conversation with his father had never left his mind; indeed, he had been haunted ever since by distant memories of his life before Jureai, people he had once known, faces he would never forget. Of all the faces he was able to recall, he still could not remember the most important; his mothers, and he hated himself for it. The ring could very well bring them together should he return to Krondathia, though he could not ever remember a family crest, he would certainly have recognised it. Enemar, his father, would never lie to him. He could answer his questions, Othello was sure of it. He would make his decision based on his father's responses to these questions. It wouldn't be much longer before the journey was over. The sky darkened a cold blue emerging, bringing with it the stars, glinting in the vast night's sky.

Moving steadily in single file, they marched on until their camp came into view, glowing like a burning oil lantern surrounded by darkness. The central fire was ablaze; evidently, the celebrations had already moved from The Arena, all the way to the Bevork camp above the valley. When the celebrating clan spotted the Hawks approaching on their bulls, they gave them the warmest of welcome, taking the reins of their mounts, helping them off their saddles. The clansmen carried their gear for them, storing it away, while the women handed them food and beverages. Vontarg made sure to keep hold of his dagger, the one with the violet hilt, as he was stripped of his gear. A young woman ran up to him, leaping into his arms, wrapping her legs around his waist like she hadn't seen him in months. He squeezed her tight, speaking softly into her ear, with a lustful smile on his face. Meanwhile, Malek made himself comfortable, sitting outside his tent, unbuckling his armour, rinsing out a small cloth to clean his face with, his dented helmet sat next to him. A man with similar features sat with him, helping him with his gear. Kenjii had leapt off his tulkan the moment he had arrived back at camp, running into clusters of clansmen with uncontrollable excitement, thrilled with all the attention he was getting; he simply couldn't quite handle it. A collection of keen men, women and young children who had not been able to attend the spectacle gathered around him. He told magnificent stories of the tournament, of the duels between Dingane and Thollin, Malek and Sarb, and Othello's battle with Kronix. He also spoke of the monsters that tormented the mighty Karn; the kylic beetles. Overhearing these humiliating stories, Karn quickly ran after young Kenjii, swiftly catching him and picking him up with one arm. They wrestled around playfully as Kenjii continued to make jokes. Karn lifted him above his head and carried him off, laughing, threatening to leave him in the fire or down a well.

"This guy is a little hero, you know that?" The clan was united in celebration, and above all else, it was a happy place to be, everyone was there, enjoying one another's company. Food was roasting over the blazing fire, soup was bubbling in large pots, and the night was still young. The following day, known as the Idle

Morrow among the clans, would be a wondrous day of reflection and relaxation before work would inevitably have to start again. It was a celebration that only came around once every three years, a night and day for everyone to enjoy together, something everyone looked forward to. Dingane and Othello had remained mounted upon their tulkans the entire time, wandering the barren plain, talking, laughing, and wondering together in the darkness. Not that the pair weren't welcome within the clan; indeed, they were the guests of honour, THE most talked about when it came to discussing the tournament. The two had been friends for years, ever since Othello's arrival as a child. They had played together as boys, trained, hunted as adolescents and fought side by side in the tournaments. Over the years they had grown close, having shared a lot of experiences; they were grown men now, approaching their thirties, and a new era dawned for them. With age, both men felt a change coming in with desert winds from the north. They had distanced themselves from the celebration, watching everyone else having a wonderful time. The cold refreshed their skin, soothing them, the darkness touching all. After a short laugh about an old memory, Dingane finally thanked Othello personally.

"I never expressed my gratitude for what you have done, not properly. Thank you for winning the day for us." Karn's deep, booming voice could be heard clearly in the middle of the camp.

"I think this one's old enough to drink now. Let's get him something to celebrate with!" he yelled, rubbing Kenjii's hair into a messy bush. A cheer arose in response. "But before he takes a sip, let me show him… NO... Let me show ALL of you how a true Hawk drinks." He took the jug of wine he was handed and tipped it over his mouth, gulping it down like he did not want to wake up for the Idle Morrow. The audience of clansmen applauded Karn furiously as he sank the contents of the jug down his throat with ease, bursting into laughter when Karn The Mighty slid off his seat. Othello and Dingane continued their circuit around the camp's perimeter, talking quietly.

"El Raud is waiting for you," Dingane noted, "You have once again done him and Jureai a great service."

"I don't think Ukthoth, Reneeia, Kollag or Kronix would agree."

"True. However, though they may not be in power, underneath all their disappointment, I know most of them would much rather have El Raud sitting in The Five-Headed Throne than Kronix." Othello stayed relatively quiet; Dingane was used to this. He usually stayed silent when something was on his mind, though his friend could only guess what was troubling him. "During The Idle Morrow we shall make some wine, you can show me how you got that broken well to work, and teach me the most important lesson in swordsmanship," Dingane suggested, looking forward to the days ahead.

"We have three years of peace now, we can all rest easy. And there is no need to thank me; we're Hawks, I couldn't have done it without you."

"Looks like we will need to make more wine to replace what is lost to the appetite of Karn. By morning, this camp will be bone dry," Dingane joked.

"Let them have their fun; they deserve it, no clan deserves it more," said Othello, who didn't appear to be in the mood for fun.

"You care about this place, don't you?" The Southlander nodded in agreement.

"It is my home. Your kindness led you to take me in when you didn't have to. I only want to see this place safe from harm."

"You have given so much back to our community; your debt has already been repaid a hundred-fold. The Bevork Clan loves you; we are the ones grateful for all you've done."

"I'd like to keep helping, in any way I can. I'll do whatever it takes for Jureai to prosper. I feel it's the right thing to do. If Jureai can find everlasting peace and unite under one banner, then its example will maybe inspire the south to do the same," Othello went on, sounding much like his father.

"I wish there were more men like you out there," praised Dingane.

"Join the party, my friend. I'll catch up with you later once I have spoken with The Sovereign." Othello trotted away to the centre of the encampment, towards The Chieftain's Nest. His friend smiled and dismounted, heading back to the revelling crowds, where he was welcomed into the celebration by his friends and fellow Hawks.

Othello dismounted his tulkan and tied it to a nearby post, before setting off up the rocky hill towards The Chieftain's Nest. In the near distance, a faint glow of candlelight was shining from the inside of one of the tents. As Enemar had promised, he had waited for his son to return. First, he would speak with The Sovereign, then he would visit his father. The Nest was a large, circular structure, far superior to any other construction around the camp. Its walls, made of reinforced trees, arranged to support the heavy roof, a shell that provided an impenetrable cover, a surface no blade could pierce, and no weather could erode. Othello knew of the creature that this shell had once belonged to; one so rare few had seen them. These sleeping creatures roamed far to the north, somewhere within the territories beyond Jureai, in the country of Sand. Giant creatures dwelled in those lands, sleeping under the dunes, rumoured to be the largest walking beasts on the planet. The chrocian titans. As big as the roof was, this shell, delivered by Sun Feather itself, had belonged to an infant titan. From within the well-lit hut came a shadow through the door; El Raud was moving around, awaiting his Champion Hawk. Othello knocked calmly and slid the door open. The one room was tidy and spacious, with an array of burning candles standing on long, thin posts. Soft wax singed and burned away, while the air was scented with sweet incense, used to keep away the insects of the night. The central fire remained unlit, however, perhaps there was no need for it with the immense celebration going on that night. El Raud, dressed in soft, luxurious robes befitting his status, heard the knocks, but ignored them and continued fiddling around with a collection of glass bottles filled with rich alcohol. The Hawk hung in the doorway, more interested in keeping an eye on his father's tent; he could see no sign of movement or the passing of shadows inside. Two other men were in this Nest; they stood formally next to a grand wooden seat. The two kept their eyes on Othello; he spotted them looking at him before El Raud spoke.

"You two may leave. I'll be fine with this man." He flicked his hand at the guards, and they bowed in unison, saluting their Sovereign. The Southlander stepped out of the way and held the door open for them. One of the guards acknowledged him as he passed by. Finally alone, El Raud handed him a pretty glass filled with the strongest smelling drink he had ever caught whiff of. "Once again, I am indebted to you for what you have done for me, the clan and Jureai." He held up his glass to Othello and drank. Othello took a sip himself after El Raud had finished, otherwise remaining quiet. The Sovereign turned away to pour another shot. After refilling, he watched Othello inspecting a collection of wooden figurines, the very same ones he had laid eyes upon when he had first arrived. They were lined up opposite each other, all part of a game called Take. The objective was to capture the board, to outwit your opponent using mental and logical strategies. The piece that Othello had always been interested in was the Knight. "The most important piece on the board, believe it or not," stated El Raud.

"Pardon me, my Sovereign, but isn't the Emperor the most important piece? He gives the orders, makes all the decisions. The Knight simply does what he is told without question."

"You haven't played much Take, have you? The Emperor is the most powerful, but even he takes his orders from The Pinnacle piece. It is easy to make the decisions from a warm room in a comfy chair. To build trust, to gain the loyalty of one's people, is a far mightier task." Othello put the piece back onto the polished board. "At first sight, it would appear that the Emperor is the most important, but in my view, each piece is as important as the rest. In order to work effectively, to win decisively, they must rely upon each other. The same principle applies when ruling over a kingdom, or a clan, as it were."

"Perhaps I do need to play more," admitted Othello, taking another sip.

"The Knight is the one who has to constantly test his courage on the field, to prove his loyalty, to risk his life for his people on behalf of the King. What I have found in my experience is that a good Knight is somewhat more essential than an entire council of advisors. A council may be well educated, but the Knight has real experience with waging war and leading men, something a ruler needs in times of trouble. Do you remember three years ago, after the last tournament, I invited you here?"

"Yes, of course."

"You still have the same look. Do you remember what we talked about?" Othello nodded. "I wanted to reward you then as I do now. It is thanks to you that I am still Sovereign; it's thanks to you that our country is safe, at least for now. I can reward you with anything you desire…" Othello stopped El Raud.

"For now? Are we in danger?"

The Watcher paced over to the table at the far end of the hut. Upon the flat surface, a map of Jureai had been spread out, weighed down by paperweights shaped like hawks. It put things in perspective; Equis really was a vast place. Looking at the map, noticing all the blank areas, Othello could see that there was still much out there untouched by humans. "I offer you rewards; you ask for none. I can give you anything this land holds, and you refuse. No matter how many times I wish to treat you with gifts, riches and power, your answer remains the same." El Raud sighed. "I mention a threat to my position, and you jump to your feet, like the Knight on the table, wouldn't you say? I only wish I had a thousand more men like you, who think the way you do, but I don't want a man of stone who waits on my every command, I want a Knight who has a life beyond his duties and obligations. No other ruler would grant you such privileges. Tell me why you behave this way?" Othello spoke his mind.

"You provide me with shelter and give me food and water. I can walk freely among your men and women. My cultural heritage is tied to those who live for greed and zeal, people who take whatever they want wherever they go, showing no respect. As much as I want to change, I will always be part of the south. I ask for nothing because there is nothing else you can offer me greater than what you have already given. You can offer me gold zeal, talon or crown and

145

but what is this next to the things that really matter? In times of crisis, people…Compassionate people don't find comfort in things of value, or precious stones. People are what truly matter. I will protect what I have grown to love from anyone. So, you see, my Sovereign, it is I who is indebted to you, always and forever, so please, if we are in danger, I'd like you to tell me." El Raud opened his arm wide and Othello came closer, standing over a detailed map. The two men studied it together as the Sovereign's voice sank lower, sounding serious and concerned.

"Xavien…You of all people should know what he is capable of. He is growing stronger, but what you know is only a small fragment of the actual truth."

"I heard from your scouts that he left Jureai and tried to begin a war with Ivulien."

"Ivulien has not officially declared war on this country. I hope they know that Xavien's barbarian war is exactly that - his war and that he does not speak for the rest of us. While he is out there and we are here, he, unfortunately, represents the entire nation, including the Bevorks" El Raud's point, was coming together. He drew back, facing the fireplace, and sighed. "We must send word to the capital of Ivulien, the city of Davune. A letter must be sent, one of the highest importance, notifying the Dovidians of our situation. I will make sure that the other clans are included; their Chieftains' signatures will be required. The letters must reach a man named Akarnal Desa, who resides in Castle Tithis. Desa is a friend of mine, and one of the highest members of Ivulien's hierarchy." He then turned to Othello, still gazing at the map. El Raud realised that this important matter did not involve the young Hawk unless he ordered it to be so. He thought to himself for a few seconds before handing down an order, knowing that no one deserved The Idle Morrow more than Othello. "I'm asking you to deliver this letter to Akarnal Desa."

"You give me this task? To travel far from home, into a land that I do not understand, to deliver a letter to a man I have never met, in a castle I've never seen?"

"Yes," the Chieftain confirmed apologetically, "This action will hopefully secure our safety from a Dovidian invasion. Those people don't waste their time, not like the gullible Norkrons from Krondathia."

"I won't go. Send someone else, a faster rider perhaps. Someone who knows the land and law of Ivulien. I am out of touch. I will stay and help protect the clan from Kronix; once healed I doubt he will heed my words I gave him today, he has always wanted to destroy us." There was a moment of silence between the two; El Raud could not deny Othello his wishes, and the young Hawk wanted answers. "As your Champion, as your friend, I know you'd never just send me away. I think I deserve to hear the truth. What's really going on here? What is it that you and the other Chieftains are so afraid of?"

"I hate to be the one to tell you this but...The real danger, the real threat to this clan... is you," explained El Raud, revealing the truth at last. Othello was visibly hurt by the words. "Xavien and his Marauders are moving; they have been moving fast ever since the tournament began. Kronix must have gotten word to him about your participation. Jureai is finished with you; the other Chieftains and I held a vote between us and our houses to decide whether you should stay, if you have outstayed your welcome? The votes came in and we lost, badly. It took all my power to allow you to even stay for the tournament. I nearly gave up the throne for you to simply participate. Instead, I levelled the playing field and allowed Kronix to compete. But you still claimed victory, which is, in a sense, the last straw for Kronix, who is in league with Xavien."

"So you have chosen me for this task to get me out of the country?"

"Only for a while; when you consider the distance between Jureai and Davune, it could...It could well buy me more time to try to save your place here. Though I do not think you will be able to compete in future tournaments," he added, shaking his head sadly. "I am sorry." Othello had to get out of the hut; his world was rapidly turning upside down.

"Where are the Marauders heading?" he asked. El Raud unrolled a recently opened letter, delivered by a courier not long ago.

147

"Here. They will come here for you during the next bright moon. You must leave…Try to understand that the real power lies in the voice of the country, not in mine alone. Had I had the numbers on my side, perhaps I'd be in a more powerful position, but I've not. We Bevorks are few in comparison with the Red Stones and Salarthians." Othello suddenly remembered his father and his words about people and their power.

"No, I am sorry for the trouble I've caused you, but it will take more than Xavien to force me to leave." Before the leader had a chance to respond, Othello exited abruptly, finishing off the glass of alcohol before he left.

"Emperors suffer too, Othello, none of them wish to see their people die on their behalf…" Othello had already gone, and El Raud was left alone. "The Knight is indeed the most important piece," he said softly, standing in the open doorway, looking out to the sky kingdom.

Othello headed back down the hill, directly towards his father's tent. The candles were out now, he noted.

"Father?" he called as he burst into the tent. He could not see much, for the centre fire had all but gone out. Piling on an extra helping of wood, the fire crackled to life, raising a warm, amber light. Othello knelt forward, he could just about make out the shape of Enemar, but he was not moving. Othello sat as still as he could for quite some time. Eventually, he pushed more wood onto the fire, as quietly as possible. Moving closer, he checked for a pulse. Othello's arm dropped from his father's neck. He solemnly pulled up the quilt his father laid under and placed it gently over his head. Resting his hand on the mattress, and closing his eyes, he came to terms with the gut-wrenching realisation that his father had passed on. Outside, the celebrations could still be heard. "Thank you for everything you did for me; I'd be nothing without you." His father's hand had closed around something in his final moments. Othello opened his fingers to reveal a ring, which fell out onto the floor. It was the golden ring with the red crest curled around its edge. The emblem was incomplete; it looked as though it was missing the other half of its crest. He wondered what the full emblem would look like if the two crests were ever re-joined and what it meant. He had to find out.

"Here you go Kenjii, *Glyph Origin*," Vontarg said, handing down a rather large, plain green book to the younger man, who was feasting on some meat next to the warm fire. Wiping his mouth and hands clean, Kenjii had a flick through some of the thick pages, noticing a series of complicated sketches and illustrations, all drawn with a skilled hand in black ink.

"This is about Glyph; the power that Sarb wielded?"

"I borrowed the book from a Vantarquinn; it took me years to absorb all of the information contained within its pages." Just then Vontarg's latest mistress came up behind him and began massaging his shoulders which ground-down his speech. "Sorry boy, she is really great at this. I will be with you in a second."

Malek was not far away, seated close to the fire, sewing something up with his bare hands. He had helped himself to some wine and enjoyed the atmosphere, even though he didn't participate in the livelier revelling. Rather predictably, Karn had passed out, collapsed in a vegetable patch while trying to juggle vegetables. Vontarg had placed Karn's head onto his side so that he would not swallow his tongue. While he was at it, he had made a wig for him using veggie leaves. Kenjii too had contributed to the decorations, sticking two carrots in each ear.

The celebration had passed its peak and was now calming down; no longer was anyone speaking loudly or acting crazy. Many came close to the central fire, while others fell back into their tents to get some much-needed sleep.

"Can you play us something?" Vontarg whispered to Kenjii.

"No, I am still trying to get the hang of some of the notes. I don't know how to play properly yet."

"Just play what you played the other night. Please? This is a night we won't see again for another three years. A perfect time to play, don't you think?"

"You were listening?" Vontarg smiled

"Of course; I hear everything. And of course, someone has to watch your back like someone has to watch mine," he whispered, glancing at Malek. Kenjii put down his wine and went off to fetch his instrument. As he walked away, Vontarg turned to his lady and whispered: "He is brilliant at this." The boy returned shortly after, receiving a few looks from the people relaxing around the glowing fire. Putting a long flute to his mouth, with his fingers set over certain holes, he played a mellow tune, both haunting and sad, yet fulfilling and comforting. The musical notes sang like the wind's breath, the waves on the waters, soothing the minds of the warrior clan, seeing couples off to sleep next to the fire. Between the tents, watching and listening quietly from the shadows, was El Raud. He folded his arms and witnessed the pleasant sight of his people, united, happy and at peace.

The ring lay on a marble table next to a single candle dripping hot wax. Othello sat alone, staring at it from a distance with his face in his hands. Someone pulled open the tent door and stepped inside, intruding upon his privacy.

"You were to be sent to Ivulien. You no longer had the chore to dig in the dust in search of water." He came a little closer. His frame was frail, his face eager; the Hawk recognised him as one of El Raud's advisors. He had never liked this man; in fact, he was probably the only thing he didn't like about the entire place. "As the Sovereign's advisor and a friend to you, I think that you should take the road to Ivulien." Othello did not answer. The intruding man noticed the ring on the table. Coming forward, he picked up the small band and slid it over his finger, smiling at the near fit. Othello stood up and found calm in staring at the yellow flame. Although he had never liked the man - always the bringer of ill news, delivering warnings and threats - he never seemed to do anything to truly help the people, not even in the simplest of tasks. Senark was his name. "Now you listen to me, nothing more awaits you in these lands. The clans no longer want you. Take the road and be gone as quickly as you came." His voice grew ever more desperate. "If you deliver the message, you may save this place from the fire, but heed my words, this place will burn, it will be destroyed by the Dovidians. Better by them than by Xavien." Othello snatched the ring from Senark's hands and threw back the fold in the doorway, letting himself out. The adviser remained inside and pinched out the candle with his fingertips.

Alone in the middle of the work plain, sitting on his favourite well, Othello listened to the far-off tune made by Kenjii, playing under the stars. Around him stood huts, half-built but sturdy structures that would last for many years. Families would live and die here, generations would inhabit them, and hundreds of children would remember them. The thought put a smile on his face. Wells, blacksmiths' shelters, shacks, and small farms were all springing up nearby, all of which he wished to see completed someday. Deep down he knew that his freedom to remain in this land compromised its innocence and safety. His choice, if indeed it was a choice, had been made for him. He knew what he had to do, even if he wished it could somehow be otherwise. In his hands, he played with the golden ring. He reached down a hand and played with the cool water that had collected in the large bowl at his feet, sighing gently.

All was quiet now. Nothing remained but the hum of insects and the scurry of small rodents lurking in the night around the sleeping Bevork encampment. The central fire was out, grey smoke drifting from the bundles of ash into the sky. Jugs, pots, and scraps of food littered the social area. Everyone had gone back to their tents and were resting comfortably, looking forward to The Idle Morrow. It was a cool night, but still warm enough to be comfortable without wrapping up in clothes. The party was over. Something moved, pacing through the camp, it was a tulkan, its reins led by a man wrapped up in a cloak, heading south, away from the clan that had made him feel so welcome for most of his life. The man paused for a moment; he knew he was being followed. Othello removed his hood and looked over at his shadowy pursuer.

"I have no choice."

"I am not here to try to stop you. I am here to say goodbye." It was Dingane, speaking quietly, with a mournful look on his face. "I knew this day would come; it feels like only yesterday that you arrived. I am sorry...About your father. Kenjii found him earlier while looking for you. He will return to the earth now, as we all must someday."

"How did you know I would leave tonight? I didn't tell anyone."

"I've known you for a long time, Othello. I know these things." They walked out of the encampment together and found an open space in the night, where they could talk without fear of waking the others.

"You've spoken to El Raud?" Dingane nodded. "Then you understand why I must go?"

"I do."

"Listen to me carefully, for you need to know this. The Barbarians, these Marauders, though far away they are on their way here. Xavien is coming..." Dingane's eyes widened at the news. "I want you to lead the Bevorks away from the camp, you've more experience on the ground than El Raud. Take them, hide in the valleys below us or take them to the mountains until the raid is over. Get the women and children out first; do it soon, every minute counts, but do it without causing any panic."

"Why are the Marauders coming here?" Othello had to tell him the truth; there was no use in inventing a story.

"They are coming for me" he admitted.

"For you?" The Hawk wanted more of an answer than that.

"Salarthians lust for power. Kronix won't leave you alone, not as long as I am with you. He has the means to do anything with the numbers he has, and his will is obeyed without question. And then there is Xavien. Xavien is unpredictable; it is only thanks to Kronix's leash that he hasn't been let loose on us in the past. Now that leash has been severed and Xavien, it would appear, has been given a new set of orders: to eliminate me. If I disappear, his mission will be pointless, and he may leave you alone, but we cannot take that risk. So, it's best we flee."

"How many do you think are coming?" asked Dingane.

"I don't know, certainly too many for us to handle. Fighting Snakes is one thing; fighting Blood Marauders is something else entirely. Get your people out of here, don't let them find you, head for a far-away encampment to bolster your numbers if needs be and hide. Jureai is a big place; it's easy to lose pursuers in the wastelands, and he won't search for you forever, Xavien is needed to lead against the Dovidians."

"OUR people. They are our people, Othello." Othello nodded, looking back at the silent camp. He belonged there, but they were not his people, no matter how hard he tried to convince himself otherwise.

Now the time had come for Othello to say goodbye, his life, his dreams, ambitions, his friends, and his home. He sensed a grip on him, as if something wanted him to stay, a feeling of resistance. Both men remained a distance away from the camp.

"Dingane, could you do me one last favour? Something important to me..." His friend listened intently. "Return my father to the earth on the slopes, and..." He paused for a moment.

"And what?" The Southlander's gaze fell on the camp.

"Don't let Xavien find you, never let him find you. Get word to Ivulien, tell their hierarchy that this war is of Xavien's doing, that the other clans share no part with Blood Marauders' activities. El Raud requires each Chieftain's signature. I know you can achieve this. Explain to the others why this has happened, why I had to leave. Tell them that the time I've spent here will never be forgotten." With that, they grabbed each other's wrists and rested their hands on one another's shoulders. Othello eventually took the reins of his tulkan and walked out into the open plain, away from the closest thing to family he had left in the world.

"HEEEY!" Dingane shouted and Othello looked over his shoulder "You never did tell me. What is the hardest lesson to learn in swordsmanship? Tell me before you go." Othello mounted his bull and yelled back:

"Let's hope you or I never have to learn it." His cloak whipped back in the wind as his mount stormed through the night, trailing a thin line of dust behind them. He knew where he was going. He was heading back to his old lands, not on a mission, and not because he was ordered to, but because he had to, to help protect those he cared about. At that moment it was just him and the open world. At that moment he was free, bound to no one and nothing.

Riding forth at great speed, tearing through the flat, dry terrain, Othello made haste across the plains of Jureai, the wind in his face. He stopped only briefly to rest. At times he caught himself examining the red-crested, golden ring; the only thing he had left to remind him of his life in Jureai, and of his late father, Enemar. He clutched it tightly, dropping it in his front pocket, pushing further south without sleep. The tulkans, a tough breed of bull, were able to travel long distances, galloping at speed for days without water or food, admirably adapted to deal with both blistering heat and bitter cold. Their hulking backs were strong enough to carry even the heaviest-set men without difficulty. During his travels, Othello kept his bull fed as best he could, keeping an eye on the animal's well-being, for they rode hard day and night, relying only on each other in order to survive. Luckily, the weather was kind to them; no sandstorms or great gales caught them by surprise. The food, however, ran out fast. Soon he was forced to use his hunting skills to survive, as well as his knowledge of the land. Out in the middle of the plains, in places that seemed devoid of all resources, certain plants did exist, ones that could provide him with nutrition for days. Othello found himself digging with crude tools and his bare hands to find potatoes that were dry and sour, but healthy. The deep roots of the plant could also be split and bitten into, to give a few mouthfuls of cool water. Tulkans were vegetarians, so the bull grazed whenever possible, crunching up thorny weeds and nettles, making short work of what little they came across. Othello quickly became close to his friendly mount, for he was loyal and never strayed far. It knew that they needed each other to survive the crossing over the hot wastelands. This routine of scavenging from one meagre resource to the next would give them both the energy needed to reach the border of Jureai safely.

The wilds of Jureai could be dangerous; it was easy to get lost, easy to get caught in a sandstorm capable of tearing flesh from the bone. Wild animals were also a concern; hyenas, if hungry enough, would call for their pack, which would stalk their chosen victims for miles and miles, before making any direct approach. Vultures out there grew to threatening sizes; they were not an immediate concern if spotted in advance, but if one was bold enough, it could quite easily make short work of a human being, plucking out his eyes before sinking its beak and talons into the soft flesh, bleeding out its prey. El Raud's last plea was Othello's greatest concern, gnawing at his thoughts every time he rested, and often enough when he was riding. He had no interest in heading to Ivulien; Dingane would send word to the Dovidians and save his clan from Xavien. Othello promised himself there and then that he would see his friends again one day. It might be years before their next meeting, but he made it a task he would accomplish before he left the world for good.

Othello planned to go through The Ledera Lands and across the southland to Krondathia's remote capital, Imrondel City. There he would seek out the meaning of the red-crested ring, far beyond The Northern Borders. First, he had to find Bane's Tree, the spot that marked the end of Jureai and the beginning of The Ledera Lands. It had to be close now, but a feeling of disorientation hit Othello, a fear he had never felt before. It cast its shadow over him; the thought of dying out there all alone, never to be found again, left in the wilderness to rot in the heat, his carcass gradually carried off by birds, hyenas, and brazen lions. Soon, however, the sweet feeling of relief washed his angst away, as the border marker came into view. Bane's Tree came peeking over the horizon. It was but a small speck in the far distance, but Othello knew what it looked like, and was glad to lay eyes upon its painfully dry, jagged branches. As he neared, he noted that a golden plaque had been bolted into the ground between its rooted feet. Upon the sign, Othello read a brief inscription…

Here rests the soul of Coppelia Velen, the people's vision.
May her visions travel yonder from this tree.

Sixth Star Caller, 890 - 908

Chapter 9 - In Search of a Face

Even the best of us make foolish decisions.

The day's work had come to an end. Isabelle smiled as the light faded and the shadows touched the trees. Her day had been long and tedious, while she could think of nothing else but the previous night. She had had no visitors and no word had come from Thao or her priests. Once again, she stood in front of her mirror and studied her reflexion. For her next incognito night out, she would hide in a coat more fitting for the cold weather. She wrapped herself up and turned out the furry collar; tying it back her hair and making it behave was a chore, for it was striking to the common folk. Picking up some of the golden zeal coins she had found yesterday, she stored them safely in her pocket, only then she remembered the envelope Thao had given her. It held her attention, laying there on the cluttered desk unopened and lonely, poking out from under a paperweight shaped into a proudly sitting house cat. It was important, originating from Imrondel City, likely containing delicate information for her eyes only. She promised herself that she would read it later when she returned. Isabelle blew a breath out into the middle of her room and the scant few candles scattered about her cabin flickered briefly before losing their flame. She opened the door, taking notice of the patrolling Glyph Wielders outside on the roads, all with bored and glum expressions. She felt a gaze upon her and turned her head back toward her room; the twelve statues locked away in the glass cabinet gaped at her as if they somehow objected to her departure. Once again, and without explanation, the key to the cabinet dropped from the lock and lay still on the floor. Isabelle entertained the idea to stay for a moment, staring right into the keyhole, but eventually took off.

Using the same sneaky methods as she had the night before, Isabelle found her way to the docking area with ease. Finding the very same boat, though this time with much less cargo, she snuck aboard under the cover of darkness. Venturing below deck, she blended in with the shadows relying more upon her ears than her eyes to sense impending danger, waiting for the vessel to set sail for Harbour's Edge.

The boat eventually landed on the shores of Krondathia and this time, with the vessel almost empty and only a few workers aboard, Isabelle was able to move around with lot more freedom. As she emerged from below, she could hear the Captain talking to some official in a smart, black uniform. She could only make out a few words and strung the rest together herself. The man's voice was sharp and sinister, not to mention spoken, so she listened intently.

"Is this the last of it, Captain? My orders have been made clear." Isabelle pulled herself up out of the hold and crouched behind one of the large, wooden crates. She did not recognise the official right away, but he was clearly upset with the Captain, a rotund man who she noted had a bottle of strong liquor stuffed in his back pocket. "Have you been drinking, sailor?" The official was clearly in no mood for negligence. The pitiful Captain was hesitant, trying to squirm his way out of trouble like a scared schoolboy. Much of the conversation was vague, but she heard the end perfectly well. "There is no room for error; these two shipments alone could be worth more than the entire city. They are not to be compromised or put at risk. One must go to Imrondel, the other to Zodias, undamaged and sealed. That is my final word, Captain. You know who these belong to; you don't want me to put in a bad word now, do you?" The Captain was submissive and shaky. "Good, I'll take that as a yes. Settled then." The official was as tall as the Captain, though not as fat. He chose that moment to take his leave, sleeking back his smooth, black hair as he walked away. The sailor walked off in the opposite direction, muttering rude words to himself, hastily pulling the bottle out of his pocket and gulping down its contents at the other end of the boat. She could not be sure, but the official had looked familiar. She felt sure she had seen him before, perhaps at meetings and other important events. If her memory served her well, he normally stayed close to The Eldor. Isabelle did not ponder on these thoughts. She put them out of her mind and focused on her mission, to reach Harbour's Edge. Deciding that the time was right to make her move, she slipped silently from shadow to shadow, heading straight for the wooded area.

As she neared the town, she could see through the thicket that it was far quieter and less hectic than the previous night. Not good.

The less social activity, the harder it would be for her to pass through. She was far more likely to be identified under these conditions. The consequences of a Star Caller breaking her curfew had no precedent, the punishments were simply non-existent for every Star Caller throughout history had been obedient. The Chosen was expected to be an example of greatness, certainly not one of defiance. These thoughts made it even harder for Isabelle to walk the streets; she had to constantly remind herself of what she was doing there in the first place; searching for a face, a man with no name. She felt a little more comfortable and at ease once she slipped in among the locals and got used to the tightly packed houses and unusual buildings that lined the sides of the roads. She walked along the open, almost empty streets, jingling the coins in her pocket. She tried to avoid attention and eye contact as much as possible, but she was still open to the people who she thought might be the face she was looking for. At times she drowned in thoughts of doubt, finding it harder to convince herself of what she was doing. Eventually, she came to a familiar site, a smallish bar with faded windows and a glowing fire within. Above the door was written in smart lettering, The Traveller's Corner Bar. At first, she was hesitant to go in, what with nearly being caught the last time by Lethaniel. Looking in from the outside, she couldn't make anything out. The windows were too misty. She opened the door and like a stranger entering unknown territory, she poked her head around the door. The pub was empty and tidy, the fire glowing red hot and the air smelling of old wood. The woman behind the bar was cleaning the work surface with a damp cloth; she had noticed the girl with the pale green eyes peering in.

"Don't worry honey, come on in, the thugs aren't here yet."

"Thugs?" The Chosen repeated, puzzled.

"We don't open for a while yet, but seeing as though you're such a generous customer, I'll make you a drink. What would you like? Another red lagoon or the regular golden ale?" Isabelle narrowed her eyes.

"You know me?" She took a seat on one of the bar stools while looking around to make sure no one else was in the bar.

"Of course I do, silly," the barmaid chuckled, wrinkling her forehead.

"How?" The maid threw the cloth away into the small kitchen behind the bar and finished her tidying, before pulling up a swivelling stool and sitting down in front of Isabelle.

"You are the girl who came in here last night, aren't you?" Isabelle had to hope that the woman did not recognise her, either way, she had no way of telling if the woman knew her or not, so she just sat there and listened. "It's good to see a pretty face every now and then. You left me a hefty bit of gold last night, and you took off so fast that I had no time to tell you. I owe you some silver." The maid fiddled around under a counter and handed over some change, insisting that Isabelle take it. "My name is Clarisa; it's nice to meet ya." Isabelle almost spilled it.

"Elle; my name's Elle." The women shook hands.

"Now how 'bout that drink?" Clarisa asked, smiling. The barmaid poured The Star Caller a drink, helping herself to a glass at the same time.

"So who are these thugs?"

Clarisa grinned.

"You're not from around here, are ya hun? The thugs from these parts are known as Tom Boyos, or at least that's what they like to be called. Really, they're just a group of oafish men, big kids in fact, who think they run the town, just because they roam as a pack. They aren't exactly the friendly type, but if you keep outta their way and give them beer then there's no problem. If you ask me, they are nothing but wannabes who're jealous of bigger gangs in Xiondel." She began to wipe down the table surface again with an old rag taken from under the counter. "What brings you to these parts? Any family, friends, a boyfriend perhaps?"

"I have friends. Never knew my father, sadly, and my mother died when I was little," Isabelle reeled off her story, trying to maintain a normal facade.

"Do you have a fella then? A big strong man perhaps?" Clarisa asked with a grin.

"No, no boyfriend." She had no time for that nonsense; her life was all about her duties as a Star Caller. Then she remembered why she was there.

"I don't blame you. If I was you, I would try to look for one in the quieter areas, like in Pura or in one of them outer villages in The Ledera Lands. Men round here are into nothing but themselves, finding whoever they can, to sleep with and abandon the next day. Lying, cheating scumbags, the lot of them, only caring about their pride, ale and who they can beat to a pulp. I see it every day. Better off without them, until that ONE comes along who changes everything, of course…Tell me more about your family. You didn't know your father?" Clarisa was very friendly, and Isabelle didn't feel the need to lie to her anymore.

"That's right. To tell you the truth, I don't know what happened to my father, he may be alive somewhere for all I know, but I do know that my mother is gone."

"I'm sorry to hear that. No brothers or sisters?"

"Nope," confirmed the Chosen, sipping on her drink. "What about you. How long have you worked here?"

"Way, way too long; about three years now, almost, but I wanna go to the city."

"Which one?" Isabelle asked, already knowing what the answer would most likely be.

"Imrondel of course; it's perfect. Clean streets, fine and affordable homes, protected by The Honour Guards, plenty of jobs going. And a nice selection of guys too, or so I hope."

"What's so special about that city? What about Xiondel? Or Davune? Their kingdoms are just as large and as fascinating as Imrondel."

161

"I believe in Starillia, and Imrondel is my home. I was born there; my late father owned a property on The Canal Side District, not too far from the palace. I hope to save up enough zeal and maybe set up my own bar or something, I dunno yet. I got a long way to go yet for those kinda plans."

"You want to do this all by yourself, Clarisa?"

"No one is going to help me; either I start now and be settled at thirty-odd or I don't start at all and stay here the rest of my life. A little extra help would go a long way, I can tell ya. I used to believe that I could do everything myself like I was something special, but...I was wrong, I need the help of another, I really do, both financially and spiritually."

"Spiritually?" The girl's choice of word sparked something in Isabelle's imagination.

"Yeah, spiritually. We go insane by ourselves."

"What are you gonna call your bar when you get it up and running?"

"I don't know for sure, but at the moment I'm thinking *Viel's*, what do ya reckon?"

"Is Viel your surname, by any chance?" guessed Isabelle, to which Clarisa gave a nod. "I like it!" The barmaid walked around and fed the fire some wood, giving The Star Caller some time to formulate her next question. "You say you believe in Starillia; have you ever met our Chosen?"

"I saw her once, a long time ago, when she was but a child, I too was young then, and I have not seen her since. I was gonna try and catch her at Penstrive, on the island, but never found the time, what with my waitress being bloody ill." Clarisa placed the rod back on its stand next to the fire and dusted off her hands. She turned back to Isabelle once she had finished "I have heard she is good looking; stick thin with hair to die for. Also, apparently, she has it all: servants, wealth, vast knowledge of Glyph, power beyond our wildest dreams. I wish I was so lucky." Isabelle sank back inside herself at the bar. She was sitting in the same spot as she had the night before and remembered looking across at that stranger, a recent memory which warmed her insides.

"Say, you're fairly good at remembering faces; do you recall seeing a man standing opposite me last night? Somewhere over there in the corner." Clarisa scratched the side of her head and squinted, trying to think back and visualise the previous night's crowd. To help her, Isabelle began to list details, using her hands to draw out a rough image. "He was wearing a hood, darkish brown hair, brown eyes…Lonesome, I guess?" Clarisa clicked her fingers twice.

"Yes, I know exactly who you mean. Funny though; I can't remember serving him, but he still ended up with an ale."

"Who was he? Do you know him?" Isabelle's curiosity was well and truly sparked, and she found herself sitting on the edge of her seat.

"Yeah, I noticed him the day before you arrived; he doesn't seem to be local or familiar, definitely not a thug. Not a bad looker, could do with a good feeding though."

"Yes yes, but do you know his name or where he is now?"

"Like I said, he's nought but a pretty face to me; I don't know nothin' 'bout him otherwise, I'm afraid. Why do you ask anyways?" Isabelle slumped back, her excitement waning, repositioning herself on the stool, thinking for a moment.

"I'm sorry, I don't really know myself. Curious I guess."

"It isn't wise to mingle with strangers, especially those who turn up and disappear as they please," warned Clarisa. "See, they could be anyone; if they're not bound to Krondathia or Ivulien then they could be Outsiders."

"Outsiders?" repeated Isabelle, realising that she didn't really know as much as she should about the real world.

"Honey, you can listen to me or not, either way, I might be wrong but I'll tell you what I think: you don't want to end up on the wrong side of an Outsider or worse a Dark Rogue."

"I've heard of Dark Rogues before, but what's an Outsider?" Isabelle questioned, coming to the end of her bottle, swirling the dregs around in the bottom.

"They used to be groups of people who lived outside the laws of…Well, everyone and everything. Even when the Norkrons took control, and the Dovidians recovered after The Never-Ending War, Outsider groups still existed. They were simply men and women with an ideal, though one that they never disclosed to the rest of the world. Their communities functioned well, without the help of the Norkron and Dovidian people, but something happened, and now I don't think they exist anymore, not many of 'em anyway…They simply disappeared."

"Just like that?"

"Just like that. One or two of 'em pop up here and there; they share no love for Krondathia, that I know for sure, and some are extremely dangerous and aggressive toward our kind." Her stories enlightened Isabelle, but now it was time to leave and look elsewhere. The Star Caller had finished her drink.

"It was nice talking to you," she said getting off the high stool and trying to hand over some silver to pay for the drink.

"No, it was on the house, keep it. It's not every day one meets such a pleasant girl. If you ever find yourself in Imrondel during the next few years, be sure to stop by at *Viel's*, Elle." The barmaid winked, then disappeared in the back of the bar. Feeling slightly ashamed at having to hide her name, Isabelle walked out and found herself back on the streets of Harbour's Edge.

Now back on the road, walking along the dark, narrow streets, she scanned ahead carefully, keeping an eye out for two things: people she knew, like Lethaniel and Thao, who would quickly recognise her, and the stranger she had briefly come into contact with the night before. She searched high and low, as best she could, though not many places were open at this time of night. A few bars were lit up, still cleaning up the remnants of the previous night's celebrations. She found herself keeping a distance from such establishments, trying to identify each person on the sidewalk. The next area was quiet; the houses remained closed and silent, the once hectic roads were deserted, not a sound of a soul could be heard. Isabelle was alone, or so she thought, yet for some reason, she always felt as though a pair of eyes were on her. It had been many hours since she left The Zodias Island and the night would soon turn to dawn. She walked ahead and found a stone clearing that led off to a crossroad. She scraped her heels along the pathway, back and forth, bored and unsettled. It finally sunk in, that this whole little trip had been a waste of time and wondered why she had even bothered to take the risk. At least she hadn't been discovered, and she had gotten some exercise. Now, it was time to head back to the boats, after witnessing the last bar closing its wooden shutters. She watched as the people disappeared from the bar in a large group, her hopes of finding her stranger, melted away. Making her way back to the dock, she passed by The Traveller's Corner Bar once again. Inside, the curtains had been drawn, and no sign of life could be seen. Isabelle did wish to see Clarisa before she left, just to talk to her before her departure, but now was just not appropriate.

"Elle!" a voice called from a short distance away. Isabelle turned and was shocked to see the barmaid standing in the street. "What are you still doing out here honey? It's freezing!"

"Yes, yes, I know. I was just on my way home. Are you alright? I know it's late."

"Hey, it's fine; it took me some time to clear the bar. It has been a busy night for me, and I was all by myself in there. How about you? I bet you've been having a good time."

"Well, I guess you could say something like that, but nothing happened worth remembering. Nothing bad either though, I prefer to look on the bright side."

"Something strange happened to me tonight, I must say," Clarisa began, "Two men came in after closing hours. One, I think, was that soldier with that famous reputation; you know, the one who hasn't been beat, the new General, the one who carries those two swords. Uhh, what's his name again?" Isabelle shrugged her shoulders, knowing full well that the girl was talking about Lethaniel, but deciding it was best to play dumb. "Anyway, I forget. So, they came in and started asking me lots of weird questions." Isabelle shuddered inside and tried to remain calm and polite.

"What did they ask you?"

"They kind of sat me down and asked me questions about last night. You know, questions like *did you see anything strange*? Or *did you recognise anyone*? It was crazy; like anyone of interest is going to come here to MY bar. However I did see that Thao guy here yesterday, he is a somebody, as The Honour Guard responsible for silencing the upheaval in Xiondel all those years ago." The Star Caller once again pretended as though she had no clue and continued to listen with open ears. "He has been here once or twice before anyway, so…Do you know him?"

"Did you find out their names?"

"Not the one with the two swords; the other was Braygon. I had a little chat with him, he is nice, although he wouldn't tell me where he's from." Isabelle was concerned that Lethaniel had been onto her antics the previous night. He was her friend and maybe he would understand if she explained the situation to him. So long as Thao didn't know, maybe she could secretly be forgiven, but she did wonder how Lethaniel would react. "Anyway, it's cold, and I must be off. See ya around."

"Goodbye, Clarisa. I'll be away for a while, but I will come back. I hope to see you in Imrondel one day."

"That would be nice. Good luck to you, Elle" smiled the barmaid, who then turned the corner, disappearing out of sight. Her fading footsteps fell silent at last, and Isabelle was once again left all alone, now with new worries to think about.

Once back at the boats, Isabelle snuck aboard as she had previously, but before she plunged into the wooden crate full of odd towels and blankets to get some sleep, she remembered the conversation between the Captain and the official. With that in mind, she decided to take a quick look in one of the other containers, curious as to what cargo they had been talking about earlier; it had had something to do with a special item. She didn't see this as a breach of trust; these men worked for The Eldor and, as he liked to say, *'she and he were one'* so effectively she was not breaking any rules. At least that is what she told herself as she pried open the crate. She muddled around in the dark, relying on her powers of touch, coming across crunchy scrolls and thick pieces of paper. Tossing them aside, she reached deeper inside and felt the cold surface of what could have been slate. Intrigued, she pulled it out, with some difficulty for it was big and heavy. Unable to see the cover and stunned by what she thought she held in her hands; her heart skipped a beat. Isabelle frantically searched for a source of light and moved away from the safety of the darkness, into the bathing yellow glow of a torch stuck in the ground nearby. Wide-eyed and scared by what she saw, Isabelle held a book that to her knowledge should not even exist. It was one of The Books from the Early Past! A volume that had been deemed lost, completely unaccounted for, for centuries. The remaining four in the series were in the care of The Eldor and his most trusted servants, The High Priests of The Column Temple. In total amazement, she opened the stone cover and flicked through the incredibly detailed pages. To her considerable frustration, Isabelle had no time to absorb any of it; voices could be heard in the distance! She quickly closed the book and dropped it back in the crate with the other bits and pieces she had removed. Jumping into her own crate further down the way, she slid back the wooden lid and remained quiet, listening to the men outside chatting and walking around on deck. From within the crate, she peered through the very thin cracks. Shadows of people passed her by. Some hovered so close around her that all they had to do was lift the lid of the crate and they would find the truant Star Caller! The most powerful woman on the planet awkwardly crunched up inside a packing box. One man said *"I swear I saw something"* though luckily for Isabelle, who lay only a few feet away, the other man wasn't so sure, and neither bothered to investigate. They hung around for a while, just talking and joking. This kind of talk bored

Isabelle, making it easier for her to shut off and get some much-needed sleep.

Early morning came and the sway of water broke upon the shore. The dim light pierced through the cracks in the crate, waking Isabelle covered in towels and priests' clothing. It was daytime and the transport boat had already docked on The Zodias Island. When she realised that they had already crossed the small channel, she quickly made herself scarce, clambering out of her wooden bedroom with stiff, cramped limbs and a sore back. No one was around, so after some careful observation, she trusted her higher senses to warn her of incoming danger; they had never failed before. Walking woozily toward her hut, she remained alert to the presence of her guards or any patrolling Glyph Wielders. She didn't always need to see them; her senses would tingle and flare up inside her whenever others who shared her gifts in the vicinity, those blessed with Glyph gave off a potent aura compared with non-wielders. Fortunately, it seemed everyone was asleep, and she was able to sneak back inside her hut without detection. She closed the door and instantly noticed a change in the air; She looked around her feet and scanned the floor, trying to spot anything that was out of order, which is when she noticed that the key to the cabinet had been placed back in its keyhole. Isabelle walked over and looked at the twelve hand-sized models behind the glass. Had she placed the key back where it belonged earlier? She couldn't remember, but she knew for a fact that one of the twelve models was slightly out of position. Unlocking the cabinet, she twisted the model of Scorpio back into its original location. Exhausted, she immediately collapsed on her bed, promising that she would dwell more on this mystery once she was fully awake. Wrapped up in her own cosy sheets, she faded into a dream.

After a short while, her door was pulled violently open. A Glyph Wielder marched in with his half staff in hand! When he saw Isabelle curled up in bed, staring at him with tiny, squinted, green eyes, he was taken aback, and muttered:

"Apologies, milady. Your escorts have arrived and are waiting outside. Please excuse my interruption." He put away his staff, sliding it into the ribbon sheath at his side, before bowing and leaving. Isabelle thumped her head back down on the pillow, trying to ignore the bitter sting of daylight now flooding the room. Thao leant on the door frame, slowly strolling in, and looked around at the mess, casting a confused look at The Chosen, currently spread awkwardly on her front, hugging her quilt and pillow, hiding her face.

"Is that how it is done now around here?" she mumbled into her fluffy pillow, suppressing a yawn. "No knocking or even a warning? You just burst in on a Star Caller while she is sleeping or dressing!? That may prove fatal if I decide to start sleeping with my long staff, Violethelm."

"Why would you sleep with your long staff?"

"If I get lonely, I suppose," she chuckled.

"We arrived nearly fifteen minutes ago; we called and knocked several times and got no answer. When all else failed, we came into the room, so not exactly unannounced. Sorry to disturb you, milady," he apologised, bowing.

"Well, you disturbed me, and you disturbed a nice dream of mine which I would like to get back to, so if you don't mind, you can give me another twenty minutes."

"You know I would any other time, but your carriage is waiting, your escorts are outside and…"

"Oh please… I thought we were leaving at noon."

"Well yes, Isabelle, it IS noon!" Isabelle opened her eyes, raised her head a little and murmured something indecipherable, sulking miserably. "I'll see you outside," Thao said, leaving the room and closing the door behind him, giving her some privacy to dress. Her floor was a jumble of clutter, and she tripped over everything trying to find her clothes and look like a great Star Caller should, pulling on her tights. She had always refused the help of maids and servants wherever she went. Not having a maid was a luxury in her eyes, but in the cities it was unavoidable. Right then, however, she really could have used the help of someone else; she was stumbling and tripping over bits and pieces, even over herself, as she attempted to pull on one of her boots. She could not find any nice pullovers, cardigans, or vest tops; even her bras seemed to have vanished! It was time to leave, but she was still fidgeting around with the clips in her hair and buckling her belt with a free hand. She had also misplaced the important letter sent to her from Imrondel, a letter she still had not read, which should have been on her desk, held firm under her sitting cat paperweight. But it was gone! Panicking, she began her search, rummaging around in coat pockets and palming through draws; she even got low down on the floor, looking for it under her desk. Thao called to her from outside; she had no time. A weight was lifted from her mind when she finally spotted it on the opposite side of her desk, not under the weight, but not in clear view either. *Odd*, she thought, first the key and now the envelope? Picking it up wearily, she pressed her nose against the paper and drew in the air around it. Thao yelled again for her to hurry up. It was times like these that she wished she could just freeze time. Sighing in frustration, Isabelle grabbed her blue coat and a bunch of her belongings, folded them under her arm and stepped outside, where a large carriage awaited her. It was larger than a standard carriage and a lot finer than most she had travelled in, being a little heavier and featuring thick, armoured walls on all sides. Thao was mounted upon his black horse alongside his two soldiers, Arthur and Scarto. Isabelle's priests were there as always, standing in an orderly line, hands together. The Glyph Wielders had long been prepared to make the journey. A separate, lighter carriage was there to transport supplies; not only food and water, but also small shelters for the escorts to sleep in at night. "Sorry I took so long," she apologised to The Honour Guard as she stepped up to enter the carriage. Arthur took the lead while Scarto guarded the rear; both were ready for a long trek. Just then, Lethaniel trotted around from the back on his fine white horse, Seridox. She didn't know HE was coming to the city! Isabelle disappeared inside catching his eyes, before Thao shut the door before Lethaniel had a chance to address her. They then set out on their path to Imrondel City.

Soon they would reach the dock and the ferry to Harbour's Edge. From the small village, they would then travel east through The Silent Vale, passing further into the lands of Krondathia. Then it would be through Xiondel City, where extra guards would join them. Crossing The Plains of Xethark, they would then traverse The Avelien River using the transports provided, already waiting for them at The Avorlian Docks. With a few days of rest and fresh supplies, the carriage would continue, heading south-east into the southland, also known as The Ledera Lands, via Korthak Bridge. From there, the final leg of the journey would take them south on a road leading directly to Imrondel City. Taking the quickest routes available to them with good weather and no delays, and stopping only twice a day for short rests, the group should reach their destination by the fifth or sixth week of their journey.

Chapter 10 - The Absent Capital

Long roads often lead to great cities.

It was him; the same official Isabelle had spied upon the night before on her visit to Harbour's Edge. She was curious as to why he had stopped the carriage on its way along the road. Unable to hear clearly through the walls of her room, she slid open a side hatch very quietly and listened. She could hear Thao's voice finishing up the brief conversation:

"It's no problem, Calias; we will deliver it safely and send you word upon its arrival."

"The contents are valuable and delicate to our Sire; it must reach the old libraries archives in Imrondel City. It is for the eyes of the librarian and The Eldor only. You must understand that neither of us is in any position to consider meddling with such materials." The official was stern but still showed The Honour Guard great respect.

"Do not worry, it is in safe hands." Isabelle saw a metal box being loaded into the back of the supply cart by a priest; it was square and large enough to hold a book; one of great importance and significance. Without a doubt, it was The Book of the Early Past she had found the night before. Clearly, the official did not trust anyone else to deliver it safely. Having finally found out the man's name, Calias, it all fell together in her head. He was one of the new officials serving The Eldor; a right-hand man to assist with the workload. Harbour's Edge soon became a distant speck behind them as they travelled to one of the most iconic cities in Equis. Thao led the way along the road, mounted upon a black stallion, followed closely by Lethaniel atop Seridox keeping his distance from the Glyph Wielders guarding The Star Caller carriage, stationed at all sides.

The day was damp and cold; the sun was shining, however, and the birds were singing, which gave the travellers something to listen to.

"I wish to talk with Isabelle soon if you don't mind?" stated Lethaniel.

"That's fine by me. What do you want to discuss?" asked Thao.

"I haven't seen her since the day I took off." The Honour Guard nodded and continued to look ahead.

"You know what she will say, Lethaniel: *I told you so*. Then she will laugh at you for not trusting her word. Star Callers are not exactly wrong when it comes to things like this... She will rub it in your face, and rightly she should, it's what you deserve," he laughed. The General trotted up passed Thao.

"The Isabelle I know would not do such a thing, but I wish to see her now. I don't think I like you anymore," he joked, shaking off the laughter of The Honour Guards.

"By all means Lethaniel, go right ahead." Thao caught the reigns of Seridox as Lethaniel dismounted and walked up to the carriage door.

Inside the carriage lay an exhausted-looking girl, tucked up at the far end on a small couch. The wobbling room was warm and luxurious, fit for the most important of people. Isabelle could not sleep anymore; her head was too crowded with repetitive questions. She thought about Clarisa and her kindness back in Harbour's Edge and wondered how long it would be before she would meet her again. She remembered Lethaniel chasing her around and almost catching her out in the early hours. She also thought about the book she had found locked in the crate; a book that to her mind, should not exist. Her eyes closed, she squinted harder and shook her head from side to side, trying to break up the troublesome whirlpool. The envelope sat there on a small table by itself, remaining forgotten and unread. She was about to go over to read it but heard someone outside, about to come in. Swinging the door open, she found herself face to face with Lethaniel, who looked like he was preparing to knock. He did not enter, thinking it rude to just walk in, so he waited for her invitation.

"Is this a bad time, Squeak?" he asked.

"No, as good as any," she conceded. "Are you going to let all the warm air out or are you coming in?" The General climbed in the moving carriage and sat down with her, resting his back upon the frame of the door. For a moment they just looked at each other. "Well well well, back from the dead I see. At least that is what some people are saying, I, however, knew exactly where you were. I hope you found what you were looking for. Did you find that place of peace, I wonder?" she questioned, shifting herself into a more comfortable position on the couch, folding her arms. Lethaniel avoided her gaze as she began to smile.

"Before you say anything, Izzy, I want you to know that you were right." She lifted both her arms up in the air childishly, as though she had just won a big prize. "You were right about Syen, about me and what I would find, but...

"I wish you would have listened to me before dropping off the face of the Earth for two years. I was trying to help you. I am the Star Caller, after all; if I couldn't see the future, what kind of Chosen would I be?"

"I'm sorry," he sighed.

"So you did find something beyond the lands with walls?"

"Yes, I did. I mean to return there one day, but now is not the time."

"Once is enough for a lifetime; you won't have time to go again, not for a while at least. Your place is here for the time being. Important matters that will soon reveal themselves won't permit you the freedom you have now; others will become your priority, and you will put them before yourself." He listened to her words but did not understand them at all.

"You're being a little vague. Care to tell me what you mean, Isabelle?"

"Nothing to worry about for the moment, though one day you will understand… Did you see it?" she continued, getting back to the subject at hand.

"Yes. It was incredible, beautiful," he replied.

"Makes you think about a lot of things, doesn't it? It makes you question and allows you to wonder. Or at least that's what I thought when I saw it myself." An awkward silence then reigned in the carriage for some time; neither had anything to say, so they listened to the tread of the wheels and the clap of hoofs on the rock. Thao was talking to his men outside; something may have been spotted on the road.

"When did you see it? I mean, you're a Star Caller, you don't normally have time to do anything much other than your official duties."

"I have not always been The Chosen, Lethaniel. Come on; you knew me when I was in your art class," she recalled.

"Oh yeah, right," he laughed, "You were good, I thought. Better at music though."

"I didn't go there willingly; I can tell you that much. Only a handful of people even know that such a place exists, and it is best to keep it that way. Not even Krondathia and Ivulien know its location. I was only five, but I remember it like it happened yesterday. My mother took me; she said there was something I had to see before I became who I am today," she explained, with Lethaniel nodding at her words. "I was taken from my family and my home to learn the complexities of ruling a country. Priests and Glyph Wielders became my parents, and The Celestial Souls, my siblings. I have spent my life reading and learning while others grew up and lived their lives freely. Since you left to find yourself over the past two years, I have been giving demonstrations around the world, like a guided tour. The last place I visited was Ivulien, in the capital Davune. The last few years have been tiresome, to say the least," she sighed.

"All for the best, right?" Isabelle shook her head.

"Maybe so, but I can never be free from this; I will always be who I am, right until I am released from my position."

"Released?" It took a moment before he understood the meaning behind the word, though he was helped by the look on her face "When not giving demonstrations, has there been anything else?" Isabelle thought back to Harbour's Edge and noticed her dark coat with the white streak hanging out of a draw in full view!

"I have been summoned to this meeting to help decide on an issue. Where I am needed is where I will be," she responded cryptically.

"That's not exactly what I meant..." A call from one of the escorts interrupted them. Isabelle was grateful that Lethaniel was needed outside, helping her avoid the dangerous line of questioning.

"Looks like our time has run out," she said.

"If you need anything, Izzy, I'll be outside." Before stepping out and closing the door, he folded up the sleeve of the dark coat, tucking it in and pushing the open drawer closed. Isabelle creased her face and rubbed her head. She then spotted the ever-annoying envelope at the far end of the carriage, finally she grabbed it before returning to her couch and ripped it open. She pulled out the contents and unfolded the letter. The seal of Imrondel was set prominently at the top of the handwriting:

-Star Caller Isabelle-

It is with a glad heart that I write to you. Your performances at Davune pleased the audiences in more ways than you could possibly imagine. I quote a Judge of The Dovidian Circle: "Isabelle gives inspiration and hope to our society." Another from The Head of Mineral Transportation: "If we have learnt anything, the bond between mortals and Celestials is strong." Isabelle, you are the most promising Star Caller since the days of Regina. During your reign you have provided us with a light brighter than anyone before. However, as wonderful as your demonstration was, it raised some concern in the minds of The

Defence Ministers and their new councillor, who still needs to be introduced and recognised in your presence. The power of Glyph and the enormity of The Holy Ultimas, the great Celestials, have stunned and shocked some of the Ivulien circle. As a member of The Xiondel High Council of Virtue, and as a friend, I must ask you to help me in this time of concern.

Our plan of action is simple: to gather together the leaders of Krondathia in Imrondel City and vote on a particular action, to let Ivulien know that our intentions in the use of our soul power does not in any way include its use as a weapon against our enemies. Milady Verano, you are to speak on our Sire's behalf. The Eldor will remain in the northern regions of Krondathia. I have arranged for you to have the best security for your journey, should you choose to accept they will meet you when you pass Xiondel. In the meantime, Thao Hikonle will escort you; he volunteered for this task, and I know that you two have seen eye to eye in the past. Thank you greatly.

Yours Sincerely,
Yespin Fquarign - High Councillor Truth

Isabelle read the letter carefully. She looked around her quarter with a feeling of impending boredom; this would be her space for a long while, her little moving, rattling house. She got up and fetched another blanket from a nearby set of drawers fastened to the wall, only to notice that her small wardrobe had been filled already, most probably by her loyal priests back on The Zodias Island. Through a crack in the door she caught a glimpse of her fine red dress tucked away inside; it shimmered and stood out among her other clothes. Her mind now satisfied with the contents of the letter, she retreated to her couch and sprawled out, ignoring her bed.

Outside on the road, Lethaniel rode along close to the door and opened it ever so slightly, just enough to see Isabelle curled up in her blankets, sleeping soundly with the letter on her chest.

"So, how is she? Any major changes?" Thao asked.

"She's exhausted, like she hasn't slept at all for days!"

"I meant has she changed in the time you have been apart?"

"I don't know. Give me more time with her, five minutes is hardly enough."

"Have as much time with her as you want, but don't get careless, remember what we are doing here" Thao reminded him assertively.

"When we reach Avorlian, do you think Mathias will meet up with us?"

"How should I know? He's been gone for a long time. The only word he has sent is to that friend of yours, Braygon. Where is he, by the way?"

"He and his company will follow within the week." Thao began to think back to that conversation they had in The Traveller's Corner Bar.

"Tell me about him; what's his relation to Mathias, and better yet, where is the man from?" Lethaniel raised his eyebrows.

"He's the old man's apprentice, I guess, the only man for the job, for he is by far the most talented and skilled. It's a long story, but in short, they are old friends who share the same ideas and have much in common. I'm surprised you haven't heard of Braygon before...And no, Thao, I have no idea where he was born. I have long given up asking, and he bears no familiar accent or accessories that might link him to a specific place. Best just leave it be, maybe one day he will let it spill."

"How did you meet him?"

"It was on the road; I was coming back from The Ledera Lands during my time away, camping out on the side of a goat path. That was about six months ago now."

"How skilled is he? What combat experience has he amassed?" Lethaniel just looked at Thao and grinned.

"He may love getting drunk once in a while, but he has more than enough experience with the sword and hand to hand, believe me." They stopped talking for a few seconds and concentrated on the pace of their horses.

"Maybe Mathias will know where he is from," The Honour Guard pondered. Lethaniel smiled to himself, thinking it unlikely, though if Braygon were to tell anyone about his origins, it would be to Mathias.

As the day rolled by, Isabelle remained peacefully asleep within the guarded carriage, while Thao and Lethaniel led the way on horseback, chatting about trivial matters and sharing the occasional laugh. The group made great time as they travelled; the weather was calm - chilly, but pleasant - and the road was clear and always empty. They stopped only once, sometimes twice a day for an hour's rest. If a good water supply were nearby, Lethaniel and Thao would take this opportunity to stop and give their horses a drink, for they were working hard too. All seemed well, yet The General sensed something odd about the ease of their journey and could not help but feel wary when turning a sharp corner or passing through where the road narrowed. He often stared deeply into the twisted woodlands, which appeared just too quiet and undisturbed. The carriage eventually had to stop for a short while on the road; one of the wheels had come loose and the men were fixing it. The Glyph Wielders were resting and preparing to continue, never straying far from the carriage door. Thao saw to his black horse, tightening the straps and refitting his saddle. There had been no sign of Isabelle since the previous day; perhaps she was still sleeping or working. Seridox was hand fed a few apples by Lethaniel, before the horse began lapping up running water from a small stream. Lethaniel knelt, also taking advantage of the source to refill a canteen. Birds were nesting in the trees above, fluttering around and singing to each other in their own language. Another tune whistled, one far deeper and far too strong for a bird of these parts to have, roused Lethaniel's suspicions. Thinking not much of it until it sounded again. He slowly stood and fastened the cap firmly on his canteen, walking toward Seridox with caution. His horse was observing something in the distance beyond the tree lines. Lethaniel strung the canteen to his saddle and stared in the same direction. All was still, and yet he kept his ears alert, listening out for that bizarre whistle, but it never sounded again. Something was out there, maybe even within striking distance? Attached to the saddle of Seridox, were a pair of sheathed swords of different lengths, with blue fabric wrapped around their handles.

"General! We are moving out!" called one of the guards. Lethaniel turned away and began to walk back to the road, from where the carriage pulled off and crunched along the rocky path once more.

"Seridox," he whispered; his mount was still staring into the thickets, reluctantly trotting after his master, who patted and stroked the horse's neck as he walked up by his side.

Elaso fiin… Blackness enveloped her surroundings! She had plenty of space to move, but nowhere to go. Except, perhaps, towards a wall in the distance, slowly emerging from the darkness. As she approached, it rapidly shifted to enclose her on all sides. Isabelle could only touch the cold stone wall with her palm, examining the familiar pattern engraved in the surface. Beneath was a series of symbols and lines cut into the smooth rock; one shape stood out, she recognised it but could not figure out where from. Taking a deep breath, she closed her eyes and pressed both hands on the wall, deep in thought. Suddenly she was jolted violently by a shocking series of pained screams ringing in her head. Her mind was assaulted by images of horrendous atrocities, crashing over her like a falling wave of rock. Her prison broke and she felt herself falling through a tunnel of wind, only to wake up, safely back inside her carriage with the fading whispers of…*An ute fiin tressa.*

Isabelle screamed as she awoke from her sleep, hot and uncomfortable. The carriage came to a swift halt and a knock came from the outside.

"Izzy, is everything alright in there?" Lethaniel called, putting his ear to the door. She slid a hatch open.

"It's fine! I'm fine, don't worry." The General drew closer, whispering so that no one could hear.

"I heard you; what's going on?"

"I'm fine," she repeated, and the hatch shut tightly, almost catching Lethaniel's fingers. He turned and shrugged his shoulders at Thao, who was watching from atop his horse. The group pressed on, a day away from the city of Xiondel.

"What was that about?" asked The Honour Guard.

"Nothing. I thought I heard something, that's all."

"Has she said anything to you?"

"No, why?"

"Isabelle has been acting strangely recently, and you seem to be on edge yourself. If there is anything you would like to share with me regarding our Chosen or our present situation, I want you to talk to me, alright?" Lethaniel wasn't concentrating, instead focusing on the area around them, having once again heard the suspicious whistle.

"It's getting late; tomorrow we will reach the outskirts of the city. In a short while we should rest for the night, don't you think Thao?"

"Agreed."

The light of the moon and stars fell through the surrounding treetops. The carriage had stopped on an open patch of soft grass, safely away from the road, almost hidden amidst the dense thicket around them. Thao was sleeping camouflaged beside a tree facing the carriage, used supplies scattered all around the place. All but one of The Glyph Wielders were asleep in their small shelters. The solitary patrolling guard walked around making minimal noise. No bird sang; only the fluttering wings of bats passing by on their hunt could be heard. The horses were tied to nearby trees, resting and grazing; except Seridox, who remained as still as a statue, haunting the woodland with his shape and glinting eyes. Ever so quietly, the side hatch slid open, scraping on its frame. Isabelle stared out into the night for what seemed like an eternity. Then the door opened. She let it swing and come to a rest by itself, giving her time and space to step out. She closed the door and knelt to the floor, easily spotting the feet of the patrolling guard. Everyone else was asleep, or so she thought. Barefoot, she trod carefully upon the grass, walking over to the supply transport, which was almost half-empty. The ground was damp and cold; the guards rested upon thick blankets and covered themselves with warm coats and travelling quilts under their shelters. She reached the smaller carriage and moved some things aside, constantly looking behind her. Finally, she came across the metal box she was looking for, which had a hefty looking lock attached to it. She grasped the lock in frustration and was about to give up and head back to the safety of her carriage, when the lock simply fell off, making a dull thud as it hit the wood below. She had no time to wonder why this had happened; either Calias had been forgetful and had neglected to secure the lock, or it had just broken then and there. Both possibilities were highly unlikely, but it was not a matter to dwell on at that moment. She hastily lifted the heavy, ancient book out of the solid container and replaced it with a flat rock she found on the ground nearby. She closed the box and steadily replaced the lock so it would not shut on her when it came to its return. With light feet, Isabelle hurried back to her carriage, but before she shut the door, she spotted Seridox spying on her, clearly having witnessed her thievery. Once inside, she locked the door safely behind her and listened for a minute to ensure she had gotten away with it. *Good thing horses cannot talk* she thought to herself. Satisfied with the silence and her mind at ease, her eyes fell upon the book, the reward for her curiosity. She placed the heavy square tome on a small work surface and lit a lantern so she could see. This was indeed the same book she had found on the docks of Krondathia. The hardcover bore an ancient mark; it was a symbol of The Ultimas and their holy power. Isabelle flicked through some pages, the thick leaves wafting a dry, earthy smell into her face. She came across a multitude of interesting topics, though there was simply too much to absorb and too much to read. It took time to analyse and understand the contents of the volume. She read throughout the night, finding things she could not even begin to comprehend. Turning over yet another page, she came across a particularly strange piece of information, which confused and worried her…

"It pointed to something unimaginable, something spiritual, hidden far away and like fools we found it; the power to destroy. At first, we had no idea of what we had found, but the more we thought about it, the greater our understanding of it became. Those who could wield it became feared and so our ability to forge an empire became a reality.

Our time shall end very soon; I will not live to see the outcome. My findings and records are incomplete, but to whoever reads this: heed my warning. A power like this should not be used; this is nought but a catalyst for war. I fear that this gift shall turn to a curse, a curse that will cripple all of Equis."

Hallow Disciple - Number Fourteen - Dated 0610 -

The ghosts of history began to creep up on Isabelle; she had read about Hallow and his diverse crew of disciples before, but this was an actual account from the fourteenth member, documented right here in this book. She read on through the dead of night, trying to put together as much of it as she could. Dates, numbers, great timelines; everything had to be considered to find order. This book was full of accounts and truths, all seemingly highlighting a warning in one form or another. That much she could gather. Another such warning caught her eye…

"We named it Omnio, though some call it Glyph. It is a mystery that we still fail to understand. Its origin is clear to some extent, but why? It appears more magical than natural. Its substance is unlike anything I have ever witnessed. In my attempt to find answers, I have crossed many paths and broken many promises. I believe that my research will show that this Glyph is linked to some higher power, a power that we should not deign to comprehend, for the sake of our future. I believe that this turn of force will lead to our doom if we continue to meddle and dabble."

Explorer - Dated 0614

The birds awoke and the sun broke through the scattered clouds. It was early morning, and still, Isabelle continued to read through the book, with heavy shadows forming under her eyes. A dim light shone through the open hatch in the side of the carriage and a brisk wind blew by. With a great yawn, she stood and stretched her back until she heard a click, then staggered over to the hatch, peeking outside. There she saw Seridox, sniffing around some of the supplies. *Knock knock*. She swiftly threw a blanket over the ancient book and opened the door to find Lethaniel resting his arm on the frame. He was dressed and ready to leave.

"Morning. I was wondering if you would like a drink and some breakfast before we head off again," he invited, holding up a hot pot of strong tea.

"No thank you, I'm not hungry," she replied, coughing as a result of her dry throat.

"You haven't eaten anything substantial for three days, nor have you breathed fresh air for some time."

"Well a Star Caller's work is never done, sadly," she protested, resting her own arm on the door frame, focusing her attention on the passing of the clouds overhead. Lethaniel distracted her by dangling and rattling the pot around.

"Come on; I've been told by some that my cooking skills in the morning are great. I promise you, Squeak, it's not shellfish stew," he teased, receiving a sharp look from Isabelle, who finally relented.

"Very well, I will be out in a minute," she accepted, closing the door, and shoving the book under the bed.

As she stepped outside, her guards stood up to greet her.

"Good morning, milady. Did you sleep well? Is there anything we can do for you?"

"No thank you, please, as you were." Lethaniel was sitting over a small fire, cooking something up; it did smell appealing, especially seeing as Isabelle had not been eating so well of late. She walked over and ducked down in front of The General. "So, what's on the menu then?" Lethaniel handed her a flat stool and they both sat around the fire.

"We have partially burnt bread, don't blame me that was Seridox's fault, eggs and... Are you a coffee or tea person? I always forget."

"You have coffee?" she asked, her face lighting up with surprise.

"I do. I bought some fresh the last time I was in The Pura Lands. It was expensive but certainly worth it."

"In that case, tea; if my guards smell the coffee, they will be all over you."

"Tea it is. We also have some shellfish stew on the menu if you would like to try."

"That's twice, Lethaniel, I still haven't forgiven you" she pouted, thinking back on the old story, failing to hold back a laugh. Thao was not at camp and Seridox still wandered around. The Glyph Wielders were getting ready to move, strapping on their clean white sleeves, and stringing together their curved shin guards and wrist bracers. Lethaniel handed Isabelle a plate of food and started to pour her a drink. One of the Wielders, ever attentive, came waltzing over to them and snatched the fork away from her.

"Hey!" Lethaniel snapped, but The Chosen just let it happen. The guard took a forkful of each ingredient and tasted it, then drank some of the tea spilling some on Isabelle's shoulder. He did apologise for the interruption after he was done. "Don't they bloody trust me?" Lethaniel wondered. "I do control an army you know!" he called after the Glyph Wielder.

"It's fine, it's fine just...Let it go, please?" she begged, putting her hand on his wrist.

"If they don't trust me, I wonder who they do?"

"They don't trust anyone; somebody checks all of my meals, so don't worry about it. Thank you." Thao was still absent; his two Honour Guards were packing up the supplies as Isabelle ate. "Your horse is very well behaved," she noted, chewing on some food.

"Yes, Seridox is his name. I wouldn't want any other companion," he confessed.

"How long has he been yours?" He scratched his head and squinted his eyes, thinking back.

"Um, Seridox belonged to someone else when we first met, his old owner died, and Seridox was passed onto me. We didn't get off on the right foot, but he is my guard, my early warning system for danger if you will. He is still young, has a good twenty to thirty years of life in him at least, which alright by me because in my line of work we rarely reach old age."

"He can sense danger?" she repeated, taking another look at the horse. Lethaniel nodded while explaining with a mouthful of food:

"He knows when it's coming, staggering really..." While she drank, he moved on to a more important subject "We are close to Xiondel now. Soon we will pass on to The Plains of Xethark, where we will meet some more escorts; hopefully, Mathias will be joining us." Isabelle's facial expression registered no change considering this information.

"This place we're in, The Silent Vale; I have read about it..." she began, trying to make conversation of her own. "This place conceals a secret, did you know? A forgotten wood and waterfall. A kind of lagoon, some say."

"Don't believe everything you read Izzy; you will be disappointed with what this world really has to offer. Besides, from what I've read, this lagoon only appears around the time that the year changes, so chances are we won't see anything." She looked a little hurt at the put-down.

"That was cold, Lethaniel, not like you to say something like that," she complained, half-serious.

"I prefer to SEE things rather than just reading about them. I hate it when secrets are left undiscovered."

"You wouldn't last long as a Star Caller then. It's sometimes comforting just to think and fantasise." She stopped talking and shrunk away, bringing about an awkward silence.

"What's troubling you, Iz? Maybe I can help" said Lethaniel before Thao marched over.

"I hope you have left some for me!? We must leave now. Lethaniel, get your gear and let's go. I hope you remember how to scout? Isabelle, if you would be so kind." Thao held something in one hand at his side as he made a move along gesture to Isabelle. The pair stood up, but Lethaniel wanted to talk more.

"Izzy?" he prompted urgently.

"Thank you for breakfast Lethaniel. I needed it." With that, she retreated to her armoured carriage, and one of her guards closed the door behind her. Seridox came walking up to his master with a bag in his mouth. Lethaniel took the bag and strapped it to the saddle. Meanwhile, Thao mounted his black stallion, and presented a slick, rusty sword to The General.

"I found this close to camp; do you know who uses this type of weapon?"

"Dark Rogues," they spoke in unison.

"It is unlikely they are on the roads, but I want you to ride ahead and make sure it is safe regardless. Just in case..." Lethaniel rode off as instructed. "Are we set?" Thao called to the guards, who were just about ready to make a move. "Right, let's move on then, shall we?" The carriage steadily moved up the slope and back on to the road, to on course for The Plains of Xethark.

187

Galloping on ahead, Lethaniel scouted the road with Seridox, looking from side to side every so often and making sure that nothing was waiting for him or the others further on. The galloping slowed to a gentle, casual canter. The air was still and there was no sign of anyone or anything, save for the rustles of squirrels and birds in the canopy overhead. Everything seemed to be fine, and the day was cool and peaceful. Seridox came to a complete halt, and Lethaniel listened out for anything out of the ordinary. Nothing happened. After a brief wait, he turned his horse around to report back to Thao, glancing over his shoulder briefly for one last look. There it was: a glimpse of a dark cloak fleeing back into the cover of the thicket.

"Go, Seridox!" he ordered, and the horse galloped back up the road at full speed, whereupon Lethaniel leapt from the side of the saddle. The speed and power of his mount gave him a sudden burst of speed, allowing him to run off the road and pursue the spy when Seridox was too big to follow, skidding to a halt on the road. Ripping his way through the trees and brambles, Lethaniel eventually came to a small opening. The cloaked figure was so close in front - at one point almost within arm's reach - but The General lost sight of him as the stalker tore through an entanglement of vines and branches. It was like the spy had simply vanished into the woodland. Lethaniel stood in the open brush, all alone, though he kept looking around, and never stayed still for more than a second. Fast feet upon dry leaves darted off into the distance somewhere yet still, he saw nothing, his senses open and alert. Before he left, he saw something on the floor; he knelt and picked up the strange ornament. Upon further examination, he figured it was a flute of some kind. A small instrument into which one blew air to mimic a birdsong. This item clearly belonged to a Dark Rogue, so he kept hold of it, sliding it carefully into his pocket, thinking that maybe it would come in handy someday. Finally, he wandered back to the road. As he mounted Seridox, who came over to greet him, Thao came around the corner with the carriage not far behind. The Honour Guard trotted up and came to a stop.

"What happened?" he asked, staring at Lethaniel, who had twigs in his hair and dry leaves all over his travelling jacket.

"I think we may have a problem…"

"What did you see?"

"You were right; someone IS here, no doubt it is The Dark Rogues. No one else can lose themselves that quickly. He got away, but I am almost certain it was one of them." Thao looked about the place, then at the carriage and came to a quick decision.

"We have no choice but to stay with the carriage; all we can do is keep an eye out. By midday, we will be out in the open on the plains. Xiondel is close." Thao continued along the road, with Lethaniel waiting until the group passed him so he could guard the rear. Dark Rogues could be all around, watching them as they journeyed. He could sense their spying eyes but could not see them. They were nearby, but why? And for what purpose? Lethaniel could only guess.

Soon the cold lifted and the sun once again warmed the weary party. As Thao and Lethaniel had predicted, it was not long before the carriage arrived on The Plains of Xethark. The secret path that wound between the woodland was left behind, and now the group was in the clear of a vast meadow of dry grass and sparse plant life. The previous days had been damp, which affected the condition of the road and softened the ground. They pushed east through the plains and did not stop for rest until it was utterly necessary. Beyond the plain, entrenched in a huge gaping ravine far in the distance, were a series of tall towers and a long stretch of wall with three mighty gates, the largest in the middle. Thao slowed his horse and held back until the carriage door was in reach, whereupon he knocked twice to wake Isabelle.

"We are passing Xiondel City, my lady!" he called. The door unlocked itself from the inside while the carriage was still moving. Isabelle hung off the side and looked out upon the city. Unlike Imrondel, which was known for its holiness, it religious foundations and gilded opulence, Xiondel was known for its more secular institutions, its iron-based industry, and it's ever-evolving, silver-dominated architecture. Considerably smaller and less fortified than the capital, it was the younger twin, The Silver City. Within the central palace of Xiliac, resided its leaders; two Councils, one higher and one lower. The High Councillors comprised of twelve members representing the virtue that originally helped to found the city. The Lower Council was constantly changing in size, for it oversaw every aspect of the population's well-being. Its membership was dictated by the people themselves, through elections. The Higher Council of Virtue were the real rulers of Xiondel City, rarely seen by the general public or, anyone for that matter; their positions were secure, having long since won over the trust of the people. Only by resignation or by death would The High Councillors lose their roles.

<u>High Councillors of Virtue</u>
Courage - Julias Tarno
Wisdom - Nenphis Esquin
Justice - Darlo Heventon
Fortitude - Souton Refefris
Honour - Marius Tilon
Truth - Yespin Fquarign
Temperance - Raven Illiard
Devotion - Arthur Thenyur
Ambition - Taktard Erien
Charity - Cillian Landris
Resourcefulness - Davien King
Peace - Barta Sage

No man was more important or powerful than the last. Each member had been selected for their ability to make a lasting positive difference. All were highly intelligent, educated and understanding of the needs of the people. The twelve Councillors of Virtue ruled Xiondel, receiving instruction from The Eldor and his High Priests, who from Krondathia's point of view spoke for the entire Norkron people. Yet, in their own way, they abided by a different code, favouring human aspects over the religion of Starillia. The twelve were responsible to Isabelle and provided great support and resources for The Star Caller, for they were for the ones, especially Yespin, who had known her since birth. People argued that Xiondel should be hailed capital of Krondathia, for it lay safe in the heart of the land. Imrondel remained the capital, however, for it was the birthplace of their beloved religion.

"It's quiet," whispered Thao.

190

"Yes, I wish there were time for a detour, maybe to stop by our homes, have a meal and a cold beer or something. Perhaps go to The Retreat…" replied Lethaniel, dreaming.

"We have our orders and a schedule to follow."

"I know, I know, lighten up Thao" said Lethaniel, tapping his back.

"You can relax once we get Isabelle safely inside Imrondel and this meeting is over and done with. Confession, I have never had a meal at The Retreat before. Do they do good food?" Lethaniel's jaw dropped in mock horror.

"Well I guess it makes sense, it is called The Retreat, that word doesn't rhyme with you Honour Guards does it?" Thao pulled a glum expression at Lethaniel "The greatest part is, is that they only serve us soldiers from the forces, so you get no interruptions from asshole thugs or stupid kids."

"I'll keep that in mind," Thao grinned.

"Trust me, you won't be disappointed" Said the General having spent many a fruitful night in that establishment.

Meanwhile, inside the guarded carriage Isabelle was studying the ancient book intently. Over the long hours and tedious days spent cooped up travelling, she had uncovered much of what she already knew. Glyph was a formidable, powerful, and highly addictive weapon, giving the user the ability to do incredible, even unnatural things depending on the type of sphere they drew from. Different combinations triggered different effects. It also had the potential to go even further, to places humans had no right to go. Much yet remained unknown about the magic's of Equis, even to the professional user. How did Glyph work? What was it made from? How was it connected to the twelve Celestial Souls? During Isabelle's years of studying this phenomenon, she had been told that it was and always has been a mystery. The ones who practised it, wielders old and new, seemed to be the problem. What worked flawlessly for some would not work quite as well for another, and so on. But what her teachers, including The Eldor had failed to mention was that its effects on some unfortunates could be painfully tragic, even resulting in the destruction of human thought, complete memory loss, schizophrenia, and indescribable insanity. The abominations who suffered such symptoms were referred to as The Cursed, while Isabelle and her Glyph Wielders were the direct opposite, known as The Blessed. A slight satisfaction came at last when she read an account stating that the use of Glyph and the effects it had on some people could be positive if understood and used correctly. Isabelle knew this to be true; for she had learned long ago that great power could destroy people and corrupt their minds, with death being the only true release. Until that moment, she had thought only a few questions remained unanswered concerning Glyph or, to give it its full name, the: *Omnio Glaphiar Spheres*. This book had opened her mind to the subject, and she now understood that even the wisest of her people had barely broken the surface of what lay within. With this information passing before her eyes, it slowly became clear that this book belonged to The Eldor and that he was keeping it from her for a reason. She was determined she would find out this reason before she reached her destination of Imrondel, giving her a window of a little over a month, perhaps longer; if the weather remained as it was and they took The Sire's Highway. On and on she read; whatever she could decode using the knowledge she had learnt in her studies; she would try to make sense of it. Turning another hefty page, she came across a language that she thought she would never have to use, it had popped up throughout and was referred to as *Englathin*; many of her priests used this language to honour the old ways, for it had been the first language created by the Norkron people. This was according to her history books which she was finding harder to rely upon. Having not eaten a decent meal for days and growing tired again, she needed more sleep before they stopped at their next destination, The Avorlian Docks, situated on the bank of a great river. Before retreating to the couch, she flicked ahead a few pages and froze when a passage caught her eyes. What she saw written there was disturbing, to say the least.

It had been several long hours, and Isabelle had not had a breath of fresh air since she poked her head out of the door to see Xiondel City. Lethaniel was eager to talk to her; he was aware of her strange behaviour, though Thao was content to fulfil his duty as a guard and offered nothing more to help with the situation. The group rode steadily onward and crossed The Plains of Xethark comfortably without further interruptions from unwelcome followers. However, the peaceful travelling did not stop The General from looking over his shoulder and checking out the flat, dry, grassy plains just one more time. He examined the small flute that The Dark Rogue had dropped; he was tempted to blow on it but thought better of it in the end. The air thickened as they approached the great Avelien River from the west. Drifting on the breeze came the distinct smell of worn stone and fresh food and provisions. Clearly, the odd combination of scents was coming from The Avorlian Docks, gradually coming into view in the distance. The facility's main function was to serve as a harbour to transport supplies to and from the nearby city, yet the base of grey stone structures was going through a time of great growth and development. The docks were a lifeline to the local population, the key to their supply and trade. Isabelle's carriage made it on to the hard road with a bump, and they approached the bustling hive of activity. The cart rolled through what was in a few years' time to become the streets of the town of Avorlian, yet much work was still required when the group passed. They saw settlements only half finished, or in the process of being constructed from the inside out. In the confusion of all the unloading and heavy lifting, the carriage had to stop before a stone wall with a raised portcullis and open gates. A rough man in a worn and weathered soldier's uniform held up his hand and walked in front of the group, stopping them in their tracks. His helmet was under his arm, and it seemed he had been expecting them, for he recognised Thao and greeted him with a salute.

"Honour Guard Thao Hikonle, you humble us with your arrival. Everything is on schedule, though we are terribly busy here as you can see. I'll apologise in advance for the noise." He glanced over his shoulder at the army of working men, pushing wheelbarrows loaded with tools and materials around the site. Temporary blacksmiths and carpenters had been set up, crafting their wares in full view, sawing and hammering away throughout the waking hours. The soldier wore armour made in Xiondel; all the soldiers stationed here were from the city. Thao returned the salute and replied:

"It all has to start somewhere. Give it a few years and this place will be magnificent. Stay strong soldier. Have the escorts arrived yet? Is there any news from Imrondel?"

"Pardon, sir, we are expecting the escorts later tonight, and your transport ship will arrive early in the morning. The accommodation has been made available to you and our Chosen." The man was clearly proud of the arrangements he had made. He took time to stare at the carriage behind Thao, hoping to get a chance to see The Star Caller, a rare event indeed for most, especially so far from her home and the capital.

"Good. Is there any news from Imrondel? I'm expecting something important you see."

"Actually, sir, yes there is. Mail came for you today; it's waiting for you in your quarters." As the two men talked, further behind Lethaniel had noticed that the work and movement had somewhat slowed, with many staring at the carriage and the surrounding Glyph Wielders. Many recognised Thao, he could hear the whispers and chatter coming from passers-by, and even up in the rafters of incomplete roofs, where builders and workers were hanging out, taking a short break to see who the important guests were. "Skyler here will lead you to your accommodations," said the one in charge. Skyler presented himself formally and dipped his head toward The Honour Guard as a sign of respect. Thao saluted back from atop his horse, having quite expected Skyler to be a woman, judging by the name. He placed his right hand on his heart and then positioned it vertically in front of the nose; this was the standard Norkron salute.

"LET THEM PASS!" The carriage pulled off under the wall and through the gate. This side of Avorlian seemed more complete, if not a little older; here lay the homes fitted out for families of the labourers. It must have been hard to live here at present. The smell was not foul, but it grew stronger as they neared the river and the many, many ports spread along the shoreline. Not venturing into the river just yet, the carriage made a hard turn and passed a row of trade and sorting buildings made of thick stone. Incoming shipments were arriving continuously; crates, boxes and nets of supplies were being unloaded and stacked high in their storage places, waiting to be sorted and distributed. The roads always seemed cluttered and tight, yet the people made effort to clear the route for the carriage. *This is awkward to travel through Avorlian,* Lethaniel thought, as he was forced to twist and turn Seridox around the crowded alleyways. Some of the horses seemed rattled; they were not used to all the noise, especially after such a calm journey through the green countryside. Seridox was not alarmed though; he was used to the way things changed around here, as was Thao's horse. Lethaniel had picked up his name over the trip; one of The Honour Guards called him Eliah. Eliah was a mighty horse; stronger and wiser than young Seridox, yet the latter had the confidence of youth and was by far the faster.

Many of the workers acted as their servants; waiting outside a tall, plain building, watching the small entourage roll around the corner toward them. They took Eliah's reins and showed him to the nearby stables. Lethaniel, however, remained mounted upon Seridox. Their supply cart was quickly emptied, its contents loaded inside. As Isabelle stepped outside, all bowed low before her. A Glyph Wielder offered his hand to help her down from the carriage, but she politely pushed it away and jumped down herself. She held some things under her arm, a few quilts, and robes.

"My lady…" She hated it when people called her that. "Your people are here to carry those for you to your rooms; do let them." The Star Caller smiled piercingly.

"If I can persuade a river to flow in the opposite direction or snuff out a fire with a breath, I can certainly carry a few things into a building by myself," she replied tersely.

"As you wish," the Wielder accepted, more than a little embarrassed. Once both carts had been emptied, they were taken for cleaning and repair. Thao kept an eye on the metal box that would end up in his room, the floor below Isabelle's. Lethaniel and Seridox trotted off as soon as they were relieved by The Honour Guard. The Glyph Wielders were given food and personal quarters in a building next door. All awaited the extra escorts to arrive so that the final part of their journey could begin. Thao had already mentioned to Lethaniel and Isabelle that they would be staying at Avorlian for the night and would start again early the next morning once the transport ship had arrived at dock six. Skyler's job was done, and he had to be getting on with other duties now. Thao thanked him kindly and they shared a moment of casual chatter before heading off in opposite directions.

Heading straight for the double bed, already set with dark purple sheets, Isabelle placed down the ancient book, wrapped up in her own quilts and a spare robe. She pulled away the duvet and looked at the stone covering. The walls of her room for the night were a cool, pale shade of turquoise. The room itself was spacious and very tidy; everything was where it should be, only nothing was contained within the furniture. The desk, drawers and wardrobe were all fashioned in the same manner as one would expect in a commoner's house; nothing too fancy, enough to serve its purpose. This did not bother her in the slightest. Upon the desk lay an unlit lantern with some other tools for holding writing equipment; some candlesticks lay about the place as well. The room smelt pleasant, with a scent of oak and musty paper. On the wall hung a large, interesting painting of the great forest of Tthenadawn. Isabelle went over to it and stared with keen eyes. As far as her geographical knowledge went, Tthenadawn Forest was the largest forest in Equis, still not yet having been fully explored. She had learnt through the stories in her books and the talk of explorers and traveller acquaintances that it was a most perilous, mysterious, and unforgiving place, holding many secrets. Within the twisted web of monstrous trees and shadow, Regina Corah had long ago ventured deep inside this forest, completely alone. There she had found a shrine to one of the great Celestial Souls; Verillas, as it was known in the old times before humans, though now most knew it as Virgo. Regina awoke Virgo, the Demi-God of Purity, a shape-shifting spectral being of the earth who loved to take different forms, and one of The Star Callers' favourite Celestials to call on. Isabelle turned away from the painting and sat on the bed next to the book, running her hand over its cold cover. Alone again with her thoughts, she got up and walked over to a set of wooden double doors at the far end of the room, near her bed, and opened them up to the balcony beyond. She could see the river she would cross the following day, just passed the pointed grey rooftops of Avorlian. A strong, cold breeze rolled in and chilled her. It was late in the afternoon, and the escorts were still to arrive; it was likely she would be expected to dine with Thao and the rest of the important Captains and people stationed there. Wherever she went, people HAD to make a big deal of it; sometimes she wished she could eat alone, in her bed or on the sofa, not having to trouble over trivialities like table manners. Food was not on her mind right now, though; she didn't want to eat, she wanted answers to the questions that clogged her mind. She walked out onto her balcony, the wind blowing through her hair. Leaning on the ledge, she looked down on the street full of people walking below. From this great height, it would certainly do the job properly, *without the worry of pain*, suggested a voice in the back of her head. Isabelle put her head in her arms, ashamed that such a thought had even crossed her mind.

The wind had picked up substantially and was still blowing in from all sides. This did not, however, affect the many boats still out on the water, making their trips back and forth across The Avelien River. Lethaniel, still mounted upon Seridox, walked upon a long, stone platform raised high above the docks at which the ships landed and departed. This stone wall stretched as far as Avorlian; almost three miles in length. To his side, opposite the docks, stood the enormous supply and warehouse buildings, where goods were gathered from the shipments, sorted, and then transported to Xiondel or The Pura Lands, the clean country of meadows and farms far west of Krondathia. He spotted the same soldier who they previously met at the gate; he was loading crates onto a cart and giving orders to a group of volunteer workers. The General moved up close behind him and called out:

"Evening, sir. Still busy I see."

"Always my friend, always...." Something then jogged the man's memory and he clicked his fingers.

"Oh, of course! I thought I knew your face, General Presian. I am Captain Ferral. The Avorlian Dock is my post. I have heard lots about you. Tell me the number. Is it three hundred; is that really all true?" Lethaniel took some time to answer; he felt flattered by Ferral's interest, even though he received this treatment all the time.

"Three hundred and fifty-seven, give or take," he boasted.

"How do you do it? Tell me your secret?"

"Intuition, Ferral. Timing and exploiting weaknesses." The man nodded before his attention was taken elsewhere, as he was called over by a few civilians; he was a busy man. Lethaniel went after him. "I wondered if you could tell me about this place, Avorlian. From what I know it's an important settlement, and from what I can see it's utterly defenceless."

"What do you want to know?" Ferral asked, giving the workers a hand with a large supply crate, sliding it into the back of a transport carriage. Lethaniel looked around; the workers were loading, and the driver of the cart was smoking and listening to their conversation.

"Feel like a break?" he suggested. The Captain didn't look like he could spare the time, but then Lethaniel presented a small box of fine papers tucked with moist, brown smoking weed. Ferral could not resist and agreed to take some time off to chat.

"I guess five minutes won't hurt," he conceded, helping himself to a generous pinch of the weed.

"If anyone asks, just say that the General needed some information," instructed Lethaniel, closing the small metal box with his one hand.

"Just give me a moment and I'll be right with you." Ferral gave the driver some instructions and caught up with Lethaniel, who had dismounted Seridox.

The two men strolled along the wide, stone platform set above the long docks. Seridox followed; there was no need to keep hold of the reins, for he was always well behaved. Ferral rolled himself a cigarette.

"Thank you. I told myself I would quit when I was eighteen," he chuckled.

"It's actually a gift for a friend of mine" said Lethaniel "How old are you now?" he asked.

"Twenty-eight. Don't worry, this will be my last one, I promise. What is it you wanted to know about the dock?"

"Tell me whatever you can about the docking points. About the ships and shipments." The other man took a deep breath and went off on a long-winded explanation, almost like he was reading a manual.

"We have a total of twenty-seven docks. Docks twelve and thirteen are currently damaged and under repair, as you can see." He pointed over to a pair of restricted areas. "Right now, four more are home to three battleships and a cargo vessel; the rest are used all day and every day to supply Krondathia and The Pura Lands. We have thirty-three transport boats, two heavy cargo vessels and four battleships, one of which is under management on the other side of the river. That is the one that will be transporting your group tomorrow, I do believe. Quite a fleet, huh?" The Captain sounded most proud of his work.

"I'd hardly call it a fleet. A transport vessel is no battleship. What do we trade here then? Tell me about the shipments."

"Our deliveries from The Ledera Lands are mostly food and other goods; the kind you can't get or grow in Krondathia. We are in business with almost everyone: Ivulien for general goods and supplies and the village of Livale is offering some interesting finds that Imrondel would love to have for its archives. Cuether, in the south-east, provides us with some great delicacies. Even the wild men in the northlands of Jureai, The Vantarquinn Clan, sell us materials and life-saving medicines. That stuff comes through here. So now you know why we are always so busy, and what with all the new developments taking place in Xiondel City, I'm sure you've heard about The Magus project?" He finally finished rolling and sealed the paper with a sharp lick. Lethaniel nodded slightly; he had heard of the massive changes underway in Xiondel and looked forward to seeing the results, but it would be many years before it would all be completed.

"We only have four battleships on our side?" he asked, sounding a little disappointed. The two men passed one such battleship, tightly moored, swaying a little on the water. It was huge; a mass of ropes and pulleys, a deck of strong wood fitted with an array of mighty crossbow turrets.

"They are the best at what they do; sinking other ships, defending our waters should the sea kingdom become perilous. It's safe to say that we own the seas. Ivulien notably lacks seafaring vessels because their shores are teeming with sharks. Those launchers you see on the sides - the ballistae - they deliver a sting like nothing I've ever seen before. Depending on the wind, and if loosed correctly, these ships can tear up almost anything, whether at close quarters or from a distance. Our battleships, however, sit idle most of the time. Seeing as we have no real use for them, they help to carry cargo and transport people to far-off locations. The ideas and engines here go to waste, in a way; there is no conflict, and these boats were designed with battle in mind. Don't misunderstand, I do not want a battle, but the question is what to do with all these instruments of warfare when wars are becoming part of history" Ferral explained, directing Lethaniel's eyes around the ship with his hand as he spoke.

"Do they have names?"

"Of course; the designer insisted that they are named. This one is called *Coelacanth* and the ones behind you at docks ten and eleven are *Teleost* and *Cobia. Cobia* is the fastest. The one arriving at dock six for you early tomorrow is named *Kathina*, after the maker's wife." He then lit his smoke using a nearby torch, and the two moved on up the platform, Seridox tailing behind, stopping to look out to the water from time to time.

"How many soldiers are stationed here? What's our defence besides the battleships?" Lethaniel reeled off his question, taking mental notes as he listened to the helpful man's answers. He felt that, as the new General, he needed to know everything there was to know about one of Xiondel's most important lifelines.

"We have fifty to sixty well-trained men stationed here at Avorlian to keep the peace and another twenty-or-so on the other side of the river. All are good men and capable of sailing the ships." Lethaniel sighed, feeling it was not anywhere near enough. "Every so often, however, you do get the occasional wise guy who tries to cross at nightfall. We seized a load of penethine just last week. That would have been destined for the back alleys of Xiondel. My men try their best to cut off the city's drug problem at the source. High-Councillor Charity has charged me and a few others with trying to quell the import of drugs, with the river being one of the most popular routes. I hate to say it, but dealers do slip by us every once and a while. We became all the wiser after The Wheat Coup, of course. Did you ever hear about that?" Lethaniel nodded.

"Indeed. Didn't the guy disguise or switch shipments of wheat for his own stuff? How many boatloads was it?"

"Forty boats; he only got caught after someone tipped us off about his location. The soldiers here are skilled, though their talents are wasted; most of the time we just break up the occasional street fight and petty brawls caused by drunken locals and silly teens. The last fellow worth remembering that we apprehended was the very same one responsible for The Wheat Coup. He was sentenced to exile by The High Councillors. The idea was that by setting an example with the biggest supplier, we would scare the others out of the drug business. Sadly, the problem still exists."

"Is something wrong, sir?" Lethaniel had stopped walking and was grinning stupidly, rubbing his forehead.

"May I ask you a question now?" Ferral asked, puffing out some smoke. "What is your interest in this place? Do you have something on your mind, General?"

"Thank you, Captain. I am sorry to have bothered you; I know you and your men are rushed off your feet. Good work. I will see to it that you shall receive more workers in the next few months." With that, Lethaniel whistled for Seridox, who came trotting over. He mounted the horse and took off for the nearby streets, narrowly avoiding another hefty load of stacked crates. Ferral flicked the rolled weed off the platform and wandered back to his post to get on with his work.

The wooden door was open; the room inside was plain, quite like Isabelle's room, with a cool and gentle breeze running through it, as the balcony windows were wide open to the light. Thao sat on his bed, an open letter in his left hand, which he read in silent delight. A knock came from the door and a soldier in uniform called:

"Sir, the extra escorts have just arrived. They are at the entrance now." Thao raised his head.

"Thank you, tell them to get fed and to stock up the supply carriages with plenty of rations, unless they want to hunt for our meals in the coming weeks. Then they should get an early night. We leave first thing in the morning. I will be right down to make pleasantries shortly." Before the guard left, he bowed to someone in the corridor who The Honour Guard could not see. Isabelle had wandered downstairs and was now hovering in the doorway, looking at Thao with the letter in his hand; he was smiling happily, re-reading the words over and over in his mind. "It has been nearly a year since I saw them. I have missed so much of his life already," he mumbled. Isabelle strolled in slowly and made for the balcony, her arms behind her back. Thao then said something that touched a nerve in her, as though he had been reading her mind over the days spent travelling. "I too wonder what my duty is all for sometimes. Do I do these things because I must, or do I do it for the prosperity of Krondathia? Or, deep down do I really do it for my son and my wife?" Isabelle remained still, listening, watching the activity of Avorlian below, with distant clattering filling the space between them. "You are not the only one to question your duties from time to time, my girl. Do not make the mistake in thinking that you are the only one who suffers. It is unwise to think so." He got back to view the letter in his hand.

"How are they both?" asked Isabelle, sitting next to him on the bed.

"Lena's fine, as is Lucion. I don't get much time to be with them, so I look forward to arriving at Imrondel."

"He will grow to be strong; like father like son, as they say. He will be as solid and as loyal as you are, you'll see." Thao stood up and placed the letter on his bedside table, but before he left, The Star Caller had one more question. "How do you do it? How do you deal with the duties that dominate your life? We only have a little time, and that time is spent serving others. How do people like us find time for ourselves?" He took a breath and began to consider her questions.

"I tell myself that I'm making a difference in this world. When so few can do what I do, I feel privileged, even if it means sacrificing so much of my time to do what is right. I am making a difference, trying to make Equis a better place. The time will come when men like me, Lethaniel, Mathias… When we serve no more purpose, and it is on that day we will know that the world, the society that we dream of and strive for has finally arrived. Your duty Isabelle, is to make me obsolete." Naturally, this made the pair smile.

"That day will come, Thao. One day." With that, The Honour Guard disappeared, leaving Isabelle alone in his room. His heavy footsteps could be heard plodding down the wooden staircase, on his way to greet the new arrivals. The day was growing dark and the shadows longer. She thought about Lucion and read some of the end of the letter; it was sweet to see his scribbled handwriting. She had failed to mention some details of her predictions regarding Thao's son; not only would Lucion be extraordinarily strong, perhaps even more so than Thao, and just as loyal, she sensed an obscurity about the boy's future. These feelings she was unsure about; she would have to spend more time with him to understand, but she would never say anything unless she was certain. She was sure, though, that one day he would be a mighty soldier and would follow his own intentions all the way to the very end. It was a future she had foreseen a long time ago, back when she was first given the news of Lucion's birth. It was a future that would not belong to her; more likely The Star Caller after her, her successor. The future was always so unclear, a fact that frustrated her to no end.

The dock lay quiet as the sun rose the next day; the river was still, and the boats remained safely moored. It was a cold day with little wind. The armoured carriage and a different, much larger supply cart were waiting with a single Glyph Wielder at dock six. *Kathina*, the battleship scheduled to pick up The Star Caller and her entourage, was yet to arrive. *Oh, wonderful! I should start doing the whole sleeping in a bed thing again*, Isabelle thought to herself, sitting at her desk with the sunlight peeking through the curtains in her room. She closed the ancient book and pushed it away from her like unwanted food. She had once again been up all-night reading what she could, trying to understand why The Eldor had kept this book hidden from her. The effects of weariness had begun to show. She wrapped the tome up in the same quilts and brushed herself down, just as a Glyph Wielder came to escort her to the dock. He noticed that the bed was made like it had not been slept in but didn't seem suspicious.

"There was no need to make the bed, my lady. There are people here who are paid to tidy the rooms," he said. Isabelle just ignored him, content with imagining where she would like to stick his '*my lady*' comment.

Thao stood at the dock with Eliah, chatting with the two other Honour Guards who had been with him at Zodias Island: Arthur and Scarto. They were equipped with light armour and standard gear, while Thao wore a battle sword at his side, the long grey hilt sheathed and latched to his belt. They waited for a little while until a small unit of able men came to meet them. They approached and came to a halt a short way down the dock. Thao stepped forward, as did another man from the new group. They greeted each other with a slight nod of the head and inspected the various soldiers. The bowmen were suited in light leather and dull cloaks for camouflage. A couple of swordsmen were dressed in a light but tough armour, all fitted for a lengthy travel.

"Good; more than I had in mind, but this will certainly do. You are under my command; all orders will come from me or The General. I have been charged with keeping The Star Caller safe on this journey to Imrondel City, but still, I will look out for all of you as best I can. Until we reach our destination, and until I relieve you, you will do as I say. Is that understood?" He paused for a second or two to hear their response. The soldiers nodded. The great ship *Kathina* could be seen on the water, approaching in the far distance. As the ship drew closer, cutting through the waves at some speed, Thao spoke again. "Are there any intelligent questions before we board?" The leading man, who looked like he had some authority, put down his saddle and came a little closer. He was nearly as tall as The Honour Guard and had a strong build, but Thao was just that little bit bigger. He had a rough look about him like he had just got off work and hurried to his new destination. His worn clothes looked more befitting of a smithy than an officer. Thao could only hope that the man's good equipment and uniform were in the rucksack on his back, or waiting on the other side of the river bank.

"Sounds fair, you being in command all of a sudden, and speaking to us as if we don't know how important an escort mission is. I have already briefed my men, Honour Guard. They will do their job without the need for your orders. And if I take any, it will be from Lethaniel, not you." Thao kept his cool, calmly telling the man how to address him.

"I am an Honour Guard of Krondathia, carrying out an order; you may address me as Sir, Captain or Thao Hikonle, soldier, if I can even call you that. You look more like a blacksmith to me, and one late for work at that. Do you want me to call you Smithy from now on? I will if that's the kind of foot you want to get off on. Or we can do this the easy way" said Thao.

"Well we are here to help The Chosen, so try to save the speeches and poor attempts at humour for someone who gives a shit…Sir."

"Is there a problem?" asked Thao, folding his arms, not in the slightest bit intimidated.

"No. No problem at all, Sir." Thao sensed an unpleasantness about this man, but didn't wonder where it came from, nor did he care to know. The other soldiers remained where they were, occasionally glancing sideways to measure Thao's reaction. "This is more than a mere transport vessel; she is *Kathina*, the true power of these waters, so try and show some respect and don't sink us while on board. Nice meeting you, and your cronies." Thao decided not to argue, so he just let it go for the time being, it was far too early, and he couldn't be bothered with anything other than the journey.

"Glad to make YOUR acquaintance, anyway," Thao said to the other escorts.

The men waited around a short while before they finally witnessed the great battleship *Kathina* coming into port. Its hulking hull, larger than all the other ships in the fleet, cast a dark shadow over dock six and the small group of observing soldiers. Its mighty, powerful sails were painted a dark colour and imprinted with the Norkron insignia of a partially encrusted jewel. Unlike its sisters, *Kathina* had mounted on its spacious deck not only the standard two but four heavy ballistae crossbow turrets. She required a crew of twelve to fifteen sailors, who now anchored the ship and made it possible for the carriage and its escorts to come aboard safely. As the planks fell onto the dock, Thao looked around for Isabelle; she was running late again. He began to walk up the plank but was rudely brushed aside by the rude officer clutching the saddle. He briefly considered pushing the man off into the water but decided it could wait for another time, preferably when a hungry shark swam up river. Soon Seridox and Lethaniel joined the group on the ship, where the latter found Thao overseeing the carriage being brought aboard, quite awkwardly despite the spacious deck.

"Hmm, more than I thought; four bowmen, some swordsmen and two cavalrymen, plus Arthur, Scarto and our Glyph Wielders. This is a good shield. Who is he?" he asked, pointing to the stubborn man at the end of the boat, currently enjoying a drink from a reddish leather flask.

"Don't know, but he seems to have a problem with me," Thao grunted, tugging on the rope still helping to pull the carriage. Lethaniel raised his eyebrows, appearing a little impressed

"Brave guy then. He looks familiar."

"Well you can keep him company, find out who he is and what authority he has. Oh, and if you could also find out where the most powerful woman in the world is, that too would be great. One last thing before you go: do you know what kind of predators inhabit these waters? Someone might well be going overboard." Lethaniel could tell that Thao was going through a tantrum this morning, so he ignored the last part and simply walked off. "FIND ISABELLE!"

The Honour Guard yelled after him, getting back to pulling hard on the rope, straining the muscles in his arms.

"I am right here, thank you very much," said Isabelle, walking around the corner with her Glyph Wielders behind her. "His name is Jerhdia, and he is quite the gentleman, I might add. Jerhdia O'Nen." Thao just looked at her with a puzzled face. "Just get to know him and try not to squabble with each other, alright? Don't make me put you both on the naughty chair." She said tapping Thao on the shoulder as she strolled by to find a quiet space on the ship. As she boarded, Seridox came over to her, and she stroked him on the nose.

"I found her; turns out she was standing right behind you all along," laughed Lethaniel. "So, his name is Jerhdia? I've never heard of him. Oh, keep an eye on that swordsman over there will you; he looks a little young, wouldn't you say?" He pointed subtly at a young lad, who certainly seemed a little out of place as if this could have been his first assignment. The Glyph Wielders came aboard, following their charge, never straying far from Isabelle's side. After a brief wait the large planks were lifted and slid onto the deck, and the ship set sail across the murky cold waters of The Avelien River. Lethaniel spotted Ferral working on the broken dock, dock twelve, with a hammer and nail. Following a quick exchange of salutes, both men got back to work.

The strong breeze was good news for the travelling party, taking hold of the open sails and pulling the ship across the water with ease. The prow effortlessly ripped through the waves, unhindered by the currents that could potentially misdirect smaller vessels. The ship was a wonder of Equis, being the largest and most spacious ever built. However, like the other battleships in these waters, it had yet to prove its effectiveness in war, but the likelihood of *Kathina* facing up against other ships any time soon was close to zero. Everyone who was to escort The Star Caller to Imrondel City was now up on deck. Thao was at the stern, talking to a sailor behind the great wheel who steered the ship. Isabelle hung off the side, looking into the water with Seridox close by and her Glyph Guards. The new unit of soldiers was gathered in front of a doorway leading to the passages and cabins below. Arthur and Scarto were walking and talking around the deck, passing by some sailors in grey uniforms. Up high in the crow's nest, a sailor with a large, unwieldy telescope oversaw the ship's route. Deciding all was well, for the time being, he climbed out of the nest and swung down to the deck, landing with a thud near Lethaniel, who asked if he could borrow the scope. The General walked to the front of the ship, nearing the very end, and stopping when he could go no further. He then looked through the glass to the other side of the river; he could see a few settlements slowly coming into view. Turning around he looked through it once again, this time toward the stern, where he spied upon Thao and tried to lip read what he and the sailor were talking about. He panned around to see Isabelle, on her way to the carriage carrying something under her arm. Squinting his eye to see more clearly, he spotted something heavy under the blankets; it appeared to be a book with many thick pages. Just then, she disappeared out of sight, and all he could see were two large black nostrils breathing in and out. He snapped away quickly, only to see Seridox looking directly at him.

"It's not polite to stare, Lethaniel," Jerhdia scalded, leaning on the railings with his arms folded and holding out his hand for the telescope.

"You know who I am?" exclaimed Lethaniel.

"I know who you are alright, and I know who they are as well! But you fellas don't know me; strange that, wouldn't you say?" The man was clearly suggesting something as he folded the telescope into itself with strong arms.

"I have seen you before in Xiondel; your name is Jerhdia, isn't it?"

"Yeah, that's right," replied the man, rather abruptly, and stepping forward. "You guys been talking about me then? What's been said?" Lethaniel turned his head away and sniggered. "I just want to know what you guys been saying, that's all." The General finally replied.

"If you MUST know, I thought it brave of you to talk to Thao the way you did. He is the leading Honour Guard; you have to realise that no one does what you did unless he feels he's something to prove to the world." Jerhdia nodded.

"I was just making it clear where we stand; he understands, I think. I have my reasons for not seeing eye to eye with his type, but I have nothing to prove." Lethaniel thought for a moment.

"Thao is a good man, and there is no one I'd rather have at my side in dangerous times, say for this beast" and he stroked Seridox "So why mock him? Especially when you've only just met him."

"I am aware of his prestigious rank. For this I respect him. I understand the natural order of things. Then again, Lethaniel, we see so little of a threat these days; I have to ask myself; do we need great soldiers like him anymore? True, they have served and triumphed in the past when the world was different, but times have changed since Regina, things have improved, so much so that maybe The Honour Guard have served their purpose. If we are in a world free of war, why then do we need those soldiers to throw orders at us Regulars?"

"You will be at the meeting?" enquired Lethaniel, having no real answer for the man's questions.

"Yeah, seated somewhere in the back, no doubt." Jerhdia sniffed and walked away, clutching the telescope with both hands, fiddling with the lens "Just don't expect me to make any speeches." With that he descended the stairs, muttering under his breath as he went. "Doesn't matter what I think anyway. Nice swords you have, by the way." Lethaniel turned away to the cool wind, letting Jerhdia walk off in peace. The small outposts were rapidly growing to his eye, and he could see the men on the other side getting ready for *Kathina* to dock. He got a grip on the reins of Seridox and led him down to the deck; everyone seemed to be ready to depart, throwing away their roll ups of weed and tightening their belts. The magnificent ship slowed, and the colourful sails were pulled up. The smaller vessels out fishing on the water made way for *Kathina* as she crept carefully into the dock. Once again, the large planks fell, and the carriages rolled off onto dry land. The new escort soldiers marched off the ship in single file; they all appeared to know each other and were greeted with fine horses. Jerhdia, leaving the ship behind them, tied his saddle down on his own dark grey mount. The Glyph Wielders stayed at the main carriage's side on foot as always. Still on the ship and looking down at everyone getting ready for the journey ahead were Thao and Lethaniel. They led Seridox and Eliah down the planks and along the road, beyond the dock and outposts. Once everyone was assembled and ready to move, the party made haste away from the outpost and into the open country of Krondathia.

The tread of the wheels along the dry, flat road softened as they met the damp dirt path. The clap of the horses' hooves was muffled as the animals and escorts distanced themselves from the boundaries of the Krondathian settlements. The group head inland, deliberately avoiding the main roads and known paths, taking a different, route where confrontations with Norkron folk could be kept to a minimum. The path sloped down, providing cover from the wind but not from the cold. The same weather pattern persisted; it continued to be annoyingly cold and frustratingly windy for a few long days. The next few days on the paths were tedious, with little talk of interest coming from the groups of men. The same bland taste of the quick and easy food wasn't enough to satisfy, and many had quickly become fed up. They made good time though, as predicted, and passed one of The Western Korthium Outposts early, without stopping for a break. The Outposts in this land were much the same as the ones built in the east of The Ledera Lands; nothing more than a small array of light fortifications surrounding a central watchtower. The guards stationed there would be Watchmen, with perhaps some Wilderness Rangers and Regulars; they supported each Outpost from a sustainable and defensible barracks within the walls. The fortification Isabelle and her entourage passed were almost like a midway checkpoint in the country of Krondathia; from here word could be sent to either of the two main cities; north to Xiondel, or south to Imrondel. Soon they found themselves approaching a view of particular interest; a vast, thick, green forest climbing the foothills of great mountains with pointed, white-tipped peaks. Further to the south, in clear sight, the sun had finally found the gaps between the grey clouds that held on to the dreary days, hiding the bright blue sky. Korthak Bridge was near, and the group would soon cross, thereby entering The Ledera Lands, the region that separated Krondathia and Ivulien, one which no one nation held claim over or indeed the rights to. The crossing soon came into view; two towering pillars connected by a mighty arch. At the highest point of each pillar flew the flag of Krondathia, its detailed sigil the jewelled broken shell visible to all. Along the stone arch, which also served as the surface of the bridge itself, the shapes of uniformed Norkron soldiers could be seen on guard; no doubt that they had received word of The Star Caller's impending passage. The bridge stretched over the daunting, rocky ravine, a vertical chasm that broke the land in two, with a river running through at the very bottom. The bridge was supported by metal bracers and secure stonework that would ensure it would stand for many generations. The river, which flooded out from an outlet in the mountains to the north, ran all the way to the sea kingdoms in the south, this was the largest waterway in existence, surpassing any other river in Equis in width, depth, and length. The river was called Serpent's Back named by one of the warlord tribes of old. The group made their way across the bridge, bracing themselves against the sudden gusts of wind blowing in from the south. One bowman had to grab hold of his cloak as it spiralled out of control, whipping around his shoulders and into his face. The door at the side of the carriage opened and Isabelle breathed in the clean air, hanging off the side as she liked to do. Lethaniel glanced around and saw her looking to the north, out beyond Tthenadawn Forest to the distant line of great mountains. He caught her eye and grinned; it was a marvellous sight to behold under the orange sun.

Once across the bridge, they would follow the river's path closely all the way to Imrondel City. Lethaniel turned his head once more; the horses looked tired and the men could do with a proper meal and rest. He leant over to Thao, riding next to him, who appeared as though he could go on for weeks.

"Let's rest; the men look tired and I could use some food myself." Thao nodded, and they continued until they reached the end of Korthak Bridge, riding between another set of identical pillars, connecting with a stone archway above. He led the men and carriages off the bridge to a spot away from the road, near the edge of the ominous forest of Tthenadawn. Dry, broken branches lay all about the place, though the grass grew long and was soft; a perfect spot to recuperate. The carriages stopped; inside, Isabelle felt a shudder as she was reading through the large pages of the ancient book. She heard the footsteps and voices of the men outside, setting up a small camp. A series of knocks from outside entered her space.

"My lady, we have stopped on the border; we shall be departing again in an hour."

"Very well, thank you," she called, rubbing her aching neck and stiff shoulders.

"Would you like anything, my lady? Some food or drink, perhaps?"

"You could stop saying 'my lady' for a start…"

"Beg your pardon, my lady?"

"I said I will be out in a minute," she grunted, standing up and putting her golden hair into a ponytail.

"Very well, my lady." The men had dismounted and were already moving around the area. The Glyph Wielders let themselves rest a little, though remaining ever vigilant as they guarded the lady's carriage. The common soldiers sat on the grass and let their well-behaved horses roam around for a while. Seridox stayed with Lethaniel. Thao and his Honour Guards spoke amongst themselves, casually discussing the route and other travel-related issues. A crate had been unpacked from the supply cart and the men helped themselves to a small buffet of meats, cheeses, and fruits. The main carriage door sprung open and Isabelle stepped outside, instantly receiving looks from the soldiers; she had not shown herself often while travelling through Krondathia, so whenever she decided to appear, it was quite the occasion. As she stepped down from the carriage, her Glyph Wielders rose, but she raised her hand commanding them to remain at ease. The other soldiers could not help but stare now but were not so rude as to gawp for a long while; instead, they continued to eat, drink and talk with one another, secretly loving the fact that Isabelle, Thao and Lethaniel were within earshot. Jerhdia came over behind her as she found a drink of water from the supply cart.

"Hello Isabelle, it's a great pleasure to see and protect you… *yadda yadda yadda*…Just getting the formalities out of the way, your presence is golden compared to this lot." He bowed his head and The Chosen smiled.

"No need for that, Mr O'Nen; remember, you have a wife to channel that sort of affection too."

"I'd rather run away with you. Do you wanna get married and have a bunch of children?" he suggested.

"Ah, you know I would, because I find you so irresistibly charming and handsome, but I am already spoken for," she giggled.

"To whom, may I ask?"

"Well, you see that guy over there…" The pair teased one another throughout the brief stop. Meanwhile Lethaniel was moving around somewhere in the background with Seridox, grumpily complaining to his faithful companion.

"I've known her for years - since we were children - and yet he speaks to her for ten seconds and gets a laugh out of her. How does he do that?" The horse merely wandered off, apparently unwilling to hear another one of his master's rants. "…I made her breakfast too."

"How is your family?" Isabelle asked Jerhdia, who now was also helping himself to some food.

"Doing well. I haven't seen them for some time, so this trip will all be worth it once we get to the city. Letty should be working in his favourite department; he already shows promise. What are your plans for when we arrive?" Isabelle was secretly delighted with the question. It felt for a moment that she DID have something to do other than her duties. She would do as she was told, and behave as was expected of her, but then just maybe, she thought, this could be a good opportunity to visit a wise and close friend of hers in one of her most frequented locations in Imrondel; The Old Library. After all, she had found out from the book, maybe it was time to get some questions answered.

"Well, I need to see someone, a friend of mine, someone important to me. My old tutor, you know. You probably know him; you know everyone, right?"

"That's right, I probably do. Listen, I will be at this meeting, so if you want me to do or say anything on your behalf, you know what to do. Remember the secret signal we practised?" Isabelle delicately used her little finger to scratch the side of her eye. "That's it, you've got it," said Jerhdia cheerfully.

"I'll use it if I'm ever in trouble, thank you. If I can find time to visit, I certainly will Jerhdia."

"And I will understand if you can't find the time. Enjoy your meal, Isabelle." With that he walked off, leaving her to eat alone beside the supply cart.

Tthenadawn Forest, an immense, largely undiscovered sprawl of trees with many stories and myths attached to it, was one of the true wonders of the world. As Lethaniel investigated the sea of greenery from where he sat, he could see that the sun touched only a tiny fraction of the floor. The canopy of trees above provided many thick layers of leaves, blanketing out most of the hot rays. At this time of year, the undergrowth at the centre of the forest would be too thick to walk through. It looked still and almost lifeless, but even from where he sat, he couldn't help but feel uneasy, as he had done the woodland paths back in The Silent Vale, where they had been stalked by The Dark Rogue. Was the stalker still watching them from afar as they ate? And if so, why? Were they still being followed by unfriendly eyes who meant them harm? These were the questions that repeated themselves inside his head.

"I think it has been long enough; we should go," he muttered to Thao as he passed by.

"You're the one who was so anxious to stop."

"Let's just move away from the forest's edge. I still think that they are watching us. The Dark Rogues, I mean." He raised his eyebrows, keeping his voice to a minimum.

"Very well, let's move out and stop again before nightfall, agreed?"

214

"Agreed," accepted Lethaniel, standing up. Just then, Isabelle came up to the two.

"Are we moving now?" She picked up on the worry in Lethaniel's face as he confirmed that they were indeed so. "Thao, could I talk with you alone please?" She avoided The General's, eyes but he took the hint and walked off to find Seridox.

"What is it, Isabelle?"

"Are we being followed by someone?" she asked bluntly. He gently manoeuvred her away from the other men, who were now up and about, clearing things away.

"Lethaniel is under the suspicion that we may have a tail."

"Who? Who is following us? Do you know? Does HE know?"

"No idea. But if we do have an unwanted shadow, it is most likely to be The Dark Rogues." He stood tall in front of the forest, shielding her from its sight, just in case anybody or anything was indeed watching. "Let's go; please get back inside the carriage," he instructed politely, leading her away by the wrist.

"Is it just one person, or a whole band of them?"

"It's hard to say, but based upon previous encounters, which admittedly are few, we are probably dealing with about half a dozen, maybe more. They like to travel in groups, so I've come to understand."

"Why?"

"I guess it has something to do with you, but do not worry. We will not let our guard down. Remember who is escorting you, and even IF, by some miracle, they manage to slip passed us, they will have you to deal with, won't they? If these skinny Dark Rogues have any sense in their heads, they will stay far enough away."

The supply cart was packed up neatly and ready to follow The Star Caller's carriage, with everyone mounting up. One soldier, however, had left some things behind near the tree line: a sword and some travelling gear. He left the group and dismounted to collect his belongings. It was getting late; the shadows emerging from within the forest had already grown darker. A disturbed bird let out a cry and flew from of its roost. The young soldier drew close, picking up the bag and sheathing his sword, only to draw it again as fast as he could upon seeing movement in the brush. Whatever it was came rushing out of the shadows after it realised it had been spotted. A great, pale arm with enormous muscle tone, greater than that of the strongest man, making Thao's arms look tiny in comparison, reached out. The mighty hand wrapped its fingers around the young soldier's head and pulled him ferociously into the darkness. His startled horse ran off, but not in the same direction as Thao and the others, who were already well on their way south.

"The Ledera Lands. Finally, we are almost there," Lethaniel noted.

"Stay vigilant, General; we still have many days and nights of travelling to go. Anything could happen," Thao warned.

"I think we are safer in the open; I don't like things that I can't see, that's why I thought it would be best to move away from Tthenadawn," Lethaniel replied, a little more at ease.

"You always had a problem with dark places, didn't you? How did you ever overcome that fear?"

"A good friend taught me how to counter it. Using the same method I applied it to my other fears, and now fear serves merely as a warning for me, one which can be easily turned off, similar to how you shut out all other senses to focus on an opponent."

"Was it really that simple?"

"It was not an easy thing to take charge of; I had the power all along, I just had to meet it head on and train to unravel the fear as if it were a knot."

216

"I guess this is one of the life-changing lessons you learnt on your travels?" Lethaniel merely nodded. "We will continue travelling south-east for a while, after which we will camp close to the river's edge and set out again in the morning. Also, I think it would be wise to station two men at a time on the watch tonight, on three-hour shifts. Agree?"

"Agreed," replied the General.

Inside the warm carriage, Isabelle could not read anymore, instead, she lay curled up on the couch. Outside she could hear the role of the wheels and the marching pace of her guards. She opened the side hatch and looked outside to the gleaming stars. Faintly she could hear Jerhdia talking to one of his bowmen.

"Purity. Virgo's was found in Tthenadawn Forest, I'm sure of it, I know a bit about it from my wife." She could only hear brief snatches of the conversation. "Fine, tomorrow you can ask her. It's kinda her thing didn't ya know?" said Jerhdia. She closed the hatch and blew out her lantern, drowning herself in darkness. Isabelle found her bed and snuggled down inside. The carriage still rocked a little from side to side, and she could hear some talk coming from the soldiers, but now relaxed and tired, she very quickly fell asleep.

Elaso fiin! Isabelle opened her eyes to the sound of gushing water; the carriage had stopped, and all was silent. She listened out for signs of movement outside, but none came. She pushed away her duvet, getting up and sliding the hatch open; the morning was well on its way. She had had a good night's sleep, it seemed, but she had also missed out on dinner. Most of the soldiers were sleeping on the floor under one-man tents, while others preferred to wrap up on the floor inside thick winter sleeping bags. As always, one Glyph Wielder had stayed awake to guard the carriage; he sat on the ground, leaning upon a wheel, using his half staff for balance. Thao was propped up next to a broken tree with his legs outstretched; his eyes were shut, but he was not fully asleep, every so often he would shake himself awake, desperate to remain alert. His two fellow Honour Guards, Arthur and Scarto, slept back to back near the carriages. The relaxing flow of the water nearby gave them all a sense of security. Meanwhile, the wind had calmed down, but still, the air remained cold and brisk. The horses too were having a peaceful time; with a few tied to a nearby tree and others bound to the supply carriages, they had also enjoyed some much-needed rest. They would be vital in their journey across The Ledera Lands. Seridox, however, was quietly patrolling the area, where he found Lethaniel standing near the river's edge, holding the longest of his blades in a black sheath. As the horse came closer, The General reached out to stroke his neck, turning around to see Isabelle creeping towards the supply carriage, carrying a large book with a stone cover. He crouched low and spied on The Star Caller. She quietly rummaged around and found the metal box; the lock was exactly as she had left it. Pulling out the heavy stone and placing it gently on the ground, she dropped the ancient book inside and closed the lid, pressing the lock in tightly, securing it properly this time. Lethaniel watched her walk back to the carriage and close the door quietly behind her. Jumping up from his hiding place, he brushed off some dirt; he knew she was up to something, but what? Should he challenge Isabelle about this? Would it be better to leave it all alone? Or should he bring the matter to Thao? Instead of rushing into a rash decision, he merely stayed where he was. *One day*, he promised himself he would talk to her about this. As he watched the sunrise replacing the fading stars, he held a necklace in his hand; it was a wooden carving of the head of a feline, a tarthais. He smiled at the thought in his mind of the person who had given it to him all those years ago. He looked forward to their meeting again once he reached the city. The men were stirring now as the birds began to sing. Jerhdia arose and came up to The General, who was now pulling the strings on his wrist bracers, taking them off one at a time.

"All was quiet?"

"All quiet. Not a sign of anything," confirmed Lethaniel, walking away, "But that's just it; invisibility is a Dark Rogue's best defence."

"If they are never seen, how do we know they even exist?"

"Very philosophical of you, O'Nen. I guess even they make mistakes sometimes."

"That's right, so we just have to wait until they do. Get some rest Lethaniel; we have a fair bit of walking to do today." The Norkron General went off to find a space and sat down, he put down his longsword and lay back, trying to sleep, but now the sun was swiftly rising, the birds would not shut up and the men had begun their morning chatter. Instead of wasting time trying to sleep, Lethaniel decided to get a drink. A lovely, undisturbed snooze would have been much better, but that would have to wait until the following night.

Soon it was time to leave, and as usual, they left way before noon.

"It's always cold when it should be warm. Hey! Throw me that flask, would you?"

"You're welcome... At least it's not raining."

"Does it matter? We will be in Imrondel soon and we will have new assignments then. I think we must have made a good impression to be chosen for this one."

"When I was given this assignment, I had to make sure that they'd got the right guy. This is only my fifth job since I became a bowman." The soldiers' conversation could be heard well by Lethaniel and Thao, who was now leading the small convoy while Jerhdia guarded the rear. Most days this was how it was; the talk was small but interesting to listen to, sometimes even humorous; no soldier was inexperienced or stupid, each man was different and good to keep as company. Between the carriages, the soldiers continued talking.

"So, are you going to knock on the door today? Or are you going to wait 'til tomorrow? Maybe you should just apologise and say that Jerhdia and I, were right?"

"Don't you bear the mark of Aquarius? Shouldn't you know your own Celestial Mark by now?"

"Alright, that's it!" The men were clearly up to something that involved Isabelle. Jerhdia tilted his weight to the right to watch the interaction, smiling as his man trot up to the carriage door. The bowman gave a rapid, nervous few knocks and The Star Caller opened. The man stuttered a little trying to get his question out correctly.

"My lady, I uhh… I was thinking..." She patiently listened to him, ignoring his nerves. "Do you know if, no, of course you know but maybe you could umm..." She put her hands together, this would take a while "..Please tell me, does Aquarius have anything to do with water? I mean, it sounds as if it should, what with the whole aqua thing going on in the wording, and to tell you the truth, one man in our group is a bit of an idiot." The question was a common one; Isabelle had been asked this many times before and was fairly used to it popping up among those who hadn't studied Starillia as she had. Thus, she answered him kindly, without a hint of judgement.

"Aquarius is an Air Celestial. The Demi-God of Wisdom to be precise, soldier." The others in the background laughed and clapped their hands, while the man at the carriage looked disappointed with himself. Isabelle knew what was going on; she had dealt with this kind of childish behaviour before and knew exactly what to say. "It's fine; many confuse Aquarius with some of the water Celestials. Even I did at one point, nothing to be ashamed of."

"My lady, I would like to ask you one more question, if I may? I mean if you're busy I can always just go away…" Isabelle laughed and nodded.

"Ask it, come on." His friends egged on, and the bowman gulped.

"What mark, what Celestial Mark do you bear?" She balanced herself on the doorframe of her carriage and tightened her lips; the other soldiers were just as keen to find out.

"Where is Jaden?!" Jerhdia interrupted. The soldiers looked about; the young man was nowhere to be seen. "JADEN!" he shouted again, moving about on his grey horse in a panic, galloping around the sides of the carriages around The Glyph Wielders. Lethaniel looked over his shoulder, Thao gave the signal to cease movement. Isabelle emerged from her carriage; it soon became apparent that nobody knew where Jaden was! Jerhdia finally returned to his men, most concerned. "Where is he?" The soldiers looked at one another.

"Sir, I… We don't know!"

"Did you see him yesterday or the day before? When was the last time any of you saw him?"

"What's going on?!" Thao demanded, trotting up to Jerhdia on Eliah.

"We have lost a man, Jaden, our youngest. Nobody knows where he is."

"Last time I saw him, we were camped outside Tthenadawn. He WAS with us then, but…He must have fallen behind," suggested an unsure swordsman.

"Tthenadawn? Are you sure?" Thao enquired urgently, to which the swordsman replied:

"Yes sir, we spoke together." Thao glanced at Lethaniel, who nodded with a serious look on his face.

"We have to go back," one of the men insisted, while Thao distanced himself on his horse, with Lethaniel following close behind, and Jerhdia too, wanting to hear what the two planned to do about this. They spoke in low tones but did not whisper. Jerhdia put the words in Thao's mouth.

"I will go back, and I will find him. I will be late, but I will meet up with you in the city. I will bring back whatever I find."

"He didn't just fall behind, Jerhdia. Who simply falls behind a carriage while mounted upon a horse that has been bred for travel?"

"Well, something isn't right, because as you can plainly see…We are missing a man!" Jerhdia grew ever more agitated "It's simple, we have two options; we either wait here for him to arrive, or I will go back and find him. Why are we spending so much time talking about this?"

"And what if you find nothing? What if the same thing happens to you? Dark Rogues could have taken him," warned Lethaniel assertively.

"If he's lost, I will find him. If he's dead…Well, I am bound to find something. Either way, I am the one who is going to be telling his parents, unless you want to do that part?"

"Jerhdia, Lethaniel is right. You must not go alone; there is probably more than one of them. Take some men and supplies and meet me later in the city. Do you understand?" With a sharp nod, Jerhdia took off with his swordsman and two-cavalrymen. Isabelle watched them gallop away.

"What's happening? Thao, where are they going?"

"They are going back to find him, my girl. We, however, shall carry on. The rest of you, guard the rear. We continue south-east," Thao ordered. Lethaniel kept his thoughts to himself; maybe it was not the rogues after all. Why would they snatch a young soldier? Dark Rogues had always preferred stealth over confrontation; none of this matched their profile.

The plans had been made. Thao and the others continued, on the path to Imrondel, while Jerhdia head back to Tthenadawn Forest in search of Jaden. A relatively uneventful day of travelling went by quite quickly, with scattered talk of poor Jaden and The Dark Rogues. The time had come to leave the sound of flowing water behind and head directly south, away from Serpent's Back and onto the final road to the capital city of Krondathia. The group soon found the hard road that would now guide their way. Travelling along the route was easy; if the good weather continued, the group was ahead of schedule and would arrive at the city gates by the end of the fifth week. Their final day on the road had come. *Knock knock knock.*

"Yes, come in," called Isabelle, and Lethaniel stepped inside. The carriages having pulled over off the road and stopped.

"This will be the last stop before the city; are you prepared? I think you should eat," he suggested.

"Yes. I have been thinking. I was wondering if you know anything about the soldier who went missing?"

"Don't worry yourself about it."

"Why not?" Lethaniel remained quiet. "I didn't even know him, but he was my guardian a young one at that. If he's dead, then Jerhdia's going to have to tell his parents that he died escorting ME!"

"He's not dead, Izzy; he either got lost or dragged behind. Even you do that sometimes, and you're well...You are pretty damn powerful."

"You know what I mean though." They both sat in silence for a while, until Izzy admitted. "I was wrong, there are dangers out there. Thao was right; I do need protection, for someone wants me dead. It concerns me greatly."

"We don't know that for sure, we will all protect you, it's our duty as soldiers."

"So if it weren't a duty, maybe everyone would be inclined to let me rot?"

"Don't say that, that's not true."

"The time will come, Lethaniel, when men will have to make their own choices for themselves, without my guidance. I've seen it, the future that is, the book is evidence enough." Only too late did she realise she had accidentally revealed more than she had meant to. She waited for the reaction to appear on his face.

"Book, what book?" he asked, having been waiting for an opportunity to bring the subject up.

"Lethaniel, my lady Isabelle, come on out, it's time to eat!" called Thao from outside. Lethaniel looked at The Chosen for an answer or explanation; now would be a perfect time, but she said nothing. He didn't know why she didn't want to let him in, and he certainly had an idea why she was behaving so strangely. Following his self-imposed exile, perhaps this was the new Isabelle; it dawned on him now that this was not exactly same girl he had known before he left all those years ago. She seemed wiser but far more wrapped up in her work. They did, of course, come from two different worlds with vastly different views. He was a General, a soldier for the army; his way of thinking was logical, and strategic while hers was ethereal and incomprehensible to most. He had no idea what training she had undergone to get where she was today. She refused to answer, and finally, Lethaniel surrendered with a resigned sigh.

"That's fine. I still think you should eat something though; you look exhausted." With that, he opened the door and went outside to catch up with Thao.

The Honour Guard was outside, digging out some of the last remaining meals from the supply cart. Both carriages had stopped by the side of the wide brick road; there was no need for secrecy now, with Imrondel less than a day away.

"What were you two talking about?" he asked, rummaging through a crate of food, and sitting down next to Lethaniel, who was staring out to the long road.

"The city - Imrondel City - the absent capital." Thao handed his companion some food, and they ate slowly and quietly. Isabelle stepped outside for a brief moment but decided to avoid the company of Lethaniel and Thao. The Glyph Wielders took the opportunity to sit her down and tend to her clothes and face; they cleaned her up and she co-operated without question. After a short final stop, the carriages rolled back onto the road for the last stretch before reaching their destination. Lethaniel climbed up on the back of Seridox the swift, while Thao mounted Eliah the strong. They stood together, side by side, and watched the carriages pass by.

"We made it. They will be expecting us, no doubt. I trust you will be on your best behaviour?" said Thao.

"I hope you were referring to Isabelle. I'd be more concerned about her than me."

"No need to worry; she is strong, this life is all she has known since she was a child. I know this is her way of dealing with pressure."

"Then you know her better than I. I don't think she truly knows me; she certainly doesn't trust me, that's for sure, at least not like she used to. I don't know her."

"That's an awful lot of thoughts you have there. Maybe you should speak to her," Thao suggested.

"I have…" replied Lethaniel, frustrated.

"No, I mean really speak to her; not to The Star Caller, not to The Chosen, to Isabelle. Ignore WHAT she is and see her for WHO she is." The words were wise and encouraging. *Perhaps he was right* thought Lethaniel, *maybe he had been going about all this the wrong way.* "Do you know what I was really thinking about?"

"Jerhdia will find him," Lethaniel replied, seeming certain the missing boy was alive.

"If not…Who? How? Why? Regardless, whoever took him will have to answer to me" groaned Thao. The two men set off behind the carriages, both torn between anger and uneasy thoughts.

The edge of the forest was dark and lifeless. The wind howled, blowing a cold gale to the east. The sun had just fallen behind the clusters of grey clouds on the horizon. Jerhdia, leading his small group of soldiers, jumped off his horse as it slid to a stop. As he reached Tthenadawn, he drew his blade and held it tight in one hand.

"JADEN! WHERE ARE YOU?!" His men also slowed their horses to a stop and dismounted, drawing their weapons; one strung an arrow to his bowstring. "JADEN! TELL ME WHERE YOU ARE JADEN!" They listened out for a response but with the wind and the sound of rustling trees, it was impossible to hear anything. O'Nen searched high and low, looking for tracks or anything that might help; his men did the same, venturing toward the tree line.

"Sir!" one of them shouted, picking up something distinctly familiar. He showed it to Jerhdia, who came running over urgently. It was the young man's sword.

"He was here. He was standing right fucking here!" Jerhdia was confused but determined; he paced about trying to make sense of what evidence the ground was telling him. "He was drawn here." His gaze then found the forest; he stared into the darkness, wishing he was a better tracker. "Jaden went into Tthenadawn," Jerhdia concluded, his fixed eyes upon the disturbed mud in the ground, bearing an imprint of the boy's boot. He went back to his horse and tied it to the fallen tree; he seemed to retain some hope, though his soldiers were nowhere near as optimistic.

"Sir, you're not going in, are you?" one wondered.

"Of course I am, and you're coming with me."

"But sir, we don't even know what happened, we don't know if he is even in there." Jerhdia finished tying his horse.

"He is in there, and it will take all of us to track him down. We may have to split up into two groups to cover more ground, so I hope you all remember how to hunt."

"Sir, can we at least wait 'til morning or for the squad behind us; they will be coming across the bridge tomorrow."

"No! We will search for him tonight, and we will find him tonight! Now, we are going into Tthenadawn, so watch your footing and remember what you were told about this place; it's dangerous, especially at nightfall." The last relenting soldier finally agreed and found his courage, tying his horse to the nearby fallen tree, securing the rope. The four men approached the forest's edge with Jerhdia in front, sword ready in hand. "Stay close behind me. Keep a sharp eye and move fast. Remember, The Shrine of Virgo is in here somewhere, let us hope she is kind to us tonight." They dashed into the forest, eager to find their missing companion alive and well.

Chapter 11 - The Scouts of Norfoon

A stranger from the past returns and treads unforgiving territory.

The weary traveller trudged on through what seemed to be endless, lifeless plains. He walked alongside his tulkan bull, his arm draped over the reins, slouching his weight forward with every long step they took together. They should have reached the borders of Ivulien two days ago, yet he had yet to pass The Crescent Forest. The empty plain gave no clues as to where he was, which had become a growing concern. There had been no sight of encampments or even roads for what felt like ages. Clearly, Othello had strayed from his intended path and somehow missed his destination. He didn't want to face the truth, but after another days walk with no further hints as to his location, The Southlander finally admitted to himself that he was lost, lost in the wilderness with no map, no provisions and no tools to hunt for food. Even if he had the necessary equipment, the animals themselves were far too scarce and weary around humans. The land was unfamiliar, nothing like Jureai, so his knowledge was limited and could not be counted upon. The bull itself was breathing heavily, feeling every footstep it took with its Bevork companion, but still, they pushed on, either south or east, in the hope of finding the slightest sign of civilisation, friendly or otherwise. Through the hard days of struggling on and the lonely nights spent in the cold without shelter, he began to experience strange dreams. He became convinced that someone or something was nearby, implanting thoughts into his consciousness; sometimes the being even whispered things to him, echoing words he did not understand. As he travelled by day he remembered segments of the conversations he had had with this unknown presence, which came to him as a friend, almost like some kind of cautious advisor, blending in with the shadows, sure to not reveal its true form. From his vague memories, he could remember that it wore a long, black coat and a wide, flat, round hat.

Occasionally, while travelling, Othello would stop and turn his head just make sure no one was following him, to convince himself once more that he was alone. He knew the dreams couldn't be real, that it had to be an illusion, a trick of the mind brought on by severe fatigue. He forced himself to ignore the strange yet wonderful mirages of cool water or the carriages that trailed by with vast supplies of food. One vision, however, both alerted and disturbed him. It was nothing more than a quick flash, a quick glance at the strange, coated stalker, which up to that point had only appeared in the dead of night. Othello caught a glare from the figure, the same one from his dreams. It wasn't the darkness of this character that caught the warrior's eyes, but rather the shining bright white mask concealing its face, and those empty, black eye sockets that could hold anyone's stare. This construct of his psyche had most certainly been following him, talking to him in the night, and now it was there! Resting its back up next to a tree, as if it had been expecting him. It gave him a quick look then disappeared as quickly as it had shown up, rattling Othello, who could do nothing but continue onward with extreme caution. One night, this black, faceless figure sat on a slanted rock mere steps from where Othello was fading off to sleep on the uncomfortable floor. He rolled over to see the being just sitting there, staring up at the night sky, basking in the light of the full moon. It craned its neck to the side and glared at him, its eyes of night gleaming under its mask. Eventually, it spoke with a discordant, deep voice that echoed dozens of voices behind it.

"I need your help, Othello…Sword-Master…We all need your help." He squinted his eyes and replied with a croaking voice.

"Why? What can I do?" The humanoid being stood up, scraping its hard boots along the rocky surface, taking a deep breath.

"It has already begun… The time is nearing once more and the Norkrons hold the key… The key to our demise… And yours. My finest elites have been selected and assembled for the assault, but none of them are best suited to the task that I need you to fulfil." Othello did not understand, his mind still hazy in his tiredness.

"Your elites? What has this got to do with me?" The Masked Entity did not answer the question right away; instead, it began to move off into the night, morphing into the darkness, untouched by the moonlight.

"My Black Dove Elites, of course, the ones who will help me bring an end to the cycle of death…Your role is unfolding and one day you will have to choose what you will become. Will you be a slave to an empire or an elite saviour? You have time, but I will be there when you decide."

"What? Will we meet again? When?" Othello shouted out into the darkness, sitting upright, now fully awake. The next time he opened his eyes, it was daylight. Dazzled by the brightness of the sky, he forced his stinging eyes shut. He could not fully remember the events of the previous night, but for some reason, he finally knew which direction he should move in.

It was a particularly hot day; the sweat ran down his face and dampened his back and neck. He itched under his clothing, which rubbed against his sore skin. Uncomfortable and frustrated with his unfortunate circumstances, he ripped open his tunic, tearing the stitching and exposing himself to the air. With a grim look on his face, he slowly unlatched the straps on his tulkan and dropped them to the floor near its hooves.

"You must go. Find others…Go…" he whispered into the beast's ear. Othello went on alone but heard the loyal bull following him. "Go - be free, my friend. If you stay, I might do something terrible…" He gently pushed its nose away to the east, or at least he thought it was east. "GO!" Othello was starving and did not want to kill and eat the animal; either way, tulkans were natural survivors so letting the beast go was not a problem. The bull grazed a little but kept turning to his Bevork, who stumbled on, eventually becoming a dot in the distance.

The land, which had thus far been dry and earthy, holding little life, now slowly became softer, flooded with moisture in the more temperate climate. The grass grew healthier the further Othello moved on. He found himself climbing a hill, but suddenly slipped down its sloping side, rolling and tumbling down the mound. Recent days had been cruel; no food, no water and the same voice in his head telling him to just keep going on: *You'll make it; you're not going to die*. Othello lay there in the mud, not wanting to move; he was weak and found it hard to stand, so he remained there for a while with his eyes closed and his defences down. As he rolled over on to his back, he realised that he had fortuitously landed right next to a source of running water; a thin stream was nearby. He gasped for air and dipped his hand in the cool water, letting it run through his fingers for a while, then he cupped his hand and drank until his thirst was quenched and his body satisfied. Laying back and allowing his mind to wander, it felt good to finally sleep peacefully. When next he opened his eyes, he knew that he had made another mistake; already the day was turning to night. Still defenceless on the floor with his head resting on the ground, he heard steady footsteps approaching. It could not be who he thought it was, could it? Or was this just another peculiar dream? No one would be out this far away from civilisation, or so he kept telling himself. He chose to ignore what he assumed was a trick of the mind, for he had heard and seen many things since the food and water ran out weeks ago. The footsteps persisted, however, and sometime later began to circle the prone warrior who woke from a deep sleep. Othello stirred and raised his head to see a shade of black walking away into the trees and disappearing; it must have been that mirage again, the reoccurring figment of his imagination. He lifted himself up and continued to travel, as if nothing had happened. Neither the lack of food and water nor the strain of tiredness would stop him. Unaware, he blindly walked into forbidden territories, lands that were only trespassed upon by those who did not wish to be found.

Something was in the sky! The flutter of wings was heard, but when Othello looked up, he saw nothing. A small shadow passed over the ground, this time he caught a glimpse of a bird; it appeared to be a dove of some kind, not a copper hawk which were rare in his homeland let alone in these parts. It was considered great luck to spot a hawk, or at least that's what was said in Jureai; copper hawks were large birds of prey that hunted snakes, though the snakes had also been known to take down the hawks. Othello missed the calls and songs they made in Jureai, he missed the food and the wine. While he was thinking about home and gazing up to try and spot the bird that stalked him, he neglected to pay much attention to the uneven ground. His boot clipped a tuft of dirt, sending him forward into a fall resulting in what would have been a humorous balancing act for anyone watching. As he caught himself, he suddenly perked up, standing up straight and alert. Facing him, was a lone camouflaged fighter, armed with a loaded crossbow, aimed directly at his head. The figure's face was hidden behind a closed, tanned helmet. The wild man edged closer, shifting his crossbow forward. Othello stayed as still as a statue; a bolt to the chest would end even the hardest man. Several mounds of dirt in the area were suddenly disturbed growing arms and legs! Men shot up out of the ground, standing up swiftly, drawing and pointing their weapons, some with crossbows, others with lethally sharp swords and long, thick daggers. Othello raised his hands very slowly, not realising the full extent of the danger he was in. The small band of men surrounded him, keeping their sights trained on him. Just then, an authoritative, commanding voice came from behind them.

"Go back to where you came from, foreigner, and stay there." Othello was about to respond but was interrupted "DO NOT turn around! One wrong move now, pilgrim, and I will bury you where you stand. Be gone and we will spare your life... Speak, if you must, in your defence; but don't dare to waste my time, for it is dear to me." The Southlander then spoke calmly.

"I'm travelling to Krondathia's capital, to Imrondel City. I have travelled west for many months, without company and in peace. Order your men to lower their weapons, for as you can see, I'm unarmed and have nothing on me." He heard some footsteps behind him, shuffling through the grass, but he remained focused on the man directly in front of him, whose face was hidden behind an enclosed helmet.

"You seek Imrondel City? What is your business there? Tell me loner, where have you come from?" came the hard voice. The men surrounding Othello, did not flinch, their fingers resting in their crossbow levers who would fire without hesitation.

"Jureai. I travelled alone." There then followed a short pause, before the interrogator spoke again.

"If you're from Jureai and you're heading for Imrondel, then you are only about halfway there. This is the edge of Fevoriel, pilgrim; land of the tulkan and home to many ancient ruins. You strayed too far south-east. Now state your business," he ordered. It all made sense now; clearly, Othello had lost his way, he was travelling south, not west in the direction he had hoped for. That would explain the lack of roads and signs. Fortunate though, that his tulkan had been set free unto its own lands; the bull would soon be reunited with its own kind. He tried to explain as best he could the nature of his business.

"This ring is linked to your city. It's one of the reasons I left Jureai." He carefully put his hand in his pocket but couldn't find the precious item. This led him to panic, causing the man in front to twitch.

"Hold your fire scout…Do you mean this?" Othello, relieved but startled, held his position.

"Where did you find this?" the voice was now closer than before, and somewhat more sincere.

"It was given to me."

"What is your name? And what makes you think Imrondel is OUR city?" Othello took a breath before answering.

"I know it because I have been there before. Look at me, look at my skin. Do you really think I have the blood of a Jurean settler? I know our kind" said Othello speaking confidently "The soldier looking right at me wears a Norkron belt branded with a Krondathian seal. Your crossbows are made from metal found in iron mines close to Xiondel. You're far from home, skirting the borders of Ivulien under camouflage suits, this tells me you're unwelcome." The man standing behind him looked over to his men one at a time, nodding, appreciating their captive's sharp eyes. "I am Othello Hawk, and you are?" The man must have given some sort of unspoken order, for the surrounding men lowered their crossbows and sheathed their swords. Othello lowered his hands and turned to see a tall man standing over him, a little over six feet, suited in worn armour, which probably looked striking when it was new. He had clearly picked up a few accessories on his way; satchels, pouches and several other belts required to hold all sorts of travelling gear. He, like the others, was dirty and stained from hiding in the earth for so long, though the armour they wore gave off a faded sheen of bronze. The one who spoke, the one apparently in charge of this unit, also wore an enclosed helmet, hiding his identity. He pointed a menacing double-edged polearm at Othello's face.

"You're a friend of Krondathia?" he asked.

"Yes, I tell no lie, Norkron." The man stepped closer, lowered his weapon, lifting his visor, revealing a face coated in dirt, a pair of colourful blue eyes, locks of dirty blonde hair and prickly stubble.

"We Norkrons must stick together. The Dovidians are many and are not to be meddled with; that is why we hide in the land, for we meddle in the light under their very footsteps. Keep in mind that this is not the northland and we are not of your clan. We seek no honour or glory; we are simply watchers by day and night... Come with us Othello; we are heading back to The Norfoon Watchtowers in the cliffs of Thnel. The journey will bring you closer to your destination." The small band of Norkron Scouts ran onward. Unsure to trust them, Othello realised he had no choice but to follow, the leader of the group still had his father's golden, red crested ring.

The leader set the pace, marching with his polearm resting on his shoulder and his helmet tucked under his arm. The others walked behind him, clutching their wide crossbows, their swords sheathed at their sides. From the front, the leader of the band signalled to Othello:

"Come here." The Southlander caught up to him "I believe this is yours." The leader handed the ring back to Othello, pressing it firmly into his open palm. "Keep heading west from here and you will reach Imrondel City. The terrain gets steep in places, but if you know your way and go as straight as you can, you'll be fine. The land will eventually flatten out and the walk will be easy from there onward; the only problem is that you will be in the open. If you want, you can travel with us, we can provide food and shelter for a night. It is your choice, but I feel I judged you too harshly back there. I hope you understand? We must be wary of everyone we come across. I've lost too many men who treated strangers with kindness and paid for it with their lives."

"You ARE from Imrondel," Othello stated.

"You have a sharp eye. Yes, we are all Norkron born; the ones you see with me are some of my best. We are strong, methodical, and able to work seamlessly as a unit. Other groups such as ours are located throughout this area; in fact, you may have already passed them without even realising it."

"We are near the Dovidian lands now, are we not?" Othello had many questions; he wanted to get as much out of this officer as possible before they went their separate ways.

"Ivulien lies to the south, though it's still a fair distance," the man answered, glancing at Othello to his left, "But if you were to continue on your present course you would certainly die of starvation or something far worse. Either way, only death waits for men in that realm of evil."

"The Realm of Theed..." Othello murmured, having heard stories of the place before, round the campfire in Jureai.

"We all know it's there, but we also know that those who go there or even venture close its borders never return. Disappearance is the happy ending to these stories, but in some cases, those stupid enough to explore Theed, or those who fancy themselves as heroes, are found later. Scouts like us sometimes pick them up, wandering the wilds, while Dovidian travellers and border patrols have encountered others,"

"What do you make of them, those that see Theed?" asked Othello. They walked a few paces longer before the leader answered.

"The few who have returned to us, who have witnessed the realm did not come back the same people. They appeared to have been afflicted by madness, something insane; we call this condition The Plagued Mind."

"The Plagued Mind?" repeated Othello, and the man described what was meant by the term.

"The last one we picked up wanted to see the realm – he didn't even cross the border - wound up completely losing his ability to communicate with us. He wouldn't stop talking to himself in a language that none of us knew; we think it was Englathin, but none of us knew for sure. We are Norfoon Scouts, not scribes. We decided to take him back, to try to cure him, to attempt to understand what it was he had experienced…"

"Well, what happened?"

"His mind was broken. Later that same night, he pulled his tongue out with his own hands and roasted it over a fire a short distance from our camp. When we smelt the smoke and detected the light in the woods we apprehended him; fire gives away our position, we have to be ghosts. He saw us surround him and spoke, this time in the common tongue, he said '*Only the pure have a chance to see, and only one sacrifice is needed to save us.*' He then slit his skin from the stomach to throat without even the slightest of screams. After that, he lay down in the flames and allowed himself to be consumed."

"How did he speak if he had no tongue?" The Norfoon Scout leader shook his head, shrugging his shoulders. "What did he mean by what he said?" Othello HAD to ask, even though he knew he would not get an answer.

"No one goes there because none ever return, and when they do, they die by their own hands."

"What's in there?"

"There was once an expedition many, many years ago; the last one before The Eldor prohibited anyone from ever going there again. A selection of the best men from around the world chosen by Freya Delmesca herself, a Star Caller before Isabelle if you forgot out history. They set out into those lands on her orders; I don't know what these orders were, for the details of the mission remain a secret to this day. What little documentation still exists is held in the Inner Vaults of Xiondel, among its other treasures. One thing I do know is that they wanted to study the realm, to find out what was in there. Some believe - and don't repeat this in Imrondel - that the answers

236

lie within; the answers to everything, all of the fundamental questions that humankind strives to answer, is found in Theed. This theory was spread by a previous generation, it is one of the reasons why the expedition was launched, to settle the debate. It was a mission of great significance."

"And the explorers?"

"Not all returned; one is still around, he works in an old library of the city, writes letters to his fellow traveller. Another disappeared a while ago, I believe his name was Ruthal. The wisest among them also lived, a Professor. Their accounts were never understood, if Theed is the place where our answers lay, it is still yet to be known. Extraordinary, really, that these men are the only men unaffected by the plaque mind; Why this is, I have no idea."

Within an hour Othello fell behind, unable to keep up with the pace. He dropped to his knees after a short while, grasping the ring tightly to his chest. He was exhausted. The leader and his men turned to see him on the floor; one of the scouts whispered something to his Commander before approaching Othello, and knelt next to him.

"Our supplies here have run dry. You can come with us or you can stay here for the silvermane wolves. Either way, it matters little to me if you live or die, pilgrim. So get up and don't fall behind again." The entire party head off as Othello stood, shaking off his weakness and slowly followed them, struggling on. One man was kind enough to wait for the stricken Bevork to catch up. He found a pouch fitted to his belt and unhooked it, throwing it to their new companion.

"My name is Faustus Deen," he said introducing himself, as Othello drained the pouch of water, almost quenching his thirst. Faustus lifted the visor of his helmet and watched him drink, taking back the empty pouch. "Our destination isn't that far away. I won't leave you behind, but please try to keep up."

Moving steadily through the thin layer of trees for what seemed like an eternity, continuing even after the sun had long set, the group eventually found a hidden track winding towards a bridge suspended above a gushing stream. This had to be the beginning of a major river. Instead of crossing the bridge, the leader jumped down the bank and into the stream, caring not about the wet and cold, disappearing into the darkness under the arched, black stone structure. The other men followed him, though Othello took his time, slowly sliding down the bank into the frigid water below. Wallowing around knee deep, Faustus called out from under the bridge:

"This way, hurry." He pointed to an opening, where Othello saw fiery lights illuminating a cave from the inside. There was a small tunnel under the bridge, dug deep into the earth. He climbed into the hole and crawled on all fours through the dank, rocky passage. Faustus patched up the opening with gathered thickets and thorn plants, also took the time to flick some droplets of animal urine from a glass vial over the grassy door. "To keep the wild out; it's just a precaution. It allows me to sleep easier at night," he explained to Othello who continued to crawl forward, further into the tunnel. The short path led to a round opening; a much larger space from what Othello could hear, though all he could see was the one torch waving around in someone's hands, creating shadows of giants on the walls. The light was placed in a pile of wood in the centre of the cave. Othello stood by and waited as the firelight grew on the gathered wood and things gradually became visible. "We will stay here 'til dawn breaks, so get as much sleep as you can. The towers are still far away, as is Imrondel." The smoke that escaped the fire was vented out through a small hole in the ceiling. The men seemed to be dropping off to sleep, except one who kept guard on the door and the leader, who sat opposite their guest, next to the wall.

"You said you travelled from Jureai; that is a long distance to where we are now. You travelled far and without company. Your strength and determination are admirable. You must have witnessed the tournament if I've kept track of time correctly?" Othello gave a slight nod, mindful of what he allowed himself to reveal. "Who won then?" The leader's words belied his curiosity, but also a hint of something more.

"The Bevork Clan were victorious, and it was a fair duel," Othello answered finally, picturing his blade scraping over Kronix's shoulder blades. A short, uncomfortable silence followed. He had found himself under a bridge in the fading light with four hardened men he did not know the names of, save for Faustus, though at least they were from Krondathia. The situation seemed safe; they were hundreds of miles away from home and did not appear to be an immediate threat to him. He found himself observing his surroundings.

"This is an old shelter; we use these as hideouts and sometimes meeting places for other tasks. This is one of many in this area, though we have hideaways like this all over the world," the leader explained.

"And what task are you working on now?"

"Commander…" whispered the soldier near the door. The leader nodded and raised his hand to the soldier before answering vaguely; clearly, there were some details that should not be being talked about.

"Observation and scouting, which of course involves a degree of trespassing." By now the light was flickering and dying, eating away the last traces of burnable wood.

"You mean spying? You're spies?" At that moment, the fire died completely, and all went black.

"Spies? Yes, that would be accurate. Spies with good reason."

Othello woke to the sound of marching that appeared to be directly above them. Thin strands of dawn shone through the entrance of the doorway near the stream and a thicker ray of light beamed down from the ceiling where the vent was. He could see a little better now; one of the soldiers had a loaded crossbow pointed at the entrance and the others were sitting quietly in the gloom, like glum statues, fully alert, all staring at the ceiling. The steps above eventually passed over them and the soldiers stood up quietly.

"Stay together, watch each other's backs and keep your wits about you, and you will be fine," whispered the leader. One scout pulled the door away from the tunnel and hopped out into the water.

They all followed, jumping into the stream. No one told Othello to go anywhere or do anything, though he followed and closed off the tunnel himself. By now the scouts were checking the way ahead, looking down the sights of their bows and looking for any signs of danger. They eventually ran across the bridge in pursuit of the men who had passed over their heads. "Stay close and quiet," instructed the leader, holding out his hand. Othello grabbed it and was pulled out from the stream and up on to the bank. The small group ran swiftly west, dispersing into a formation unknown to the newcomer, who had forgotten his hunger and need for energy for the time being and remained focused on keeping up with the others. They had long since abandoned the road and the ground seemed to be rising, growing steeper, slowing the men down. Soon the unit came across a ledge set in a stone wall overlooking a road below. The scouts again made sure that the area was safe before signalling to their leader, who was coming up behind them, grasping his double-edged polearm as if he expected to use it. They knelt on the ground; some removed their helmets, revealing their faces for the first time to Othello. They all seemed so tired and pale, but they had the appearance of rugged veteran soldiers with experience. Faustus looked like the youngest of the bunch, around twenty-eight, maybe thirty years old. A scout's job was not an easy one; alert and ready all day every day, always conscious of being discovered or pushed into immediate danger. How long these men had been out here in the wilderness on the borders of Ivulien, not far from Theed remained a mystery, as did the identity of the leader. They remained still, passing around a crude-looking brass telescope taking turns to look through it, analysing the situation, not saying a word. "Mercenaries..." muttered the leader.

The large band of mercenaries marched through the trees, their footsteps orderly as if they were one. The scouts hiding in the hills could see them clearly from above. The invading unit, lacking any type of matching uniform or weapon, apparently had a single leading Commander, who stood out from the rest, wearing sophisticated, expensive armour, armed with a longsword. *Too expensive and too smart for any contract killer to get his hands on*, thought Othello. The leader of the Norkron Scouts took an unspoken liking to another one's helmet, round and topped with two long horns. The unit marched as an army would, and there were enough of them to make a decisive blow against the smaller band of scouts and their settlements in Thnel.

"They are marching south; this is definitely the same group that passed over us earlier. They are a clustered unit of about fifty to sixty, mercenaries of unknown origin. Their Commander - the one in black - he is not one of them, looks to be Dovidian, though the one with the horned helmet certainly is a wild card, definitely part of those marching, must be their Captain or the one who pays'em." The Norkron Scout leader slumped down behind the rock and sat thinking to himself. One of his men kept watching the mercenaries, marching gradually out of sight, using the roads and not the short passages, which suggested that they were not familiar with the land.

"Sir?" a scout asked for instructions.

"No, we will stay our course and make for The Norfoon Towers. From there we go to Quenethia, where we will assess the situation." As the scouts dashed off, Othello looked back in the direction of the mercenaries, before hastily following The Norfoon Scouts over the rocks where they found a path leading through a small range of hills.

As before, they travelled fast, running as one through the trees, across open grassy meadows and through streams. They were never caught off guard, always vigilante. Days turned into nights, nights became days and still, they left no trail. Othello followed them; he knew that they knew the way to Imrondel City, so before he would make his own path, he would make sure he knew where he was going. This leader knew the land well and was very proficient when it came to navigation and evasion. Another long day of solid jogging, aching joints and a starving belly was coming to an end when in the distance before a clear blue sky, there appeared a valley of grey mountains, their tips lost in a mist of cloud. The sight was a refreshing one, and a long-awaited touch of excitement gently relieved Othello. The land was changing, finally. The first step in his journey was almost complete and the thought of reaching Imrondel was now growing larger in his mind. As the group got closer, he stopped and noticed that they had abandoned their main path; they were now heading towards a small but thick, green woodland across an open plain of grass to the north. Othello caught up with the soldiers, who were slowing down and talking quietly amongst themselves. Eventually, they came to a complete halt; two soldiers loaded their crossbows, another drew his sword and the leader faced Othello.

"You are who you say you are, aren't you?" he asked in a demanding tone.

"I am from Jureai and my name is Othello, you know this and I…"

"You could be a liar, Othello. Which is why we cannot trust you to go any further with us. Allowing you to join us for a while is one thing, but showing you our next route is entirely different, the risk is too great, you understand? I'm only thinking of my people."

"If that's how it is then I should be on my way," accepted the exiled Southlander, turning around and walking away, back to the path. Faustus came up close to the leader and muttered a few words in his ear.

The scout leader whistled "Othello" he called. The wandering warrior stopped and turned around. "Do you know how to use a sword?" Othello nodded. "Do you know how to fight?" Before he could answer, the leader came up to him and handed him a spare sword that had been latched to his back. "You might need this. Keep going west in that direction." He advised, pointing out the route. "You will have to pass over some rocky terrain, but I am sure you can handle it. When you see the road, take it, and follow it to Imrondel City. Also, if you see any vents in the ground along the way, they are hideouts like the one you were in before. If you do find any, there may be some supplies stashed inside. You're welcome to help yourself. In the event of meeting other Norfoon Scouts, show them the sword I gave you and say I have granted you safe passage."

"Thank you for your help, I will not burden you any longer. Good luck."

"I hope you find what you're looking for" smiled the older man, walking back to his Norfoon Scouts.

"What is your name?" asked Othello as he prepared to set out alone; that question had been itching at him for days, but now he HAD to know. The leader turned.

"I am Mathias Sious, Commander of The Norfoon Scouts" One of the men under a helmet waved, while Faustus saluted Othello, placing his right hand on his heart then swiped it vertically down the centre of his face. Beyond the woodland, nestled deep within the ravine, Othello could see part of a mighty tower of wood and stone. The Norfoon Watch Towers were evidently located there in those mountains, though the path to them lay hidden in the woodland ahead, into which Mathias, Faustus, and the rest of the men, disappeared inside. Othello was alone, with only his thoughts for company. The sun was going down, sinking behind the mountains. Many a cold, lonesome nights under the stars lay ahead. He soon found the path and resumed his course west, hoping to find Imrondel while he still had the strength. The blade he had been given was of a high quality, a relatively short, one-handed sword with a black handle, it must have been a fine instrument in its earlier days. Night had now begun to set in, and the lonely traveller pushed on. As he walked on in the fading light, his memory travelled back to a time long ago, when he was growing up in Jureai, among The Bevork Clan.

El Raud stormed into his hut, full of his unpacked belongings. Some of the most important things were already lining his shelves, while the larger items and relics were stocked up the corners of his chamber. He poured himself a drink from a large glass and downed the amber nectar in one go. Enemar then entered without knocking, receiving a quick glance from the Chieftain, who began to pour his friend a glass. El Raud creased his forehead and concentrated.

"Has the boy received any training? From you or any of your Captains in Imrondel?"

"A little from me" admitted Enemar.

"What about when you were living in Xiondel; could he have been tutored by one of your men there?" El Raud was rushing through the questions in his excitement, not really thinking about them too carefully.

"Othello was too young, still a baby while I was in Xiondel. Imrondel is all he knows. He has received no real training; this I promise you."

"So what we saw him do just then, to some who have been in practice for years, that was self-taught?" The silence was answer enough. El Raud sniggered and poured himself another glass, though he didn't drink right away, instead, he stepped away from the small stand and slowly paced around his quarters. "I have something in mind, my old friend. I think you should be the first to know..." Enemar took a sip and listened to El Raud's plan. "Othello shows extraordinary talent, not just in fighting others but also in the Jurean ways, our ways. Most human beings are naturally kind, I've always believed this, but when he sees someone he could benefit or help in any way, he does whatever he can, without consideration of payment or reward. Not only has he already earned the respect of the clan, but he has taught us that not all Southlanders are how we thought them to be. Education is the key to The Bevork Clan's growth, education and..." El Raud fell silent and Enemar leant forward, eager to hear what came next. "Maybe Othello should compete in The Pit...Let rumour reach Kronix's ears of the boy. Let us unleash him upon the Salarthians. I have no doubt he WILL succeed, and when he is victorious, the Bevorks will take the throne. Jureai will rise after our victory; a new order of balance shall be established. Our order." Enemar liked the idea and nodded enthusiastically. They clinked their glasses together, unaware that Othello had listened to the whole conversation from outside.

Chapter 12 - The Palace of Imrondel City

A great capital city, yet far from its own home.

The carriage rolled smoothly down the road in the sunset, toward the great city of Imrondel. Beyond multiple rings of solid walls, the glowing tops of wonderful towers peaked, and over yonder taller towers of greater proportions lightly caressed the sky kingdom. The Palace of Imrondel City was known as Norisis, the heart of the city, the centre of local life and the grandest gathering of all its structures. The Golden City dwarfed that of its silver brother Xiondel, struck not with cold iron artistry but graced with an ancient kiss of Celestial spark. Heavily protected around its outer rims, as wild as a fruitful forest built from stone and metal with holy hands, cherished by its dear Norkron populous, Imrondel was the birthplace of the faith Starillia, the capital of Krondathia home of the Norkron people, a place of prayer, worship, forgiveness, rejoice, and refuge for all people's and cultures of Equis. All were welcome

The procession was soon joined by many decorated guards mounted on horseback. They were in valiant uniforms, equipped with some of the finest gear the Norkron world had to offer. Greeting their visitors, they marched alongside the armoured carriage, following a traditional routine, holding their great spears vertically as they passed through the giant city gates tarnished with a silver sheen. The horsemen were members of the famous Thunderhoof Riders, a unit with a complex history involving The Tulkan Knights. Lethaniel recognised their banner, which was held high, attached to their pikes; it was of their own unique mark, sewn into their tunics and forged into their armour, a decorative mark that depicted a horse's hoof, wrapped in a bolt of lightning, the latter signifying the devastation of their famous cavalry charge. Atop Imrondel's walls, the soldiers lined up the walkways and saluted as the carriage drew closer. Isabelle's arrival was anticipated and welcomed, for hundreds of citizens were flocking from behind the walls to see her carriage. Imrondel was renowned for fussing over Star Caller entrances, no city did it better. A memory of when she was fourteen never failed to draw pleasant sensations, when the armies of Krondathia had gathered just to welcome the blonde beauty after a long trip away to Pura. She had been showered with millions of flower petals before entering each gate, trumpets blew, and performers danced around her all the way to Norisis. Behind the city walls was a dry moat, large enough to manoeuvre units of men and anti-siege weaponry through comfortably. The moat was more like an armed trench, not a welcoming sight at first glance for such an iconic city but considered by most in power including Isabelle, to be necessary. The line was known as The Defensive Trench, its purpose to fend off invading forces should a siege ever take place. Threats of conquer were a thing of the past, the last major attack on any Norkron city had taken place centuries ago.

The carriage came to a halt, waiting for one of the many tall, formidable-looking portcullises to open within the inner wall. As it ascended with a rattling creak. Thao rounded up his men and the other armed escorts, while Lethaniel hung back upon Seridox and listened.

"Well done, all of you, I mean it, well done. I know some complications have arisen, but they will be dealt with in good time. We have arrived, our Star Caller is safe, rest easy. Mission complete; your names will be prioritised for further assignments. Get some sleep in a bed tonight, have a drink, visit family and friends, That's an order. Tomorrow you will meet at the barracks at noon for further duties. Dismissed." The men dispersed; some headed straight into the city, while others stayed within the trench and dismounted. Thao's Honour Guards stayed put and let a young boy through when he asked politely to see the new arrivals.

"Excuse me, Sir! General Presian!" he yelled, getting Lethaniel's attention. Taking off some work gloves that were far too big for his young hands. "You were with the escort party, right? With Isabelle? I am Letty O'Nen; my father was with you. It's great to meet you finally, Sir, it really is." He held out his hand, hoping for a handshake from The General. Lethaniel gladly shook it from atop Seridox and started to explain to Letty about Jerhdia's whereabouts.

"Your father is... He will be arriving here shortly, probably with the next group that's expected tomorrow, the *uh*, Seventh Company," he improvised, referring to Braygon's own unit.

"It's alright, I know that's not the real reason, but I will buy it just to make things easier for you," the boy accepted, surprisingly cheerful, understanding that Lethaniel could not tell him everything about recent events. The General smiled at the pleasantry and nodded. It looked odd to see such a young boy working among the soldiers and engineers of Imrondel, dirty and coated in grit as if he was actually involved in a heavy-duty line of work, for which he clearly had neither the strength nor the qualifications to do so. At only fourteen or fifteen, he was too young to do most jobs here anyway, but clearly, he was doing simple tasks for someone. Lethaniel couldn't be sure, but he admired Letty's individuality. Most other boys his age were off playing and fooling around, chasing girls or breaking things. This one, on the other hand, was working and learning from wise men all around him, educating himself and listening to those who knew better. Letty's attention was then drawn to Thao. "You're The Honour Guard everyone always talks about, aren't you? I've never met you in person. How do you do, Sir?" Letty cleaned his hands off again with his gloves and greeted the older man, who was almost five times his size. "My father has talked about you before."

"Really, what did he say about me?" Thao asked, sounding surprised.

"He says you're a great man, my mother says so too." Lethaniel raised his eyebrows at Thao, just as surprised as he was.

"That's good to hear. I certainly got a different impression, but maybe it's just me," Thao laughed, thinking back to his first encounter with Jerhdia. Inside the carriage, Isabelle was listening in while lying down on her bed, resting a palm on her cheek. She had spoken to Letty before and knew he was quite a charming young lad. The conversation outside brought a smile to her face. She rested her hands behind her head and continued to listen.

"Is she in there? Can I talk to her now? Does she have her long staff, Violethelm with her?" the boy eagerly asked, looking anxiously around at the carriage.

247

"Not today, little guy, maybe some other time. We have been on the road for a while, so she is very tired. Besides, it looks like you've got lots of work to do," encouraged Thao.

"You're right; swords and arrowheads don't make themselves. Just tell her I said hello if you would. Oh, tell her that I've started to learn the languages of those who came before us, and I bought a book on the workings of Glyph energy." Once again Lethaniel pulled a shocked expression.

"I'll tell her, don't you worry, my boy, I'm sure she'll be proud of you." Letty picked up a box of bits and pieces and head for a forging area in The Defensive Trench.

"Letty! How did you know me?" called Lethaniel, curious.

"It was your horse at first, then I saw your two swords, they are my father's greatest pieces, I hope to be like him one day." With that the boy head off further down the murky trench, moving out of sight. Thao and Lethaniel looked at each other, chuckling.

"I like him," said The General.

"Agreed" said Thao, before knocking on the side of the carriage. "You hear that?"

"Yes. Charming lad, isn't he?" Isabelle said from the inside of the carriage, tending to her toenails.

Lethaniel drew inspecting the hilts of his longsword. It was of a unique design made for him, perfectly fit for his hand, a weapon for a General; it even matched the armour he wore, the suit that currently waited for him in his quarters at home. He could remember the day he received the swords like it was yesterday, but he had never realised that Jerhdia had made them himself. He put aside the sword and followed the carriage toward the city centre.

They exited the Defensive Trench through one of the portcullises. Once the carriage was safely through, the iron gate rolled down, the sound of ticking chains ringing out as it shut tight, lodging itself within a set of grooves in the paved stone floor. Casually, the group made its way toward the residential quarter. They crossed an open area of well maintained, lush, green gardens tended to by peasants, gardening folk and even some priests, all of whom worked with a sense of commitment and care. In the middle of this small garden, in a large, square, stone courtyard stood a fine statue of the leader of the Norkron people. The depicted Eldor was looking up, holding out his hands to the skies above. The historic centre was the heart of the city, by far the most luxurious and spectacular part of the capital; its golden crown jewel, made up of the tallest and finest collections of rich structures, all coming together reaching for the sky kingdom. These wonderful, shining towers connected via webs of elegant bridges, was The Palace of Norisis.

Imrondel's infrastructure had been grounded into districts. There were five of them, one being The Holy District where the teachings of Starillia were nourished. The Star Gardens were found within this district, in the shadow of The Eliendras Cathedral, a smaller recreation of The Column Temple. Ringed around The Holy District was The Canalside District, along this giant moat the Norkrons diverse hospitality industry thrived. The Military District, the smallest quarter of the five districts, was cordoned off, almost its own separate entity of the city where the Norkrons housed every form of its forces, from Regular units, Thunderhoof Riders, Norfoon Scouts, Visarlian Knights and Honour Guards, here was where the cities fist grew strong. The largest district was The Living District. Unlike its military counterpart this district was not confined to one block, rather it a vein that spread throughout the city. Some parts were wealthier and larger than others, served to house the Norkron populace, providing schools, hospitals, educational institutions, and markets to fuel the economy.

Districts of Imrondel
The Holy District
The Canalside District
The Military District
The Central District
The Living District

Already it was getting late, so many of the people had made for home, though some children continued to play their games on the streets. Some of these youngsters noticed the carriage passing by but did not make a fuss about it. The roadsides were lined with stone houses, their inhabitants locking up for the night, while shops and markets alike lay quiet. Streetlamps burned oil, fuelling white lights to illuminate the way, attracting humming insects. The carriage head for The Holy District and approached Norisis growing out from a circular island ringed by the canal, along the canal Norkrons could take pleasure in the sight of their glowing palace while enjoying delicious servings of the best food and finest drinks. Imrondel was almost self-sufficient, but most of its luxury goods were imported from far-off countries and provinces, such as The Pura Lands to the northwest, which made huge contributions of grain, wine and other fine things that the city needed to keep its businesses alive. Imrondel also traded with Xiondel, directly to the north. It had business with Cuether and Davune, the Ivulien capital home to the Dovidian people in the east. Unlike The Palace of Norisis, Davune's own royal residence, Tithis, looked more like a fortress or an old castle from The Age of Six.

The carriage crossed over the southern bridge curving over the canal. The side hatch slid open when they reached the other side and Isabelle's face appeared; she wished to share some words with Thao before they separated.

"Thank you for your company, Thao, as always it's appreciated," she said gratefully.

"It was a pleasure to travel with you again. I hope it won't be the last time," he replied. The Honour Guard slowed Eliah down to a halt while the carriage kept moving. His task was complete.

"Do me a favour: go see your family and spend some time with them. I order you to do so!" said Isabelle, falling back inside. He watched as The Thunderhoof Riders escorted the armoured carriage toward The Palace of Norisis. Like with The Priests of Starillia, Thao could not help but empathise with The Star Callers situation, he knew, he could see it with every look with every fake smile, Isabelle was rotting.

"So, do you wanna grab a beer or find something to eat before you turn in?"

"No thank you Lethaniel, not tonight. I have been given an order straight from the top" Thao gently pulled on Eliah's reins taking him down a well-lit road of the city, the clatter of hoofs on concrete beneath him.

"You look tired," noted The General.

"Why did you call our Chosen, Squeak?" Lethaniel sided a smile.

"Grab a beer with me and I'll tell ya" said Lethaniel.

"Take it easy Lethaniel, I will see you at the briefing." With that, Thao rode away. Free of duty for the rest of the evening, Lethaniel head back the way he had come, jumping off Seridox to walk the lit streets, hoping to grab a quiet drink somewhere and enjoy his own company. Unfortunately, the inns and bars were teeming with life, citizens would only bombard him if he were to stroll on up with Seridox who had somehow garnished a greater reputation than he had at this point. Instead, he and Seridox moved away towards the east end of the city. His home was in a secluded part of Imrondel, far away from the cluttered housing areas and distant enough from noises of the military. The lamps along the sidewalks lit his way, giving him the chance to see into every house he passed, each one dark and still. Either its residents were sleeping soundly, or they were out drinking and eating like most others. He was more interested in keeping his head at the ground, listening to the hum of the wind and the tapping of a slight rain coming in from the west.

Further ahead he saw someone walking toward him followed by the echo of hard heeled shoes. The movements this lady made were all too familiar, as was the shape of her shoulders, her hips, and legs. It was her! As she passed by one of the glowing lamps, he became certain. She too caught a glimpse of Lethaniel, further up the path, if not sure on the man, it was Seridox without a doubt. She took her hands out of her coat pockets; General Presian froze under one of the oil lamps and waited for her to approach; she entered the light with him, revealing her delighted face. She rushed to him and leapt into his arms adoringly. They embraced one another very tightly under the bright, white light. The rain fell harder, the water droplets illuminated by the lamp, but it did not matter; nothing mattered to the two at that moment.

"You said you would be back soon. You have been gone too long. Ever since that day… Where have you been? Why didn't you write to me?" she cried; her words were sad but her voiced belied a relieved joy. He held her for a few seconds longer before he spoke; she was so warm and alive, her long hair tied back and tucked inside her coat, it smelt wonderful.

"I am sorry. I really am. I had to go away for a while, but I am back now. I'm not going anywhere." He squeezed her tighter and she squeezed back. "I am not going to leave you, Eva" he promised. This is what he had been missing; the feeling of her around him was what made all his responsibilities worth it.

"Damn right you will be!" she exclaimed, placing her hands on his chest, feeling the necklace under his worn riding jacket.

Knock Knock Knock. The door opened and Thao was welcomed inside. Before he settled for a well-deserved rest, he embraced his wife.

"I missed you."

"I wasn't expecting you home so soon," smiled Lena, "I would have saved you some food if I had known you would be back at this hour."

"It's fine. Apart from being very tired, all is the way it should be. You have no idea how good it is to be home…How are you? How is our son?"

"We've been very well; you wouldn't believe what he has been up to though." She had clearly been looking forward to telling him this story. Intrigued, he sat down in a chair near a wooden table. "I was worried at first but then I remembered what your mother told me about you, all those years ago," Lena began, kneeling in front of her husband and leaning on his knees, "Your son found the key and got into the basement a while back..." Thao looked at her and grinned very slightly, not knowing whether to be concerned or excited. "I have caught him down there many times, taking an interest in certain things that belong to you, your armour and your gear. I think he likes it; he talks about you every time we sit down to eat. He asks lots of questions and I think it will be best if you answer them. He is curious as to what it is you do for a living. I was thinking..."

"What were you thinking, my love?"

"I think it is time for Lucion to know some things about his father. There is only so much I can tell him." Thao took her hand and stood up, facing a bookcase. He slid his fingers down the spine of a book; the name read *Raising an Honour Guard*, and he distinctly remembered his own father reading it when he himself was growing up.

"He cannot know what I've done. I will never put that armour on again."

"And you won't ever have to if you don't want to. I am not asking you to dig up the past. I am not asking you to forgive yourself, I've already tried that... Just, while you are here, be a father to our son, that's all I am asking. You do not see him very often and he needs a man in his life, not any man, but the best, and you are the best one I know." Thao nodded, giving his wife a kiss.

"Besides, I need some time off from being a mother; it is tiresome work, perhaps I can wield the hammer and you can wield the rolling pin" she teased, snatching the wooden pin up and holding it to his throat!

"Looks like you got me in a sticky spot here" said Thao.

"I've ways of disarming the greatest Honout Guard that ever lived" she smiled.

"No no there is actually something on the rolling pin Lena, I can smell it" said Thao, taking the pin away, it dripping with syrup.

"That's my poison" and Thao sucked the sweet nectar off his fingers, as he considered his wife's words.

"I don't want him to end up like me. One day he will find out about my history and what I have done. It cannot be erased like I want it to be. My actions are part of history, and for that I am ashamed. All Lucion has to do is look in the correct book and flick to the right page or meet one of the members of a family I destroyed" Thao lowered his head, feeling the weight of his shame "I won't blame him if he grows to hate me and The Guard, honestly, I'd be concerned if he doesn't."

"It's not complicated, Lethaniel; she's a Star Caller, we can only imagine what is going on in her head. Think about how much pressure you were put under and extend it by a thousand. It's called empathy soldier boy, don't forget it" said Eva, playfully.

"I've not forgotten" said Lethaniel, bringing about a pause.

"I heard what you did to Syen," said Eva, her tone diving into something more serious.

"I overreacted. It was foolish and ill-advised, I know that now, but you are right. You're always right..."

"Of course I am" and she took a look over her shoulder, then back at Lethaniel, "Seridox agrees with me." The magnificent horse followed behind the pair, staying with his master wherever he went. "Where is Isabelle now?" Eva asked.

"At Norisis; it was a long trip and we lost a soldier on route. We have men out there now, searching for him."

"You lost a man?! Who? What happened?" Lethaniel, being a General, thought twice about disclosing anything to her; he had already said too much.

"We have reason to believe we were being followed by Dark Rogues from the moment we set foot in The Silent Vale, then I don't know what happened, but we think we lost our man near Tthenadawn."

"Do you think it was the rogues?" Eva asked.

"I do, but then again, part of me tells me otherwise. Something tells me this is different. The Dark Rogues are notorious for mass thievery, organised raids and generally breaching the peace, even arson when they get crazy or feel like they must revolt, but they have NEVER been known to body snatch. It makes no sense, or maybe it does, I just don't know where to find my answers." He still found himself unable to complete the puzzle stuck in his mind.

"Could it have something to do with The Chosen?"

"I hope not, but something is definitely going on."

"I have always asked you one thing, though you probably think I am being ridiculous - if anyone can defend themselves it's you – but please, be careful when you're out there. Do it for me. I don't want to hear one day that you won't be coming home," she pleaded softly, touching his arm.

"And I always tell you not to worry about me," he replied with a smile.

"You know, when I found out that you had disappeared two years ago, after that time in the courtyard with you, I really thought you would never return. Being a General meant everything to you, didn't it? You worked so hard for it, and when Syen landed the position, I wished I had said more that night."

"You said enough, don't worry, more than enough to wake me up. But in order to make a difference, one that people can see, one must be in a high position of power. A Regular or a Norfoon Scout cannot make waves to topple empires; If I could be that man, if I could be the superior, I could bring some good to this world," he explained.

"I disagree" she said with a moan "I think any one of us can make a difference" she said.

"In order for one's voice to be heard, elevating your position grants you advantages" was Lethaniel's response.

"Tell me about your voice Lethaniel?" he had never been asked this before, his ideas made sense inside his head but voicing them, he need a moment to collect his thoughts.

"We're living in an uncertain time. Many believe Isabelle will deliver the utopia, she shows promise, graced with an aura unbeknown to any other Star Caller. We have come so far, we have reached so high, we are almost there! Though there are some who are scared, fearful of the change that is coming and will do all they can to prolong our journey. I serve to stop them."

The rain was falling a little harder now; the drops became heavy and rolled off the slanted, stone rooftops of the nearby houses. Streams ran through the streets and puddles started to rise.

"Thank you for walking me home, Lethaniel, you didn't have to. You must be exhausted," Eva said with a smile, one foot on her doorstep.

"I wanted to. I'm sorry I'm not around as much as I used to be."

"It can't be helped, but if you want, you can see me again tomorrow night?" His mind raced but could not remember his schedule off the top of his head causing him to hesitate. She shrugged her shoulders "No? Maybe another time then" she sighed, unlocking her front door.

"I'll find you once my duties are done, I promise." Eva stepped away from her front door and joined him at the bottom of the steps.

"You know where I live, I finish work when the sun begins to set, I will be here at dusk. I'll wait for you." She gave him a warm smile and disappeared inside her home.

Lethaniel hovered around outside for a moment. It was so good to be back.

"Come on Seridox, let's go home."

Isabelle stepped out from the carriage with a handful of belongings and it immediately pulled off towards another part of Norisis to be cleaned, sorted, and unloaded. Under a grand platform held up by dozens of giant stone pillars, shielding the carriage park from the rain, was a fine carpet of gold leading to an arched entranceway. Guarded from left to right by Glyph Wielders and Thunderhoofs, Isabelle walked the carpet passed a fleet of fine carriages much like her own; The High Councillors of Virtue, the leaders of Xiondel City had already arrived. Isabelle was greeted by three familiar faces, waiting at the archway, dressed in similar, smart outfits that looked tight around the chests, but loose at the sleeves and waist.

"Lady Star Caller. It is so nice to see you. The leaders are assembling, we look forward to your words of wisdom." Isabelle bowed low to the men and addressed the one who had spoken.

"Thank you, Yespin Fquarign. It's a pleasure to see you too." He smiled and held her chin gently as she arose.

"No need to offer me such pleasantries, young lady, come you must be tired."

"I only grant my pleasantries to people I know who deserve them, High Councillor Truth," she replied, returning the smile, catching the eyes of the others behind him.

"I do believe you've met High Councillor Charity, Cillian Landris?"

"Yes, we have met before, briefly. Nice to see you, Cillian"

"And this is Taktard Erien, Ambition. To the best of my knowledge, you have not encountered each other before."

"No, not properly anyway, but I am sure we can be friends"

"These two will be filling you in on recent events and the current situation. I am sure you have an idea already about what is happening?" He put his arm around her as they walked inside through the palace doors.

"It's the Dovidians; they are frightened. Frightened of me," she clarified.

"You sound quite sure of yourself, my dear. Do you know something we do not?" Taktard and Cillian followed them into the main hall, where The Palace Guards closed the doors behind them.

"Please, Yespin, I wish to see all the letters you and the other twelve have received from the Dovidians, I also need access to Freya's records, she spoke in Ivulien many times, I'd like to read up on her experiences. If you could gather all of this together, I would be most grateful. I would like to work on it now, as soon as possible, if you don't mind?" She stopped at the end of the hallway; the three councillors had already come to a halt. "Does there seem to be a problem Councillors?" she asked, raising her eyebrows.

"No, no problem, Isabelle. I can see and hear a change in you. As vigilante as ever and you've barely even begun your reign as a Star Caller" praised Yespin, stepping forward, holding Isabelle's gaze with his own. "Get some sleep tonight, Miss Verano, tomorrow we will work on what you have requested." Isabelle considered this over a deep breath, nodded and pulled a smile. Led by Palace Guards to her rooms, she asked.

"Pandora?"

"Playful and well" said Cillian, unexpectedly, and Isabelle retired to her quarters.

Isabelle. Isabelle. Elaso fiin Isabelle. Darkness drowned her. A prison of stone engraved with markings enclosed her as thunderous storm arose from a viscous violet wind, a wind that took her, spiralling her senses into myriads of confusion, unable to tell if she was falling or soaring. A jolt broke through her back and awoke her from slumber, and she slipped into a bath of pain and discomfort. Her chest ached with every beat of her heart. *What did it all mean?* Fully awake, sitting up in a dark yet luxurious bedchamber, she could have sworn she had heard a voice during this last frantic episode, like someone was crying out her name. The light of the moon crept in through the open window, the breeze rolling in cooling off her hot skin, though sweat still ran down her forehead and trickled down her neck, making it uncomfortable to stay under her sheets any longer. She felt around the middle of her spine where the jolt had pulled tender muscles and winced when she felt a bruise. When confronting the mirror there was no mark upon her, no damage of any kind but the dream was frightfully real. The torment inside her mind, kept her on a wide couch in the corner, keeping her from the warmth of her bed. Isabelle sat alone in the dark, curled up, fighting a strong, pulsating headache circulating around the whispers of; *Elaso fiin, Isabelle.*

Chapter 13 - An Advisor and A Teacher

Everyone needs help sometimes, even Star Callers.

"Where are we going?" young Lucion asked.

"Don't pretend like you don't know. Your mother and I feel that it is time for you to start making your own choices; you may be young, but this is where your story begins," Thao replied, leading the boy down a set of steep, wooden steps. The early morning light found its way through the small side windows fitted in the wall, though it grew darker as they descended. "Your mother loves you son, as do I. We Norkrons are free to travel when we please. Free to read what we want, to express how we feel and free to love who we love. We also have the freedom to work, and to build, few realise this last freedom, it is often forgotten, but it is important for us to remember our place, our purpose. The lower classes who are rarely noticed, have jobs that must be done, cleaning our streets, cooking our meals, stabling our horses, making the blankets we sleep under, these people are important, it's easy to forget yourself when you've risen so high, easy to forget the things that really matter. Everyone who works deserves respect because they, in turn, help us do our jobs, they help me do mine. It has not been an easy journey, but together Norkron civilisation has succeeded in creating a stable economic system. I do what I do best, using what is available to me, but I could not craft such tools myself, I need an armourer for that. I enjoy coffee, I love your mothers cooking especially the way she bakes our bread, but have not the know how to do these things myself, or know how to grow the coffee beans that put me in a good mood. I Do you understand, Lucion?" The boy nodded. "The ability to choose, travel and socialise when and where we please after our duty is done is our freedom; as long as you give something back, society will repay you for your hard labour." When they reached the basement, Thao knelt in front of his son. "Freedom is not free; the price we pay for the illusion of freedom is high. Tell me, Lucion, what do you think I do?"

"You're a soldier." Thao smiled.

"I am more than just a soldier, my son," he replied, standing up, a giant compared to Lucion, who had to strain his neck to look up at his father. Thao disappeared into the darkness ahead. "I am going to present you with a choice, just like my father did for me at your age and his father before that, and so on, but only you can make this decision. If you need more time to make it, I'll understand. Remember what kind of world we live in." Lucion could not see his father, but he stared bravely at the darkness. "I am an Honour Guard, Lucion. More than just a soldier, more than one who just serves and protects. I am the leader of a unit of five hundred men; more are in training. We devote ourselves entirely to the protection of justice. It takes more than knowledge in combat, which can be quickly picked up; it takes a lifetime of discipline and devotion, to obey without question and to fight without the burden of fear or thoughts of retreat. Will you devote yourself? Will you become an Honour Guard? Will you wield the hammer, Lucion?" Thao unlocked and slid open a door on rails. Light burst into the room. Hung upon the walls were the helmets of former Honour Guards, arranged in order from oldest to most recent, each showing small signs of improvement and modification as time had progressed. Placed upon weapon racks were the tools of The Honour Guard. The weapons included war hammers, battle swords, wall shields and great spears. Large boxes contained smaller gear and accessories, sealed, and stacked one on top of the other. In the centre of this room, was a broad mannequin, fitted with Thao's famous Organix Armour. Below it rest The Hammer of Justice and The Shield of Protection, the finest suit of armour any soldier could ever hope to earn.

"Yes! I want to become an Honour Guard." The boy had clearly made his decision, and much sooner than Thao had expected.

Isabelle ran through the empty streets of Imrondel. The early morning was cold, and it would be hours before the citizens were up to start their day's work. She emerged into an older part of The Holy District. The buildings there here were bulky and square with a unique sense of history and age upon them. Finally, she stopped for a breath outside The Old Library, the largest such institution in this district. Its stone of bronze glowed in the thin light creeping through the clouds. Its windows were arched, tinted with a multitude of crystallised, sparkling colours. Catching her breath with deep gasps of air, she opened the tall door using its heavy handles. She let the door go once she entered, and it slammed shut behind her with a loud thud, disrupting the peaceful silence in the vast, empty space. Her steps echoed on the hard floor. The sun was now rising and shone through the windows, creating marvellous patterns of light upon the many thousands of books, stacked, and sorted upon the huge, wooden bookshelves. "Anyone here?" she called when she detected movement behind a bookshelf to her right. She caught a shadow coming closer to her and waited for it to confront her. As it approached, Isabelle realised it was not who she had expected. It was a boy, quite tall for his age, with an odd dress sense; nothing like the other boys of the city. He was holding a stack of books with one open in his hand. The Star Caller recognised this volume, *Knowing the Formulae*; she had read it herself when she was in her early stages of training. It covered the workings of Glyph; the material and content within its pages was far too complicated for a child of his age to comprehend, it even stifled her in some chapters

"Hello there. Can you tell me where I can find The Librarian?" she asked politely. He pointed to a spiral staircase leading up to the highest level "Thank you." Reaching the third floor, she walked from aisle to aisle, going through a process of elimination in her mind. Finally, she saw a trolley stacked with books waiting to be replaced on the shelves, about halfway down the aisle. A ladder was leaning on the shelf opposite. As she reached the trolley, she picked up one of the books and flicked it open. To her delight, it was exactly what she was looking for.

"An amorphous form. How it can rage and how it can ravage its prey so mercilessly. A giver of life, yet also a reaper of souls. Consuming everything that meets its touch until ash and dust fill the air. I did nothing but breathe and take in the inferno's fumes. Fire; the first true tool and weapon of mankind. The core power to everything on this planet, the breath of life. We should be thankful for its existence. The flame of Aries, the first son of our Star. A Celestial made of unquenchable fire. A ghost of the flame perhaps? As real as you and me, Aries' fire is alive. Its power, oh how I envy it, oh how I wish I did not want it. Maybe I'll learn this God's history, but only if I tread very carefully. I must visit The Amber Islands."

Note of the Ninth Star Caller - Melisa Nightsky

"Melisa was a poetic one, wasn't she? Extraordinary indeed; a late bloomer when it came to Glyph and a hard mind to understand, but she had the gift of an artistic streak, just as you do..." began the man opposite her, holding a heavy stack of books as he balanced atop the ladder. "They called her The Illusionist from the age of fourteen when she tricked a crowd of people into thinking day was night and night was the day, all with a cast of her own design that she called a Solar Flare. Ironic that she had the last name of Nightsky; often life is stranger than fantasy." He put the volumes back on the correct shelf, slotting them in neatly one at a time. He wore small glasses and dressed like a gentleman in well fitted clothes, suitable for one so wise and educated as himself. He was much older than Isabelle; old enough to be her father in fact, but he was not frail, he still had a strong back, bright eyes, a full head of hair, a wealth of experience with a variety of cultures and an intellect not to be underestimated. "You don't look well, Isabelle, you're not eating; even a Star Caller must eat." She handed him the book as he came down the ladder; he pushed up his glasses and checked the spine. "No no no, this book belongs somewhere else, further down on aisle twenty-eight, I think. Fancy a stroll?" He stepped off the ladder in front of Isabelle, who was just a little shorter than him. They walked together through The Library, as The Librarian pushed the trolley while Isabelle followed and talked

"It's nice and quiet here today. How has work been lately?" she asked with genuine interest.

"Oh, it has been going very well. I look forward to each lecture; the children are always keen, and I try to help them as much as I can. Most of them are smart, though others need that little extra push on occasion. Unfortunately, the real lessons I want to give cannot be taught so easily, they must find those ones out for themselves. Mistakes are unavoidable and inevitable, sadly. I know! I was young once too you know." They arrived at the correct aisle of The Old Library. "No guards with you? Or are they waiting outside?" He began to scan for space for the book he held.

"There are no guards, Master Eran. I came here by myself." She knew this was a wrong move. Eran stopped his search for a moment.

"Isabelle! That is exactly what I am talking about, making your own mistakes. I guess one must learn somehow, though, I doubt you will be punished if you are found out; no one knows how to punish our Chosen, I believe. It's unheard of." He found the space and pushed the book into it. Now his attention was fully focused on The Star Caller. "I have been working all morning and I am in need of a refreshment I think you too could benefit from a drink to."

"Yes, actually, that would be great."

"Splendid, meet me downstairs; I have a few more books I need to fetch first. Tea? Or maybe something cold?"

"I was thinking some liquor would go down nicely," she joked, receiving a wry smile from Eran. "Tea will be fine, thank you, Master."

"The Honour Guard respects his fellow man, being stronger than and far superior to any other soldier or civilian who ever lived. His true power comes with restraint; never should an Honour Guard show dishonour in his ways. Should he demonstrate weakness, however, then he is no better than the enemies who attack and prey on the frail. The Honour Guard's true strength is reserved only for when it is necessary. Compared to the Norkron army we are few, but more than enough to make a difference on the outcome of ANY battle, no matter how hopeless it may seem at the time. When an Honour Guard looks on a war with fear, doubt, or uncertainty, then he is no real Honour Guard." Thao was giving Lucion his first lesson, sitting on a balcony overlooking the city of Imrondel. Having memorised fragments of the speech his own father had given him, he now passed this knowledge on to his son. Flocks of birds flew by in their hundreds, struggling against the wind. Thao and Lucion were in one of the towers of Norisis, a retreat intended for Honour Guards alone, a place where they could find peace and rest from duty. The boy leaned over the balcony and stared out across the fine view. The two had the same shaped shoulders, one of the traits Lucion had inherited from his father. He still had much growing to do, but he would reach his father's size eventually.

"When can I start fighting? When can I begin training?" he asked with enthusiasm.

"To be an Honour Guard, son, you need more than just proficiency with weaponry; it takes discipline, might and willpower to become one of us. One of the hardest lessons to learn is how to use your logic, how to acquire wisdom and access it when required. Most of the time, your intelligence is the key to overcoming your opponents, not the sword in your hand or the shield in the other. You wouldn't think it, but claiming victory comes mostly from outwitting your enemies, luring them into a position where you can exploit their weaknesses and exercise your own strengths. It's a far better tactic than resorting to pummelling your foe's face into the ground. But most of all, it takes courage to admit to your failings, to admit to making your own mistakes; that is the only way to improve. It's easy to wallow in self-pity, though by all means if the defeat is that great then let yourself go for a while, but always with the intention of arising anew with a fresh outlook. Understand, Lucion, that failure is an essential lesson and you must learn from it at every turn, instead of letting it defeat you. Not only must you grow strong on the outside, but on the inside as well. Become better than what you were before, evolve; be the great example. It is said from a Glyph Wielder's point of view that wisdom and intelligence overcome physical strength. This I believe is true, we strive for to have both."

"I am never going to fail. I will always win," vowed Lucion, admiring the skyline.

"I remember saying the same thing once. I know a man who hasn't fallen to the blade of another. People talk of his reputation all over this city. He is very skilled, but his time will come, and if he survives the outcome, he will wake up to the realisation that we all must fall in order rise."

"Could you defeat him?" This was an excellent question and one which certainly silenced Thao for a moment. Thinking it over, he assessed his chances should he ever have to battle against this man.

"It's hard to say, Lucion. Our styles are completely different. I guess he would win if we were set toe to toe, in a setting he is most comfortable with using swords, but in the thick of battle, commanded by your wits and raw instincts, no one topples your Dad." Grinned Thao, baring his teeth.

"What if you were to use your hammer, would you win then?"

"My hammer is only used when people really piss me off" he growled "It's best not to think about challenging or comparing yourself with your allies, Lucion, for they are the ones you should be able to depend on, who you should trust, and so they should be granted the very same treatment from us."

"Have you made mistakes?" Lucion was full of questions.

"Yes, I have, I've had to learn like everyone else. Our mistakes shape us into who we are; only my mistakes were... Unforgivable..." Lucion began to wonder. "Don't worry about that now, my boy; you will learn someday, you will taste the bitterness of defeat and the thrill of success. It's not easy, son, people have died to try to pass these tests, but not without purpose." Lucion did not understand this; his father noticed his confused expression. "If one should die during his training, it only shows us that he was not worthy to call himself an Honour Guard. It has happened before. It's a horrible way of filtering out the unworthy from the worthy, but such is the cost worth paying, for if the weak mingles with the strong on the field, the structure of your defence, shatters" he explained. His son once again looked out over the city, catching sight of the flock of birds, perching upon rooftops then diving down and flying into the streets below.

"Who defeated you?" Thao didn't want to answer this, for the answer would shake only dishearten him, for it was Thao's own father, who crushed him. Fortunately, Lucion didn't give him time to respond, relieving him of the responsibility. "Is there anyone stronger than The Honour Guards?" Thao looked down and nodded very slowly.

"Unfortunately, there are. Physical combat isn't advised against those who wield Omnio; standing toe to toe against a Wielder of this highly destructive craft is almost suicidal. The Glyph Wielders aside, Lethaniel has battered a handful of my Honour Guards in training. Mathias is another; he uses a lengthy polearm, if he were here, I would take you to him. Thankfully, they are ALL on our side. I suppose there are some in Quaith who might stand a chance, and a few warriors from Jureai, but not many. It's safe to say that The Honour Guards are the true soldiers of Equis."

Isabelle and Master Eran sat in the seating area of The Old Library, on the first floor. The seats were big and comfortable, made from leather which had been softened and stained with a shade of red wine. Warm rays of sunlight shone through the tall windowpanes. It was quiet throughout the halls, for it was still quite early in the morning. Eran prepared a silver tray while Isabelle spun around on her chair. Outside, the city began to stir; a few people strolled by, heading for work. A cat sat on the window ledge outside, casting its shadow inside, licking its furry paws. As The Librarian prepared the tea, he said:

"So, Isabelle, how may I be of assistance? It has been a while since I tutored or advised you. I gather you have been busy of late?" She stopped swinging around on her chair and steadied herself with her legs.

"I need your help Master, actually."

"You have lots of good people for that, my sweet girl, who am I compared to them?"

"You're a Master; the best there is, I do not care what others say, it's true. You are the only one who will understand me. Please, keep this between us. You probably think I'm acting like a child..." Eran put the tray down on the table set between them and poured Isabelle a glass.

"No, I don't think that; we all need help sometimes, even Star Callers. According to a good friend of mine, another Master, he says *'Sometimes all a person needs is to listen to themselves.'*

"I've heard that before, only sometimes I feel it necessary to share things with others, those I trust."

"I hope you like the tea; if you can guess where it's from Isabelle before you leave here, I will not only be impressed, but I'll put a star on your nose like I used to… Now, stop dancing around the subject, what seems to be the trouble?" He too sat down in his chair and got comfortable, ready to listen, ready to be of service. A squeak from a trolley's wheels rang out from somewhere deep within the maze of bookshelves; it was the boy from earlier, selecting some books, reading as he went.

"Eran, you spoke of Melisa Nightsky. She is many generations old, one of the finest of my line, yet you speak of her as if you tutored her yourself."

"Word spreads fast in Equis, this is something that has always been true, passing from one generation to the next. Through the same word I learnt what they are calling you: The Conductor. I hope you like it because it's something that has definitely stuck," he laughed.

"Yes, it is alright, I don't mind it. Makes me feel like I know a little about music, which of course I don't!" she said.

"It is important to document everything we know and everything we have learnt. As a human race it is vital to our growth; to understand the past is to understand the future. The Eldor understands this all too well. I've read everything there is to know about Melisa, I see no reason why we would not get on had we been born in the same era."

"Tell me more about Melisa please," Isabelle requested. Eran put his hands together and began to explain, holding back on asking his question. *Why did she want to know about Nightsky?*

"Melisa, the ninth Star Caller, also known as The Illusionist. She was a bright one, and she also did a little poetry in her spare time; it shows through in some of her accounts. When it came to learning about Glyph, she was a late bloomer and could not grasp it as easily as those before her. When she was able to manage it, however, without a primary source, something changed in her."

"What changed in her?" Isabelle asked, drinking from her glass, keeping the mystery of the tea's origin in the back of her mind.

"Nothing came of it; fortunately, the change was subtle. She lived out her days in peace, to the age of fifty-one, I think, or fifty-two. But if the circumstances had been different, maybe we would have seen another side to her." She looked at him in disbelief. "Yes, you must believe it Isabelle; even The Star Callers can be corrupted. Why wouldn't that be the case? You are trained to think that you are ideal, moulded into perfectionists, but in the end, we all are indeed a part of the same species, we all suffer, we all have vulnerabilities. You need the same things as any other girl of twenty-seven."

"Twenty-six, actually," Isabelle pouted.

"My apologies, my dear. I hope not to offend but you are unique, but ultimately no different to anyone else."

"Have any other Star Callers suffered? Have any broken the rules, or worse, rebelled?" she asked, knowing she would get a straight answer here; Eran had never lied to her. He thought about the question, as knowledgeable as he was it took him some time to gather his wisdom concerning The Star Callers.

"To my knowledge, no Star Caller has ever been known to break the rules or worse rebel, but not everything is written down. It's true that some had their faults, but if I recall correctly, they all served admirably and fulfilled their duties as leaders, as the mothers of Equis." Isabelle suddenly felt ill, as if she had dishonoured her line and all before her; she felt singled out and alienated. Eran looked at her troubled face and leant forward, a frown creasing his lined forehead as he raised his greying eyebrows "Between us, remember. I can't help you if you don't tell me what's really on your mind." He sat back and let her answer in her own time. Isabelle eventually spoke again, but it was not what he had expected her to say.

"Master, what are Visions? Where do they come from and why do I have them?" asked Isabelle, biting on one of her nails.

"A Star Caller's power doesn't just come from Glyph pearls. Star Callers are spiritually superior and much about them remains unknown to us. Part of being The Chosen is figuring out these things for yourself. The answers are in you. Visions, as far as we know, come only to Star Callers, though some people claim otherwise. Visions can be mistaken for dreams or nightmares; some find it hard to tell the difference at first, but the main difference is that a Vision is real. A Vision is a glimpse into the future or past. Star Callers can use this ability to see what's coming and act upon it, if necessary, to change the future. But you asked me why you have them and where they come from? No one truly knows the answers to these questions; we can only speculate. The *Stardust Ideology* is a good place to start, but the first step is defining it, as I just did. All one can do is use their knowledge to make an educated guess. Guess, experiment and then compare with what we do know, against things like our laws of nature. If your experiment disagrees with nature, it's wrong." Isabelle nodded her head as he spoke. "It's a mystery, my dear, that is a fact, but I am confident the answers will be revealed in time." It did not answer her question, but it gave her some comfort in a small way. Maybe her Visions of late were nightmares; maybe she still had time to act. "Have you had a Vision that forecasts an ill future? If so, what can we do?" Eran asked.

"I don't know but let me explain it to you first. It's quite peculiar." Before she could begin to explain, he interrupted her.

"Why don't you show me them?" he suggested.

"No! I can't do that, Master Eran."

"Why not? Didn't Freya teach you how?"

"She taught me how when I was nine, but that was a long time ago. I have only Vision Channelled once and it hurt. I don't know if I can control it. Don't make me do it," she pleaded.

"Of course I won't Isabelle, no one should be made to do anything they don't want. Vision Channelling, from what I am told, is dangerous to Star Callers who have not yet fully mastered it. Freya told me so herself, if you're not confident, keep it at bay."

"What did Freya say about it?"

"Remember the first time you felt that sudden surge of Glyph power run through you?"

"How could ever I forget that feeling, Master?"

"Imagine it again, but a hundred times stronger… Now, talk to me about your Visions. If you're not confident enough to Vision Channel, explain them to me as best you can."

Young boys stood on the soft earth, ordered into lines in the yard. They all wore woven helmets and thin, wooden vests held together with thick corks. Armed with wooden canes and small, round shields, an older supervisor inspected the boys, patrolling up and down the ranks, showing the young lads how to hold the training sticks and shield effectively, before giving the word to fight after a short demonstration.

"We train in The Military District, a section cordoned off from the public. We do this for psychological purposes, to preserve a good morale. The less our good citizens see of our forces, the better. Units of soldiers marching the streets, drums up tension so we're strict with keeping our men inside this district as best we can." Thao explained to Lucion watching the boys fight amongst themselves.

"Who would want to attack us?" asked Lucion, raising an intelligent question. Thao moved his son away from the training yards as he answered.

"You'd be surprised, the biggest threat usually comes from within, rather than the outside. If Imrondel City or Krondathia were to fall, it would most certainly break from the inside first, which is why it is important to treat your people with respect. History has taught us this lesson; learn from our history and you will be prepared for the future. Even Honour Guards depend on others around them, Lucion; everyone has a place and a job to do, not everyone should be a soldier, not everyone can be soldiers, this is not a shameful admittance, it's important to show people the respect they deserve, always remember that."

"Even if it's a tax collector?" Thao grinned.

"Especially if it's a tax collector."

"Mother hates them."

"Yes, yes she does" chuckled Thao.

"Did you practice here?"

"Yes, I trained here intensely for years. I trained with your grandfather; he taught me nearly all there was to know about fighting. Fighting in the wind, under the heat of the sun, in the thick pouring rain and the freezing cold, he was always the stronger man. I never thought I would surpass him. He watched me fight the strongest of soldiers, he was there every time I got knocked down and beaten to the floor," Thao recalled, staring at a patch of dirt on the floor, remembering how it taste and how much blood he spat into it.

"You fought your own father?" Thao nodded and Lucion's face turned glum.

"It will be the same for you…" Thao said, resting a hand on his son's shoulder, "But not for a long time yet."

"I have been having these Visions for some time now. They don't come every night, but after each one, it gets worse. I don't know what they mean; whether they are linked or if they are all pieces in some bigger picture. I am afraid of talking to The Eldor, I am afraid of saying anything to anyone because if the message is dire, I could be responsible for a widespread panic. Yet I can't ignore it, it could be important."

"I will check The Star Caller records again, to see if any others before you have experienced what you have, though your Visions do seem unusual," Eran admitted. He topped up Isabelle's glass and his own. The tea was hot and very refreshing, but still, she could not pinpoint where it had come from.

"What do you think the Vision is, Master?"

"I don't know yet; it's open to interpretation, but I will look into it. My advice would be to try to see it through. Next time you are in there, stay there, for as long as you can. Maybe something more will be revealed. Train yourself to remain in your dreams. I have plenty of books on how it can be done."

"There is something else. '*Elaso fiin*'. What does '*elaso fiin*' mean, Eran?" she asked, slowly drinking her tea. The elderly man went silent. His face seemed to slip into shadow as he stared at her. These words had triggered something in his memory, something dreadful, it was in his eyes. He eventually spoke:

"*Elaso fiin... Elaso fiin...* Freya spoke these words. The language is old, much older than Englathin that most of the priests speak today. I mean, there are only a few of places I have seen it written before, and those were the old ruins Hallow dug up in Fevoriel all those centuries ago. Only some can speak it, and when I say some, I really do mean only a mere handful. It's an impossible language of symbols and signs, it takes years to master. I have also discovered it when attempting to read it in The Books of the Early Past."

"The Books of the Early Past...What does it mean, Master? I need to know," there was a hint of desperate urgency in her voice. Eran raised his eyes and told her what it meant.

"It means '*Find me*'." A chill ran through her; someone was reaching out to her, someone speaking an ancient language was asking her to come forth through her dreams. She stood up.

"You said Freya said the same words?"

"Before I say anything more, you must promise me you will remain calm." She nodded but did not promise anything. "Freya spoke those same words to me both before and after I returned from an... Endeavour... Though her state of mind was broken, far beyond repair by the time I returned to her. Her mind was ruined; she barely knew who I was when I walked into the room and sat with her for the final time. To see someone you love suffering so much that they cease to breathe... I will never forget. You must remain in control of your thoughts, Isabelle. Remain true to yourself."

"The Readers know this language; Where are they now?"

"They are in Xiondel City." Isabelle cursed silently. "Beware; The Readers are indeed knowledgeable, but they also use their gifts without restraint. They will tell you things that maybe you were better off not knowing. I think you should consider other options before seeking out their help. There is no guarantee that they will answer you; no one has gone before them twice; it is against our laws. You should know this," Eran said frantically, walking away, not wishing to continue this conversation any further.

"Master?" called Isabelle.

"I have a friend in Xiondel; you may remember him, he is a Master, a man who I trust entirely. His name is Atheriax, Professor Caleb Atheriax. He specialises in a range of topics, including historical, architectural and prophecy studies. He has the finest record on paper when it comes to educational accomplishments. Before you run off to The Chronicle House to confront The Readers, risking yourself in more ways than I can't even begin to comprehend, I suggest you pay him a visit first."

"I remember him. He attended some of my demonstrations when I was a teenager, he went over several of his books with me. Haven't seen him properly since." Isabelle felt like she had touched a nerve in Eran earlier on by mentioning The Readers. "Is he smarter than you, Master?" Her question was a little childish and easy to answer for The Librarian.

"His list of qualifications surpasses my own, a mere list can't measure intelligence, but it's a very good indicator of one's intellect but, what he sees is far beyond me" Eran said, mulling his answer.

"I can't picture anyone silencing you in a debate Eran. Caleb can't be more intelligent than my favourite librarian" she smiled, putting a hand on his shoulder.

"You are too kind Isabelle. If Atheriax is in the city, corner him, arrange a meeting, show no mercy, because I guarantee you he'll be busy, with a schedule like his, you need to be two people, I don't know how he does it."

"Master, thank you," she smiled, walking next to him.

"I wish I could be of further help. Please, be careful with what you say from here on in, share this information only with those you trust. Wherever you go, whoever you meet, be careful; even around The Readers if you ever meet them again" he warned with a sympathetic touch.

"There is more than just '*elaso fiin*' but I cannot phrase it." Isabelle proceeded to the bookshelves, her heels echoing with every step. Engraved on a beautiful golden plate, at the top, were the words *Omnio Glaphiar Sphere A - Z*. She looked around the shelf, investigating a noise and saw the young boy reading another advanced book, another one that Isabelle had struggled with during her training. Eran directed her away, so the boy could be in peace. "What is his name, Master? How is he reading that book? I barely understood it," she asked hastily.

"Easy, my child, his name is Adarmier, one of my young students," he answered, almost at a whisper.

"He has a mild Glyph scent; I became aware of it when I entered the building, but at first I figured it was coming from another Glyph Wielder in the area. Is he a…?"

"Yes, is it so hard to believe?" Eran interrupted with a question. "He's the youngest yet, I think. Younger than you, I believe, when you first started learning and younger than one of your predecessors who held the record for a while… Blast! What was her name again… Coppelia! That's it, Coppelia Velen, the one who died tragically at eighteen. So gifted for her age it was unheard of, experimenting on The Stardust Ideology, following up on Hackney Beau's research, if I remember correctly."

"Burned by her own flame is what I read, Master Eran," said Isabelle, while he encouraged her to read the accounts written by Ursula Cerrin, Coppelia's successor.

"Adarmier is much younger than Coppelia was when she experienced her first surge."

"Master, it can be dangerous for a boy of his age to be learning about Glyph in this environment. How did you get the approval from Gaia?" She then looked at the man as he drew a devious grin. "Master…" she sighed, a little disappointed, shaking her head.

"That makes two of us who have broken a few rules. Our mistakes will hopefully remain hidden; we're all guilty of something Isabelle. One day I will take him to Gaia, this I promise. In that academy Adarmier Elpin will shine, he is already capable. I am confident in his abilities. I've seen what he can do; he can already use the Omnio spheres without a primary source element close by. He will break new ground," he predicted; his words reflected pride in his student, but Isabelle thought only of the negative side, of what could happen to him or what he could become should he become dependent on the Omnio.

"While in training to become a Blessed, you run the risk of becoming Cursed. Keep an eye on him, if he shows any symptoms. You will come to me at the earliest time" said Isabelle, pressing the seriousness of the matter.

"Tell me, my girl, how are your own skills progressing?" he asked, diverting the attention away from the boy. They stopped walking and Isabelle gave him a look, sensing a doubt in his tone.

"I have some questions about Glyph. Questions that I thought had been answered, but I was wrong, and they need revising from a book you have in your possession. Maybe you can help me?"

"I am sorry to interrupt, but my drink has gone cold. Would you be so kind?" He held out his glass. She nodded kindly and smiled at the test, gripping the tumbler between her index finger and thumb, all the while maintaining eye contact with Master Eran. Her eyes shone green as the Glyph within her stirred, focused in the tips of her fingers and the tea, grew hotter. She blew away the steam before releasing her hand and took a step back, her eyes returning to their normal state of pale green. "Ah, that's better" said Eran taking a sip. "I've heard it's easier to blow fire, tear down a bridge or raise water

276

rather than do something useful. You have great control over your gift; I hope you keep it that way." She did not react; her mind was focused on something else.

"The book, Master; where is it? I want to see it."

"Long ago, before the time of the first great Star Caller, Regina Corah, the one who awoke the twelve sleeping Celestials, Equis was an extremely violent place. Mankind was divided into six factions: Liarath, Desaru, Renasark, Muligoro, Dovidian and we Norkrons. Each tribe sought power, wealth and dominion over the world. Chaos and confusion reigned, fuelling endless grief and constant misery. Battles raged, thousands died every day, whether by the sword or the brutal aftermath of war. The race for conquest was relentless. When the clash of swords was finally silenced, the warlords dreamt up new ways of destroying one another; they began targeting the innocent, usually by poisoning lakes and rivers, attacking farms and cutting off their fresh food supplies. This, Lucion, is a piece of history most prefer to forget. Evidence of The Never-Ending War can be found in any library. Master Eran is the man to find if you seek a thorough understanding; he will tutor you as he has helped teach The Star Callers, Freya Delmesca and our current Chosen, Isabelle Verano. He also holds lectures; you will one day attend them three times a week. You must learn about the ages Equis has lived through, the first being The Age of Six, after which came The Time of the Warlords." Lucion was handed an open book by his father; it depicted the tribesman of the six factions, fighting on an open plain, driving swords and spearheads into one another, spilling buckets of blood over themselves and the earth beneath their feet. They were met with horses and fire; arrows flew into the air and struck down anything in their way. "The wars did eventually end; only after entire generations had been lost, did hope reappear. Even the blood thirsty lose their taste for battle and the tribes gave up their crusades for domination. I do not believe that account of the historians; I believe that the tribes grew fearful of The Honour Guards' wrath and declared a truce once they knew they were outmatched. Global law and order were born soon after the rise of The Guard. We fought many battles and triumphed each time, winning the land for the Norkron race. Finally, we were able to move forward in peace." Thao and Lucion stood in front of a great painting, depicting the end of that brutal second age. The Honour Guard leader of the time, who led the final charge had just won the final battle upon The Plains of Xethark, right outside Xiondel City. This leader of the legion held up a flag above a heap of fallen enemy corpses, with a look of utter glory on his tired, battle-scarred face. His remaining Honour Guards walked upon the bodies and raised their arms high, celebrating one of the most famous victories in Norkron history.

"What happened after that?" Thao sat on a bench behind his son and answered the question.

"The tribes surrendered, and a peace treaty was signed. Men became equal and the fighting ceased. Incredible really; the day before they were ready to slice each other up, and before they knew it, the signature was scribbled on a line and the shattered tribes dropped their swords and picked up shovels, ready to rebuild. Not all converted to the Norkron tribe; some opted to remain independent. This was a new age of freedom, an age of construction and formation, making up for all those centuries lost to the carnage. It was also an age of discovery. The Awakening Ages followed The Time of the Warlords. Regina was born in direct accordance with the predictions of Hallow, who was deemed crazy until the event; he was half-mad, but he knew his archaeology. Regina brought faith to the world in the form of Starillia, and raised each Celestial Soul from first to last, travelling the world to find their secluded shrines. Starillia bound us Norkrons together; the religion united us from the foundations laid by that of The Honour Guards." Thao stood up, taking a break from his lecture, and having a drink before continuing. "Remember the ones who chose to remain independent? While the Norkrons were praying and worshipping spiritual beings living in an ethereal plane, the other tribe were re-constructing their own civilisation. They forged themselves into a position of power to negotiate with the west. A conflict now would undermine our progress and compromise our enlightenment, so we learned to draw peace instead of the sword, learned to live together. They kept their lands and birthed their own culture taking up sanctuary in the eastern lands that we now call Ivulien. Today their people survive as the Dovidians."

Adarmier was reading a book in complete silence by the window. He occasionally stared out to the streets, deep in thought. Meanwhile, Eran and Isabelle patrolled The Old Library together. The Master led her to his quarters, hidden behind a plain, oaken door, with his name engraved in gold upon a plaque fixed to its centre. The room was filled with shelves, each stacked to the rim with books. It was untidy; evidently, he had been working on something important; either that or he was simply an untidy person. Isabelle noticed piles upon piles of old papers and open books upon his desks; none of it looked particularly interesting to her, just a myriad of words. It reminded her somewhat of her own cabin back on The Zodias Island, only this room made her own look organised. They stepped inside and Eran sat down behind his desk.

"Close the door, would you?" She shut it quietly and turned around, standing opposite him. Approaching a shelf at random, she picked up one of the many books with the name Tudor on the spine.

"I thought these were all destroyed," she observed, picking up another and flipping through it.

"Not all of them. Sometimes Tudor's works are the only words I can trust in moments of uncertainty" Isabelle strained her forehead but did not say anything in response. "I would appreciate it if you could forget you have seen his works here today. I told our Sire all the copies were destroyed. People do not like what he writes; they find it offensive, and I need to find better hiding places."

"He writes about reality," protested Isabelle.

"People would rather believe in a fairy tale than the harsh truth; just one of our species' many failings. However, the truth can be damaging to ill-prepared minds."

"Yet it's fine to lend materials to Adarmier?"

"The boy can handle the truth. He would rather that than a lie." Isabelle nodded in response and placed Tudor's books back in place. She had to remind herself why she was now standing in the office; time was limited, and she had to be getting back soon.

"Well, do you have it or not?" she asked, folding her arms.

"First tell me how," the Master insisted. Isabelle hung in the doorway, tapping the back of her heels on the floor; he wanted to know how she had obtained it, she guessed; there was no point in lying, so she told him everything.

"It wasn't guarded. They wanted it to be, but there was a changeover after we left the island. It was locked away in one of our supply carts. One night I took it when everyone was asleep. No one saw me, besides a horse. I replaced it with a rock to imitate its weight until the day came when I returned it. I am no thief, but if I wanted to, I could have kept it." His silence suggested that he was not quite as amused by her actions as she was; maybe she had gone too far and misjudged his tolerance. She could see this was a serious matter and so changed her tone of voice, clearing her throat. "To my knowledge, Hallow Diases, unearthed FIVE books from certain burial sites in Fevoriel hundreds of years ago. The Eldor, our Sire has four in his possession; I have seen them with my own eyes. He has always claimed that the other was lost, unaccounted for, likely destroyed with time, but he had it in his possession all along," she spoke defensively ready to raise her voice further should Eran argue with her. Yet he didn't; he continued to listen, understanding the point she was making. "He lied to us, Eran. He lied to me, to you, to every man, woman and child in Krondathia and that's not the worst part. The real question is WHY? Why would he lie about it?" Isabelle wished The Eldor was here right now when taking a breath; she would get the answers from him. She sighed and ran her fingers over her forehead, posing another question before Master Eran could say anything. "Are there any more of these books?" Eran sat staring at her face, unable to answer right away. She placed her hands down onto his table as if she wasn't being assertive "That book contains something, something that he doesn't want us to see. He wanted it hidden for a reason, Master, and I don't think it was just so he could boast to his friends that he had collected the whole set." Eran smiled softly at his young student's wisdom. "You know, don't you? You know the reason why! Are you going to tell me, Master?" He cradled his face in his hands and sighed.

"Why don't you tell me? You know too whether you realise it or not. You read it on the road, in the dark, with a candle nearby, when the moon was high," he guessed correctly. He did know her well after all. Isabelle pulled up a seat and patiently waited for the librarian to explain, but he just sat there, eyes fixed on hers.

"Master, I have made many journeys and seen many things but I…"

"You've journeyed, have you?!" Eran quickly butted in, his face a picture of shock. "What do you know of journeys? The world we live in can be read about, studied, talked about, even destroyed, but few have really made a journey and learned just how harsh the laws of the land can be. What lies beyond our roads and the hidden paths you've travelled is nothing compared to what is really out there! The things you've seen and the experiences you have gained are meaningless in comparison to those who have really journeyed." He looked to his right, at a big square map of the world of Equis. "There is much yet to be discovered. You are an unbalanced Star Caller Isabelle, you are reckless and rightly so, you are a mere student in the eyes of many, you fear this, you fear this but you should not, for we all are students in the eyes of someone, people we idolise, people we admire. Discovery is a fearful and often damaging process, the question is not why, it's how much? How much is the cost of knowledge?" She sat silently for a while, sulking like a child having just been shouted at.

"My faith has been shaken, but I believe it will see me through the darkest of days. If you've learnt something, I demand you tell you me what you know. Show me the book" she insisted.

"It arrived yesterday, late at night. An Honour Guard delivered it. I was as shocked as you when I learned that all five books had been accounted for, but I was sworn to secrecy. Understand, Isabelle, that I am hesitant about who I voice my discoveries to, there are some things that people simply should not know until materials are thoroughly understood. Meddling with such powers can get people killed. We have done terrible things to each other when poisoned with ignorance. Some myths should remain myths, no matter how true they might be."

"Who wrote The Books of the Early Past? I found our language, Englathin, contained within."

"It's open to speculation, but some say the first explorers or arguably our predecessors wrote them. As for the documents in Englathin, there are many languages that are lost and passed on with the passage of time. Englathin isn't entirely ours; it's derived from another language, and that one from another, and so forth. Maybe we learnt it and adopted it for ourselves. Time is a killer, but it can mend things in such ways that we finish the puzzle ourselves, even if it is incorrect," he explained cryptically. Isabelle nodding along. The great explorers Hallow and his followers had discovered The Books of the Early Past, written by the first explorers, who had spoken mainly Englathin, and the Norkrons had later adopted it as their language. But something else gnawed at her, the art of Glyph. "I am glad you came, Isabelle, talking to you has actually educated me a little. All will become clear in due course, especially if a man or woman hungry for answers is on the trail" said Eran.

"Master, can I see it?"

He stood and moved around behind her. "Sorry, could you give me a hand, please?" Isabelle got up from her seat and moved the heavy chair in the corner. Eran removed the discreetly cut patch of red carpet and handed it to her. He pulled away some wooden boards and there it was! Together they lifted it out and placed it gently on the desk.

Thao opened the door to his house and let Lucion run inside and up to his room. He left the door open for the breeze to come in and Thao grabbed an apple from a wooden bowl on the table. Next to it lay a beautiful bouquet of flowers. Lena silently shuffled downstairs in a blanket.

"I didn't hear you leave, but I heard you last night; since when do you talk in your sleep?"

"I'll ask myself next time my head hits the pillow" he said, taking a bite.

"How did it go today?" Thao finished chewing a mouthful and replied:

"He has made his decision." She shuffled on her chair, using the blanket to cover herself further.

"So soon? What if he changes his mind?" Her voice was filled with concern for their son.

"I don't think he will change his mind, Lena. See for yourself..." Thao stepped aside and pointed outside to the interior courtyard. Lucion was out there, charging around swinging a wooden sword, pretending he was a great hero, slaying winged demons by the dozen. Thao raised an eyebrow as he watched the child play ferociously. "What's wrong, Lena?" She was finding it hard to swallow the truth.

"Don't hurt him, don't make him hate you," she warned.

"He will hate me, at least for a while. That's how it usually works. I hated my father for a time when he gave me my first scar. Don't worry, I will go easy, but he'll have to learn. Would you rather it be by my hand or that of someone without mercy?" Lena lowered her face; Thao thought she would protest Lucion's decision, but she didn't, instead, she raised her head with a smile.

"Make sure he doesn't hurt you! I couldn't take it if you got hurt again, not like last time." Thao folded his arm with a grimace and tried not to think back to that incident.

"I will teach him everything there is to know, Lena."

"No Thao...WE will teach him everything there is to know. I am his mother and he will live a life of joy as well as a life of honour." How Thao loved this woman dearly.

"This book is ancient, Isabelle. One of the five Books of the Early Past. The Eldor kept it hidden for a reason. It dates back to before The Awakening Ages, well before the first Chosen, Regina Corah. Its writings speak of the finding of the first ruins of our ancestors, the discovery of their temples and the ones who unearthed it all, the ones who set out on their great journey of discovery;

Hallow and his disciples," Eran spoke clearly, studying the book intently. Isabelle did the same, saving any questions for later. For the time being, she let the man speak. "This book documents the discovery of the Omnio Glaphiar Spheres, including speculation about how they work, how to use them efficiently and what types exist. It's ALL here, written in code, in the same way a magician keeps note of his parlour tricks in case someone gets hold of his notebook. It also speaks to us of the twelve; our Celestials."

The Books of the Early Past
Atlas
Luminaries
Biological Organisms
The Ancestor's Temples
Ultimas

They both leant over the book, drawn in by its archaic aura. The volume was large, heavy, bound with a rigid front cover made of rock. The spine was soft and spongy, the paper thicker than usual sourced from elderly trees. An engraved marking upon the cover read *Ultimas*. The symbol looked sinister and triggered a reminder of her Visions.

"What about the warnings, Master? Many accounts that have originated from knowledgeable men, even some of Hallows own disciples, have warned us about the use of Glyph. I was told that it was a gift; if one was able to wield it with skill and confidence, he or she was a Blessed One, with a strong mind and spirit." Eran licked the tip of his finger, keeping his eyes on the book and turning over one of its pages. There he saw one such account, a sincere warning, written in dark red ink springing up off the page. As always, he prioritised logical thinking above all else.

"Some say that Glyph can have a reverse effect on people, giving the wearer unprecedented, unrestrained abilities, turning a blessing into an addictive curse from which you cannot escape. This is not a fairy-tale, Isabelle, this has happened before. We sometimes refer to Glyph Wielders as *Blessed Ones* or the *Blessed*, but we also have a name for the other ones, the ones who turn out wrong, those who crave damage, taking pleasure from the destruction of others: *Cursed Ones*," he explained and Isabelle nodded, recounting some of the stories she had encountered. "The Cursed Ones are spread across our historical timeline, each one suffering the same fate as the last, long before they became too strong to handle and control. Understand that if The Cursed are given enough time to manifest their power, then one can only assume that even a high-ranking Wielder, or even a Star Caller for that matter, might find it extremely difficult to overcome them if they were opposed. Once one becomes Cursed there is no cure; the sentence of death is the only option we have. But do remember, Isabelle, that men fear what they don't understand and for a long time we knew little; we found everything so quickly after the book of Atlas was studied and revealed to us the signs. It's only natural that many in this period became fearful, drawing wild, uneducated speculations regarding Glyph and The Celestial Souls."

"Are The Cursed stronger than The Blessed?" Isabelle asked bluntly. Blinking once very slowly, she turned her head to Eran after a few seconds passed without an answer. She looked back at the book, realising that he didn't know. "Then what about this part?" She pointed to a passage. "The Celestials? What about the twelve Regina raised from their sleep? What does this mean, Master?" The physical passage looked as disturbing as its contents; the sentences were written in black, scribbled ink like a madman had scratched it down, his last message to the world before meeting his fate. Eran read it using a magnifying glass:

"In the face of rejuvenated Deities, we are nothing but a rotting compost farm of shadows, blood and bone. Deluded as we are, we've fooled ourselves into believing we are divine. What faiths we have created to consolidate our fears of death are lies. Death is inescapable, inevitable, forever constant and our time is coming to an end. Those who we perceive as our saviours are our destroyers. No one will survive the reckoning to come, not even our holy judges, for even they await certain destruction at the hands of the shattered shells they once inhabited."

The Librarian stood up straight, taking a deep breath. Isabelle did the same, making eye contact with him. Eran removed his glasses and pinched the top of his nose. Even the Master, renowned for his historical knowledge, found it hard to fathom the message scribbled across the page. He would need more time alone to research the entire book.

"Master…What does that mean? Why is this book full of warnings and predictions of danger? I think you know but you don't want to tell me. Do you?"

He closed the book and threw a blanket over it, just in case someone decided to walk in, then sat down and began to speak his mind. "When The Celestials were raised from their shrines, Regina gave to the world a wonderful thing. Not only did she feed us the imagination of Starillia, giving the Norkron race a path, she gave us the comfort of another world; the idea that when you die, it is not the end, life continues in another way. She gave us hope and belief in those harsh times. She eliminated fear and brought our kind together, she created the faith," he stated, tapping the table with his fingertips, thinking carefully about his next sentence. "Isabelle, I think it would be wise if you kept this knowledge between us. For now, at least."

"What? Master, the people have a right to know, this book is littered with warnings!"

"No! You have a right to know, and now you do. That's the way it should stay," Eran insisted seriously, pointing at her as he spoke.

"But why?"

"Let's focus on what we know, for now, let's break it down." He began to list off the facts, using his fingers to tick off his points one at a time. "No one else in this world can call upon the Celestials; if what this book says is true, then only you can bring about the devastation it predicts. Should you sit back and decide not to Star Call, then they will remain forever stuck in their ethereal plain." Isabelle understood the point being made; "A sword was only as dangerous as the wielder my Chosen, keep the weapon sheathed, and it cannot harm anyone. The last time you Star Called? How did the Celestial react? Did the entity behave malevolently?"

"I didn't detect anything out of the ordinary, Master, Libra was calm" replied Isabelle. Eran was already in the process of preparing another point.

"What if this writing belongs to a faithless believer? A madman, or worse yet, a Cursed One undergoing his inevitable, declining transformation? You are The Chosen; only YOU have the ability to pull The Celestials into our plain, no one else can wield such powers. What you do with your gifts is up to you." His arguments all made sense to her, taking the weight off her mind. "If you feel that history should be rewritten, if you feel that changing our belief so drastically in one afternoon is the right course of action, then who am I to tell The Chosen otherwise? If that is indeed your decision, then so be it. But I beg you Isabelle, be patient, give us time to discover the truth. We have achieved peace amongst ourselves. We have a functioning world and a great society thanks to your line. Would you risk its collapse when we are so close to finding paradise in Equis, because of what this old book says so, for what this crazed man or woman has scribbled down?" They sat quietly together until she stood up. "I am all for the truth, Isabelle, but to disclose all we know about our Celestials at the whim of a madman would be irrational. Should more evidence be given to these claims I will gladly look further into them and inform you."

"The Eldor says, that '*to understand the past is to understand our future.*' One day it may be too late to go back on what we've done. One day I feel that we all will be forgiven for our mistakes. I can't make mistakes. You said it yourself; I have this ability to Star Call and I do so at my own accord." Eran said nothing. Isabelle relaxed her neck, rubbing it with her hand

"Thank you, Master, you have been most helpful, but now I must be getting back before anyone discovers my absence." She opened the door, but before it closed again, she turned back one last time. "I trust your words, Master Eran. What is it you told me all those years ago? You said it often to me most of all, whenever I was under immense pressure."

"That one day, all of us will rest eternally. Life is nothing more than a trial to be fulfilled, once that is done, we slip away, never to return," he reminded her. Isabelle smiled, setting foot out of the door, finally feeling ready to hazard a guess.

"It's Cuethen, isn't it? The tea comes from Cuether." Eran smiled back and corrected her:

"Livale, actually." He still had one final warning for her. "Isabelle, please put all of this behind you and think about it at the opportune moment. You have the present to think about now, stay focused on those who walk amongst you. Once we decipher more of the book, maybe then you can make an educated decision on what to do. The leaders are gathering as we speak, and you are to be there on The Eldor's behalf. Your words must be convincing, and your mind cannot be pondering over ancient texts and old prophecies. I will dig deeper, for now, let me worry about this. We will talk again." She left The Old Library at some pace; she had to get back to her quarters in The Palace as quickly as she could. The morning was coming to an end and she had work to do.

Chapter 14 - The Red Dance Partner

Free time is more valuable to the hard-working than the lazy.

Later that afternoon.

Lethaniel stirred in his bed; he was still half asleep as he rolled over, taking the sheet with him. His place was untidy, uncared for, with his clothes flung everywhere and his few plants turning a pale, dry brown. A soft breeze drifted into his room, while a thin light from the outside world crept its way in through the balcony doors. He savoured those last few moments in bed before eventually pulling himself out, dragging his feet across the floor, catching his foot on the tray of silver pots and plates he had used the night before. His body was hard and toned, though his skin could have used some sunlight; it lacked its usual healthy glow. There wasn't much he could do; every day he was required to wear a uniform or his armour, both of which shut out the sun's warming stare. He had little fat on him; his figure was well-built yet lean. He lacked the honed physique of Thao, who was loaded with muscle and might but made up for this with his swordsmanship. He picked up his clothes in a feeble attempt to tidy his room, throwing them on his bed, stubbing his toe on a tray in the process, and then resigning himself to the disorder. Finding a jug of water on the floor, he pushed opened his balcony doors and stepped outside, half-naked in the open air. Around his neck was a loose string necklace, at the end of which, draped over his torso, hung the wooden carving of a fierce feline. Taking a large gulp of stale water, he washed it around his mouth and spat the dregs out over the edge of the ledge. Lethaniel stretched until he heard that familiar click from his left shoulder, then stretched the other side. His house looked out upon a rich estate full of tall houses with fine, black rooftops and white stone architecture. All housing areas in the city had similar features, though some expressed an element of individuality in their own fashion. Lethaniel's house was the last on that road, occupying the highest lot on the slope. Of all the dwellings in the area, his was the most run-down and neglected; it could have done with a fresh coat of paint, the windows on both levels needed a good cleaning and the patio had become so overgrown with weeds that it looked like a lawn at first glance. His other house, in Xiondel, was much the same; left alone as if abandoned, with few possessions inside, mainly due to the risk of gang-related theft rampant in that city. Such problems, however, did not exist in Imrondel, so it was safe to enjoy the pleasure of possessions both valuable and sentimental. Lethaniel yawned as he saw a familiar looking man a few houses down, on the right-hand side of the brick road, enjoying a morning smoke. He caught the man's eye and acknowledged his presence by holding up his water jug. The man took a drag from a small roll-up of weed, flicking the remains over the edge of his own balcony, and waving back. Lethaniel signalled for two minutes with his fingers and retreated inside his dark, unorganised room. He grabbed and threw on some warm clothes, the first he could get his hands on, again stubbing his toe on the tray, which he really should have moved. Leaving his house, he met up with his friend down the road, who strolled outside cheerfully as his famous neighbour approached. He offered Lethaniel a smoke, but it was refused. The young man looked roughly the same age as The General, though at that moment a little scruffier and lot more hung-over.

"Lex," nodded Lethaniel.

"How are things going? I saw you get back last night with Seridox. It must've been late; not like you to sleep way into the afternoon, people like us have usually done more in the early hours of the morning than others do in a full day."

"Sometimes I catch a break Alexius."

"In your current line of work? Hah! I hardly see you anymore, and what little word you do send my way is only bloody boring military talk, full of hidden agendas and shit," grumbled Alexius half serious, scanning his friend from head to toe, awaiting an explanation.

"Don't complain; you know what I do, some things I can't talk about to anyone, not even assholes like you who I go way back with."

"I'm just saying that you could make my job a lot easier if you let me in on some of your shadowy missions. I have a job too, ya know, believe it or not."

"I'm surprised you were able to get up in the morning and get there on time," laughed Lethaniel, rolling up his sleeves. "Did you walk into the interview eating or smoking?"

"Both!" chuckled Alexius "I'm the best there is, and you know it. I'm your go-to guy, am I not?"

"That you are, but you know how secrecy works Lex."

"We are all on the same side, *General Presian.* By the way, congratulations on that promotion; does this mean I have to call you General or Sir from now on?" he laughed.

"Only when my friends are around, make me look good with a salute to go with it…" groaned Lethaniel, barely hiding how glad he was to be back in such good company after so long apart. "Where are we going?"

"Thought you might want a late breakfast. I know this great place in The Canalside; you'll love it. Opened just last year, great food, great drinks and this one waitress who has a great ass! You have to see it, it's mesmerising."

"I get it, Lex, calm down."

"I'm buying of course; I know you're low on funds." Lethaniel laughed at the sarcastic comment and they continued down the wide road. "I'm not calling you General and saluting, you only get one, try to make me do both in one sitting and our friendship is over."

"You'll do what you're told asshole"

"I'll refuse?"

"Then I'll put you on potatoe peeling duty for a month."

Isabelle was exhausted from a significant lack of sleep and nutrition. She had spent half the morning tutoring young Glyph Wielders and researching timelines from the histories in her spare time, refreshing her memory on Hallow Diases and his most famous discoveries. Going against Master Eran's advice to let things be she had to learn something, anything that would get her closer to the truth. Tiredness had finally taken its toll and now she rolled over onto her bed, lying there flat on her back, overloaded with all this new-found knowledge. All her life there had been mysteries surrounding her, things she just couldn't figure out. Usually, when confronted with these difficulties, she would find comfort in the things that she did know. Now, however, they gave no such consolation; even the established truth didn't seem so clear anymore. It troubled her being in this state of ignorance, unable to break free of the cage within her head. She lay there for a while, trying to sleep, but it didn't work, she had to be elsewhere soon, to give more tutorials. It had been a long time since anyone had called for her or even knocked on her door, but the anticipation of being disturbed was never far away. Her thoughts dwelled on Xiondel City and her next meeting with The Readers; and the fight it would take to be granted a visitation. She went over the questions she wanted to ask them in her head, mostly about her strange Visions. What was it that the ancient writings and warnings really spoke of? How was Glyph linked to the great Celestials? What about their human predecessors? Why had they disappeared so suddenly and mysteriously? Most importantly of all, she would visit The Eldor again and confront him with her new findings. The next few months would be long and tedious, she predicted, yet she couldn't help but feel a longing for something else, a craving not in her head, but in her heart. Isabelle got up, moved to the window, and pressed her head against the glass, trying to ignore her worries and confusion. She stared at the free birds flying by outside, clearing the tops of the triangular buildings over the glorious Golden City. She unlocked and pushed open the tall window and peered over the edge. It was very long way down, long enough to do the job. She quickly closed it again before the thoughts enveloped her, startled upon hearing a knock on her door. It was a priest, wanting her to get ready for the next class of student Glyph Wielders. She had not the time to notice the hooded figure with a handheld telescope, watching her from a secluded alleyway in the street below.

A woman carrying two trays came over to Lethaniel and Alexius, sitting down outside *The Soup Kitchen*.

"One soup special and bread…"

"Thank you, petal," said Alexius.

"And one cooked potatoe salad with a side serving of stringed beans. Thank you, gentlemen, enjoy your meal," she spoke cheerfully and toddled off back to work. All the while Alexius was captivated by her wide, wiggling hips.

"Mmmm slow down and I might tip you," Alexius muttered as soon as she was out of earshot, clutching his mug.

"Thought you had no more zeal on you?" Lethaniel teased.

"I don't. Who said I would tip her in zeal? I'll meet her out back in ten." They both smirked and tucked into their food.

"You were right," said The General, looking around, wondering why Alexius had ordered the soup. Lex had never been keen on soup and this was a soup-oriented place; it seemed he had changed a little in their time apart, though not that much.

"Yeah I know, it is quite splendid, isn't it?" He swirled his soup around with his silver spoon, while Lethaniel just grinned and shook his head.

"No argument there, I usually visit The Retreat but this place gives it a run for its money."

"If it wasn't for the kids running about hurting my brain, it would be perfect" said Lex, as a couple of loud children darted passed him, knocking his elbow. Lethaniel dug into his potato with a knife and fork and started to mush it together before eating. Alexius rested his spoon down and took a gulp from his mug, only restarting the conversation once his throat was clear. "I heard you ran into some trouble with those bloody rogues, I would think that you and certainly Thao could handle a few chicken shit thieves?"

"These aren't regular thieves, Alexius, they are Dark Rogues. The last thing they are is chicken-shit. Their tactics put our own law

293

enforcement; to shame; we rarely see them these days but… They are here."

"Fucking cowards, the lot of them. Step into the light and fight for fuck sake, sadly I don't think I'll be around to see the day" moaned Alexius, spooning up some soup.

"I think I have figured out how they communicate with one another," Lethaniel explained, crunching up some red lettuce in his mouth.

"How?" Alexius asked, blowing on his hot soup.

"Bird calls."

"Bird calls? You're joking, right?"

"Why not? It's better than shouting to one another. I found some kind of flute in The Silent Vale; I believe The Dark Rogues use this apparatus to communicate." The General sounded pretty sure of himself as he broke up more potatoe, mixing it with some beans.

"Bird calls are a thing of the past Lethaniel"

"The Dark Rogues have perfected the method in a way we could not," said Lethaniel, sounding encouraged.

"Well, what about the fact that you came back with less than half of your squad?"

"You know I can't speak about that, so can we get off the subject? I'm sure you will be made aware of the situation soon enough."

"I like to know a bit beforehand; you know me, I like to walk into a shit storm with my eyes open" A lady eating on the table next to him looked across, disgusted with his use of language. "What's with the attitude anyway, Leth?"

"It's still early and I didn't get much sleep last night" replied Lethaniel, faking a smile. Alexius squinted, and turned his spoon around the rim of the bowl, slowly.

"Have you spoken to Miss Grey?" Lex had been correct; as soon as he mentioned her name Lethaniel's eyes flared.

"I saw her last night," Lethaniel muttered before getting back to eating, leaving Alexius to pursue the conversation

"And?"

"We will talk again today. We're growing apart. The more time I spend away, the more I lose touch with my life here in this city. It's different now and I can't help being leagues away on a regular basis. I miss the times I spent with her. How has she been, anyway?" Alexius took a breath and told Lethaniel the truth.

"Her father died two months ago. You missed the funeral. She is grieving, though she hides it well. Better than I did when my old man passed on. I destroyed my liver when she... She just... She's stronger than most, I think. She does miss you. I don't think the gravity of the loss has hit her yet, but at some point, it will, and you should be there when it does. I should have sent word to you about this sooner, but I thought she would have done so herself. So I did nothing; it's better to talk about this stuff in person?" Lethaniel agreed, nodding his head, drinking some more. He felt saddened by the ill news. Eva's father was a good man and had always liked Lethaniel; even though they didn't talk much, there was a friendship there.

"We used to write all the time, about anything and everything. I'd even start on the second letter having just sent the first, we were that close. Now I get nothing, she never writes anymore... And neither do I. I want to, but I stop myself. I don't want to hound her; I want her to want to write me, you know?" The General's face had dropped; he no longer foresaw future with Eva like he once did, which troubled and pained him deeply. Alexius could see this but stuck with the subject. Talking through these things was always cathartic.

"She doesn't seek anyone's help, people change" When Lethaniel said nothing, Alexius piped up, after wiping some soup away from his mouth "You're not blaming yourself, are you? Her father died of natural causes, he went peacefully in his sleep one night, how she deals with this is on her, it has got nothing to do with you."

"You're right, it's got nothing to do with me" murmured Lethaniel, suddenly losing his appetite. Eventually, they moved onto other matters.

"The councils are assembling. The Courts of Imrondel, The Higher and Lower Councillors of Xiondel..." Alexius stated, smiling at the thought of the rare occasion. "This is the first time in a hundred years. I can only wonder what it's all about." His tactics were transparent, but nothing was forthcoming from Lethaniel. "Have you been to Ivulien of late?"

"Not recently, you know how long it takes to get there."

"It's grown, far more advanced in comparison with our cities. I'm only going by Isabelle's recent reports and what I saw six to seven months ago mind. Speaking of which" Alexius felt around in his back pocket "I got you this, thought you might like it." Alexius placed a small, brown leather bag on the table in front of Leth. Lethaniel put down his cutlery, cleaned his hands with a white napkin and picked the object up, unwrapping it with care. "I picked it up outside Menathig Keep in Ivulien. The guy said he didn't need it anymore and sold it to me for half its price" he said, lighting up another roll of smoking week, using the small, golden flame encased in a lantern in the centre of the table. Lethaniel noticed his supplies were low.

"Do you know what this is? You know I can't use these things! I'm just not receptive to it" complained Lethaniel.

"Not that you need more power anyway you sword wielding maniac, but that one is meant to be lucky, quite rare apparently; in fact, no one actually knows what type it is. Maybe you should study it, it could be something special" laughed Alexius, puffing out some smoke. Lethaniel merely raised his eyebrows. "Just keep it with you asshole, I'll feel like I've done something good for once. If not, I'll take it back and give it to my niece, Keira"

"I'll hang on to it forever and ever, if that would make you any feel better? Thanks," smiled Lethaniel, putting the item in his pocket and returning to his food.

"It would actually" said Alexius, taking a long drag on his roll up. Lethaniel then remembered something in his own possession.

"Oh, that reminds me, I got you something too." As he pulled the small, tin box containing weed and smoking tools from his pocket, Alexius's face lit up with excitement.

"I didn't know you smoked! You've had some already, how dare you do this to me?" he joked.

"No no, I offered some to Ferral in exchange for some information about The Avorlian Docks," Lethaniel explained, and Lex thanked him for the gift. The waitress walked by them again, once more hypnotising Alexius with her rear end. She noticed him staring, though she clearly didn't mind the attention. Lethaniel wasn't stupid and quickly got the message that Alexius and this waitress had a thing for one another; it would explain why his friend hung around this place so often even though he had no interest in soup. He just needed an excuse to be there with her. Once she was out of sight Alexius's mind cleared.

"I wish you would tell me where you disappeared to after that incident with Syen," he moaned. "Look, I know this is your day to rest, you don't have many, but maybe you could come to the barracks with me today?" Alexius suggested, sounding serious.

"If this is a trick to make me fight you again, then no. I'm getting tired of knocking you to the floor. One day I may actually kill you by mistake."

"Hahaha! No, it's not a trick, it's about something important, something that maybe you need to hear and see." Lethaniel glanced around from left to right, observing the people sitting at the other tables and whispered.

"Can't you just tell me now?"

"I think it's best if you are there. Later tonight, at the barracks, it's important" and Lethaniel reluctantly agreed. Alexius never usually took life seriously, but when he did, it was often serious.

Thao and Lucion stood in the backyard, preparing to strike each other with wooden sticks shaped like swords. Lucion rushed forward, poking and swinging, no method to the madness of his technique. As predictable as it was, Thao timed his defence well and blocked the stick effectively, driving his young son gently away. The boy tried the same thing again and again, not learning from his mistakes, although over time he did channel more aggression into his attacks. Once again Thao had predicted this would happen. With no effort at all, he blocked the delicate attacks and pushed Lucion over with his foot. The boy pulled himself together and held his sword out, waiting for his father's advance. Thao stepped forward and made a few light but sturdy swings, moves that wouldn't harm or injure, but fast enough to force his son to react. He was able to trip Lucion after the second swing, his shoulder hitting the ground first. The boy held his leg where he had received a graze. Thao came closer and tutored him:

"Now you would be wounded if this were a real blade. In the event of injury during combat you don't have time to see to wounds, however painful they might be. You have to block out the pain for as long as you can until the fight is over, mask it if you can so your opponent cannot tell you're damaged"

"What if I was bleeding?" Thao helped his son up off the floor.

"You hope it is not fatal" said Thao "First lesson, conquer yourself, the real battle takes place in your head. That voice that panics, that tells you to flee, to cower and please for mercy, this soft voice you need to replace with one of courage. Stay in control, reserve your fury, fight like you have an infinite supply of strength EVEN if you are using everything you have. Fool the mind of your opponent and bless yourself with an unbreakable interior" Thao handed back the wooden sword and backed away. "Second lesson.

Always remain defensive, never lower your guard; attacking lowers your own defences exposing yourself to the swift and cunning. Do not give your opponent any ground or advantage, adapt your methods to fit the situation. Being able to change yourself to suit the scenario can mean the difference between a victory and defeat. Now, I will attack, watch me and be ready." Lucion sucked in a deep breath as his father came at him once again. This time, the boy allowed him to come closer and rolled forward passed Thao's hip, finding himself within striking range. Thao, however, moved and blocked his swing, sending Lucion to the floor yet again, his strength colossal compared to his son. It was as easy as using one hand to grab and throw him by the collar. "Because you are a child, rolling around may seem appropriate, it happens all the time in the stories, but on the field against men who want to kill you, this is very ill-advised unless you're a specialist."

"I'm sorry, father."

"Don't apologise. I' am far bigger than you; you are small, so speed is your friend, sometimes being agile is a key factor. Did you know boys as old as you used to kill bears, using their own size and weight against them?"

"How?" curiously asked Lucion.

"They'd lure the charging bear into traps, deadfalls they'd call them, littering the pits with long spears. Bears would often stand over their prey, rising onto their hind legs to intimidate threats, but upon their fall a single spear is all it would take" Thao smiled, smirking at the imagery, and roughed up Lucion's hair.

"You aren't a bear" Lucion pointed out, making Thao laugh.

"Think of me as an armoured bear then" Thao teased, playful jabbing Lucion's side. "If you can avoid it, always hold your ground son, you will increase your chances of survival. Remain on the defensive. Avoid expending more energy than is necessary. Believe me, many soldiers fail in this regard, and that is what makes them weak; your stamina runs dry quicker than you think especially when carrying a suit of armour, so learn to conserve it. Now, no more rolling around, no running and jumping, no backing down, let me see you in a defensive stance, let me see you stand as tall as a mountain. Hold your weapon close; it is an extension of your arm." The two practised for hours, perhaps Thao pushed Lucion too hard, but Lucion always obeyed, listened, and learned, never fell down crying or speaking back in anger. Lena watched the pair, in secret from the upper floor of the house, the bond between them was strong.

"Are big guys harder to fight than the small guys?" Lucion asked, taking a breather.

"Large opponents intimidate inexperienced fighters; no doubt about it, nature dictates this. What you will find is that big fighters tend to rely too much on their height and weight, nourishing an air of confidence which gives them an edge, both physically and psychologically. This tends to be enough to defeat most of their opponents. Over time they get used to winning, not through skill, but simply by intimidation. It's important not to underestimate anyone, and I mean anyone! It's always those you least expect who turn out to be the ones who surprise you. Smaller opponents have the advantages of speed, agility, flexibility, deception, stealth and explosive power; they use these techniques to create their own fighting styles, which are nearly impossible to predict. All these tactics are lacking in bigger men. Understand that the greater you are in size, power and strength, the weaker you are in speed and agility. Every advantage is also a disadvantage. The idea is to use what you have to the best of your ability, and to train yourself to battle opponents of all physiques, now, let's go again."

Inside a warm conference room within The Palace of Norisis, lined with bookshelves, desks in the far corners and several large comfortable chairs, a third of The High Councillors of Virtue of Xiondel City had gathered for refreshment. They strolled around the rich, colourful room deep in thought, relaxing and discussing important matters between themselves, occasionally taking advantage of a buffet of local delicacies. Suddenly the double doors of the waiting room opened and Yespin Fquarign, High Councillor Truth, walked in. The four other High Councillors looked at the man as he entered; one was walking around with a book, reading silently; his name was Julias Tarno, High Councillor Courage. Two others were seated in chairs facing each other around a wooden table with a glass surface; they were Cillian Landris, High Councillor Charity and Taktard Erien, High Councillor Ambition. The last was helping himself to a plate of food; his name was Darlo Heventon, High Councillor Justice. All were smartly attired in subtle blacks and opulent golds. Worried looks covered their faces. Cillian made eye contact with Yespin, and made a suggestion regarding their concerns:

"We should wait, at least until the others arrive. You know we don't make decisions unless we all consent." He leant back and waited for the response.

"We will make no such decision" Yespin agreed.

"Where are the others? In the future, we should all travel as one for such matters of importance." Darlo interrupted with his mouthful.

"We never travel together, for our safety and for the safety of others; you know the risks, Landris."

"Thank you for that information, Darlo," replied Cillian "But Yespin you still haven't answered my question"

"They're on route; days separate their carriages, but they will be here soon. Have patience, Cillian" Yespin took a seat near a window. "The meeting will take place as soon as the leaders of Xiondel have assembled. I am merely asking for your views on the matter now. How do we answer the Dovidians?" The small group of High Councillors pondered the question and it was Darlo who answered first, this time free of food.

"I guess we can only look at it from their perspective. How would we feel if the situation were reversed? Their argument is fair, I say. They should be afraid of such things; I know I am at times. What would we do if the Dovidians possessed such power, all in the form of a single woman?" he asked. Taktard, a good-looking man with sharp eyes and fine, black hair, spoke next.

"It is not our power to control. We are all for laws and politics. Over the long, uncountable years the Celestials have lain dormant, it has been clear that only one can work with them: our Star Caller. The Chosen is in control whether we like it or not."

"Where is she now?" enquired Cillian.

"Aren't YOU supposed to be with her?" responded Yespin.

"I think she is in her quarters or teaching a class; she has also been complaining about chest pains and headaches to the physician. The Palace Guards are with her" informed Taktard.

"If we were going to go to war with the Dovidians, with the Celestials at our side, wouldn't we have already done it by now? Not that we have any dispute with Ivulien, but perhaps the Dovidians should ask themselves a few questions before they start raising an alarm and accusing us of misuses of power. We don't know everything about Starillia yet."

"You're right there Cillian," a voice called from the furthest part of the room "We don't know everything; in fact, we know next to nothing about the potential of Celestial power. I think it would be unwise to even consider the use of The Star Caller's gifts as a form of offence. From what we have learned about Glyph, I imagine it would be like fighting an ant with a sledgehammer. Total overkill!" opined Julias Tarno, High Councillor Courage.

"All I am saying is, why the sudden interest? They never raised any concern before; Why now?" Cillian posed.

"It's Isabelle... She is very promising, showing the Celestials in a new light," Darlo pointed out, "She gave a demonstration to the Dovidians not long ago." Yespin then spoke again.

"We should talk to Isabelle; let her know how we feel. Taktard, I think you should find her. She may be teaching, so check the classrooms or the Glyph Domes. If not, she will most likely be catching up on her usual habits."

"And what are they?" asked Taktard, getting ready to leave the room. The others quickly found the answer to that question.

"You know, sleeping" said Yespin.

"No, I'll go find her," volunteered Cillian. "What exactly are we going to talk to her about?" he asked before departing, one hand on the doorknob.

Isabelle kicked open the door to her room, carrying with her a towering pile of books and papers. Her hair was frizzed, as though she had been struck by a bolt of lightning fired by one of her cocky, male students. Her eyes were sagging, hungry for rest. She carefully placed down the heavy volumes on the floor and went to take off her blue hooded long coat. Her arms constrained within the cumbersome sleeves, the pillar of books toppled over, crashing down like a besieged tower two of which lost the grip of their pages held in the spin, spilling all over her floor. Tossing her coat aside she fell forward, bouncing onto her soft bed. Rolling over onto her back and staring up at the ceiling, she dropped off to sleep almost immediately.

Having slept for an unknown period, she awoke to find her cat, Pandora, a silver tabby sitting on her chest, staring at her with those big, beautiful, green eyes of hers, purring lovingly, padding her claws over Isabelle's pullover. "Ah I wondered when you would show up" said Isabelle, stirring out of slumber. The sun was still in the sky, so it couldn't have been that late. The troubling thoughts found their way back to the front of her mind, through her thumping headache. She needed more rest and someone to talk to; someone wiser than Eran, as crazy as that sounded, though she did not believe that Professor Atheriax was as knowledgeable her old teacher, from what she could remember, Atheriax was a hard man to read, like he was two different people, feeling like she had to build repour over and over in the short times they had been together. Thao, as thoughtful as he was, was her guardian, not an advisor. Her priests acted as guides, but if they discovered how she truly felt and what she was up to, they would certainly notify The Eldor or other officials; these types of actions wouldn't do her any favours, she could lose the trust and respect of the people, something she was not about to risk. Lethaniel always remained an option, but the risk of him being able to handle such a secret was too great; not that she didn't trust him, she just didn't think him the type to talk to about spiritualistic things, he dealt with issues in a more physical head on sort of way. The Eldor, of course, could never know of her true troubles, there was no telling what he would do. His power was not spiritual or magical like her own; his was founded on political lessons. She had hoped that Eran would be able to help her with these matters, but now she had seen him, she only wanted to go back to his wonderful library and continue their debate. Unfortunately, her tortured mind and her responsibility to Norisis prevented her from moving a muscle. With almost all avenues of assistance exhausted, she could only think of one more she could turn to in confidence. A great companion and a good friend of hers. Isabelle's eyes dropped to the one clawing at her top.

"I have an idea Pandora" she clicked her fingers, "How about YOU become The Chosen for a while? And I'll do what you do for a while. Maybe we can take it in turns!?" She stroked her cat's shiny, silver coat. Pandora purred happily at the touch of Isabelle's fingertips. "But if you like the job as much as I imagine you would, I will understand if you want the position permanently…" *Knock knock knock.* "Go get the door, Pandora. Isabelle needs sleep now," she groaned. Pandora twitched her head toward the door as another knock came from beyond the wood, though she nothing but give Isabelle the order to get it.

"My lady? The Xiondel High Councillors are here to see you," a voice called. Isabelle lay there in silence; "Isabelle, it's important, can you answer the door please?" Finally, she opened the door to find one of her guards, with Cillian Landris standing behind him, leaning on the wall in the corridor.

"Come in, High Councillor Charity," she smiled tiredly, opening the door wider for him and only him, pushing it shut as the guards tried to enter. He thanked her as she sat down at her desk.

"Good sleep?" he asked, making an educated guess from the state of her bed and the shadows under her eyes.

"Yes, it was, but I must say that with all the travelling recently, I am starting to get used to the sound of the road and the comfort of a bouncing carriage," she replied, lying through her teeth.

"Well I am sorry to hear that, the carriages stationed below on the ground floor are the best in Krondathia, built to absorb the bumps in the roads all in the wheels" he said, before being quickly interrupted.

"Am I getting a new carriage, Cillian? Is that why you have come to see me? If so, I'm grateful. Or am I going to be dragged off to another location leagues away?" Pandora rubbed herself up against Isabelle's leg as she raised her eyebrows at her visitor, waiting for a response.

"The other council members and I have been talking, and I think it would be best if you came with me to the lounge. It's about the Dovidians and the demonstration you gave in the Ivulien capital, Davune," he spoke in a very persuasive manner.

"Right..." It looked like she would be entertaining The High Councillors during her nap time; a frustrating prospect to say the least. "I will be down in a minute. I would like something to eat before I start talking though, if you don't mind." Apparently, Cillian had already been made aware of her strange eating habits, as he told her:

"We have food prepared downstairs. I will tell them you're coming, whatever you need." He opened the door wider, about to leave when Isabelle spoke to his turned back.

"Tell the guard to feed Pandora, if you would? She likes chicken."

As she was changing into something more fitting for the meeting, she caught sight of a peculiar figure down in the city through her open window. She didn't know why that particular person caught her eye, but the cloak they wore was dark, their face covered by a worn riding hood. The shadowy visage seemed to be staring right at her! Whoever it was could not possibly see Isabelle from that distance, it was too simply too far, but still, she sensed the pair of eyes upon her. It made her feel uncomfortable. The figure walked away along the small Northern Bridge just outside The Palace of Norisis, just as she began to stare back. *Such a dark and weathered figure*, she thought as she changed, occasionally checking the bridge from her window, in case the stranger had returned. As she turned around, she noticed that the door was wide open. And a Glyph Wielder was standing right there, pretending not to look as she changed! "What!?" she demanded as he swiftly looked away. Isabelle sighed and smiled, standing there in nothing but a small bra and her trousers. "Have you not seen a half-naked Star Caller before? Don't you have a woman?" She flicked her wrist and the door slammed itself shut. "Bet she can't do that on a whim," she whispered, appreciating her power. Finally, content, she looked at herself in the mirror embedded within her wardrobe, but couldn't hold a gaze for long, her appearance really wasn't her main concern at the moment. She made her way downstairs through the rich palace escorted by two Glyph Wielders. Priests, honoured soldiers, maidens, and people of Norisis glanced at her when she passed by in the hallways, waving after her. She arrived at the lounge and threw her hair back over her shoulders. It felt so good to be free of its elastic ties.

Knock knock.

"Do come in!" Yespin's voice called, and Isabelle opened the double doors and entered the room. Once again, all eyes fell upon her immediately. She ignored the men's admiring faces, as she was far more interested in the buffet in the corner. Her stomach moaned, but she did not go for anything just yet, not until she had dispensed with the usual, boring pleasantries. She closed the doors and turned to face five of the twelve High Councillors of Virtue. *Funny*, she thought, these men ruled a city of thousands and thousands of people, the top minds in their fields, and all except Cillian were at least ten years older than her, but it was her words that were truly important to Krondathia. "It's good to see you fully rested. Have you settled in alright? Your quarters are just as you left them, as you requested," spoke Yespin, breaking the silence. Isabelle was not fully rested, far from it in fact, but she ignored the matter.

"Thank you, Truth. Yes, everything is fine," she replied with a faked smile. The food looked too tempting to ignore, she immediately strolled over to the buffet and started to nibble at anything that took her fancy, the chicken appealed right away. "I am aware of your feelings about Starillia; I know that you don't put much faith in it and that you... Sometimes work separately from Imrondel, but I never quite understood why, Councillors?" she enquired, taking a bite out of a chicken wing.

"We simply don't rely on twelve otherworldly spirits to see us through trying times. True, they are powerful and just as real as the human race, but we simply believe that the human spirit is stronger than they are, milady. The Celestials have led us this far and solved many of our problems, but have they built our cities and homes for us? Have they healed the sick and sheltered the homeless? Do they bless every child that is born, destined for a long, healthy life? Do they fight disease? Do they make this world a better place to live in, Isabelle? No. Human hands and human labour have and are making those things happen every day, while more than half of the population clasps its hands in prayer and worship." She had heard this argument before, but she didn't dispute it, not yet, she bided her time, nodding slowly as he spoke, the chicken was delicious! She sat down as Yespin went on and on and crossed her legs. "Human spirits build the future Isabelle, not the Celestials." Finally, it was her turn and she crushed his argument.

"The human spirit sure likes to take its time, doesn't it? Before Starillia, Equis was a place of green fields, sunny days, picnics, and rainbows. Don't waste my time Yespin, the Celestials inspired unity" said Isabelle, ripping some chicken meat off the bone.

"You are aware that the meeting has been called? It will take place next week, hopefully, depending on the haste of the other council members, who are on the road as we speak. The meeting has been called because of the Dovidian response to the demonstration you gave the last time you were there. Please take the time to read this letter, Isabelle, upon your request this is the last of it" said Yespin, coming forward, handing her an official message from a Dovidian associate, its purple wax seal, branded with the face of Tithis, broken in half. She brushed the crumbs from her hands before taking the letter, swallowing her mouthful of food and began to read...

Krondathia

Friends, be not intimidated by the contents of this letter. The words expressed herein were not written out of anger or jealousy, but rather humiliation. Impressive was the demonstration your Star Caller, Isabelle Verano, gave us. Ivulien found itself envious and overwhelmed with awe in the face of one of your great Celestial Souls. I am sure that Isabelle's intentions for this blessing are simply to make the world and the cities we thrive in a better place to live. They certainly have shown your Norkron people a path to greatness.

Such a power, so vast and unknown, strikes us with the whip of fear. If this gift were to fall in the wrong hands and turned against my people, whether now or in a hundred years, we fear that the results would be catastrophic for the world we live in. We beg that you be aware of our own people's feelings, to be wary of what you hold in your possession. My courts agree that some action must be taken to prevent the abuse of this Star Calling technique and Glyph Wielding ability.

We look forward to your response to this letter and hope that we can come to an understanding with regards to the future use of Omnio. We would greatly appreciate a swift reply to quench our concern, for the weather is turning colder, much faster than anticipated. Summer has never seemed to settle in this age.

Ivulien bows its head to your nation with great respect and friendship, as it always has done since the ending of the second age of Equis.

With the greatest of respect to your Sire. Your High Councillors of Virtue, The Courts of Imrondel and your gracious Conductor, your Chosen, The Star Caller, Isabelle Verano the 23rd.

Sincerely, Akarnal Desa

Once Isabelle finished reading, she looked up at Yespin and addressed the obvious:

"So, they are afraid. When I used to be afraid, I would hide under my bed. What can we do?" The room lay silent for a few seconds as she glanced from Councillor to Councillor.

"Can you tell us what happened in Ivulien, Isabelle?" asked Taktard from across the room. "That may help us to better understand this message," he added when silence wanted to fall once again.

"Did anything feel strange? Or out of place? Anything at all?" questioned Darlo, folding his arms, ready to listen. Isabelle leant forward in her chair, putting her hands together in thought. Her fingers touched the tip of her nose as she pondered, she did not know what they wanted from her, and she could not remember anything out of the ordinary when she had Star Called in Davune.

"I remember Ivulien as it was five years ago; nothing but a grey city back then, with not much going for it. Now it has changed, gentlemen; something beautiful and colourful has arisen from something cold and rigid. It has transformed into something wonderful. The Dovidian Circle of theirs that once led Ivulien, has reduced in size. It seems that it takes but a handful to manage their country, unlike we who apparently require many. Ivulien is focused on development and progress; it sure is on the right path…" She rubbed her forehead, pressing her fingers into her skin, trying to keep their attention while ignoring her rising headache. "When I performed the ritual in their Crystal Dome, there were a lot more people observing me than I had anticipated. One man stood out; I must admit; he looked like he went unseen by everyone else but… I saw him, Councillors. He hung close to Akarnal Desa; he was youthful, with a piercing gaze. He didn't look like he belonged, is all I am trying to say, gentlemen. I had plenty of space and all the time in the world to perform the demonstration. Other than those details, I don't remember anything else. I'm sorry." The High Councillors remained silent. This time Yespin made eye contact with Cillian.

"I am to understand that you called upon an aerial Celestial; the soul of Libra?" Isabelle raised her eyes at him.

"Yes. Liranous… or Libra if you prefer the modern term."

"Why did you call Libra?" Isabelle frowned, disappointed in him for not being able to figure that out for himself.

"Libra, one of the three airborne Celestials, gives the mark and the blessing of balance and equality. I thought as we are allies with a… complicated history… I thought Libra was the best of the twelve to go for. A way of letting them know that we all are all still on the same side." Isabelle took a bite out a sandwich, feeling she had spoken well. She started talking with her mouth full, forgetting her common courtesies. "Did I do something wrong, Councillors? Why the long faces? Should I have called upon Capricorn, who is all for independence? Or Aries perhaps, the Celestial of War? I believe that would have made a huge impression on them; Wouldn't you say? Maybe we would have had a lot more than a letter sent to us if I had done so." Cillian hid a little grin at her snarky attitude.

"How did Libra behave inside the great Crystal Dome?" Yespin pressed on.

"Libra came to me as he always does; emerging from the roof of the world, from the heart of the sky kingdom, shrouded in cloud and mist. As spacious as The Crystal Dome is, he would have found it impossible to find a way inside without ripping the roof off with his talons, let alone fly around the space within. No, he flew around outside making some passes, spreading his mighty dragon wings. He spoke his own tongue; a wail the likes of which no one in Ivulien had ever heard before, shrieks of a language uttered by the elements. After that he disappeared, taking off into the sky, evaporating into the air from whence he came. The audience reacted graciously as they always do, but some of them did have eyes filled with dread, not awe! You know this; it's all in the letter. I don't know what we can do to put their minds at rest. Being afraid, to my mind, is no excuse; let them be afraid because let's be clear, aren't we all just a little bit fearful of the Celestials, especially when one enters our plain?" She raised an interesting point, despite getting rather flustered by the feeling of having to take care of everything herself.

Isabelle hastily stood and returned to the buffet, starting to pick and choose again until she turned around to a collection of bewildered adults. "What do you want me to do? I've done all I can. If the Dovidians want me to perform again then I will gladly carry out another Star Call to end this pointless dispute. Only on the condition that I can travel with Thao again," she insisted, jumping ahead of herself rather than formulating a better plan. Yespin spoke for the others:

"That's just it: we don't want you to travel anymore, not for a while. Your place is here, for now, it seems. It has been some time since we last saw the Celestials; we wondered if you could be so kind as to perform for us."

"You want to see them? You want me to Star Call? There is nothing to be afraid of stop looking at me like that."

"I thought you just said they make you fearful?" Taktard noted cleverly.

"I've spoken to them, Councillor Ambition. I know them and I assure you all that The Celestial Souls are kind. I am not fearful of them, but I understand why there is a sense of terror when I pull them from their plain. They are misunderstood, they have instincts like wild animals; it is natural to fear those bigger and stronger than us. Know that they respond to me alone, for I am the Star Caller, they would never do anything untoward" she explained in a reassuring manner.

"I know, Isabelle; that is why we would like you to perform. Today, if you would? We can clear your schedule for the rest of the afternoon if you accept" Yespin offered in a kind voice. She sat down and chewed on something crunchy while she considered. Eventually she nodded, agreeing to the idea. Of course, she would perform in exchange for receiving the rest of the day off; she was overjoyed, in fact, but made a note to hide her happiness.

"Alright, I'll do it. Who is my audience? I warn you, gentlemen, that some performances are not suitable for *children*, so if any are to come along, be sure that they are ready for quite a show." She chose her words carefully.

"Just us, Isabelle, no one else, no youngsters. Just Landris, Darlo, Taktard, Julias and myself."

"This will be a brief Star Call; this rules out performing outside of the city. I'll do it in a Glyph Dome" she said, mentally preparing the details. Yespin agreed silently as the other High Councillors of Virtue began to look a little excited. Tonight, they would see a Celestial Soul; not amidst the roars of a crowd of thousands, but a private viewing, up close and personal. The Chosen remained quiet and professional, though she sensed their anticipation. The Councillors began to leave one by one, making their way to the nearest Glyph Dome in The Holy District. She had one more question to ask, and it was by far the most important one. "Yespin!" He glanced at her face and she sat back in her chair, tilting her head to the side. "Which Celestial do you want me to call into Equis? Only one soul may be called upon and drawn into our dimension at a time, and only one may be in any one place at a time. The rules of my line are clear."

"I shall leave that choice to you, my lady; you have wiser judgment than I in such matters. You are The Conductor, after all." Isabelle nodded, making a quick decision in her mind, tapping her fingers on the armrest like keys on a piano. Yespin left her alone in the lounge with the food she would destroy in a moment. She was no lady at heart, she was no one's lady but her own.

Lucion strayed too close to his father and Thao responded by throwing him aside with next to no effort. The boy began to let his frustration get the better of him, swinging violently and uncontrollably. Thao could see the anger in his son's eyes and stopped the attack quickly with his own wooden sword, forcing the boy to the ground once again. Lucion did not get back up this time; instead, he stayed on the floor, fed up and miserable. Thao sat next to him.

"What kind of father would I be if I allowed you to win? If I lulled you into a false sense of confidence, you would become prideful and overconfident in yourself. This would eventually lead to your undoing. Lethaniel suffers from this somewhat;

overconfidence is his weakness. Sure, he has never lost a fight, but he does not respect his enemies well enough, making the grave mistake of underestimating them. Lethaniel believes he is above everyone else when it comes to swordplay, and he has certainly earned the right to express that level of confidence, but it's only a matter of time before he learns one of the hardest lessons.

"What's that?" asked Lucion, grumpily.

"Defeat, and the defeat usually comes at a fatal cost" said Thao, lowering his head to Lucion. "What kind of soldier would I be if I were defeated by a child in my own back garden?" he laughed, nudging his son in the shoulder, trying to draw a smile from him.

"You're too big! You're too strong for me! It's not fair!" complained Lucion, crossing his arms and pouting. Having heard the commotion from the kitchen, Lena stepped towards the yard where her boys were training and watched on in silence. For the moment they remained unaware of her intrusion.

"It's not fair? What if a soldier were to say that to his enemy on the battlefield? Do you think he would be spared? War is not about fairness, but, tis rare when men prefer to fight on an even keel. Once upon a time, Lucion, I found myself disarmed; my sword had become lodged in a tree and I pulled so hard on it that I snapped it at the hilt. My opponent had the advantage, but what came next I was not prepared for."

"What happened?"

"He threw away his own sword and we continued. Beware of men like this; if an opponent endangers himself for the value of honour, then he will likely be highly trained, dangerous and... Dare I say it, confident in his ability to win" Lucion suddenly remembered why he had become agitated in the first place.

"But you are bigger and stronger than me! What chance do I have of winning against someone like you?" he argued, now having regained his composure enough to look his father in the eyes.

313

"We are practising son; this is about learning. Do you think that I have not fought bigger, stronger, faster men than I? It's not about size or strength. It's about your will, it's about holding on to courage, in here" and Thao tapped Lucion's forehead. "That's what makes the difference between a good and a great soldier. Giving up on yourself during a fight is the last step before you are slain. Do you understand?" Lucion lowered his head, listening but not saying anything. "I am not expecting anything from you. I am simply teaching you to use your head."

Lena looked from the window and smiled at the sight of father and son sharing moments together. Lucion would never forget these times. Thao stood up and helped the boy to his feet.

"No one can defeat you or Lethaniel," stated Lucion, grinning once more.

"If only that were true. Lethaniel has a few lessons to learn himself, but there is not a better swordsman in the city, in all of Krondathia for that matter. Not yet anyway, but someone will inevitably rise to take his place, this is the way of things. Tomorrow we will train again, and you will notice that you have become just a little bit wiser. Now pick up the swords and run inside. Tell your mother you hit me, she'll be proud."

The sun shone throughout the day, until grey clouds invaded the blue sky of the afternoon, casting their bloated shadows over The Holy City of Imrondel. The people went about their lives, as usual, shopping and strolling the streets, meeting up with friends and family, eating, working, and gathering at open pubs and cafes. People of all types; men and women, young workers, farmers, shop owners, soldiers, blacksmiths, potters, sculptures, tailors, architects, teachers, tutors, Glyph Wielders and politicians all walked the streets in peace. Every day was a busy day in Imrondel. The crowds diminished as the darkness grew and the stars appeared. The barracks of The Military District lay silent and almost deserted at this hour. Lethaniel was navigating the inside, traversing a wide corridor, and heading down some stone steps into an open training area. Beyond the yard, a pale candlelight was coming from a room directly ahead. He knelt on the edge of the court, tying his bootlace,

314

not noticing the not so subtle movements in the shadows behind, stalking him. As he was preparing to stand, he spotted fresh boot prints in the grit; he then realised! The shadow jumped out at him from behind, noisily alerting him to its presence. Lethaniel reacted fast and grabbed the handle of the wooden training sword, kicking the legs out from under his useless stalker. The attacker lay on the floor, panting through his grinning mouth, for he had been holding his breath before attempting a strike.

"You would not make a very good assassin," panted Lethaniel, helping Alexius to his feet. "Cowards put a knife in someone's back."

"I thought I'd try a different approach; no one can beat you head on, so I mixed things up a little," and they shared a laugh at the logic.

"It is late and I have somewhere to be. Why are we here? If it's a lesson you want, talk to a Captain in the morning or join in with some Regulars," suggested Lethaniel, but Alexius stepped inside the room with the lit candles, illuminating a few large pieces of paper and a map ravaged by time. The General gave the chart a brief, uninterested glance; he was more interested in looking through the doorway, back into the life of the bustling city. "What do you want me to see?" he pressed. Noticing Alexius's solemn face, he put aside all thoughts of Eva for the time being, and looked a little harder at the map, trying to see its importance. He stared intently at the documents next to it and further unrolled the map. Alexius held it open for him, allowing him to study it more carefully, moving his eyes over the layout, while reading the headlines of some of the papers. "The Dovidians... Why are they preparing to march upon the northlands?" he questioned, having dropped his casual tone and used his General's voice.

"From the looks of things, Ivulien is threatened by Jureai and its five clans. I don't think it's war, but it could very well escalate. The Tournament of Leadership took place recently. The Chieftain of The Bevork Clan, El Raud, was victorious once again. Do you know of their ways, Lethaniel?"

"Yes, I understand how they select their country's Sovereign. Every three years they hold the tournament; whichever clan is victorious acquires or keeps The Five-Headed Throne for another term. I've been hearing rumours, rumours which are growing more numerous by the day; the clans are growing restless. They long for change in their Chimera Order."

"Did you hear of the warrior of the northlands? The one even Kronix himself cannot defeat?" Lethaniel continued to stare at the maps; he had a vague idea of who Lex meant.

"You mean Xavien? Why would Kronix fight his own Champion?"

"I didn't say Xavien, he is nothing more than a blood-crazed mercenary-for-hire, a monster, or as the northlanders call him, a Demon Man. No, I am referring to El Raud's Champion, his cherished warrior, supposedly never defeated... Just like you." Lethaniel was puzzled.

"I am in no mood for stories, Lex, so make your point and let's be done with this. Why are the Dovidians in a feud with Jureai?"

"It is a great distance to Jureai; scouting takes time these days and I received my information from Norfoon. With El Raud's Bevork hunting forces, Kronix commanding Xavien the Demon Man who supposedly can't bleed and this unknown warrior who quite simply doesn't fall, I'd say that is quite a formidable force marching against the Dovidians northern territories."

"So we go to their aid?" snapped Lethaniel, picturing Eva waiting on her doorstep.

"I am asking you to put it before the council when they are scheduled to meet. The scouts of Norfoon have done their job, successfully remaining undetected and sending us a clear warning. I too have done my job, by notifying you of these incidents. It's your turn now Lethaniel."

"I doubt the Courts will allow this. The Dovidians should send word for help if they need it."

"Word spreads fast in Equis, as you know, but we need it to fly faster this time. Maybe time will kill us, who knows? I have no specific count, no size or measure of this northern strength in Jureai, not yet… The next package I receive may not be maps and writings, but the heads of our Dovidian allies in baskets. Where do you think these clans will turn to next when our Dovidian allies have been conquered? We should focus on looking for Northlander spies scouring our lands. If ANY are found in our regions, I recommend they be seized and detained immediately, with interrogation to follow as always," suggested Alexius. "If they seize control of Ivulien, we are looking at a struggle which could last years, decades even if they aren't smart enough to act now. I don't know about you, but I like the world we live in as it is, alongside Ivulien, not set against the east. We are so close to Equis being made whole. Isabelle will deliver our paradise soon. We must stop this rebellion at the root. With your approval, I will issue the order for all soldiers and official citizens of Krondathia to restrain any Northlanders sighted in or around our lands." Lethaniel studied the details a little further before stating his commands.

"Issue the order. I will stand by the action and address the courts when the time is right. Do it tonight" he sighed, signing the official document. From that moment on, all Northlanders would be taken prisoner if caught wandering or spying around their borders.

Isabelle's door was opened by a guard. She ordered him away and stepped inside the room, where the sensual scent of ocean pearls hung in the air. A little light had been lit for her in each corner of the tidy room. She raised her hand a little and twisted it around, the warm candlelight in the room brightening with the action of her wrist, the flames glowing stronger. She lifted off her top and draped the fabric over the back of a chair. The image of herself in the mirror stared at her as she approached the large square wardrobe. She gently let the door swing open and placed her hand inside the space, feeling the shimmering touch of her beautiful, fiery red dress. Carefully she released it from the hook and hugged it against her chest. Pandora sat on the nearby desk watching her mistress with those colourful green eyes, reflecting the candle flames.

"Isabelle, it's time. Are you ready, my lady?" called a voice from behind the door. She turned to the mirror, looking deep within herself and spoke.

"I'm ready." Hearing the footsteps drift away, further down the corridor, she continued in little more than a whisper: "But, are you ready, my dear High Councillors of Virtue?" The candles extinguished themselves, their flames drowned out falling into an emerald shade, for Isabelle's eyes were alive and shining.

The High Councillors of Virtue had been true to their word and granted Isabelle the rest of the day off, though what they failed to understand was that she had not been relaxing during this supposed free time. The Chosen had been psyching herself, preparing for The Star Call. Five of the twelve rulers of Xiondel City stood in a perfectly round, stone chamber; A Glyph Dome, this was where people would practise with the Glyph pearls that emitted Omnio energy for The Blessed to harness. The gentlemen gathered around a centre stage. The chamber itself, carved from black and bronze rock would have been pitch black had it not been for a basin of fire and the gatherings of lit candles lining the walls. The display the men were greeted with gave Yespin a clue as to which Celestial Isabelle would be Star Calling. She had been in and out of the room all day, preparing it for the arrival of the Demi-God, making the area presentable and perfect. The Glyph Dome was fit for at least a hundred people, but tonight it would accommodate five. Taktard and Darlo stood whispering together near their front row seats. Julias was also seated on one of the flat, stone chairs closest to the stage, which were more like sets of steps leading higher and higher toward the top of the stone room. The chatter quickly quietened down to silence. Cillian, High Councillor Charity, sat down in front of Yespin and leant back to him, asking:

"Did she tell you which Celestial will be visiting us this evening?"

"No, I left that decision up to her. I am confident in her wisdom" catching a sigh in Cillian, Yespin addressed him "You doubt her?"

"I don't doubt her abilities as The Chosen. I've seen her power first-hand before, and it is most impressive."

"So what's troubling you, Charity?" asked the Councillor of Truth.

"I feel like her power is misplaced. She's enough well to end poverty, yet people still go hungry. Your arguments are sound Truth" Yespin nodded his head slowly as he answered.

"And so are hers. It was indeed The Celestial Souls that delivered us from chaos and gave us a path. If it hadn't have been for the first Chosen, Regina Corah - the one who Hallow had predicted would come, would bring us Starillia and awaken the twelve - our world would be a very different place and neither you nor I would exist. Isabelle is a pawn of Starillia, the wealth it accumulates becomes its property, and Isabelle receives a slice. She has power Cillian but not enough perhaps to overturn the ways of the faith that is if she wanted to spark rivalry with the religious sect, her aptitude doesn't suggest this intent. Be patient, Cillian, embrace our peace and be thankful for it. We will witness a spectacle tonight that many would pay handsomely to see."

"Where does her slice go?" Cillian questioned, squinting his eyes, keeping his voice down to a whisper.

"Isabelle is always looking for answers, so most of it goes to education and to the works in Fevoriel; there are many buried temples and tombs in those lands, which may hold answers about our predecessors. She funds Livale, on the borders of Tthenadawn Forest, where artefacts lost throughout history are being uncovered. Old Druidic objects are the most common; you should go to the museums and see them for yourself. Her generosity has also helped to fund major developments in Xiondel, her donations have been most appreciated, and she keeps little for herself. I cannot believe you didn't know of her contributions to, well… Charity." Cillian sat quietly, put firmly in his place.

"Why is this the first I have learnt of this?" Yespin smiled.

"Isabelle doesn't make her donations public; she doesn't feel the need to do so, but we know it is her. She has already won the people's love simply by spending time among them as often as she can. She has easily surpassed the popularity of Freya through her focus on children's education. Each Star Caller has excelled in comparison with her predecessor, but no one has ever been better than Regina, and I mean no one; she was the greatest who EVER lived. The only way to surpass her is to bring about utopia" Truth sat upright, shifting his weight on the stone step.

"What is it?"

"I get the feeling she does too much for the public and not enough for herself; it's one thing to be selfless and another thing to be neglectful. Sometimes I get the feeling that Isabelle is growing weaker." Cillian looked back at the stage, he had more arguments left in him, but now was not the right time to express them, that time would come in due course. The other Councillors sat down and awaited The Star Caller, for it was time for the performance to begin. The Glyph Dome sank into silence, a lonely moth fluttering passed the tall, double doors as they opened as one, creaking painfully on their tight, stiff hinges.

The Star Caller stepped inside, dressed in lethally red attire. Her golden hair was tied into a top knot; along her arms were wonderful wrist bracelets and rings decorated her fingers. She walked with grace toward the centre of the round stage, her black, high-heeled boots sending echoes throughout the dome. The Councillors let their eyes wash over her in awe. As she climbed the stages steps. The Celestial she was about to call upon whispered words into her ear, thanking her in advance for the invitation to another dimension. A gentle breeze breathed over the fire burning in the wide silver basin and waft the robes of The High Councillors. Isabelle's ruby red dress hung thinly off her shoulders and trailed behind her like a ghostly red shadow. With all eyes on her, she stood in the centre of the stage, holding her long-staff, Violethelm, close to her side, focusing her thoughts on the act she had practised repeatedly for years. She breathed deeply. Her chest moved in and out, in and out, as she built up the energy needed to perform. The ritual was about to begin.

Isabelle closed her eyelids dashed with a purple tint and raised her head, lifted her arm and flicked her hand to the side. The double iron doors slammed shut with a deafening thud, extinguishing every flame in the room in a heartbeat. From the darkness rose an amber light, like that of a summer's sunset. She remained in the centre of the stage, arm held high and relaxed, feet close together. She performed her swaying, snaking her shape in an alluring hypnotic way, all the while keeping her eyes closed. Lowering her hand down close to her thigh she wove together delicate steps. Slowly she raised Violethelm in her right hand in rhythm with the flow of soft music coming from somewhere in The Dome from a band. Isabelle left her spot and danced gracefully following a circular path while bodying circular motions with her hips and lifting her legs high, endlessly twirling. The gentlemen watching the ritual were shocked; none having known she was so flexible, able to speak to her limbs so fluently without debate. Her balance never faltered as she danced to the swirls of music, allowing her conscientious to be absorbed with the winds of hymns, rising into a cyclical storm. She shut herself off from everything around her, from the entire world of Equis and all her worries, crossing in and out of the realm of the ethereal, the realm where her Celestial waited patiently, surrounded by darkness and a heavy, blue mist. The drifting lilt of the music was her only guide now, Isabelle moved like a river meandering around a rock, straightening her staff and sliding her curves around it like a boa constricting its helpless prey. Her face remained calm, her mind focused on the ritual, but her body appeared to be moving by itself without any conscious input. Her eyes remained closed, the Glyph within dictating the fluidity of her curling legs and twisting arms. Skipping her way back to the centre of the stage, rolling into a great leap, she dropped into a crouched position upon landing, with Violethelm balanced vertically. Her ruby red shadow trailed after her, settling around her feet. Not a sound could be heard from the councilmen in the room, boiling with joy and anticipation. The candles sparked and the small flames grew tall into shining pillars of light.

The basin of fire burst with a blinding flash! A brightness dazzled everyone but Isabelle, whose eyes had only now opened, revealing a fire of emerald within. She arose, returning to life matching the temper of the music, exploding into a rage of

321

movement only the inferno could dance to. She spun as viciously as an angry tornado in an open field. She tapped her feet and turned her legs on the spot, all the while twirling around, releasing her limbs into a series of spiralling kicks, constantly circling the stage. Her arms made use of her staff, spinning rapidly around her wrists. Isabelle swung around the edge of the stage, tailed by a gleam of green flame emitted from her eyes. Picking up speed, she dove into a forward roll and flipped herself into the air! The councillors gasped at the height she was able to raise herself and danger of what a misstep would bring to her. She moved like fire in the wind, the beauty of her leaps almost inhuman. The dress that trailed after her seemed to turn and move by itself, acting as her inanimate dance partner. The Star Caller leapt into the air and rolled into a ball, landing on her feet, slipping Violethelm into a hole at the far end of the stage. The staff stood vertical and the soft melody stopped with a thundering thud. A slower tune arose from the shadows, the candles glowing blood-red, the basin of releasing swarms of fireflies as the fire ascended outward, curling and coiling into The Dome only to plummet like a waterfall, splashing back down into the basin of searing heat. The loving melody floated and crept into the ears of the observers. Isabelle had gripped the attention of her audience; she would have to die to break their attention now; none of them could physically look away from the spectacle. She paced around Violethelm seductively, exposing her thighs, giving the gawping Councillors a treat. As the melody grew ever quieter, she grabbed the tip of the staff where the clouded, lilac orb was indented into the helm, pulling something out. The music grew to a crescendo and The Chosen leapt into a series of back flips, coming to a stop in the centre of the stage. Her palm outstretched her hand convulsed with the effort of trying to pull something from the orb. As the magical sphere reacted, so did the basin of fire; something was coming through! The Councillors could just about make out a string of web, a trail of mist running from her hand to the orb. The web then shattered as Isabelle made her final pull! She lost concentration for a fraction of a second as she noticed something beyond Yespin; in the shadows of The Dome was a sixth onlooker! An uninvited and unwelcome guest. Lured in by Violethelm, she pulled the staff from the hole in the stage; reclaiming her tool, part of her since she chose it from many others. Isabelle twisted herself on the spot, the melody repeating itself in time with her steps and leaps. The music told a story, though there were no sheets to read from, the musicians had long since become one with their instruments, just like The Chosen was one with her Glyph. She was in control of how long the music would play; indeed, there was no set time for the ritual, rather it was depended on how long it took her to accomplish. With a deep breath, she turned and javelined the staff high into the air. Time slowed down, the men watching on as the staff fell through the air into another groove at the opposite end of the stage. The end landed perfectly in the hole and steadied itself, only wobbling ever so slightly. Her dress sank to her sides as a light gust blew followed by a moment of peace. Isabelle stood completely still with her head held high, her eyes delicately closed shining through her eyelids. Was the ritual over?

Yespin managed to fill his lungs with air and release some words just as Isabelle burst into flames, the fire engulfing her entirely. Darlo shouted out in horror:

"VERANO!" but was held back by Taktard. The fire reared up and wailed. A few of the Councillors looked at each other in panic; was this a horrible accident or part of the ritual? Yespin could barely see The Chosen, apparently encased safely inside the blazing shell, standing normally, arms at her sides. His heart rate calmed as he saw that she was in no danger. He could see her mouth moving through the breaks in the flames; she was talking to someone - or something. *What was she saying?* The inferno gave way, opening like a flower in the warmth of spring and then whisked itself away, disappearing into the air along with the flowing notes of the accompanying melody. Suddenly, all was quiet and still. Isabelle toppled onto her front, using her fingertips as balance, her red dress once again falling to the floor, only this time... Nothing happened. The girl collected herself exhausted, breathing like she had been drowning. The Councillors sat there, stunned; even Cillian looked uncomfortable in his seat. Darlo sat down, a bit embarrassed about his outburst earlier, hoping that the others wouldn't make anything of this later over drinks. Yespin stood slowly, realising the ritual was over, and called out to Isabelle, finding to her feet, shaking off her fatigue.

"A fine display, young Isabelle," he praised, clapping. "That was rather more than what we expected, I'm sure, but where is The Celestial Soul? Why didn't it come?" Isabelle raised her strength to talk, sharing her voice with another occupying her mind, a voice only she could hear.

"He is here. He is before you. Behold the pure fire." A few droplets of sweat ran down her forehead, streaks of loose hair had escaped their ties and dangled over her face. Vapour evaporated off her shoulders and the pores in her neck. She took a long, deep breath of air, noticing the moth dying on the floor, its wings burning, sizzling away. She pointed to the basin, her finger glowing with golden rings, and then relaxed her arm to her side. Her eyes, still emanating a glow of green, she was more interested in the moth, roasting on the floor. Yespin stepped down from the seating area and on to the stage, feeling a sudden rush of heat as he approached. The closer he became, the more difficult it was to walk, as if he was passing through a hot mist. Still, he edged toward the basin.

"Careful!" warned Isabelle, "Be slow with your movements, Yespin. Do not touch anything or you will burn up in an instant." She picked up the little moth in her hands, enclosing it in her palm. Yespin peered inside the smoking basin and saw charred rock and a dying fire. He glared again at Isabelle, who stood still on the stage, her back to him as she cradled the moth. Once again, he inspected the basin; the dying fire was starting to find life once more, so he stepped away, a little startled by what he had seen inside. Darlo called out impatiently:

"WHICH CELESTIAL?!" This outburst did not sit well with the soul that had made the journey to the human plain. From the basin behind Yespin a thick, yellow stream of fire arose, lighting the entirety of The Glyph Dome. A wide column, a rising stream of golden flames grew a web of wings and unfolded a tail of fire. Isabelle spoke the ethereal tongue, a language heard only by Celestials and The Star Caller.

"The Phoenix? You've always adored this form." The men in the room knew nothing of the conversation between them, only the creature engulfed in flames having materialised into Equis before their very eyes, could understand her. "Maybe something a little smaller if you don't mind, my sunlight son?" she requested of the Demi-God. The fire left its wings behind and transformed into a large serpent, coiling around the curved wall of the chamber. Isabelle

324

faced The High Councillors of Virtue and spoke aloud, this time in the common tongue: "BEHOLD... THE PURE FIRE... ARIES! CELESTIAL OF WAR!" The serpent, made entirely of a controlled inferno, slithered around The Glyph Dome, around Isabelle. "May I?" she asked Aries, and the Celestial agreed, allowing her to touch him. The flames burned purple as she gently stroked, the radiant heat having no apparent impact on her. Aries was her friend after all; he would never harm The Chosen. The Celestial leapt into the centre of the stage, taking on yet another form. It trotted in the form of a ram, with long pointed horns and a whipping, crackling tail. The ram moved around slowly, staring at the council members, one at a time. The Councillors stared back, restrained by fear and powerlessness. Isabelle strolled over, her palms together and knelt in front of Aries. The two exchanged whispers which the men could barely hear nor understand. Aries galloped away from her, taking flight, turning into a fiery comet, and launching itself into the heart of a tiny candle flame in the corner of the room. The Councillors had forgotten to breathe while in the presence of Aries and managed to contain themselves as the smoke cleared away. Isabelle opened her hands and the moth crawled out on to her fingers, fluttering away, blessed with the use of its wings once again. She watched it fly, and then looked down to the Councillors, still struck in awe. She gave them a look like nothing had happened. Her irises paled back to their normal colour, the Glyph storm inside her was as calm as the sea, and her heart ceased to pump so violently. "Hmph!" She muttered, pulling Violethelm out from the groove in the stage and bound down the stone stairs, wiping the sweat off her brow, flicking the droplets away.

It was late and Lethaniel realised he was in trouble. He sprinted through the streets, The Palace of Norisis overlooking him. The large building, he ran up to was already closing for the night and people were coming out with delighted smiles on their faces, all talking about the grand act they had just witnessed in the theatre. Lethaniel sighed and felt sick as he breathed heavily, cursing to himself. He waited outside on a damp bench, taking note of every person that left the place. Before the doors were closed by the guards, one last person exited. He saw her standing there, looking beautiful and innocent in the night, but she was cold. Standing up, he approached her slowly. Her face said it all when her eyes fell upon his.

"I am sorry, I meant to come by, it's just..."

"It's alright, Lethaniel. I understand; you had to work. You're an important, although you've always been important to me," she said in a soft, understanding tone of voice.

"Did you go alone? I mean, did you see any of your friends that may have taken you in?" asked Lethaniel.

"No, I guess everyone else will go another night, but I saw it and I would like to see it again someday."

"Eva, I'm sorry. I truly am. Maybe we can make arrangements for tomorrow?" Before she could even respond, he changed his mind. "No, wait, not tomorrow, in three days' time perhaps... maybe. If I can talk with Thao, I could possibly re-schedule" overlooking a light sigh. Eva tiptoed down the steps and stood next to him, shoulder to shoulder. "Can you tell me about it?" he asked from a wince.

"I am so glad you're home. I wish you all the best in your career as General; I know you won't fail the people." Lethaniel's heart sank; He swallowed, but his mouth was dry, he needed water and quickly.

"You were the only thing keeping me going, you know that right"

"I know, so were you" she said.

"One day there will be no need for men like me, will you be there when that happens?"

"I don't know, how can I answer that?" she said, squeezing her eyes.

"Don't" he said as she came a little closer and held his hand, he was unable not to grip her fingers, pressing it to his chest.

"I wish I could go back to that place, to those moments we shared, I held onto them for as long as I could, hoping that one day they would grow, but I can't hold on anymore, I let go a long time ago. I'm sorry." She let go of his hand and kissed him lightly on the lips, before finding her way home.

"I'm sorry about your father…" She stopped momentarily on the road but did not turn. "I'm sorry I wasn't there for you when you needed me. I should have been."

Lethaniel lost count of the hours that drifted by, he found himself splayed out on a bench that overlooked the canal, fiddling with his wooden pendent of the feline, laced around his neck.

The High Councillors had left, and the doors had shut tight. Isabelle removed her hair net and her curls fell over her shoulders. She could have sworn she had seen someone in the shadows while she was performing, so she returned to The Glyph Dome to investigate. She listened carefully for quite some time, for a noise or the shuffle of fabric, yet nothing came to her ears. Was there another presence in the room? She sensed movement in the surrounding darkness. Whatever it was it had not been infused with Glyph, otherwise, she would have picked up the scent. She had no reason to be afraid; she was The Chosen, a great Star Caller with immense amounts of power at her fingertips. So why then was she so reluctant to venture into the darkness? "Seal this door, do so now" she ordered.

"Yes, milady," the guard said, bowing his head. She was joined in the hallway by more of her Glyph Wielders who escorted her back to her room in The Palace of Norisis.

Chapter 15 - The Tower Cell

Some days after Isabelle's performance, on the eve of the assembly.

In the quiet of the early morning, the gates of Imrondel opened for a band of galloping riders. They traversed the smoggy Defensive Trench and rode into the gardens on the stone paths. The riders dismounted and were greeted by one of the gate keepers, while their horses were taken to the stables for feeding. One rider was left alone, almost avoided, like a rabid stray dog or an unwelcome guest. Alexius walked over to the new arrivals, puffing out some excess smoke, and met up with the armourer.

"There he is. People told me you were on route with The Star Caller, but when you didn't arrive with the rest... Welcome back to Imrondel City, Jerhdia," he beamed, shaking Jerhdia's hand.

"The days have been rough; summer I think, has decided to pass us by and spend its time elsewhere." Indeed, recent days had not been warm; the daylight hours had been brisk. Jerhdia refused the offer of a roll-up, so Alexius closed the tin of smokes and shoved them into his pocket. It was only then that he noticed the strange man upon the horse, the outcast. He gave the man a brief glance before looking back at Jerhdia, who spoke with a hint of urgency: "I must talk with Thao. Take me to him now, would you?" Alexius ignored the request, for the time being, instead, he leaned into the armourer and whispered:

"Who is that? Is he one of your men?"

"No, I don't think he's from around here," replied Jerhdia.

"Is he from Jureai then?" Alexius asked, noting his tanned skin.

"Yeah, I think so; he wears the cloth of a Bevork." Alexius inspected his surroundings. Without warning an armed group of Regular soldiers rushed in and surrounded the rider, using their sharp spears to block his way, ushering him and his horse up to a stone wall. "What is going on?!" Jerhdia demanded, making his way toward the guards, arresting his travelling companion, pulling him off the saddle of his horse, binding The Northlander's wrists with rusty shackles. "What's going on? What are you doing with him?!" Several guards restrained Jerdhia before he could intervene.

"Let the armourer go," ordered Alexius, who then explained the situation, the new laws concerning visitors from Jureai found in The Western lands.

Lena was preparing a meal in the kitchen, surrounded by healthy, blossoming herbs and plants. She occasionally glanced outside to check on the progress Thao was making with their son in the yard; she wondered how long it would be before Lucion would want to move on to the real training areas in The Military District. She sighed; even after days of practicing morning, noon and night, the boy still attempted the same predictably aggressive moves against his father. He tried too hard and was knocked to the floor each time. *Knock knock.* Lena went to the door, pulling her hair back into a ponytail as she opened it. Thao was unaware of his wife's disappearance and continued as usual in training.

"Your swings are long and ungainly, giving me far too much time to act against them," he criticised.

"So I should strike quickly?"

"Yes, but make sure it's a hard, decisive blow; don't hesitate, never hesitate, hesitation gets people killed. Often you can defeat the more inexperienced fighters just by watching their faces and noticing when they lose focus. Now, again my son and this time try not to think about hitting me and just bloody hit me!" As he readied himself to absorb the impact of the strike, he noticed Lena coming outside. Blocking Lucion's strike and forcing him back, he turned to his wife as she spoke.

"Mr Marsay wishes to see you."

"What does Alexius want?" asked Thao.

"Jerhdia has returned to the city, and he has someone with him you may wish to speak to." Thao nodded, aware that the day's lessons would have to finish early.

"We will have to cut it short today, Lucion. I apologise but remember what I told you. Daddy has some important work to do." He rubbed his son's head and handed the wooden sword to Lena as he passed her on his way to change, leaving her alone in the yard with Lucion. The boy looked ready to fight her too; she smiled and stepped into the yard with him.

"You don't want to see what I can do," she joked, looking at the end of the wooden stick.

"Can you fight?" Lucion asked, spinning his own sword around childishly in his hands, fumbling the handle, dropping it only to quickly pick it up.

"Of course I can," she replied, taking a few gentle swings from her son, able to block them easily each time.

"Are you good? What weapon do you use?" Lucion had never heard anything about his mother fighting. He had received plenty of training from Thao; now it was Lena's turn to offer some insight.

"I can fight just as well as your father; in fact, he would probably say I am the better fight."

"Really? You are better than Dad?" She nodded, twisting her wooden sword around Lucion's.

"I prefer to fight my battles without resorting to violence. Your father has his way of resolving problems, I have my own." She could tell by his expression that he did not understand; he just wanted to practise his sword work. Lena stopped blocking his attacks and lowered her training stick. "Overpowering your foes with brawn has its uses, but there are other ways to fight without spilling blood. You will learn about them in time" she winked, exaggerating her prowess in a clearly playful manner.

330

"So do you use a dagger or bow?" Lucion misunderstood, Lena laughed and knelt in front of him.

"I use the greatest weapon in the world…" Lucion was now intrigued. "Far stronger than a hammer, sharper than any dagger and even more precise than an arrow fired from the finest bow."

"Is it… Magic? Do you use Glyph?" Lena shook her head.

"There is an even better defence than Glyph…" She touched her finger onto his chest, giving him his answer. "Your father is right when he says fight with your head. Your mind can tell you when to charge, your mind can tell you when to run. It can strategise, plot, deceive and decode, but your heart is where your real voice truly lies. Listen to it when all other voices are spent, follow it, it will always know what to do." She stood up and took the wooden sword from him. It was time to eat.

Thao followed a band of soldiers through the city streets, absorbing many glares from passers-by. They came to a large building with an arched entrance way built from white stone, a Norkron banner hanging from the centre. The men led Thao up a passageway of hundreds of steps which merged into an open walkway overlooking a grand view of The Golden City. Below them was a country of shapely rooftops with rivers of Imrondel's citizens flooding through the streets. Norisis had the tallest of towers, casting their shadows over the other districts in the distance. At the end of the walkway was an oak door, the escorting soldiers waited outside for Thao to enter along. Sitting behind the door was Jerhdia and the others who had travelled with him into Tthenadawn Forest, to look for the missing boy, Jaden. Thao swung the door to a close, shutting out the light; he had been anticipating this meeting.

"Did you find him?" Jerhdia shook his head and pushed Jaden's sword and his few belongings from under the chair. Thao picked them up and examined them.

"We ventured into Tthenadawn Forest and scouted for two days," said Jerhdia.

"And what did you find?"

"Nothing but what you're holding." The armourer stood up and put his hands on his hips, pacing around, waiting for Thao to speak, but he never did, he just looked at the belongings, asking the same questions Jerhdia had been asking for days. "We did manage to track something else in those woods; something big…" This captured Thao's attention; Dark Rogues were the first thing that entered his mind. "Tracks led us deep into Tthenadawn; it was strange, I've never seen prints as large as this…" Jerdhia scratched his chin as he tried to describe what they had seen. "They looked human, but we could not be sure. We abandoned the search on the second day, it was a hard decision to make. We all cared for Jaden, but that forest can turn into a labyrinth. Stumbling into the unknown and losing more men was the last thing I wanted, so I gave the order to withdraw." Thao sat down and placed the equipment next to him.

"Does the loss of this soldier affect our situation?" Jerhdia scowled at Thao. "If Jaden is alive and The Dark Rogues pick him up for interrogation, that cannot bode well for our current circumstance regarding the Dovidians, can it? Does Jaden know of anything important?" Jerhdia ignored the questions and continued his story, saving the arguments for later.

"That's not all we found. When we started our return journey to Imrondel City, we came across someone, a man. He was riding upon Jaden's horse; we nearly put four arrows in him on sight. I think he is from Jureai, a Bevork Clansman, his skin is well tanned, his cloth was light and there is a tinge of a northern accent in his voice."

"Where is he now?"

"Don't worry, he has been detained. Soldiers seized him just outside The Defensive Trench. Alexius oversaw the arrest. He refused to talk, or even defend himself for that matter." Thao felt it was a good time to explain the new law.

"An order was issued that any suspicion of foreign scouts must be investigated. Ivulien may be facing an impending invasion from the north. We are simply taking precautions, Jerhdia. What do you think of this Bevork?"

"He seems harmless; he didn't make a fuss while travelling. I think we should release him as soon as possible, caging him up as we did without food, water or explanation as to why we arrested him seems a bit inhumane to me..." Thao nodded in agreement. "Now if you don't mind, I have other matters to attend to." Jerhdia walked to the door, taking his missing man's gear on the way. "It doesn't affect us or our immediate situation, Honour Guard, but I assure you that his family's lives will change forever after I deliver the news today. I assigned Jaden to this task; I will take full responsibility for his loss and apologise profusely to his parents. Not that apologies will heal the family's wounds, but it's better than not saying a word." With that, he stormed off down the hall. Thao stood and asked the other soldiers where he could find the prisoner.

"Inside The Prison Towers," one answered.

"And what is the Bevork's name?"

"Othello, Sir...Last name Hawk"

"The rest of the Councillors are close; last I heard they were about two days away. I hope this meeting will actually solve something, rather than simply creating more problems like usual," said Isabelle, stirring her hot tea as she walked next to a trolley full of books in one of the narrow aisles of The Old Library. "Thinking about it, it has been a long time since the leaders from Xiondel and Imrondel City gathered together like this. It's almost like they've no need for one another anymore... Hah! Competitive natures and alliances, they all clash eventually I guess."

"It does beg the question, Isabelle; the cities are allied despite the bickering relationship of their citizens, we are united and prepared to stand together, but against what, exactly? Either way, it's your voice we listen to. You will be expected to speak on The Eldors behalf at this meeting. I hope you have been preparing your words carefully, words that will reach the minds of politicians, noblemen, mayors and ministers," replied Eran, slotting some books back into their gaps. They continued along in the pleasant atmosphere, bells ringing outside from distant towers; today the city was bright and alive with many thousands of people flocking the streets. A few walked the halls of The Old Library, seeking shelter from the intense sunshine. Those who passed, acknowledged Isabelle with small bows and smiles, making space for her to move by comfortably. She walked with her head up high, arm behind her back, the other hand clutching her tea.

"I cannot say I have prepared any speeches just yet, but I have an idea of what I wish to say."

"Care to share?" prompted Eran, juggling a handful of books, getting ready to climb up his extendable ladder.

"I will not give up the power of the Celestials; there is no way they can prevent me from using Star Call. As a matter of fact, they cannot stop me from using any of my gifts, whether it be Vision Channelling, Skin Burning, Whispering or any of the others. For as long as I live, I will always be a Star Caller, cutting me off from my abilities and practises would be cruel…" Eran seemed to like the first part as he continued to work. "I cannot see Krondathia sharing its secrets with Ivulien either. Our treasuries in our Inner and Outer Vaults of Xiondel and The Safe Houses of Imrondel, our riches and wealth… I doubt any of it is of interest to the Dovidians, so what can we offer to put their minds at rest?" She continued to flick through the book while Eran paused for a moment. He jumped down the metal steps, surprisingly agile for his age; he had thought of a solution that would resolve the matter, but couldn't bring himself to tell her, not just yet. He looked at her to see if she had noticed the change in his facial expression, but she hadn't.

Just then, the front doors of the library opened and a group of young students came flooding inside, all holding books and fancy, black satchels. They were dressed in their traditional uniforms, bearing a strong resemblance to Eran's librarian outfit; a loose, black robe, light grey tunics, and a green sash. The Master had a golden sash, a pure white robe and silver tunic, but otherwise, they looked very much alike. The students made their way to the common seating area and sat at their desks beside a wall inset with colourful windows. One came over to Eran; she spoke of her work and showed him a page in her notebook. She did not notice Isabelle right away, sipping her tea. It was only when the young girl made her way back to her friends that she turned around, shocked to see the most powerful woman in the world not twenty feet away.

"You're welcome to stay, my dear," the Master said to Isabelle, who was thinking about her own years as a student, how she had grown up studying with Eran and the other tutors, who simply couldn't compare to him. She could remember his lectures, twice a week in her schedule. He never used to get cross or frustrated, because his lessons were always captivating and thought-provoking, people wanted to be there. He would use a large, square blackboard that he could roll around on squeaky wheels. Isabelle remembered it as a child, she used to dread the sound of the approaching board, but now she loved it. She had fond memories of being called upon to draw on it, to solve equations or to highlight certain passages from books. Speaking in front of the class used to frighten her, standing up alone in front of all those judging faces brought on terrible episodes of anxiety. Stage fright was something she had had to overcome, but with Eran's help; she could stand before an audience of any size without making a stutter.

"I will stay for a little while if that's alright. What are you teaching today?" she asked, putting the book she had been flicking through back on the trolley. He chuckled at the question, amused at the irony.

"Omnio. Magic studies. Your favourite, I believe. These are some of my most dedicated students." Isabelle raised her eyebrows.

"Only because it was easy, and I didn't have to try…" Eran gave her an accusing glance. "What?" she smiled, and they both laughed quietly.

"Don't make me call you up to the front for talking in the back like I used to," he warned. With that, he began his lecture. The students stopped gossiping about The Star Caller in the library standing only a few feet away, leaning on a nearby bookshelf, her bare arms folded. Every once in a while a student would turn their head to get another look at her, to look at her face, to try to spy the invisible aura that surrounded her, the aura that had grown and grown, ever since she picked up her long staff during the ceremony where she was hailed as The Chosen. Behind her stood Adarmier, who was reading the spine of an interesting book he had found, though he had many others under his arm. She found it incredible that he had the time to read so much. He looked about the same age as the other students; she wondered if he required the same tutoring. Maybe it was time to properly meet this young lad.

The wind blew cold against the Prison Towers. Like many such structures in Imrondel City, the Krondathian flag flew proudly at the very top, strung to a lengthy, iron pole. Inside the prison, along a dank, narrow hallway, a row of four prison cells lay quiet. An irregular hole had been knocked into the wall at the far end of the passageway, allowing entry to an uncomfortable draught of air and a single ray of light, which beamed in diagonally onto the stone floor between eroding iron bars. Two prisoners occupied this tower, each to their own cage. The crime rate in Imrondel was so low and the justice system so efficiently swift, that those who dared to commit offences were quickly caught, tried and punished, serving their sentence in the top of one of these towers, paying back the community through time and labour, depending on the offence committed. Torches lit the hallway, drops of water running down the sides of the damp, rocky walls, the only sound being the scurrying of insects infesting the soggy, dank corners of the cells. Othello perched upon a nook in the wall, head down and miserable, wondering why he had been arrested and locked up without reason. He missed his village, the warmth of the sun and his friends in Jureai. It was cold here in this part of the world and no one had truly seen him, but at least he had made it. He sometimes had to remind himself why he was there, why he had travelled for so many months. The ring his father had given him brought with it, fond memories; that was his true purpose, to find out its origin. From the shadows of the farthest cell, something crawled out, dragging its fragile weight over the unclean floor. It had no need to use its legs; it had not used them properly for so long they had become useless. The old prisoner's clothing was hideous; shredded and stained with muck and grim. The prisoner edged his way to the bars, looking through them at Othello, sulking in the opposite cell. The older man's hair had grown long, rinsing itself with a natural oily conditioner, having long since collected families of hungry lice. His voice was dry and sickly; he no longer had a full set of teeth, so his speech was slurred as he babbled scratchy words, some being too hard for Othello to decipher.

"You..." his whisper was long and drawn out, which gripped The Northlander's attention. "You are not from here... Or maybe you are, just been away, have you? Far away in the north?" His laugh was short and sounded painful. Othello did not respond. The prisoner pulled himself up and leant on the bars with his bony shoulder; coughing roughly, spitting out blood and wiped his mouth with his damp sleeve "Why are you in this place, boy? They only reserve these cells for dangerous men. Why are you in here?" Othello maintained his silence. "Are you a traitor, lad? A murderer? Or did you dare to speak? Telling the truth will get always you locked up in here, heh heh," he laughed again, finding something amusing about the situation. He had clearly lost his mind. Othello stared at him in confusion and finally replied:

"You're delusional. I'm not a boy, look at my face, I'm almost thirty."

"You're still just a boy, compared to me you have barely lived..." Othello stared at the rocky space between his feet. "You don't look like a murderer. I can tell what kind of person a man is by his eyes, what they've seen, what they've had to witness. Your eyes have seen violence, but you are good. You are no traitor either... But then neither am I. I am here because of..." He stuck out his wart ridden tongue, "This!"

"You were put in here because you spoke a word?"

"Hahaha! A few words strung together actually, boy. I think it added up to a sentence or two in total, but I never killed anyone who didn't try to kill me first. All that you've heard about me before you got in here is a lie. I tell everyone who sits where you are, but they don't believe me, no one does." He spat out more blood and wiped it away with the same portion of the sleeve, smearing red across the side of one cheek.

"I've not heard anything about you, I've only just arrived. What did you say to get yourself locked up in here?" asked Othello.

337

"I don't remember, and it doesn't matter now, but I was put here by them who's in charge."

"I haven't said anything, I do not even know who is in charge, I've not met their King" said Othello.

"Then you are here for a different reason. If I were allowed outside I might be of more help but I have not left this tower for some thirteen years. Thirteen years they've kept me here, only to silence me, to silence my words. They know nothing and refuse to accept the truth, the real meaning that I figured out, that I found in that… land… That land of nightmares. The only way they will let me out of here is if they cut out my tongue and chop off my hands, though they already got one," the prisoner snorted, holding up his left arm for Othello to see. His left hand had been mutilated, with just a few fingers remaining, hanging off a fragile wrist bone. The decrepit man lay on the floor of his cell with his legs splayed out like they too had been broken. Othello noticed hand-crafted, stone figurines, crudely made from fallen rocks inside the cell. Distinctive marks had also been scratched into the wall; drawings of mountains with suns rising between them. The drawings were detailed considering the few materials the prisoner had to work with. He also spotted a bird's nest sitting in the higher reaches of his cell, in the driest corner. "What are you looking at, lad?"

"Nothing… Who are you? What truth do you speak of?" whispered Othello, trying his best not to draw the attention of the guards hanging around outside. The prisoner smiled, revealing a set of yellow teeth. He slumped his head against the bars, his skin so thin it looked like it would tear.

"You really wish to know? You wouldn't understand, boy, but someone else might… Another who will come to share this cell maybe. As I said, only the dangerous inhabit these cells, and in the future we will need dangerous men and women, to fight the wars we cannot. Maybe one day real heroes will unwrap my legacy, those who have knelt before her and returned. I knelt before her, my boy; I knelt over her bones, the bones of her, the first… I remember when I was once called a Master. I remember many things, extraordinary things. I was so close, but… We thought it best to leave when we had already gotten so far. It seemed like the best plan at the time, because of that land… That land wants you dead. It wants you to die, wants you to suffer. It wants you to go mad. If you can gaze upon the realm and live to talk about it, strange things start to happen, impossible things start to appear. When you cross the boundary, something changes; the real world recedes to be replaced with insanity. It's rumoured that only one can walk that plain without being hunted by giants and attacked by the violet storms, only ONE is unaffected by its cruel nature. The rest of us are exposed to whatever is in there. I heard something talk to me, calling me from the darkness, but I had not the strength to go on by then…" His words made no sense, though he was clearly growing more and more upset as he spoke. "I can still hear it! I can still hear him! He wants me back… LIKE WE HAVE MET BEFORE! Somewhere." Othello was cautious about asking questions, afraid they'd lead to more nonsensical ramblings.

"And what is in there?"

"Something… horrible. Something unreal, I made maps, I did, maps of the nightmare plains and death-defying, twisted, clawed mountains…" He continued to speak in riddles of a place Othello had never heard of. "Before I entered the nightmare… I had travelled to the hidden city, frozen in ice, buried under layers of snow. 'Tis a place of death, corruption is drawn there, but if you get to it, if you get to that place under the shadow of the ankle, evidence is what you will find, evidence is buried there. You'll see them! You'll see those who came before our kind…"

"Buried in snow you say? Far to the west of Jureai the altitudes rise, and snows fall. I have heard stories of a mountain the size of a thousand cities. A sea, set in ice, a creature dwelling in its depths… I do not know of this nightmare place you speak of, but I know you must be referring to Maire, a country frozen in the snow." The prisoner chuckled heartily.

"You're a sharp lad, but not sharp enough. I speak of places men dare not travel to, but I've seen them, and escaped them." A tally of the man's days of imprisonment had been scratched away in the wall in his cell, now showing nearly fourteen years. Othello decided to ignore further more of the prisoner, resigning himself to the fact that the poor fellows mind had turned to rot. He stood up and placed his hands on the bars, resting his head on them with greater pressure. "If only you could see what I saw. The truth that surrounds us, choking the religion. I know that one day man will discover the truth and finish what I started. It will begin with these drawings I have made. Sometimes the guards give me paper, this paper will lead the way, you'll see, you'll see. I made better maps a long time ago, but they took them from me. These scraps are merely copies, copies of the unknown that will guide the chosen one to salvation and peace. First, you must help me get out of here though," he said, scrambling to his feet to reach Othello's eye level, stuffing the reams of paper behind a loose rock in the cell wall. "Help me, please! I have been here for so long," he begged Othello, who merely shook his head.

"I'm in the same position as you, I can't help. I'm sorry."

"Hand me that!" The old man pointed to The Northlander's midriff.

"You want this? It's only a leather belt."

"Yes! It will help me escape this place for good." Interested in seeing what the plan was, Othello undid his belt and threw it to the rotting prisoner in the far cell.

"Thank you. Thank you, kind sir," he praised while pulling the belt tight, testing its durability. "What is your name, boy?"

"Othello. How do you plan to escape the cell?"

"Mine is Toshore. MASTER RUTHAL TOSHORE! FOR THE THOUSANDTH BLOODY TIME! I am pleased to meet you Othello." Seemingly unaware of his random outburst, he reached through the bars, attempting to shake his new best friend's hand, but had offered the foul stump. Toshore crackled out a loud laugh cut off with the opening of the tower's door. Toshore hid the belt and skulked back into the shadows from whence he had come, picking up a rock, the very same one he had used to mark his walls. Grunting to himself, he began to scratch something on a smoother surface of stone. The Honour Guard that entered was more interested in

Othello, who did not flinch as the man of mighty proportions approached.

Isabelle sat at the back of the class in a larger, more comfortable chair than the students, who had to settle for wooden, fold-out seats. Eran was teaching them about the birth of Glyph, where it came from, bursting out from rivers of mana inside the earth's crust, forming spouts of energy, also known as Glyph fountains or springs. As he spoke, he gestured with his hands, pointing at his blackboard with a feather pen, fielding a stream of questions from his fascinated audience.

"Is The Cavern of Mana real, Master? Do you know if it exists?" Eran knew the ripple effect questions like these had in his class, and before he had a chance to quell the excitement, hands were rising and his students were firing.

"What about Druids, Master?"

"What about The Pearl Caves, the Pinching Imp?" "The Remedy Keeper and the sunken city petrified in crystal?" The queries all seemed to originate from the stories they had read about or had been told as infants, stories that connected lovingly with Eran's lessons.

"I have heard these rumours before" Eran slid the quill behind his ear and rested his back against the frame of his blackboard. "Explorers, some of whom are my former students, have long endeavoured to find proof of such colourful stories and returned with questionable but sketchy fragments of evidence. This 'proof' debunked by some, idolised by others, does not meet Gaia's standard, meaning it is not up for debate, but last time I checked, we're not in the halls of Gaia, we are in a far greater place than that, are we not?" said Eran drumming up slight laughs and giggles from among his students. "None of said explorers have come back from their travels having witnessed a myth for themselves. For argument's sake, The Silent Vale is nothing more than woodland; would you all agree?" The class nodded, mumbling amongst themselves, but ultimately siding with Master Eran. "A former student of mine returned to me last year, claiming that the rock he was waving around in front of my face came from the formations surrounding the waterfall of Nightfall's Lost Lagoon itself. I'm sure you've heard of that one; a lagoon so beautiful, so mesmerising where The Vale opens up when the night is at its darkest, where nature is at total peace with itself, where the water sparkles at the merest of touches and the star blooms glow brighter than ever before." His description even had Isabelle hooked. "The outside world is temporarily frozen in time, unable to break the boundaries of the paradise you've stepped into. Ten out of ten to this student for bringing back EVIDENCE instead of just his word, but the rock was nothing more than a rock. I could find the exact same thing outside my house. He couldn't lead me to the lagoon; he couldn't give me instructions on how to investigate this myth further, no, apparently, he had just visited the place and could provide nothing more than his word and the rock which was just... A rock..." The students looked a little disheartened. "That is not to say that such myths do not exist, there is a reason to still hope, it's nice to believe and wonder, it's nice to fantasise about stories and tales from books. I was once like you, a dreamer, but we all must learn how to think long before we start involving fairy-tales, inserting them into the gaps of history, or using them to explain away mystery, can only stifle our progression and wear down the critical thinking skills." He caught Isabelle's eye at the back of the class. "Never stop asking these questions, study your answers and do your best to debunk your theories, otherwise the world will do it for you?"

"You mean Equis will humiliate us if we get it wrong?" said one of the boys sitting at the back.

"Maintain a mental line between fantasy and reality my children; by all means, don't stop reading fairy-tales, it's important to indulge, just be sure not to get lost in there to the point that you start believing it's true. Fantasy can be a dangerous tool. Enjoy it, but do not start promoting false accounts as fact." He took the pen out from behind his ear and dropped it upon his desk, having come to the end of his little speech. "I'll give you a week to finish the assignment I set you, pose yourself an impossible question and come back and tell me about it, but please keep any rocks to yourselves guys, I have enough of them in my collection..." They laughed generously at his attempt at humour. "Delving into the unknown is useful, imagination is an ingredient as to what drives us forward as a species." One student was leaning back in her chair, only partially listening while fiddling with a small shard of glass, which Eran noticed, it reflecting the light. He pointed and the others turned to look. "Jayna!" The girl jolted upright, startled by the sound of her name being called. "What are you holding there?"

"It's a magnifying glass, sir," she replied, twiddling its handle in her fingers, holding it up for all to see.

"There, that is a perfect example. At some point in time what you are holding HAD to be thought up, it HAD to be designed and it HAD to go through a process in order for it to end up as a working end product, for use by people who desired a closer look at things. Everything you see here - the desks you sit at, the spines of your books, The Star Caller's long staff and my wonderful chalkboard - everything you see had to be imagined, designed and built to serve us. That includes Eliendras Cathedral, The Palace of Norisis and Xiliac all the way up to The Column Temple."

"What about The Column? Didn't someone - or something - else craft the temple, Master?"

"Well spotted and how right you are. It is indeed true that we found The Column Temple through the efforts of our explorers; we did not build it ourselves, which begs the question: *who did*? As for the temple itself - now here is an interesting fact you may or may not have heard - it actually looked different hundreds of years ago during the first years of The Awakening Ages. The temple is moving, my young students, it's unfolding..." None of them believed him; instead, a mellow eruption of laughter and whispered doubts filled the air. "Seriously, the temple is twisting itself, block by block, little by little, less than a millimetre a day, the blocks are rotating, and it has been proven. Freya Delmesca was the first to notice its slow spin when she was outside, around the side of the wall. She found tiny mounds of dust gathering at the base and, apparently, a bird's nest had fallen off a ledge that had been there for months. The bird's nest story isn't all that compelling on its own; nests fall all the time, after all, but how do you explain the accumulation of dust? Master Atheriax confirmed years ago that the temple is, in fact, twisting on the spot, with each block seeming to move at a different rate. Why? We don't know why... What history tells us is that Regina was the key to finding this temple, the world was a very different place back then. She opened doors for us when no other could; she unlocked secrets inside the temple when she herself was denied entry by the men in power. Secrets of twelve shrines dotted all over the world; she discovered those too. She was the first Chosen, the one with violet eyes Hallow predicted would come. Hence the name of the third age: The Awakening Ages. The Celestial Souls act as our guides; The Column Temple is their home. But she didn't learn everything in her short time; she simply set us on a path, one we are still journeying along, to bring forth an idyllic society, the utopian world. Anyway, enough of that, we are getting off topic. Don't let wonder throw you into peril. Some people believe that vaults of Glyph DO exist deep inside the planet, but I warn you, I urge you not to go looking until you learn all there is to know in the classroom. Your mind is your greatest tool and sharpest weapon, use it wisely. Surely you are aware of such great adventures, adventures of discovery and exploration in our world that have met cruel ends; perhaps this is the price of exploration, it's a perilous life. Know that the world IS dangerous and a lot of it remains unknown. The world's mysteries sometimes are best left at that. In any case, we are searching for facts and truths. Learn about what we know and master it, understand it and then move on to the next issue." He then drew detailed diagrams of mana fountains and the formation of the Glyph pearls themselves. The matter was explained as properly and professionally as possible, but even with Eran's wise words, some of his explanations were a little vague. Where did the Glyph find its power? What was it made of and why did Glyph flow through some humans better than others, giving them great strengths and sometimes massive weaknesses? And most importantly, why did Glyph bless some and curses others? The lecture was all too familiar to Isabelle; sometimes she felt very tempted to answer some of his questions and launch her hand up in the air to interrupt the class when no one else would.

She sat there, listening for a while, growing impatient, but then she saw Adarmier, moving around on the higher level of The Old Library. She got up and left the area quietly so as not to disturb the class. Making her way upstairs to the young boy, she didn't quite know what to expect from him, only that he seemed to be very much interested in the workings of Glyph. She was alerted by his Glyph scent, her green eyes lighting up very, very briefly when she sensed it. Her irises faded back to normal as she ceased to use her Tracking ability. He did not appear to notice her approaching him. He appeared tall, smartly dressed in a sharper, more professional uniform which he had customised himself. With his fine, healthy, black hair, dark brown eyes and eyes that pierced Isabelle's the moment their gazes crossed, she knew he was different, just as Eran had said. He was reading a book in silence, sitting comfortably on the floor.

"Hello there. What are you reading?" Isabelle asked kindly, sitting down next to him on the floor. The boy did not seem moved by her presence, which instantly got him off to a good start in her mind. She was used to everyone gasping, keeping their distance, questioning or not being their true selves around her. Adarmier was simply indifferent to her presence. He turned over a page and put the book down face-up so she could see the cover. Unsurprisingly he had been reading about Glyph. "Some days ago, I saw you reading a far more complicated book than that one. Were you reading it for pleasure or are you just interested in the workings of Glyph?"

"Did you read it for pleasure?" he asked, "Or do you read such books because you are genuinely interested?" Adarmier responded with his own questions, without a hint of hesitation. The boy looked her in the eyes as he spoke; he was very direct and fearless.

"Probably not, if I'm honest. If I had taken a different path I would likely be just like any other girl in the city. I'd have a job, I'd live in a house with my cat or my husband if he could tolerate my weird habits. So no, I probably wouldn't have gone near them even if I had the choice," she replied, adopting a lighter tone of voice.

"So you don't believe in destiny?" She pouted her lips, pondering the question, but before she could answer he elaborated. "Some people believe that the next Chosen, or Star Caller, reveals herself to her predecessor, that there is no other possible path for her, that it's just fate. Others believe that she is groomed for the position. Moulded and selected..." Isabelle had heard of these theories before and knew how to counter them, though she was patient enough to let Adarmier finish. "If I had to guess, I'd say you would believe in the latter theory." She liked the way he thought and smiled; it had been a long time since anyone had raised such an interesting topic, a topic that she had to spend time thinking about.

"Looking at it the way you do, giving me a choice between theory one and theory two, I'd say yes, you guessed correctly, grooming was an essential part of my progression. But if you look at it the way I see it, I'd say you were wrong."

"Could you explain?"

"Certainly." she folded her arms and legs and relaxed her neck, staring at the ceiling, searching for the correct words to use. "I was moulded, you could say I was groomed for power before I met Freya, after accidentally demonstrating my gifts to my unsuspecting mother. I was then taken to meet The Chosen of my time and don't ask me how, but Freya just knew I would be the one to take her place. Wouldn't you agree that the events that took place leading up to that choice could have been my destiny all along? Even if you train or are shaped that could very well be the path to revealing yourself…Understand?"

"That does make sense. I think," he sounded reluctant to agree, as though his mind had been left a bit boggled.

"When I went to meet Freya, I learned that she had already named her successor. Until I came along she would have been the next Star Caller, supposedly. There are strong arguments to support both theories you've shed light on, but if there can only be one Star Caller at a time, then it's always been my fate to be what I am today, and that is unchangeable because here I am."

"What happened to Freya's initial successor after she learnt that she was not to become The Chosen?"

"If only I could turn back time, that would be one of the first things I'd find out. Adarmier, it has been a pleasure to meet you." Adarmier took hold of her hand and shook it lightly.

"Lady Star Caller, you can't turn back time, but you can bend it; you just need to know when." Isabelle felt ashamed at her knowledge being undermined by a young boy; he was speaking to

346

her as Eran would. To avoid humiliation, she had to choose what she said carefully because this boy was smart.

"I can bend time you say? Can you tell me how? It could prove useful, you know."

"You can see into the future, can you not, with your Visions? As it goes, you may have the opportunity to alter it if it comes to pass before you. Your Visions allow this foresight…"

"Visions do not come to you on demand, nor are they ever in order."

"A Star Callers Mana flow is different to that of a normal being's; it's what separates you from me, why you have Visions and can call upon the great twelve Celestials that Regina awoke. It's the reason no Glyph Wielder will ever be as powerful as you. It's not foolish to think that it's probably the reason you were selected as a Star Caller in the first place, because you had a more potent Glyph scent... I read a book by a man named Tudor; his research on the Omnio Glaphiar Spheres goes far beyond anything ever imagined; it even touches upon its TRUE origin. It's fascinating. It's called *The Omnio Philosophy*."

"I've heard this story before, as have many men and women. Tudor died some time ago. I agree his works are infinitely intriguing, though most of his books have disappeared, but don't believe everything you read," she advised, feeling slightly hypocritical for she gained most of her knowledge from books and believed far more of what she read than was advisable.

"But Isabelle, don't believe everything you're told either. Most of Tudor's books were destroyed after his discoveries; does this mean we are not able to accept what he found? Or are we just incapable of realising it or accepting it ourselves?"

"I admire your thoughts and your passion for study, but you must accept what the wisest of us all taught."

"And what is that?"

"Belief. What you believe in or what you choose to believe is all that matters. It's a dangerous idea but it holds value," she quoted. "A wise one told us that, Adarmier. Do you know who it was?" His first thought was Regina Corah, but he wasn't sure, so he shook his head.

"I don't know... Was it Corah?" Isabelle smiled; he was incorrect.

"I think it was my mother actually; you might have heard it in a different context, but my mother instilled in me the knowledge that people believe what they want to believe, regardless of any arguments to the contrary. This method of thinking has led to our greatest discoveries, our greatest triumphs and revealed our most spectacular flaws. I placed my belief in my power and my core, in doing the right thing and sticking by it no matter what others told me. I am sure your mother lectures you from time to time, as all do their sons and daughters, a feeling you have in your heart, a voice you must listen to and follow. Mine did all too often..." The boy did not answer. She spotted a diagram of the cross-section of a Glyph sphere in the book he was reading. Adarmier studied the page, no longer making any attempt to engage in conversation. "You know what sphere that is?" she pointed. He took a very quick glance, lowered the book, and answered:

"Elemental Draw. Common. Located at every fountain. It grants the power to draw upon the elements, to bend them to your will. Once able to draw upon a primary source with ease, it won't be long before the holder finds the aggression of the fires and hurricanes within themselves to wield without the presence of a nearby source. Though this process takes time, it's a learning curve all who want to be Glyph Wielders must take." Isabelle nodded; it was a textbook answer, he was clearly well-read and confident in his words. She fished around her blouse and took out a golden locket that hung from around her neck. Adarmier was attracted to its golden glow and returned his attention to her. She opened it up and there, resting within its frame, were four Glyph pearls. She picked out a shining yellow pearl.

"My first set, given to me by my mother. I don't need them now, they are useless, but they did help me when I started out. Normally

I would pass them on, but I carry them with me, for safe keeping. I may even pass them on to my successor when she reveals herself to me." The boy shifted a little closer to her and picked up the golden locket, staring into the yellow pearl's centre, witnessing a whirlpool of liquid clashing around inside, at war with itself.

"This pearl grants power over water, doesn't it? What about the other elementals; fire, earth and wind?"

"I was not given them until later on in my training; water was my first element and preferred choice if I'm honest." She put the yellow sphere back into its slot and picked out a shining, blue sphere. "Do you know what this one is?" He looked inside it as he had before, holding it up to the sunlight. He saw bolts of electricity sparking within, jolting violently.

"This is Somite Strength. It enables the wearer to increase physical strength and agility. Depending on a person's physique, Somite Strength can work in a variety of ways. For you, I would say this gives you greater stamina, granting you speed and direct focus; your Star Calling performances require such attributes." *Another model answer*, she thought, *well remembered and again well spoken.*

"That's right, it certainly does." Isabelle placed the blue sphere back into the golden locket and closed it. Downstairs Eran was still teaching his class, though he did briefly stop and notice the pair of talking and laughing on the higher floor.

Thao pulled up a small wooden stool and sat in front of Othello, leaning on the doorway of his cell.

"What is your purpose here?" The Honour Guard began the interrogation. The prisoner did not answer. "You're from the northlands, so I am told, the red wastes of Jureai. Which clan are you with?" Thao suspected Bevork, but he wanted the man to talk. Again, however, he did not answer. "Withholding information is a serious matter; you could be here for a very long time until we get to the bottom of this. So you are going to answer my questions or am I going to let you sit there for a week to think about it, and two weeks after that if you refuse again and so on until you talk" he threatened, having experience in dealing with difficult people. Othello had no intention of staying in that cell and broke his silence.

"Where I am from, we talk to each other, we show respect, and to do this we must know each other's names. I've not been shown respect and heard no names, just hostility towards me. Is it like this everywhere? Why have been locked in your cells? Cells where I am told house only the most dangerous men are sent. I've not threatened you, yet I am here, locked in a tower, why?" Thao cut right to it.

"I'm all for respect, but I have reason to believe you've killed one of our own." Othello had no idea what Thao was talking about; his face showed his puzzlement. "The horse you rode upon to get here; how did you acquire it?" The captive sat back down on the nook in the wall and rubbed his hands together, eventually answering with the truth; he had no reason to lie.

"I found it grazing, its rider was lost so I took it to ease my travel to your city. A man named Jerdhia intercepted me; he was peaceful, but the men with him used force. There must have been some confusion, mostly on my part. I think I would have made the same assumptions as those men, and Alexius." Thao found Othello familiar, as though he had met him before. The way he sat and spoke triggered something in his mind, the way he rubbed his hands together; he felt like he knew him.

"The law is different here; it recently changed, and it concerns men like you. I imagine the first thing you noticed was the weather? It's supposed to be summer, believe it or not." Thao broke into a smile. Othello grinned in response when finding common ground, the weather was behaving more like the latter part of the year. "My name is Thao Hikonle, Commander of The Honour Guards of Krondathia. I apologise for the threats, but the laws have been passed and I must obey them."

"I am Othello, of The Bevork Clan. My rank is non-existent here, though hopefully, that will change in times to come." With the pleasantries aside, Thao had finally made some headway with the prisoner. He knew the man was no threat, he had met killers before, this was just a traveller in the wrong place at the wrong time.

"Before I can let you out of here, Othello, I would like to know a few things. You say you're from Jureai, but I can see you were not born there, you've not their blood. You're from our lands, aren't you? You must have moved?"

"I left these lands a long time ago; my father took me away to the north, while my mother stayed here. I have not seen her since."

"Why did you move away?"

"It was my father's decision; he never said why but it must have been of great importance. I never liked the city, so I happily went along with him. He died not so long ago. With him gone and my clan safe, I returned here, though this place is different to what I remember." Thao found a key inside his pocket.

"I'm sorry about your father. I don't know why, but I trust you Othello, you seem true to your word and I hate liars. You are welcome to stay in Imrondel City for as long as you please. Behave yourself or you'll be seeing me again under similar circumstances." He unlocked the door and held open the exit of The Prison Tower holding cells. Othello took one last look at Ruthal, clinging to the metal bars, waving goodbye with his bony fingertips. The wooden door slammed shut the moment Othello passed through.

"Why has that man been locked away for so long?" They walked down a rough, dank, stone corridor; Othello could see a few guards talking to one another while guarding the cells.

"That man is in there for some severe crimes. It's what he deserves."

"I can't see how merely using your voice can be held against you so badly," Othello protested.

"He is not in that cell for something he said; he has said nothing to my knowledge. What I do know is that he killed six men and burnt down their farms for his own gain, that's why he is locked in that cell." Thao opened the door and held it open for the freed prisoner.

"Ruthal told me he was detained for what he had said! Not for the murder of any sort, he must be…"

"Ruthal?" Thao interrupted. "His name is Hendrice! We have no one called Ruthal in our tower cells." Othello, did not understand.

Eran's lecture was over. The students picked up their belongings and left while searching The Old Library for The Conductor. The Master wiped the board clean and rolled the whole thing away to where it belonged. Isabelle came strolling out from behind some bookshelves, holding a book of her own; she came up behind Eran and tapped him on the shoulder.

"I would like this one, please," she said childishly, twirling a curl of her hair with a finger.

"I didn't notice you leaving."

"How was it, any potentials?" He looked at the book she had given him and slid on his reading glasses.

"The students are eager to go traipsing off to any godforsaken place, looking to solve mysteries we've been puzzled over since the dawn of time."

"Hmph can't blame them for trying…"

"They are keen but inexperienced, my girl. Out there in the wilds, far away from Krondathia and Ivulien, lies nothing but uncertainty. The unknown is dangerous ground. I fear for anyone who attempts to leave the boundaries of Equis. Why do you want this?" he asked, referring to the book she had handed him. "You already read this when you were thirteen."

"Adarmier said it would explain some things; he said that revisiting our roots from time to time is a good exercise. You know me, Master; I accept advice only from those I trust, and I trust Adarmier, he is not a threat, but… wait up Master!" she called, as Eran had made distance between them without her realising.

352

"Please, Isabelle, I am not your Master anymore."

"My roots as Star Caller are married with The Readers, I've not resigned my endeavour but please…" she said, following him into his office. Eran could see she had been thinking hard and losing sleep over the matter, so he waited for her to finish. "I don't know if the Readers will be able to help me, I don't even know if I'll be granted access to them. Professor Atheriax is a very hard man to reach; no one seems to know where he is half the time, but I have written him a few letters, hopefully, a response will come soon. I plan to bring this new information about the warnings in The Book of the Early Past to The Eldor." Eran came close and put his hands on her shoulders.

"If that is what you feel is right, then so be it. Prepare yourself for the unexpected." She dipped her head, and he handed the book back to her after he had stamped it. With a few words of thanks, she began to walk out of his office, pausing in the doorway and looked back briefly.

"Eran?" He raised his head. "What happened to Adarmier's parents?" The Librarian sat back down in his sturdy chair, taking off his glasses.

"Adarmier is an orphan." Her face dropped.

"What happened?" Isabelle leant on the door frame, wanting to hear the story.

"His mother was young, a little younger than you are now, far too young to have children, she just wasn't ready. His father was one of my friends, who excelled in his understanding of Glyph, an instructive tutor; he was very wise and very intelligent. Adarmier takes after his father…He was a good friend…" She slowly wandered back into the room as he spoke. "Sadly his gift with Glyph grew to be an obsession; he couldn't stop using and using. He became remarkably skilled at wielding the power held within the pearls. Unfortunately, he showed early symptoms and he soon fell; he became a Cursed. It overtook his life and his little secret obsession was soon made public to the guards of this city. His wife hated him for it and tried to protect her son, hiding him here, keeping him inside this very office, away from her crazed husband who wanted to flee with them at his side. He killed her with his Glyph, tearing her apart in an attempt to find his son…" Eran got up and pushed aside a small bookshelf, revealing the mark left by a fierce flame in the far wall of his office. "They call him Ramskull. The conflict raged, spilling out into the streets of Imrondel." Isabelle was shocked and felt appalled with herself for bringing up this subject with the poor boy, though if he felt the pain of loss, he certainly hid it well.

"What stopped him from getting Adarmier?"

"That I don't know. Only the boy knows what happened in here between him and his father, before the guards raided this place, having heard the screams of his mother. He was eight when this happened; it has been six years since the incident."

"What happened to his father?"

"After abandoning his son, he had the whole city coming after him; Glyph Wielders, Visarlian Knights, even Thao's Honour Guards. He killed many of them; swords are no match for Glyph. He was eventually stopped at the gates by a small army of high-class Glyph Wielders, who had no option to react with force… Adarmier was left alone in the world. He never talks about it, not to anyone, not even me. I looked after him for a while, then he went to live at the orphanage permanently."

"Where was I during all of this chaos?" she asked, feeling as if she should have been here to deal with the situation.

"You were off giving demonstrations around the world, doing what Star Callers do best. You wouldn't believe it, but incidents like this do occur from time to time, which is why it's important that we keep an eye on EVERY Glyph Wielder we have in training today, and take every precaution necessary to prevent such atrocities from happening again. Sadly, the only method we have for dealing with Cursed Ones, however far along they are, is… unpleasant, to say the least."

"Who notified the guards about Adarmier's father's condition?" Isabelle narrowed her eyes at Eran, almost immediately realising the answer to her own question. "You did it! You betrayed him!" At heart, she knew he had done the right thing, but she was still shocked.

"He was a madman who delved too deeply, who lost his mind. Glyph is dangerous; you have control over yours, but some simply do not. Cursed Ones still haunt parts of this world and they are far deadlier than any Honour Guard, Knight or Dark Rogue. It's even argued that The Cursed Ones are capable of growing far stronger than The Blessed, developing new techniques, pushing themselves to horrifying new levels that no sane person would ever dare approach. That's why it's the law to turn these men and women into the authorities if they show the symptoms, at any age. The Eldor cannot risk The Cursed wreaking havoc in his cities again. Adarmier's father is the perfect example of a good man falling to Glyph... I did what I had to do and I have no regrets." Despite her criticism, she knew she would have done the same.

"I see. Thank you for telling me the truth, Eran. Have a fine day."

"Watch yourself out there, Isabelle; the wind has really picked up." She bowed and exited The Old Library. Eran was left alone; he closed the door and locked it. Then, very slowly and with steady hands, he pulled The Book of the Early Past, out from under the floorboards. He touched its cold, stone cover, gazing into the strange symbols of holy power.

Having just been released out into the cold wind of the city, Othello stood to wait for Alexius, who came jogging down some steps. He had to speak up, raising his voice to shouting level in order to be heard, for the gale was blowing hard.

"Everything checked out. You are now a citizen of Imrondel again. Here is your new address; sorry, but it's the best place going at the moment. Here are some essentials for you and your place, and two day's worth of food." Alexius handed Othello a backpack of fresh clothes more fitting for city life than his Bevork gear, a piece of paper with his address written and a bundle of filling foods from the markets. "I am sorry for the trouble we caused you, Othello. I wish you the best of luck here. Take care of yourself. Oh, and by the way, the sword you had has been taken to the barracks in the north-eastern part of the city; if you want to you can still pick it up, it's yours." As Alexius turned to leave, anxious to get inside away from the harsh wind. Othello called after him.

"Wait! What am I supposed to do now?" Alexius shrugged his shoulders.

"Find a job, you work and pay your way like everyone else, or become a Regular. Stop by the barracks in The Military District and join up; the forces will take care of you if you won't. It's all up to you now; I can't help you anymore" Off he went, running down the road into the city, latching arms with a waitress, patiently waiting for him. Othello looked around, bending down to pick up his food and tucked the package under his arm. He read the paper flapping in the wind and turned around, setting off to find his new home. Stumbling about in all directions, he read the paper again to try and make sense of it. He could only guess and find his own way now. Surrounded by tall buildings, their appearance completely foreign to him, he walked the streets, fighting against the bitter weather. He managed to get the attention of a lady who was closing her fruit stand; she told him roughly where his apartment was located. He plodded on slowly, staring at the far-off towers and The Palace of Norisis in the distance. Finally, he saw where he needed to go; the stone paving led away from the city centre and marketplaces, toward The Living District. As he made his way into the quarter, the space around him seemed to narrow significantly. Square roofs loomed overhead; the building area was basic here compared to the richer estates he had passed by earlier. Generations of inhabitants living, cooking, cleaning, and fighting had left the once-fine stone walls more than a little beaten down. The vibrant colour of the place had long since faded into grey. The air tunnelled through the alleyway, making it even harder to push against the wind. Eventually, Othello came to an opening and was glad to find that his address was not in one of those narrow alleys. He turned his head and saw a boy laying in the gutter; nothing but a pile of bones, shivering in thin rags under a stained blanket. Othello was stunned; no one was helping him, he was completely neglected, alone and abandoned. He hurried over, but the boy appeared afraid of him, trying to move away feebly.

"What are you doing on the floor? You have to get home!" The boy coughed; his throat was so dry he couldn't even speak. "Oh wait, hold on, hold on... Here, have some." He took out a flask of water and helped the boy gulp it down. He was clearly ill with an infection. He shuffled around the backpack and wrapped a blanket around the boy who refused to talk. "There you go, it's fine. Come on, I can offer you shelter... I don't think it's far from here." The boy shrugged Othello's hands away, ripped the blanket off him and darted off. "I am not going to hurt you!" he pleaded, holding out a hand as the boy ran away, not looking back. Othello could not help but notice the Norkron folk, looking at him as if he were a madman. His appearance alone was odd enough. He picked up his belongings and left the street, ignoring the onlookers. From a nearby road, Eva had witnessed the entire event. She had been watching him from a distance and continued to follow him as he navigated the city streets. Eva stared at Othello as he tried to find his bearings; he was obviously lost. She jogged up to him through the wind; he noticed her coming toward him but didn't say anything.

"You look lost," she called, the wind whipping away most of her words.

"I am trying to find this place here," he replied, handing her the piece of paper Alexius had given him. After a brief moment of thought, she recognised the address and directed him using her hands.

"Follow the road down this way, take a left and then a right. That will be your street. It should be clear from there on."

"Thank you, citizen," Othello said, sliding the paper back into his pocket.

"You're welcome." As he set off on his way, she shyly flicked a lock of hair away from her face, studying him from head to toe, but his appearance, his manner reminded her of someone else.

Chapter 16 - A Chance Meeting

**The time has come, the leaders have assembled,
and Isabelle is ready.**

Isabelle reviewed the letter from Akarnal Desa, her associate and closest friend in Ivulien. She sat at her desk, tired, with Pandora purring on her lap. She had not prepared a speech, just ideas of what she wanted to say. It would all depend on what was said by the assembled courts and councils and in what order. With luck she would get away with not saying anything; at least then she would not be held responsible if something bad came of what was decided. This was a childish way of thinking though; not to contribute to the meeting would be foolish for someone in her position. Clearing her throat, she headed for her window, holding Pandora close to her chest, her mind never let to rest. Maybe it was time to reveal the secrets that The Eldor had kept from everyone, to speak her mind and expose her feelings about Starillia? This would be a daring move and not even she could predict what would happen. Instead of dressing in typical Star Caller robes, she dressed appropriately for the matter at hand, opting for a feminine suit in formal, muted tones. There would be a lot of important people in The Council Chamber today; some of the most powerful politicians in the world. Every leader, every court member, every Commander and Captain of both cities' armies. The Priesthood would be present; they had arrived earlier in the day to represent the followers of Starillia. The only man of significance who would not be present, was The Eldor. He had to look after the rest of Krondathia while everyone else was here in the south. The Sire trusted The Chosen to speak for them both, often stating that he was the father of Krondathia while she was its mother. The tension was building, mounting upon her shoulders. It was hard to concentrate as she ran through a few sentences in her head; she didn't like them. This frustrated her greatly because it would be HER that everyone would be listening to, people would bicker but would fall silent when she shared her thoughts. It felt like she was back in her school days, on a morning a presentation was due, and she wasn't ready for it. She tried once again to formulate a suitable opening for her speech, but gave up halfway through, needing a cold glass of water. It was strange; all her life she had been told she was special, ever since the day she was hailed as the next Chosen, but she didn't feel righteous or holy right now. Her teachers had taught her how to harness her power and refine her abilities, making her the woman she was today, though she didn't even feel powerful. Adarmier's words crept back into her mind; was she destined for this role, or was she simply chosen by system built by men? Apparently, no other woman in Equis could handle her tasks, not until the next Star Caller revealed herself. She had yet to begin her search for a successor; she was so far behind with everything compared to those who had reigned before her, who appeared to have handled their duty perfectly. In a few hours, the meeting would begin, and action would be taken.

Othello lifted a heavy, rattling box off the floor, sliding it into the back of a transport cart. He closed its back door and banged twice on the side.

"Alright, it's ready to go. Take it away," he instructed the driver, and the cart pulled off, following one of the main roads of the city. Somewhere behind him, a loud, heavy container hit the concrete paving and sprayed its load of fruit and vegetables all over the pavement. He went over to help tidy up the mess. "The crates are meant to go inside the carts, Mr Frost," he pointed out, picking up an apple that had rolled to his feet.

"I'm sorry, the lid broke off," apologised Frost, hastily replacing the contents.

"No need to apologise; you've provided us with nutrition, and I've had nothing all day. Catch!" Othello tossed the man a loose tomatoe that had rolled on the ground. Ethan Frost caught it in one hand. Once the crate's contents were packed up again, they sat down to eat on a nearby bench beside a towering shipment of boxes waiting to be loaded. Opposite them, people streamed by; there was never a quiet day in the city, not unless rain fell, or gales swept in. Only the most extreme conditions would affect the relentless hard work of the city.

"Extra shipments will be in soon; we are in for a long day, Othello. Rumour has it that The Dark Rogues keep taking our carriages along the lonely roads. Every cart they steal means more work for us. Annoying that" moaned Ethan.

"This is simple work; it could be much worse. At least we are outside," Othello replied optimistically; he was new to the job but had already gotten used to the tedious routine.

"I was thinking about trying my hand in the barracks; I signed up not so long ago, they are still recruiting soldiers for training, you know? Maybe you should come with me and sign up too?"

"You want to become a soldier? Not you too... Come on, look around, there is enough work to be done in the city as it is. One more man with a sword won't make any difference here."

"You'd be surprised what one man can do." Ethan refused to be discouraged by Othello's words.

"I heard that soldiers are a dying breed anyway. There is no conflict here or anywhere, as far as I know, say for a few rumours, so where's the need for armoured men?" Even as he spoke, The Northlander remembered the state he had left his previous home in; on the edge of disaster, the merciless bandits preparing to attack. He pinned his hopes on Dingane, trusting that he would lead them to safety, away from the terror of Xavien.

"Maybe you're right; let's hope it stays that way. I don't plan on becoming an Honour Guard or a Knight like Lethaniel, but I just want to be able to serve on the line with others, to be there in the moment for history to remember. There can be no greater way of giving back to the country that raised you, sheltered you and looked after you. What do you think?"

"That's an interesting perspective. A bond is formed when people are given a common foe to stand against; a bond that only exists when great dangers arise. I understand, I get it. This bond brings those involved closer together." As he spoke, he was remembering The Tournament of Leadership. "The bitterest of rivalries between men can be settled or even forgotten when someone else shows up to kill them both... Just don't ignore the fact that you don't have to suffer or risk your life on some distant battlefield to repay the privileges you were granted at birth. There are far better ways to give back without the hassle of, you know, dying in agony at the end of metal."

"I guess you're right, I just want to join for a term or two, to learn to fight properly," replied Ethan, who then went silent for a short while.

"Who is Lethaniel? I've heard his name crop up several times since I've been here, but I have no idea who he actually is." Ethan cleared his throat and answered:

"Lethaniel is a great Knight; the best Knight in the whole army. He has NEVER been defeated, he truly is a perfectionist with his sword; no one has ever even landed a blow upon him, no one has even come close..." Othello raised his eyebrows, impressed. "Extraordinary really. Even as a boy, during his training, no one can recall ever knocking him to the ground. He prides himself on his undefeated record. I would like to meet him properly or better yet, meet the man who does manage to outmatch him." Despite his outward display of interest, Othello's mind had shut off the moment the word sword was mentioned. Finishing off his apple with a final bite and spitting out a seed, he stood up and threw the core into a bin across the road. His aim could not have been more perfect; it didn't even bounce off of the sides, though he did nearly hit a woman walking passed. She caught Othello's eyes and he apologised silently, putting two hands together. Just as the two began to recognise each other, the half-eaten remains of a tomatoe came flying through the air, and splattered on the outside rim of the bin.

"Oh shit! Sorry," Ethan called to the young woman, her eyes shut as tomatoe juice dripping down her cheek and nose.

"Good throw, though your aim needs work; a little to the right next time," Othello advised. The woman took her leave after flicking a seed off her chin, though she did look back a few times as she distanced herself from the pair of slackers, glancing at the man with bronze skin. "I recognise her. I saw her when I first arrived here. Who is she?"

"She walks passed here every day on her way to work. I think her name is Eve or Eva or something. She's a beauty, isn't she?" replied Ethan, getting back to work. "That was a brilliant throw by the way, perfect shot," he added, measuring up the distance between themselves and the bin.

"Thank you. I hit my target each and every time, without fail," Othello stated, sure of himself, but his friend sensed an element of luck to the first throw, so he called him out on it.

"Are you sure about that?"

"Yes, I'm sure; I don't take a shot unless I know I can hit it. When the wind is blowing strong, that's when things can become tricky, but I hit my targets nonetheless."

"Go on then… Prove it, right now," Ethan challenged, scooping up a couple of pebbles "I want to see these in that same bin within ten seconds."

"Oh please…" groaned Othello.

"Come on, make the throws; no one's watching. I'll buy you lunch sometime if you can get all three in." Othello shrugged his shoulders; the other man was not backing down.

"Alright," he finally agreed, weighing up the rocks in his hands.

"Should we put a real bet on this? You know, make this a little more interesting?" Ethan suggested, rubbing his nose with the side of his thumb, folding his arms, keeping his eyes on the bin over the road.

"I wouldn't do that…" began Othello, hitting the target with the first projectile, "because…" the second flew into the bin, ringing the metal within, "you'd lose that bet." As the last pebble flew through the gap, Othello dusted off his hands. It wasn't luck after all. "You owe me lunch" Othello grinned. "With rocks, it's all in the wrist, but when it comes to launching swords long distances, the strength comes from the shoulder" They got back to work the moment the next transport cart rolled up in front of them, stopping in the middle of the road. "She was looking at me, right?" considered Othello. His mind wandered throughout the day, mostly focusing on, going over the fine details of her physical appearance. Her hair was dark, long and flowing. She was tall, slim but not frail, and the motion of her legs and hips was inviting. He found it hard to focus on anything other than her, which troubled him; he had never thought he would find a Norkron woman so interesting, they were usually all so shallow and superficial, lacking self-respect, jumping from one man to the next without a second thought. The Jurean women he was accustomed to were the complete opposite, selecting their partners carefully and remaining with them as long as their love was reciprocated. A different world entirely.

Inside the spacious Council Chamber, hundreds of large seats fitted with black leather surrounded a circular platform in the centre. Over the years some of the chairs had worn and torn in places typically at the edges but most were fine, shiny, and smooth, their arm and backrests carved into shapes resembling flowers with long petals and sharp leaves. Men, glorified with titles, power and authority had always assembled in this chamber to discuss important issues that arose in Equis; it had been this way for centuries. Now those who had been invited to the meeting were flooding in, filling up their designated seats. Then followed the twelve High Councillors of Virtue, the highest authority figures of Xiondel City, gathering in one of the far corners of the room. These well-known men were draped in loose robes, with small, tight waistcoats underneath, preferring neutral colours, mostly whites, greys, even silvers. Sitting in the seats below them were The Lower Council of The Silver City. Amongst the politicians were the heads of the Xiondel army, which had not been called upon for its services in a long while. Commanders and Captains of all of Xiondel's regiments found their seats, including Uther Sreton, Captain of the Unicorn's Minions, also known as The Thunderhoof Riders. Another was Taylon, Hyrax, leader of The Tulkan Knights. The two high-ranking Captains kept their distance as they sat; they shared a horrific history, and any citizen who had lived through the strife of the last civil war knew all too well that these two would never see eye to eye. The Courts of Imrondel consisted of dozens of men, seated directly opposite their counterparts from Xiondel. They appeared socially awkward and unapproachable to anyone save for their own kind. Joining them in the middle of The Council Chamber were The Priests of Imrondel and those of The Zodias Island, deep believers in Starillia and truly dedicated to its cause. This included the three High Priests from The Column Temple. Sitting quietly behind the courts was Jerhdia; one of the greatest builders and craftsman of both cities, these engineers or men of the cog were called Meks. Thao was not far away; he needed no introduction, his fame and presence preceded him, as did that of Lethaniel, who was lingering in a corner, a few rows down, his face was pale, as if he had just surfaced. Alexius was a few rows above him, feet planted upon the backrest of the chair in front of him, supporting his head with his fist. Master Eran shared a bench with other tutors from around the city; they greeted one another with friendly handshakes and pleasant small talk. Master Atheriax had been sent an invitation but had failed to show, few were surprised at his absence. Many could sense a certain tension between the two sides of the room. Everyone had mingled before finding their seat, greeting, and clasping hands, but The High Councillors of Virtue and The Courts of Imrondel had remained separated. With their differences of opinion regarding how to rule Krondathia, with all the different viewpoints gathered under one roof for the first time in a hundred years, it all put a strain on to one's allegiance. Inevitably, at some point, this strain would crack, and the men would feel the urgent need to speak out, for here was the place where battles were fought. Only The Star Caller had to arrive before they could begin.

The stone chamber fell quiet, everyone ceased their talking and arose to their feet, as the great doors were opened. The Glyph Wielders marched in, setting up a perimeter in the centre floor, each man standing upon circles imprinted around the rim of the stage. Isabelle was the last to step into the chamber her green eyes lit with an emerald shine, rotating her wrist ever so slightly at her side. The heavy doors behind her were locked tight at the will of her mind and the stares proceeded to follow her down the aisle right to the centre stage where a Glyph Wielder waited, holding a silver seat out for her before a table. Isabelle seated herself and once she did, everyone took to their seats with her. Whispering something to one of her associates, she handed him the letter from Akarnal Desa.

Isabelle's associate would be the first to take to the floor and clearly read the letter loud and clear When he finished, whispers echoed, murmurs fluttered from around the room. He placed the letter back onto the table and slid it in front of Isabelle. A member of The Court of Imrondel wished to speak, so he stood. Isabelle didn't recognise him, a lot of these faces she did know, but those she had not the pleasure of meeting, alarmed her. He spoke with a raised voice:

"We are aware of the contents of Desa's letter. Word has reached our ears and we have informed the people who are present in this room today. We are here now to ACT on the situation involving our friends in the south-east, our Ivulien allies."

"What do they want from us?" called a man from Xiondel.

"They simply lack knowledge. We should share with them OUR cherished faith? Send our wisest priests to the eastern lands, bringing with them the teachings of Starillia? Spreading the word of our holy doctrines would only improve and strengthen our position." Imrondel had been the first to have their say; the talk centred around their concerns while Xiondel contingent remained somewhat quiet and reserved.

"You'll often find that men fear what they do not understand, councilmen. With a little more knowledge our priests could deliver to them, this may very well settle the dispute, for now at least," announced a Court Member.

"If the Dovidian people were at all interested in the beliefs we hold so dear, they would have joined us in the coronation, in tradition, in ceremony centuries ago." This comment came from a member of The Lower Council, speaking loudly from the very back of the chamber. The ones who had something to say stood up when they wanted to speak and only sat again when interrupted or upon finishing their contribution. At times some disobeyed the rules, causing hectic moments. Each idea was accepted gratefully, but still, no genuine solution was forthcoming, no idea bold or brave enough. Isabelle made a mental note of what each man said. Gradually, she pieced together a portion of her speech, constructing it as the meeting progressed, building upon a few key statements she had memorised. As men clashed and began to talk over each other, Thao and Lethaniel's eyes met, their expressions glum, their frustration building over their inability to understand what was being said. Nothing would be resolved if they continued to speak out of turn. Both men, as well as The Chosen, knew that order had to be restored, somehow.

"He is right. The reason they fled and made peace during the second age of The Never-Ending War was BECAUSE of how powerful WE as a nation had become! Sending priests to the Dovidians now to increase the spread of Starillia would be a waste of time," opined a member of The Lower Council of Xiondel.

"It was not Starillia they feared! Starillia was delivered to us AFTER The Never-Ending War. That victory belongs to our Honour Guards, not Starillia, for it was unknown to us at the time. As a Lower Councilman of Xiondel City..." the man from Imrondel hissed the name, "It would be wise to get your facts straight before you embarrass yourself." This did not sit well with Xiondel; several of the city's representatives stood up in protest at the man's attitude. Naturally, this was countered by their counterparts with ill-advised comments made in abusive tones. One particularly distinguished gentleman felt it was his turn to contribute to the debate, which was increasingly losing its focus.

"Have we all forgotten the historical facts?" Yespins posed his question to not one sect, but to the room "Have we forgotten our accomplishments?" Master Eran leant forward in his chair and rubbed his chin, listening intently, for he could debate with the best of them. Unlike many in the room, he had a mind of wit, charm, and confidence that would break the most gifted of speakers. "We Norkrons as a tribe, as a people, over the ages have achieved feats greater than all others. We ended the war, we birthed Starillia, we co-exist given disagreements. We've given rise to women, ended tyranny and abolished slavery." Eran fact-checked these statements as they were given; what Yespin said indeed was true, but if one knew history as well as Master Eran, he could have listed off a few more, and delivered them instilled with love and a sense of pride. "I am led to understand that our very own Conductor, our great and talented Chosen, gave these people the privilege of a grand demonstration. This happened some months ago, with great success

I hear. Word of Isabelle is everywhere in Equis, word in this realm spreads fast. Sending preachers of Starillia to Ivulien may give them a better understanding of what the religion is about, but this would only be a temporary solution; the Dovidians would soon be knocking on our door again. This won't solve the problem it will only stall their concerns. How do you eradicate fear?" Yespin asked, ending his thought-provoking speech with a question. For the religious followers in the chamber – The Priesthood and The Courts of Imrondel - this meeting was all about promoting the spread of Starillia, while Xiondel, who generally favoured secularism, wished to keep the practising of this religion within the Krondathian borders. Isabelle watched as a verbal tug of war took place between the two parties, all the while wondering when it would be her turn to speak. How long would it be before they would involve her? She knew what was going on; both parties were arguing their own case, and she was the judge they would eventually turn to, to see where her opinion came down, and whoever she sided with, she'd make friends and enemies.

"Would the councils in this chamber consider the possibility of granting Ivulien and its people another demonstration? Perhaps it would prove the peaceful nature of our intentions. Maybe our Conductor, if willing, could return to the east and deliver them a spectacle the likes of which even we have never seen," suggested a man from Imrondel.

"What do you suggest she do beyond what she has already done?" cried Darlo Heventon, High Councillor Justice, in response.

"Demonstrating perfect Glyph technique is her area of expertise. I will let her decide on her own approach, but I was thinking she might Star Call again, only this time with two Celestials." Roars of dissent and support erupted simultaneously. Many spoke out against the notion while others applauded the idea. Isabelle now had no choice but to intervene, but she could not speak with the present racket. She subtly drew the attention of her associate sitting next to her and whispered in his ear. He got to his feet and held up both his hands for all to see. Silence once again reigned and finally, Isabelle was able to contribute to the debate, though she did not stand.

"Star Calling is no easy task outside The Column Temple, gentlemen. It has taken me twenty years to perfect the methods required for each Celestial, and even I struggle at times. If it were as simple as reading a passage while being aware of what foot to put forward first, I'd do it far more often. It's a debate in itself, just like the one we are having now, but it's expressed in ways that go beyond the power of words. It's physically and mentally draining, sometimes exhausting me to the point of collapse; nothing is more strenuous. I want you to understand that fact, it's a fatigue greater than that of your usual fatigue, one that non-wielders will never understand. Though I must express this is somewhat irrelevant, the fact is that Star Calling a single Celestial is a task, but Star Calling more than one has never been tried, I do not know anyone capable to perform such a trial. It's dangerous, likely impossible even for a Star Caller." Her words were clear and well-understood by most, though some less educated on the subject, mainly the secular groups from Xiondel, wanting to know the reasons for it being impossible. "I repeat, no ritual has been designed for such a Star Call. Each Celestial requires his or her own routine, some are more physical than others. Like I said, it has taken twenty years of dedicated practice to perform them." Isabelle had them, they were patient enough to allow her to take a breath "Let us not forget, a Celestial is a superpower; two entities governing elemental powers, sharing the same space may not be a wise a move... These are the first rules one learns when becoming The Chosen..." She began quoting the three initial rules set in stone by Regina, the spiritual mentor the Chosen's line. "Rule one: Star Calling during an existing visitation, while another Celestial inhabits our plain, forbidden. Rule two: Contravening the first rule in any way, shape or form is forbidden. Rule three: Relaying orders to a Star Called Celestial while it inhabits our plain, forbidden. In short, I cannot give them orders when they are here, I can only whisper in their ears." Master Eran felt immense pride for her ability to immediately silence the room, demonstrating that they weren't the all-powerful masters of the universe they fancied themselves as.

"Then return to Ivulien, call upon a Celestial that better demonstrates our peaceful cause," suggested the same man from Imrondel.

"The Star Caller called upon the might of Libra last time. There is no other Celestial Soul that expresses friendship, loyalty, and equality more than this creature. Get your facts straight before you embarrass yourself next time," yelled a Xiondel official.

"Then maybe it is time we sent her to Star Call upon something with a little more fire. My lady Isabelle, Aries should come forth. Let Ivulien know just how powerful we can be with The Celestial Souls at our sides. We should send a new message, an informed one: WE Norkrons, the people of Krondathia, rulers of the west, are in control of Equis!"

"That would be most unwise!" exclaimed Nenphis Esquin, High Councillor Wisdom. "It would be a completely irrational action to take. How dare you threaten the east?! If we are to demonstrate again it should NOT be through the power of Celestials or Glyph magic. Waving what could potentially be a massive destructive force in front of Ivulien will only intimidate them further, if not provoke them into acting in a manner no one could predict. What the Dovidians want is a further show of allegiance, proof of our commitment and allegiance to them. We should not play with our powers to scare or to justify our measures, especially in front of a nation that is near twice the size of our own. How dare you say such things? You owe us all an apology." This sent a ripple of concern through The Court of Imrondel, though Nenphis sat back down to widespread applause. Yespin then stood up to speak again.

"Gentlemen, the Dovidians are not our primary concern..." People stared incredulously at this new information. "Some of you are aware that the northern tribes of Jureai are advancing south from their lands, crossing Ivulien boarders. They have already pushed beyond River's Finn. This problem is evident enough and, as with the eastern allegiance issue, we must attend to this right now. We have received word from Commander Mathias Sious. The Norfoon Watch Towers have confirmed reports that acts of barbarity have been directed at outlying Ivulien settlements. Innocents have already suffered at the hand of the one called Xavien and his pack of Blood Marauders. Merciless killing is taking place as we speak. The ideal Equis Isabelle will deliver us can never arrive while such atrocities are taking place. If the Norkrons are to rise to our highest potential, if we are to be successful and deliver paradise for our future generations, where every society, every man, woman, and child can live free, then action must be taken to eradicate upheaval! We must rid ourselves of those who live evil NOW! Rid ourselves of twisted individuals such as Xavien..." Thao and Lethaniel glanced at one another; if there was to be a mission to eliminate The Demon Man, it would almost certainly fall upon them to deal with it. "Let us address this issue of invasion!" With that, Yespin sat back down as applause arose, mostly from the Xiondel contingent. Taktard Erien, High Councillor Ambition, decided to speak next;

"I would like to hear from the one who brought this knowledge forth; he should stand and announce himself. We must hear from him and the one who will volunteer to take up this responsibility, to cleanse the sinister and to keep Equis a world of peace." Heads began to turn as people began to search for the one who had delivered the news. "Would the one who gave us this information please stand and tell us your story?" Taktard remained standing until the individual made himself known, but no one came forward, at least not right away. Mumbles and whisperers circled the chamber. Lethaniel rolled his eyes with frustration and looked over his shoulder, making eye contact with Alexius, slouching in his seat a few rows above. He was busy rolling up some smokes, sealing one with a lick; he had made ten so far and had them balanced on the backrest of the seat in front of him.

Suddenly Alexius realised that everyone's attention was focused on him! He quickly put down the cigarette next to the others and stood up, dusting off his hands.

"Hi guys, how are we all doing today?" Lethaniel's face, fell into his palms. "I'm Alexius Marsay..." It was hard for him to concentrate with all these men and gawping at him, not to mention The Star Caller herself. "I am the courier, or rather I was, that's how I started out anyway, but what I do is I manage cargo. I work on transportation and see to the distribution of resources, making sure everyone gets a share of everything they need..." rambling, he caught sight of Lethaniel making a sly hand gesture, twirling his finger around in a circle, urging him to get to the point, and do so quickly. "But I also make sure that private business remains private. Don't kid yourselves, gentlemen, we all have secrets." He rested both hands on the seat in front of him as he continued his speech, knocking a few of his smokes down the collar of the man sitting in front of him. "I recognise some of you in this room today; I know you all trust me to make sure your letters are delivered safely, and thanks to you I can afford anything, so we are good. You know, I went out with this stunning woman not so long ago..." Thao coughed, Lethaniel's eyelids fell but Isabelle just laughed. "If I hadn't my house and nice things to impress her with then I'd be one unhappy, frustrated guy right now, so thank you, your zeal is greatly appreciated..." Many men in the room were no doubt wondering if this man speaking was even supposed to be there. "I am personal esquire to The High Priests, a handful of Honour Guards, Visarlian Knights, Captains and you Commanders, and yes I did receive word from Mathias, and yes, as High Councillor Truth said, the reports have been confirmed. We do have a problem, guys. Unfortunately, I'm not a military man, I didn't take that route. I think it's stupid, but you don't need to be a military man, or a soldier for that matter, to understand what kind of a man Xavien, this Demon Man is. Simply put, he is a fucking monster. Even if I were a soldier, if I were Mr strong man Honour Guard over there..." he said, pointing at Thao "From what I've seen in the reports about this man, I wouldn't hold it against anyone if they ran away pissing their pants. I'd think twice before undertaking a mission to quell this threat." For someone less educated than most sitting in the room, Alexius knew how to hold their attention and get across a serious point, albeit long-windedly. "Lethaniel Presian trusts me with sensitive material; he is the one who now will take the floor because my throat hurts..." The man in front pulled a bent roll-up from out of his collar and handed it to Alexius. "He is our new General...Leth, take it away." Eran initiated an applause, which quickly spread, and Alexius sat down and opened his hand out to Lethaniel, gesturing a go ahead. Heads turned to the far corner, they found Lethaniel, who was not exactly as prepared as he thought. Many of these military officers had not even met their new General, a man without any real wartime experience, just an undeniably impressive undefeated run in combat. Lethaniel had feared he would have to give his presentation concerning Jureai and Ivulien here today, instead of in the barracks where he would have preferred.

"People of Krondathia: Wise priests, politicians, military men. I'd like to thank you all for coming here; I realise that many of you have travelled great distances and this is the first time I am speaking to many…"

"Spare us the introduction General; we know how grateful you are to be amongst us. What do you propose we do about the invasion?" called one particularly impatient fellow sitting opposite Isabelle. She knew him from somewhere; it didn't take her long to remember his well-groomed face, neatly combed black hair and dark eyes. He was Calias, a man who always seemed linked to Starillia or The Eldor in some way. He must have been one of The Sires most recent new hires; for she had not read about any endeavours or escapades of his. What she did know was off the books, carrying out a secret order, entrusting Thao to deliver one of The Books of the Early Past to The Old Library in Imrondel City and another crate to The Zodias Island. She knew one had contained the book *Ultimas*, but what the other crate contained she had no idea. It must have been something valuable. What was Calias doing here? What was his authority? Lethaniel hesitated; with all those faces looking to him for an answer, he found it hard to focus, the heat was drying his throat and taking its toll on his calmness. He needed some water, but none was available

"Sorry, yes, of course, I'll get right to it…" He shuffled some papers around as he collected his thoughts. "I have a proposal at hand, an idea to halt this attack. If this council will allow me, I will tell you what I have in mind."

"Are we going to aid the Dovidians, General?" A court member yelled from somewhere in the room.

"Yes…Yes, we are…" His response was met with general approval from his audience, but a ripple of disapproval was enough to halt him. Calias was about to speak out; Isabelle could tell by his face that he would protest so she intervened before he could say anything.

"YOU MAY PROCEED!" she called over the top of him, seeing that Lethaniel was in need of some assistance. With the help of Alexius, Lethaniel set up a tripod to support the scroll he was now clumsily unravelling. It was a large piece of thin fabric with the map of the world imprinted upon it in dark inks. Some areas were highlighted in red, which Lethaniel had carefully added himself, to help demonstrate his strategy. He took a deep breath and moved to stand beside the chart. When he was ready, Isabelle gave him the go-ahead to begin his presentation.

"The information we have from Mathias is vague, but it's enough to work with. What we do know is that The Northlander Clans have indeed invaded The Ledera Lands and are attacking the outer Ivulien settlements as we speak. Dovidian people have already been put to the sword and many more are at risk. We must learn what Xavien is capable of, what he wants, and soon. Understanding an enemy makes them easier to assess, and in turn, easier to destroy." He paused for a second having gripped their attention. Lethaniel's nerves had settled and his mouth was not so dry anymore; he now felt calmer, maybe it was thanks to Isabelle or perhaps he was just getting used to talking in front of large crowds. "Whether or not the Dovidians want our help is irrelevant. They are still people, our fellow human beings, who can benefit from our assistance. True, we have had our conflicts in the past, but that is history, those days are long gone, and if we were one day surrounded by enemies, I would feel honoured to know that Ivulien stood by our side."

"Get to your plan, General. We are still waiting!" Calias called out, hurrying him along. Isabelle scowled at the man and then glanced back at Lethaniel.

"Lives are on the line. A strategy has been carefully devised with the help of Thao Hikonle and my Visarlian Knight, Captain, Rayn Lebourne. We have decided to use one of our older tactics, basing an assault on the element surprise. We will hunt them down, lure them from their fortifications and overwhelm them on all sides, giving them no chance to escape and re-group. However, we have learned from Mathias's report that these guys don't like to sit still; they move swiftly and efficiently, which is why before we set the trap we must study their movements, figure out where they will be and then execute. From that position, surrounded by Norkron soldiers even Xavien, as horrid as he is, will have to choose between death and surrender" Lethaniel paused for a moment, sratching his forehead lightly with his little finger "There are plenty of places around those areas suitable for such a tactic. It is just a question of finding them. If all goes to plan and we pull this mission off, which

373

I'm sure we will, we can end this little rebellion in a day and avoid the fuss of cleaning up petty pockets of resistance." Thao caught Lethaniel's eye, silently agreeing with the plan, as did Isabelle. "I am addressing the military personnel in this room: Captains, Commanders and Officers, if you have a better idea, please do not hesitate to speak. A good contribution could save lives, I am new here I recognise this." No one spoke up; apparently, his own plan was convincing enough. Approaching the map, he grasped a thin pointer, using it to further outline the strategy. "We will march east and arrive at The Norfoon Watchtowers in the peaks of Thnel, near the border of Ivulien. There we shall join up with Mathias and his Norfoon Scouts, they will be perfect for tracking down the invaders and will provide us with the best possible vantage points from which to strike. Terrain is important; we need to use it against Xavien, who is used to wastelands and desert plateaus. We have the home field advantage. We shall send our Norfoon scouting parties further east and north, even to the coastal cliffs in the south if necessary, and flank them wherever possible. We will use the element of surprise and stop them in a single encounter... If their numbers are significantly larger than our own, we have devised a second action, using an effective tactic. Even Xavien and his Blood Marauders need to eat; a large group cannot depend on hunting alone to sustain themselves. What few animals do exist in those parts are predators themselves; the rest of the local wildlife will be going into hibernation or will have already moved elsewhere to avoid the cold weather. Which means that The Blood Marauders will be using the common pathways that trail through the wilds. These routes have been mapped by our Norfoon Scouts and will make things easier for us; we will simply cut off their supplies and starve them out." So far so good; he had heard no protest or argument, suggesting that there was no better way to deal with this invasion. Uther then stood up and Lethaniel acknowledged him. The grey uniformed man was heavily built, much like Thao. Uther was Captain of The Thunderhoof Riders, an experienced rider in the horse army of Xiondel, a man renowned for his loyalty and reliability. He was not one to speak out of turn, nor was he known for being particularly aggressive. His question was predictable:

"Does Xavien use any form of transport? Would we be going up against footmen or mounted warriors?"

"Mathias's report doesn't mention Xavien using mounts, and I doubt they have the knowledge to navigate beasts through a foreign land. These men, from what I've read, are savages who look out only for themselves, moving from place to place, pillaging and looting. Men like this can be beaten."

"You sound sure of this, General," stated Uther, sitting back down.

"Pretty sure, yes."

"Tell us why?" called Calias.

"Because I've heard that they eat horses, they enjoy the taste, and rumour has it they see flesh as flesh and would even rip apart and consume a human being without hesitation or remorse. That's the kind of men we are dealing with." This time Thao stood; for a second Lethaniel dreaded the question, but it was not in Thao's nature to undermine those he respected. He was a veteran, a gentleman when not on the field and THE most capable fighter in the room, barring Lethaniel with experience on his side.

"What size of force are you planning on sending to the east to stop them?"

"I will be going with less than half of my Visarlian Knights. I will stop Xavien myself. Rayn Lebourne will remain here as acting General, and await further orders if required."

"Less than half?"

"Yes, I believe that's all the Knights I will need for this mission. We will enlist the help of a unit of Regulars from Imrondel, The Norfoon Scouts when we arrive, and any Wilderness Rangers Mathias has at his disposal."

"I'll leave Scarto behind to take charge of my Guards while I'm gone assisting you in this endeavour. They are at your Command if you so wish, General Presian. Krondathia will see this threat dealt with swiftly," announced Thao, bowing his head.

It was decided. An agreement had been reaching concerning one of the matters at hand. Thao and Lethaniel's Visarlian Knights were to travel east to investigate and aid Ivulien however they could against the horde of Blood Marauders. Lethaniel made his way back to his seat with his belongings. His duty of addressing the audience was over and a course of action had been settled, so he could now relax for the duration of the meeting. Though he had no desire to travel again, even in the company of his own men and Thao, who he trusted unconditionally, he knew that many cold, lonely nights lay ahead of him, nights of pondering and re-evaluating his future. The road ahead would stretch on much longer without the fantasies of being with Eva; she had kept him going, kept his heart warm, to which had died long ago, all but remained was a hole, a void which had to be filled with honour and duty; He gripped his wooden carving, his calm interrupted when Calias stood and addressed him directly.

"Visarlian Knights AND Honour Guards. That's a formidable force to send against mere savages, General; some of our finest in the land. Couldn't you simply send more of the lower classes of soldier for this mission? The cost of sending Regulars would be far less and the results would be the same." Lethaniel was amazed; after his speech, he thought that Calias would have understood the plan of action and that no more talk about it would be required, but he was wrong, obviously, because Calias was still unsatisfied.

"I heard no objection earlier," he replied.

"The people in this room may agree with you, General, but I think it's overkill, akin to squashing an ant with an axe. Don't you think you are overreacting? We have many, many Regulars itching for the experience. Why not send a legion of them, instead of risking our finest?" Lethaniel tapped his board pointer into his palm thinking of a way to silence Calias, who was after immediate results. He wanted absolute peace like every other man in the room but was going about it in a callous manner. Lethaniel's plan would be costly; it would take far longer to prep and execute and there was no guarantee it would work, but fewer lives would be at risk. Calias's method, on the other hand, was to go for certain victory with higher stakes in terms of human casualty. Imrondel had thousands of

376

fighting men to spare. The General sat back and folded his arms before speaking again; he had to pick his words carefully in order to silence the man and win over the courts again for they seemed to fall into Calias's camp.

"There was a battle once; it took place a very long time ago, between a handful of brave Norkrons and an invading army of thousands of Desaru tribesman…" Thao knew what was coming and smiled sharply; he admired Lethaniel for choosing this historical story for his defence. "The Norkrons were overwhelmed, they hadn't eaten or slept in days, going against the Desaru head-on would be suicide, a five-year-old child knows this. We all know the result of this battle; we wouldn't be here today if those Norkrons hadn't prevailed. I advise we do the same as those men; we should pick the setting of our victory, visualise the scenario before it happens and adapt swiftly if necessary, exploit their weaknesses and coordinate an offensive. It's wise not to underestimate our enemies, Calias. What you suggest is almost certain to work, but how many lives will we pay for the victory? How many mothers will wait on sons never to return? I don't want to lose any men, and if we plan this assault carefully and prepare prudently, then a bloodless victory is possible. I cannot make a promise that everyone will walk away from this; we are dealing with very violent men, after all, people will get hurt. These men have grown up in a harsh, unforgiving environment, their weapons are crude and less refined than ours, but this does NOT mean that they will be pushed over easily. We have more information suggesting that there may be several other lone warlords to be concerned about. I'd rather win risking few than win risking many. The Regulars are tough, solid ground troopers and I do not wish to knock their abilities; they serve us well, they are the backbone to my army, but my Knights and Thao's Honour Guards to this day have yet to be matched. I trust we will get the job done and you will have your results." Calias didn't respond immediately, instead choosing to confer with another man sitting next to him. Isabelle heard them whispering; it was off-putting, but she could not help but try to overhear them. She could make out some of the words they were saying, but not enough to string together full sentences. The decision was final, despite the shady man's protests. Isabelle rested her arms on the table; it was time now to get back to issue concerning Ivulien and Starillia.

Othello heaved another heavy crate off the floor and slid it into the back of the cart. The day had been a busy one, with an early start and an even later finish. Even the boxes seemed to be getting heavier as time went by; Ethan was already struggling by midday. Shortly after, he began to lose his stamina and actively avoid the heavier crates, leaving them for Othello. Othello knew what he was up to but didn't let him know that he was on to him. Load after load came in without a moment's rest. Every time they finished a batch of crates, thinking that it would be the last, dusting off their hands and hastily hydrating themselves, another load was brought in to be sorted and loaded. The work was unbelievably tedious, though Othello was fuelled by the reminder of Eva. She had been on his mind ever since he had nearly hit her with the apple core; he had spent the meantime wondering what she was like, whether she was bright and ambitious, what her interests were and countless other concerns. Such fantasies distracted him from his work to the extent that he made mistakes from time to time, making an idiot out of himself. Luckily, he was able to mask his clumsiness while Ethan tested the weight of each crate.

"The last one, off you go!" Assuming there were no more crates left to lift, Othello turned to his co-worker, only to see one final box, left suspiciously alone in the middle of the road. This crate was longer than the rest and required two men to lift it. "Why has this one been left out?" he questioned, pointing with an outstretched finger.

"That has to go to the barracks. See that insignia on the side? It was shipped in by Xiondel; its seal is similar to Imrondel's, only more detailed." Ethan and a few other loaders hovered around as Othello inspected the crate, waiting for another delivery to arrive. He pulled on the crate with both hands and lifted off the lid. Inside was a neatly stashed assortment of weapons. These shields, swords and spears were different to the style used by the enforcers in Imrondel. Othello removed a kite shield branded with a red seal of Krondathia; running his hand over the metal, he picked it out and fitted it onto his forearm.

"I like this!" he exclaimed, testing its flexibility in his hand. "It's light, but sturdy at the same time; it could easily be used as a substitute for a melee weapon."

"Put it back," warned Ethan with a hint of concern in his voice, "We are not meant to open any of them." Othello agreed, slid off the shield and placed it back into the crate. "I think these are meant to replace the old model," noted Ethan.

"Why? What's wrong with the square ones?"

"I don't know, I guess the military just thinks they look better." Othello raised his eyebrows in response.

"Both types of shields are effective, as are the swords I've seen being carried around. With the spears, on the other hand, there is room for improvement." He pulled a wooden pole from a nearby stack, followed by a metal head from the crate. The weapons were thin, taller than a man by a fair number of inches, just as spears should be. Othello held it like a guard standing on duty, gripping the head of the spear in the other hand, comparing the two. "Notice anything?"

"Well the head is missing for starters..." laughed Ethan. Othello lowered the wooden pole so his colleague could get a closer look, yet he still failed to grasp the point.

"The head of the spear is too large and heavy for the pole!"

"Yes, but the heads are lethal, look at them! You don't want to be on the receiving end of that!" Ethan was by no means wrong, but he still didn't really understand.

"You don't want to be on the receiving end of a fist either..." replied Othello. "These poles are too thin for the metalheads. Thrust this into a man or an animal and it's very likely to snap off or become lodged inside. Last thing anyone wants to be doing while in a life and death encounter is searching around for another means of defence." He closed the lid with his foot and Ethan stamped it shut.

"Maybe you should tell someone about the design flaw," he suggested.

"When you're standing on that line you dream about with all the others who foolishly want the same thing, I recommend you have a spare sword at your side." With that he strolled away, awaiting the next load of crates. Ethan would remember this lesson, but he remained puzzled as to how Othello knew so much about weaponry. This was a man with more than a few secrets.

Inside The Council Chamber, a decision still had to be made with regard to the Dovidians. Arguments had flared, the abuse had flown across the room in all directions. Tensions had long since boiled over and everyone wanted to be heard, to have their say. Thao and Lethaniel were sat right in the middle, caught in the crossfire of the heated debate. Eran, however, was not involved; he just sat there, arms folded, waiting for the squabbling to cease. He was above these pointless shouting matches. There was another who took no part in the mayhem; Alexius sat back in his chair, feet up, with a lit smoke in his mouth, casually puffing out rings like he was in a bar or outside his house. No one even cared about the presence of smoke in the room; everyone was too busy screaming at each other to notice. In Isabelle's mind, this debate was over; the patient, logical pragmatism of the men had long since given way to their egos and greed. It was becoming abundantly clear that she would have to settle it. So much for getting through this meeting quickly and easily. She shook her head, trying to silence the echo of foolish men's words in her mind. Picking out Jerhdia from within the crowd of argumentative politicians, she gave him the signal, stroking the side of her eye with her little finger, upon which he gave her a wink and stood up. Making his way down to the floor, he pulled a small horn out from his deep trouser pocket, the kind used to signal a retreat during battle. Isabelle plugged both her ears before he blew, the deafening groan resounding throughout the chamber. *That shut you up* he said to himself, taking the horn away from his lips.

"Crazy fucker!" yelled Alexius, having nearly swallowed his roll up.

"Arguing over each other and not paying attention to what is being said will solve nothing, gentlemen. Our Chosen has something to say, and I suggest we listen. Go ahead, kid," Jerhdia invited before jogging back up the stairs to his seat. This time Isabelle made her way to the centre of the room to speak. Certain words came to mind, words that would almost certainly break Starillia's support in Krondathia. She hesitated before she uttered; maybe the blasphemous speech could wait? She did not want to be responsible for any hurt or worse a breakdown in society, not when the city was in such good shape. So, she held her tongue for a few seconds, re-evaluating what she wanted to say.

"Gentlemen, it has been riveting listening to you speak, so orderly and so affectionately to one another. I had my doubts the moment I learnt about this conference; who wouldn't? We are not peasants, we are not primitive, we are Norkron..." As her words came to her, she found she was turning slowly on the spot, trying to address everyone in the room at once. "Norkrons deciding the fates of many..." Her eyes fell on Lethaniel and then Thao. "Some of whom I know personally, people I'd rather not see so far from home, and dare I ask; What is home? I think the root of the problem lies with those who have lost touch with the foundations of our great society. To those of you who have, I have a question for you: What does it mean to be Norkron?" No one answered her; no one was brave enough to venture a response. In the far corner, Alexius shot up his hand, thinking he was back in a classroom. She noticed him out of the corner of her eye but pretended she had not. On she went, answering her own question, which had been her intention all along. "We are a race that was pushed to the very brink of extinction... But we survived, we reconciled, we were victorious, and we must not forget what we have accomplished, everything we have overcome, together or individually, we all matter. Every time a foe has set out to destroy us, we have proven ourselves triumphant time and time again. The civilisation we have built out of the ruins of our past has come from an unbreakable will, devotion, and a fierce grasp for life, to survive, to take our rightful place in Equis. That is what it means to be Norkron, that is what sets us apart from any other nation, we survive..." The room was unsettlingly still and silent. "We are the most powerful nation in the world, with Equis in our hands, and yet we cannot keep ourselves calm and open-minded when in the company of our own. How can we expect to remain at the strength we're at when in the presence of the Karthians, the Dovidians, The Chimera Order, The Fawn of Damalesque and Fevoriel when we cannot even hold a formal discussion? This situation is unacceptable. No one leaves…" She pointed at the door, her eyes lighting, freezing a layer of ice around its hinges "…Until we have come to a decision." She made her way back to her seat as her irises faded back to normal. "If you cannot hold an orderly discussion, consider this. An order of twelve watches over us, twelve Celestials who command the fires that keep us warm, provides the very water we drink and the air we breathe, they chose us to hold their mantle, the utopian world awaits, I choose not to faulter, I will deliver, but I need your help." Calias could always be counted upon.

"A Star Caller who fails to translate the Celestial voice is a level of incompetency I am unwilling to tolerate. I am inclined to meet a man like Xavien with a heavy boot, with the full weight of our proud army behind it, rather than a measly force that may be in need of reinforcing in the weeks to come." Isabelle was equipped with a response, to Eran's satisfaction.

"I trust Lethaniel will thwart this invasion swiftly, chairman, his record is flawless, match it with my Honour Guards I've no reason to doubt their capabilities, nor should you. Soon this rebellion will be behind us and the reconstruction of Krondathia can begin."

"Reconstruction? Don't you mean reformation, Isabelle?"

"Both, I have you know"

"Reformation of what, exactly?" His questions were intrusive and inconvenient, but they needed to be answered. She took a deep breath; she knew her next sentence would not go down well, but she had to be brave.

"Reformation of ALL our military services." Calias smiled as the uproar arose all around him, from the military personnel present in the room to those who were in partnerships with, they all arose in protest.

"Your service has my respect and gratitude my friends" said Calias, bowing to the angry mob, hurtling abuse Isabelle's way, the worst of which was Calias's sneering smile. Never had she been heckled in this way before, never had she met such a solid opposition. Hadn't these military men not seen this coming? With the abolishment of war, what purpose would her forces have? Isabelle reassured them with the only card she had, a card already undermined by Calias.

"The Celestials will always watch over us my Norkrons. Their strength outmatches that of any army. We can always depend on them."

Nothing would make Lethaniel happier than to one day permanently sheath his swords, though he understood the concerns the military personnel had when faced with this proposition. It would have been an unprecedented event to drop Krondathia's forces, to be replaced with something no-one could figure. Thao remained silent, drawing the same conclusions as Lethaniel, this was after all everything he had been fighting for, but never expected such drastic action to come around so fast. Torn between his sense of duty and his faith, his silence spoke volumes.

"Greatness comes from the ability to avoid wars. The Celestials prophesise this; we must look to our faith" she urged, speaking into the commotion. "But until that time, our military will resolve this conflict in the east and see that is done so quickly. No reformation will happen until our utopian dream is further realised, please gentlemen." The Council Chamber grew somewhat calmer to Isabelle's withdrawal, their panic understandably so. The removal of such Norkron pieces, pieces which had granted them power in Equis would be left open for the taking should Isabelle fail to deliver the promises of a Star Caller. "I would never leave Krondathia naked without certain assurances in place. Our power comes from our armies, we're right to rely on such forces in times of uncertainty and we'll continue to do so until the prophecy is fulfilled. My power comes from my faith, I believe the world is ready to unite, I believe we are capable of unity. Let us see these events through together, let us talk solutions." Isabelle fell silent and allowed herself to relax. Calias, on the other hand was not put to rest.

"Apologies my Star Caller, I only fight for what is best" said Calias with a well-reasoned tone of voice. Isabelle kindly acknowledged this. "The Lady Star Caller wants solutions. I feel like I have one being a student of history myself" acknowledging Master Eran. Isabelle connected the dots; she was unaware that Calias had been a former student of his.

"What do you have in mind, Calias?" Yespin demanded.

"As we are in the habit of honouring the older methods, I feel this may be appropriate" He glanced at Lethaniel briefly, "I say we do as our Requorn fathers had done. Let us design a treaty, offer our Dovidian allies a gift demonstrating our friendship and assuring them of safety. Let us spread the wings Starillia's teachings to the country of Ivulien."

"A treaty? What would the document declare? Peace was made centuries ago," Nenphis pointed out.

"We will write a new treaty, together" said an enthused Calias "An unbreakable one that will secure the bond between Norkron and Dovidian for as long as this world lasts." Curious were the people in The Council Chamber, intrigued they were about his propositions that had historical weight that built success.

"And the gift?" questioned Cillian, raising his voice which had been near enough silent all the way through the meeting.

"Our father of Krondathia can rule these lands alongside us. I propose we send our mother to Ivulien, to love and to hold them as she has done us." No riots or heckles had flung, Calias's solution resonated, like a plague it spread agreeableness throughout the room to a rising applause. "TO ANSWER THE IVULIEN CALL! TO PUT THEIR CONCERNS TO REST! WE WILL SEND THE STAR CALLER TO SPREAD THE WORD OF STARILLIA!" called Calias, cementing the proposal to thunderous applause, an applause Thao was not a part of. Jerhdia glanced at Lethaniel sitting a distance away with a muddled expression in his observations, as was Alexius taking in a hefty draw of rolling weed. It mattered not what any of them thought; it looked like the council had already made up their minds, but it would inevitably be put to a vote. Eran had sunk into his chair, his head in his hands. He had known this was coming but had lacked the courage to warn Isabelle earlier. She sat alone at her desk with her hands together. It was a good solution, she wasn't about to deny it, just a shame it had to come at a heavy cost. Her duties were to continue if the vote passed, only she would be in a foreign land far from home.

"This can't happen!" Lethaniel muttered to himself. The meeting was as good as over; some had even started to leave, though they were going nowhere until Isabelle unfroze the door, yet she sat motionless at her desk.

The hard day's work was over. The last cart trailed off into the city, leaving Ethan, Othello and a few other loaders behind to clear up and clear out. As Othello dusted off his hands and approached his loaders, they moved away from him, forming into groups; it was obvious that he was being purposefully ignored. Maybe it was due to his foreign style, his long hair, his tanned skin, the way he spoke or pronounced certain words, replacing modern day terms and phrases with old-fashioned ones, or it could have been the fact that he was still a stranger to them. Ethan had become a fast friend, being the only one opening up to him and engaging him in conversation. Eventually, the loaders scattered. He did not appreciate this; things had indeed changed since he last was here. Men in the city were working for gain, to purchase things for themselves or put their earnings towards poisoning their livers. Most men didn't work to make the city a better place like they used to do; they did it because they simply had to, and in some portions of the city this had begun to show. Women were the same but preferred the men to work while they stayed home; most wasted huge amounts of time on their looks, dressing up like a porcelain doll for every leering cretin in Imrondel to obsess over. This concept confused Othello; to him, it was a dog eat dog world, everyone seemed to be focused on themselves and meeting their own ends regardless of who they hurt in the process. *Not like Jureai* he thought. In Jureai, a man or woman could go to sleep after a hard day's work knowing that their village or camp was a better place to live. Each clan member knew they were a part of something grand and their efforts were rewarded by others, with respect and the promise of peace at the end of the day. Love between two people in Jureai often lasted many years, it was a beautiful thing to behold, something to be cherished and allowed to blossom; very few couples became separated, stronger as a family, encouraging men to be men and women to be women, not like here where it was absolute warfare. The Bevorks believed in a richer way of life, where a beautiful world took time and effort to achieve. A Bevork Clansman didn't gather, build or fight for themselves; they would do it for the benefit of everyone. Their treasure wasn't just the talon in their pocket, but it was the drinking water they retrieved from a river, or the love and friendship of another. El Raud, Reneeia, Ukthoth and Kollag believed that if this way of life was to continue, eventually their ways would spread and the paradise that everyone strove for would soon come to pass. It occurred to Othello that Jureai would soon be a haven, a perfect place to live in should it carry on its traditions. *Nothing like this place,* he thought. Looking around at the grey surroundings, he felt depressed by the lack of colour, betrayed by his father's words. What he had left behind, seemed all the more special; It had gotten cold quite quickly. He wrapped up in an extra blanket he found on a nearby bench.

"Where are YOU going in such a hurry?" he asked Ethan, who was clearly eager to get away.

"To the yards in The Military District; my Commander is not to be messed with. Apparently, he was a former Honour Guard. I am in training now, you see… Are you sure you won't join me?"

"I am sure."

"I will be there again early tomorrow before we start another day of loading. We'll be learning how to handle swords," Ethan related excitedly, hoping this would convince Othello, who did nothing but nod once, picking up the tools left on the road. "Have a good night!" called Ethan, waving as he walked off down the street, catching up with the other loaders, leaving Othello to his business. A few left around him stretched their arms and backs, complaining of the meagre pay they would receive for the highly strenuous work. Othello felt no aches and no pains; these men knew nothing of real labour. The previous nights had been uncomfortable, lonely and cold; the small supply package given to him by Alexius was almost at its end, so Othello finished what he was doing and made off across the road, heading toward a certain district in search of a nice, hot meal. Ethan had told him that loaders were given one free, full meal a day, so there was no need to worry about zeal. Along the road, he spotted a horse carrying a man riding at a dangerous speed toward the city gate, which he shot through without stopping.

"What was that all about?" he wondered to himself.

"Chosen. Star Caller. Mother. Conductor... Ivulien...Why me?" she moaned, leaning on her window, looking out on all the free people below. The votes had been counted and recounted several times, her path was decided, and she had agreed to it; for it was backed by the people and seemed the right course of action to take. Calias's proposal was sound and part of being a Star Caller realising one's selfless, making the right decisions for the benefit of others, but it hurt. It had hurt to think of the life ahead of her in Krondathia, now it was worse! There would be no peace, not for a very long time, no time however little for herself to enjoy. Isabelle would be the first Star Caller to live out her days in a foreign country; as such she would certainly make her mark on history and be studied over the centuries to come, this part she didn't mind, for she wanted to do great things. For Isabelle, her entire life was one of servitude, dedicated to the faith, a constant commitment to its laws and teachings. She would be sent to Ivulien, the country of the Dovidian people, to spread the wings of Starillia, to educate those who did not know about the twelve Celestials. Visitations to Krondathia would be required, but her home base would be in that of Ivulien. Looking out of her window, she spotted the courier speeding off out of the gate, taking the news in writing to Ivulien. It was all for real now; there was no stopping the message unless she suddenly learned how to fly at ridiculous speeds. She felt powerless, even for someone in her position and with her powers, the weight of her responsibilities crushed her chest. As the horseman left her sight, a series of knocks came at her door. "Who is it?" she said coldly, hoping it was someone bearing refreshments.

"Only me, young one..." Polite and respectful as always, it was Master Eran who did not enter until invited in; of course, his arrival was always warmly welcomed.

"Please come in Master." He stepped inside and closed the door behind him gently. The day had grown dark though it was still early in the evening. Pandora crept around the room and made herself comfortable on the desk, proceeding to wash behind her little, pointed ears. The room lay silent for a short period of time. Isabelle did not move from the window, so Eran came a little closer.

"You can say something, you know." He knew the difficult position she was in but could not truly put himself in her shoes mentally, no one could. She did not respond, instead, she continuing to stare out of the windowpane, thinking to herself. Eran sat on the bed facing away from her; he looked at his nails and said: "I want you to know that I am proud of you. I thought what you said in there was very brave." This drew the slightest of smiles on Isabelle's face, the warm air that escaped her mouth clouding the cold glass of the window. She still did not to move from her viewpoint, however, opting to allow Eran to continue. "It seems times are changing, or perhaps they changed a long time ago and we did not notice until we were all in that chamber, sitting across from one another." Another silence reigned for a while. Pandora stopped washing, almost as if she wanted to listen to what was being said. When Isabelle failed to open her mouth, the cat lost interest and got back to her preening. "Very well..." Eran was about to leave, assuming she just wanted to be alone.

"Master..." Isabelle murmured quietly, hoping he would stay longer. "What was she like?"

"Who?"

"I remember her; we spent time together, but I still do not think I truly knew her, not like you did." It was only then that he understood.

"Freya was capable, Isabelle, strong, powerful and kind, just like you. I was envious, I won't deny it, but a lot were back then. She was a very pleasant woman to be around, more than just a gazer; beautiful she was, a born ruler, but she... Lost something along the way."

"Why did she choose me?"

"She was very fond of you from the moment the two of you met. She never did state a specific reason as to why she chose you as her successor, though I am sure it is documented somewhere, but I think it was your approach to life. You saw things the same way, like mother and daughter; you remain calm and reserved when confronted by obstacles. I think that's what attracted you two to one another," he concluded, hearing a faint sigh coming from Isabelle. "She died too young. That's what is so magnificent about you; you grew and developed without much tutoring, learnt things with little guidance. Picked up skills few could without a teacher. You mastered the ways of Glyph, the ways of The Chosen so quickly with very little prior knowledge. We all watched on with amazement as you became the woman you are today."

"How did she die?" This was an unexpected question for Eran, who put his hands together and attempted an answer, nonetheless.

"You were noticed early when you arrived here in this city. Freya was still young when she named you her successor. As you know, another had already been named as her successor. Your presence, however, changed Freya's" he explained.

"I remember; Freya died in pain. I still hear her screams sometimes, echoing through the corridors of Norisis. You weren't there for her, Eran. Why weren't you there when she was screaming?" she enquired, rubbing the back of her neck with both hands.

"She had sent me away to accomplish a task… Her passage to the next life, if there is one, was not easy. She had become ill but made the time to instil in you what it meant to be a Star Caller. Before she died, she prepared you to carry on her legacy. I know you miss her; she helped you at the time of your mother's death, you became close, confided in each other, and then she too had to leave you alone in this world."

"I've been alone ever since." Old feelings and distant memories shuffled themselves to the front of her mind. Sad feelings, regrettable feelings. This never-ending sadness allowed her to appreciate what everyone had done to help her climb this far; the sadness of lost loved ones kept her alive. Freya's lessons were nothing but thoughts and feelings now; they faded with each day that passed, becoming less and less real in her mind. Worse yet, her mother was among these fading memories. It seemed that the more she delved into the mysteries of Starillia, the more memories of Freya and her mother she lost like it was consuming her entire being.

"You can still say something. You can still change the future."

"No!" she exclaimed sharply, turning her back to the window and putting her hands on her hips. "This is how it's meant to be, for the good of all. The decision has been made. It's not about me, it is about the future. Ivulien can only benefit from the teachings of Starillia; all it demonstrates is how to be better people, how to strive toward a pure society. We cannot falter in this. I cannot falter in this. I'll bring the faith to them and make them see." Eran nodded and continued looking around the room.

"I have been doing some reading, looking into research involving your Visions. I found something of interest." He withdrew a few pieces of paper from his pocket; old, crumply documents, nothing significant to look at. Isabelle had been hoping for more and looked at him in disappointment. "Read them if you like, but don't get your hopes up. Maybe it will help you understand a few things."

"How long do I have left here?"

"You have enough time. When the Dovidian leaders arrive to sign the treaty, you will make your way to your new home with them. You know Akarnal Desa well; he will accompany you. Anything you need, you go to him."

"He won't replace you. You will always be the best." Eran smiled, wishing she could stay; they had been through so much together, yet he had to leave, to find his way home, to eat and to sleep though the whole night.

Once again, she was left alone. She spotted the sheets of paper on her desk; *so kind of him to help*, she thought, she would miss him dearly when she had to leave. It wasn't too late, but already Isabelle felt tired; she yearned for the comfortable escape of sleep and the chance of beautiful dreams like she used to experience. Yet even the privacy of sleep was compromised; the same strange darkness and disturbing Vision haunted her wherever she went. The stone prison that entrapped her, the screams of people, the tormenting whispers destroyed her appetite for rest. *"Elaso Fiin an ute fiin tressa"*

"What do you mean!? Who are you!?" she moaned aloud as she sat upright in her double bed, the sheets sticking to her legs. Getting out of bed was cold and uncomfortable, but she needed some fresh air. Opening her window wide to the grey sky lingering over the silent city, she leant out and looked down from the considerable height. There was, of course, one way to escape all of this, one way to escape this prison. Biting her bottom lip, she felt the sudden urge to let herself go. "I can't," she whispered to herself. A sad cry alerted her from behind; a worried little voice coming from her feet. She felt claws tugging at her nightdress. Pandora was at her ankles looking up at her with those big green eyes of hers, full of sadness and worry. Evidently, she knew that Isabelle was in distress. Coming to her senses, she closed the window and picked up Pandora, holding her close. Outside the city was shutting up, the lights being extinguished, the last few inns and bars now closing their doors for the night. Isabelle didn't notice, for it was very dark, but someone could see her, someone was spying on her from the streets below.

Othello had just finished his meal. Placing his knife and fork together on the plate, he sat back in his chair, taking his time with his drink, relaxing outside in the open air next to one of the canals. He listened to the hymn of the water, the sound of others talking around him, socialising, gossiping, complaining as always. It was only then that Othello noticed that people were still steering clear of him, keeping at least five feet away; no one was even seated in his vicinity and he couldn't figure out why? As far as he knew, he was always polite and considerate with other people, he made the effort to talk to them, but still, he received the same strange, cold neglect from almost all with whom he came into contact with. Some kept their distance entirely. The women of the city tried to hide their attraction towards him; they would follow the majority and keep away, yet some could not help but inspect him from head to toe. He was well-built, after all, with chiselled facial features and a generally healthy appearance. He was not packed with muscle, but he had some weight to him, filling out his lean figure nicely. With a brief feeling of surprise, he suddenly spotted the very same woman he had been thinking about at work earlier in the day. Eva was leaning on a rail, looking out across the canal, was also enjoying the cool, calm evening. She had spotted him earlier and had been constantly trying to catch his attention, but Othello had been far too interested in eating and drinking. Now she caught him moving over to her slowly, and she quickly looked back at the water, controlling her nerves. She had wanted this to happen, but never thought it actually would; his mere presence took control of her hands as they began to shake so violently that she had to grip the rail tightly. He did not come too close but joined her leaning forward over the water. Eva had to say something; she was interested in what she saw and could only hope that his personality matched his looks. During her twenty-five years, she could spot a good man from a passing thought.

"It's a nice night, isn't it?" The inn behind them closed its doors with a loud bang.

"It certainly is," he replied, "Apologies on behalf of my friend today." She had to stop to think for a second, but then she remembered the messy incident and laughed.

"Oh, it's fine, people throw fruit at me all the time. Although a girlfriend did find some in my hair. Next time throw something I actually like, it would save me packing lunch." As she spoke, she edged her way a little closer to him along the railing.

"You don't like tomatoes? The tomatoes here are extravagant." Eva caught onto his strange accent, a cultured voice but entwined with someone from the north.

"You're not from around here, are you?" She had clearly been observing him; He was all so familiar somehow like she had known this man for a long time. Othello looked at her with raised eyebrows before she continued. "Your skin is darker than most others, it kinda glows."

"Thank you," he beamed.

"Your speech is -I don't know - it's foreign, but only slightly… Stop me before I say something offensive, please!" She was now facing him, becoming more and more confident as the conversation progressed.

"Would you like to know my name?" he asked. Eva blushed.

"I would, I guess it would help."

"My name is Othello." He held out his hand to her, though she appeared hesitant to take it. "Am I doing something wrong?" he wondered, looking at his hand, hoping she would accept his friendship. Finally, she shook it.

"I am Eva. How do you do?" There handshake lasted a little longer than usual. Othello's grip was strong, his hands were rough, and he returned to leaning on the rail overlooking the canal, taking a drink of ale as he watched the water.

"So where are you from, Othello?" He did not answer right away, instead, he took another drink of ale while she made her own guesses. "You're from the north, aren't you?"

"I am but there is more to the story" Eva was not dim-witted; she was an educated woman with a sharp eye.

"You're part of one of the clans?" Othello hid how impressed he was. "Your hair has a braid in it, I sell something similar in my shop. They come all the way from Jureai. Which clan did you belong to?"

"Guess" he teased.

"No, I don't know them all, tell me? Wait, you're part of the good kind right?"

"What do you think?" asked Othello, and Eva drew closer and asked the strangest of questions.

"Open your mouth"

"What?" grunted Othello.

"Open your mouth I need to see" she insisted. Othello opened his mouth wide as she gave her inspection, onlookers stared but the pair did not care what was happening on the outside.

"Well your tongue is not forked, I can relax, phew, you're not poisonous" and she breathed a sigh of relief.

Othello scratched his forehead, tucking a few stray strands of hair behind his ear. "Salarthians do not have forked tongues girl, that's not how it works, nor do the Red Stones have horns. I'm a Bevork."

"You're a Bevork man, huh? I've heard of them, good hunters."

"Indeed so" he agreed.

"Were you a hunter Othello?"

"For a little while, but mainly I was…" Othello held his tongue for a moment, feeling it right to keep his title of champion a secret "… Mainly I was a carpenter."

"A carpenter?" she repeated, though without a hint of disappointment. "What kind of things did you make?"

"I put together chairs, tents, bows, arrows, spears, made a few wells. It's tiresome work but rewarding all the same."

"Are you paid handsomely in the north?" she asked naively.

"Bevorks rarely reward their own clansmen with talon; many of our clan do not barter with it at all; our rewards aren't so material."

"The other clans do. I assumed Bevorks did the same."

"That's right, they do. Every culture today is based upon the growth of wealth. Bevorks are different, we build upon different foundations."

"So what is this remarkable foundation made of, Othello?"

"A place to live in peace. Opportunity to pursue one's passions. Respect. A sense of purpose in this world, a vision on the horizon we can work toward."

"Somehow I don't think that would work without gold. It's nice to speak of such things, but few would share in that dream," Eva argued.

"That is what it means to be Bevork. We've already begun; we've already started but one day our settlements will come together, the other clans will see the benefits and the horizon will glow a little brighter. Norkrons are not the only ones in search of an idyllic society; there are other ways to achieve it."

"How?" she asked.

"By building it yourself, on your hands and knees brick for brick. Creating it one little piece at a time" Othello gently took hold of Eva's shoulders and turned her to see the grand, the enormous Palace of Norisis, the hear of The Golden City "Even that once fit into the palm of your hand Eva." Othello retuned to his ale as Eva, strangely enough squeezed her fingers together, pressing them into her palm.

They continued to lean on the rail together, looking out upon the specks of lights dancing over the water's surface. The stars were bright, and the night was calm and quiet. Eva and Othello continued to talk well into the early hours, discussing a wide range of topics. Unfortunately, their beds called them home. Having enjoyed the time they had spent together, they said good night.

Chapter 17 - The Sire and The Messiah

Far west in the lands of Krondathia, two men discuss their plans for the people of Equis.

The Eldor sat in the dark main hall of the empty Cathedral, the midnight moon having fallen behind the roving clouds outside. Dressed warmly in a thick, white cloak, the old man sat next to a table lit by blazing candlelight. Suddenly his attention was drawn to a struggle outside. Unperturbed by the sound of slicing and screams from his guards, which quickly died down to deathly silence, he pulled back his hood, revealing his face. The door swung open slowly with a long creak. The Eldor remained still, staring into the candlelight, knowing full well who it was and why he had come. As the door slammed shut, the intruder strolled confidently into the room, sheathing his curved sword.

"I grow tired of this waiting," he complained as he approached. "Our plans are already in motion, Ivulien is waiting. I hope for your sake, for the sake of your people, that you have news I want to hear." The Eldor replied without a hint of intimidation in his voice:

"The situation is delicate. I have my best, most loyal man on the matter. Calias will sway the minds of men in that chamber, I swear it."

"It's not the men I fear, it's that woman. Your Star Caller is the problem. I saw her again at the demonstration some months ago; fortunately, I don't think she recognised me. She has far more power than I had imagined. Physically, she is strong, like all Star Callers should be. Isabelle must not be allowed to compromise our plans." The man was young and slightly built; he had entered like a shadow, dressed as a twilight assassin. His hair was plentiful and fine, reaching his shoulders; his skin was smooth with the radiance of youth. His bright eyes, however, told a different story; they had apparently prematurely aged through the horrors they had witnessed. Judging by appearance alone, The Eldor guessed the man was in his early twenties, but he couldn't say for sure, he could have been younger. All he knew was that to cross him would be a dreadful mistake; an unfortunate few had done so before and ALL had ended up in a cold, early grave. The man in black pulled back his white hair with both hands and strolled to the half-open window opposite his host, staring out at the night sky, smiling subtly in anticipation of what was to come. The Eldor could see his sword, intimidating even when safely concealed in its hard sheath. The old ruler did not feel comfortable with the silence, so he asked a question, breathing in deeply.

"Nonetheless, our plans are underway. You will have your victory. Does your chain of command know of your strategies?" The man in black was silent, fixating on the dark sky. The Eldor looked over at him, twisting his head around, taking care to mask his dread. "They do not know, do they? This is your campaign…" He just about made out a slight shake of the young man's head, an almost invisible sign of disagreement. "Who sent you? Who leads you?" Once again, his questions went unanswered. Growing desperate for answers, he spoke again, only this time it came across as a plea. "Does it have to come to this?" Finally, the man responded, in a sinister tone of voice.

"The time is right. We finally have enough strength. After all this time, things are happening at last. Retribution is coming to Krondathia; for all your wrongs, for all your foul deeds and endless greed. We want vengeance, *Sire*, but it's not just about that; this war is necessary. Krondathia must be destroyed and the Norkron race eradicated." He turned away from the window to look the elderly man in the eyes as he continued. "It is true that the Salarthians attacked the Dovidians first, but no matter. All it took was a little persuasion and bargaining; we promised them land, wealth and of course a purpose in Equis. Once Xavien and his Marauders fulfil their part of the deal, we will unite as one and crush them forever. There is no place in Equis for this Demon Man, or for those who follow him, but in the meantime, we can make use of him. The Ulgorans wanted more. They wanted the living, breathing slaves once the war is over, to rebuild their mountain kingdom that YOU destroyed during the rise of your people." He pointed an accusatory finger at The Eldor. "I will not allow slavery, but their homes will be rebuilt. Our ranks are further bolstered…" The Eldor did his best to stand strong and brave; in his mind, he was afraid and could not help but feel beaten and manipulated by this young man, "… with the aid of Ulgor, the Salarthians, Blood Marauders and our Mercenary allies. It would seem pointless to resist us now."

"Ulgor?" muttered The Eldor, desiring an explanation and quickly receiving one.

"An ancient tribe from the mountain caves; they call themselves men but... I would say they are more akin to ogres, brutish and clumsy. Yet what they lack in intelligence they make up for in might. Cruel even toward their own kind... I am interested to see what Goro and his sons do to any of your soldiers who stand against us. They are as anxious as I am to get moving."

"This is outrageous! You plan to betray Ulgor as well as Xavien's Marauders? You risk too much! You'll end up dead, boy!"

"Calm yourself, old man. No one can kill me. After this war is over, neither of us wants to see Xavien in power, so it's in both our best interests to eliminate him and his kind from the situation. As for Goro and his Ulgorans, well... They have no interest in land; they have agreed to fall back into the mountains once they have seized their slaves. They will take no slaves, I promise you that, but they will obtain a workforce that you will provide. I cannot see them following through with the agreement; it's likely that they will become greedy, just like Xavien. Once their purpose is fulfilled, I will deal with them myself if they do not comply. The High Councillors of Virtue will be forced into submission after they receive the news of our victory over their greatest city. Xiondel will be unable to resist once Imrondel has been crushed; what is left will be used to pay off Ulgor. You nearly destroyed Ulgor Crown Mountain; it is only fitting that you help Goro rebuild the world you devastated."

"Listen to me, Messiah: my men will not bow down to you, nor will they surrender so easily. Men will die and I must appear to be actively working against you."

"It will be quite a display, don't you think? All of your men comfortable under a false sense of victory. Only death awaits those who dare pit themselves against me. I give you my word; people will die, but this is for a greater cause, sacrifice has never been so necessary. Future generations will look back on this age in centuries to come and they will be thankful for the choices we made today, what we did to save ourselves and prolong the future. And let's not forget what you have done to save yourself… All the lies, the deceit, all those people you put in the dark." The Eldor looked disturbed by Messiah's way of thinking; he was on a different level to anyone he had met before.

"It is a weakness to be so confident. I warn you: don't underestimate my soldiers." He held up an object, which Messiah took eagerly; it was a white key with an oval head, inscribed with a series of words written in the old language of Englathin. "The key to the city" said The Eldor, dangling it from his fingers "This is what you came for?"

"It's the final piece. Your soldiers do not concern me. I don't think you quite understand, old man. If I fail, my master will simply find another. It won't end until we succeed, never! We are destined to win. I am still waiting for you to fulfil your promise of new weapons. I have received nothing and that makes me nervous. I hope you're not considering backing out."

"It's not our fault; the roads are dangerous; the shipments we send you are going missing. We cannot find the ones responsible, though we suspect The Dark Rogues are to blame." Messiah's face dropped at the mention of the notorious thieves.

"Dark Rogues?" he repeated, rubbing his forehead. "Toula… The next time I see him will be the last time." The Eldor sat quietly, letting his visitor talk. "With or without your ranged barrel weapons, the plan is already in motion. I couldn't stop it even if I wanted to. Prepare for loss, Sire. When the day of defeat comes to your General, it won't be me who he will bow down to," Messiah stated, heading for the door.

"What of Isabelle? She can still stand in your way if she learns of your intent. Her senses are far more attuned than her predecessor, Freya."

"Has she named a successor?"

"No… Not yet."

"She will be dealt with in time; we have an agent more than willing to *take care of her*," Messiah assured him, quickly regaining his confidence.

"Are you mad? There are none who can match Isabelle!"

"Don't be so sure about that sir, the one of whom I speak has taken the study of Glyph to unprecedented levels. She will kill your Star Caller. Isabelle will fall. Who knows, they might even recognise each other, it hasn't been that long since they parted ways. Your role has already begun, old man. When this is all over and your flag burns and turns to ash, you will step down when I order you to. Keep me informed of the situation; all must go to plan, otherwise, there will be consequences." He pulled open the door and vanished into the night. The Eldor breathed in heavily; the ordeal was over, and it would be a while until their next meeting. Messiah was no more than a messenger sent by his anonymous master in Davune. It was true that the Ivulien power structure was changing. The Eldor knew all of their names, a task made easier by the fact that they were significantly fewer than the key decision makers of Krondathia. As far as he knew, the Dovidians were planning an attack to take back what was theirs and to deliver a crushing blow to all who opposed them. He knew it was coming, but he was not the one overseeing the defence strategy. If Calias was successful in his role then part of the deal was already complete. Whatever the Dovidians were planning, this move would make it far easier for them to finish their campaign. Messiah did not suffer fools; he was cunning, not the sort of man who made mistakes. The Eldor feared him and had to remind himself each and every day; Why he was taking such action and why he was siding with the enemy in the shadows? In the name of saving future generations, was the story he told himself, prolonging humanity's existence in Equis was a lullaby he sung to send him off to sleep at night.

Chapter 18 - The Man under the Hood

The mind is fragile.

Priests, politicians, ministers, and nobles had been visiting Isabelle's quarters all day, to wish her a safe trip and a profitable future in Ivulien, and to thank her for all the happiness and elation she had brought to Krondathia. She had to assure The High Priests that her work would continue, that she would carry on serving Starillia with as much passion, vigilance, and dedication in Davune than in Krondathia, which would become her new home. The notes and documents Eran had given her a few days before was atop her bureau; she had yet to study them. Pandora received a lot of attention from some of the children who visited, constantly purring and always in a playful mood. With all these visits and farewells, Isabelle had anticipated the arrival of the few in the city who were truly close to her, but they had not yet come. Thao had not visited, though his wife Lena had, which was a most pleasant experience; they spoke mainly of Lucion. Isabelle was curious to know how he was progressing, but she never revealed how she truly felt about him. There was something unpredictable about that child; his inner self unclear to her. Lucion had the chance to grow into a mighty servant of Krondathia, but there was also a shrouded side to his personality building within him, a side that might grow to represent everything Honour Guards worked to destroy. Thao would be there soon, but for the moment he had business in The Military District with Lethaniel; they and the other Captains and Commanders had to arrange a strike team for what was being called *The Barbarian Raid* mission. Jerhdia was also absent; she looked forward to his visit, he always had a relaxing aura about him, a charm she found curious from the opposite sex. Late in the afternoon, she had arrived back at her quarters after a dinner with the three High Priests. It felt good to be alone, free from the bombardment of questions surrounding the prophecy and teachings of Starillia; she had heard it all before and frankly was tired of it, tired of raising a fake smile it hurt to do so. She could only wallow in mysticism for so long before her head began to ache, without the ability to voice her stress, it bled into a sickness that took away her fire. About to keel over, she steadied herself, having had something to eat, she felt it was time to read what Eran had provided. At first glance, she knew that the document had been pulled from The Star Callers' archive in The Old Library. She recognised the names of the callers who had come before her, listed in order from first to last.

Star Callers 0718 - 1511
Regina Corah the 1st
Ashleigh Hauckos the 2nd
Hackney Beau the 3rd
Anazerath Relarnd the 4th
River Lye the 5th
Coppelia Velen the 6th
Ursula Cerrin the 7th
Ebony Heart the 8th
Melisa Nightsky the 9th
Atira Unasia the 10th
Selphie Olopoly the 11th
Iris Senatre the 12th
Kiera Atalisa the 13th
Melony Vel the 14th
Scarlet Siatas the 15th
Liandra Liola the 16th
Stella Verl the 17th
Penelasio Floras the 18th
Angelica Helii the 19th
Lexi Enil the 20th
Thespany Kayla the 21st
Freya Delmesca the 22nd
Isabelle Verano the 23rd

Isabelle held several documents in her hand but was most interested in this. Chills of awe crawled up her spine as she read the list. These were remarkable, historically significant women, each unique, supremely talented Omnio artists, flawless servants of their faith. Before she could move on to the other bits and pieces Eran had lent her, the door flew open and slammed into the wall.

"Knocking is the polite thing to do, Calias," she said without even raising her eyes from the paper.

"I just came by to see how our Chosen was doing, if you don't mind. What are those? You're a little old to still be revising, aren't you" he teased, reaching for the papers she held, but she pulled them away from his grasp.

"They're not for your eyes!" She quickly threw them in the drawer and closed it.

"Of course, how rude of me. Even a Star Caller such as yourself must be allowed some privacy," he smirked, making himself comfortable in her room. Pandora remained in her favourite position on the desk.

"A little privacy would be nice; I have much to prepare," she hinted, urging him to leave. Calias began to fiddle with some of her possessions, annoying her greatly as she sat on the end of her bed. "What is *your* service to Krondathia? You're not just a court member, are you?" He folded his arms and responded indignantly:

"I serve The Eldor, Isabelle. I do what I am told to do. I don't upset the order, I maintain it."

"Maintain it? Even if it means carrying out foul deeds under the shadow of night when you think no one is watching? Deeds that should be made known to those with authority, people like me?" He ceased his fiddling.

"What is it you think you know, Isabelle?"

"I know enough"

"Do you know what a pawn is Isabelle?" She stiffened her back, unsure of how to answer the question "Of course you do, you of all people should know what it's like to have pawns. You have the most pawns on the board."

"Get to the point and then get out Calias. I've already grown tired of your nonsense!" she demanded, rising from her bed, and holding the door open as he continued to plod around her room, scuffing the carpet with his black shoes.

"I can tell you yearn for them; you yearn for the attention of the lowest common denominator, and even they care not to prioritise a visit."

"Is this why you came? To tell me that which I already know? Don't muddy the water Calias, don't pass this off to one of YOUR pawns, I saw you conducting your business in the dark. The only thing worse than a sleaze is a sleaze who pleads innocent while his hand is in the jar." He came close enough to whisper but spoke as normal.

"What do you know about my conduct?" They stared at each other, face to face; she could feel his warm breath on her nose. She stood up to him, raised her chin and placed her arms behind her back.

"I know of the book, the one you've tried to keep secret. I can understand why you kept it hidden from the general populace, but not from me. Why?"

"The answer to that is simple, call it trust, we do not know if we can trust you with what its pages hold" he stepped away, leant out into the corridor to make sure no one was within hearing distance of their conversation. "Starillia is fragile; it's not the rock that most people believe it to be. Maybe in some years, we will finally shed light on the truth and let you in; they say you are the most promising Star Caller since Corah, but frankly, I see no promise in you. You may be worthy in the temples, but not here, not on the outside, and that is where you conduct your affairs, in the temples. The book is yet to be properly deciphered, I am sure the warnings inked across its pages are nothing more than the whims of a madman, but should this book fall into the wrong hands it could be devastating to our way of life, would certainly give The High Council of Virtue something to throw at us. This is not acceptable, and it must remain hidden to prevent our people from tearing apart what we have worked so hard to build over the ages, our people are animals, animals that need securities. I strive to maintain that security; I maintain the order and that is what I will oversee. You are a mouthpiece, do your country a favour and say the right things, keep them away from each other's throats."

"The Eldor is in on this too, isn't he!? You want me to spread the faith knowing full well we are not in full possession of the truth. Well I ask you, which is more important; A foundation built upon truth or that of a lie? Calias I am talking to YOU!" she yelled, alarming him. He had had enough of her talk and without hesitation, rushed over to her and grabbed her by the mouth, pushing her up behind the door so no one outside could see, talking into her face.

"Listening well Isabelle." He pushed her harder against the wall, squeezing her jaw shut. "You will not speak a word of this to anyone, not here nor in Ivulien, you will perform your duty as is expected, if not for yourself, but for your pawns. Your Honour Guard and that boy General may find themselves walking into an ambush one day while patrolling supposedly safe borders. The Librarian may one day drink the wrong water or suffer an unfortunate accident on his ladder, your armourer friend, the one you flirt with may not see the rusted scaffolding joints supporting a tall walkway…" His eyes met Pandora. "Even your cat will meet the hounds. I have the authority and believe me when I say…" he came in close to her ear and whispered "… We are watching you, Isabelle, we've always been watching your kind throughout the centuries and we've become remarkably efficient at removing noisy pieces…" he pulled away from her ear and spoke back into her face "…Now behave, understand that you are not in charge and don't make me do anything I don't want to…" He released her and backed away, his tone returning to normal. "There was no reason for my visit; I only wished to meet you properly before you left and to wish you well. I enjoyed what you said yesterday, I learnt something, good day." He adjusted his collar and left her with a crooked smile. Isabelle sank to the floor and kicked the door closed. Almost instantly a few of her guards came running, knocking frantically on her door.

"Milady, are you alright? Can we come in? Is there anything you need?" She didn't answer, instead just sitting there in silence, her foot on the door, holding it shut. She buried her head in her arms, hiding in the darkness.

A biting wind invaded the night. The moon, a frozen orb in the sky, gleamed down upon the lonesome towers of Imrondel City, a sparkling labyrinth of lights dotted about the gloom. Millions of stars

405

glinted in the vast sky above. No matter how low the temperatures had dropped, it was still a beautiful night to behold for those on the ground. The city basked in the glow of the moonlight; some of its streets lay eerily illuminated while others remained drowned in shadow. Nocturnal animals scuttled about in search of food, scavenging and scrounging whatever they could find. Owls perched on rooftops and high statues, periodically swooping down, and snatching up small critters. Bats preyed on the insects drawn to the oil lamps, while cats patrolled the streets like guardians of the night, the dominant predators when the sun went down. Despite the cold, none were dissuaded from hunting. Most humans had retreated indoors to the sheltered warmth of their fiery stoves, but others, the silent ones who didn't want to be seen, wandered the streets. One such young man leant next to the bridge outside the quiet Palace of Norisis, his hood up to defend against the cold. He stared into the calm river, losing himself in his thoughts, hypnotised by the rhythm and flow of the running water. In his hands he held a slightly curled dagger; he was using its pointed tip to pick dirt out from under his thumbnail. Echoing footsteps alerted him to the presence of another, waking him from his trance. He saw a woman in a long, blue coat running over the bridge in a hurry, though she did not see him. Curious, he followed her, sheathing the dagger in a concealed sheath strapped to his wrist. He did not expose his presence to her, content to merely keep an eye on her from afar. He could not make out her face, but he knew her hair was long and blonde for it danced out from under her hood. She seemed to be heading toward the wall of Imrondel, the boundary of the city's territory past The Defensive Trench. One of the many portcullises along the wall had been left open, which meant not everyone was out of the trench, and few were still working, or guarding. The Main Gate was shut tight as always at this time of night. She found some stairs leading up to the walkway at the top of the main wall. Her shadowy stalker followed, making no noise as he crept up the stone stairs. The man under the hood kept his distance as he ascended the final stone step, moving out into the openness of the walkway, his cloak flapping around his shins. He saw her standing above the main archway, teetering dangerously close to the edge. A fall from that height would result in crippling injuries at best, most likely death. The wind could take her at any moment. He made sure the dagger was secure in his sleeve as he edged up behind her, trying his best not to startle her. Approaching as close as he dared, he looked up at her standing on the highest part of the wall. He could tell that she was crying or at least had been recently judging by her sniffles and rapid breathing. She tried to calm herself down, thinking about what she was there to do. Her unseen follower put his hands in his coat pockets and called out softly:

"Pardon me for intruding, I don't usually follow strangers but from here it looks like you're going to jump off a wall." She heard him but didn't see him, she focused on the paving stones far below her. He continued in a soothing voice, coming a little closer. "Something I learned when I was growing up, is that no matter how dark life gets, giving yourself those moments to vocalise your thoughts often lets you see the root of the problem. Before you do what I think you're about to do, I was hoping we could have that talk, perhaps there is something I can do?"

"Can you turn back time? Can you take away what I am? Can you remove my chains of burden and give back my voice!? If you can do ANY of that then you might be able to help me, if not I want you to go away" she ranted angrily. As he hesitated with his response, she got back to looking off the wall at the wide, flat road below. Clearing his voice, he eventually replied:

"Ah! I am sorry. I can't do any of those things, but I…"

"Then leave me to my business and go!" she snapped rudely, pointing away with an outstretched finger. He didn't leave, instead got gradually moved closer.

"I can't do those things milady…" and she hissed at the phrase "… but maybe we can figure out what went wrong and understand exactly why you want to jump off a wall! After we do that, if you still feel like you need to end it, I will leave you alone, I promise, I cross my heart…" he drew an 'x' on his chest as she looked down at him. "I hope that you will come down from there first though, so we can avoid the possibility of you accidentally slipping off, you don't want to land on your feet from this height."

"What do you mean?" she demanded.

"Well, you see, most people who fall great heights don't actually die instantly when they hit the ground, they tend to live on for some time in unbearable agony, unable to move having shattered their bones, slowly bleeding out from the inside, it could take a while. There are a few people around, they would likely hear you shriek and would make every effort to see you live. You will never walk again, someone would have to feed you or fit a tube down your throat, you get the idea" he explained, with a relaxed demeanour. She didn't turn around as she lingered close to the edge; the wind only had to pick slightly, and she would be gone. The young man edged closer to the stone wall and looked over the edge. Measuring it up and down in his mind, making an educated guess. "Yep, I'd say it's a fifty-fifty chance that you'd die from this height. I mean, the ground is hard and flat so the pressure will ALL be focused on whatever part you land on. If you want to go quickly, then I suggest a nosedive, but even then, I can't guarantee it won't be painless. People have survived things that should have killed them a thousand times over but manage to pull through, it is a funny old world. I hope you know how to do a nosedive, the technique takes practice, though I've heard that seconds before impending death the body's reflexes take hold and it tries to do whatever it can to prevent damage. So you may execute a perfect nose dive, only to break form last second" he warned, glancing up at her with a humorous look.

"Ugh! Will you just be quiet whoever you are and leave me alone!" she snarled, trying hard to ignore everything he had just said. Of course, he didn't obey her command, he hung around for the time being, shuffling around in his coat. He decided to try something else, another method of persuading her to come down.

"I remember when I was little, my friend and I were playing around near this deep ravine; we liked to drop rocks and other bits of junk over the edge and watch them fall all the way down. Anyway, one time my friend got too close to the edge and fell in. I thought that he was a goner, you know? The second I saw him fall my mind went blank; the shock takes you first. I never thought I would see him again. But in fact, he had been saved by a root in the side of the chasm, growing out from the earth. I managed to get some rope and pull him up to safety. He told me what it was like when he was falling…" The man paused his story and waited for a reaction, but received none from the woman, although she did appear to be listening intently. "He said it was regret. Regret that he had not lived, not done all those things that everyone should do: seeing the world, swimming off the shores of Sapphire Views, learning to ride, seeing a Celestial, wandering Crescent Forest, kissing that girl he liked... Regret it was, and fear, this is all that went through his mind and he had only been falling for two, maybe three seconds. It's an odd combination, but funnily enough, the two combine well." He looked like he was preparing to walk away. "If you want to be alone then I will leave you alone, just... I know it doesn't really matter now, but my name is Teo." He held his hand out to her, but she did not take it. "Very well then. Nice meeting ya. You were probably a lovely girl; shame you've decided to waste your life." With that, he walked away, his hands in his pockets. The lady on the wall suddenly turned her head and shouted after him:

"Wait! Have we met before?" Teo stopped and turned.

"No. Not properly anyway." Then it hit her; she knew where she had seen his face before.

"You... You're the one from the bar..."

"I am indeed him. So sorry if I scared you. Like I said I don't usually follow strangers; I was just curious as to where you were going in such a hurry." His tone was polite, everything she had imagined it would be when she first saw him.

"My name is Isabelle. I..." She had already begun to stutter, so he quickly interrupted her:

"Maybe you should get off the wall." Teetering on the edge she gripped the walls walkway and jumped down onto his level, pulling back her blue hood so they could become properly acquainted.

"I am Isabelle Verano."

"Teo Liolas, pleasure to meet you. How are you doing?" his smile was infectious, his aura a kind one as they took one another's hands. Isabelle noticed a mark around his neck, stretching all the way up to his ear. It looked like a burn of some kind. She was about to ask about it but decided now was not the right time for such a question, so she put it out of her mind.

"Liolas… Is that…"

"No, Isabelle, it's not; first of all, her name is Liandra *Liola*, mine is *Liolas*, so no relation there. Trust me, I've heard it all before." She was impressed that he apparently knew a little about the sixteenth Star Caller, not something she was used to.

"You looked bigger when I first saw you," she observed. Teo lifted his arms then dropped them by his side.

"And you looked worried and confused. Then again, I guess it's not every day a Star Caller goes for a drink by herself, is it?"

"I thought you were one of The Eldor's servants, spying on me or maybe worse." She could not help but feel a sense of unease, what Calias had shared with her had stuck.

"Does The Eldor deal with those types?"

"I don't know anymore; yes, I guess. Everything seemed so simple just a month ago," she groaned, her eyes falling from his.

"Don't worry you can speak your mind" he said, his hands sliding into his coat pockets as they distanced their way from the wall's edge to Teo's delight. *Mission accomplished*, he thought; by the looks of it, she was not going to leap off and make a bloody mess outside the gate. They head down the stone steps, through The Defensive Trench and into the great courtyard. Isabelle hesitant about what she shared.

"Is that why you decided to jump? Because things got complicated?"

"I'm sorry, I don't know what I was thinking, but I don't think you would understand; Star Callers lead… Different lifestyles to others, very different." As she spoke, she realised how harsh that sounded; she didn't know how wise this man was, and his life could have been a wreck too for all she knew.

"Tell me. Maybe I can help you after all, huh?" he suggested kindly.

"I have to be getting back now. I apologise for disturbing your evening, Teo," she smiled, kicking herself inside. He stood there looking at her with those deep eyes of his; she didn't want to leave the encounter like this. She couldn't ignore the troublesome feeling, and oddly enough she felt like she could trust him, so she began to speak of her life in vivid detail. "I… I have been having some trouble recently and I thought everything was clear to me, but my life, if you can call it that, has taken a turn and I'm not ready for it. People always demanding and wanting things from me, guards are always on my back, servants working round the clock invading every space I keep. I can't help everyone as much as I want to and there are times when I only want to help myself, but I can't even do that without feeling guilty. Going around in circles is what I do best." She turned away and looked up at the stars. "I am never allowed to be myself, just this image, this impersonation of someone I am pretending to be all of the time. This pretend-me is what the people expect a Star Caller to be like, but I feel something else. It's true, I have power and I have been blessed with this Glyph…" and her eyes shone gently "…but I never asked for any of this. My real self is lost, I have forgotten who I was before and it…Kills me."

"Not lost… Everyone changes over long periods of time. That person you were is still in you somewhere. People grow, becoming better versions of themselves. If you do not like this lifestyle, why not just walk away? Don't you have a choice? Isn't that a part of what being Norkron is about? Star Caller or not, you are still human." No one had ever suggested that option to her.

"It's not that simple. Only I can do what I do, walking away from the responsibility would undoubtedly cause chaos, as much as I often loath my position I understand selflessness" she said to herself as a silence took hold of them both. "What is it you do, Teo? You're not a soldier, are you?"

"Not exactly, but I will protect what is mine as much as it is. You don't have to be a soldier to be able to fight. I'm not exactly from here," he answered, revealing little, noticing her deliberate changing of the subject.

"Why did you come to Imrondel City then?"

"Why did *you* come here?"

"I came here because… I came here because I was ordered to," she replied.

"I thought leaders were supposed to give the orders," said Teo pointing out the obvious.

"Even your leader must obey at times." They continued to walk the path towards Norisis. The night was still brisk and chilly, but it mattered not to the pair strolling alone.

"Who says you're my leader?" Isabelle stared at him, though she didn't feel nervous or cautious for she could see he was only teasing. "I could be from Ivulien or Fevoriel, in which case you technically have no power over me." He was right in a way.

"I don't think you're from Ivulien; most of the Dovidians who lived here have now left the city and headed home, Ivulien has made some interesting strives. I will look into this further, when I've the time."

"Why?"

"Because I am the Chosen; I have a responsibility to my people."

"But the Dovidians are not your people, whereas the Norkrons are, aren't they?" he responding knowingly, forcing a grin from Isabelle.

"You're enjoying this, aren't you?"

"Very much so," he answered with a smile.

"I try not to break people up into factions, I try to see people as people, whether you're Dovidian, Norkron, Jurean Karthian, we're more similar than dissimilar"

They came to the bridge before The Palace of Norisis. They had been talking for a long while and now it felt like it was time to turn in, but before she did, she wanted to say one last thing.

"I want to thank Teo, I am truly sorry for my behaviour."

"You have nothing to apologise for; I didn't drag you down from the wall, you hopped down yourself, remember."

"Goodbye, I wish you goodnight." As she head across the bridge toward her The Palace, he got back to what he had been doing; staring into the flowing water beneath the bridge. "Teo! You're not leaving the city anytime soon are you?" she called back.

"Goodnight, Miss Verano" he replied, waving. They parted ways; one disappearing into the night, the other wandering into the bright lights of The Palace.

"I will lead the scouting party out a day after we reach The Norfoon Watch Towers. Hopefully, we will meet Mathias; he knows the land and his assistance could save us days of scouting. Thao will devise a strategy based on the location and numbers of the barbarian raiders; he has volunteered to lead the first charge against them. If we are in a position to negotiate, then that overrides any attack plans we have. Personally, I don't wish to talk with these men of bloodlust; they deserve what's coming to them," Lethaniel announced to Alexius who was patrolling close by, listening intently. "What's on your mind, Lex?"

"Braygon contacted me today; I told him what was about to happen…"

"And?"

"He wants to be a part of it. I would recommend that he joins you on this mission."

"That's what I had in mind, he's an experienced traveller and a Captain, besides, he knows Mathias better than any of us."

"Good call" agreed Alexius "Let's try to make this thing quick." The two were almost home and they stopped outside Alexius's house.

"When we reach the towers, scouting could take weeks, I hope you're prepared for some rough nights. Some of the terrain up there is only accessible by foot, so we are going to have to thin our numbers out dangerously to cover the entire area. We could lose men just looking for them" warned Lethaniel.

"Don't worry I'll bring my hiking boots" Alexius said with sarcasm. "If I told you I knew someone from the northlands, someone able, would that help you in this task?" Lethaniel needed little time to respond; his face lighting up at the suggestion.

"A friendly Northlander could prove most useful. Do you really know one or are you fucking with me again?"

"Jerhdia ran into one while looking for Jaden, his missing companion. Maybe this Northlander can help us."

"He's here in the city!?" and Alexius nodded.

"He works down at The Distribution Centre, loading and unloading supplies and materials. I can find him tomorrow and bring him to you if you'd like? I think he'll appreciate the time off, he never stops, reminds me of you" said Alexius, rolling a smoke in his fingers.

Chapter 19 - Knowing A Star Caller

Some people need very little introduction.

"It was just his aura Master; he didn't hide who he was just to be nice, he spoke and listened to me in an honest way. Most of all he didn't seem afraid of me, unlike everyone else in this city…" Isabelle babbled happily and then realised what she had just said, quickly correcting herself. "How rude of me; I know YOU understand me, Master. You probably know me better than anyone. It's just strange to meet someone who can express themselves so freely to me instead of the usual, formalities. You grow to notice it and it gets tiresome."

"I don't understand you Isabelle, I don't try to understand anyone anymore."

"What do you mean, Master?" she asked, jogging a little after him to catch up having fallen behind in her daydreams.

"Just when you think you know someone, they will go ahead and surprise you, or worse, betray you. It has happened before. People are unpredictable and always keep secrets, the best of us are guilty of it, I certainly have some I'd not wish to share." The look in Eran's told her that something life changing must have happened a long time ago in his past. There was still a lot she didn't know about the man; she often wondered how he had come to be granted the title of Master. What had he been like when he was her age? What kind of lifestyle had he lived before he decided to settle down and start tutoring others? Eran was wise and learned; he spoke from personal experience and wove them into his lectures, this method enthralled young minds and kept them hungry for more. She felt sure there was a story here worth telling in the future, but for the time being, it seemed he would keep his past to himself. "I'm sure you still have a few secrets locked away in there Isabelle. Thoughts you keep only for yourself? But I advise you remain cautious around the withdrawn, those who withhold and divert, it is likely they are hiding something if they display these behaviours consistently" he said, smiling. "Oh don't look so worried, Isabelle. This Teo fellow, is he from Krondathia? Is he a Norkron?"

"No. Well, I'm not sure," she muttered.

"Does he work in one of our cities?" he continued, overtaken by curiosity.

"I don't think so," she replied, scratching her head, realising what the questions were leading to.

"Could he be from The Pura Lands? Or from one of the Outer Villages of The Ledera Lands? Men from those parts often seek enlightenment in this city."

"Maybe, I didn't ask." Eran pushed a book back onto its shelf, a mild look of surprise on his face.

"Well, my girl, looks like he understands you an awful lot and you seem to know everything about him..." he responded with sarcasm. "Is he a soldier, do you think?" he went on, as he began to climb up a wooden ladder with an armful of books. She moved to help him, handing him stray books from the trolley below as they continued their conversation.

"I don't think he has the steel to be a soldier. I mean, who knows, he could be, but he didn't look like one. Most soldiers in my armies speak in a certain way, act in a certain way and all have delusions of themselves. They all want to be heroes; that word gets thrown around so often these days it's lost almost all meaning. From my observations, most men seem to feel like they have something to prove to the world or at least to their superiors. It's sad. If only they knew what being a hero actually meant, what it entailed and how difficult it is to earn the status... I fear if they really knew how to be a hero, they would cower at the cost. Heroes, from what I've read don't want to be heroes."

"You don't need to be a soldier to be a hero, Isabelle, I hope you realise that? The word can be assigned to anybody, truthfully speaking, but I do see where you're coming from." They had had a very similar conversation a long time ago, when she was a teenager, they could have talked further about heroes, but really all Isabelle wanted was to talk about Teo.

416

"He doesn't have the build of an Honour Guard, far from it. They are walking mounds of muscle. Nor does he have the qualities of a Knight," she began listing off her observations.

"Could he have the skills of an assassin? They have no use for titles; it's not something they parade around either. No doubt about it, assassins are light, swift and just as deadly as the highest echelons of our armies." Isabelle pursed her lips. "Could he be a Glyph Wielder?"

"No. I didn't detect a Glyph scent. He has never used or been exposed to high levels of Omnio."

"Could it have been a very weak scent?" Eran suggested.

"Weak scent or not, they are still traceable. My mind wasn't completely with me at the time, but if I see him again, I'll make sure. Still, I would say no, he does not use the spheres."

"Soldiers come in many shapes and sizes, my dear; some of the best in history originated from small, out of the way towns and distant farms, young boys most of the time, with hopes and dreams on their backs, who went on to make a mighty difference."

"He shows no world-weariness or scars on his skin; almost every soldier has had a near miss, save for Lethaniel, of course. I see no violence or threat in him and that is something I don't find every day." Eran's face found puzzlement.

"No scars?"

"A slight burn around his neck but, no scars" she replied, raising an eyebrow.

"So you have removed his clothes and checked him all over, have you?" This prompted a cheeky grin from Isabelle, and she flicked Eran's tiny, grey notebook at him. "I am only teasing you, my dear. From what you have told me I would say he is a pleasant boy of the city, and they aren't easy to find, I agree. Most are just out to prove something like you said and end up failing miserably or

417

making silly mistakes rather than great changes. In this day and age, where war is non-existent and the villains of the world run alone and afraid, as they should, heroes - Excuse me, a better term would be *good fighters*, with morals and ambition - find themselves struggling to prove their skills. Going back to the subject of heroes and good versus evil, if you will, the key ingredient in making a hero is a villain. Without them there can be no hero, there can be no good set aside from evil. I'll tell you now, the LAST thing Equis needs right now is a villain or some enemy with strong devotion and capability; the last one in this world was not... How can I put this, not so easily stopped. I'm sorry, I know I ramble on..." Isabelle smiled and looked at the floor, excited about what the next few days would bring. "Be cautious though and remain aware as I said; some people, most people, in fact, are not what they seem. I don't mean to be cruel but should this friendship of yours go any further for any reason, your position and credibility could be put in jeopardy. Do yourself a favour and walk away Isabelle, leaving it at a pleasant encounter. At least then no one can get hurt." She dropped her hand to her side and flicked her wrist, the notebook she had thrown at him flew back into her hand.

"Here is your book, Master." She tapped it on his forehead. "And this is for being so kind to me." She gave him a quick and friendly kiss on his cheek. "Chances are we will never cross paths again, Master I would not worry; there are over three hundred thousand people in this city, most go their whole lives without meeting more than a few thousand," she said as she began to head for the exit. Her guards were waiting outside.

"Isabelle!" She stopped and turned. Eran came up to her and spoke in a low voice. "I have been going over some of the text in the book; it took me all night to decode a little of the language, but I found something interesting... A short passage." He paused, debating whether or not to tell her.

"What did it say?" she whispered.

"I found that this particular piece of text turns up more than once. I can only read a little of it to you, and I'm not entirely sure what it means, but maybe it links to the...."

418

"What does it say Eran? Tell me. Please." He recited what he could from memory.

"Only one so bold can end all chaos and strife, for the time has come for us to step gracefully aside. By nature's fury, they will be sent to do her deeds and deliver us the justice and purification required to nullify our travesties..."

Isabelle hung her head. Clearly, this passage was important, for it had shown up many times in the book, and Eran had felt it necessary to relay it to her. THAT was what concerned her most of all.

"The Readers, Isabelle? Or maybe you need to find another Master. Atheriax will be able to help you. I am out of my depth here. Have you tried asking your Counterpart? Have you tried using Inner Peace?"

"I was going to discuss it with my Counterpart, Master, but I believe she will say the same thing as you. Atheriax... He is a hard man to reach and when he is available it's usually only for a very, very short period of time. And if I may say so, Eran, I believe you are the greatest Master in this world; it's a rare status to achieve." He shook his head in disagreement, but she was adamant about her belief. "Say what you want, think what you want. Master Atheriax is nothing next to you. It would be interesting to see a debate between the two of you, though you both seem to agree on many subjects. As for The Readers..." She rested one arm on a nearby bookshelf and rubbed her eyes "...Distance prevents me more than anything Master, along with one other reason; no one is allowed to go before them twice in a lifetime, Star Caller or not. It's a long-standing rule. The Readers reside in Xiondel, in The Chronicle House; they have no desire to return to Imrondel. Travelling confuses them and can be dangerous. Watched and surrounded by a hundred guards, day and night, there is no chance I can slip by for a private visit without anyone knowing. The only other way is to confess everything I'm feeling to The Eldor or The Courts of Imrondel, which could be just as dangerous for me and might lead to more trouble for the people too. The last thing I want is for them to lose faith or trust in me for having such nightmarish Visions, Visions I cannot understand. I could send word, perhaps," she pondered, removing her hand from her head, coming to a quick conclusion.

"I would rather you talk to your Counterpart and then have an audience; it's a small chance but if anyone can help, it's them. Only The Readers would know this language fluently, only they would be able to put the contents of this book into context and help you decide what is best. I fear that they are your only hope now. This is important; if your feelings are telling you something is wrong, then we are all in danger," he warned.

"Impossible; aren't we forgetting that the Dovidians will be here to sign the treaty in a matter of weeks, after which I will be taken to Ivulien?" Isabelle walked in circles. "Eran, YOU must go before The Readers and present them with the book and my case, make them listen to you!" His face said no. "Why not?" she demanded impatiently. He sighed, feeling unworthy before her.

"This is your endeavour, your mystery to solve, not mine. I can only advise you and help you where I can, as I've always done. Only you, young one, can understand the games of The Star Callers, not I."

"You've shown me so much already. I can't do this alone. I need your guidance and the knowledge of The Readers." A never-ending river of problems was sneaking up on her; troubles she was scared to face alone. "I cannot do this without you, Master."

"You know as well as I do that The Readers see more than what meets the eye. When I look at you, I see many things, most others would say the same, but The Readers, they see what we cannot. In your presence, I may appear as something significant, a Master, a teacher, the man in The Old Library…"

"A friend, actually," she interrupted.

"But before them, I would appear as something else; a result of an exceedingly long equation, an incomplete man who has not yet fulfilled his true purpose. Who knows how they function? Your Star Caller presence is different to everyone else's; you and only you can make them listen."

"Please Master," she pleaded one last time, though she knew he spoke the truth. Eran took a deep breath, he had always done what he could for her, but this time it was far beyond his control. It was hard to look into those green eyes and refuse her on such an important issue, but he had no choice but to do so.

"Have you forgotten that it may not be in your power to change things after all?"

"What do you mean?"

"I suggest you look into The Book of Findings before you face the Imrondel Courts or The High Councillors of Virtue. Knowledge is one's greatest weapon in situations like these. I wish you well, Isabelle. You have a difficult path ahead."

"The Book of Findings; that's Regina's journal, right? The story of her journey, the arrival of the first Star Caller?"

"It looks like your time is up. Study her rules. Learn from the one who made you what you are," he urged, placing one hand on her shoulder. One of The Glyph Wielders held open one of the double doors. "You know where to find me if you require my assistance. I will be here most days. Good luck with the people today. What is it, seven hundred or nine hundred?"

"Thank you again, Eran, as always I shall leave here a little wiser than before. Six hundred is the estimated turn out." She head toward the door. Adarmier watched her leave from his seat next to one of the windows, reading as usual.

Inside a war room centred on a table piled high with stacks of maps and old documents, along with the odd mug of tea left out from the previous night, Lethaniel and Thao sat waiting for Alexius to show up with his mystery man from Jureai. It wasn't like Lex to be running late. Also, in the room stood one of Thao's Honour Guards, Neraal, one of his best men. Seated in the corner was Rayn, Captain of the Visarlian Knights, Lethaniel's second-in-command. The door slid open and The General stood to greet The Northlander he had been expecting, but Alexius entered alone.

"I could not find him! He was not where he should have been, there are delays on the roads and transportation has been late. He must be using this time to take care of other matters. Dark Rogues have been reported; they robbed the food convoy sent from The Pura Lands and made off with carriages containing our weapons from Xiondel. They took care of everyone in their path, though some are still missing. Othello could be anywhere in the city, Lethaniel," he panted; he had been running from place to place all morning. He had always wished for a faster and more convenient means of transport than the usual horse. Lethaniel sighed, while Thao put his feet up on the table, rest back in his chair and drank some more of the cold tea in his mug, swirling it around in his mouth.

"This is my favourite part of the city" said Eva.

"Why is that?" Othello asked.

"Because it's quiet here and at night the view is fabulous. You can see everything, especially The Palace that is lit up. I used to come here when I was little. It's a good place to get away from everything," Eva explained. The two had reached the top of a towering building that housed countless families in small apartments. They had found the highest balcony on the highest floor and worked their way around it using a ledge no more than a foot wide. Desperately trying to avoid looking down, they had then used the same ledge to jump on to the roof of the building opposite. In these empty, spacious surroundings, Othello had found his own place on the square roof while Eva leant her elbows on the surrounding wall, looking out over the city while rubbing her neck and shoulders. A wordless calm fell over them as they realised how little they actually knew about each other. Eva was the one to break the silence. "Thank you for coming," she said, resting her head in her hand.

"You're welcome."

"You came by so willingly, may I ask why?"

"People seem to be afraid of me here, they keep their distance, but when some have had a few ales, they become hard to ignore, like yourself for example"

"I wasn't drunk when I came up to you. I had been drinking but I wasn't…waaargh, waaargh!" sputtered Eva, making what she interpreted to be drunken noises.

"You almost fell into the canal, TWICE!" Othello pointed out.

"I can handle my drink just fine I'll have you know!" she giggled, folding her arms.

"Where I'm from, we make our own wine, it makes the ale and such here seem like water. Maybe it's a good thing I didn't bring a couple of casks with me, it would do wonders to you."

"The first wine I had was with my Dad. I was eleven, I saw him drinking alone downstairs one night. I sat next to him and he poured me a small glass…" Othello listened politely as she told her story. "I hated the taste, like a strong vinegar. Guess he was trying to put me off" she said having found a fond memory.

"Didn't work very well, did it?" Eva smirked.

"I did wonder why he chose to drink at such strange hours. It didn't take long for me to realise that it was his way of dealing with the passing of my mother."

"How did you cope?"

"I didn't. Someone came along out of nowhere and helped me, let me into his life, talked me through it. He became… a very close friend, he still."

"What happened between you?" Othello sensed a deep sadness coming from within her, as good as she was at maintaining a strong façade, he saw through the subtle cracks.

"We still talk, but his occupation requires him to travel, to risk himself, so I rarely ever see him anymore. As I spent most of my youth grieving, he became the only friend I could relate to, the only one I could share my feelings with; no one else seemed to care about one another or only wanted me around when they needed something." Remembering his conversation with Ethan, Othello did not want to hang in silence, as close as he was to his own father empathy was easily found.

"The pain never quite goes away, you get used to it. I am sorry for you loss."

"Thank you," she murmured.

"May I ask how?"

"I don't know. He worked so hard for me; with my mother already gone he raised me all by himself, it must have been hard to take on three jobs and maintain a relationship with his child in Imrondel. He taught me how to read, how to cook, we had a lot of fun doing things together, no matter what time of day it was, he was always there. He taught me how to always make a good first impression, taught me the importance of work and how to spend my free time; he never stopped caring and he never gave up on me, even when I was upset with him for the most ridiculous of reasons. Strange, the memories I have, I sometimes struggle to picture his face."

"Think of a moment you shared together, think of the drink you had when you were eleven, think of the times he sat you down to read" suggested Othello, allowing Eva to pull a wide smile.

"A long time ago, when I was about seven years old, we were out fishing, and I was playing with a ball. I really loved this ball, though I don't remember why exactly. I remember throwing it, it hit a tree and bounced into the river. I started crying and screaming, I could not part from this ball, it was mine; so silly, I know but my father dove in, swam over and fetched it for me, he lost a boot, and some zeal all for a stupid ball..." She laughed as she recalled the memory.

"What of your mother?" asked Othello, having heard little of her.

"We never talked about my mother. She died when I was only four, her face is a blur. I wish I'd had the chance to get to know her."

Her attention then shifted entirely to Othello. He had adopted Norkron culture, having ditched his Northlander dress sense in favour of a more local outfit. Had it not been for the bronze skin and the length of hair he would have blended right in. The way he stood, however, the way he looked at her would always be send her into a spiral; she was sure that they had met before and couldn't help but see it in everything he did. "I saw you help that boy in the street; that was very kind of you." Othello nodded, scratching the side of his jaw in mild sways of embarrassment.

"He didn't seem very appreciative, I only tried to help. Where I'm from, that would never be allowed to happen."

"It's just how it is here; some have no one to blame but themselves, some just get no luck. I know it's unfair, it's worse in Xiondel City, believe me."

"I see, but I don't understand." She moved closer and explained:

"There are refuge points dotted around this city for people in need; think about it, Othello, you couldn't have looked after him if you wanted to. You work all day, you need to pay for the roof over your head and for the food that keeps you going. Another mouth to feed is a huge responsibility." He nodded but still had more to say on the issue. "But the kindness is admirable."

"There are no homeless in Jureai; we live off the land and everyone is taken care of, born with a sense of purpose. The people here need a horizon, one not made of prophecies requiring prayer, something they can build toward a Bevork touch" he liked that idea, any mention of his clan lit up his face. Eva felt a certain warmth sitting there beside him, a sense of security while on their roof. She gripped his arm with one hand.

"I remember you telling me about it. I want to know more about Jureai and why are you here? Where is your family?"

It was midday and the sun was already shining over Imrondel City. People gathered and queued in their hundreds outside the solitary, but grand Eliendras Cathedral with a mighty steeple, located in the centre of The Star Gardens in The Holy District. The beautiful flowers were in blossom, spreading out their wide, lustrous petals, absorbing as much sunlight as possible. Summer had been brief; some days were glorious but most had been cloudy with downpours of rain. Many predicted that the next winter would be a long one and would more than likely arrive early. Isabelle stood outside the closed doors and confronted those waiting alongside her priests and two guarding Glyph Wielders, observing the crowds that had gathered. From a spiritual point of view, Eliendras Cathedral was the heart of Imrondel, though for any military perspective The Palace of Norisis took priority. The people of Imrondel had flocked to The Holy District, to see The Star Caller. Isabelle presented herself in a beautiful long dress, with ribbons in her blonde curls that fell over her shoulders. Visitors would come to her one at a time, bowing their heads in awe and respect, and would then receive a gift and a few words from her and her priests. Some were rather hesitant to approach her or even look her in the eye. A few were fearful of her and her abilities, but wanted an audience nonetheless, for the respect would always be there. Isabelle would always touch their hands, hear what they had to say and offer what wisdom she could share. Many brought gifts that a priest would collect in a round, terracotta bowl. After a brief visit with The Star Caller, people received a package, its contents ranging from medicines to charms, or even blessed earth and water from the birthplace of Regina Corah. The previous year they had handed out blessed earth from Tthenadawn Forest, home of Virgo or *Verillas*. This year, the primary gift was medicine. A shipment of grain had recently been found to be contaminated, which had spread throughout The Trade District. Children had been affected most of all, showing signs of fever. Though not fatal it was of growing concern. Later in the day, Isabelle was still meeting with people; it had been several hours, and she was beginning to grow tired, though the last man she had just seen too, the blind one with a funny accent, calling her a blonde beauty, tipped her toward the need for a drink. She whispered a few words to a priest on her right and he informed the crowd that she would be taking a moments rest. Isabelle was temporarily free to walk through The Star Gardens that surrounded Eliendras Cathedral. Her thin, light dress trailed after her as she walked the paths that cut between the green. This crowd was somewhat understanding of her absence and left her in peace, happy to wait for her return, but a Glyph Wielder had to restrain a man who had had one too many ales and caused upset in the queue. The Star Garden grounds were big enough to enclosed The Cathedral, and from within grew a symbolic flower called Starlight Blooms. They were a mysterious species; during the day time, they would attract insects with its marvellous scent of vanilla, while at night their white petals would light up and glow softly in accordance with the stars in the sky above, in cosmic tune with the stellar rays. Isabelle sat down on a paving stone beside a particularly large cluster of the flowers and ran her finger up a stem to feel the soft touch of the petal.

"You did recognise me then, though in the moment I was pretending I couldn't see you" he said, lying down behind her, hidden by a hedgerow, out of sight of The Glyph Wielders taking note of where The Star Caller was. Isabelle was delighted to see him again but did not act or show any sign of excitement, for she was still being watched.

"I did not know you were a religious man? Actually, I don't think you are at all religious." He grinned as he played with one of the blossoms in his hand, putting his nose to it, taking in its pleasant scent of vanilla. He was not looking at Isabelle, but she was staring at him. "Why did you come here, Teo?" He hesitated to answer but did eventually.

"Hmm… Oh, I came for some enlightenment."

"Right, has nothing to do with the free medicine?" she kept her voice above a whisper, and was sure to keep an eye on her guards.

"That and the chance to touch your hands, my lady. Do you moisturise, because I was wondering…"

"Tell me, Teo, do you have little ones who have fallen sick?" she asked, interrupting him.

"No! How old do you think I am?" he demanded in a show of mock offence.

"Old enough. Remember, I am a Star Caller, boy. Learning is what I do. Understanding and knowing people is part of the profession."

"How can I forget that? You can't even travel to Ivulien without hearing your name pop up somewhere."

"You're smarter than you look," she joked, twirling a blade of grass around her finger.

"You're not as dumb as you look either," he replied, grinning as he looked up at the sky avoiding her gaze.

"What did you say?" she said, raising her voice a little over the safe limit.

"Nothing...." Isabelle widened her eyes at him, again noticing discoloured streak around one side of his neck.

"Not all blondes are thick, Teo!"

"I didn't say they were thick" he replied, pretending to be on the defensive.

"Yes you did!" she answered.

"No, I said you were dumb!" Isabelle shook her head.

"Aren't they the same thing?" she asked.

"You tell me I'm not the Star Caller" Isabelle threw a twig at him, catching him in the face. "Glad to see a smile on your face Isabelle. I know you're going through a time but there are still some things to laugh about."

"So why are you here? Besides wanting to call me names," she asked, the sun on her face.

428

"We need all the medicine we can get our hands on." Isabelle looked at him strangely.

"What do you mean *WE*, Teo?" Just then, he heard the approach of one of her followers and rolled closer toward the hedge under the shade to avoid being seen.

"Milady," a Glyph Wielder began, standing behind only her a few feet away.

"I'll be right over" she said, and he made his way back to Eliendras.

Pretending that Teo was not even there, standing up and brushing herself down, she whispered quietly:

"Will you be around later? I must get away from this crowd."

"Most certainly," replied Teo quietly, from under the hedge, removing some loose leaves from his face.

"I'll see you later then," she said, walking away with pointy cheekbones.

"Catch you later, blondie," he giggled, her cheekbones growing firmer. Returning to her hand-outs, Teo mysteriously disappeared without her seeing. Where he had gone and when, baffled her.

Othello told Eva a story about Jureai, telling her of the people he knew, his friends Dingane, Karn, Vontarg and the silent but loyal Malek. He told her of the tulkan herds that passed through the land annually. The copper hawks that soared overhead and nested in the canyons. He hadn't shared such a conversation with anyone since he left The Northern Lands. Eventually, he explained the tragedy of his father's slow demise. Eva listened as he spoke, occasionally chipping in with a light-hearted joke to compare his experience to her own. Othello never mentioned anything about the struggles between the clans, the fierce hate between the Salarthians and the Bevorks or the dangerous situation with Xavien. The Tournament of

429

Leadership, Kronix; all of this he left out and chose not to tell. They were slowly making their way back to The Trade Distribution Centre where he worked.

"Your world and way of life sound very fulfilling," she stated, picturing it in her mind.

"As long the Bevorks remember their foundations, I'll always think of it as home." A question then popped into her mind; they had now reached the centre and it was time for Othello to get back to work. Empty carriages were arriving, waiting to be loaded with supplies. Countless crates had been stacked high on the pavement. Ethan and the other loaders were already hard at it; he spotted Othello in the distance, noticeably surprised to see Eva standing with him. The woman every loader had seen but had not the guile to speak to.

"I have one more question for you; I can't make sense of it in my head. You returned here when your father passed, but for you to leave a place so suddenly, leaving all you love behind? It doesn't make sense to me. I could have easily fled to my real home in The Pura Lands, but I never felt compelled to do so, the pain would follow."

"Perhaps it would be easier to show you…" Othello never wore the ring to work, nor did he carry it with him in his pocket "…It's harder to explain" he noted Ethan talking to Alexius outside the blocky grey building which was The Distribution Centre. Eva knew they were pressed for time.

"There is a gathering tonight in The Star Gardens; I was wondering if you are to be there?"

"OTHELLO!" shouted Alexius, having been directed over by Ethan. "Othello, we need you over at the barracks, it's important that you come with me right now." He was not alone; two guardsmen of the city were also present. Othello turned to Eva.

"Be at The Star Gardens," she suggested, touching his arm and then swiftly head off passed Alexius.

"Hello Eva," he said.

"Hello Lex, how are you?"

"I'm very well. Yourself?"

"Just peachy. Glad we could catch up"

"Likewise," she replied, fully aware Alexius was on duty and had a job to do. She disappeared out of sight along the road, blending in with the crowds. Leaving Othello with Alexius.

"Why am I needed at the barracks?" he groaned, eyeing the two guardsmen.

"On special request of General Lethaniel and Thao Hikonle, it's best you come by, trust me." Othello remained where he was, still maintaining the an expressionless, uncaring face, the one he pulled when he was arrested; He agreed, and was escorted to The Military District.

The density of buildings lessened as they neared The Military District, far from the homes of Imrondel. The sky was now clearly visible for there were no high-pointed towers or dominant buildings to block it out. A small fortress in itself, the district was home to a series of barrack bases. They walked under a portcullis and through a heavy gate; this was where the military council convened. Othello took note of the many training pits to his left and right. Men were training with wooden weapons of all shapes and sizes, fitted with light armour and shields.

"Wait here," a guard said to him. Alexius went ahead alone. Standing among the soldiers of Imrondel who passed him by, Othello could not help but think of his own skill and naturally compared it to the skills he saw all around. He observed some of the soldiers fighting, examining how they fought studiously, how the triumphant celebrated childishly after knocking his opponent to the ground.

"Stand up! Stand up! You're a fighter, so fight me, damn you!" a tall, menacing Commander shouted at a fallen rookie nearby. "How can one so weak be in this army?" The Commander then thrust his foot into the side of the man who wailed in pain, clutching his side.

"That's Barthul; his methods are somewhat different to those of the other Commanders of this barracks. He has been warned before about his harsh ways..." Alexius had returned and noticed Othello staring. "I don't think he will be here much longer. He was once an Honour Guard but was discharged for obvious reasons."

"Why was he allowed to become an instructor in the first place?"

"It wasn't my decision to make, nor was it Thao's or Lethaniel's. I guess it had something to do with the fact that he teaches one important lesson."

"Which is?"

"He instils hate. I wouldn't stare at him if I were you, or it will be you who is dragged through the dirt."

"He shows no skill..." Othello muttered under his breath.

"I'm sorry?" Alexius said, not catching his words.

"Nothing." Othello took one last look at Barthul, who returned the stare before continuing to humiliate and bully the rookie.

The crowds finally started to show signs of thinning. Isabelle was diligent to meet with as many as possible, but the que was a hundred people long. Teo must have left long ago, though she kept a sharp eye out for him. Grim clouds drifted overhead, heavy and bloated; The Priesthood began to clear things away and move under the cathedral's archways. Rain put a halt to many things in the city and the people knew this, though it didn't actually start right away. Isabelle gave her farewell to the crowds, who had to be moved along by the Glyph Wielders. Those who hadn't been seen were promised a visit later, at the festival. There would be a gathering that evening in The Holy District to honour The Celestial Souls' great influence and power over humanity, a long-standing tradition among the Norkron people, stretching back to the time of the very first Star Caller. Starlight Blooms would be glowing brightly under the starry night if the weather was kind and each person in attendance of this festival would free a candle upon a tiny flower float and let the currents of the canals guide it around The Palace of Norisis take until their flame burned out. From Imrondel City and Xiondel to The Pura Lands and the far north where Reneeia Talaka dwelt in her mountain home with her Vantarquinns, candles would be placed at sea or let loose into the sky in soaring lanterns. This was a key tradition for the followers of Starillia, a yearly tradition of worship and merry making, anyone who was anyone would take advantage of the free ale, the food, music, and dancing. Isabelle backed off when relieved of duty, retreating inside Eliendras Cathedral to grab a moment for herself, while her priests attended to the crowds and cleared away the tables.

Safely inside the cathedral Isabelle pulled back her blue hood. Beneath her feet was a wide stone floor patterned with entwining elements. In the centre of the round stone hall was the seal of Krondathia surrounded by the insignias of each Celestial Soul. Each Celestial was also given its own pillar within the cathedral, stretching up into the rafters to support the roof where they met in the middle. From this middle curvature, hung a chandelier ringed with hundreds of shining candles. Idols - much like the ones she kept in the cabinet within her hut on The Zodias Island - were placed on a solitary grandiose table to the side, partly hidden in the shadows. This was a place of peace, much like the magnificent Column Temple yet smaller in design, influenced by the Celestial home. She approached the shadowy table and gently inspected the stone idols of The Celestials. Sagittarius, God of Chance, was a Fire Celestial whose shrine lay at the heart of a hidden peak among The Mountains of Ophiadras. Pisces, God of Compassion, was a Water Celestial whose home was found out at sea amid the unforgiving waves. Rumour had it that an ancient settlement known as The Crystal City could be found easily from the shrine, though those who dared to look, were all lost, never to be seen again, having ventured beyond the known realms of maps. Taurus, God of Culture, was an Earth

Celestial, its great shrine located on the border with Jureai to the west, near River's Finn. Gemini, God of Communication, was a twin Celestial of the Air, with a shrine atop one of the mountains of Lienoth, near Ivulien. As she was handling the figure of Sagittarius, considering tapping into her Inner Peace, to commune with her Counterpart, she noticed a gap in their ranks; one had been picked up and taken away. She put the idol down, its weight thudding against on tables surface, and set out to investigate which of the twelve had been stolen. Isabelle turned around, startled upon hearing a noise behind her. She was not alone in Eliendras after all!? It must have been either the sound of one of her priests or a stray rodent, a lost bird maybe, something was here. That same eerie feeling came over her again, that higher sense that all Star Callers possessed, the same reaction she had experienced in the Glyph Dome when she gave the brief performance to the Xiondel High Councillors. Teo stepped out from behind a wide pillar, holding the missing idol in his hands. Relief filled Isabelle as the threat dissipated.

"You shouldn't be in here!"

"These are incredible sculptures. Can you tell me which one this is? I mean, you were right, I'm not really a religious person, but wow, these are beautiful! This one is my favourite though."

"This place is reserved for a select few; it's forbidden for common folk to enter. I'm sorry, but you must leave," she urged, trying to sound assertive but it was wasted on him.

"Common folk?" Teo looked around and shrugged his shoulders. "I'll let you know if I see one" he said, getting back to examining the sculpture "Who makes these things? I could use a paperweight" he smirked, ignoring her concerns. She walked over and stood by him having given up trying to move the man. She took one glance at the sculpture in his hand and identified it.

"Skarapio…"

"Say what?"

"That's Scorpio for you *common* people. Scorpio, God of Passion. Scorpio is a Water Celestial Soul. I've called upon her once,

434

when I was nineteen, back at The Zodias Island." She then pointed to certain parts of the model and explained a little bit about the creature. "She is a Goddess, Teo, she can manipulate the hearts of men and women with her eyes, she could enslave should she so desire, but that is not where her real power lies, controlling men is a talent all beautiful women possess." He cleared his throat and replied:

"I heard of a woman who resembles Scorpio, a Chieftainess in the northlands."

"I've heard these rumours too and I believe them to be true. Her name is Talaka; she leads The Vantarquinn Clan." Isabelle turned the idol onto its side, returning to the subject of The Celestial. "Her wrath is greater than her passion, believe it or not. You would never learn this lesson from her personally, for you would be dead in an instant, but take it from the one who knows her best. Mess with her children or the ones she loves, and you will see wrath like no other as you face The Lady Scorpion with her deadly sting." The idol depicted a woman, elegant and tall, but on her back was the plated armour of a fierce arthropod warrior. A long tail with a deadly tip curled around her, concealing her chest and hips.

"It sounds as if she is to be feared, despite being the Goddess of Passion? Something isn't right there, is it?" Teo questioned, moving from Isabelle's side, and tossing the priceless idol up in the air, leaving it for her to catch.

"Uhhh… She is NOT to be feared, you have nothing to worry about around her. Actually, she is the most devoted and caring of all The Celestial Souls, with the possible exception of Cantonos. I remember when I first spoke with her though…" Isabelle went to the table and put the idol back in its rightful place.

"What mark are you? What's your Celestial?" Teo asked curiously, fiddling with another priceless artefact of some kind.

"I was about to ask you the same thing," she said, raising a narrow eyebrow.

"Isn't there a way to tell instantly?"

"There is; there are two ways to know what mark you bear." She expected a question from Teo at that point, but when he remained silent, she made things clearer. "I can either learn from the person or I can use a method which Star Callers call *The Skin Burn*."

"The Skin Burn? Sounds painful," he winced.

"Oh, it's not painful; all I have to do is run my hand above the particular area where the mark is located, and it will light up like a candle." She smiled, for this test was fun to perform. "From learning one's mark, I can then quickly assess a person's character, it helps me to predict their actions and understand their personality before I counsel them," she explained.

"Is it a reliable method?" he asked, feeling a tad vulnerable; he didn't like the idea of her knowing so much about him so fast.

"It's not entirely solid; there are some who have surprised me, but it is a good starting point when it comes to learning about someone's nature. Don't worry, I won't Skin Burn you, unless the person gives consent it's forbidden."

"Didn't you say this place was restricted? I'm surprised you're letting me stay a while." At that moment Isabelle put an end to the innocent chatter and moved on to a subject he did not expect.

"You are standing in a forbidden place wearing a weapon and yet I haven't raised the alarm. Why do you think that is?" Teo raised his cloak a little, revealing the weapon concealed beneath.

"You saw it? I bought this from a merchant outside Xiondel; apparently, it originally belonged to Toula Winduece." She checked it out again, sensing that he was concealing the true nature of the dagger.

"Toula Winduece? That bandit! I think the salesman was having you on with that one," she laughed.

"What? Why?"

"Oh come on Teo, now who is being dumb? It's a nice story to have under your belt but all of Winduece's possessions are long gone. He was caught trying to break into The Outer Vaults of Xiondel; that happened a year before I was even born."

"Is that all?" Teo replied, folding his arms, bored with the history lesson.

"No, actually, if you want to play games with me, I'll play too; He was a bastard bandit, a murderer and a terribly, foolish thief? The vaults of Xiondel cannot be breached not without six keys; The locks themselves are designed to prevent the use of picks and will break if the slightest miscalculation is made. He was caught and killed publicly after his arrest in fourteen eighty-four, on a Wednesday, early in the morning in front of a crowd of hundreds," she recited a passage memorised from a book she had read.

"Did the man who was hung beg for his life?" She nodded. "Did he kiss the flag of Krondathia, fall to his knees and confess his crimes, shouting out his innocence before he died?"

"Yes, yes he did. I can't say I approve of the death penalty, but some crimes are just too great to ignore," she answered, wondering how he had known those details.

"Do you know why he did all those things?" Teo asked, smiling strangely at her.

"Because he wanted to live; everyone cherishes their own life." It wasn't a perfect response, but it was her best guess.

"Do you?" Teo's question was indeed poignant. Isabelle was silenced! "The man who was hung WAS innocent, Isabelle. The Eldor's guards failed to capture the bandit Toula after they spotted him near the vaults. Unable to face The Eldor with their failure they picked up a man off the streets, dressed him in thieves clothing and handed him over to be hanged in Toula's place." Isabelle rubbed her face, she remembered a time when she would fall back on The Eldor's unbreakable word, now, however she felt more inclined to believe to story of Teo's.

"That does not explain why you wear a weapon, Teo," she said getting back on track, Teo continuing his patrol of The Cathedral.

"I feel it wise to have some form of protection at hand. I have my blade you have your Glyph which is FAR more devastating than this puny little thing. Wouldn't you agree?" She dipped her head. "You didn't raise the alarm Isabelle because you're a Star Caller, there is not much in the way of what we know, who can match you." From under the light of the chandelier he shrugged his shoulders with a childish attitude, knowing she could not come back from his statements.

"I am a... I am an uh..." she hesitated, but finally whispered, "I am an Aquarian."

"What was that?"

"I am an Aquarian; my Celestial mark is Aquaria, Aquarius, the God of Wisdom."

"Air Celestial, huh? Nice," he grinned, getting back to fiddling with the various priceless golden ornaments in Eliendras. Isabelle had expected the usual confusion caused by an Air Celestial having a name related to water, but apparently, he already knew.

"Would you like to see my mark? I can demonstrate The Skin Burn if you'd like." Teo immediately became more interested. "Come here," she instructed softly, using her fingers to usher him over, which he did cautiously. She gently pulled the dress strap over her shoulder aside, revealing some bare skin. Her eyelids fell heavy and when they opened again, they were shining, her green irises having lit up. Teo stepped back a little; if she were a sword she would be drawn right now, if she were a crossbow she would be loaded.

"Whoa... Easy," he said, as if afraid she would hurt him.

"It's alright, I'm in control." Her palm hovered over her left shoulder, just above her breast, where Teo spotted a very shallow, very defining light emanating from under her hand. He carefully moved her hand away so he could see what was going on. There he saw her mark, clearly visible and glowing, burning under her skin.

Just as she had said, it was that of Aquarius, two small waved lines parallel to each other, searing hot but emitted no heat. He went to touch it but immediately drew back. "It's fine. Go on," Isabelle said softly, and he did so, his hand guided by her own. It felt ever so slightly warm on the tips of his fingers. The glow of the mark faded fast, soon turning invisible when Isabelle's eyes returned to normal. She pulled the strap back over her shoulder, and covered herself.

"That's probably the strangest thing I've ever seen," Teo admitted.

"We all have a mark somewhere under our skin."

"I know a little about the Celestials and Glyph, but much of it still confuses me."

"That makes two of us. There are many things that I don't understand. I seek help but help is limited when you've stumble across a Celestial toy box."

"But you're a Star Caller; The Readers selected you because you are gifted..." She stood there and nodded, so far so good. "You can call upon them! The Celestials. No one else can, don't you hear them?"

"Wouldn't be a Star Caller if I didn't" she said.

"What do they say?" She rolled her eyes, turning to face the table with the sculptures.

"They say many things Teo, though it's sometimes hard to understand the tongues of these Demi-Gods, but one thing IS for sure."

"And what is that?" he asked eagerly.

"They will always be here for me; they will never leave my side or answer to anyone else as long as I live. They grant me my power, I guess, giving me purpose." She stroked one of the sculptures delicately. "Fringe groups of Starillia that grow smaller by the day, say these Gods are not Gods at all, that they're otherworldly creatures with the power to appear Godly. I have to go looking for literature that undermines Starillia's claims, literature translated by authors who as whimsical as our jesters or at least, they're perceived this way by the populace" she spoke like a philosopher.

"You're talking about our predecessors, right? And their ruins that lie all over the place?"

"I am. Why they disappeared is another story. I've asked The Celestials about their disappearance and their answer is always the same. They do not know. The Celestials are only what they are today because of us Teo; remember, our predecessors knew them, I guess they worshipped them and cherished them as much we do. If you want proof, all you need to know is right there. Just look at that!" She pointed at a framed scroll on the wall, which featured a list of every Celestial Soul, even including their ancestral names.

Celestial Name - Element - Form - Celestial Gift - Trait

(Capradius) Capricorn - Earth Celestial - Ibex - The Runes of Insight - God of Independence
(Arieth) Aries - Fire Celestial - Chimera - Phoenix Blood - God of War
(Liranous) Libra - Air Celestial - Condor - The Cloak of Flight - God of Equality
(Pelios) Pisces - Water Celestial - Manta Ray - Breathing Pearls - God of Compassion
(Verillas) Virgo - Earth Celestial - Fairy Witch - The Angelic Elixir - God of Purity
(Lothos) Leo - Fire Celestial - Throne of Kings - Kingly Gifts - God of Pride
(Jewl-Akus) Gemini - Air Celestial - Twin Angels - The Geminian Mirror - God of Communication
(Skarapio) Scorpio - Water Celestial - Scorpion - Lotion of the Arthropods - God of Passion
(Tarlathos) Taurus - Earth Celestial - Tuskan Spirit - Gold Dust - God of Culture
(Sargintos) Sagittarius - Fire Celestial - Centaur - The Burning Blossom - God of Chance
(Aquaria) Aquarius - Air Celestial - Dragon - The Wisp Collar - God of Wisdom

(Cantonos) Cancer - Water Celestial - Crab - The Necklace of the Crustaceans - God of Emotion

"So you have the Celestial Gifts in your possession?" asked Teo

"Some of them... Not all. They have popped up on numerous occasions around the world. A simple farmer from Sapphire Views in The Pura Lands once had in his possession The Breathing Pearls of Pelios."

"Which one's that?"

"Pisces, Teo, keep up. Once The Eldor knew of this relic's location, he met with this peasant personally, giving him land, wealth and a title in exchange for The Pearls. He is growing obsessed with gathering them all; they are priceless relics. These gifts are the stuff of fairy tales. Men spend their lives looking for them, many even dying to learn of their locations, but those who succeed in making headway or happen to be lucky enough to retrieve one, are handsomely rewarded. The High Priests of Equis believe that once they are all accounted for, the world will be a far safer place to live, but that is only the belief of men. I can't see how gathering twelve artefacts together in one place will solve anything, but it's something we are working on, nonetheless. Wishful thinking comes to mind. Some look to me for guidance, they hear about my Visions and assume I can change it. I never know what to say. The future comes to me in fragments."

"I'm sorry but I don't think I am the one you should be talking to about this; I can't perform miracles or wield great powers like you, the best I can do is draw a pointy stick" and he revealed his dagger.

"You would be surprised what one can do when one least expects it. I know a young boy for instance, who goes to The Old Library every day. He doesn't need tutoring; he knows too much already, he is special and one day he will grow up to be someone strong and wise, a true master of the Omnio Glaphiar Spheres. I was never like that; I was disciplined into becoming a Star Caller, groomed as it were. If I had the same choice now, I would be a very different person. Don't you see? I am not special, I am only special because they made me special, perhaps in the same we idolise our Celestials."

"Don't talk like that; you can wield Glyph like no other!"

"Funny you should say that; Freya was teaching another before me..." Suddenly the door thundered open and sprang into action. Her Glyph Guards came marching in with several priests behind them.

"Milady, it would be wise of you to inform us of your whereabouts in the future!" one announced as if something tragic had just occurred.

"I was no more than five feet away, so if you would please leave me in peace, I'm trying to pray..."

"As you wish, my lady, if there is anything I can do?" The little priest backed away outside timidly. As the Glyph Wielders closed the doors Teo came back into view, standing with his back up to the wall.

"Nice moves; they would have locked you up for a long time if you had been caught in here with me."

"Is that all? I wonder what the price would be if I was caught inside The Column Temple!"

"Armed guards arrested a fellow some time ago and held him for several weeks just for speaking ill of Starillia. He claimed that The Celestials were false Gods and that our ways are untrue and sinful."

"Maybe he was telling the truth," suggested Teo.

"He disappeared after he was set free. I think his name was Hendrice." Teo was moving around slowly, occasionally making eye contact with Isabelle as she talked, though he seemed more interested in the other rooms of The Cathedral.

"So everyone must believe, is that right? Or they will throw you in prison if you speak your mind." His argument was fair, but Isabelle was knowledgeable on the subject; she had been studying and answering such questions for most of her life.

"It's not that you can't speak your mind; the Dovidians of Ivulien don't believe in Starillia. What Hendrice said was blasphemous; he spread lies, ruined property that belittled a priest in public outside a place of prayer. For that he was arrested and released soon after with some counselling; that sounds fair, don't you think?"

"Then he just up and disappeared?" Isabelle nodded and Teo raised his eyebrows.

"Stop thinking so much, you're making me nervous."

"I'm sorry, my Star Caller." He was still wandering in and out of rooms as Isabelle watched him from the corner of her eye. "You know so much, but so little," he said cryptically, fiddling with his necklace of a silver owl.

"I know quite a bit actually," she replied with a confident grin.

"More than the others?"

"What others?"

"The other Star Callers," he explained, tilting his head; he too had heard of her great reputation, how she was apparently the most talented since Regina.

"There aren't any other Star Callers; I am the only one. Until I find my apprentice, I'm alone," she stated.

"And who will that be?"

"I don't know, I've not met her yet."

"I understand all Star Callers must be women, right?" She nodded her head.

"Why?" Isabelle had predicted the question.

"It has something to do with our...It could be because of...It must be an inherited trait only women possess" she answered clumsily.

"It's alright not to know" he said, apologetically on her behalf, as Teo continued to explore.

"So where are you from?" she asked, turning to face him. He stopped and looked at her too. "What do you do, Teo?" He was about to speak when two great thuds came from the door.

"Milady, we need you outside! We are preparing for the celebration." Isabelle opened the door and greeted a priest.

"Alright, I'll be outside shortly." She began to close the door, but he put his hand on it, stopping her from sealing the gap between them.

"I am sorry, milady, what we need is inside." The doors opened and a multitude of priests and Glyph Guards made their way in. Isabelle couldn't stall them; Teo would be discovered! She braced herself for his discovery. "If you would kindly make your way outside, milady, a carriage will take you to The Palace so you can prepare." There was no sign of shock or struggle. "Milady Isabelle, is something wrong?" She caught herself observing the ceiling and dark corners of Eliendras; where could Teo have gone?

Othello entered the war room and was confronted by Thao, who he recognised from the prison interrogation. He took some seconds to examine the men's faces. There was Neraal, The Visarlian Captain, and Lethaniel, The General he had heard so much about. He awaited introductions from everyone but was met only with cold looks from around the room. Othello did not know what they wanted from him or what they expected to see, but it felt awkward. Even though he had never met Lethaniel before, he knew who he was instantly by looking at him. Such a man with such a great name had to be of a certain calibre. In the back of the room The General had been eager to meet this Northlander, but now could not shake off a sense of threat. He could tell that this man who stood before him was no commoner; his eyes read the room, his posture strong and unchanged among great men. Thao also sensed a rift between the two, a sense of imbalance.

"Gentlemen, introductions all around before we begin. My name is Thao Hikonle. Over there is Neraal, one of my best. The two you saw outside are Arthur and Scarto. Scarto is my second. This is General Lethaniel; he commands the Visarlian Knights and controls our army's movements. Next to him is Captain Rayn. We are the ones who will be leading the strike force against the invaders in the east."

"Invaders?" Othello repeated.

"Yes, The Barbarian Tribes have invaded Ivulien territory. Were you aware of this? I understand that you spent a fair amount of time in Jureai?" Thao addressed him directly. "We don't know precisely how many have invaded or why. We know little of their methods and tactics. But what we do know is that they are merciless having already killed many innocents. We cannot allow this to go on. They must be stopped."

"And what has this got to do with me?" Othello questioned, looking grim. Thao paused and took a moment to look at the others in the room, before getting straight to the point.

"We wondered if you could advise us on how to deal with this sort of threat? You know of their tactics, sharing them with us would be a start."

"Battle tactics?" Othello asked, feeling that the request was a little vague.

"The more information you give us now, the better we can understand what it is we will be going up against. How many are typically in a hunting party? What weapons do they carry? Where would they most likely make camp? Most importantly who commands them and why? These are the kinds of things of things we need to know."

445

"How would I know who commands them? How would I know any of this? I was part of a workforce"

"What kind of man were you in Jureai?" asked Neraal, placing his hands on the table. Lethaniel moved his eyes back to Othello, watching him closely as he answered the questions. The man seemed to be on the defensive; Lethaniel saw a glint of anger in his eyes, a rush of emotion the moment Jureai was mentioned. Somehow, he felt he could relate to this; many a time he had felt that same anger and had to control it by clenching a fist at his side. Othello took a deep breath and replied reluctantly:

"I was a builder. I helped the people gather food and water. I put up many huts and tents. I also built wells for my clan, something I am immensely proud of" Othello ignored the light flutter of laughter "I made wine and maintained the farms. I was a worker, what more do you want?!" Thao raised his eyebrows, Rayn made ey contact with Neraal like this had been a mistake. Lethaniel noted Othello's fist, as tight as his was when facing off against a challenger. Thao held his hand up for silence.

"It seems we have summoned you for the wrong reasons; for that and on behalf of my men, I think an apology is in order."

"No need, good day to you" said Othello, bowing awkwardly to more snuffled laughter coming from Neraal and Rayn.

"Would you consider joining us?" asked Thao, shaking his hand at the subtle laughing.

"As a soldier? No, you have plenty of them to win any war!"

"Not as a soldier, as an advisor. You look capable; if you're skilled enough with a sword then certainly you can carry one, a means of defence will likely be necessary during a mission like this advisor or not, you'd require some armour too" spoke Rayn. Othello despised the thought of wearing Norkron armour.

"Sorry, but I am not one of your soldiers nor a wise enough advisor. You are wasting your time."

446

"Would you at least think about it? Three meals a day, standard pay plus bonuses depending on your dedication and what information you can provide. It's a good offer for what has to be done." Othello opened the door and left abruptly, not swayed in the least by talk of remuneration. Thao looked at Lethaniel who followed out of the door, annoyed and ashamed by the poor outcome of the meeting. They could certainly have handled it differently.

As Othello was leaving the barracks area, entering the training yards, he once again passed commander Barthul, thrashing another one of his men with a rod across the lads back. Othello continued on, pushing his way through lines of soldiers practising to march. Briefly, he turned to see Lethaniel catching up to him. Barthul had pulled his recruit off the floor the moment he spotted Lethaniel.

"If you're here to offer me the land or zeal, I am not interested."

"I don't want to offer you anything. You aren't the sort. I know, because I am the same and know when I see someone who shares these values." Othello slowed his walk and let Lethaniel catch up. "I'm sorry for the behaviour of my men; they still believe all men can be bought or manipulated easily. We usually handle things differently. It won't happen again."

"This city is corrupt; I realised that on the first day I arrived. How do I know that you are no different from them?"

"This is not Jureai. Did you expect Imrondel to be the same as your country? It is different, but once upon a time we Norkrons were just like those in the north. Time has just changed things is all."

"Sell your story all you want, it won't change my mind. Krondathia has more than enough power to deal with this problem, you don't need me."

"I repeat, I am not selling you anything; I just want you to listen, for a moment, if you would?" Othello stopped, as did Lethaniel, noting his appearance. They were of the same height and shared the same body frame. Othello's skin was bronze, his hair of a longer length and straighter. Lethaniel's skin had not seen as much of the sun and his hair was shorter and curled towards the tips. "My name is Lethaniel Presi…"

"I know who you are, General; your reputation is widely spoken of," interrupted Othello, who now turned around. "As is your skill with swords; they say you are undefeated?" Lethaniel smiled and held his hand out, which Othello took.

"I am not corruptible, I can see what is worth fighting for and it's not out of a desire for gold or reputation; though even you must understand that in Krondathia zeal is what makes the world turn; gold and silver pays soldiers to save lives, it pays farmers to keep growing the crops we need to feed the working families, engineers, fishermen, architects, teachers, tutors, gardeners and so on. One day, Jureai will prosper like this land did once all those long years ago and it too will change, hopefully for the better, hopefully becoming something more than you see around us." Othello nodded slowly and Lethaniel began walking back to the barracks. "We will pay you whether you like it or not; use your earnings however you wish. Save enough to grow old in health, to die somewhere warm; gold from around Equis makes this possible. The men in the barracks are not asking for your help, but I am. There is nothing more worthwhile than knowing you saved someone's life. People are suffering out there Othello, help me? Let's do business together and part ways when it's done, that's all I'm asking. You don't like the city, this mission will take you back east, where we will see things not many have the chance to see. I'm offering you an opportunity to do something for others. It's your choice Othello, I hope you make the right one."

"My name is Othello Hawk" Lethaniel acknowledged him kindly, liking the sound of it.

"You say you can make wine; maybe you can show me how? It would save me having to buy it every day." Lethaniel winked and waved as he headed off.

Chapter 20 - Flowers and Moth Meadows

Everything we do on this planet, for good or for evil, has an effect.

The sun had fallen below the horizon and the sky was darkening, the air growing colder with every passing minute. The clouds had decided to rain elsewhere, blessing Imrondel with a clear, starry night. This was fortunate, for the people of the city were celebrating, honouring Starillia, giving thanks for The Celestial Souls' power and influence over humanity. The name given to this tradition was The Festival of the Awakening. All around the world in large cities and towns, small villages and even the places that were not large enough to merit a dot on the map, people would be coming together to celebrate, even The Vantarquinn Clan in the north joined in the tradition in their own way. Xiondel City was not as holy as the capital, but it was still able to host immense, fantastic celebrations and parties in honour of The Celestials. However, wherever The Star Caller happened to be, further devotion would be dedicated to the event. Next to The Eliendras Cathedral, surrounded by The Star Gardens, the gathering of Norkrons was steadily growing. The area was bustling with excitement.

People flocked to The Holy District, to The Eliendras Cathedral built in the exact centre of The Gardens. They were luscious, cut perfectly square, flourishing with colourful flower beds. All were carefully trimmed and tended to, day and night. The gathering crowds took care not to disturb the blooms, for they were sacred, holding great respected from among the people. The food and fires were located along the stone pathways that split the fields into blocks. As usual the wine was flowing, and ale was being served alongside juicy meats, wholesome seeded breads, and fresh vegetables. There was plenty to go around, the atmosphere was pleasant, music was playing at the banquet and The Star Caller was mingling with the people, receiving gifts under a vast, white tent near Eliendras. Isabelle was smiling and seemed to be enjoying the celebration. The turn-out was higher than expected; it was a remarkably busy time. Jerhdia walked among the people like the simple working man of he was. He too had come to witness the spectacle, to enjoy a few drinks and a bite to eat. Dressed in his rough working uniform, he had had no time to change into something smart, instead, he had just left on his stained overalls, heavy boots and thick gloves; this was his usual look of a mek, a valued workforce people appreciated.

Before entering The Star Gardens, Thao took a long look at the scene, assessing the situation before moving in; he did this wherever he went and by now it had become second nature. When he did eventually enter, he was followed by Neraal and Arthur. They wore no visible weapons or armour for it was not needed on such a festive occasion; The Star Gardens were attracting a lot of attention, people were moving freely and socialising with one another, with everyone appearing to be having an enjoyable night out. Armed guards were scarce, however; from a General's point of view if an enemy were to launch an assault upon the easy-going city, then tonight would be the perfect night to strike. Lethaniel greeted the men as he too walked in, accompanied by Captain Rayn. People watched on with a slight sense of trepidation as these great names drifted through the crowds. Lethaniel queued for a drink before the large barrels of ale like everyone else, helping himself to a tall mug and a leg of meat to the right of the barrels. As he walked along the path, eating and drinking, he saw Braygon, sitting at a table with some friends Lethaniel had never seen before. Braygon stood and they tapped their mugs together.

"General Presian, it's good to see you here. It's a grand night, is it not?"

"My friend, I thought you would have contacted me sooner."

"You're not the only one who is busy right now; the city is full of rumours, talk of an invasion, talk of The Star Caller and Dark Rogues at our door, and of a Northlander joining your ranks? I have been hearing much" said Braygon.

"Word spreads fast in Equis. I hear you wish to join us in our mission," began Lethaniel, biting a piece of dripping meat off the bone and continuing with his mouthful. "I hope you have kept up with your swordplay. We also may need your help with another matter." So delicious he had to lick his fingers.

"Let me guess, does it have something to do with my fascination with history? Do you hope that I'll provide you with a walking tour of the places you deem fit to ransack?"

"Could be; your history may prove to be of some use."

"History is always useful, General; you wouldn't think it is, but it has the power to help you get out of very tricky situations," Braygon spoke from experience.

"I was thinking you could help us find Mathias and convince him to lend us some support and maybe a few of his Norfoon Scouts?"

Braygon put his arm around Lethaniel's shoulder, moving him away from the table, away from the listening ears of his friends. "Mathias will take little convincing, he may be a bit stale but his allegiance to Krondathia remains strong, I am sure of it. In a few weeks, perhaps a month, we will be on our way away home, to return TO THIS!" he shouted, and raised his arm to the crowds and The Star Gardens with the great Eliendras Cathedral ringing its bells from the steeple. "Ale and celebrations! Who knows, this may very well be the last time you draw your swords again, what a thing to say. Are you anxious to enter the field once more?" asked Braygon.

"We are on the brink of a new age, a new world order is coming, let's pray our services become a distant memory on our return." The men tapped their drinks together once more, in hope of this, and drank to the future.

"You must excuse me General; someone has just arrived, and I would very much like to speak with him. Have a good night." With that Braygon disappeared into the crowds, leaving Lethaniel alone in time to spot Eva in line to see The Star Caller, who sat upon a highchair dressed in white livery woven in vines of gold to suit her status. She was surrounded by priests who managed the que, a unit of Palace Guards circled the vicinity brandishing long spears and a pair of Glyph Wielders were to her left and right. Lethaniel ditched the scrap of meat, downed his drink, and went over to catch Eva, after she had shared some sentences with Isabelle.

"I thought you weren't coming," Thao remarked, smiling at Lena inside a neatly fit, backless dress, dyed with a wash of sunset colours.

"I changed my mind." Arthur knew his presence was not needed here; As he walked away, Thao called after him:

"Arthur, keep on your guard but feast well tonight, enjoy yourself." Arthur bowed his head casually and moved off. Neraal too faded into the crowd and Scarto joined the married couple, sliding a tray of drinks onto Thao's table.

"Keep on guard? Against what, exactly?" Lena questioned, holding her husband's waist.

"Honour Guards never let their guard down. Besides, if he's on duty then that means I don't have to be," he smiled, getting closer to her, kissing her on the forehead. Scarto handed him an ale "Where is Lucion?"

"He is with Rosetta, so long as she is on duty, it means I don't have to be" and she returned the kiss. "I found him reading today."

"Reading what?" Lena took the ale from his hands and had some for herself.

"Some of those dusty books you keep on the shelf downstairs. When he is not outside trying to clock you or me over the head, he is inside reading books that weigh almost as much as him." Studying Thao's face for a reaction "Are you proud of him, or worried? I find it hard to tell with you."

"Oh, I am certainly proud of him. I just did not expect this much commitment so soon. Give him time and discipline and no doubt he will make a great Honour Guard one day. Yes, I am proud of him" Thao answered with complete honesty. The couple then embraced one another again, dancing slowly and swinging slightly to the rhythm of the mellow music being played further up the path.

"I look forward to the day he becomes your equal, I look forward to the day when you hand him your hammer and helmet, but most of all, I look forward to the day when you drop your weapons for good" Thao reared his head away from hers "I know you have your doubts, but people are talking of a new age, one where men of the sword, will find a new purpose" she said into his chest.

"I was never handed my father's weapon; He died in battle when I was young; he always said to me; *Be all you can be, do right by others and never fall in shame, fall in honour*. My mother never understood this, she even fought him on it."

"Then your mother and I share something in common. I don't understand it either, this glory, this obsession with battle, bloodshed and death. To fall in battle, how can that be glorious? There is nothing glorious about it, someone snatching your life away from you! It makes no sense." Thao did not answer her directly but instead tried to calm her with comforting, reassuring words, in a tone he reserved for her alone.

"It's not obsession, it's the honour of giving yourself over to what he feels is good, and right."

"Don't let me raise Lucion alone. Fleeing the field to fight another day is a fair trade."

"My father did not choose his fate, nor will I, nor will Lucion."

"Then promise me I'll see you again, promise me you'll sit with me in old age from beneath the earth or on it? So long as you're next to me."

They wrapped their arms around each other, Thao sealing the promise.

"Master! Master Eran!" Braygon called, catching up with The Librarian among the crowds. "I meant to come by earlier, I am glad I caught you" he said cheerfully to his old tutor.

"Mr Augiene, I heard you'd arrived in Imrondel, no doubt you'll be heading off again knowing you" noted Eran.

"Yes sir, I cannot sit still."

"No need to address me as sir dear boy; we aren't in the classroom anymore. Have an ale, let's find a table. What can I help you with?"

"I am accompanying Lethaniel and Thao on their venture east to The Norfoon Watch Towers, to quell this rebellion" Braygon explained, moving aside some of the empty mugs and bottles left on the nearest table.

"You'll be serving alongside our greatest Honour Guard and the new General; these men are the finest we have. You are no stranger to this breed, I hope you're ready?"

"I am sir, I mean I am Eran" Braygon corrected himself.

"I am to understand that you were an apprentice of Mathias after you left my class, his only protégé." Braygon nodded, finding it hard not to feel unworthy next to great people like Lethaniel, Thao and Mathias, living icons of the day, whereas no one knew about Braygon.

"Can I get you a drink of ale Master? Or a yellow pond perhaps?"

"No no, I turned from that path a long time ago, but thank you for offering. Instead, I will have something which doesn't lead to a loss of equilibrium, however tempting a yellow pond sounds; sooner or later they will be off the market, their fruits have begun to grow scarce," he replied.

"I should cease the drinking too, alas Master, as you said all those years ago, we're allowed at least one bad habit." Eran chuckled.

"How can I help you Braygon?" Braygon took off his brown jacket and folded it under his arm.

"Do you remember when you taught me how to identify an enemy?"

"I seem to recall it."

"On my way here from Harbour's Edge, I travelled with a small company. We took the shortest route through the woodland, through The Silent Vale. Master, there was no doubt we were being watched!"

"Watched by whom?"

"The Dark Rogues. I saw one wrapped in camouflage, blending in with the night. They used bird calls to communicate with each other."

"Are you sure it was a Dark Rogue? They don't normally step out of the shadows. You're aware of the saying; *If you think you saw a Dark Rogue then you never saw a Dark Rogue.*" Braygon recited the last part along with him.

"I am positive it was them Master, yet they did not attack or show any sign of threat. They just watched us from a distance, from within the thickets, from the tops of trees and from mountain ledges." Both men remained quiet for a few seconds with nothing but the sounds of other people's laughter and conversations filling their ears. "It's very strange and it got me thinking. Why do we hate these Dark Rogues? When was the last time they stole anything? Or is it just because they choose to live outside our laws? Our Commanders tell us they are our enemy and that we should apprehend them on sight. Men train themselves to hate as soon as they are told to, but what if we're wrong about them. Who are our enemies Master? What if..." Eran took his turn to speak before Braygon had finished.

"There was an incident that happened not so long ago; it involved trade carts and carriages, one containing a batch of Xiondel's weapons, it was taken. The men and horses are still missing; the soldiers who reported the incident believe this was an act of The Dark Rogues, it was far too organised to be bandits or common thieves, they men were fast and efficient."

"I heard this too. What do you think?" questioned Braygon, taking a drink.

"Equis is full of schemers, stories without valuable context convoluting the truth, making it hard for men like us to uncover the facts. Something is certainly happening, forces are at work, could be the old world making a last ditch attempt to cease the inevitable coming of a new age. Soon we will see Braygon, soon we will see" said Eran, resting an arm on Braygon, standing up. "Come by the library, we'll talk further, in the meantime, enjoy yourself."

Eva stood out from the mass of people; a bright flame among a parade of shadows. She received her gift from The Priesthood and was asked to move along, to allow others for their chance to meet The Chosen. To Lethaniel's delight she emitted a glow when spotting him on the concrete path.

"You made it!" she said bouncing over.

"Did Isabelle share some kind words with you, or did she leave you bewildered like she does most?" Eva laughed a little and replied:

"No actually, she uh… She made sense this time."

"That's worth drinking to wouldn't you say? What am I getting you?" offered Lethaniel.

"Something red, something really red, I'm feeling red I don't know why" she teased. Lethaniel crunched his face.

"We better get you something red then." Eva linked her arm around his and they wandered through the crowds to the nearest open bar.

Isabelle had just attended to another one of her followers, an old man who had waited for some time. It wasn't long now before she would address the people with news of the present and future. Her speech had been prepared by The Courts of Imrondel City, but she would always go off the script and talk for herself to an extent, she couldn't help it when wrapped up in the flow of enthusiasm. As she turned her head to see to the next person, a sense of defensiveness crept over her. Calias stepped forward and bowed to The Priesthood.

"My good priests," he greeted them before turning to Isabelle "My lady." Isabelle controlled her irritation and spoke as if nothing had ever come between them.

"Calias, so wonderful of you to come. I hope you're having a grand evening."

"Isabelle, your warmth can be felt throughout the garden, you look ravishing tonight my Chosen." He took her hand and kissed it before the eyes of The Priesthood. "May I steal this fine lady for a quick moment, I'd like to make sure Isabelle has the speech on the tip of her tongue" he spoke like a gentleman when addressing the priests, who did not see a problem with his request. Isabelle gripped his hand tighter and allowed him to pull her onto her feet. "Thank you, gentlemen. I will return her in one piece, don't you worry" said Calias, in a charming manner. The priests spoke to the few remaining devotees, explaining that she wouldn't be away for long and Isabelle, hand in hand with Calias, walked a path alone, unaware that they were being followed by a hooded figure. When they were clear of the crowds, Isabelle abandoned her politeness and let go of his hand, shrugging him away.

"You are a good actor; I'll give you that. What is it you really want with me?"

"To check in, to make sure we understand one another. Be a good girl and say what you have to say tonight, and everyone stays nice and safe." Isabelle stopped in her tracks.

"You've nothing to fear, the words I read will faithful, my belief in Starillia is as strong as your desire for control."

"I need not desire it, control is my business Isabelle, I build it, I maintain it, and if not me, then there are others waiting in the wings. It's an order you see, a necessary order."

"One that has been exposed, how long do you think your secrets will stay secret now they're out?"

"You misunderstand, you're not the first and you won't be the last. Look over your shoulder, do it now Isabelle and do it quickly and discreetly." As she did, she spotted three men playing cards, tossing some zeal into a growing pile in the centre of the table. "They aren't really making bets they are my shadows, and they make sure that I am your shadow. If I fail to carry out my tasks or in the event of my disappearance, the consequences are dealt onto those close to me…" Isabelle's blood ran cold "…So if you were thinking of ways to remove me or stepping out of line, someone dear will pay for it. Keep that mind little Star Caller and do as you're told" he advised, tapping her cheek gently with three fingers. Isabelle caught a glimpse of a silver ring on his finger, which bore an emblem of Krondathia. "Now, lets get you back safely in time for your speech, I'm looking forward to it" he held out his hand for her to take which she had no choice but to squeeze. As they made their way back to Eliendras, they passed the three innocent gamblers, drinking ale, dealing cards, and not acknowledging Calias or The Star Caller.

The people gathered before a stage, brightly lit with braziers on either side. Lethaniel and Eva were among the crowd conversing comfortably, Eva sipping back on a drink so red it could have been mistaken for blood. Though now they stopped talking, their attention drawn to the stage. Thao and Lena were also among the dense crowds, along with Alexius, his hand around his waitress girlfriend's waist. Braygon hung around at the side, not too far away from Master Eran and Jerhdia who drank some strong liquor from a black bottle. All of The High Councillors of Virtue were scattered

458

throughout; Isabelle could easily pick them out from her elevated position. Yespin, High Councillor Truth stepped up onto the stage and the talk among the people, settled. The band that had been playing mellow music with their strange, stringed instruments stopped to the sound of insects and burning torches. The breath of the wind and the crackle of fires was all that could be heard and Yespin, addressed the people.

"Krondathia! What a pleasure it is to see you all, gathered here tonight in celebration of Starillia. I won't hold your attention long, I understand who you'd rather see up here as much as it pains me to admit, I know I'm not that special to you, I'll be as quick as I can" said Yespin acting an upset posture which raised a laugh from the audience. Clearing his throat "It isn't easy being a leader. It isn't easy when people look to you for answers when you do not have any or turn to you for a decision to be made that puts others at risk, especially those that we love. I admit that the past few weeks have been difficult; no doubt the next few will be even harder. I refer to what has been rumoured, it is true that the east is under attack." Those in the crowd who had doubted the stories looked at one another and whispered quietly among themselves, some even spread faces of shock. "You will be pleased to know that any deliberation on the situation is over and a plan has been formulated. Give thanks to The General and the soldiers who put their lives in danger, to give you the liberty. Let us thank all those who protect us, who keep us safe, and most of all, to make sure that our great way of life continues as it has since the elder days. Here is to you, to the protectors, to the shields of this land!" he raised a glass "To the shields!" Yespin called. The crowd mimicked his action, holding up whatever drink they had at hand and drank. Eva gently nudged Lethaniel in the arm; she knew he was a part of this and drank to him, staining her lips with her vibrant red beverage. "Let us hope that this is the last endeavour our soldiers have to face; that this time next year our soldiers will be serving US the drinks instead of drawing their swords demanding one…" A rippled of laughter fluttered through the people. "Thao Hikonle, if you are out there, please forgive me," Yespin shouted, searching for the mighty Honour Guard.

"NOT A CHANCE!" Thao wailed.

"Now! The moment you have all been waiting for. I present you someone who requires no introduction. Somebody who has been itching to talk with you this evening. The one you all came here for. Krondathia, my Norkron people… I present to you… Star Caller Isabelle Verano the twenty-third, OUR CHOSEN!" Before he had even finished saying her name, the crowd lifted their joy into calls of praise and wild cheer. Those still seated stood up for her; those already standing raised their mugs and glasses. Yespin bowed before Isabelle as she stepped to the centre stage handing him her blue long coat. The crowd continued to applaud, whistling, and chanting her name. She stood there for some seconds, smiling, blushing, and taking in the adulation. Lethaniel prodded Eva in the arm and remarked:

"I know her; made her breakfast once." Eva shook her head from side to side, grinning at Lethaniel's childish behaviour.

"Shut up, you!" Isabelle raised her hand to the crowd and they eventually allowed her to give her speech. It was at that moment that Othello turned up, wondering what all the fuss was about, laying eyes on Isabelle for the first time in years, who was not a small child anymore as he had vaguely remembered, but an adult of enormous power.

"It's a remarkable sign that so many of you have shown up here tonight. It tells me that you care as much as I do for the well-being of Starillia. It gives me strength, and I thank you all for your infinite love, your hard work and support." The crowds once more burst into applause. "Yespin was kind enough to thank those brave men who risk their lives in the wilds to keep us safe, I too raised my glass. I, however, wish to thank all of you today, with all my heart, for making this country whole, for believing in Norkron power and the force for good it so truly is." She held her hand up again, requesting quiet so she could say more before another eruption took place. "You are what makes this country work! You are the ones who have delivered us the cities, the homes, the protection, and freedom we need to march into the future. You have given Krondathia everything, I wish I could reward you all with your heart's desires, your dreams but… But I…" Yet again the crowds showed her how much they loved her, filling the air with overwhelming positivity. As they hailed her with praise, her inner voice made itself clear: *Only they do not know, they don't know the truth, the lies we have told, the layers of deceit burying the truth. If not now, when will they learn?* Her face turned noticeably glum. She stopped smiling and started to pace the stage, like her sense of presence had run out and all that was left in her whittled away before all those eyes looking up at her. Eran, among the crowd, moved his stare from side to side, trying to see if the people had noticed the change as he had, but they were too busy relentlessly cheering her on. "Please, I must ask you kindly…" her attempts to calm them were of no use. What should have been heartfelt, became an annoyance "…Please Krondathia, there is more I have to say…" They didn't stop "…I must go away!" The atmosphere, so recently warm and comfortable, sank into a strange aura of wonder drenched in sadness. In that one moment, Isabelle had thrown away her people's happiness, she could see it in their faces; she could sense their dampened blue spirits. It was here that she abandoned the old speech she had revised earlier and proceeded with her own. "For how long, I cannot say. I must go away to spread the word of Starillia. It seems my work and ALL The Star Callers before me, our work is done." The crowds remained as they were "I will leave to bring peace to far off countries, to share my glorious tales, to tell other peoples of the world I left behind, and I'll miss you dearly in those moments. What we have accomplished here, is just the beginning. It is time to move on, to move on and spread the wings of Starillia so that everyone may benefit from the unification it brings. My journey will start in Ivulien, I'll give the Dovidians a touch of Celestial intrigue, one which I'm sure they will adore as much as you have. From there, I will head north to Jureai, where we will teach The Chimera Order things, things they never thought possible." She spoke radically, from the heart and from her own dreams. Her words became excited and joyful, the crowds enveloped by what she had to say. Isabelle could not know if she was winning them over or pushing them further away, but at that moment it did not matter, she had to continue. "If my strength wills it, I will head west to the forests of Damalesque, I will meet The Fawn and together we'll merge our great societies." She could not help but pick out the upset faces, not stirred by her speech. "Norkrons, Norkrons do not despair, I beg you, for this is a joyous occasion, one that I'd like to remember graced with happiness and celebration. Do me this last honour, let me leave this land the proper way, the Norkron way in style…" with her fierce smile, the others mirrored her "…And when I return, let it be to this ground, to this

461

very spot where we delivered…THE! UTOPIAN! WORLD!" As she uttered those words, she raised both arms to the crowd for an embrace, welcomed with a thundering roar filling her with the fire of ambition and a nourishing sense of pride. "Enjoy this night Norkrons. The Celestials command it!" she shouted, hopping off the stage, immediately caught by High Councillor Truth. She was met with a loving mob enriched with smiles and kind words, wishing her luck, wishing her all the joy in Equis, she could not help but lose herself in the thick of people, absorbing their passion for her and for Starillia. The band changed its tunes to dynamic rhythms and so the dancing grounds were drawn. Isabelle managed to clear herself of the crowds, slipping away from the celebratory Norkrons. She washed her face using a bowl of water near her seat; it felt immensely refreshing. She splashed even more water into her face and rose, unable to find her hand towel.

"Oh, Cillian Landris, thank you" she said, drying her face with the towel he passed her.

"I hope you know what you're doing," he said, before walking away, to where the crowds grew thin.

"Why does my intuition tell me that you're somehow involved in this grand scheme?" Eva asked Lethaniel, raising an eyebrow. He just grinned at her, flicked the cap off a bottle and took a sip of beer. "When will you be leaving?"

"Soon, but I'm not going alone. A whole party of us will be heading out together, and we will return together. Only this time it will be different; when I get back, when all this is done, hopefully, I'll be returning to a place where my services as a General are no longer required, and the challenge of finding a new line of work can begin." Eva returned to her thoughts. He knew she was worried for his safety; she didn't even have to say anything to him anymore, he just knew by that look she gave, when her eyes seemed to harden. "Don't worry about me. I'll be fine," he assured.

"Are you taking Seridox with you?"

"Wouldn't leave without him."

462

"Don't forget to stock up with plenty of water. Remember to eat at every opportunity. Stop and rest often. When you do rest, be sure that a trusted man is posted to keep watch over you..." Lethaniel nodded, having heard this many times before "...Keep your swords close and don't..."

"Eva!" he interrupted, halting her lecture, allowing her to take a breath. "I will come back, no one can put me in the ground."

"Be sure that you do" she murmured softly, finishing her drink, setting it down on a nearby table and began to mingle.

"Eva, wait" Lethaniel caught up to her and handed her a handkerchief "For your mouth it looks like you've been gnawing on someone" he said.

"Good night. See you soon" she said after wiping the red juice away from her lips. Lethaniel swallowed his heart and wanted to find Alexius, only he could get him drunk in thirty seconds flat.

The stars were out but the moon remained hidden behind unmoving clouds. All around Eliendras Cathedral the Starlight Blooms were in full flower and glowing wondrously. Around the sides of the gardens, the celebration was becoming more intense by the minute. Fresh barrels of ale were rolled in and fireworks flew into the sky, leaving behind them a furious flurry of colourful explosions. Master Eran spent most of the night at his table, talking with his students who could not wait for next week's lecture on Glyph. Alexius was gone, drunk out of his mind where he had passed out mid-sentence, and was being loaded into a wheelbarrow by the waitress, who wheeled him way through the people to deliver him home safely. Lena sat on Thao's knee, chatting at a table, drinking together. Occasionally, someone or groups of men would interrupt them, would want to shake Thao's hand, or even buy them their next round. Lethaniel, having abandoned Alexius unable to understand a word coming out of his mouth before he was carted off and out of the district, bumped into Letty who was as always happy and keen to talk to him about Isabelle, about his two swords, about his trials and his journey to becoming a General. Braygon, hung at the open bar, talking to strangers, and enjoying the night.

Othello and Eva found one another amongst the festival, spotting each other almost simultaneously through those who were dancing. The crowds would disperse soon, they would be heading over to The Canalside District. The Priesthood and The Glyph Wielders were already handing out flower boats along with small candles, candles to be placed in the centre of each model float.

"Hello" Othello greeted holding out his hand. Eva slapped it aside and wrapped her arms around him. He held her there, close with one hand over her soft hair. "What was that for?"

"For sharing a rooftop with me." When she pulled away from him, his eyes fell to her mouth "Oh yes, sorry, I've been eating human flesh." Her comment only widened his eyes as she vigorously cleaned with the handkerchief. "That was a joke Othello, it's alright to laugh" and he gestured the *phew* sign of relief.

"This festival, what is it all about?" he asked.

"Shhh, don't let anyone hear you say that!" she giggled. "It's The Festival of the Awakening. It happens each year. We come together in celebration, to give thanks to The Celestials Souls. Isabelle is soon to pray to them in that Cathedral…" and Eva pointed to Eliendras "…She receives a gift from them. Those flowers the priests are handing out are not star blooms; they are far too delicate and treasured to treat as such, so we create models of them into little floats. We place a candle in the centre and set them adrift in the canal that circles Norisis," she explained.

"One of the clans of Jureai, the Vantarquinns, they celebrate this tradition. They place flames in small balloons and release them from beneath a foot of a mountain with a mighty shrine carved into its side. It is quite beautiful" he recalled.

"Othello, are you feeling alright?"

"Yes, why wouldn't I be?"

"Being so far from home, in a different place, new people, new ways… Different city, different everything. You must get lonely, right?"

"This was once my home. It is different, so much has changed I barely recognise it, it has lost a certain magic. I cannot even find my way back to my old house" he stated, masking disappointment.

"Is that why you left Jureai? To rediscover your roots" Othello knew he had forgotten his father's ring, it was hidden in an envelope in a chest of drawers at his empty place. "I know how that feels, it's the time Othello; time takes everything away." Trying to catch his eyes she said "I feel like I've have met you before, as impossible as that sounds, I feel like I know you" she insisted, growing more and more sure of herself.

"You must be mistaken."

"How old are you Othello?"

"I just turned twenty-eight. I was in no position to celebrate. I was on my way here, facing almost certain death. The road was long but I made it in the end, with some help," he explained, referring to his loyal tulkan and Commander Mathias.

"Yes, of course, you travelled here all alone, all that way. It must have been difficult?" The people had started to move off to The Canalside District, to place their candles in the water circling The Palace.

"We should be heading off too," Othello suggested.

"No… Wait!"

"What's wrong?" he asked as she looked up at the moon, hidden behind clouds.

"Yes… Maybe we should go, but another way perhaps" she said with excitement.

"Where do you want to go?"

"You want to see some magic? Come with me!" Eva grabbed his hand, leading him away in the opposite direction to where the crowds were flocking. Othello snatched up a stray candle having been left on a wooden bar table, but Eva did not notice. They quickly separated themselves from the people to find a spot of their own.

The people swarmed around the canals that circled the huge Palace of Norisis. Thousands had gathered for the occasion, indeed most of the city was in attendance. Many wished to place a candle in the canal for the Celestials, mostly children, for their minds were young and new to the tradition.

"Let us begin!" Isabelle announced once everyone was ready, stepping forward to lower her lit candle into the cool flowing water. Her flower boat was a lot more decorative and elaborate than the rest, designed to stand out. Hers was the first candle to be placed in the water, sailing gently down the wide waterway. The Norkron people then followed in Isabelle's example. Soon the canal was shimmering with a mass of candle lights, a galaxy of swirling fire stars. Isabelle took time to observe the glow on the faces of those who took part. This was her twenty-sixth festival; the tradition was the same, but the feeling differed from those prior. The turn-out of people was far greater than in previous years, this also would be her last festival in Krondathia; next year she would have to come up with a new idea for the Dovidian people in their own capital. While the people were casting their floats with the help of her priests and Glyph Wielders, she backed away from the canal and further onto the pavement. She turned around having thought she heard something only to catch a scream, slapping a hand over her mouth "Teo" she hissed her whisper, being sure to stand formerly, having caught the attention of a priest noticing her. "You scared the life out of me!" she whispered, gasping for air.

"You're twitchy tonight"

"I can't be seen talking to anyone at the moment." Teo stayed quiet, blending in with the crowds, moving from her left to right.

"But if you have any plans, I would gladly…" Teo interrupted her before she could finish; he did indeed have plans.

"Behind us, through the alley, the one with the barrel," he whispered.

"What have you got in mind?" she asked, slyly looking over her shoulder trying to catch a glimpse of him, though he had already disappeared. She hung in that same spot for a little while longer, looking for a chance to slip away. As soon as her priests were occupied with a hoard of fanatics, she backed off toward the alley with the barrel at its entrance. Quickly, she darted inside, remaining there for a moment just to be sure she had not been noticed. Finally, convinced she had successfully snuck away, she proceeded further down the way. Her priests were not the only ones watching her, her guards were also alert, so she had to be careful. When she got to the end of the alley and emerged out on to the opposite street, she looked around for Teo, but there was no sign of him.

"I enjoyed your speech," he praised, coming out from the darkness behind her.

"How did you do that?" she demanded to know, hands on her wide hips.

"You have your tricks, I have my own, Lady Star Caller. You walked straight by me and didn't even notice" he teased.

"Not that. I mean how did you escape The Cathedral, with all those guards around? What did you do? Where did you go? There was nowhere to hide!" She gave him time to respond, but he merely grinned and looked away toward the dark rooftops, avoiding her gaze. "So, you liked my speech? This one was a little short, I think." Teo scratched his chin.

"It was inventive." Incidentally, he had also witnessed her private talk with Calias.

"So what are we doing here?"

"I thought you might want to get away for a little while?"

"I must be back at the cathedral soon, to talk to the Celestials."

"Isn't that the same as finding Inner Peace? Another Star Caller ability?" Teo questioned.

"Not quite, you are referring to something else entirely." She took a breath before explaining "We have many abilities, one of which I am sure you're familiar with, is Vision. There is Vision Channelling, which allows us to pass our Visions onto others. Inner Peace allows us to focus the mind, to take an inward journey inside ourselves to meet our Counterpart, the kindred spirit that represents our soul in a silent otherworldly place called Limbo. This is difficult to master and navigating Limbo when you get there before it collapses, is another feat altogether, but when you meet your Counterpart, you can learn a great deal about yourself, and you return to your physical body enlightened. You already know about Skin Burn, and then there is the ability to talk directly to the Celestials in prayer, which is what I will be doing today. It is called Whispering and tonight one of the Celestials will answer; it's also a tradition that The Star Caller receives a gift. I wonder what it will be this time," she blabbered excitedly.

"And what gifts might you receive?" He asked, putting aside the more important question of; What her Counterpart was or resembled?

"Last year I received a…" She paused to think.

"Go on," he urged, interested in learning more.

"Last year I received an idol, a small statue of a woman, or at least I think it was. Honestly, I do not know what it represented, but it is kept inside the temple where The Eldor keeps it safe, along with all the other priceless treasures."

"I want you to take this." He presented her with his slick-looking dagger, safely sheathed.

"The Celestials have enough treasure Teo."

"It's not for them, it's for you."

"For me? I don't understand?"

"There is so much you do not understand, well understand this, it will keep you safe."

"I can't accept it Teo" He shrugged his shoulders.

"Why not?"

"Because it's a steel weapon!" she pointed out.

"It is indeed, plain and simple, everyone in the world knows the language it speaks. Keep it with you, just in case."

"In case of what? In case I forget how to use my Glyph?! Come on, Teo, that's not going to happen."

"In case you need to lean on something reliable. Maybe you will need something made of steel." Equis had spoken the language of swords and shields longer than it had spoken Glyph.

"Fine, I'll take it?" and she reluctantly took it.

"If you're in danger, so are we all" her friendly demeanour turned to shadow. Teo pulled up his hood and turned the other way, marching down the road. Just as she was about to call after him, she heard a familiar voice:

"Isabelle!" yelled Lethaniel. "What are you doing down here? They want you at the cathedral. Let's go!" As she head back to the canal, Lethaniel spotted Teo. Curious, he began to follow him. Noticing this, Isabelle tried to distract him.

"Lethaniel, it's this way," she insisted, trying to get in front of him, but he pushed her lightly aside.

"Go back to Eliendras, Isabelle; I'll meet you there in a moment," he promised. She stopped and observed as he began to jog after Teo. "HEY! WAIT!" he shouted. Teo, hidden under his cloak, burst into a sprint. He was fast on his feet, but Lethaniel was anything but slow. Soon it became clear that the fittest man would prevail. The General saw the stranger turn off into another cramped, dark alleyway. He stormed around the corner and found himself in the dark, facing a dead end in the form of a flat, stone wall, with no sign of the hooded man. He couldn't help but feel like he had been here before, in The Silent Vale. A noise, a scrape of leather on rock echoed above him, and he caught a glimpse of dark fabric passing overhead. *How had he climbed up so quickly?*

Teo and his two companions, fitted from head to toe in black and brown camouflage, remained still and silent on the rooftop, waiting for their pursuer to leave, which eventually he did. One of the young men was built, carrying a heavy set of muscle under thick leather armour, a solid man of power, and strength. The other was of a slight build, his features were hidden behind a stretch of cloth covering the lower half of his face, he gathered up the rope that had been used to lift Teo from the ground.

"What's wrong with you?" he whispered.

"What do you mean?" replied Teo quietly.

"Cutting it a bit close, weren't you? You do know who was fucking chasing you?"

"That's rich coming from you, Draygo!" Draygo finished reeling in the rest of the rope and glanced over at his companion for further support.

"He's right Teo. Do not depend on luck, because it will not last. You are taking too many risks; it's amazing Isabelle hasn't caught on to you."

"That's why I have you guys to watch my back, right? Right, Riagel?" Teo repeated. The men looked at each other and then returned to gather up the rest of the equipment. Draygo darted off and leapt from a nearby rooftop, leaving the other two behind.

"What if Draygo and I were compromised Teo? What if we were unable to support you?" questioned Riagel. "Don't answer, you'd be going toe to toe with a man who has never lost a fight, not a situation you want to find yourself in." Teo shrugged his shoulders and protested.

"Says you! You've been in far worse situations than this. I've heard the stories about you two; I find it incredible that both of you are still breathing considering the shit you've faced. You are either seriously smart or incredibly lucky. That was an easy getaway Riagel, no need to fret about it." Teo tried to step by his superior but was halted by a sturdy hand, no one walked passed Riagel.

"You are missing the point kid. There are reasons why we are still alive; you are thinking only one step ahead of the game, when the trick is to be so far ahead you can't fail. If we had been compromised, you'd have been dragged to The Prison Towers by now for interrogation and I'd be heading back to Tthenadawn with one less man." Teo had nothing to say, so like a naughty student, he stood there taking a lesson from Riagel who was almost a foot taller than he was. "We are a team, but if shit starts to fly and the alarm is raised, I look after myself, Draygo can take care of himself, he has proven himself fuck knows how many times. We've done it before and survived; Why?"

"Because we are always ahead" They said this together.

"Don't make me repeat myself to you again Teo; one day you will be on your own, I hope you'll be ready" warned Riagel, pulling his hood over his head and fetching a polearm.

Othello and Eva were alone in the gardens, though the Norkron people would soon be returning for the final part of the celebration. Usually, it was forbidden to walk inside the gardens, but Eva ventured into them barefoot, taking care not to harm a single petal.

"It's different when you're with them, isn't it?" she asked, keeping an eye on her footing. Othello remained on the wide, stone path, hesitant to break the rules when he was so new to the city. Eva was dressed in a lovely, grey dress with a jacket to keep herself warm, while he was still dressed in his baggy work clothes, heavy boots included and wrist bracers. "Come on, come over here. No one is watching," she urged. He removed his footwear and stepped out into the garden; as he did so, a tingle ran up his spine. It certainly was a pillowed feeling to be among the flowers. "They say that these blooms are linked to Starillia or even the life of the planet. Somehow, the roots gather nutrients from Glyph energy, you know, the same stuff that gives certain people powers. That is what I read anyway. As long as they glow brightly, it means that everything will be alright, as if they are in touch with the land itself, like they are actually aware of what is going on around them. As long as things remain peaceful, they will continue to shine" she explained, approaching the middle of the large, square garden with Othello tip toeing behind. "It's very strange, wouldn't you say?" She stopped when she got to the exact centre; the sounds of people could be heard faintly in the distance, far away near The Canalside District. Othello suddenly remembered a similar story that he was sure she would like to hear.

"Have you heard of The Moth Meadow?"

"No, I've never heard of such a place."

"The moths that nest out there, their wings are resplendent with colour, while in the twilight they shine, emitting a soothing light from their wings. If you disturb them while they are nesting in the thickets of long grass, they disperse in a scintillant swarm. It is written that during The Never-Ending War, they appeared to react to strife. While the world was on its knees, the moths of the meadow stopped shining and instead, they coloured themselves grey with patterns symbolic of death and pain. Yes, it is strange and even disturbing in some ways, but it's reassuring when you see those lights."

"Who told you this?" she asked.

"El Raud, my old Chieftain. The elders of Jureai, who have travelled and experienced more than any other, they've stories far greater than I could ever tell. When I was growing up, my head was filled with such tales; they weren't fairy tales to me, but rather things that could come true, you just needed to know where to look. I wanted to see for myself, but... My life was different then, and all I see ahead of me now is work without meaning."

472

"You're so secretive all the time," she complained. Usually, it was a trait she appreciated in a man, but it was possible to have too much of a good thing. "It sounds like you miss your home very much. Why don't you return?"

"I will, one day, but not so soon. I left for the sake of those who raised me. Looking at these lights now, reassures me that my clan are alright." She finally saw warmth coming from his eyes like she could trust him. This was what she had been waiting for before moving any further with him.

"I would like to see it one day" she murmured, staring into his eyes.

"I know you would like it" he replied, allowing her to get closer. Othello wrapped his arm around her waist when she drew a little closer, running a hand up his chest. The moon finally unveiled itself, and the flowers picked up the shine, holding the white orbs glow. Locked in a loving embrace in the middle of the garden, Othello and Eva shared an intimate kiss surrounded by a mist of white light.

"When you next take a trip to Moth Meadow, if you feel like you want some company, I'll happily join you," Eva suggested, drunk on the rush of affection she had not experienced in a long, long time.

"I'd like that," Othello replied, his brevity for once being a result of positive emotions. She smiled before they lost themselves in the moment again; soon they would have to steal away, for the crowds could return at any moment.

"It gets cold at mine" she clutched him a little tighter. He responded with another kiss softly, and gripped the back of her head, pressing her into him. "Alright, good," she stuttered, pulling away, taking his hand once more "You can keep me warm at mine, it's this way" said Eva, leading the way in a hurry.

The Festival of Awakening was ending. The children were tired, and the adults were merry, some of them were too merry dreaming of their beds. Isabelle was escorted to the doors of Eliendras Cathedral where her priests and guards awaited. She removed her coat, pulled off several necklaces and bracelets and handed them to a nearby attendant. Teo's dagger was concealed neatly in the folds of the blue long coat. A High Priest robed in ruby red approached and placed a stunning white tiara over her golden head. Once she was handed her majestic long-staff, Violethelm she was finally ready to enter Eliendras Cathedral. The doors were opened for her and she disappeared within. General Presian was standing close to Thao outside.

"So where was she?" whispered The Honour Guard.

"Not far away," answered Lethaniel, considering telling Thao everything - about the hooded figure and Isabelle's recent behaviour - but he decided against it. It was neither the time nor the place. Thao suspected that he was hiding something, but lost the chance to voice it, when Lethaniel stepped away to the priests and began talking to one of them. Thao and Lena could not make out what he was saying, but it appeared to be important, concerning The Star Callers livery.

"What is he doing?" wondered Lena.

"I don't know." One of the holy men bowed to Lethaniel and went off to fetch someone or something, leaving the General alone with Isabelle's possessions. "Lethaniel is no liar, but I'm sure he's hiding something."

Inside the cathedral, a quiet and ominous atmosphere reigned. Isabelle knew that all the rooms were empty, but she could not shake off that unmistakable feeling of being watched. Maybe it was Teo who made her feel this way or perhaps it was Calias, who never seemed to be too far away, but she knew for a fact that neither man was in there with her. She entered the central room, stepping between the twelve pillars. The candles that had been placed in their tall holders by her servants earlier were slowly dying, giving off a waning orange glow. She still needed the light, so without looking she pointed at the weak flames gathered in the corners one at a time, and they found their strength once more. She knelt next to the central seal and closed her shining green eyes, preparing to begin her prays.

One second felt like an hour, an hour a day, and there in the darkness of her thoughts something was different; a sense of danger and misplacement, a feeling of distortion coming from somewhere in the world. It felt like she didn't belong here at all, that Krondathia was no longer her home, nor was Ivulien for that matter. Her home existed in a place far beyond both countries, beyond Equis even, in a place long forgotten and far out of reach of anyone. What she saw she could not explain, but what she recognised was the voice that whispered *Elaso fiin* was growing louder and louder. She forced herself to open her eyes, shaking off the mild effects of paralysis. There, under the shadow of The Cathedral, was some kind of anomaly. A shape arose from the floor, a smoky apparition that quickly morphed into a distorted humanly contorted shape. Was this an enemy? Should she run or welcome this hazy visitor? It moved lifelessly toward her, bereft of features. As the being left the shadows, so too did its form. The apparition lost leaving her trembling with sweating palms. The Star Caller fell to the floor and gasped, only to hear something hovering above her, it was a bird of black feathers.

Chapter 21 - Daggers and Thieves

You are what you are. One week later, on a beautiful day in Imrondel.

"Krondathia has tasted the grief of war and bloodshed. I covered our history in last week's class; I know you were all there..." Eran lectured, walking between the desks in his classroom in The Old Library, tapping the shoulder of a student who had buried his head in his textbook. The other students laughed a little, then got back to listening. "All civilisations rise, will inevitably fall or go through reformation and reconstruction. Why? Because once they reach the pinnacle of their achievements, when complete order has been established there is only one place it can go, and that is to the route of chaos. This is can be applied to our own lives, when you reach your potential it takes a level of responsibility to maintain it, otherwise you too will fall from grace."

"So what about us, Master? Are we at our peak as a society?" one student asked, his young face bright and optimistic.

"It is difficult to say, but I will try to answer," Eran replied, clearing his throat, mustering the best explanation he could. "I'd say we are indeed nearing our peak. We have a long way to go before we start looting the streets, tearing down buildings and clawing at our neighbours' throats."

"Wouldn't you say that we are smarter than that? Don't you think that these times are different to what has come before? The utopian world is coming." This query came from somewhere in the back row. Eran removed his glasses and perched on the front of his desk.

"You were at the festival, weren't you? I saw some of you there..." Some of the class began to feel a little uneasy, having assumed they had gotten away with their covert partying. "No need to worry, your secret is safe with me. It would take you openly drinking in my class under my very nose for me to get upset. Now, to address your question, you mentioned intelligence, who are we smarter than exactly? Norkron, Dovidian, Karthian; whatever nation you are from, we all fit under the same banner; we are all of the same species. As for the utopian world, our Star Caller and those before her, have been trying to find a loop hole from this inevitable cycle, to try to break away from this rise to order and the fall back into chaos, our species cannot walk this path. We have to break from this pattern now or we risk losing everything as our species progresses through the ages."

"If we were made aware of this decline early, surely we would be able to halt it?" a young girl questioned.

"How right you are, it is not usually an instant collapse; it's like a rot, an erosion. Normally the process is slow and tedious, the civilisations sinks lower and lower, bit by bit each day this infection eats away at the foundations until the pillars that support our kingdoms snap! You'll know a snap when it happens, and I recommend on that day social order breaks, flee!" His words were not encouraging, he drew from lessons taken directly from the history books. "It would be nice to believe that we are somewhat superior to others, but unfortunately, we are all just animals who created fire and melt iron. We share the same weaknesses as any other: greed, jealousy, hatred, revenge, all of which are traits we can do without because they are what eat away at our society." A student then raised his hand and Eran pointed to him, giving him permission to speak.

"Are we all doomed to fall victim to this cycle?"

"I'd say it helps to be aware of the problems that exist and to understand them. Only when you've a thorough knowledge of the process can you act accordingly to solve it" answered Eran overjoyed with the interest his students were showing; he could not remember the last time a class had been so invested and involved in one of his lectures.

"What if a society is unified Master, but its only chance of survival is to spread, and to drain the resources of another who is unwilling to share?"

"I'd question that societies consumption rates, you may have a unified country but that does remove the problems of food, water and space distribution. It's a slightly different issue but…When a civilisation is in immediate danger of extinction, threatened by another civilisation in this case, a sure way to stop the invasion is through force and what does force entail?"

"Resistance!" they replied in unison.

"Exactly, and resistance can lead to war and that is what we must try to avoid because it would not be a gradual erosion, it would be like experience the snap!" said Eran, clicking his fingers.

"How would we fight a war today, Master?"

"Humans are adept at fighting each other; it's one of the things we know how to do best. Destroying people's lives comes naturally to us, we needed to show a level of bloodlust to pass natures test. As for how we would fight today, we would use similar tactics as our warlords during the second age. Our weapons have become more advanced, such as the invention of the armour-piercing crossbow. Our siege engines have become far more refined, able to throw heavier projectiles further distances at smaller targets. Glyph has certainly changed the Norkron way on combat. As we speak, we are working on hilts and scabbards that trap burning Omnio energies to create swords and polearms, made not of metal, but harnessed spectral forces. As of yet, no one has succeeded with this new method, but one day someone will perfect it. Chemical formulas have advanced so much that we can treat wounds and diseases otherwise fatal a century ago. We can build cities like Imrondel and Xiondel, all of these examples are testament to expansion in knowledge and power, but what we always seem to return to is war." He began to wrap up the lecture, spotting Braygon hanging in the doorway in front of the light. "Finding ways to prevent conflict is something we will cover next week. Tomorrow we will be looking at those who profit from war but for now you're dismissed. Those of you who have assignments the deposit box is outside my office. Thank you very much and enjoy the rest of your day." As the students packed their bags and began to leave, Eran had a drink of water from a glass resting on his desk, looking up as Braygon who approached, standing aside for the students leaving The Old Library. "Braygon Augiene! I did not expect you so early, no hangover?"

"I wish it was a hangover, shut out the light and lay still, easy fix, but something has happened" Eran sat down in his chair and put his hands on the table.

"Is there a problem I can help you with?"

"Master, it's The Chosen; some of us are growing concerned for her well-being, and her behaviour."

"The last time I was with her she seemed very well. What with all the duties she has to attend to on a daily basis and her responsibilities as a Star Caller, not least of which is looking after an entire population, I think she is doing rather well. The occasional odd moment I'd say is only natural considering the pressure."

"Yes, Master, but she seems arrogant and stubborn when it comes to performing the simpler tasks."

"Have seen her of late?" Eran asked, raising an eyebrow.

"No, Master."

"I will speak with her, she often comes by, will that put your mind at ease?" Braygon rubbed his chin and took a few steps back. "Where is she, Braygon?" he asked, necking back the glass of water.

"At the moment, Master, none of us know. I was actually hoping she would be here with you." Eran set the glass down with a concerned look on his face.

"No need to panic. I am sure she can look after herself; she is our Chosen after all. Who else knows of her disappearance?" Braygon shrugged his shoulders in response, thinking to himself for a second.

"Myself, Lethaniel and a few of her Glyph Wielders, who are currently out looking for her." Eran stood up and walked towards the window, observing the beautiful day outside.

"She's not here. If you find her first, I would like you to bring her here, we can then tell her guards that there was a simple

479

misunderstanding and that she was reading quietly upstairs this whole time." Braygon understood, and bowed his head in agreement, having had a similar idea himself. He made for the door, but as he put his hand on the handle he turned once more.

"Master, the festival; has she said anything to you about it and what happened in Eliendras?"

"No, nothing at all. You'd best get moving Captain if you are to find her first, Braygon."

"What did you do? Did you eat it?" laughed Isabelle.

"Oh, I had no choice. I mean, I was sitting directly opposite my superior and his wife, who had slaved all morning over this meal. It was a blend of all the ingredients that make me wretch, all of my worst nightmares mixed into this one bowl of soup. The colour of it alone was enough to put me off. There was no bread or water available to wash it down with, that dinner made me the man I am today" explained Teo.

"I guess it's important to make the right first impression and be polite, even if it means enduring pain, or in your case the taste of cauliflower, broccoli, cheese and peas. It sounds very nutritious if I may say so," she giggled.

"I can deal with cheese and peas, but the other two I have no chance against," grinned Teo, shaking his head. They were sitting in a rather secluded part of Imrondel City, along a long, winding road that rarely saw many people and was used mainly as a short-cut for supply carriages. Teo sat under a broken window leading into an abandoned warehouse, while Isabelle leant up next to a wall in her dark coat with the white streak. She cleared her throat and spoke again:

"I'm not too keen on sausages, personally" she added.

"What's wrong with sausages?"

"They're disgusting. I am fortunate though in my palette, Star Callers are expected to eat everything that is put in front of her. I can deal with most foods but sometimes I have to really focus on the *chew chew chew and swallow as quickly as possible* method, followed with a rich red wine, that way I avoid the embarrassment of belching in front of people of power, expecting you to be the one to deliver paradise in Equis."

"What do you say to something like that? Where does someone like you go for advice?"

"Welcome to my world Teo, the list who can help is rather thin" she said, holding out a hand and counting down. "I've a rather wise librarian, an Honour Guard, let's see a mek, his name is Jerhdia and The General, Lethaniel and Pandora. Their knowledge is limited and their time is scarce so, I read."

"Pandora, what does she do?"

"She's a good friend of mine, keeps me company."

"Right, does she work here in the city?" Isabelle slowly nodded her head and replied hesitantly.

"Yeah, something like that." Before he could continue his line of questioning, she decided to change the subject completely "Are you from Xiondel City by any chance, Teo?" He looked at her and considered the question before responding:

"Yeah, something like that." Avoiding her face quickly as she narrowed her eyes, he got back to studying the concrete floor.

"I thought I was close then" she said.

"Close to what?"

"I thought you'd let something slip. I know next to nothing about you," she complained, folding her arms, hoping that her sulking would compel him to tell her a little bit about himself. "Star Callers can normally read faces; we're intuitive, sensitive, some of my line were even able to read minds. We are disciplined and…"

"Tell me something I don't know," Teo interrupted.

"My practises in this regard are small, I'd rather you tell me a story." When she turned back round to look at Teo, he had completely disappeared. She remained there for a short time wondering just where he had gone and why. As she began to make her way up the road, she heard a sound of approaching footsteps, so she backed off to feel a firm grip on her arm. It was Lethaniel! Before he could begin to talk to her he also was alerted by the metal footsteps. At a moment's thought, he put his hands onto her shoulders and moved her further into an alley and pushed her behind a nook in the wall under the cover of darkness. He joined her as several Glyph Wielders passed by them, who failed to notice them in the shadows. Only when they had gone did Lethaniel let her go; she owed him some answers.

"Isabelle, what are you doing? You're needed at The Palace. You were not in your room, not in your study area, nor were you in Eliendras. People are out looking for you, including Braygon, who is also required elsewhere; we have a mission to organise, possibly the last one we ever set out on, it's important we get this right. We've not the time for this!" He had been concerned for her safety and had already traversed half of the city searching for her. Finding her was a great relief, but there was still much more that concerned him. Isabelle tried pushing passed him, but he firmly stood his ground and got in her way.

"I needed some air and some space." Her half-hearted excuses would not suffice.

"For the whole morning?!" he groaned, to no defence. "Are you going to talk to me? I only want to help."

"Well by keeping me here you're not helping anyone, so if you would please move…"

"Do you want to tell me about this?" He pulled on the sleeve of the dark coat, the one with the white streak running through the hood, the same one he recognised when she had broken her curfew. "Very well, can you tell me about the book?" She stared at him as if he had been reading through a personal diary. "I saw you take it, Isabelle." When she could not give him a reply, holding his face with a look of shame, he slowly stepped away from her, giving her some room to breathe.

"Have I changed so much in our time apart that you cannot find it in yourself to trust me?"

"I don't know, have you changed Lethaniel? I trusted you enough to keep our secret, secret and so far you've been true to your word, but whether or not you've grown and parted yourself from your sporadic behaviour is another question entirely. It makes you dangerous and unpredictable, or are you going to leave it up to me to find out how far it goes?" she answered defensively.

"I'm not asking you to do anything Isabelle" said Lethaniel, crossing his arms.

"I have an answer if you really want to know, people just love to talk and hear about themselves day in, day out, but when confronted with someone like me, who has the ability to break down one's psychology, you'd be surprised how many of them stick around. People do not want to know who they really are or what they are capable of, most people are afraid and only wish to hear what they want to hear, to see them through the day."

"Isabelle, there is no need to…"

"With you it's easy to see what you're going through. You put on a brave face, you hide your trauma extremely well, but it's still there, isn't it? Have you not figured it out yet, Lethaniel? Why I keep myself away from you? It's because the truth hurts and like you who walls up his truth this city does the same, it's not built on a foundation of honesty like it should be, it's built on lies and is cemented by fear. You're afraid of losing, you're afraid of losing control, but Lethaniel, we never had control, not you OR me." They backed away from each other.

"Is that was this is for…" and he handed her an object, wrapped in a white cloth "…To regain control?" Isabelle unwrapped the cloth revealing the dagger, Teo's dagger.

483

"Where did you get this?" Not that it mattered, she had been caught, but Lethaniel, humoured her.

"I found it among your belongings outside Eliendras." Isabelle wrapped the dagger up and slid it into her pocket.

"That's a Dark Rogue's dagger Isabelle, sharp enough to cut through flesh like it were butter." This new information smacked her straight in the face. "You don't have to tell me anything, Isabelle, you're The Star Caller, I'm your General, if that is all you want me to be then so be it." Lethaniel left the alley muttering "Find your own way back to The Palace and make sure no one catches you with the blade of the enemy, consequences might be severe." He left her in the alley, alone with nothing but her thoughts.

Chapter 22 - The Bird in the Rafters

A vague message.

It had been several days since Isabelle had last seen Teo and all sorts of things were running through her mind. She had been attending meetings and going over scriptures with her High Priests for most of the day, learning techniques of how to relay religious text with otherwise a secular group of people. The Dovidians were as intelligent as the Norkrons in a traditional sense, though they perceived things such as religion in a different manner. It would be up to her to debate and to teach their intellectuals on a daily basis of which they had many, about Starillia from her new home in Ivulien. The work would be constant; she would have to master the finer points of lecturing in addition to just performing demonstrations. Inviting Celestials from the ethereal plane of Lunas into Equis would not be enough to satisfy the people of Ivulien; she would need to do more and be vigilant about her message of utopia. Her shoulders began to ache as she hunched over some papers given to her by Master Eran a short while back, stored in her chest of drawers. They had been salvaged from The Star Caller records in The Old Library. All hand-written by various Star Callers of old, recording their respective Visions. Isabelle's Vision had not changed; it had only progressed becoming more unfathomable. She paused for a moment to bemoan her situation; it seemed the more thinking she did of late, the less progress she was making, even with the assistance of Eran and his wealth of resources, she always hit a brick wall. It wasn't just her Vision that concerned her, but also the horrifying texts found within The Book of the Early Past, the fifth volume in the series called *Ultimas*. Ancient symbols were scattered through its pages, seemingly devoid of any meaning or logic. They appeared to be messages, vague warnings regarding the power of the Glaphiar Spheres and The Celestial Souls. What did it all mean? What did it all point to? It hurt to think, so she did what anyone else would do in the situation and took a drink from the mug of strong tea set down beside her. Standing up, she walked over to the window. The day seemed mellow enough for those outside at least; her own world was troubled and shaken. Isabelle almost felt like sneaking off again, but such a plan would not be in her best interests. That reminded her; she owed Lethaniel an explanation, as well as her appreciation for his discretion concerning her behaviour. Isabelle's line of thought was interrupted by a knock at the door and she quickly pivoted around to see who was there? This would be her tenth visitor that day and probably not the last.

"Yes?" she called, and the muffled voice of one of her guards replied from behind the wooden door:

"Milady Star Caller, word has come from our furthest outpost that the Dovidian entourage is on its way."

"Is Desa with them?"

"All of the Ivulien leaders are on their way, this includes Akarnal Desa. You are also required downstairs."

"Of course I am," she muttered under her breath. She took her time preparing herself not feeling any urgency. Her long-staff, Violethelm was in the room with her, its purple orb fixed into the head of the five-foot golden pole, leaning up against the wall beside her wardrobe. For safety's sake, she now placed it inside the wardrobe and covered its head with a thin blanket. Strange, she had never done that before. Before she left her room she looked around for Pandora, but she was nowhere to be seen.

Lena stepped outside into the yard where Lucion and Thao had just finished training. She picked up one of their wooden swords, left piled on the dusty ground, and out of boredom she began to pick her nails with the end of it. Her hands were worn and dry, her nails brittle and beaten. She noticed her husband standing at the edge of the yard, staring out at the city, watching as the warm sun fell between Imrondel's array of towers.

"He is ready…" She turned her focus from her nails to him. "He is ready to move on from our back yard. I've taught him the basics, given him a head-start, drilled into him a soldiers routine and left him with words of The Honour Guards."

"So soon? Are you sure?"

"You know where he must go, where he wants to go," he replied, rubbing the back of his neck.

"Are you sure there is nothing more you can teach him here? I mean, he knows how to use a sword, but what about the spear and the shield? What about all the literal work and his training on the..." Thao shook his head; she knew already that Lucion could no longer keep learning this way, she knew that once he reached this stage he must move on to larger schools, built to transform boys into men, men into soldiers and soldiers into valiant Honour Guards of Knights of Krondathia. It was Lucion's time and they both knew it.

"He must go to the academy. I will talk to Scarto, he will make the arrangements." He thought back to the day he had left his own home to further his studies; back then he would never have expected to become one of Krondathia's finest warriors. "He is not going away forever; you will be able to see him once, maybe twice every year. Soon he will stand where I stand, with his own life."

"He'll be alright, won't he?" Lena tried to be brave but needed that little extra assurance.

"He is our son, of course, he will" Thao replied with pride. "I will give him my sword and everything else in due time."

"Even your armour?"

"The Organix Armour? No, he will have to earn it, though hopefully not in the same way as I."

"You did what you had to do my love. You ended a civil war, one that claimed thousands of lives. I know my words won't change the way you feel, but you didn't do anything wrong. You followed the orders necessary and thanks to you, more people are alive today, had it been allowed to carry on, who knows where we'd be" Lena could not penetrate his hard face, like he wanted to feel the pain, like he needed to. She kissed him softly, then left him alone with his view of the city. Lena had done all she could for Thao and for Lucion, but now she had to let them both go, at least for a while.

As Isabelle entered the large sitting room, she could see what was going on. A delicious buffet larger than the last had been laid out on a long dining table. She hesitated to enter, for Calias was currently helping himself alongside a few other court members. When she saw the welcoming faces of Yespin and Taktard, she entered and greeted them. After exchanging pleasantries, Yespin handed her a letter.

"For your eyes only. It arrived late this afternoon." Thanking him, she took the letter and found a relatively private space in the sitting room. Calias had been watching and now stared rudely as she opened the envelope. Pretending she hadn't noticed, Isabelle turned her back to him and read what was written.

Star Caller Verano

I am glad to hear all is well in Imrondel City and that you have performed so graciously during your stay there. I have never doubted you, Isabelle; I am also sad to hear that you will be leaving us for the cities of Ivulien. As much as I want you to stay in your homeland, I think it would be a bold and wise move to travel to Davune and spread Starillia's wings. All of this is hard to come to terms with; no Star Caller has ever made her home outside of Krondathia. This is history in the making and I believe what we are about to undertake, will only strengthen the civilisation of man.

Remember Isabelle, we are leaders, we must accept our responsibilities, however hard it may seem and wherever our paths may take us. I've been charged to care for Krondathia in your absence, I shall not fail you, I am willing to make that first step.

I have seen the future in my dreams, I've seen the end of your journey, and when you come full circle, we'll behold a world together that embraces Starillia, a world united under one banner. Such a dream to have, I wish I could share it with you, I wish you could see what I see as far away as it seems, but together we'll take that first step, and together we'll rest after the last.

My heart goes out to you my child. You are ready.

Eldor, Kastius Greylion

The letter bore his signature and seal, it had been written by his own hand. After reading the contents, it dawned on her that her perception of him had changed dramatically over the past few weeks. There was a time when she had held great respect for him; she had always thought of him as a mysterious, holy leader with many gifts. It had always seemed evident that The Eldor was wise and powerful and that no one else deserved the position more. Yet, it felt now that his mysticism and great attributes had worn off. She was now beginning to realise that he was just a regular man. The letter made her feel no different about the current circumstances. She returned to The High Councillors at the dining table.

"May I ask what it said?" requested Yespin, helping himself to some shellfish stew, a dish that contorted Isabelle's face.

"That I should go to Ivulien, that I'm ready to move on" she replied vaguely.

"We will miss your company, Isabelle. I have been told that the Dovidian leaders are on their way; an entire entourage it seems. It will be quite the occasion."

"Akarnal Desa is with them, he made growing up without a father bearable. I look forward to our re-unification. "

"When he and the others arrive, they will revise the treaty written by our prefects, they may request some alterations in which case, their stay may be extended. When they sign our treaty, you'll leave with them." Isabelle forked up some chicken and popped it in her mouth as Yespin spoke. "We summoned you here for two other reasons."

"I think I can guess what they are" said Isabelle playfully.

"The people need to know what happened to you inside Eliendras Cathedral. It is customary for Star Callers to reveal what

489

they are shown, as well as displaying the gifts they have received," explained Yespin.

"And the other reason?"

"For your company; it will be a long time before we see you again, soon enough our time here will end, and we'll be on the road back to Xiondel. Our cities may not always see eye to eye, but we're still Norkron born and so are you. Your absence will be noted" said Yespin, as Isabelle picked at the buffet. Yespin and Taktard found their comfortable leather seats and waited for her to join them, though she was reluctant to do so, for it was only a matter of time before they pressed her. All they wanted to know was what happened inside The Eliendras Cathedral, she suspected their praises that smoothly ran off the tip of Yespin's tongue, had been somewhat accentuated. She took her time in deciding what she wanted to eat and drink, noticing that Calias was directly opposite her, across the table.

"You should try these," he suggested, pointing to a plate. "Caught off the shores of Sapphire Views and sent here by the demand of the hierarchy. Because of their rarity, they are too expensive for the lower classes of Krondathia to enjoy." He held up a red prawn, placed on top of a slice of wheat bread smeared with a tangy looking sauce. Isabelle had tried the delicacy before; they were juicy and very tasty, apparently, they were served best at the Retreat in Xiondel City, a restaurant reserved for military personnel. She was so appalled by Calias's attitude that she decided to challenge him.

"Please excuse, I've a problem with fish."

Calias bit through the shell of a prawn and loaded up a few more on his plate "Your friends are getting impatient..." he mumbled while crunching up flesh "...Are you going to tell them what happened in The Cathedral? We are all dying to know."

Isabelle could not fake a smile for him, she had built a plate for herself to pick from and said under her breath "Careful Calias, you wouldn't want to choke on your food now, would you?" She poured herself a glass of wine and found an empty seat in the corner, closer to Yespin. "Where are the others?" she asked, setting the plate on the armrest.

"In their rooms in the palace. Raven Illiard, Marius Tilon and Nenphis Esquin are returning to Xiondel City tomorrow. Taktard, Darlo and I are staying here for a few more days, spending the time with you whenever we can. Souton Refefris and Julias Tarno are heading for Cuether on business, to meet with Minister Vou; he has a couple of youngsters who want to be considered for Glyph training." Isabelle's interest faded in and out, sipping the fruity red wine. "Arthur Thenyur has already departed and is on route back to Xiondel; the drug problem there is worsening, the crime rates increasing. He feels he must be where he belongs. As for Davien King and Barta Sage, they will be heading to The Pura Lands shortly, also for business-related matters" Yespin explained.

"Aren't you forgetting someone?"

"Ah, Landris. High Councillor Charity has been given some time off."

"Why is that?"

"We feel he has overworked himself; he needs some time to rest." *That makes two of us* thought Isabelle. "The young man is under stress. His duties will resume in Xiondel." Isabelle recalled what it was Cillian had said to her on the night of The Festival of The Awakening. She hoped she really did know what she was doing. She valued Cillian's advice over the other High Councillors.

The time she spent with the two councillors was pleasant enough, but as it grew darker outside, more important business had to be attended to. She could no longer steer the conversations away from the matter, having been doing for an impressive amount of time. Taktard was the one who finally asked the question:

"It's not that we want to be too forward with you Isabelle, but the people are wanting an answer, we want an answer. If they don't get one soon, rumours will spread throughout the city, people will start making their own assumptions as to what happened. I'm sure you agree that this is not a favourable outcome." Isabelle smiled and lowered her head.

"Taktard is right; if the people are not informed, they may assume the worst, last thing we need is a panic sprouting from an ill-informed populous" it was Yespins turn to refill their drinks, he topped Isabelle's up "Time to tell us what happened in Eliendras, Miss Verano?" The bottle was poured empty into Taktard's glass, he set it down on the coffee table and sat himself down, ready to hear her report. Isabelle had not the stomach for anymore wine as she fondled the glass's stem around her thin fingers.

"What if... What if I didn't know what happened?" Yespin and Taktard found what she said, hard to fathom. "I need more time to understand the message in its entirety before I address the city. I would not want to misinform them, or you." Isabelle's green irises found her red wine, she tilted the glass in a circular motion, watching the rich red rim the lip of the edge. "You've always supported me. Can you buy me a little more time?" Yespin leant back and scratched the back of his neck.

"Whatever our Star Caller needs." Isabelle sighed with relief and thanked them.

"How much time do you think you will need?" asked Taktard.

"This time tomorrow, I'll find you with an informed understanding."

"And if you cannot find the meaning to the message?" asked Taktard, border lining a demanding tone of voice as Isabelle pulled on her blue coat and slid the hood over her head.

"I'm sure Isabelle won't let us down, Taktard. Isabelle, I bid you a goodnight. Do alert The Palace Guard in the other room, they will take you back to your room" said Yespin, remaining seated.

Isabelle left the room and closed the double doors behind her, there were no guards present, they were in the other chamber next door, Isabelle could see them having removed their helmets participating in banter and a helping of some fine liquor in black bottles. Backing up away from the chamber door, she took off and ran through the deserted hallway and made for the exit of The Palace downstairs. Trotting down hundreds of marble stairs, through wide corridors and round bends she passed few people, so used to her presence here, spotting her marching from room to room was nothing out of the ordinary so they thought nothing of it, especially when Isabelle met them with a glowing smile. Getting passed the sentry guards however on the first floor could result in a problem if caught on these lower levels without an escort. They were not looking for her, so she had the advantage to dart by, it was also close coming up to supper and a shift change enabling Isabelle to make methodical moves. Sneaking from pillar to pillar, taking care to be light on her feet through open areas, she fell into a quiet reading room she knew was being refurbished, and took from the door hanger a priests robe. Inside the dark study she heard the faint tap of rain on the pane of a glass window. Pushing the window open, she was skinny enough to slide out, legs first, landing into a flower bed just outside. Rain was on the way; cool drops pat her face. Adjusting the hood, she made from shadow to shadow, she would have to hurry toward her destination if she were to avoid getting soaked from head to toe.

Knock knock knock! Isabelle was about to hammer on the door again when it sprang open, enveloping her in yellow light and a draught of air scented with paper. Her face dripping wet, the rain was consistent, manipulated by the swathes of wind.

"Isabelle!" exclaimed Master Eran holding a mug of tea "Do come in," he invited and stepped aside. Isabelle entered, wrapped up in the robe of a priest. Inside, his house was warm and welcoming, there were several bookcases filled to the brim with books next to each of the four walls, a small library in that of itself. A large desk fit nicely under the staircase, a cosy place where he occasionally worked well into the early hours. Some partially eaten bread and a few empty mugs had been left on its surface next to some aged candles. Eran tended to the dying fire and managed to get it going again. Pouring two mugs of his favourite tea, he sat down in a wooden chair opposite Isabelle, who had exchanged the stolen robes for a blanket. "In all my long years Isabelle, no matter what the problem is, I've found that tea sobers unruly thoughts."

"I'm sorry for disturbing you like this Master" she apologised, holding the warm mug close to her face.

"Ah not to worry. I wasn't sleeping, I was reviewing a lecture that I am due to give tomorrow. You're welcome to stay for a while."

"Thank you." They listened to the fire and the wind outside.

"Does anyone know you're here?" She shook her head and Eran sipped his tea.

"Master?"

"If anybody else had found you, they would have gone to an authority, and you'd be judged" said Eran, having been paid a visit by Braygon.

"I know" she said, undoubtedly agreeing.

"The entire world would know by now. Your reputation would be jeopardised, and the people's faith would be weakened..." he then leant forward "...But it was not just anybody, was it? It was Lethaniel."

"I owe him my thanks. In fact, I owe him a lot more than that," she admitted.

"Is that why you're here?" She took her time in answering.

"No" she said. "It's the bird, Master. The bird in the rafters."

"That's what you saw in The Cathedral?" She nodded once more.

"There was something else though, a being of some sort, an apparition..." She tried her best to explain but could not find the right words to keep her in the world of the sane. "It was not a person. It was something else, something elemental, something unreal. It was there; it came towards me. It told me things."

"What did it tell you?"

494

"It's a she" somehow this drew a smile "I could tell by the way it walked, the way it moved, it was a she."

"What did it tell you, Isabelle?"

"The same old thing: *Elaso fiin an ute fiin tressa. Elaso fiin. Elaso fiin.* I whispered to The Celestials and felt nothing, but then the bird appeared when I opened my eyes. It stared at me, a bird with black feathers that should have been white. A black dove... It was a black dove. I know what I saw."

"A black dove," he whispered.

"The dove looked at me for so long. After I left the room, I returned later to see to it, but it had gone." Eran scratched his short, white beard. "What is happening?" Isabelle needed an answer, anything! But Eran was unable to deliver anything of substance.

"Maybe Master Atheriax can offer you more than I can. He's your best option."

"Atheriax was last seen departing Xiondel, heading for a site in Ophiadras, he is not an option, Master" said Isabelle having received recent word from someone on his behalf.

"Set up a meeting with The Readers, you've a small chance, but you'll never know if you do not try."

"What if I'm denied access, Master, where then do I go?" she questioned, feeling lightheaded.

"You've only a final option if the prior fail, not one I'd recommend or encourage, I just hope you're granted clearance" he said, drinking some more tea.

"What is the final option?"

"Get your answers by any means necessary" Eran set the mug on the table after finishing. Isabelle did the same. "These signs are mysterious, reminiscent. Review your work again when you have the chance, and do not worry about the people or The High Councillors, I will speak to them for you" he assured.

"You're the best Master, always have been." She sprawled out on the couch, her speech slurring. "I can't see myself in my own Visions. Do you know why?" She had barely finished speaking when she fell into a deep sleep, leaving her question unanswered.

Lethaniel woke up in his bed early in the morning. He dragged himself up and went through his usual routine. His room was a mess, but a manageable one in which he knew where everything was. A few frames hung on the walls with beautiful paintings of distant locations; one depicted a battle fought long ago. Hanging off its frame was the necklace Eva had given him; He unlocked his balcony doors and stepped outside to a mild breeze, which felt good on his face, freshly shaven. He noticed Alexius out on his own balcony a few doors down, flicking away the remnants of his morning smoke. As usual, they met at the end of the path, where the estate of fine houses ended. The two walked down the road towards the nearest place that sold breakfast. Alexius rolled up another and final spoke.

"Good morning."

"Morning," Lethaniel replied, once again refusing his friend's offer of a roll up.

"Any news?" asked Alexius, popping it into his mouth.

"Received word from the courier we sent out to check on the Dovidians' progress. They should be arriving within the next week."

"What about Mathias, any news there?"

"Nothing. I'm tempted to go up there myself and find out what's going on."

"I was thinking the same thing" and Alexius widely, stretched his arms and bent his back.

"Are the plans set? Is everything ready?"

"All is set, Lex. The only thing stopping us from setting out right now is my order."

"I think I can guess why," groaned Alexius, and they both looked at each other thinking the same thing.

"Othello could be a useful resource, he lived among the clans for years, know their ways. I am going to talk to him again before we set out. Maybe I can change his mind."

"Have you offered him..." Lethaniel interrupted, having already made the necessary steps.

"Yes, he is not interested in land or wealth; his cares go deeper, which makes it harder for me to recruit."

Isabelle opened her eyes as the morning light crept in through the closed, green curtains. The nearby fireplace had completely died out, and the smell of charred wood tingled her nose. Then she realised where she was and where she was meant to be! In a panic, she pushed away the blanket that had been set over her sometime during the night and hurried frantically to the door.

"Don't panic, young one, they know you're here," Eran assured her, coming down the wooden stairs, fully dressed and ready for work in The Old Library. "You fell asleep on my sofa last night. One minute you were here, the next you were gone. I didn't want to wake you. You were exhausted." Isabelle breathed a sigh of relief.

"Where would I be without you Master?"

"Don't mention it. Would you like something to drink?" She accepted gratefully and sat back down next to the fireplace, poking the ash with a brass rod. "Something to eat maybe?" Eran called from the stove room.

"No thank you, Master, I must be heading back soon." She continued to play about with the ash and thought about the bird she had seen in Eliendras. She abandoned her crusade to break up the charred log in the fireplace and stood, to have a quick look around Eran's house. The desk under the staircase had been cleared, leaving a flat, polished, wooden surface. She scanned the bookshelves and pulled out a book about birds. Opening it, she flicked through the pages and admired the detailed drawings, she didn't expect to find anything to do with her bird in here, but it was worth a study. Surely Eran would have been able to give her answers last night if the species had been listed within its pages.

"I have been meaning to ask you, how have your Visions been?"

"The same; I still do not know what they mean, though I will find out soon, hopefully," she replied. "You're teaching a lecture today, may I come along? I must do something important before I run out of time."

"Of course you can come along, Isabelle. You'll probably know everything I am going to teach but be my guest."

"I've been meaning to give something to someone, a friend of mine," she said, moving to the window and gently siding the curtains to peer outside. The ground was damp and fat droplets of water rolled down the windowpane. "Are there people living in Imrondel City without windows?"

"Quite possibly, but Imrondel is not the problem these days. Xiondel has many, many issues that need dealing with," replied the Master.

"Long ago they called Xiondel The Glass City, for everything passed through it: knowledge, power, wealth, wisdom and faith. It was a wondrous city at one point in history, but now, now it is falling into slow decay."

Chapter 23 - High Hopes

Acting on impulse.

Othello and Ethan lifted the last crate together and loaded it into the back of a supply carriage with a sizeable trailer. These boxes would be sent to the town of Cuether. It had been an unusually busy morning at The Trade Distribution Centre, with men and women running all over the place. Carriages coming and going, the heat of the day rising and falling, getting under everyone's skin. The last load of supplies destined for The Pura Lands, Xiondel City and Cuether had been intercepted by Dark Rogues; this was the reason why there was so much more work to do, they were behind. Imrondel had to make up for the lost cargo and do so quickly if the Norkrons in those far off places were to see the goods in a reasonable time.

"I wonder what's in these crates," Othello muttered.

"Can't even take a peek, I know. These ones are locked up well. No one can break these locks," Ethan replied, tapping one of the hefty padlocks with his foot. Othello read the details recorded on the small document nailed to the wooden crates...

Shipment Load - 141 / 300
Departure Base - Imrondel City Trade Distribution Centre
Destination - Cuether
Cargo - Twenty-Four Wooden Crates
Contents of Cargo - Building Materials; Work Tools; Long Wood; Slate Rock; Glass Panes;
Requested by - Minister Vou

"Interesting. Still requires a signature from The Peacekeeper. Nothing inside these but building supplies, mostly, and work-related tools. Strange..."

"Why is that strange?" Ethan asked.

"Why would The Dark Rogues want to get their hands-on building supplies? From what I've heard they live in the woods."

"Something doesn't add up there, does it?" Othello thought for a bit; maybe he could pry it open quickly and pretend it was damaged. "Who cares? The sooner we get this done, the sooner we can go home," continued Ethan, sounding happy at the idea of finishing for the day. The soldiers that were to escort the extra supplies had nowhere else to go for the time being, so they hung around in a group on the side of the road, near to where the loaders were working. The military men were bored, sick of the heat and worst of all, full of themselves. The two loaders worked solidly through the morning, without break or rest. Ethan wanted to finish early, while Othello was most certainly looking forward to the evening, getting up that morning had been difficult due to the activities of the night before. It would seem that Ethan had grown stronger since Othello's enrolment as a Regular soldier. His training was paying off and it was beginning to show; his stamina had increased, and his arms had become toned, defining the muscle. The cool breeze certainly didn't hinder the work of the loaders, offsetting the harsh effects of the beating sun. Ethan stood by the driver of the carriage, filling out some forms on a clipboard using a feathered pen. "Good day to you sir. Have a safe trip." Othello slid in the final crate along with another loader, raised the flat door and locked it shut, before tapping on the side of the full carriage. As he turned back to Ethan, he couldn't help but notice the painful looking bruises on his arm. They waited for another supply carriage to arrive and Othello took this short break as an opportunity to talk to Ethan. Even though he had gotten stronger and fitter, he was looking a little worse for wear. Othello had noticed him struggle with certain movements while lifting the heavier crates, large tools, and concrete blocks.

"What happened to your arm?"

"What… Oh, that, it's nothing. My instructor is a former Honour Guard I think, he doesn't allow for mistakes or look too kindly on those who fail to uphold a sword routine. He has a way to deal with failures," replied Ethan.

"Your instructor did this to you!? He shouldn't have done, it's against regulations. What use are soldiers who can't use their arms? Why did he do this?" Ethan rolled down his sleeve to hide the bruise; he appreciated Othello's affection but didn't really want the attention to draw on him. The bored soldiers were watching the pair talk.

"I messed up during methods Othello. Methods are when you learn a particular type of…"

"I know what methods are Ethan, no need to explain," he interjected, rolling the sleeve back up, to take a better look at the damaged skin.

"Othello, it's nothing really," insisted Ethan, as his friend examined him further.

"It's not only your arm that has been bothering you, is it? I've noticed. If you push yourself too hard, you'll break. It doesn't take much to cripple a person, all it takes is the right knock in the right spot and that person is no longer a threat. I've seen it happen. The worst thing is that when the damage has been inflicted the person who received the blow is aware he'll be crippled for life. Your instructor should know this," Othello spoke seriously, from experience.

"My instructor said that when you're out on the field of battle, pain is a burden we all must deal with, that pain comes later. I'm thinking of this as training and mental preparation," Ethan explained, making excuses for himself.

"Look around my friend; we are loading food, tools and building equipment in the middle of a functioning city. Eva tells me, even though she doesn't believe it herself personally, that soon there will be no need for soldiers, that Equis will become whole."

"She refers to what The Chosen has proposed, I believe that day will come eventually Othello, but for now, I think we have a lot of work to do. This paradise people are talking about is in our sights. It will be one fine day when The Military District is torn down to make room for more substantial things, but it won't build itself."

"Yeah, I agree; think of the number of crates we will have to shift then. Come on, I am getting you to a healer. Where I'm from we had a remarkable healer," ordered Othello, wishing he could pay Vontarg a visit right now.

"We don't call them healers here," remarked Ethan, and Othello scratched his forehead, feeling a little embarrassed.

"Oh, what do you call them?"

"Medics, or doctors." Othello went off and had a word with another loader; he simply said that he would be gone for a little while to find a medic for Ethan, just to have a quick look at his arm. The loader agreed and Othello began to walk off, away from his post; needless to say, this got the attention of the nearby soldiers who had been standing by watching the workforce all morning.

"You! Where do you think you're going? You've got work to do," one called out, glaring at Othello with a fair number of his men behind him; all were suited up in the standard silver armour, these were Regulars of Xiondel's army. Othello looked around in confusion; was the guard talking to him? All the work had been done as far as Othello could tell, and the loaders were simply waiting for the next supply cart to arrive.

"I am going to find someone; my friend's working with one arm here. I won't be gone long, but I think it's best he gets it checked out," replied Othello. The soldier took one look at Ethan.

"He has been working well enough all day, he can last, now get back to work yourself. You aren't allowed to be leaving your post" the soldier spoke rudely, getting the attention of the other loaders who never spoke out against anyone of authority, not wanting to run the risk of getting a complaint filed against them, or worse, suffer a beating. No one wanted any trouble. The soldier sat safely within his fellows, surrounding him and viewing Othello, sucking back on bottled beer, drinking from an opened beverage crate with no Captain in sight. Othello double checked that all the work had been done, up until the arrival of the next supply caravan, this they did not appreciate, some of them noted his appearance in a degrading manner. The delivery was obviously running late, this would be the perfect time to fetch someone to look at Ethan's arm who was encouraging Othello to let it go.

"I am still going" said Othello, removing his work gloves while moving along the stone road. The guard however, swiftly stood up, leaving the safety of his boys who stood at his side, blocking Othello's path, pushing him back a few steps. They all had swords sheathed at their sides, and some had kite shields strapped to their backs.

"Are you fucking simple? I am the soldier, you're a loader. Get back to work or I'll drop you like a sack of shit!" Othello said nothing; instead, he just stood there as the soldier got into his face, chest out, standing over him. It did not have the effect he wanted, for Othello was not phased or giving him an inch.

"Let me pass, I won't ask again," warned Othello, tightening his hand into a fist of rock.

"You're the one who comes from the northland" said one of the other soldiers, wagging a finger at Othello. "Yes, you fucking are, we heard about you. Fancy bumping into the only one with a fucking attitude problem." The soldiers joined in the mockery, one flicking pieces of a dry cracker he had been eating at Othello, who took it, squeezing his wrists one at a time.

"Dust dwellers and dirty fucking mud wrestlers the lot of them, fucking animals" cursed the centre soldier taking his eyes off Othello to enjoy the joke. Unfortunately for him it would be the last thing he would say for some time.

Like lightening Othello lunged at the soldiers with a fist that could break a wall. He smashed out the soldiers two front teeth and dented the bridge of his nose with the one punch, dropping into the ground, spitting out blood and pieces of teeth. One of his mates drew his sword and went for Othello, grabbed the hilt of the weapon and with all of his strength twisted the man's wrist around and pulled the soldier's arm out of place, up taking a manoeuvre he had learned in the fighting pits; the squeak of steel, the crack of bone, followed by the shriek of pain sent a clear message to the other Regulars, a message of *Don't fuck with me!* Othello now had possession of the sword and pointed it at the others, his favoured stance. He looked down at the broken guard with no sympathy and stepped over him, to find a healer or a doctor as they were called in these parts. Tossing the sword aside, the soldiers sheathed their blades and gave Othello as much room as he wanted. The loaders watched him leave, unable to talk until he was out of sight.

Isabelle had made her way back to The Palace and climbed the long stairway up without meeting a single person along the way. She entered her own room and expected Pandora to welcome her, but as it would appear, she was elsewhere. She took a key out of the drawer, knelt beside her bed, and reached under, pulling out a wooden chest. Using the key, she opened it. Inside were various bits and pieces, including some of her favourite books, one entitled *The Helter Spiral*, covered with a few strange necklaces and pieces of intricate jewellery. Through her travels and experiences, she had collected as many memories as possible, to help remind herself of where she had gone, what she had seen and who she had met with each piece having a story behind it. The most recent of memories was the dagger given to her by Teo, The Dark Rogue. She moved aside some of these things and lifted out an arm's length, unscathed black box. She removed its lid to check if its contents were all in order, it was. Satisfied, she took the black box and closed the chest, pushed it back under her bed with her foot. Guards escorted her out of The Palace as usual and followed her wherever she went; in this case, it would be to The Old Library. She had something to deliver, a job to do before she left Imrondel. As she distanced herself from the palace, Teo spied upon her, disguised under a hooded cloak among the other citizens walking to work.

Othello returned with several 'doctors' who immediately saw the disabled soldiers and rushed to them. The other attended to Ethan.

"Othello, how did you do that?" said Ethan, casually as the doctor touched the bruises, assessing the damage.

"Who is your instructor? I want to meet him," Othello replied, ignoring Ethan's question.

504

"His name is Barthul. Are you interested in joining the Regulars, Othello?" Ethan asked with a slight grin on his face as the medic bandaged him up. Othello did not respond, but his face did lighten up after Ethan mentioned the name, Barthul. "So tell me about you and Eva?" Before Othello could say anything, two guards and a Captain took him by the arms and pushed him up against the nearest wall.

"They say that you are the one responsible for this?" cried the Captain.

"I am!" answered Othello.

"Then I have no choice but to arrest you on the charges of…"

"HOLD that sentence Captain. Witnesses here reported what happened and it was not the fault of this man" said Lethaniel.

"I've got two of my boys crippled, one will be eating through a tube for six months because of what HE did" the Captain argued, pointing at Othello.

"He was acting in self-defence. Your boys are in dire need of discipline and further training, I am suspending the whole group from service until they meet a qualified level and I am thinking Captain, of including he who failed to intervene" Lethaniel held out his arms, shrugging "It's your call?" said Lethaniel. The Xiondel Captain dropped his defensive tone, and hesitantly agreed with The General.

"I'll enforce your order" he said.

"Be sure you do Captain" said Lethaniel, placing his hands on his hips as he walked away, pulling one of his boys by the collar, hustling them together.

"Thank you, Lethaniel" said Othello. Lethaniel acknowledged this with a respectful nod.

"I apologise for their behaviour. As hard as I work to eradicate these shits I never seem to get them all."

"You have come for my answer, have you not?" enquired Othello.

"Walk with me." Othello followed Lethaniel away from The Distribution Centre; even though there was still much work to be done, Lethaniel's authority was not to be questioned. They walked through the gardens and passed the gardeners who tended to the green with rakes and other tools, they head toward the great wall of Imrondel, making small talk as they went, conversing about Othello's techniques. Their conversation steered back to topical concerns. "So you've thought about what I said? What's your answer?" Lethaniel asked, looking directly at Othello.

"I'll do it General. I will accompany you and Lethaniel smiled.

"Glad to hear that Othello, welcome aboard" and they shook hands.

"I would like to know some things if that is alright?" asked Othello.

"We usually disclose this information as a group, but fire away Othello."

"I want to know who is threatening us. Which Clan or faction has you taking to arms?"

"We know they're from the northlands; they travel light, fast and spare no one. We have yet to link them to any one group of The Chimera Order" answered Lethaniel. To Othello, it sounded like Xavien, The Demon Man, which warmed his heart. If he were invading, then he and his Blood Marauders would not be hunting The Bevork Clan. "Our Norfoon Scouts put their number at around fifty to a hundred, but there could be more, we are certainly preparing for the likelihood of more. We'll counter the invasion with with Visarlian Knights, Honour Guards and those stationed with Commander Sious at Thnel. Our army will remain in Imrondel" Lethaniel specified.

"Terrain?" from the way Othello spoke, in such a military manner, armed him with clues as to his history, he had definitely spent time around soldiers.

"We shall be travelling east until we reach the mountains of Thnel, also known as The Livale Peaks. From there, we will find the Norfoon Watch Towers." Othello knew this place but had never been there; he had only passed it during his long trek from Jureai to Imrondel. The pair came to the top of the wall. Othello looked out to the bleak weather and flat grassy plain outside the city. "We leave as soon as the Dovidians arrive for our Star Caller, after they sign the treaty; we will slip out at nightfall, and ride till morning." Lethaniel explained. Othello leant on the wall's edge, still admiring the view, enjoying the wind on his face. "Is there anything else?" Othello turned, remembering something.

"I want to be a Regular, a Regular in Ethan Frost's unit." Intrigued, Lethaniel had to confirm Othello's decision.

"Under Barthul?" Othello dipped his head in certainty. Lethaniel took a moment and gazed to the stretch of city. "Alright, if that's what you want, you'll have to address me accordingly" said Lethaniel. Othello seemed to appreciate this. Lethaniel slid his hands into his pockets and asked. "What part of your order do you represent?"

"The Hawk, General"

"Interesting" Lethaniel whispered "You must know El Raud?"

"I do"

"And the Chieftainess Reneeia? Do you know her and the others?" asked Lethaniel. Othello paused before he answered.

"Yes." Noting Othello's guarded tone, Lethaniel joined him leaning on the wall. Their shoulders perfectly aligned. They listened to the wind and the work of the men below in The Defensive Trench. "What you did today was wrong." Othello looked at Lethaniel. "Those men might have deserved what happened, but as a soldier, as any great soldier would tell you in Krondathia, staying your hand

507

rather than forcing it, is a true test of a man's power. It is easier to answer in bloodshed, than to respond with mercy."

"Men should be punished for their crimes" Othello said in response.

"There are times when this is true, drawing one's sword is sometimes necessary, but Othello, greater men are those who settle their differences without the use of steel. How are men to change if you leave them crippled?" Lethaniel tapped him on the shoulder pushed off the wall's walkway. "You may be instructed under Barthul. You and Ethan may take the rest of the day off. Be at the barracks tomorrow at daybreak. I'll let your superior know of the transition and Barthul to know you're joining" he said, trotting down the steep stone stairs, leaving The Defensive Trench. Othello, however, stayed at the top of the main front wall, taking in the fresh air.

Isabelle told her guards to wait outside while she went into The Old Library. She could see that Eran had already begun his lecture, his deep, cultured voice echoed through the great hall. This time the number of students had doubled. Master Eran acknowledged her entrance who made a subtle upward gesture, signalling that Adarmier was somewhere upstairs. Isabelle walked passed the students and toward the iron, spiral staircase where she made her way up to the highest level. It rattled as she climbed the stairs, her boots tapping upon its metallic surface. Finally, she reached the top floor, not quite the attic of The Old Library but was the highest level for sure. The light wasn't perfect up here, it appeared darker and the entire floor felt constricted and closer to together. The dust shroud was thick and made Isabelle cough; the dust could only be seen through the few rays of light that beamed down through small, triangular windows fitted high into the slanting ceiling of the building. The light above completed a circle upon an open space of floor, somewhere behind this bright warm light, sat Adarmier, reading as always. Isabelle approached and stood in the centre of the light, where she knelt and put the black box on the floor between them.

"They don't allow students up here. Eran says they are not ready for what the pages in these books hold," murmured a glum voice from the darkness.

"Eran thinks very highly of you, as do I, Adarmier" she said, looking directly at him.

"It feels good to be noticed, doesn't it?" he noted, turning a page in the dark.

"Sometimes," she replied.

"It feels good to know that I am not like them"

"Like whom?"

"Like everyone else. The other students talk about me, laugh at me for being different. Do you know what I say in my defence?" He closed his book and left her to her response.

"What do you say in your defence, Adarmier?"

"Nothing, because they won't understand. Not until their lives become prisons due to their poor choices. I pity them." Isabelle, rest a hand on the black box.

"I have something for you, Adarmier, something very valuable, someone such as yourself will appreciate." She pushed the box toward him; he came closer and was now under the beam of light with her, he knelt to the floor and clicked open the lid. As he lifted the lid Isabelle saw a sudden change in his face, one of awe and amazement. "That was mine. Given to me by the twenty-second Star Caller, Freya Delmesca." Adarmier placed his hand upon the most beautifully crafted half staff he had ever seen in. "Go ahead. Pick it up, she needs a new wielder," she told him as he carefully placed his hands under it and took it out of its case. The half staff itself was grand to look at; black but reflected a blue tinge with an essence of shimmering silvers. Towards its point, it entwined around itself and curved into a leaf's edge. In length is was as long as a man's forearm, weighing as much as knife. The texture felt good against his skin, as hard as marble. Adarmier held the half staff would he be in a

509

defensive pose. Isabelle stood up and checked his composure, using her hands to even him out. "Yes, this half staff suits you," she remarked, straightening Adarmier's back and neck while circling him like a mother would her child. "The sheath is in the case; wrap it around your waist. Look after it, keep it at hand, respect the energy that will pass through it, and one day, it will save your life and the life of another close to you. I promise" she touched his shoulder "I am sorry, about your mother, I wouldn't wish that pain on my greatest enemy." She had to leave and made for the spiral staircase.

"Isabelle!" said Adarmier, still in awe over the staff. "This staff is meant for your successor, a girl no doubt, the one who will one day take your place as Chosen. I will never be those things" he protested.

"No, you won't, but it feels good to break a rule now and then doesn't it?" They broke into a smile "Keep it with you, farewell." She left The Old Library without disturbing Eran during his lecture.

"Back to The Palace, my lady?" one of the guards said.

"To Norisis" she confirmed. As they made their way back, Isabelle caught sight of something familiar, a movement following them from her right and then from her left. Aware not to alert her guards, she kept her eyes and senses open. When she looked passed the people or down the separate roads, she spotted nothing. She would check individual faces and could have sworn she saw Teo spying on her from under his hood. Seizing her opportunity, she split from the designated path and down a separate road, the guards didn't even know she had gone until a few seconds later when they realised she was not following them and broke formation to find her, and soon they would.

"Isabelle!" called Teo, coming from around the corner, slowing down from a run. She backed away from him, putting many feet between them. "Isabelle! I need to talk with you."

"STOP! Don't come any closer. Stay there!" she warned, interrupting him, her eyes flashing green. Teo waited for her explanation. "Is it true?" she asked.

"Is what true?" he questioned.

"Don't play with me Teo, I am tired of hunting for the truth at every bend. Tell me, please" she cried. His silence was his response. "I guess it makes sense" she said, her anger transforming into humour. "How could I have been so stupid?" Teo stayed quiet as she deconstructed her recent travels "You unlocked the lock, didn't you? The lock on the metal box that contained the book, right?" Teo gave the slightest of nods. "You must have read my letter too, in my cabin on The Zodias Island? I could have sworn it had moved" the deduction of evidence continued "You were following through The Silent Vale. Lethaniel was right, it must have been you inside The Glyph Dome when I gave my performance to The High Councillors of Virtue and no one but a Dark Rogue could have evaded capture when cornered, say inside Eliendras?"

"You are a terrific dancer" said Teo, his only response.

"What about that burn around your neck! What is that all about? A close encounter perhaps?" That mark had been annoying her ever since she had seen it. When she mentioned the scar, his eyelids fell softly. "Why did you lie to me?" she asked, drunk on disappointment.

"I did not lie, I chose not to tell you Isabelle, there is a difference." Enraged she doused the Glyph boiling inside her veins, her eyes rising into light, only to quickly fade.

"Did you kill the boy because he spotted you?" Teo's face did contort into something of confusion when faced with the accusation.

"We didn't kill anyone" he said with a stern voice.

"WE?! You mean there are more than one of you here?!" she shouted "Do hurry, there is something of a time issue here" hearing her guards relaying orders to search the road they were on.

"Yes, we! My wing is nearby watching but you'll never catch us Isabelle" the guards metal feet were drawing near "The only way I'll see a cell tonight is if you stop me." Teo saw the flicker of green in her eyes, the surge of Glyph coursing through her like she would unleash it at any moment.

"Isabelle!" one of her guards called, catching up to her "Where did you go?" The guard called to the others, signalling she was safe.

"I'm sorry I must have fallen behind and got a lost, this city is so big" she said, putting a hand to her brow in embarrassment. "Take me back to the city would you" she ordered, and they left the street.

Othello did not return to his cold place, instead he walked through a richer estate of Imrondel. The houses were neatly spread apart, and some had their own gardens of notable size. Taking to a set of steps Othello entered a house and was greeted with the smell of intoxicating herbs found in the north. It smelt like home. Putting down some goods in the hallway he found Eva, sleeping face down on a soft feathered bed and quietly perched next to her, listening to her therapeutic breathing. He wanted to join her but had not the heart to disturb her dreams. Taking off his top, he removed his work boots and laid next to her, gently caressing her bare back with the tip of his fingers, her skin as smooth as silk, her scent as sweet as alyssum, her warmth as radiant as a sunbeam. She stirred in her sleep, almost awake.

"Hello there. I am sorry to wake you" he whispered in her ear.

"It's fine, as long as it's you," she whispered rolling onto her back beneath him. Othello did not stop his flowing touch and glided over her hips. "I like your style, you woke me up just to send me back to sleep again, right?" and Othello nodded, transfixed on the muscle tone of her midriff. "I'm no fool, Mr; I know what you're doing," she blissfully giggled.

"I'll stop if you like. I'll let you sleep while I cook you something to eat" he said, taking his hand away.

"No, keep doing what you're doing for a little while" teased Eva "And don't worry about cooking for me, I've something bubbling for you in the stove room. Hope you like it."

512

"It smells very familiar" said Othello, having eaten such meals in Jureai.

"It was my first attempt so be mindful of my feelings" she said, hanging her arms around his neck.

"Even if it's revolting, I'll lie to your face and say it's perfect" said Othello, kissing her passionately.

"We can always go out if you're that disgusted" she laughed "Come on, let's eat, I can tell you how I was almost swindled for half my zeal over a herb worth less than a piece of silver" and she jumped up onto her feet and offered her hands to help Othello.

"I had an interesting day myself Eva, you might have to brace yourself."

Chapter 24 - Rules to Be Broken

Telling the truth and standing up for what you believe in makes you more of a human being, but that doesn't mean it's always right.

Lethaniel threw down a short letter onto the large table inside the strategy room of the barracks. The letter landed in front of Thao who glanced at it from his chair, leaning over the paper as he sliced through an apple with a small cutting knife.

"The Dovidians must have passed The Western Korthium Outpost by now, when they pass a rider will be sent to us to speed word, standard procedure Lethaniel it will be fine" said Thao, not sounding overly concerned as he crunched up a sliver of fruit.

"Why would a member of the court write to us if there was no need?" Lethaniel argued, pacing from left to right his hands on his hips. Thao sighed.

"Because they are itching for progress" hissed Thao. Lethaniel was in no mood. "So, the Dovidians are late General, don't let that impulsive head of yours get the better of you, I know what you're like..." said Thao waggling the knife his way. "It's a large entourage, we've had rain, it looks as though winter will arrive early this year and it's a different land for them, not what they're used to, far more troublesome terrain wise, so just relax will you." The General gave him a scowl and continued moving around the room. He reached for the letter and read through it quickly squinting his eyes, but still, it did not sway him. "We're heading east soon need I remind? Our men are prepped and assembled for The Barbarian Raid; All that is left is the go ahead, which is down to you, or me once I get sick of the sight of you...Lethaniel they will arrive, Desa will sign and leave with our Chosen. Stick to the plan" advised Thao.

"You're right. I'll give it one more day. I will inform Calias who will inform our Sire" said Lethaniel, writing up a document, folding it and sealed it with a wax stamp.

"That's my boy" said Thao nibbling on the core of the apple. "Doesn't Alexius usually deliver your messages?" he asked, as Lethaniel pushed open the doors to leave the room.

"Yeah, but he is still drunk from the festival. If anyone else called it as it was I'd tell them to not set foot in this barracks again, but because he is so fucking brilliant at his job he scores a pass" answered Lethaniel, handing the response letter to another courier. Lethaniel gave him some instructions and off he went. Thao cleaned off his hands with a cloth and joined The General outside, his arms folded, looking out to all the squads of men training in the cold yards sectioned off for units to exercise and run methods, with their squad leaders setting the pace. Lethaniel could remember this part of the day very well, he once being in their shoes, he knew how tedious and how boring it could become lapping the district, forcing yourself to do that one extra lift or push-up in the mud all before your first coffee. Some trained in knife throwing and target practices with crossbows putting bolts into marked, dummy targets. Other units paired off and wrestled, or trained with other weapons made of wood, advancing their skills move up the ladder of status. One particular unit of Regulars caught Lethaniel's stare.

"What are you looking at?" asked Thao, attempting to see what Lethaniel saw. However, Lethaniel didn't answer. Thao soon realised and watched with as much interest and curiosity from the doorway as The General.

The training men, dressed in their regular clothes, had lined up, backs straight and attention forward, facing and listening to Commander Barthul, discharged from The Honour Guard, renowned for his unorthodox ways in training his units. The turnover rate for Regulars under Barthul was higher than any other squad leader, yet those who survived his trials often turned into reliable disciplined soldiers. Barthul was taller and stronger than every man in his squad; naturally, he would be, for he had the bones and the build of someone who would pass for an Honour Guard, he was even a little bit bigger than their Commander, Thao Hikonle, although unlike Thao who commanded respect and honour, Barthul inspired dread. He stood before his men, looking down upon them with his brutish bald head displeased with his units assembly after they had just completed a lap around the district not even given the time to dress into Regular undergarments. The men were sweating, panting, their legs burning, doing their best not to look Barthul in the eye for too long, doing their best not to look like they were avoiding his stare. He wore a thick, black leather vest, his arms were mighty, pale and bare, arms that would rival the strength of a bear.

"Pitiful, the would-be soldiers of this city who cannot even run a district without keeling over. Though I guess you pathetic skid wipes are not all to blame, it's that meat sack of a woman you call your mother, and the bundle of brittle twigs that she let penetrate her are the one's responsible for your miserable lives. By The Celestials what happened to the men of Krondathia?" he moaned as he patrolled up and down the lines of his unit. "I can smell your stink. I can taste your fear it's repulsive, you reek of it, the lot of you." He stopped his patrol and gently pointed his finger at his unit having arrived at an idea for their day in the yard "You're not men today, you understand, you're not men, you're a centipede, and like that filthy insect you will work together and do as I tell you. You will run where I tell you to run, lift what I tell you to lift, fight who I tell you to fight and if I want you to take a shit in front of the whole platoon, you will do exactly that. Failure to comply will result in pain to each and every one of you. Don't be the shit stain that condemns your squad, because I'll make time for each of you" said Barthul with a fiendish grin, baring his white teeth yet one in the corner of his mouth was missing. When he shouted it made the odd man flinch in his position, but not Othello who had not picked up a sweat. When Barthul had his back turned to the squad, the men seemed to take in as much air as they could, doing their best to recover from the lap. One man, who had walked the last part of the way turned up late and tried sneaking into a line at the rear of the unit. His hopes of Barthul not noticing fell like a sack of bricks as Barthul spotted him and made his way over! Pushing through some men, one was Othello and Ethan, Barthul looked at the dishonest man while grinding his teeth. "It's your lucky day men, this volunteer will be the example should you fail to follow or keep up with the rules. Barthul grabbed him by the collar with his huge fist and pulled him to the front of the squad. He lifted his hand up with his own so all could clearly see, Barthul picked out the man's middle finger, looked into those terrified eyes as he enclosed his fist around the finger, and snapped it backwards! As easy as it was to break a twig. The bones split through the man's skin and a scream shot out into the sky.

Lethaniel and Thao had watched from the high ridge at the barracks from a distance. "That's it! Have Barthul arrested and detained; he will no longer train these men. I've warned the fucker before, but he carries on" angered Thao, calling over Neraal to apprehend Barthul.

"Wait, Thao!" snapped Lethaniel. Thao ordered Neraal to hold. Othello, broke formation and made his way through the squad.

"May this be a lesson to anyone who tries to cut corners or break my rules. For every rule you break, I'll break a finger" Barthul kicked the crippled man writhing in pain on his knees at his feet "Empires were not founded on the backs of men like this, his kind are the ones that let them topple."

"No, but they remember" said Othello and Barthul homed in on the voice.

"Who are you?" Barthul's mind caught up to him and he remembered. "Ah yes, you're the new one, little huntsman playing soldier" scowled Barthul coming close to Othello; he was a head taller and much larger in every way, yet Othello, did not give anyt ground, and let Barthul measure him up from head to toe, he drew in so close he could feel his warm, unpleasant breath on his face. Barthul stared at him, searching for Othello's fear but to his disappointment, The Northlander stared right back. "What are YOU going to do dust-dweller?" insulted Barthul grinding his teeth in his mouth and Othello remained stationary. Losing patience Barthul gripped Othello as he had done the other and threw him into a rack of wooden training swords. Thao was about to step in, but once again, Lethaniel put his arm in the way of his path, watching with anticipation. Othello lay on the floor, buried in weapons, and picked himself up. Barthul found his own, stood across from Othello and granted him a fair challenge for not cowering. "Your balls are bigger than most, I can respect that, so I'll give you a chance to pick up a sword and fight me." The squad's eyes fell on Othello, who did indeed pick up a training sword, examined it for a moment, and tossed it at the feet of Barthul.

517

"None of these swords feel right, I'll pass" said Othello. The squad had lost their formal pose and watched the pair like they watched a show, and a tingle of humility crawled up Barthul's spine. "Pick up the sword or I'll thrash the whole squad after I beat you into the ground!" cried Barthul, spitting anger. Othello squeezed his wrists one at a time as Barthul closed in to break him.

Othello slanted himself to the side avoiding Barthul's predictable, right hook and threw his own fist as fast and as hard as he could across Barthul's face, taking a shocking blow he had never felt before. Othello grabbed his head with both hands, giving himself leverage to knee the brute in the groin, putting Barthul on his knees trying to contain the pain with a gripped hand. Othello did not hesitate and followed up his attack with an uppercut, cracking against the chin of Barthul putting the squad leader, a former Honour Guard into the mud. Barthul's nose streamed blood, his was cheek bruised and a few teeth were missing, but he was not out cold to Othello's surprise, so he waited patiently for him to find his feet. Othello picked up a wooden sword and flicked it over and caught the would-be blade "All too fucking easy" he muttered and swung the hilt against Barthul's skull, finishing the job and dropped the splintered training sword. Lethaniel's eye's met Thao, stoking the bristles of his black beard.

"I am sure a courier is on the way right now to enlighten us," Isabelle said, rushing quickly on her feet through the rich hallways of The Palace, followed by several people, including Darlo Heventon, Taktard and Yespin.

"The courts have already informed Lethaniel of their concerns" said Yespin. "We're expecting a response today."

"Then we shall wait and see what Lethaniel has to say, won't we councillors? But I don't expect his response will be anything we didn't already know" replied Isabelle.

"If the Dovidian's do not show what do you think will be our next course?" asked a follower squeezing through Darlo and Taktard.

"Umm I'm not sure" she laughed "They seemed rather keen on coming, let's be a little patient" she said, seeing off other questions and comments "Gentlemen" she spoke over the group, addressing them all "I've just spent all morning reviewing the treaty, I understand you're concerned with the lateness of Desa but until they arrive or we receive word, there isn't much we can do, but I am sure Lethaniel is on it. Now if you excuse me, I've a meeting to get to. Good day." Her Glyph Wielders stood in the way of the parade on her order, blocking the corridor on the flick of her wrist, giving her the freedom to walk alone.

The squad was put to one side as doctors carried away Barthul on a stretcher. Othello sat on the floor, away from the group with two heavily armed guards next to him while Lethaniel argued with Thao in the doorway of the barracks, both men tried to keep their voices at a bare minimum.

"It had to happen sooner or later. We did warn him Thao, you even warned with a discharge, yet he did not stop" assured Lethaniel.

"When he comes around"

"IF he comes around" Lethaniel corrected.

"We'll patch him up and he'll serve time in the tower cells followed by rehabilitation, only when he is cleared will he begin his life as a civilian. Agree?"

"Agreed. I'll make it happen" said Lethaniel, mulling over something else. "I knew it, I knew Othello had skill, it's in the way he moves even in the way he speaks. He tore through two Regulars from Xiondel like they were nothing, now someone like Barthul. I recognise that confidence, I know his method I too use it. I was wrong to ignore it. I'm thinking of giving him the squad."

"Fighting is one thing, leading is another Lethaniel" Thao was sure to make eye contact "You know this better than anyone" Thao's protest was fair.

"Barthul had been pierced before, years ago. Othello spotted it and knew to exploit it." Thao sighed, rolling his eyes, giving in.

"You are the General, I will leave the decision to you, Lethaniel, but as your second, and as your friend, my advice would be to be patient, keep your eye on him further before granting him power" he warned, disappearing inside the barracks with Neraal.

Isabelle sat at a long table in a wide room. She sat with several other men who helped run the city; they were in charge of things with minor significance next to what Isabelle was concerned with, but it was a meeting she had been putting off for far too long, and just wanted it done. They talked and argued amongst one another about trivial matters, during their petty debate she made out like she was interested. In between answering the odd question, they passed over to her, she daydreamt, sometimes having to snap herself out of a trance. Time didn't seem to move and the list they had to get through was pages long. She began to list the things she could have been doing, things with so much more value, like apologising to Lethaniel, she had already worded it mentally a hundred times in the past half hour. Or she could be saying her goodbyes to Master Eran, Jerhdia and Thao, to all those who had been with her and protected her from the beginning. Her thoughts dwelled and came back around to Teo, the man who had not a desk to leave a letter on, the man who had no address or a square on a schedule. It dawned on her that maybe she would never see him again, the feeling hung taking her attention off the meeting.

"What do you think we should do, Isabelle?" Asked a gentleman from across the table, bringing her back to reality.

"Hmmm?" she murmured, wide eyed and embarrassed. "Oh, yes uhh, I agree, we should follow with standard procedure" she replied, hoping her answer would fly, and it did to her relief. She sat there in her seat, emotionless and hollow, thinking hard about what the future held. Staring into her reflection coming off a metallic jug used for pouring milk she could not help but smirk at the state of her face. She angled the way she sat, in an attempt to fix the distortion, but no matter how hard she tried, no matter what place she came at the jug, her face would not line up, and formed into something

520

grotesque. "Gentlemen!" her knees hit the underside of the table, spilling the milk "I am sorry, but I really must depart; something has come to my attention. You all seem to know what you are talking about and do not require my help. If you do require some assistance High Councillor Truth is right down the hall. Please excuse me."

"But Isabelle, we haven't even come to a decision yet," one man said as she departed. She would wait until sunset to find The Dark Rogue. Isabelle created a loose course to follow. If Teo and his group were out there, they would find her, all she had to do was make herself easy to find.

The barracks was almost empty. The men had returned to their homes and were probably feasting at this time, reminiscing about how Barthul met his match at the hands of Othello, spreading word. There was one man left in the training yards; it was Othello standing in the middle of several stuffed mannequins, mannequins used for crossbow practise. He had found a collection of swords that hung on a wooden weapon rack and refined his skills; the swords he had worked with had been sunk blade-first into the ground, he took a liking to the longswords, swinging each one he pulled around his hand and wrist skilfully with fluidity. When he finished handling the blade, he would slide it into the mud and found another to repeat the process. It was mesmerising to watch. Othello thought he was alone but Lethaniel had been keeping an eye as he worked from the barracks. When his time came to head for home, he joined Othello, leaning next to one of the stuffed dolls as he twirled a short around, striking his target in front of him with lethal precision. Had the doll been real, any one of these strikes would have been fatal.

"Those swords in the ground will require sharpening" Lethaniel noted, spotting the pillars of swords in the ground.

"Why do you want to make me a squad leader, Lethaniel?"

"Why did you accept?" Lethaniel replied, cleverly. Othello smiled and continued to practise with his sword. "Barthul has been removed from his position, he won't be coming back. The squad needs a man to lead them. I think you are the best candidate." Lethaniel explained as Othello continued to strike the mannequins.

"Is that it, no lecture, no discipline?" questioned Othello, ceasing his training.

"I'm not going to lecture you or detain you, you've done nothing wrong, the Xiondel soldiers was an act of self-defence, as was Barthul. Squad leader is a promotion, my second advised against it, but I am The General, and I see strength in you" Othello smiled, getting ahead of himself before Lethaniel stepped forward, entering his space "But I need you to understand something Othello; when I give an order I expect it to be obeyed, you're not a hawk anymore, you're a Norkron, and Norkrons watch each other's backs, my men's lives matter to me, perhaps more so than the mission, I will not endanger them anymore than what is required and in order to do that I need men to obey. Perform well during these raids and I'll consider granting you a Captain's rank; this comes with a healthy salary and your own quarters in the city. Alexius will fill you in on the details if you have any questions," explained Lethaniel as Othello nodded slowly.

"Oh I've just the one, if this is supposedly out last mission, what need would I have of a new title?" Lethaniel smirked.

"Until I get the order to hand up my swords we go about business as usual, but first comes our task" he grunted.

"Something on your mind General?" Lethaniel pulled out one of the longswords from the ground.

"The men on this coming mission, I've served with them, I know them, some I can even call close friends, you are not, and this little stunt has made me nervous. I know because I've done similar things" Lethaniel shared, opening up a page of his past he'd rather tear out.

"What happened?" At first Lethaniel took a moment to consider sharing anything more with Othello but decided to create some rapport.

"I was made General by default. A man named Syen Kaaz was selected initially. I thought that if I proved I could take him on with sword in hand and win, I would somehow be reconsidered for the promotion, I was wrong, that's NOT the way we do things here, this is not a tournament" noted Lethaniel, catching Othello's eye as he paced between the mannequins.

"What happened to Syen?"

"He was never the same person after I crushed him. I hear his name here and there, but I haven't seen him for some time. I hear he took up the bow, but, not much else." The pair fell silent, Othello took up a defensive pose. "We'll find you a weapon before we depart. Of the swords you've pulled, I would choose this one" suggested Lethaniel and he tossed it to Othello before heading off out of The Military District, to his lonely house at the end of his estate.

Squeezing his palm around the handle, getting a feel for it, Othello whispered, "I agree" and he launched the blade at the furthest mannequin. It spun through the air and planted itself in the doll's chest.

Slipping away was easy; it had almost become second nature to her now and she used the same methods as before. She knew the shift patters and routines of the chamber maids. The sun was swiftly falling behind the clouds; the wind was fighting against her as she jogged to her destination. Isabelle could only hope that Teo had not left the city, she'd have no way of knowing if he had and that was most frightening. Her pace quickened when she climbed the steps leading up to the wall of Imrondel, hoping to see him there. When she reached the top, her hopes faded, the space was empty! Although her trip was not completely wasted, she admired a beautiful sunset and lost herself in the myriad of light, bursting from behind a broken wall of white clouds. Isabelle took a few steps closer and leaned on the chest high wall, mesmerised by the beauty of the sky kingdom. Fitting it seemed for her last night in Krondathia. The sunsets in Ivulien would be undoubtedly be different, especially from the tops of Davune, from its walls and stone towers brandishing their banners of violet and black. Something soft rubbed up against her leg! She took her eyes off the dynamic sky to see what it was. "Pandora!" she whispered, shocked to see her so far from The Palace of Norisis, but of course, Imrondel City was Pandora's back garden after all, and had been since she had found Isabelle as a tiny kitten. Isabelle lifted Pandora up on to the wall she leaned on, and they watched the sunset together. Pandora curling her tail.

"I am going to miss you," she said, scratching her cats head lovingly. "Look after the place while I am gone." Pandora alerted to some movement behind them. The cat stared at the intruder, which made Isabelle curious. It was Teo! Isabelle tried sorting out what she wanted to say in her head, but the speech had disorganised itself, coming at her too fast and backwards. She looked back at the sunset, doing her best not to blurt anything out. Luckily for them both, Pandora was the one to start off the conversation and meowed loudly.

"So you're leaving?"

"Tomorrow. When they arrive" she replied brusquely. Teo fiddled with his sleeves and she stared at him, with nothing to muster, wondering if a dagger was strapped to his forearm.

"Listen, Isabelle, I want to…"

"Are we alone?" Isabelle's question jarred his speech. Teo considered how he would respond. He chose the truth.

"No"

"Where are they?" Teo held his gaze and took a breath.

"Nearby"

"Can they hear us?"

"They're watching, but they cannot hear us" he assured. Isabelle nodded, satisfied while she observed her surroundings, searching for clues as to where The Dark Rogues were! There were some men in the trench, she could hear them work, yet they were out of sight, there were a few guards posted along the wall's walkway, too far away for them to notice her, and they were dressed as men of

524

Imrondel. "Lethaniel reported sightings of you in The Silent Vale; was that you?"

"We were with you all the way, I got closer than I should have" he said. Isabelle slumped back on the wall and stroked Pandora. "We didn't kill anyone, Isabelle."

"Then who was it? Who took Jaden?" Teo grew closer and and put his hands on the wall, to think.

"They're from Ulgor."

"Ulgor," she repeated, the country west of the frozen lands of Maire.

"Yes... Ulgorans, ogre men. They're huge, very strong, very tough anywhere from eight to ten feet tall, three to four hundred pounds and they have moved into the south" he described.

"Why would the Ulgorans threaten us?"

"We do not know yet, we're unsure if this is an isolated incident or is organised but one was stalking you along your route to Imrondel; my companions and I found its tracks in Tthenadawn Forest. It was responsible for Jaden's death. They don't make great assassins Isabelle, they are sloppy, unclean, messy, they leave plenty of evidence behind for us, but they do know how to keep a distance and eyes on a slow-moving carriage. These ogres can walk for days and not tire, they can lift a man without much burden and can withstand wounds fatal to us."

"Were they trying to kill me?" her question almost gained a laugh from her, she was The Star Caller, keeper of mighty abilities.

"Ulgor drones are not bright, the select few that float around at the top their hierarchies would still benefit from books. It all figures, Isabelle in a stupid kind of way; an ill-educated enemy of Krondathia, with little knowledge of the Norkron capabilities, only they would be foolish enough or be duped into making an attempt on your life. But nothing happened, which suggests other things," he said.

"Such as?"

"Either it panicked and hesitated when it was detected by your soldier and all this was just a horrid misunderstanding or it was sent to watch and evaluate the scenario, similar to what a scout is tasked with doing, and reports back to the one in charge" Teo explained.

"Why were you following us?" He hesitated in answering. "You're not here to assassinate me, are you? Dark Rogues aren't stupid like Ulgorans, but they would make excellent assassins. Why are you here?"

"We are here for you Isabelle…" Isabelle didn't move; she needed more from him. "Our orders are to look out for you. To make sure you made it here safely," he finished.

"That's a lie," she concluded, not at all convinced.

"I didn't expect you to believe me, and I understand. Whenever something goes wrong you, Norkrons blame it on somebody else, you rule out all other possibilities and pin the guilt on outsiders. The Dark Rogue wing I am involved with are NOT to blame. We are not your enemies, but Krondathia always needs an enemy to shift the blame and focus its hatred upon. If the hatred is elsewhere, then there is no need to hate itself from within. Your Peacekeepers are a lot of things, but they did this, to preserve your people and themselves, to maintain the order, that's all that matters to them. Don't worry, we've our eyes on them as well as you."

"Explain to me about the Xiondel supply carriages then? All that cargo! You were reported to have taken it" Isabelle accused.

"Your scouts must have their eyes tested because none of us were there on that route at that time. We arrived, to see your men being dragged off by Ulgorans along with the carriages, but it wasn't us. I repeat we are NOT your enemy Isabelle. We suspect that someone on your side is shipping new weapons to a foreign enemy of Krondathia. Another wing of Dark Rogues intercepted weapon carriages, taking it off the Ulgorans in the middle of the night, and stashed them deeper inside Tthenadawn Forest, to make sure they stayed out of the wrong hands."

"If you hate us, Teo, why do you side with us?" asked Isabelle. It was an intuitive question; Teo had not been expecting it.

"There are far worse people out there than Norkron. We attempt to leave aside biases and fall in line with what is right."

"I must find some information on Ulgor," she said taking in a breath.

"You won't find any" snapped Teo.

"Then I must tell somebody about this."

"Isabelle, that will not help now, remember you are being watched and not just by us, but by The Peacekeepers, they can make your life very difficult."

"I am the Star Caller," she spoke confidently.

"I know, but the situation is out of your hands, pieces are already moving. Play ignorant and obedient for the time being, stay ahead without them knowing and work from the shadows" without even realising it he had gripped her arm, he released her and retreated to the wall, where Pandora stared at him. "Nice cat. What's her name?"

"Teo, I'd like you to meet Pandora, Pandora this is Teo."

"Ah, I remember, this is one of your closest friends" said Teo, tickling the cats chin.

"How can I work from the shadows when even the shadows themselves have eyes?" Teo had an answer.

"Put yourself in their shoes. Learn how to think like them, step in the role of someone who does not want to be found, keep in the forefront of your mind what it's like to be searching for someone, keep smiling, keep obeying and wait for your moment. You may want to leave a Star Caller mentality behind, Isabelle if we're to get through this."

"I can't do that, Teo." Both were momentarily silenced by her comment.

"I am going to disappear. You should too," he suggested, hearing the voices of workers inside The Defensive Trench growing louder. Isabelle nodded and began to walk down the steps with Pandora in her arms. Teo let her leave peacefully; it would be the first time she would depart before him. Isabelle turned her head before getting out of sight; she saw him put his hands on the wall again, looking out across the plain outside of Imrondel. She smiled, then left.

Chapter 25 - The Question

War is made in such ways.

It had been a long night and day for Isabelle and an even longer night for Lethaniel. The Dovidian leaders were now alarmingly late. There had been no word from any of The Korthium Outposts concerning the whereabouts of the entourage. If riders had been sent, they would have reported in by now. Action was being made today! Isabelle waited outside some stables for someone; she was close to The Military District and her guards were standing by her as always. She waited impatiently and fidgeted with the bangles around her wrists. Lethaniel saw her from a distance as he approached. The Knight was dressed in a dark, leather tunic; plate armour fashioned to his status had been strapped around his wrists, shins, and shoulders. He had been up before dawn, preparing all through the morning, leaving orders, giving instruction, informing his crew and the hierarchy of his plan. Finally, as the day's sun was setting, he was ready for travel. As he approached the stable, he acknowledged Isabelle, but did not engage in conversation; instead, he pushed open the stable door and walked in alone. Isabelle waited for a few seconds outside, sensing this glum behaviour of his, and then marched in after him with a stern look on her face, catching him up halfway down the long stable corridor, full of fine horses. Uther sat near a stable, tending to a grey horse, he saw Lethaniel coming.

"Is he prepped?" Lethaniel asked.

"Indeed General, as ready as he'll ever be, he's beautiful" replied Uther, saluting Lethaniel as he passed by, and bowing quickly when he saw Isabelle following him and gave them some privacy.

"This feels familiar" she said, siding a smile.

"This time it is different Isabelle. Last time was about me, the situation has changed" he replied, getting ready to leave.

"Are you travelling alone?" she asked.

"My party is assembling" he answered, checking the straps around his wrists.

"And who will be in your company?" Lethaniel took a breath.

"My second, Thao Hikonle. Jerhdia O'Nen, the mek, he made a request to come with us but I was considering him anyway, we'll need his expertise. The Captain of the Seventh Company, Braygon Augiene. My esquire Alexius Marsay and one other, a specialist who knows the ways of Jureai who may be able to help us track down the invaders efficiently. Our reinforcements will meet us in the east, once we make contact with the Dovidian entourage." His answer was sound enough.

"You're talking about The Northlander, the Bevork, aren't you?" she concluded, putting a hand on her hip.

"He is very skilful and can be of use, Izzy, I made him a squad leader after he toppled Barthul. He knows how to hunt and how to track." She shook her head from side to side, she disapproved, and he wondered why?

"All you see in him are his skills with a sword, don't you? You don't know what he's really like."

"Actually, Isabelle, I do," he replied, with a certain fatherly tone in his voice. Isabelle widened her eyes at him. "He's not materialistic, he finds value in the things that really matter and will fight for that, a way of life Othello found in Jureai. I see great potential in him, Izzy." Lethaniel turned. Feeling confident in his analysis and continued to get Seridox ready for travel. Uther had done a grand job in fitting the blue saddle to his back, and the headgear to the horse. Isabelle remained quiet; she didn't show it, but she began to feel worried for Lethaniel's safety, she didn't want this to be the last conversation they would have, so she had to tell him the truth, she had to warn him.

"Word spreads fast in Equis, Lethaniel. I showed you a path years ago and you took it, you will walk so many more, I know it. Stop seeing the world as a grid" she advised.

"It's the training Iz" he replied, "If it's not a grid then what is it?" she came a little closer, resting a hand on a stable door.

"A river" she whispered and Lethaniel drew a sigh.

"Two minutes, and then I am leaving" and he gave her his full attention.

"Othello is broken, a battle rages inside of him, a storm that exists in all of us and when it overwhelms us, we shelter, retreat and lick our wounds but not him. Othello is a fighter, in this world and the other, and when it takes control, what he once perceived as good, decent, and moral will distort and warp into something terrible. Your ears and eyes betray you, what your mind tells you cannot see what the heart knows..." Lethaniel's face remained solid as Isabelle's was water "...I am not certain myself of this myself, his storm is rising, his rage manifesting, as if he is searching for something, and I don't know what. The problem is, I've felt this before, in someone else the same battle was waged." Lethaniel did not know what to think, to him he heard her like she was reading from a piece of ancient text, written by someone with an incomplete vision.

"Where have you encountered this before, Isabelle?"

"Inside you. You will go one way; he will go the other" Isabelle pressed her forehead; the Vision had been hard to see. "The future is hard to see, it's unclear but I think... I think that one of you is going to die!" Isabelle did not know how he would react to the news; she understood that maybe she should have fully worked out what she had seen in her Visions before revealing anything, but Lethaniel was leaving now.

"You think that one of us is going to die?" he repeated, doubt in his voice.

"He will endanger you and your men. I'm sorry, I had to say something, I hope I am wrong"

"A Star Caller is never wrong Isabelle, you know what they say" said Lethaniel, quoting a famous phrase.

531

"I will try to contact you if I see anything more. It could be nothing, but I spoke to you last night, through a dream or some kind of astral projection, you were wounded, we were covered in dust and it was dark. Later I see you in a great cave, that's where it ends, where a part of me dies and you never find the power to forgive yourself." Lethaniel held his hand up, stopping her from talking. "I know you don't believe a word I am saying, sometimes I don't even understand it, but trying to make sense of this is my burden, I am The Star Caller."

"I try to understand you Isabelle, I try, but it's impossible. So many paths, so many routes, so many choices intertwining and separating, how can anyone have the slightest idea where one's journey leads? As you said it's a river, and as beautiful as this vision is, I trust my grid, it may not be perfect, but I can see the outcome" detailed Lethaniel. "Othello is coming, I need him to fight our enemies."

"Who are our enemies Lethaniel? It seems they're growing. Watch out for one another out there, beyond the walls is a wild myriad of beauty and danger, do your best to distinguish one from the other" she said, giving her final warning. "Ride safe."

"Goodbye, Isabelle, I will see you in a few months." With that he trotted off, leaving Isabelle alone in the wind.

"No, you won't," she whispered, as Lethaniel disappeared into the stone city. The sky was dark, but the wind was warm, the night was young perfect for a hot meal and a cold drink with some friends, but not for a Star Caller, her guards would make sure she would find her way back to The Palace of Norisis.

Eva and Othello stood side by side in their special, isolated place upon the rooftop. It was growing darker and Othello had received his orders, he had to be making his way.

"I must go," he said, touching her back, finished his wine and set down the glass on the wall Eva rest her hands on, leaning over to see the street below. "I like this" it was his candle, the same one he snatched from the festival, wrapped in a star bloom she had picked and embalmed so it would not age. "We'll light it when I get home."

"Home?" she questioned.

"Here" he said, siding a smile, caressing her cheek with the outside of his finger.

She enjoyed his touch as long as it lasted, the sense of protection and safety-filled her whenever he was around, always she felt comforted in his presence, always she felt secure. "Be careful" and she kissed him.

"There is one thing I must ask of you; it's just a small favour."

"Yes, of course, anything," she smiled, holding his waist.

"I want you to look after something for me, something that belongs in this city and not out there. It's important to me, it's one of the reasons why I left Jureai," he explained. Her face was open and eager to help. Othello pulled out something from his inner tunic pocket wrapped in a light grey cloth and placed it in her hands. "I have yet to find out its meaning, but when I get back maybe we can investigate its origin. It was my father's…" She held it in her hands "…Keep it safe for me please." Moving away, he turned to leave the rooftop.

"Wait… Othello!" she cried, rushing toward him, for one last moment. She wrapped her arms around him, embracing him tighter than usual. He returned the affection, knowing that it would be many months before he would touch her again before he would lay with her and hear her voice. "I will miss you." It was time for him to leave.

"I will miss you," he whispered.

Othello left, leaving her alone in the night. From atop her roof, she watched him depart until he was out of sight. The weight of the object, wrapped up in a cloth in her hands, felt curiously heavy. She unwrapped it to see what it was Othello wanted to be kept safe. When she pulled away the last fold of cloth, she saw the glint of a golden band with a red crest in its centre. She gasped upon identifying the piece. It was a twin; the other half belonged to another. She held it up to the night sky, to try to illuminate its features. Without a doubt, it was what she thought it was. Then and there it all made sense to her; the mystery behind Othello was solved! She HAD to stop him. She HAD to talk to him before he left the city.

The portcullis was reeled open and Lethaniel, atop Seridox, trotted through The Defensive Trench. He looked from side to side and saw the city's mighty catapults and anti-siege weaponry being rolled into place; he also saw stacks of swords and all kinds of weapons that had been transported in very recently. Spears, bows, shields, and thousands of arrows lay in wait to be sorted. The Defensive Trench was large, large enough to support Imrondel's soldiers on the walls and provide heavy fire from its catapults for support. The last attack upon Imrondel had been well before Lethaniel's time, so much of the equipment was old and hadn't been used for a long while. The Main Gate, made of thick, cold iron slabs of metal, was heavily locked from the inside to keep invaders out; never had it been breached, but the outside had seen off attacks in the past. Men working in the trench began to open the gate. The first step was to pull apart the lengthy, metal girders with rattling chains. The girders slid aside with difficulty, screaming as they were dragged. The gate itself was then opened by several burly men, who used detachable levers, they fit these levers into neatly made grooves and pulled as a group. As the doors were opened to the grassy, empty plain, Seridox walked out of Imrondel City carrying Lethaniel on his back. Both were ready for the travels ahead. Lethaniel didn't have to wait long before Thao showed up atop Eliah, his great black steed that had seen the blood of battle before; he was no stranger to war and had the scars to prove it. Thao stepped outside the city and acknowledged Lethaniel listening to the hymn of the night. The wall of Imrondel reflected some of the moon's light, giving it a glistening, pale white shine. Alexius, the esquire, was next to arrive on horseback followed by Jerhdia, the armourer, the man responsible for building most of the defences all around them. They joined Lethaniel and Thao on the plain in front of the city, Jerhdia greeted The General but ignored The Honour Guard. Braygon was on his way riding into the trench waving to the group atop a brown horse.

He was an experienced man for his age, only twenty-seven, a traveller, a Captain and a man with a secret, his homeland was unknown, a mystery most in the unit wanted solving.

"Have you travelled this far east before?" Thao's question directed at Braygon, the newly arrival.

"I have seen The Towers of Norfoon before; If we are not picked up by Mathias or his scouts on the boarders of Thnel, we may risk a dangerous journey" replied Braygon.

Alexius took a drink from a pouch of water; he swirled it around his mouth and spat it out "Are we all here?"

"No" said Lethaniel, "One more is coming." Just then, Othello came galloping up to them; his horse had been prepped for travel just like the others, and he seemed confident in riding the horse familiar to Jerhdia. It had belonged to Jaden; as Othello was the last one to arrive, receiving odd looks from Thao and Alexius. Jerhdia greeted him with a pat on the back and Braygon stretched his arm over to him, where they engaged in a friendly handshake. "We ready?"

Lethaniel gave instruction to the doormen behind, to seal Imrondel for the night. Their travelling began and the group rode over the stone paving. Braygon was about to pass Lethaniel only to be stopped.

"Braygon. I don't know what we will find out there but... Whatever we encounter, I just want to be sure that..."

"I got your back, Lethaniel," Braygon interrupted. "Just remember your morals, remember your training and get all of your men through this alive" he added, keeping his eyes fixed on the road straight ahead of him.

"Keep an eye on Othello for me?" asked Lethaniel nearly at a whisper.

"Why?" Isabelle's words of warning came flooding in. "No reason, just keep an eye, he's not from here." Lethaniel tugged at the reins to get ahead of the men and gave his first set of orders. "Stay on me, anyone needs to stop urgently raise it with the man in front and pass the message along. WE RIDE EAST! Let's move out!" With that, the men sped off over the plains at full speed in single file. Lethaniel led the way with Seridox, clearly, he was the fastest horse of the group. Then came Braygon, Jerhdia and Alexius, who rode hard. Othello and Thao trailed behind but kept up with the group. The night was warm and they enjoyed the whip of wind through their hair, the breeze on their faces. Their objectives, to find the Dovidian entourage coming for Isabelle, and to rendezvous with Mathias at The Norfoon Watch Towers nestled in the mountains of Thnel. Once stationed they were to prepare to meet the invasion and to eradicate the threat coming from the east. Only when these objectives were cleared would they return to Krondathia, to enjoy the beginning of a long and lasting peace in Equis.

Eva gripped the portcullis bars and shouted out to the nearest man.

"YOU! HEY! Has Othello left?" The young lad working nearby heard her and came closer.

"Who?" he asked, dusting his hands off.

"Othello! Have Lethaniel and Othello left yet?" she asked again, fearing the worst. The boy looked very young to be working, he looked even younger to be working HERE!

"Yeah, you just missed'em, not sure when they will be coming back either. Won't be for a while I guess. I know because my father went with them. Sorry missy," he finished, getting back to work. Eva slumped on the bars and cursed to herself. She turned away and began to walk back home, noticing another woman hovering under the shadows of a nearby shelter. As soon as she saw her face under a blue hood, Eva instantly bowed low and addressed her Chosen appropriately.

"My lady Star Caller," she spoke humbly, sounding a little nervous.

"Who are you?" asked Isabelle.

"My name is Eva Chennela Grey, my lady, we spoke at the festival."

"Please stop bowing and let me see your face silly" laughed Isabelle, stepping closer. Eva rose and stood up straight. "Eva Grey... Of course, I know you. The General has mentioned you on more than one occasion."

"Isabelle, I don't want to take up your time. I'll be on my way."

"You're special to him, did you know that?" Isabelle asked. Droplets of rain fell from the sky; it would be pouring soon.

"Yes, yes I know; we have known each other for a long time, nearly all our lives to tell you the truth," responded Eva. She suddenly felt foolish; of course, The Star Caller knew this.

"So have I. I always knew he would make a great soldier, but perhaps General is too much for him. Still, I wonder if he will ever become what I sense in him... A Hero."

"Oh he is a hero, through and through" praised Eva, confident in Lethaniel.

"What did you want with him before he left, Eva? It seemed urgent." Eva wanted to answer, but hesitated. Isabelle looked up at the sky to the falling rain, her eyes bled a bright green, reflecting off the droplets of rain keeping the pair dry as they shared some stories. It wouldn't be until much later, when Isabelle would fall asleep in her bedroom, where she would see something, where she would experience a Vision as clear as she saw Pandora, sitting on the window ledge, staring out into the night. Something had happened recently, she sensed; something life-changing that resonated inside Eva. She would do her utmost to meet with her again.

The riders felt the falling rain; it would not affect them immediately as they galloped east together. The rain would, however, make the ground soft and slippery. The horses would have to reduce their speed when it came to abandoning the stone road and riding across the grassy plains. They sped along the main road of Imrondel for an hour before slowing the pace, allowing their horses an easier gallop. As always Lethaniel led the way and the others followed. The rain began to sting and make riding difficult. Jerhdia pulled a balaclava over his face. Alexius already wore a cloak that came with a detachable hood, he made good use of it to minimise the pins of the water. Braygon lifted his soldier's helmet from his saddle and placed it on his head. Lethaniel, Thao and Othello had no means to deal with it, so they did their best and rode on. It wasn't long before they came to a crossroad, the road splintered off into three different directions. Further east was the prospering town of Cuether and the shores of The Isle Line. North was Tthenadawn Forest and Korthak Bridge, while south led to perilous and dangerous terrain called The Dross Marsh, where wild, slumbering creatures lay in wait under the swamps dark surface for lost unwarily travellers. Lethaniel steadied Seridox on the spot, to find his bearings and navigate. The others caught up and awaited instruction.

"This way. It's this way!" shouted Lethaniel and Seridox darted off the road and into the darkness. The others followed him and quickly made themselves scarce in the dead of night.

Day broke and the rain had calmed but fell lightly from grey clouds, making it uncomfortable for the riders who had been travelling all night across the plains, at a steady pace. Further ahead over the distant mountains grew a curving, colourful rainbow reflecting the sunshine. The air was fresh and clean, the ground was flooded, and water arose over the tips of the grass, drowning it. The horses, having broken off into a random formation during the night, were now walking in single file again, with Lethaniel in the lead and Thao at the rear. There had been no talk during the night travel, and now day had risen, the appetite for talk rose with it.

"I think it's time we rest, don't you think? Let's find higher ground" Alexius suggested.

"No, not yet. A Korthium Outpost is not far away. We will rest there," he replied. Alexius sighed quietly and helped himself to his own supplies of dry crackers and cold spring water. It was a beautiful

538

day indeed, was a morning to wake up to during time off work, with a warm body next to you, rather than be working or travelling long distances. The surrounding fields and meadows shone with moisture, the distant hills and far off mountains seemed to go on forever. These mountains cast great shadows upon the land. Othello turned his head around to Thao admiring the view.

"Do you know where we are, Othello?" asked Thao, wondering how much his new companion knew about this region of Equis.

"This is the place no one owns, a land that separates Krondathia from Ivulien" Braygon interjected, deciding to assist Othello with his answer.

"We're in The Ledera Lands, Othello. No one nation holds claim over it, but small parts are owned by certain factions. The lines were drawn by ancient battles and fallen heroes. Imrondel, was built on such territory and we consider it part of Krondathia, even though Krondathia is far from here."

"We should be nearing the outposts soon. Are you tired?" asked Thao.

"I'm fine, but my horse may need to stop" said Othello, paying the horse some attention, stroking the side of its head. "I heard an outpost is nearby?"

"The outposts? The Korthium Outposts, nothing much to it really. Shelter, food, a watchtower and a barracks. All defensible of course, within a ring of stone. It's no fortress, Othello. You'll see when we get there." It wasn't long before signs of an outpost started to show, a mud path lay before their horses' hoofs and small stacks of used supply crates and junk heaps polluted the area. Then a Korthium Outpost came into view as they broke through the woodland; a stone ring, just as Thao had described, though the ring was damaged, chunks of the wall had crumbled and as a temporary solution, wooden supports had been fitted. Thao was right, it wasn't much to look at, but the impressive watch tower in the centre grew tall and by no means was it a flimsy structure. The barracks was not nearly as large as those situated in Imrondel City, but it still had all the requirements for the soldiers stationed here. Other small settlements had been scattered around, homes and stables for horses, though the stables could do with tending to. A malnourished farm was nearby outside of the wall and a lonely broken well battered by the elements. Guardsmen manned the entrance as the group approached and Lethaniel waved to The Korthium Guardsmen who called over to his senior officer. The riders dismounted and their horses were taken by the guards, outfitted in Imrondel armour. Lethaniel wasted no time.

"Welcome to The Eastern Korthium Outpost, General," a Watchman greeted.

"No sign? No word soldier?" asked Lethaniel, and the Watchman shook his head.

"What about the other outposts north and south of here?" queried Braygon.

"We must assume a delay and wait upon…"

"No! It's too late for that, no more waiting" groaned Lethaniel "The people are growing impatient; our Star Caller is growing impatient. We're to make contact with the Dovidian entourage, to find Desa, put them on their way and head to Thnel" said Lethaniel firmly, standing taller than the Watchman.

"Very well General, stay as long as you like. I understand your company will be arriving shortly?" Thao confirmed this and the Watchman left them to their business. Lethaniel looked at his riders and came to a quick decision.

"Rest yourselves men and eat something, we'll be moving out shortly." He walked off to check on Seridox; no doubt the men who led him off to the stable had closed the stable door AND tied him up. Seridox hated being tied and locked in, but it happened everywhere he went like he was suddenly a normal horse. The others dispersed to find some food. Othello sat on a chair close to a dying fire with a pot heating over it. He leant back on the flimsy chair, stretching out his arms and legs, not noticing a nosy guardsman nearing him.

"You're here for the dirt dwellers causing trouble in the east, aren't ya? I've heard the rumours," the miserable-looking, grimy guardsman asked. Othello stared back at him in disgust.

"Yes," he replied, noticing the filthy stains on the guardsman's armour. He had gritty, long hair which desperately needed a wash and patchy stubble like he had attempted to shave but had given up halfway through. Not a pleasant type of man to sit with, but he had been here for a long time it seemed, and could not read people's faces.

"Kill one for me would ya? Teach'em a lesson. Them tribespeople need to be wiped from our land for good. If I could, I would travel with you fellas and give you a helping hand with the sword work, if you know what I mean. Heh heh heh." Othello was grateful that this man was not accompanying them; he also knew that he was not worth the time to dispatch right here and now.

"Do you know something about it?" asked Othello.

"I heard it was them Northlanders invading us last. Who knows what they want and why they came, but they make me sick thinking they can kill us and get away with it!" Othello patronised him with a sharp grin, hoping he would notice his bronze skin and connect the dots.

"That was only a rumour though, right?" Othello questioned.

"Aye, but I tell you, I know it's them from the north. Dirt dwellers… Should stay in their lands and never cross Bane's Tree." He spat out a glob of thick saliva to the ground as he finished talking, then offered Othello some of his drink from a grotty mug. Othello politely refused; not that he couldn't do with a drink, but he would rather be thirsty than sickly.

Lethaniel sat alone, a short distance away from the social areas at a flat, wooden table outside the run-down barracks and pulled out a map of the surrounding area. Eating a crust of bread, he reviewed the terrain, searching for faster routes if any into Thnel, and studied possible roads the Dovidians may have lost themselves on in their

541

travel. Alexius found him and joined him, sitting opposite with a mug of ale in his hand.

"Little early for that, don't you think?"

"I'm thirsty," Alexius protested.

"Drink some water then? Or boil up some water for tea, they also have some coffee beans here, which IS a huge surprise."

"I'll have one later," said Alexius, taking out his tin of rolling weed. "What are you thinking about General?"

"Look here..." Alexius leant further over to see clearer. "The Dovidians must have come this way, so we have to scout all other possible routes if we can't find them along the fastest road from the east. I think it will be best if we split up along this path here or around here to scout a wider area" explained Lethaniel, pointing the plan out with his index finger. Alexius scratched his chin and offered his thoughts.

"That's a lot of ground to cover. Two parties I reckon, in groups of three." Looking deeply at the small, square map, they both examined it together, Alexius drinking his ale, Lethaniel pulling his bread apart.

"I was thinking three parties, two per group..." Lethaniel considered, "If you can help me come up with a better strategy, Alexius, then I am all ears, my friend."

While Alexius and Lethaniel worked on a plan of action, Jerhdia was making his way up to the top of the watchtower, ascending the hundreds of wooden steps, spiralling around the stone brickwork of the tower's wall. He reached the top to find it empty. Bows and quivers of arrows lay about the room, along with a half-eaten plate of food and empty goblets. This outpost had not seen action for a long time. The soldiers stationed here must be bored with their duties, so they had to make the most of the ale shipment when it arrived every month or two. Krondathia couldn't afford to have intoxicated Watchmen in their outposts, so the supply was rare.

542

Jerhdia looked out through the open gap to the east; he saw nothing but the vastness of The Ledera Lands. He saw seas of green grass upon the open plains, rows upon rows of distant grey mountains with icy, snowy tips. He took a closer look through a small telescope balanced on a brass tripod, facing outward. Meanwhile, below, at the foot of the tower he spotted Thao, feasting on some food. The meaty broth looked greasy and unhealthy, but it was salty and delicious.

Braygon patrolled the perimeter, talking to a Korthium Guardsmen who seemed to know a little bit about the history of the tower. Alexius and Lethaniel were still discussing the route when Othello came over to them; he had grown tired of sitting with that smelly, grimy guardsman who kept pestering him about the northlands.

"When are we moving out?" he asked Lethaniel.

"Right now. Find Jerhdia and get your horse. Let's go," ordered Lethaniel, folding up the map with a clear plan in mind.

"You heard him, Othello, lets gear up," said Alexius excitedly, walking toward the stables and Othello followed, refusing a smoke Lex had rolled.

They assembled and left The Korthium Outposts. Othello was the last to leave. When they were clear of the ring of stone they picked up the pace, galloping over green fields and around wide thickets housing waterholes. Lethaniel came to a halt after a large stint of solid riding. The ground and terrain stayed very much the same, the sign of rain clouds were forming again, only this time they were right above their heads. Their excitement and anticipation of this mission had gradually worn away, ever since they had left the comforts of Imrondel City, their task became ever more real. The others gathered up behind Seridox and awaited their Generals instructions.

"We'll cover more ground if we split into two groups. Braygon, Othello and Jerhdia, you will head northeast and scout as far as you can. Report anything suspicious. We have to know what happened to the entourage. Alexius, Thao and I will head directly east. We will meet up on the plains outside Cuether at sundown. Don't be late, be thorough and stay together" ordered Lethaniel.

"If you find them, stay with them. See to it that they find a safe route to Imrondel. Send one of you to notify us of the situation. We will do the same if the situation is reversed, agreed?" spoke Thao and all nodded.

"Good luck, gentlemen," wished Lethaniel. Without any further questions, they obeyed and swiftly rode out, eager to find the lost entourage, to find Akarnal Desa.

Braygon's group scouted far and wide, finding no sign of the Dovidian leaders. No tracks or evidence of passage, either the entourage came this way and left no tracks at all, which was impossible, or they took a totally different track which looked more real with every passing minute. The weary day drew on with no results. Boredom and self-doubts had settled in.

"Braygon! Braygon!" Jerhdia called to Braygon further ahead "They didn't come this way. Let's pull back, it's getting late." Braygon looked on ahead, hoping they were just round the next bend, but alas, just the dirt path and tall green bushes.

"Maybe they are just over the next ridge" said Braygon with optimism. Their horses were getting restless with all the stopping and starting; they wanted a stable and some fresh water. Braygon looked at Othello for backup, but he remained silent as he had been throughout the trip.

"Braygon, come on, let's go. It's time to meet Lethaniel anyway. Look at the sun," the armourer insisted. They turned around and rode back to the meeting point.

Further east, Lethaniel rode hard upon Seridox. Like the other group, he had found nothing, it didn't make any sense. Lethaniel eased up and Seridox slowed into a walk. Thao was close behind and gave Eliah a breather too. Alexius did the same, slurping back some spring water. The rain clouds above their heads were getting thicker and darker. Soon they would burst and soon everything would be drenched. The sound of thunder fell, signalling their que to pull back. As they casually trotted through a small thicket of bony, leafless trees, their thoughts began to run.

"How far away is Cuether?" asked Alexius.

"South, further that way," said Thao, waving in its direction.

"What's it like there? I've never actually been."

"See for yourself when we get there Alexius. It looks as if we are spending the night under Minister Vou's watch," he replied, confirming the plan with Lethaniel with a simple nod. "What is wrong Lethaniel? You haven't said a word in hours." Thao noted, riding up next to him.

"I feel like the longer we are away from the city, the more danger we will find ourselves in later. It's just a feeling, one I am trying to trust" he answered, being a little vague.

"This is what we do Lethaniel," replied Thao, though the remark didn't help in the slightest.

"The idea to hang up my swords, is an attractive prospect Thao." The big man suddenly held up his hand, signalling to stop.

Several arrows had pierced a nearby tree, one of which was bloody and broken. Alexius immediately grabbed his sword hilt but Lethaniel calmed him down, resting a hand on his. Thao approached the arrows and pulled one out; the arrows were flecked with a yellow feather. He presented it to Lethaniel and then Alexius. None of them had anything to say. They split and scouted the grounds and to their horror, spotted something over the next hill. "Look! What's that?" Alexius pointed. Thao, Lethaniel and Alexius drove their horses forward, pushing them hard. Seridox speeding out in front. Smoke arose from the carnage and their search was over. The rain clouds finally collapsed, and rain fell upon them and the fallen bodies littered around the wreckage of the Dovidian entourage.

The caravan lay in the road, pillaged and destroyed. No life remained of any kind. The carriages had been ransacked and the horses that transported them were gone. The bodies of the Dovidian leaders lay on the ground; judging by the pools of blood the attack had happened recently, Thao predicted a day or two ago, in which case the attackers could still be lurking nearby. Atop the hill, two Dovidian men had been tortured; hanging from a wooden pole bound by wire, their hands and legs tied together, their flesh flayed and their heads missing. As the rain began to fall, so did the blood thin and run down the corpses. Lethaniel, Thao and Alexius heard galloping horses riding toward them. It was the others; they had finally arrived having caught up to the group. Jerhdia dismounted swiftly and drew his sword, investigating the area alongside Braygon, who checked some of the dead. The Dovidian leaders had been killed; some of the faces they even recognised. Lethaniel stayed quiet and felt the chill of death upon his shoulders. Braygon continued to scour the area, rolling over the bodies, checking their identities, searching for something, anything that may give them a clue as to who was responsible. Jerhdia rummaged the insides of the carriages; they had been cleared out by whoever did this, nothing much remained but wreckage. Othello hung back on his horse behind Thao as the investigation took place; checking the arrows, sure to know they were not loosed from Bevork bows.

"Who did this?!" cried Braygon, knowing that none of the group had any answers.

"It must have been The Dark Rogues. Damn those crafty bastards!" yelled Jerhdia, jumping to conclusions.

"Let's not forget why we are here. What about the invasion? It could have been done by the foreign invaders," Alexius suggested.

"There is no way that they have invaded this far inward without us knowing, no way," insisted Lethaniel imagining the geography in his head.

"If The Norfoon Towers are still ours, Lethaniel is right, Mathias would have warned us, but we do not know of their condition" said Thao.

"It wasn't Xavien," Othello put in.

"What makes you so sure? It could have been anyone," Alexius pointed out.

"I know because these fallen men still have their skins and jaws. I won't rule out Salarthians but it's unlikely they were involved," replied Othello, bringing about a sudden pause. Alexius gave the newcomer a long stare, who returned the look.

"It must have been Dark Rogues; who else could it have been, huh?" Alexius spoke, apparently now in agreement with Jerhdia.

"It was enemies of Krondathia. We can all agree on that. Men who are not keen on peace" said Thao. Lethaniel trot into the wreckage upon Seridox, his hooves soaked in blood. Among the corpses, he spotted the miserable body of Akarnal Desa, Isabelle's old friend.

"Who are our enemies?" he muttered to himself, thinking about what she had told him the last time they had seen one another. Thao heard these words but chose to let them go for now. "Thao!" Lethaniel called, about to ask for guidance, rallying his men together.

"This is how it begins. Ask yourselves what it is you fight for? Because whatever it may be, it's on the line." The wind whistled, the grass blown aside, haunting the grounds. They realised with heavy hearts and crushed spirits that the events of today would change everything. There would be no going home any time soon, this mission was not as simple as it once was and their next move would be critical.

"What do we do now?" Alexius asked, the question on everyone's minds. A black dove sang upon a branch of a nearby tree, grabbing the attention of Othello. It looked to him. The dove, that strange and wonderful black dove, was perhaps a witness to what had happened here. A shame that it could not speak.

- END OF VOLUME ONE -

THE ANCESTRAL ODYSSEY

THE UTOPIAN DREAM

Teaser

Time ticked by slowly. Days dragged on at a snail's pace. Isabelle read and researched in her carriage as she made her way to Xiondel City, rolling along the fastest route, known throughout the land as The Sire's Highway. Lethaniel took his group north as he had planned, to try to locate the threat that existed in the wilds, or even in the valleys of Thnel themselves. His Visarlian Knights had eventually arrived; they were a day late, which put Mathias a little off schedule. The Visarlian Knights were spread out evenly among the towers, some caught up with Lethaniel to provide him with further support, and the others head east and offered Thao and his platoon some aid. The Honour Guards had been posted throughout Thnel, they lifted the morale of all men wherever they went, for they were the elite martial force of Krondathia. Mathias kept watch over the towers, working mostly from inside of Lockheart. The extra hands made it slightly easier for everyone stationed there, taking much of the pressure off the commanding officers. The Norkrons were outnumbered had their intelligence been accurate, spread alarmingly thin through the valley, they had made the best tactical choices available to them, and with Lethaniel and Thao being among them this raised their chances at success greatly should an assault be made, but none ever came.

The Norkron men worked tirelessly together but despite their best efforts, all parties and scouting groups failed to return with results of any value, their empty hands testimony to the elusiveness of their enemy. This was quite accurate to what Mathias had predicted in the briefing the day Lethaniel had arrived, though he wasn't expecting any immediate results, he was expecting something given the reinforcements. As it stood, not a single track had been found, not a single sign of anything untoward. The invaders were cunning indeed.

A fortnight went by and still, nothing had been found, two weeks of watching and waiting, two weeks of hiding and staying painfully quiet. All that time spent moving under the cloak of night, bitterly cold and hungry without an end in sight. Laying low in muck and discomfort became routine. On the plus side, none of the scouting groups had encountered any silvermane wolves or worse, bears. The bears of this region had been rumoured to grow abnormally large and were known to wander from place to place in search of food. The waiting was growing unbearable for some of the men. Alexius had been without a smoke since they had left the tower, and the cold air wasn't letting up, save for the odd afternoon of respite when the sun was at its highest. Lethaniel was with the group stationed furthest north. He now decided to head east, moving into the larger, thicker woodlands where the trees would offer some shelter, and maybe, just maybe, he would catch sight of a barbarian camp. He figured that if he and his men were under the watch of the enemy, seemingly randomising his search pattern might throw them off. Othello had been useful and had spotted subtle signs of Jurean warrior activity, although nothing alarming or worth reporting back for. Food and water had to be carefully rationed. From the day they had moved up north their supplies had been tight, so whenever possible they would hunt for nourishment in those harsh conditions.

Night had fallen, and all was quiet and still. Nothing moved but the tops of the tall trees, swaying in the brisk wind. It was a bitter night indeed; the stars were hidden behind the clouds, as was the white crescent moon. The moon had provided light on many nights while scouting, but in its absence, Lethaniel was the first to notice the difference. He could hardly see anything from his position. He and his group were nestled in a ditch six-foot-deep, surrounded by plants and conveniently arranged bushes. The horses had been given camouflaged warm coats, though at night the horses rested together, hidden by the men. Many nights had been spent without conversation, listening took over; the sound of the land became music, poetry reaching the ears of the Norkrons. Every so often, Lethaniel would get a sudden feeling, if he thought something was not right or if he suspected something was up ahead, or if the music of the world was displaced, he'd investigate. At times like these, he would ready himself for an encounter by gripping the hilt of his sword, but there never was anything to find or confront. It felt like waiting for ghosts or hunting the invisible. Mathias's warnings were long forgotten, and the urgency felt on their departure from the tower now felt massively overstated. Something was out there however, something was roaming wilds and whatever it was, it couldn't remain secret forever.

Another week drifted on by and still, there was no sign of anything. No sound of footsteps or the tell-tale call of a Commander, much the same as yesterday and the day before and the day before that, not even Othello could spot any differences in the wild landscape. Lethaniel was first on watch tonight, standing in a trench as deep as a grave, his head peering just over the black mud ledge, sheltered by plants for green camouflage. His reflexes were sharp, and his wits were on edge, itching to make a move. Othello couldn't sleep, so he stayed on watch with Lethaniel that night. They waited together, listening to natures poetry. Braygon was asleep for now; he had been on watch the previous night. The few Visarlian Knights in their company were also sleeping within the shelter of the trench, all wrapped up in thick, dark blankets. All the men wore their armour and would wisely not take it off unless ordered to, when not inside the safe zones of Thnel. Quietly, Othello edged forward to Lethaniel and whispered,

"Anything?" Lethaniel took a while to answer; he was transfixed by the blackness of the shadows up ahead beyond the ominously swaying trees. Was something watching him from that darkness? Or was it just his overactive imagination? He could have sworn that a man dressed in black was out there, mocking him and his men's efforts.

"I don't know. I think something is up ahead. I thought I saw movement an hour ago. If what I think is true, then we are not hidden, we are being surrounded as we speak." Othello watched as well for some time with Lethaniel, but he couldn't see anything, their eyes could only see so far before being shrouded by the darkness.

"Let's hope that you are wrong," prayed Othello. A half hour of silence went by before Lethaniel spoke again.

"Do you miss Jureai?" he whispered; his eyes still focused forward intently.

"Sometimes..." Othello began, struggling to prepare a proper answer after such a long time spent in silence. "Living so far north would not be the same now. I've learnt so much here. My father always said something like this would happen; that before paradise could reign, chaos would have to befall us." Lethaniel hoped with all his heart that this would not be the case; that this invasion would be cut short, that he could go home and see Isabelle fulfil the prophecy.

"I am sorry for your loss Othello," whispered Lethaniel, eyes unflinching.

"We've all lost people, it's because of loss and tragedy we can find new meaning in life." Lethaniel listened carefully to Othello as if he had never properly listened to him before.

"What happened to your mother Othello?"

"I have but a few memories of her, but those memories are clouded with anger and confusion. Imrondel City is a different place now," he said, remembering to speak at a whisper.

"Why did you go to Jureai?" Lethaniel's eyes were now on Othello, and not on the darkness up ahead where they really should have been.

"My father's choice."

"Like what?" Lethaniel was curious to know, he began to fit his memories of his own life around Othello's, what he ended up with was a similar story. Othello's vague descriptions filled in some of the gaps in his own hazy past.

"He gave me a ring. I don't have it on me right now; I gave it to someone back in the city, for safe keeping. I don't mean to sound disrespectful Lethaniel, but if I had to leave Krondathia, she is the only part of that place I'd want to take with me."

"Who? Who is this woman you speak of?" asked Lethaniel.

"Do you know Eva Grey?" Lethaniel twisted his whole body around to face Othello, and in his anxious flutter of excitement, his voice rose above a whisper

"How do you know Eva!?" At that moment, a far-off glint of light lit up one side of Lethaniel's face, the bellow of a horn found his ears, throwing him completely off topic. It was a distress call from one of the towers in the distance. A Knight then shouted out,

"LOOK!" and pointed south, toward The Norfoon Watch Towers in the valley of Thnel. Lethaniel whipped his head around and witnessed, to his horror, one of the towers exploding with fire, the conflagration at the base quickly incinerating the structure from the inside out. The thick, brown smoke belched by the tower blotted out a fair portion of the sky.

"It's begun!" Lethaniel growled, a hint of resignation to the inevitable in his voice. A bombardment was taking place, the air was rent by echoes of crashing and the thunder of fiery comets colliding against the Norkron towers. His Visarlian Knights needed no orders, they leapt from the trench, ripped away the surrounding shelter and made for their horses nearby. Lethaniel immediately mounted Seridox. Braygon was up and vaulted onto his horse, as did Othello.

9 78